With over one hundred recordings, Brendan Graham's songs have enjoyed success across the world. He is composer/author of two winning Eurovision Song Contest songs 'Rock 'n' Roll Kids' (1994) and 'The Voice' (1996). 'The Voice' features on the soundtrack of the Pierce Brosnan movie, *The Nephew*.

A former basketball international, and a recipient of Australia's Lansing Bagnall Award for business studies, he has for many years been an activist on behalf of composers. He was Chairman of IMRO, the Irish Music Rights Organisation, for a nine-year period to 1997, during which time he was appointed to FORTE, the Government Task Force, to develop Ireland's music industry. In 1998, Ireland's Taoiseach, Bertie Ahern, T.D., cited Graham's 'outstanding contribution to the Irish music industry'.

Born in County Tipperary in 1945, he lived in Australia for five years before returning to Dublin, where he is married with five daughters.

The Whitest Flower is his first novel.

D1280870

'This is truly an extraordinary book, an epic in the true sense. Ellen Rua, the central character, is clearly discernible, through her struggles, her journeys, her ultimate overcoming of her sufferings, as the personification of Ireland. She is the keeper of its culture, its music and language, its spirituality. She is its voice, even when the impossible choices which faced people at the time force her to be complicit in the destruction of her own language . . . Ellen is the quest for Ireland's spiritual soul tossed between the old and the new religions. She is also the resurrection of the new Ireland rising out of starvation and disease, the embodiment of the hope that kept our people going.'   AN TAOISEACH, MR BERTIE AHERN, T.D.

'Ellen does represent Ireland. She represents many Irelands, the one that suffered, the one divided, the Ireland consumed with shame and guilt and silence, but ultimately she represents an Ireland that survived both here and through its people in other countries.'   *Irish Times*

'*The Whitest Flower* is a disturbing, challenging, and rewarding read, which puts our history in context and through Ellen Rua O'Malley reminds us of the beauty of a pilgrim life well lived.'   FR. BRIAN DARCY, *Sunday World*

'History painted with a broad, dramatic brush. It's cinemascope, a large screen, covering as it does the west of Ireland, Australia, Canada and Boston. Graham evokes so well the true human tragedy, the loved ones, friends and neighbours dying of hunger, disease, the wasted survivors managing to get passage to the New World and the faint promise of a new life. Definitely epic material here. It's meticulously researched, telling not only the story of the Famine and the Irish but also the heartrending plight of the Aborigines. The sickness and sadness of the disease-ridden Grosse Île is magnificently covered as is the racism and prejudice the southern Irish faced in the land of the free. It's also a generous and balanced novel.'   *Tuam Herald*

Brendan Graham

THE WHITEST FLOWER

HarperCollinsPublishers

HarperCollins*Publishers*
77–85 Fulham Palace Road
Hammersmith, London W6 8JB

This special paperback edition 1999
1 3 5 7 9 8 6 4 2

First published in Great Britain by
HarperCollins*Publishers* 1998

Although this work is based on real historical events
surrounding the Irish Famine of 1845–52,
the main characters portrayed therein
are entirely the work of the author's imagination.

Lyrics by Brendan Graham
©1998 Acorn Music Ltd/Warner/Chappell Music Ltd
Reproduced by permission of International Music Publications Ltd

ISBN 0 00 651050 7

Set in Linotype Sabon

Printed and bound in Great Britain by
Clays Ltd, St Ives plc

ACKNOWLEDGEMENTS

This book started with a song, literally. In fact three connected songs. Then in August 1996, through a series of disconnected events I found myself in the Boardroom of HarperCollins*Publishers*, London, telling the story of Ellen Rua O'Malley to seven people . . .

Along the way many people in many countries have helped me in very many ways to bring Ellen's story to where it now is.

To them all I am deeply grateful.

In memoriam – John McDougall, HarperCollins*Publishers*, June 1998.

BRENDAN GRAHAM, *Dublin, August 1998.*

IRELAND: Thanks to An Taoiseach, Bertie Ahern T.D., for the quotation he kindly gave which is contained herein; to Avril Doyle T.D., former Chairperson of the Government's Famine Commemoration Committee; Brian Collinge, and in particular Alice Kearney, Dept. of An Taoiseach have been of ongoing assistance throughout. I also express my appreciation to the British Embassy, Dublin, for its co-operation. To the two Arts Councils of Ireland, North and South, who administer the Tyrone Guthrie Centre at Annaghmakerrig where much of the writing was done; Resident Directors, Bernard Loughlin and Mary Rogan-Loughlin, and the wonderful people there – many thanks for all your kindnesses. Special thanks to Cathy Armstrong, Dublin Heritage Project; Robert Poynton, Session Clerk, Abbey Presbyterian Church, Dublin; John Paul II Library, National University of Ireland, Maynooth. Thanks also to Rev. James Brogan, Ormond Quay and Scots Presbyterian Church; Stephen D'Arcy, RTE; Peter Folan and Betty Magill, Mater Dei and Clonliffe College Library; Michael Jacob, Teagasc, Peatland World, Bog of Allen, Co. Kildare, and Kevin Lyster; Angela McGee, Project Co-ordinator, Leixlip Heritage Environment & Culture Project; Tom O'Byrne, Druid priest; Fr. George O'Sullivan, St. Brigid's Parish, Cabinteely; Margaret Powers, Cork Central Statistics Office; Fr. Brendan Supple P.P. (R.I.P.) and Fr. David Boylan – former chaplain, St. Mary's Parish, Maynooth; Church of Ireland Theological College (RCB) Library, Dublin; Orla Foley, Maynooth Public Library; National Library of Ireland; Nicholas Carolan, the Traditional Music Archive, Dublin; Ivor Hamrock and Jerry King, Mayo County Library, Castlebar; Galway County Library. Tom Gillespie, Editor, *Connaught Telegraph*, Castlebar, for making archival material available. I am indebted to Peter Mantel, the current owner of Delphi Lodge and likewise to Maurice Nicholson, owner of Tourmakeady Lodge, and to Aishling O'Donnell for the guided tour of the latter; the Famine Museum at Strokestown facilitated me on more than one occasion and I express my gratitude to Jim Callery and the people there. Special thanks, too, to Margaret E. Ward, and to Kevin Whelan. I express my gratitude to Ed Heine, Managing Director Warner/Chappell Music U.K., and to the people there who were enthused about Ellen's story from the start. To local historian Carmel Laffey, Clonbur, and to Bridgie O'Malley, for each, in their own way, preserving what has gone before, *buíochas*. Special thanks to Nick Pedgrift for sound advice, as ever; and to Clare Ramsden, healer. To my colleagues at IMRO, the Irish Music Rights Organisation, in particular to Chief Executive, Hugh Duffy. As well as the foregoing, there were a number of people who were crucial in their support. Sandra Ní Gharbháin had the misfortune a few years back to find me amongst her students at Irish Language night classes. She was the gate-keeper for the Irish words and phrases throughout this book. *Buíochas*. A special thanks to Donal Synnott, Director, The National Botanic Gardens, Dublin, for his valued help with matters botanical, and on the Gardens in the 1845–8 period. Thanks also to Curator Christy Crosby, and to Michael Higgins. Jarlath Duffy of the Westport Historical Society, was similarly of important help with regard to the West of Ireland. Vincent Comerford, professor of Modern History at the National University of Ireland, Maynooth, was supportive throughout the writing of this book. For his helpful suggestions and corrections with reference to the historical context I am very grateful. Kim Mullahey, my researcher, deserves special mention. No task was too big, no detail too small. Like clockwork the information requested arrived every fortnight over the past two years.

To Gibson Kemp, and Stuart Newton, for the door half-opened. To Adrian Bourne, Managing Director of HarperCollins Trade Division, who opened it fully, and who with his colleagues sat and listened to Ellen's story – *Míle buíochas!* I do not have a literary agent and have had no prior dealings with the book publishing industry, but from Chairman Eddie Bell downwards, HarperCollins U.K. have been outstanding in the support I have received. Patricia Parkin, my editor at HarperCollins, I thank most sincerely. Firstly for coming to Ireland to visit the places where the story is centred; for her encouragement in the early days of the book and her skilful guidance in the latter days, and for being impassioned about Ellen's story. A very special thanks to Anne O'Brien for all her hard work and care, and for having an unfailing memory for a careless sentence or word – even 220 pages ago! Also to Mary-Rose Doherty for her patience during the final 'housekeeping' and to Georgina Hawtrey-Woore who completed the editorial team.

LIVERPOOL: Thanks are due to Reg Greene, author of *A Race Apart: the History of the Grand National*; Joe McNally, Sales and Marketing Manager, Aintree Racecourse Company Ltd.; Eileen Organ, Supervisor, Liverpool Record Office, Central Library.

AUSTRALIA: Thanks to Prime Minister John Howard, for the quotation he kindly gave which is contained herein. My thanks to the following, who were of assistance before, during, and after my time there: Kate Alport, Curatorial Officer, Dept. Anthropology, South Australian Museum; Phil Gordon, Australian Museum, Sydney; Prof. Eric Richards, Faculty of Social Sciences, the Flinders University of South Australia; Sydney author Sue Woolfe; Ilse Wurst, Project Officer & Susan Duyker, Archivist, Sydney Cove Authority; Migration Museum, Adelaide; South Australian Maritime Museum; June Bernhardt, Adelaide Hills Tourism, Hahndorf; Barossa Visitors Centre and Barossa Valley Public Library; State Library of Victoria; John O'Brien, Melbourne; Barrie Hitchon, Christine Farmer and the HarperCollins team, Sydney; Tony Fisk, and HarperCollins, Auckland. Special thanks to Richard O'Brien, Irish Ambassador to Australia, Edward J. Stevens, Australian Ambassador to Ireland, Russell Jackson, Former First Secretary, Australian Embassy, Dublin; Lynn Collins, Curator, Hyde Park Barracks Museum, Sydney. To Barossa writer, Peter Fuller, and Geoff Schrapel, Director, Bethany Wines/Chairman, Barossa Winemakers, for their suggestions and corrections to the Barossa section of the story. Shirley Hartman, Tom Trevorrow and the Ngarrindjeri people of the Coorong. In particular, George Trevorrow, for exposing me to such a rich and spiritual culture, for his help with the Ngarrindjeri vocabulary, as well as suggestions and corrections to the text in the Coorong section of the story – an ungune.

CANADA: Thanks to Prime Minister Jean Chrétien, for the quotation he kindly gave which is contained herein. Without the generous assistance of Québec-based author, Marianna O'Gallagher, I could never have visited Grosse Île in the first place. Her two books, Eyewitness: Grosse Isle 1847 (with Rose Masson-Dompierre) and Grosse Île: Gateway to Canada 1832–1937, both published by Livres Carraig Books, Québec, are outstanding testaments to those times; to those who fled the Famine to Grosse Île, and to the many French-Canadians and others, who cared for them.

I express my deep appreciation for all her help, and for proof-reading this section of the book for historical accuracy. To Hugues Brouillet and Parcs Canada for facilitating me 'out of season', and to my guide on Grosse Île, André Couillard De L'Espinay . . . Je vous remercie de tout coeur.

Special thanks to Michael Phillips, Canadian Ambassador to Ireland, Public Affairs Officer Evanna McGilligan, and in particular to First Consul, Patricia Low-Bédard.

Thanks too, to Colleen Williams, Statistique Canada, Ottawa; Musée de l'Amérique Française, and Musée de la Civilisation, Québec.

UNITED STATES OF AMERICA: My thanks to former Ambassador to

Ireland, Jean Kennedy Smith, to Stephanie Schmidt, Irish Hunger Commemoration Coalition, Tenafly, New Jersey; New York author Peter A. Quinn; United States Senator and author Tom Hayden, California; Celtic scholar and musician, Eileen Moore Quinn, Dept. Anthropology, Brandeis University, Mass. Special thanks to Steven Jaffe Ph.D., Senior Historian and Associate Curator, South Street Seaport Museum, New York; Marie F. McCarthy, University of Maryland for allowing me to preview her forthcoming book, *Passing it on: Music in Irish Culture*, Cork University Press (March 1999). I owe a debt of gratitude to Michael P. Quinlin, author of *Guide to the New England Irish*, and founding member of the Boston Irish Famine Memorial Committee, for all his assistance while in Boston. I am also grateful for his helpful comments on the Boston part of the text. Thanks also to Collette Quinlin.

My daughter Niamh, not only put all of my original hand-written text onto word processor, but all the re-drafts too! This was in between organising trips, meetings, and generally co-ordinating all my efforts over the past two years. Without her work, this book would never have come together.

Finally, to my wife and family for all their forbearance and patience over the course of this book.

Buíochas óm' chroí.

The story of Ellen Rua O'Malley is just that – a story, but what she and her family experienced is largely based on actual recorded events of what happened to the poor in Ireland during the Famine years. I have, too, tried as accurately as I could, to portray the Ireland of the times in which Ellen lived – the places, the political, religious, social and cultural background. Similarly for Australia, Grosse Île and Boston.

For omissions, mistakes of fact, and novelist's licence, I am totally responsible. This should not in any way reflect on the very many diligent people who helped me with research material and whose work and suggestions were invaluable in creating the historical backdrop to *The Whitest Flower*.

CONTENTS

Ellen's Country

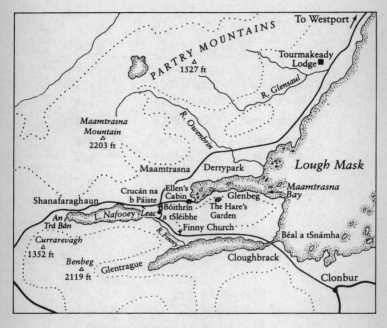

.... *Areas showing ground above 360 ft*

An Trá Bán	lit. The White Strand, known locally as The Silver Strand
Béal a tSnámha	The mouth of the swimming place – now called the Ferry Bridge
Bóithrín a tSléibhe	The little road over the mountain
Crucán na bPáiste	Burial place of the children
Leac	Ellen's 'rock'

Note: Maamtrasna in 1845 was in County Galway.
The County boundaries were redrawn in 1896. Maamtrasna now
resides in County Mayo.

Ellen's Journey

IRELAND

Westport
Lough Mask
Galway
Dublin

CASTLEBAR

CLEW BAY

Achill
Island

Clare
Island

ATLANTIC
OCEAN

Old Head

Westport
Quay
Westport Bay
WESTPORT

Louisburgh
Kilsallagh
CROAGH
PATRICK
2483 ft
Murrisk
The Reek

PARTRY
1270 ft
MOUNTAINS
Partry

SHEEFFRY HILLS
2476 ft
PARTRY
Tourmakeady
Lodge

MWEELREA
MOUNTAINS
Doolough Pass Rd.
Doo
Lough
1527 ft

Mweelrea
2645 ft
Delphi Lodge
Ben Creggan
1370
Ben Gorm
2275 ft
R. Bundorragha
Aasleagh
Falls
R. Owenbrin
R. Glensaul

Maamtrasna
Mountain
2203 ft

Lough
Mask

Killary Harbour
Leenane
Devilsmother
2096 ft
Maamtrasna
Ellen's Cabin
Leac
Derrypark
The Hare's
Garden
Maamtrasna
Bay
Béal a
tSnamha

Lough Nafooey
Currarevagh
1352 ft
Benbeg
2119 ft
Cloughbrack
Clonbur

See detail on opposite page
for this area

BOOK ONE

IRELAND

1

Ellen Rua O'Malley woke and immediately made the sign of the cross on herself. At the 'Amen' she pressed the thumb and forefinger of her right hand to her lips, then gently laid the hand in turn on the heads of her husband and three children. Unaware of her blessing, they continued to sleep – Michael, her husband, nearest the wall as was the custom; the children on the other side of the still-warm space she had occupied.

Her benedictions complete, Ellen moved quietly to the door of the small cabin and stepped out into the dawn light of the Maamtrasna Valley.

Roberteen Bawn, from his vantage point at the window of his parents' cabin, watched Ellen appear. His mouth slowly widened in anticipation. This was the fifth morning in a row that she was up and about while all others in the mountainside village slept. All, that is, except for Roberteen.

The boy was pleased with the illusion of intimacy conjured up by this notion. Ah, it was a bit of luck he'd had five mornings ago: if that mangy, flea-infested thing his father kept for a dog hadn't disturbed him with its persistent scratching he would have slept on like the rest of the village. Roberteen allowed himself a congratulatory smirk. From that first time he saw the red-haired woman slip away to the lake, he'd had the measure of it all. He'd known instinctively that she would repeat the ritual – rising each day with the sun as it appeared over the top of the mountain, brightening the dark waters of Lough Mask – and he would be ready, in his position by the window.

Roberteen pressed closer to the cold stone of the window ledge, trying to keep his breathing under control. If his father – or, worse still, his mother – woke and caught him spying on the wife of Michael O'Malley, he'd be dragged by the ear-lug down the mountain to the priest in Finny. A chilling image of Father O'Brien denouncing him from the pulpit entered the boy's mind. But dragged to Finny or no, he could not drag himself away from the window and the sight of the red-haired woman that filled his eyes.

Roberteen followed her every move as she straightened to full height on leaving her cabin. Good – he tensed with delight – she wasn't wearing the shawl. When her bare arms reached out to the sun it was as though the sun came to her, its light playing on the dark red hair that earned her the name Ellen Rua – red-haired Ellen. As she reached back with both hands to loose the tangled mass of hair, she turned her face in Roberteen's direction. He drew back sharply, and waited a few moments before inching his face to the window opening again. She was standing with her back to him, looking down the valley towards Lough Mask. He could see the white nape of her neck where she had pulled the hair forward over her shoulders. She mustn't have spotted me, he thought, rubbing his hands together.

At nineteen, Roberteen Bawn was ripe for marrying. His mother, Biddy, was forever telling him so. 'Oh! Roberteen,' she would say, 'if only you could get a girl like Michael O'Malley's wife – she'd knock some spark o' sense into you.' If only she knew!

Ah, with such a fine woman for a wife wouldn't he be the talk of the valley – and of Finny and Tourmakeady too – just like Michael O'Malley was.

Intent now on what the red-haired woman was doing, Roberteen's thoughts broke off from his mother's intentions for him. Ellen had not moved for some time now. She stood very still, gazing at the lake or perhaps at Tourmakeady far down along its western shore. Planning and scheming, most like; the red-haired women were notorious for it, and this one's head was full of ideas she'd got from her father, the Máistir.

He turned again to check on his parents. Still sleeping. Good, he was all right. When he turned to look at Ellen again, she had moved slightly. Suddenly it struck him. Sure, he should have known right away by the way she was standing so still, her hands joined. She was praying, that's what she was at!

This deflected him momentarily. It wasn't a right thing to be looking at her that way, and she praying. But, then again, maybe she wasn't praying, just looking at the lake and dreaming . . . dreaming of songs and poems and stories and all them things the Máistir had put into her head as a child.

His conscience thus salved, Roberteen remained where he was, watching.

Ellen felt the sun move down her body, searching her out, nourishing her with the warmth of its rays. It was difficult to pray this morning. It was always difficult on the mornings after the nights when she had turned to Michael, and, from deep in her throat, drawn out the soft, low words he loved to hear. It had been thus these past five mornings – ever since 15 August, Our Lady's Day. It was almost as if the two strands of her love – her deep spiritual love of God and her deep physical love for Michael – should be kept apart, should not touch each other.

She put all other thoughts from her mind, giving herself up instead to this wild place on the mountain. Before her the Mask spread out, its myriad islands sparkling like emeralds in the August morn. Though her village lay on an arm of the Mask which extended just inside Galway's northern border, Ellen nevertheless regarded herself as a Mayo woman – both her parents being of that county. The other arm of the Mask embraced the far side of the mountain, reaching back towards America Beag. Nothing there now but a few fields and empty cabins. The first one to go left back after the famine times of the 1820s, the Máistir had told her. Then the dollars from America came, and the next one left. One by one they followed like links in a chain, until they were all beyond in Boston or New York. So they called the home-place America Beag – 'Little America'. Strange, she thought, only the odd one had left from anywhere else about the place.

From across the lake she could hear the dogs of Derrypark yelping for their morning scraps, their hunger echoing over the still waters of the Mask. Her eye wandered on along the far shore towards Tourmakeady, where Pakenham the landlord lived.

She had seen him once at the fair in Leenane. He had smiled and nodded at her, struck by the way she stood out from the crowd. She, without acknowledging him, had moved on, but not before she had heard him bellow at one of his lackeys, 'That girl, who is she? No, not her, you fool – that one over there with the red hair.' She was gone from earshot before the lackey had time to reply.

Not wishing to darken this fine morning with thoughts of Sir Richard Pakenham, or any other landlord, she redirected her attention to the valley. The garden of paradise could not have been more beautiful than her valley of the lake, framed by the towering Partry Mountains. Her eyes took it all in, just as they had taken in the sudden movement in Roberteen's cabin. The thought of young Roberteen brought a smile to her blue-green eyes. The next time she came across him, she'd look him straight in the eye – let him know that she knew, the little whelp! And he not even the height of her shoulder. Some hard work drawing turf up the mountain would temper the rising sap in him. If Michael suspected Roberteen of spying on her, he would give the lad a thrashing and a half. But she wasn't about to tell Michael. She would deal with it in her own way, and in her own time.

She let her eyes rest upon the patch of land between the staggered row of cabins and the lake shore. She always saved this scene, the most important of all, until last. There, just below the *bóithrín*, were the lazy beds. Underneath these long raised mounds of earth grew the villagers' sole means of existence: the lumper potato. The growth was luxuriant – the best she'd seen in years. Down below the green stalks and the little white flowers bobbing this way and that, the tubers themselves were ripening and fattening, getting ready to be lifted.

Ellen praised this fruit of the furrow. She praised the dance of the morning sun. She praised the earth and all its gifts. This would be a good year. They would work hard and, maybe, with God's help, they would be able to put a little by after the rent had been paid.

She looked back at the cabin and thought of her sleeping family: Michael, one arm unconsciously reaching for her; the twins, her darling *cúplín Ellen beag* – 'a pair of little Ellens', as the villagers called them. Katie, a six-year-old bundle of fun and mischief, and next to her, or rather intertwined with her in a jumble of arms and legs, Mary. Quiet Mary, so different from Katie, but the two of them lying there as if they wanted to be one again. Patrick, two years older than Mary and Katie, slept a little ways off, as was proper for male children. If the girls were the reincarnation of

Ellen, then Patrick was a young Michael in the making: dark of hair and feature, typical of the 'Black Irish' found along Ireland's western shores – a living testament to the Spanish Armada's visit to Galway in 1588.

'Our children are our hope,' the Máistir used to say. Would her children be allowed to realize the hopes of their parents – the hope of release from the tyranny of landlords, the hope of freedom from English rule?

Aware that her thoughts had strayed from prayer, Ellen corrected herself and returned to the traditional format of petition and thanksgiving to the Creator. Then, pleased at having reconciled herself with her God, and pleased with the blessings He brought, she strode happily alongside the mountain stream to the point where it entered the elbow of the Mask.

As she bent over to splash some lake water on her face and neck, her thoughts once again turned to last night. How she loved the strength of Michael's arms when he pulled her to him; the smell of the turf and the heather in his hair after he had been a day at the mountain; his eyes, shining out through the dark at her, riveting her very soul.

At thirty, he was four years older than she. Was it ever nine years since they first met? She had just turned seventeen and the Máistir had brought her to the Pattern Day Fair at Leenane. She'd seen Michael watching her – unlike Roberteen, he'd done it openly, like a man should – and she had known at once he would come for her. Before the week was out he called to see her father. Ellen remembered the way the feelings stirred inside her on seeing him again. In no time they were married. She was scarcely over her eighteenth birthday when Patrick was born. Then came the double joy of Katie and Mary. And then nothing.

Though they still loved each other passionately, God had not blessed them with any more children. At first, this hadn't worried her unduly, but after a few years she began to wonder if she was barren; if it was a sign from God that she and Michael had loved too much.

She longed for a big family. As an only child, she had grown up wishing she'd been surrounded by brothers and sisters, like the other children in the village. At twenty-six she was still young enough – not like Biddy, who was too old to have any more after Roberteen was born. Children were a blessing from God and Ellen Rua wanted to be blessed again.

Eventually, somewhat against her better judgement, and without telling Michael, she had crossed the mountain to the hut of Sheela-na-Sheeoga. Sheela had delivered Ellen's first three children, but the valley women rarely went to her now. It was rumoured that she consorted with the fairy folk and changelings, hence the name Sheela-na-Sheeoga – Sheela who is of the fairies.

What Ellen learned from her secret visit to Sheela-na-Sheeoga served only to trouble her further. The old *cailleach* had asked some questions of a personal nature, laid her hands on Ellen's forehead and stomach, and then shuffled off into the darkest corner of her cabin. It sounded as though the old woman was mixing something, all the time a-muttering away in words which Ellen did not recognize. When Sheela-na-Sheeoga finally emerged from the darkness, she anointed Ellen on the forehead, on the tip of her tongue, and over her womb, with a strong-smelling herbal brew.

'Nothing ails you, *craythur*,' she said. 'You are young and you are strong. When the whitest flower blooms, so too will you bloom.' She had paused then and moved closer to whisper: 'But the whitest flower will become the blackest flower and you, red-haired Ellen, must crush its petals in your hand.'

Before Ellen could respond, the woman made a gesture of dismissal and said, 'Now, go home to your husband, Ellen Rua!' And with that she had ushered Ellen out of the cabin.

Once out of sight of Sheela-na-Sheeoga's hut, Ellen had spat out the vile-tasting mixture on her tongue and, with a handful of grass, cleansed the places where it stained her body. But the riddle the old *cailleach* had set her proved harder to get rid of; it had preyed on her mind ever since.

And now it seemed that all the old woman's doings with herbs and spells was just nonsense. Ellen's prayers remained unanswered. There was still no sign of a younger brother or sister for Patrick and the twins.

Now, as she sat looking for answers in the deep waters of the Mask, Ellen caught sight of her own reflection. Something about

8

her face seemed different. She bent down closer, peering into the mirror of the lake's surface, trying to find an explanation for the sense of trepidation and excitement she was feeling. This was more than the exhilaration of a fine August morning, the effects of the sun, the shimmering lake. Kneeling in the shallow water, she lowered her head until her hair draped over the Mask's surface. The breeze rose. The water flicked at her face and tendrils of hair floated about her, red-eeled, seeking release. Then the breeze died and the waters settled to their previous calm. Still Ellen waited and watched, face to her face's image. Seeing into herself.

First, it was a slow realization, sweeping silently over her body as the early dawn swept in over the valley – unnoticed until it was there. Then, with growing excitement, she knew – the face in the water knew – that this morning, after six long years, Michael's seed had at last taken within her.

She was carrying his child.

'*Moladh le Dia*,' she whispered to the radiant face in the water. '*Moladh le Dia*,' she repeated before lifting her face and her wet hair heavenwards.

She remained thus, silent in thanksgiving, for a few moments. Not daring to be too overjoyed, she resolved not to tell Michael yet. She'd keep it to herself until the month was out.

Roberteen Bawn watched transfixed as Ellen turned to make her way back up from the lake. Drops of water glistened in the sun as they fell from her hair. The loose-fitting shift she wore now clung to the contours of her body, accentuating each movement. Yet she seemed not to notice as she paused by the side of the stream, silently raising her head to heaven.

While his mouth and throat were dry with excitement, the unruly mop of blond hair which framed Roberteen's face and forehead was ringed by beads of perspiration. 'A curse on the woman!' he muttered under his breath as he wiped the sweat from his eyes. 'She's the very divil!' Gripping the outside of the window ledge, the boy hauled himself up until his legs dangled above the cabin floor. Now he would be able to see her better.

Too late, he heard the swish behind him as his mother's broomstick whacked squarely against his frenzied backside.

'Get down outta there, you dirty little blackguard!' Biddy yelled, while laying into her son with the broom. 'I'll give you spyin' on that poor woman! 'Tis at your prayers you should be' – she landed another whack on him – 'droolin' over another man's wife!' Again the broom found its mark, harder now, to emphasize the seriousness of his lust. 'Go on, get out o' the sight o' me, or I'll not be responsible for you!' she threatened, making one last lunge at Roberteen, who was already half out the door and headed for the mountain.

But his irate mother knew she was too late. Roberteen Bawn, her fair-haired son, had already sinned over the red-haired woman.

David Moore, curator of Dublin's Botanic Gardens, marvelled as the sunlight fell upon the vibrant reds and yellows of the rose gardens, then shimmered across the lily pond. His daily rounds, notebook in hand, were a constant source of delight. What better position in life could one aspire to? Working under God's airy light, bounty and beauty on every side, entrusted with the pursuit of scientific knowledge and the furtherance of God's work in creating new hybrids of plant life. Fine gentlemen and their ladies, out taking the air in his gardens, nodded to him, acknowledging his handiwork, and his treatises on matters botanical had won plaudits – even from Kew.

This morning he had every reason to be pleased: his roses were abundant in their growth and in the full bloom of botanical health – no sign of greenfly. He made a note for McArdle, his outdoor foreman, to prune them back harder next year. Turning the page, he scribbled a reminder to write to Pakenham at Tourmakeady in response to a letter he had received from that quarter. Pakenham wanted to know how to deal with blemishes afflicting the pride of his extensive rose gardens, a *Rosa chinensis* – the Jenkinstown Rose, forever immortalized by the poet Thomas Moore in his song, 'The Last Rose of Summer'. The curator thought it likely that Pakenham's problem was a product of the poor soil in the West, but he would consult his reference books and consider it further before replying. Moore's own specimen was flourishing and showed neither spot nor blemish of any description.

Satisfied with the condition of the rose gardens, Moore moved on to the vegetable 'patch'. Every kind of vegetable known to be capable of cultivation in the Irish climate was grown here. As curator, he carefully monitored growth under varying weather and tillage conditions, and conducted experiments with sulphides and phosphates to ward off diseases.

'God's day, Mr Moore,' he heard, and turned.

'Ah, yes a good morning, indeed it is, Canon,' he replied to the sprightly old rector who frequented the gardens on a daily basis.

'My most important appointment, as I always say. A good constitutional, in the company of the Lord, combined with a visit to my faithful congregation *botanicus* in your fine gardens . . . That's the thing, eh, Moore?'

'Yes, Canon,' the curator replied unenthusiastically.

The good Canon Prufrock, having delivered himself of his prescription for a healthy life, began to saunter away, muttering to himself in Latin. But his ruminations were interrupted by an anguished cry behind him. Alarmed, he turned to see the curator bent as if in pain.

'What is it, man, what's the matter?' he asked, hurrying back to Moore's side.

'It's here! It's here!' The curator gesticulated, unable to find words to describe what he had seen.

The old cleric stooped to examine what manner of dangerous, disease-carrying creature had caused such agitation in the taciturn Scot.

'Why, I see nothing there except the makings of fine healthy potatoes glistening with God's morning dew!' he pronounced, adopting a tone which indicated that he thought Moore had taken leave of his senses.

'That is no dew! Look at it – feel it. That, Canon, is the blight. Have you not read of it in the journals? Introduced from America, it has wiped out the potato crop from the Low Countries to Northern France. Now it is here in Ireland – and may God have mercy on us all!'

'Will it be of . . . of such a consequence?'

'Consequence! If it takes root here in Ireland, this murrain will wipe out the entire potato crop in a matter of months. With two million acres – one third of all tilled land – given over to its cultivation, well over half the population is heavily dependent on the crop. Of those, some three million souls rely on it totally. This could be the biggest disaster Ireland, or the Empire itself, has ever experienced.'

'But what is to be done? Is there nothing you . . . ?'

Moore had not registered until then the awful burden which now rested upon his shoulders. As curator of the Royal Botanic Gardens it was natural that he should be looked to for a solution to this calamity. Sounding more composed than he felt, he began to outline a plan of action: 'Firstly, I must alert the Lord Lieutenant. He, no doubt, will inform London with utmost expedition so that the Government can mobilize its resources to avert a catastrophe. Here, in the gardens, we must immediately find a cure. We must prevent this blight from taking root in Ireland, whatever the effort, whatever the cost.'

'God will provide,' Canon Prufrock said tremulously. 'God will provide,' he repeated. And then, almost *sotto voce*, he added: 'If it be His will.'

Slowly and deliberately, David Moore opened his notebook and recorded the first occurrence in Ireland of a blight which was to leave a trail of death and desolation, and forever change the lives of Ellen O'Malley and her little family:

Late Blight – Lumper Potatoes
Royal Botanic Gardens, Dublin.
Twentieth day of August, 1845.

As Ellen walked back up towards the village, an unseasonably cold chill swept in from the lake, catching her about the neck and shoulders. She shivered, and for a fleeting moment the old *cailleach*'s strange prophecy echoed through her mind. But Sheela-na-Sheeoga's words were drowned out by the *rí-rá* coming from her neighbours' cabin. When young Roberteen emerged, scurrying up the mountainside like a scalded cat, she laughed and relaxed. Then smiled, thinking all the more of her new condition.

2

As Ellen re-entered the cabin, Michael was rising. He watched her incline slightly to negotiate the door and the fall of her breasts brought back to him all the urgency of last night. Framed in the doorway, the sparkling August morning behind her, she seemed to glow with light and life.

Silently Michael gave thanks for this woman, the most beautiful he had ever seen. Tall, like the warrior queens of old, she carried herself differently from other women, her bare feet clenching the ground, knowing it was of her and she of it.

In her face strength as well as beauty was held. Her high, well-formed forehead 'a sign of intelligence' according to village lore. And those eyes – it was like looking into the waters of the Mask: a mixture of green and blue, forever drawing you in, deeper and deeper. Her lips were wide and generous, not thin-lipped from whispering about the place like some of the other women. Sometimes she laughed a little laugh when he kissed those lips. He never knew whether this was encouragement or shyness at his advances. Whatever it was, it made him all the more fervent in his desire for her. And when she laughed fully and threw back her head, revealing the mysteries of her mouth and throat, then he was completely lost to this woman – his red-haired Ellen.

She caught his eyes, and, knowing what he was thinking, cast her gaze to where the children were still sleeping.

'*Dia dhuit*,' he said.

'*Dia's Muire dhuit, a stór*,' she whispered, returning the customary greeting and blessing.

'It's time to wake the little ones, Ellen,' he said softly.

At her gentle touch, the still-intertwined twins were up in an instant, tumbling into her waiting arms.

'*A Mhamaí, a Mhamaí*, what will we do this morning?' they insisted simultaneously.

'Wait a minute now,' *Mamaí* prompted, 'the first thing we do every morning is . . . ?'

'The prayers, *a Mhamaí*. But what then?' said they, undeflected by their mother's question.

'Sshh now, and kneel down. Patrick, are you ready?'

Patrick rubbed the sleep from his eyes with his knuckles. He did not go to her as his sisters did, but she reached over and put one arm around him drawing him towards her. He was growing, she thought. He gave her a quick look and a sleepy smile, and she nodded back understandingly. They didn't need to say much between them. It was the same with Michael – more the silence than the spoken.

Together they all knelt down and, for the second time that day, Ellen crossed herself. Then she led them in the first of the morning prayers while the children, somewhat at sixes and sevens, joined in sleepily behind her. Katie, as always, elbowed Mary at every mention of the name of the Mother of God. This drew a similar elbowed response from Mary, coupled with, 'Sure, you're only jealous 'cos there's no prayers for Katies.' Ellen, fixing them with her most baleful glare, ordered Katie to lead the Hail Mary. This Katie did reluctantly, annoyed at having to give praise to her twin sister's name. 'Now, Mary,' Ellen said when Katie had finished, 'you will say the Act of Contrition.' Mary considered that the Act of Contrition applied more to Katie than to her, and in consequence gave it plenty of emphasis for her sister's benefit.

Some semblance of prayerfulness was restored when it came to Patrick's turn. He was getting to the age where 'O Angel of God, my guardian dear . . .' seemed childish. Katie and Mary might still need guardian angels, but he was big enough to go to the top of the mountain by himself. Nevertheless for a quiet life he fell in with the part required of him.

Finally Michael concluded the morning prayers with the petition: 'Keep us from all sickness and harm this day for ever, and ever, Amen.' Then, having started the day off properly, he went outside – 'To see what class of a day is in it.'

The others, meanwhile, had their own rituals to attend to.

Patrick cleared the night ashes from over the glowing turf and fetched fresh sods for Ellen to show him how to build up a new fire. Now he watched as she took the longer, narrower pieces of turf and stood them on end, balancing the top edges against each other for support, so that they encircled the smouldering embers of yesterday's fire.

'Always leave plenty of space between them for the breeze to get in and fan the flame,' she advised. 'Fire means life – never let the fire go out. When the fire is gone, so too are those who tended it.'

Patrick was too young to fully understand what his mother was telling, of what it meant to her to pass on the old ways she had learnt from the Máistir. But he knew from the way she held her face close to his and fixed him with those eyes that it was an important thing she spoke.

Mary and Katie, meanwhile, were up at the spring. For protection of both spring and playful water-carriers, Michael had laid two flat slabs of stone over the rock where the spring emerged. Forgetting the task at hand, Mary and Katie now lay on those slabs studying their reflections, fascinated by their sameness, and trying to find some feature in one that was not replicated in the other. Eventually a shout from the cabin below reminded them what they were there for: to bring back a pot of water. So they scampered back down – the lift in the land now being in their favour – pulling the pot this way and that between them, and spilling half the water in the process.

Thus began their day, like most every other day in the valley.

Then it was time for 'the Lessons'.

Ellen's love of learning came from her father. A former priest, he had left the priesthood when he fell in love with her mother, Cáit – a great scandal, and still whispered about in the valley. Subsequently he had become a hedge-school teacher or 'Máistir'. At his knee Ellen had learned to read not only in Gaelic but also in English. She had picked up a smattering of Latin, too. And he had taught her the history of Ireland, and the Kings and Queens of England, and told her of the far-off places in the world where the people spoke strange languages and followed strange customs.

In the evenings they would sit across the hearth from each other and he would pass down to her some of the old *sean-nós* traditions

– the songs, stories and poems from the Bardic times. 'The spoken tradition. It comes from my father's father's time, and his father before him. Keep it alive, Ellen, *a stór*,' he would say. 'Hand it down to your children, as I hand it down to you today, child. It is what we are, what formed us.'

Love of tradition and love of education. They were his great legacies to her. 'Come what may,' he would tell her, 'tradition and education will always stand to a person. It's tradition that keeps the people strong and true to themselves, and it's the education that will free them in the end. Never forget that.'

But her father's greatest gift to her was love. She remembered how he would reach out his hand to her across the hearth's space between them. And when she went to him he would smile and clasp her to him. His hand would then find her back just below the shoulder blades and caress her there in small circles of comfort. Then she would hear him softly murmur into her hair, 'Ellen, *mo stóirín, mo stóirín rua, mo Ellen rua*.'

Now it was time for the education of her own children.

'Tell us again about Cromwell and the Roundheads, and when he drove all the people "to hell or to Connacht",' said Patrick, showing signs of following his father's nationalistic tendencies.

'No! Do the lesson about our cousin "Granuaile",' Katie piped up. Her choice – Grace O'Malley, the chieftain's daughter who, three hundred years earlier, had ruled the Connacht coastline from Clew Bay, dispensing with her enemies as quickly as her husbands – suggested a liking for the idea of independent womanhood. Katie particularly enjoyed hearing how, when summoned to meet with Queen Elizabeth I of England, Granuaile had considered it to be a meeting of equals.

'And what about you, Mary – what would you like?' prompted Ellen, knowing that the quieter twin would never put forward what she wanted, being content to let Katie make the running.

'I like the story of the children who were turned into swans,' Mary said.

How like Mary it was to pick 'The Children of Lir', the most childlike and the saddest of all the great legends of Ireland.

'All right, then. Patrick, fetch me the *traithneens*,' Ellen instructed. Patrick darted outside and was back almost immediately with the three blades of grass he had plucked. He handed these to his mother, who put them behind her back, rearranging the stalks in her hand as she did so.

'Patrick, you first – draw a *traithneen*,' she said, presenting the three blades of grass to him.

Patrick made his choice. Next it was Mary's turn, and then all eyes were on Katie as she whisked the remaining blade of grass from Ellen's hand.

'Who has it? Who has the shortest *traithneen*?' cried Katie, wanting to know immediately if it was she who would get to choose the subject for this morning's lesson.

'I have it!' Patrick shouted excitedly.

Cromwell had drawn the shortest straw.

Ellen waited for the children to settle, then began her story: 'Before Cromwell's time, two hundred years ago, the Catholics who lived in Ireland owned three-quarters of the land. But the King of England, who was a Protestant, wanted to take all the good land away and give it to the landed gentry. They were the descendants of people who had invaded Ireland and settled here, and they were Protestants too. When they were good and did what the King asked, he gave them big castles and lands in Ireland' – Ellen could see Patrick bristling with questions, but she continued – 'and took it away from the Catholics who didn't want to obey him.'

'But why didn't they fight him?' Patrick couldn't hold back any more.

'Well, they did. And there were a lot of Catholics – more than there were Protestants. Then, over from England came a big army . . .' She paused before posing the question: 'Led by whom?'

'Cromwell!' shouted Katie.

'Yes, that's right, Katie. Now, Oliver Cromwell was a bad and wicked man and he hated the Catholics. He beheaded King Charles first, and then came to Ireland to kill the King's supporters here, the Royalists. They were mostly Catholics. But Protestants, too.' Ellen interrupted herself for another question: 'What were Cromwell's soldiers called?'

'Roundheads.' This time Patrick asserted his pre-eminence in matters military.

'Yes, Patrick, good. They were called Roundheads because of the big round helmets they wore on their heads to protect them from the swords of the Irish. So, Cromwell and his army of Roundheads marched through Ireland, and they went into the villages and murdered all the men and the women, and even little boys and girls. Everyone was killed.'

Ellen could hear the intake of breath, as three sets of eyes widened at this terrible telling.

'That was a very bad thing to do to all the little children,' Mary ventured, horrified at the thought. 'And them not doing any harm at all – being only small like me and Katie.'

'Yes it was, *a stóirín*,' Ellen said gently, 'and the reason Cromwell did that was because he was afraid that if he killed just the big people, then the children, when they grew up, would remember this and make a big army to kill him back. Also Cromwell wanted to get the land, so he had to clear out all the people who held the land. That's why the Roundheads knocked down the poor people's houses and burnt their crops – so that nothing was left, no trace of them at all. It was as if they had never been there. Then Cromwell sent word that this would be the fate of any Catholics who stayed on their lands. He wanted to drive them over here to the mountains and the sea, over to the poor lands of the West. "To hell or to Connacht" he said he'd send the people – and he did just that, the devil.'

'That's why we're here on this mountain, with only a little *bitteen* of land and bog to keep us,' said Patrick, repeating a favourite phrase of his father's.

'That's right, Patrick,' Ellen replied. 'That's quite right. The old people – *seanathair mo sheanathair*, "my grandfather's grandfather" – were driven back to this valley, to the rocks and the stones, by Cromwell. So always remember this . . .'

Three heads craned forward.

'It's all to do with the land – everything goes back to the land.'

'And he hung all the priests too!' Patrick was warming to the subject now.

'He did,' said Ellen. 'He put a price on their heads and the "Shawn a Saggarts" would hunt them down for money. Then Cromwell would hang them in front of their own people. One of his generals once said of a place that there was "neither water enough to drown a man, nor a tree to hang him from, nor soil enough to bury him in." Now, wasn't that an awful thing to be thinking? They say Cromwell was the most hated man ever to set foot in Ireland, and the people haven't forgotten – he still is.'

While Patrick would have listened for hours to stories of Roundheads and hangings and the like, and was waiting to hear tales of his own particular hero of the times, Patrick Sarsfield, Katie and Mary were beginning to tire of the foul deeds of Oliver Cromwell. Their tiredness coincided with the sound of Michael returning, so Ellen cut short the lesson with a promise that tomorrow they would draw the *traithneen* for Granuaile or the Children of Lir.

As she ushered the children outside, she wondered to herself whether she and Michael might now have been 'strong farmers' on the fine rolling plains of County Meath, had Oliver Cromwell not driven their forefathers to plough the rocks and bogland of Connacht.

She wondered how their lives might have been if the Roundhead leader had never installed Pakenham's forefathers at Tourmakeady Lodge.

When the children were out of earshot she muttered to herself, 'Cromwell – a curse on his name.'

Ellen had decided that she would tell Michael she was carrying his child on the homeward journey from the Sunday Mass. She always felt uplifted after partaking of the Eucharist, but this Sunday would be extra special because the God of all creation would be within her, side by side with her unborn child.

A month had gone by since that morning at the edge of the Mask when she had discovered she was pregnant. Everything had gone well with her since then, and more and more she felt the surge of new life strong in her. For some reason she had fallen into the habit of thinking about the new baby as 'she'. It wasn't that she particularly wanted a girl; another pair of labourer's hands to look after them in later years would be equally welcome. Only God could decide, she told herself – but still, she just knew the baby was a girl.

There was no breakfast to be prepared – they would not break the fast before receiving Holy Communion – so Ellen was able to spend longer than usual getting the girls ready. She started with Katie and Mary, giving their hair one hundred strokes each with the silver and bone brush that the Máistir had given Cáit as a wedding gift. After her mother's death, the brush had passed to Ellen. She never used it without recalling her father, reminiscing with that faraway look in his eyes:

'I would sit there of an evening while the shadows moved across the lake and the *meannán aerach* would swoop down through the sky, his wings making the noise of a young goat, and I would watch your mother as she stroked her hair one hundred times with that brush, drawing it through the strands till they were like gold-red silk of the finest ever seen. And she all the while a-crooning in the old style, a soft *suantraí*. She never counted the strokes at all, but she was never one more nor less, because many's the time I counted them myself,' he would recall, longing for those days to be back.

Now, as she stroked Katie's hair with her mother's brush, Ellen felt part of something, conscious of her role in carrying on and affirming the simple beauty of the lives of those who had gone before.

Patrick had dressed himself, and was now lacing up a pair of old boots which Michael had worn as a boy. Ellen smiled at this handing down between father and son. Yet another connection between then and now; crossings and linkings, always there, always reminding.

When she had finished with the children, Ellen took down her good red petticoat and dusted it off. Not a bright red – more the colour of autumn leaves. Surprisingly, it did not clash with her hair but merely added to the radiation of colour which seemed to encircle her. She had already brushed her wild *dos* of hair into some semblance of order and it now cascaded, loosely bound, at the back of her neck. Finally she draped her shawl – dark green, as her eyes – over her shoulders. This would cover her head on the journey to Finny and for the duration of Mass.

Michael, his Sunday cap perched jauntily over his black curls, watched approvingly as his family emerged from the cabin. Some of their older neighbours had already begun the trek, and they could see them in twos and threes negotiating the steep path that ran alongside Crucán na bPáiste – the burial place of the children.

To their right lay the dark beauty of Lough Nafooey, and above it the mountains, like steps in the September sky running all the way back to Connemara. Ahead of them, Bóithrín a tSléibhe wound its way over the crest of the mountain to Finny – the village on the banks of the river which connected the Mask and Lough Nafooey. Everything bound together, thought Ellen, fitting so well. Just like a family.

'Katie, come back here!'

Ellen's reverie was broken by Michael's warning shout as the child careered dangerously close to the side of the mountain. For a moment, Katie looked hurt. Then, breaking into a big smile, she raced back to her mother.

'I just wanted to get these for you,' she said, gifting to Ellen some purple and yellow wildflowers she had snatched from the edge of the mountain.

'Thank you, *a stóirín!*' Ellen smiled at Katie's burst of generosity. 'Now, take my hand. You, too, Mary. Hurry up now, we mustn't be late for Mass.'

As they made their descent, Father O'Brien emerged from the church. He looked up at the mountain track, seeing his people gathering in to hear the Word of God.

Among the black-clad figures of the old men and women, the sun seemed to pick out the tall figure of Ellen Rua O'Malley as, hand in hand with her twin daughters, she hastened down towards the church. Father O'Brien wondered what fate awaited them, given the news he must shortly break.

Deep in thought, the priest went back inside to make his final preparations for the Mass. Since Archbishop MacHale had stationed him at Clonbur, he had come to look forward to the one Sunday in a month when he said Mass here at the little church-of-ease in Finny. He loved this place and its people. Here in the midst of the mountains and the lakes, he heard the voice of God much more clearly than in the suffocating cloisters of Maynooth. And the French professors of theology there had taught him little compared to the peasants hereabouts with their humility, their gratitude for the precious few gifts bestowed on them, and their forbearance and dignity in the face of an unrelenting struggle for survival. On the Mass Sunday they flocked to the little Finny church. Some walked the near distance from Kilbride, but others faced more difficult journeys: skirting the edge of Lough Mask round from Glentrague, or climbing Bóithrín a tSléibhe up and over the mountain from Maamtrasna.

He wondered what they thought of him, the 'new priest'. This would be his biggest test so far, and he did not want to fail them. But how was he to tell the peasants and mountainside cottiers who made up his flock of the news he had learned on his recent visit to the Archbishop in Tuam? What hope had he to offer them, what alternatives? None, he thought, except faith in the goodness of an all-providing God. Or, failing that, hope in 'thy kingdom come'.

At least he could advise them to dig early rather than waiting until October to lift the potatoes.

Even so, maybe he was already too late.

When they reached the church there was still fifteen minutes to go till Mass. As was customary, Ellen, the two girls and Patrick – the latter with some resistance – went and knelt on the right-hand side of the aisle, while Michael, having doffed his cap, joined the men on the left-hand side.

Ellen thought that Father O'Brien looked a bit on edge as he took his place in the pulpit. He was nice, this new young priest from Clonbur. He had time for everyone, and he wasn't all fire and brimstone as some of the clergy were. He had a holy face which shone with an inner light throughout the Mass and particularly at the Consecration. His hair was dark brown and neatly kept, in the way of clerics, but his eyebrows were the darkest she ever saw, darker even than Michael's. She was tempted to look across the church to where Michael was, but knew she mustn't – the old ones would be watching her, and she mustn't give scandal by looking across the aisle.

'*Gloria in excelsis Deo*,' Father O'Brien intoned. Ellen liked the way he said the Latin. It was as if his Western brogue left him when he spoke the chosen language of the Church.

The Máistir had studied Latin in the seminary at Maynooth and had taught her enough that she could follow most of the Mass. But she thought it a cold language. Latin didn't have the life, the earthiness of the Gaelic tongue and was only slightly ahead of 'the narrow language of the Sasanach' – as the valley people referred to spoken English – which had neither poetry nor music to it.

The sermon had started. She had better listen instead of wandering in her mind. Father O'Brien had a habit of picking out a member of his congregation and fixing his eye on them when he spoke.

In fact, Ellen needn't have worried. Father O'Brien had come to the conclusion that eye-contact might work in the cities, but the people here were generally so shy and in awe of him that it just served to embarrass them. During last month's Sunday Mass in Finny, while preaching on the Sixth Commandment – 'Thou shalt not commit adultery' – he had happened to catch the eye of Roberteen Bawn. The boy had looked as if he would bolt from the church. And he just a harmless enough young fellow, unlikely to be up to anything much under his mother's hawk-like eye. Yet Father O'Brien was in no doubt that his sermon had seriously unsettled young Roberteen. Today he would be more circumspect in the use of his eyes.

He spoke to them in Irish: 'Today, my dear people, instead of the usual sermon, I have something to read to you.'

Ellen began to feel uneasy as the priest began. Then, as the sermon continued, all the feelings of warmth, life and light which had filled her that morning seemed to slowly ebb away.

'The Archbishop has, in his wisdom, decreed that all priests in the Archdiocese should today lay the following information before the faithful. The Archbishop cautions against panic, but because of the dependence of so many of the people upon the potato crop he considers it prudent to advise you of the information to hand.'

At these words, there was much shuffling of nervous feet in the church. Father O'Brien pressed on in the same emotionless voice, careful not to betray the unease he felt inside:

'While there is no conclusive proof of the arrival of the potato blight in Ireland, the advice the Archbishop gives, having consulted with some experts in this area, is that it would be wise not to delay the digging of the crop until October but to lift the potatoes immediately.'

He paused to let the message sink in.

'I would therefore suggest to you that when you return home from this Mass, you should immediately commence digging your crops. The Archbishop hereby grants you all a special dispensation so that this work can be done today.'

This was serious, thought Ellen, as frightened whisperings filled the church. To work on a Sunday was to bring seven years' bad luck; it went against the strict code of the Catholic Church regarding the observance of the Sabbath. She drew the children closer to her. The rest of the congregation looked as fearful as she felt: wives and children turned in their seats, seeking reassurance from husbands and fathers across the church.

Father O'Brien raised his voice to make it heard above the commotion as he read from the copied extract given to him by the Archbishop: 'The *Dublin Evening Post* of ninth September reports that: "There can be no question at all of the very remarkable failure in the United States, and with regard to Holland, Flanders, and France, we have already abundant evidence of the wide spread of what we cannot help calling a calamity."'

The priest read on, translating into Irish as he went: '"It is in the densely packed communities of Europe that the failure would be alarming and in no country more, or so much, than our own."' A deathly silence descended on the church. Father O'Brien wet his lips with his tongue before continuing: '"But happily there is no ground for any apprehension of the kind in Ireland."' Ellen, along with the rest of the congregation, exhaled a sigh of relief. '"We believe that there was never a more abundant potato crop in Ireland than there is at present, and none which it will be more likely to secure."'

'So you see,' Father O'Brien concluded, 'the picture is not yet clear. On the one hand, if you lift the lumpers now, they will not be fully grown. On the other hand, if you do not lift them for another month, they may be diseased.

'Considering everything, the Archbishop's advice is as follows: when Mass has ended, you should go immediately and dig your potatoes with all haste. Now, we ask the all-knowing God for His guidance and, if it be His Divine will, that the crops might be saved. May God bless the work.'

With these words Father O'Brien returned to the liturgy of the Mass.

As the people filed silently out of the church, Ellen had a bad feeling about what she had just heard. The priest was very nervous. Maybe he knew more. Was he holding something back so as not to frighten the people? As soon as they got home she would go into the fields with the children to help Michael lift the potatoes.

On the way out, she paused to cross herself with holy water. A figure in black stood waiting within the corner of the porch. Waiting for her. With a start she realized it was Sheela-na-Sheeoga.

'The blessings of God and His Holy Mother and the Infant Jesus, be on you, Ellen Rua. I see you are in bloom,' she said in a half-whisper.

Ellen made to move on. She did not want Michael and the children – or the priest for that matter – to see her talking to the old *cailleach*. But Sheela caught her by the arm.

'Be not hastening away from me now, Ellen Rua. Wasn't it yourself who was quick to hasten to me over the mountain, not a woman's time ago?' she said, her voice rising. 'Remember the words I spoke to you then: "When the whitest flower blooms, so too will you bloom." Go now with your husband, and lift the fruit of the whitest flower.'

Ellen looked at the crease-lined face beside her. Of course – how could she not have seen it? The whitest flower was the flower that blossomed on the lazy beds. It was so obvious, she had missed it.

'But the whitest flower will be the blackest flower,' Sheela-na-Sheeoga continued. 'And you, red-haired Ellen, must crush its petals in your hand.' She paused, gauging the effect of her words. 'Remember and heed it well, Ellen Rua.'

Ellen instinctively drew her hands about her body where her unborn child was. She could read nothing from Sheela-na-Sheeoga's face; the old woman's eyes stared back at her, ashen and grey, like a dead fire. Ellen was about to ask what the riddle meant, and if it had something to do with the news they had just heard, when she heard footsteps approaching. She turned her head for a moment and when she looked back again Sheela-na-Sheeoga had vanished. In her place stood Father O'Brien.

'Was it waiting to speak with me you were, Mrs O'Malley?'

'No, Father, thank you. Just thinking a while, wondering what's to become of us all.'

'I don't know . . .' Father O'Brien said. 'We must pray and put our faith in the hands of the Lord, He will provide.' Then, echoing the words of the old *cailleach*, he advised her: 'Best go home now, Ellen, and take up the potatoes with your husband.'

Michael was waiting outside. He knew by the way she pulled the shawl closer about herself that something troubled her, but Ellen said nothing.

Eventually she broke the silence: 'Michael, do you think that the priest is right about the potatoes – that they'll be bad, that the bad times are surely coming?'

'Well if they are itself, I still don't think it's a right thing the priest said, to lift them today, on a Sunday.'

Ellen looked at him, understanding his reservations about 'Sunday work' – a taboo that went back generations.

'Well, if it troubles you, Michael, then we'll wait. The children and myself will gather for you in the morning,' she said.

They were approaching the crest of the hill. It was there, with their valley opening out before them, that Ellen had planned to tell Michael about the child. But now the time seemed all wrong. The bad news from the priest, the meeting with Sheela-na-Sheeoga, had created a sense of foreboding that was somehow bound up with her being pregnant. To talk about her pregnancy under these circumstances would, she felt, be harmful to the baby in some way. By her silence, therefore, she was protecting her child.

Suddenly, as if coming face to face with a force beyond which they could not pass, they both stopped walking, stunned at the sight below them in the valley.

There in the fields were the men, women and children who had left the church before them. All furiously digging for the lumpers, pulling them up by the stalks, shaking them free of the earth, twisting and turning them – until as one they joined in a great mad shout that rose up to greet Ellen and Michael where they stood:

'They're safe! They're safe! Praise be to God, the potatoes are safe!'

3

Next morning Ellen was up early, as usual, only to find that Michael was ahead of her. Quickly she tended to the children. The Lessons would have to wait. There was more important work to be done.

It was a bright September morn, with just the hint of autumn chill in it – a good day for the fields. Together they set out for the dig. Michael carried his *slane* – a kind of half-spade used for digging out potatoes. If you were skilful enough in its use you could lift the tubers without damaging the next cluster along the lazy bed. Ellen and the three children each carried a *sciathóg* – a basket made of interlaced sally rods. The lumpers would be placed in this rough sieve and shaken to remove any excess clay.

They weren't the only ones out in the fields. Obviously, despite the Archbishop's dispensation, some in the village had decided to respect the old ways and not work on the day of rest. But they were in the minority: in the fields adjacent to their own, Ellen and Michael could see where the lazy beds had been dug the previous day.

They were fortunate, she thought, having the two acres. Most of their neighbours had only the 'bare acre'. An acre, even with a good crop of potatoes, could not keep a family of five for a year. May, June and July – the 'meal months' – would be especially hard. The previous year's crop would have been eaten, and it was too soon for the new harvest. Families who had no savings and couldn't find alternative work to see them through were forced to get credit to buy meal or potatoes. She would have hated that. The credit came from 'strong farmers' who had saved money, and who then charged a pretty penny in interest to borrowers. These *scullogues*, as the people called them, would not lend money to those who were most in need of it, for the very poor would never have the means by which loans could be made good. The destitute had to rely instead on the support of their neighbours, or go begging.

Michael was already at the first lazy bed and had sunk the *slane* down into the earth under the potatoes. He carefully levered up a slaneful of potatoes and clay. Nervously Ellen watched him bend and tug the plant from the loosened earth. He shook it vigorously and then wiped away the remaining clods of clay from the tubers, examining them intently. Then he turned the plant in his hand, studying the three or four potatoes which dangled from it. He turned to her as she approached.

'*Buíochas le Dia* – they're sound.' He held the plant out to her. 'Here, look for yourself.'

Ellen examined it carefully. There was no sign of disease anywhere to be seen. She looked at him, the smile creasing her face. He caught her by the shoulders, the laughter of relief wild in him, and brought her to her knees with him. Together, there on the earth amongst the lazy beds, their food for the year to come now safe, they thanked God for His bounty.

Michael dug while Ellen, Patrick, Katie and Mary gathered and inspected. The lumpers were smaller than usual because of being lifted earlier. This was not unexpected, and therefore no cause for alarm. At one point, Katie raised a scare when she yelled out, '*a Mhamaí*, this one has black on it!' But it turned out to be just an exceptionally large 'eye' on the potato.

What an ugly plant the lumper was, Ellen thought to herself. Squat and uneven in shape with what looked like smaller versions of itself stuck on here and there like little misshapen heads. The lumper wasn't sweet like the cup and the apple variety of potatoes the Máistir had once brought back from Castlebar. But it was floury when boiled well, and, most important of all, it was hardy and grew in abundance.

While she waited for the children to return from emptying their baskets, Ellen plucked one of the tiny flowers from an upturned potato stalk. She had never before taken much notice of the 'whitest flower'. Like the grass in the field, it was just there from year to year. Now, however, it had assumed a new significance in her life. She twirled the stem slowly between her thumb and forefinger. It was quite beautiful. Fresh and frail, its tiny petals, white as snow, formed a perfect ring around the yellow centre. Strange, she thought, the stark contrast between the beauty of the flower and its ugly fruit.

What secret did this blossom hold for her and her unborn baby? What harm could lie in this tiny flower? In keeping with the old woman's riddle, she crushed one of the petals between her fingers and brought it to her nose. Ugh – its smell was not at all sweet; nothing like the smell of a flower. It had no perfume, but smelt dank and unclean, like an uncooked potato. She dropped it to the ground and rubbed her fingers in the earth to cleanse them of its stickiness.

'The whitest flower will be the blackest flower,' Ellen said to herself, wondering.

All day they toiled in the field until twilight fell over the valley, hushing the sounds of the day. Michael did most of the digging, with Patrick being given an occasional turn at 'man's work'. Gathering, inspecting and ferrying the baskets full of potatoes to the cabin was woman's work, in Patrick's eyes. But he understood the urgency of what they were at and pitched in willingly, doing whatever was required.

On one of the trips to the cabin, cradling the heavy *sciathóg* between her hip and the crook of her arm, Ellen caught sight of the fair head of their neighbour's son coming towards her. A mischievousness took hold of her. She set her basket on the ground and waited for Roberteen Bawn to draw near.

'*Dia dhuit*,' she bade him, friendly-like.

'*Dia's Muire dhuit*,' he returned, happy to see her.

He was about to continue walking past her, abashed at finding himself so close to the object of his desires, when she said, 'Wait a minute, Roberteen.'

He turned towards her, his fair skin pinking at the cheekbones. Was the woman going to shame him here in front of the whole village?

'Roberteen, I wouldn't be stopping you from your work,' she continued, an air of earnestness about her, 'but it's long the day has been, and the cradle of lumpers here getting heavier with each passing hour. Would you go by Michael and tell him I need his help – these lumpers are the weight of rocks?'

Roberteen looked at Ellen warily. He had consciously avoided conversation with Michael since the morning his mother had caught him spying on Ellen. This is some scheme of hers, he thought. The basket wasn't that heavy, especially for a fine strong woman like her. Sure, weren't the children carrying them up all the time. What was it she was up to? She must have told her husband about him watching her and now she was after sending him to Michael for a thrashing. She had that smile on her – full of divilment, she was. He looked at the creel of potatoes on the ground. It dawned on him then – a way out.

'Sure, Ellen, isn't Michael busy lifting the lumpers from that fine field you have? What would he be thinking of a man to be running messages to him, bothering him, if I didn't lift a hand to help you – me being a neighbour? I'll bear them up to the cabin meself for you, Ellen, with a heart and a half,' he said, delighted with himself. The red-haired woman wouldn't catch him out like that! Emboldened, he didn't wait for her assent but picked up the basket and set off for the O'Malleys' cabin. He had got out of that one well. Now he could walk with Ellen Rua, and no one to say a word to him, only thinking what a fine good-natured fellow he was. Why, with all her schooling the Máistír's daughter still couldn't outwit Roberteen Bawn.

Had he been less self-congratulatory, and thought to look over his shoulder to gauge Ellen's response, he would have seen the mischief sparkling in those eyes he was always dreaming about.

As they walked she chatted amicably with him, showing interest in his prattle and being grateful to him for his kindness. He found it hard to look straight at her, but was conscious of her nearness and the power she seemed to have over him. He couldn't wait to tell her about all the work he was doing with the turf, and how he would soon live up to his father's reputation for doing the work of a man and a half. But somehow the words all came out in a tumble and he wondered if he was making any sense at all to her. However, she didn't seem to notice and, the times he did look at her, she smiled at him, which set him off talking ten to the dozen again.

When they reached her cabin she asked him to put the creel over in the corner next to the hearth. He did as she asked, but when he turned to leave he found that she was leaning against the cabin door, having closed it behind her.

'Now, Roberteen Bawn, my fair-haired boy, I'm very grateful to you, very grateful indeed, for sparing me the task of carrying that heavy load. Will you not wait a while and take something with me?' she coaxed seductively.

'No, no thanks,' blurted out an alarmed Roberteen.

'Sure, it's in no hurry you are, Roberteen, and himself won't be home yet a while to thank you for your kindness to me.'

The thought of Michael arriving to find the door of his cabin closed against him, and he, Roberteen, alone in the house with Ellen, sent the fear of God through the youth.

'I have to go now . . . the work . . . my father.'

'Faith, Roberteen, I'll be thinking you have no regard for me,' she teased with mock hurt in her voice.

Dar Dia, he thought, if anyone hears her, I'll be ruined. Then involuntarily he heard himself say, 'No, no, Ellen. It's not that, it's not that at all.' She had him all flummoxed now.

'Well?' Ellen drew the word out slowly. 'Sure, that would be a terrible thing for a woman to hear, and she walking to the lake every morning, and throwing her head to the sun for a man to be looking at her, and he not having any regard at all for her. Wouldn't it now, Roberteen?'

Why was she doing this? If only she'd stop it and let him out. She was trouble, all right. He'd never bother with her likes again, as long as he lived. A red-haired woman was nothing but trouble to a man, nothing but trouble, and this one was the very divil.

'I have to go now . . . I have to . . .' he spluttered in panic, thinking that not only Michael but the whole village would soon know he was in here, alone with her.

'Well, I'll not be the woman to stand in the way of a man and his work,' said Ellen, feeling some sympathy for the state he was in – and he, after all, only a simple *gasúr*, for all his nineteen summers. 'But it's a queer thing, all the same, you running off that way, and me offering you the hand of friendship only to have it dashed back at me again.'

She stood away from the door and he bolted for it. But she was quicker, and again he found his way out blocked by her.

'Now, one piece of advice to you, me fine *buachaill* . . .' she said, her face now close to his.

The smell of her womanliness, her talking to him this way – she was confusing him. Doing it on purpose. His plan had gone all wrong.

Sensing she might have gone too hard on him, Ellen changed her tone. 'There are plenty of fine young single girls out there, waiting to be taken off their fathers' hands, for you to be watching a woman that's married and with children nearly as old as you are. Isn't that so, Roberteen?' She was not scolding him now, just stating this in a gentle, matter-of-fact way.

The boy looked at her, his light blue eyes filled with a mixture of infatuation and sheepishness, and she regretted having taken it so far with him.

'I'm sorry,' was all he said.

'I know you are, Roberteen,' she said, reaching out and touching his arm. 'You're young – there'll be someone for you, you'll see.'

He did not respond. She wondered whether she had underestimated the depth of the feelings he carried for her. Maybe to him it seemed more, much more, than just the sap of youth running wild in his body. Whatever – she decided not to prolong his agony any further.

'You should go now,' she said. 'We won't say another word about this, or the other thing – the mornings – to anybody. It will just be between the two of us.'

The boy didn't lift his head as he went out past her. She waited a while and then called after him, so others would hear, 'Roberteen! Thank you for carrying up the *sciathóg* – it was getting too heavy for me.'

As the door of his own cabin swallowed him into its safe haven, Roberteen Bawn was grateful for that.

After the Rosary had been said and the children were asleep, Michael spoke to her.

'I saw our neighbour's son carry the *sciathóg* for you today. I'm thinking he has a longing for you, Ellen,' he teased.

'Ah, sure, he's only a *gasúr*, it's just the summer madness that's troubling him. The long cold nights of winter coming in will knock

32

that spark out of him!' She laughed, and drew closer to Michael. Then more seriously, she asked: 'But what of the potatoes, and this blight?'

'Well . . .' Michael paused. 'We didn't find any blackened ones at all today. We'll dig again tomorrow. I'm thinking maybe we should lift them all out.'

Ellen considered this. If they dug up all the potatoes now, they would be small. There wasn't enough room to store them all, so they'd have to sell the excess immediately, but the price they'd get would be low on account of their size. After the rent was paid, there'd be nothing left. If they left the crop in the ground until the later dig in November – 'the people's crop', as it was called – the lumpers would be full size. There wouldn't be the storage problems, and they wouldn't have to sell them below price. But were the blight to strike, the second harvest might be ruined. And so would they. It was too big a risk.

She turned to Michael and put her hand to his cheek. 'You are right, a stór,' she said, full of love for him. 'We should lift them all now. Somehow we'll find space for them.'

'You know,' he said, his dark eyes aglow for her, his hands reaching for her hair, 'it was a joyful sight for me today to see you and the children beside me in the fields. The two small ones sporting and playing, and Patrick, wanting to do me out of a job of work. But most of all,' her husband softened his tone, '"twas yourself, Ellen, singing your old songs on the breeze, tending to the children, bending and picking all day – without ever a want or a word of complaint. You were like the sun itself come down to earth all fiery and bright. Happy any man would be, Ellen Rua, with you next to him in the fields.'

Ellen went to her knees in front of him. She took his two arms in hers.

'Michael, my love, I've something to tell you. The Lord and His Holy Mother have blessed us again.' She got it all out in one mouthful.

'You don't mean . . . ?' Michael's face lit up.

'Yes, I do – I am with your child a month now.' She said it like a girl, her face shining up into his. He looked back at her, the pride and love bursting out of him. He had always wanted more children

33

with Ellen, but had almost given up hope. After all, it was six years now since Mary and Katie were born. Not that the whisperings in the village worried him – three being a small number of children. No, he wanted more children for their own sake, and now his prayers were answered. Never mind what times lay ahead, he, Michael O'Malley, would provide for all his children, and any more that the good Lord would send. He caught hold of her.

'Rise up, Ellen Rua, rise up! It's not for you to be on your knees to me, or to any man. I knew it was a sign from above – you with a song on your lips and the sun come down from its highest Heaven and it dancing around you all day like you were the very centre of its world,' he declared, holding her to him. 'I just knew it!'

In the days that followed, they continued to work in the fields: lifting the potato harvest; inspecting the tubers for signs of blight, of which there were none. Late into the night they were cleaning and drying the potatoes, then storing them in their cabin for the winter ahead.

In other years Michael had stored half of each harvest in a pit near the cabin, and the other half, which was for more immediate use, in the cabin itself. This year he decided not to take the chance on outside storage because of the danger that the murrain might attack the potatoes in the pit.

This decision posed a problem, for the amount of potatoes requiring storage was almost double that of a normal year. Even though the lumpers were smaller than usual, it was going to take some ingenuity to fit them all into the two loft areas which ran either side of the cabin from hearth to door. The potatoes had to be laid out on beds of straw to keep them dry and well ventilated. So Michael and Ellen devised a way of stacking the lumpers to roof-height, taking care not to bruise them, and interleaving each level with straw.

Then it was time to bury the seed potatoes for next year's crop. These tiny tubers had to be kept in the earth because it was the only way to preserve them until it was time for planting; thus Michael had no choice but to place them in the outside storage pit.

All in all it was a good week's work for the O'Malleys and most of their neighbours. Some of the villagers had decided to take a gamble and leave a portion of their crop in the ground for the later harvest. Debate raged in Maamtrasna as to the merits and demerits of each course of action, both sides convinced that theirs was the right way. The general mood, though, was one of optimism for the year ahead, and thanksgiving that everyone in the valley had some sufficiency of food for the long winter months to come.

So it was that the much-relieved villagers decided to hold a *céilí* celebrating the harvest the following Sunday night at the place where the roads to Maamtrasna, Derrypark and Finny met.

At eventide people drew in from all over to the *céilí*. Father O'Brien turned up; not so much to keep an eye on proceedings, as his predecessor might have done, but to see his people enjoy themselves. Before he had gone to the seminary at Maynooth, the young priest had been well able to step it out with the best of them in a set or half-set of jigs or reels. Mattie an Cheoil – 'Mattie Music', as he was known – brought his squeeze-box accordion over the road from Leenane, and Michael took down his fiddle and bow. They were all there: the O'Malleys, the Joyces, the Tom Bawns. Even Sheela-na-Sheeoga crept down the mountainside to be at the '*spraoi agus ceol*'.

When Ellen and the children arrived the *céilí* was in full swing. Michael had gone on ahead to 'tune up'. Ellen well knew that part of the 'tuning up' applied not so much to the fiddle as to Michael himself, and involved a sup or two from Mike Bhríd Mike's poteen still. Well, he deserved it, she thought.

Laughter and merriment mixed with the music, ringing around the mountainside and down to the Mask, floating over the lake's surface and then fading into each corner of the valley. Ellen's head was swirling with it all and the loveliness of the mid-autumn evening. *Meán Fómhair* – middle harvest. How apt, how poetic it was, the Gaelic name for September.

'To think our language and music were driven underground by the Sasanach – the harpers hung high for playing the old songs,' said Father O'Brien, his words echoing her thoughts. 'And why are you not dancing, Ellen Rua?'

'Well,' she said, 'with Michael making the music, and the young ones to mind . . .'

'Oh, come now!' He caught her hand. 'Step out a jig with me – I'm a bit out of practice, but . . .'

'No, Father, I . . .'

He looked at her. Such an outstanding beauty; even in her peasant's clothing, she could have turned many a berretted clerical head in the cloisters of Maynooth. That rare combination of strength and engaging humility. He had seen her at Mass – you couldn't help but notice her – kneeling upright, intent and attentive throughout, except now and again to throw an eye on one of those errant twins. When she received Holy Communion, she closed those dark-green eyes and you just knew she truly believed she was receiving the Body and Blood of Christ. He had seen many holy and pious men, but none so transfigured as she was in the presence of God. He had heard tell that her mother, Cáit, had also been renowned for her piety and beauty. She had died in childbirth. The infant, a young sister for Ellen, had also been lost. It had almost broken the Máistir's heart. And what grief it must have been for the young Ellen to lose the mother she loved.

'Is there something troubling you?' he asked. 'Last Sunday at the church . . . Sheela-na-Sheeoga?'

'No, Father, there's nothing troubling me, nothing at all, that isn't a good thing.'

There – she had given him a clue. The young priest pressed her no further. Though his priestly studies had been of death and rebirth rather than birth itself, his upbringing in rural Ireland had given him a finely tuned ear for the half-said and the unsaid.

'Well then, Ellen,' he said gently, understanding her circumstances, 'if you won't dance, at least you can't refuse to sing. It's time we had a song.'

When she didn't refuse, the priest approached the two musicians and spoke with Michael. They cut short 'The Siege Of Ennis', much to the dismay of those re-enacting the famous siege through dance. The mutterings of discontent quickly subsided, however, when Father O'Brien shouted, 'Quiet now, please, for a song from Ellen Rua.'

A few calls came for different songs, but she would sing Michael's favourite: 'The Fair-Haired Boy', an old song of love lost through emigration. Ellen sang, unaccompanied, in the *sean-nós* style. This primitive style allowed the singer great flexibility – using notes around the melody line other than those which were correctly of the melody. Some *sean-nós* singers favoured much ornamentation, which displayed their vocal skills. Others, like Ellen, preferred to remain faithful to the original melody, letting the beauty of the song speak for itself.

Father O'Brien was glad that these old songs survived in the West. Like storytelling, they formed an important part of the oral tradition of Ireland. Not that the Church had much time for the old ways, many of which were considered to be leftovers from the pagan days. But these songs were neither Christian nor pagan: they were songs of the lives and times of the people.

The priest's thoughts were interrupted by the first notes of Ellen's song, cutting through the absolute stillness the crowd had accorded her.

> Oh, my fair-haired boy, no more I'll see
> You walk the meadows green . . .

As always, when she sang, Ellen would close her eyes, and go deep within herself, particularly when singing a *goltraí* – a sad song – like this one was. She would think of Cáit, her mother, from whom she had learned the songs and the art. She would think of Ireland and the great misfortune of its people, and she would think of Michael, her great love.

'Hope with the sadness of no hope – love with the lament of lost love,' was how Mattie an Cheoil described her singing.

So the story and air of the fair-haired boy, loved and then lost, became merely a vehicle for Ellen's own feelings. She revealed herself most when she sang. This somehow connected the singing with those same deep places of the heart in her audience. Every so often between verses, she opened her eyes and looked at Michael. His gaze remained transfixed on her throughout, as he struggled to understand the turmoil of emotions which her singing raised in him.

The young priest too stood motionless, awed as if in the Divine Presence, marvelling at how true she was to the melody, not needing to embellish it just to show she could. Being true – that was the quality she had, this red-haired woman.

Ellen opened her eyes and looked at the crowd. In the background she caught sight of Roberteen – fair-haired Roberteen – hanging on her every word, the sorrow of unattainable love etched on his young face. For the briefest of moments their eyes met and she gave him the flicker of a smile. Then she closed her eyes again and continued to sing, drifting away into the depths of her song.

> Your ship waits on the western shore,
> To bear you o'er from me,
> But wait I will e'en to heaven's door,
> My fair-haired boy to see.

She had scarcely let go of the last note before the crowd began to cry for more.

But the magic of the moment was short-lived.

'What the devil is going on here?' The belligerent voice of Sir Richard Pakenham cut through the applause. Accompanied by Beecham, his agent, and three constables, he rode into the centre of the crowd.

'Lazy swine!' he shouted at the revellers. 'More interested in merrymaking and drinking than tending to my land. Blight is forecast – you should be on your knees praying!'

Mike Bhríd Mike tried to take advantage of the commotion to slip away with his jugs of poteen, but Pakenham spotted him. 'Constables – seize that man!' he ordered the Peelers. 'I won't have him selling that devil's juice they call poteen to my tenants!'

Mike Bhríd Mike, his progress hampered by the two large jugs of illegal brew he was carrying, was no match for men on horseback. The constables quickly apprehended him.

Then Pakenham turned on the priest: 'And you, Father, a man of the cloth, encouraging this wildness, this law-breaking – what have you to say?'

Father O'Brien stepped forward. 'These people have done no wrong. Nor are they savages to be ridden down and rounded up. They are people of God who have worked hard all week saving their crops from the blight so that they can pay the extortionate rents you exact from them. This is their innocent enjoyment – can you not leave them even that?' Having been well capable of matching the most fearsome of the French professors in Maynooth, the young priest would not now be faced down by a Protestant landlord.

'Popery and Pope-speak, that's all you priests ever have so as to keep the people enslaved to a Church which takes their last few pennies after paying their lawful rents. Did not your own people rise up against the high tithes demanded by your Church to baptize, marry and bury them? Shame on you and your kind, Priest! Cromwell was right: "Hang them high, and hang them plenty!"'

At the name of Cromwell, a muttering arose from the crowd. Pakenham jerked his horse round. 'Silence! And you there – music makers!' he sneered at Michael and Mattie an Cheoil. 'You call this caterwauling music? Neither form nor grace to it. I know you, O'Malley. Fine time to be fiddling! Mark me, if the rent's not on time, I'll have you and that fiddle of yours out on the road, and you can diddley-i-di-diddle-i to the moon and the stars all you like, then, with no roof over your head.

'Now, Beecham, let's see what else we've got here in this happy little gathering, besides a priest, a lawbreaker, and a pair of tuneless musicians. And, of course, the singer,' he said, pulling his horse around in front of Ellen. 'Beecham, is this the sweet thrush we heard, whose notes floated across the Mask to greet us as we rode here?'

Beecham's reply was drowned out by the landlord's command to Ellen: 'Step forward, woman, till we see you.'

Ellen moved forward. The children gathered into her, afraid.

'Ah, a thrush with fledglings,' Pakenham continued, leaning forward in the saddle. 'Methinks I know this red-crested thrush. What is your name, woman?'

'Ellen O'Malley,' she said, not proffering the usual 'your Lordship'. This was not missed by Pakenham.

'Ah! I see!' he exclaimed, looking back to Michael and then turning once more to Beecham. 'A fine little nest of songmakers we're raising here, Beecham – don't you think?'

Beecham muttered again, but this time a 'yes, M'Lord' could be distinguished.

'Well, we'll see what sort of music you lot make on empty bellies, and what jigs and reels you hop to when you present yourself to me over the next few months.

'And you, Priest, stick to your popish spells and incantations, and don't meddle in my affairs.'

The priest did not respond to the taunt as Pakenham kicked the stirrup into the flank of his mount, emphasizing the threat. The mare responded with a high whinny until he jerked her around again to face Ellen.

That one's trouble, Pakenham thought to himself. There was a defiance about her and that husband of hers not found in the other wretches – except for the priest.

Ellen stood, never flinching before the horse which, goaded by Pakenham's rough use of the bit, bridled in front of her. She could see Michael tensing himself, ready to jump in if insult or hand was laid on her.

Pakenham addressed her again: 'You'll sing for your supper yet, my red-haired songbird – mark my words!'

Ellen's eyes never fell from his for a second. But for now she would keep her peace.

Eventually Pakenham broke the moment, calling over his shoulder: 'Come, Beecham, let us away from here and back to Tourmakeady, to whatever modicum of civilization is to be found in this damned country. For now we will leave these scoundrels to their dancing, but they'll dance all right: any riotous behaviour on my lands, and dance they will – at the end of a rope!'

Ellen watched as they rode off towards Tourmakeady. Mary and Katie were in tears at either side of her, frightened by the menacing attitude of both horse and rider. Patrick meanwhile had moved slightly in front of her, instinctively stepping into the role of protector.

Suddenly, a shout rang out from the retreating landlord. 'The devil! I've been struck. There he is – up there! After him! I'll have his hands off,' they heard Pakenham order his escort, all the while holding a hand to the back of his head where the well-aimed missile had caught him.

A cheer went up from the crowd, but Ellen was concentrating on the drama unfolding on the road below them. A movement caught her eye and for a moment she had a clear view of Pakenham's assailant. There, in the murky shadow of the mountain, was a figure clambering up where no horse could go. The figure stopped and turned to look once, not at its pursuers, but back towards the villagers. Back towards her.

Ellen saw a young face exhilarated by the chase, and by the revenge exacted for the insult to the red-haired woman. Then the face was gone, and Ellen knew that the fair-haired boy would escape his pursuers.

The following day Michael came running to her, down from Bóithrín a tSléibhe. 'Ellen, the Church – Lord Leitrim has torched the thatch of it again! A curse on him, I'll wager Pakenham put him up to it this time!' he cried out.

'You'd think he'd leave the House of God alone,' Ellen replied. 'That's a few times he's tried to burn it since Father O'Brien refused the keys to him.'

'Well, the priest is right,' Michael said. 'Even if Leitrim owns the church, no man is God's landlord. He can torch it now, but one day himself will feel the torch of hell for it. We'll see how he'll landlord it below there!' And he laughed.

It was true, Ellen thought, the landlords owned everything, even your religion. And they tried to own the people, not only their little bit of land and the *botháns* and whatever they produced, but their bodies and minds, too.

'The landlords own everything,' Michael said, echoing her thoughts.

4

Ellen was in the middle of the morning lesson with the children when first they heard it. The shout seemed to come from faraway, and Ellen, thinking it was the men in the fields calling to one another, paid no heed but carried on with her story. She was busy explaining to a very attentive trio of pupils how the potato first came to Ireland, why it seemed to have overrun the whole land, and as a result why this blight was so serious. It had been Mary who had raised the question. Indeed, the topic for today's lesson was hardly surprising, given that so much talk recently, from church to crossroads, was about the blight.

The children listened enthralled as Ellen told them about the jungles of South America and the great river 'longer than all of Ireland'. She told them of the Indian tribes who first grew the potato in the mountains, 'long before the time of the infant Jesus'. Then she told them of the men who sailed across the world in great ships from Spain – sailed for a whole year to reach the lands of the Indian tribes, and how those men took the mountains and the great river from the Indians, and put their own names on them.

'But it was not the Spaniards who first brought the potato to Ireland,' she told them. 'It was an Englishman called Sir Walter Raleigh. He would sail to all the far-off countries and bring back gifts for the Queen of England, and it was he who brought the potato to County Cork almost two hundred years ago.

'At first there were many different kinds of potato grown in Ireland, not just the "lumper". But you remember I told you about Cromwell driving the people to the poor land out here in the West?'

They nodded.

'Well, when the people had only a little land on which to live, and the land was poor, they had to find a potato which would grow where other types of potato wouldn't. That was where the lumper came in. Even up in the boggy lands on the top of the mountain, where nothing much but turf and heather grows, your father has the lumpers growing.'

'Why didn't we pick those ones?' piped up Katie.

'Because they're our little secret, and we want to leave them another few weeks. Anyway, we haven't room to turn in here, with potatoes on every side of us.'

The shouting outside had grown nearer, and now there seemed to be more voices added to the clamour.

'Sit still here for a few minutes until I see what all this *rí-rá* is about,' Ellen told them. Then she ran outside.

What she saw sent a chill through her. Coming up the *bóithrín* from the direction of Glenbeg was a group of men and women, all of them clearly distraught.

''Tis here, 'tis here!' they shouted. ''Tis back behind in the Glen. The blight, God's curse on it, has come down on us at last.'

As they drew nearer, Ellen recognized Johnny Jack Johnny to their fore. She ran down the *bóithrín* towards him. All around her the cabins of Maamtrasna emptied of people as the villagers rushed to hear the news they had dreaded.

'Johnny, what is it?' she demanded.

'Oh, woman,' he answered, his voice broken with the news he bore, ''tis a terrible sight indeed. Last night the fields were green with fine healthy stalks. This morning they're as black as the pit of hell.'

'Overnight?' she said, reaching out for his arm in disbelief.

'Yes, Ellen Rua, one night and every last one of them was gone – black and sticky with the smell of death on them.'

Johnny Jack Johnny held up his hands: they were coated with a stinking black substance – the likes of which Ellen had never seen.

'But didn't you lift them like the priest told you?' she asked.

'Some did, but most didn't. Sure, we kept watchin' them day and night, and there wasn't a sign on them. They were the best crop ever – ''til now,' the man said, shaking his head.

'And are they all gone?' Ellen wasn't going to let up. There must be some hope – there had to be.

'Every last one of them that was left in the ground is gone – like

43

we never put them down at all,' Johnny Jack Johnny said discon-
solately, the murmurs of despair from those around him rising in
a chorus of lament for their lost crops, and for themselves.

'God's pity on us all. What are we to do with the long winter
bearing down on us?' Johnny Jack Johnny asked of no one in
particular, knowing no one could answer him.

By now the villagers had heard the worst. Those who had not
lifted all their potatoes rushed to the fields. Without waiting for *loy*
or *slane*, they tore into the lazy beds with their bare hands, hoping
against forlorn hope that this blight hadn't reached here, hadn't
come the extra five or six miles up the valley to Maamtrasna.

Ellen watched as one by one the frenzied diggers recoiled from
the lazy beds, nothing in their hands save a mass of putrid black
matter. The people remained where they were, immobilized by
despair – fields of dead men, kneeling.

Like the contagion itself, grief spread among the stricken people.
Some threw themselves upon the source of their grief, the diseased
lazy beds, in desperate supplication, digging their fingers deep into
the cruel, unresponsive earth.

Ellen, too, was seized by panic. She couldn't think straight. Her
first instinct, as always, was for the children. Somehow she got
her unwilling legs to move, slowly at first, then running to the
cabin, taking what seemed an eternity. She drew them to her. All
three were sobbing, terrified of what was outside their cabin door
without being fully sure why, but caught in the hysteria that swept
on every side of them. Darting devils of sound that shouted and
hissed at them of death and destruction.

'Shssh now. Where's your father?' she asked.

'There he is!' Patrick punched his finger urgently towards the
mountain, glad to speak, glad to break through the tears.

Ellen followed the line of Patrick's finger. A number of shapes
were hurtling down the mountain at a dangerous rate of descent.
Ellen could just about distinguish Michael, Roberteen and Martin
Tom Bawn, half running, half sliding, knocking stones and shale
before them, as they careered down to the village and the awaiting
calamity. By now the cries of despair had dissolved into sobbing
and the keening normally reserved for the wakes of the dead.

Michael ran straight to the cabin. Through the dust and sweat,

Ellen could see the fear on his face. Neither of them spoke, only bundled their small family closer in to them.

In the fields, husbands, wives and children did the same, until everywhere were hapless little bundles of people cut loose from life. Hopelessly hanging together. Each thinking the same thought. Wondering when death would claim them.

Fear driving his body onwards, Michael O'Malley for the second time that morning climbed the mountain. This time the ascent which normally took him a leisurely forty-five minutes was completed in twenty-five. He was the first to reach the ridge. Behind him was young Roberteen and, a ways further back, Roberteen's father.

Michael ran across the soft peaty ground, avoiding the swallow holes. His eyes were fixed on a small dip to the far side of the marshy area, where a few years ago it had occurred to him to try out some seedlings from the lazy beds below. The hardy lumper had grown well here and he had gradually extended the area of this mountain crop of potatoes. The natural fall of the land conspired with the planters to keep what was planted hidden from view, safe from the landlord's prying eyes. Only his next-door neighbours, with their own crop growing alongside Michael's, knew of this place. Each harvest-time the three of them would spirit away their secret crop, under cover of dusk, to their cabins below.

Michael found it hard to understand why more villagers hadn't followed their example in reclaiming some of the wasteland to provide a little extra food for themselves and their families. Perhaps they had been deterred by what had happened over in Partry. There Pakenham had discovered his tenants' secret potato patches, and had rewarded their enterprise by levying extra rent. 'This extra ground which I have allowed you to cultivate in justice demands extra rent,' he had told them. 'How could I be seen to act even-handedly towards all of my tenants, as any good landlord should, if I were to grant additional acreage to some, and not to others, and all paying the same rent?' So those who had worked harder, and made good land out of bad, were even worse off than before.

Here, on the far side of the lake from Tourmakeady, they were well away from Pakenham and the prying eyes of his toady, Beecham. The crop should be safe from the landlord, at least.

Michael slowed down just before he reached the dip where the potato patch was. Roberteen, still running, came up behind him. Together they stood on a lip of ground overhanging the dozen or so lazy beds, waiting for the older man to catch up with them. When he did, the three of them continued to gaze down on the stalks blowing hither and thither, gusted this way and that by the mountain breeze. Each was reluctant to make the first move, holding back the moment when they must discover that which they most feared.

Roberteen was the first to say it. 'Look, Michael – look there, on the leaves.'

But the keen eyes of Michael and the older, silent watcher had already taken in the white substance which lay fleece-like on the green leaves. It was almost beautiful, glistening in the half-light of the October sun. Like mountain fog – a will-o'-the-wisp that hadn't lifted.

Michael had never seen its like before. He looked first at the others, then slowly stepped down on to the patch. He went to his knees beside the nearest lazy bed and gingerly reached over to touch the mysterious mist. It felt as it looked – soft and dewy, yet sticky too. He tried to brush it from the leaf, but unlike the dew it did not melt with the heat of his hand. He took a closer look. This furry down was growing out of the green veins of the leaf. As he made to examine it, the smell that accompanied the rot assailed his nostrils. Panic setting in, he plunged both hands into the mound of earth, frantically searching for the hard uneven roundness that would tell him the lumpers were safe.

But there were no lumpers, just a stinking mass of putrefaction. He withdrew his hands in disgust, staring in dismay at the foulness dripping from his fingers.

'They're lost!' he shouted.

The watchers, still and silent until now, jumped down beside him.

'God save us, Michael – what is it?' Martin Tom Bawn asked.

'I've never seen the likes of it before today . . . It looks and smells like the very melt of hell,' Michael whispered.

''Tis an evil thing, surely,' young Roberteen added. 'A fearful evil thing,' the boy repeated in hushed tones.

'And is there nothing at all down there, Michael?' the older man asked.

Michael did not answer. Instead he said, 'We have to be quick. What we'll do is this: Martin, you start on the beds at the far side, and turn every bit of them – maybe there's some can be saved. Roberteen, you start there in the middle and work towards your father, and I'll start here and work in towards you.'

The three men set to their task without any great heart, but knowing that they must do it. If a few potatoes could be saved, it might carry their families just that bit further through the winter.

What was most frightening, thought Michael, was the speed with which the blight had struck, and then spread, destroying all before it. He noticed, as he worked along the lazy beds on his hands and knees, that the white fleece on the leaves was already rotting, turning each leaf into sodden decay before his eyes. He worked more furiously, trying to outpace the run of the rot. But the result was the same. No matter where he dug, the blight had been there before him, waiting for him, waiting to cover his hands with its black clinging cloyingness.

The more diseased potatoes he uncovered, the more the stench of them filled the air about him, until his body recoiled from carrying on. But carry on he did, as did the others, desperation driving them to turn every last handful of earth, to uproot every last stalk.

Time after time they were defeated, but still they persisted in the heartbreaking task. It was as if even one good potato would be a sign of hope. A sign that all was not irretrievably lost.

Fate, however, did not afford the three diggers even that slender thread of comfort. When they finally finished, they remained on their knees, aching and blackened, united in despair.

'It can only be the work of the devil himself,' Michael finally said.

The others nodded. Then all three silently raised their heads in grim prayer to the glowering heavens.

It did not seem to them that the heavens listened.

*   *   *

Ellen and the children waited for Michael at the foot of the mountain. The wait seemed to go on forever. Black rain clouds gathered over the top of the mountain, throwing dark shadows down its side. Feeling Katie and Mary shivering against her, Ellen had just decided it was time to bring the children inside when Patrick shouted, 'No, wait – there they are!'

She strained her eyes to the place where the three men should have been, but whether they had stepped into shadow or one of the many little crevices, she could not make them out until minutes later they breasted a rocky ridge.

They were making slow progress. At first Ellen thought that they must be dead weary, the way they weren't looking up at all, trudging head-down, keeping close together.

When he caught sight of her, Roberteen ran on ahead, anxious to be first with the important news. 'It's the same above as below,' he said.

Then she saw the look on the faces of the other two men.

'Every last one of them is gone . . . gone into a stinking mess of pulp. Not even a beast could eat them,' Martin Tom Bawn said to her as he approached.

She looked at Michael.

'It's not good, Ellen – not good at all,' was all he could say.

5

'Damn his impudence!' Sir Richard Pakenham slapped the letter he had been holding. 'It is impossible to get an honest answer out of this new breed of scientists without also getting a lecture.'

The master of Tourmakeady Lodge threw the letter from Dublin's Botanic Gardens on to the walnut-topped writing desk at which he was sitting. That dashed Scotsman, Moore, should never have been made curator. What were those eggheads at the Royal Dublin Society thinking of – appointing someone who took two months to reply to a simple question about roses? And when he did deign to reply, it was to pronounce the soil at Tourmakeady possibly 'unfit for roses in any event'.

And Tourmakeady Lodge with a garden full of roses, the finest this side of Victoria's palace.

He tugged at the bell-rope. Where was that serving girl? It was long past tea-time. Didn't anything work in this accursed country?

While he waited, the landlord picked up the *Mayo Telegraph*.

'More tirades against landlords, I expect,' he mumbled to himself, knowing by now the editorial stance of that newspaper on such matters. Wearily he put it down again without reading a word, and picked up the *Mayo Constitution* instead. At least the *Constitution* would give him a non-papist view of local events. An account of Daniel O'Connell's recent visit to Castlebar caught his eye. 'The Liberator, indeed! The last thing we need here is him and his damned Repeal movement exciting the populace.'

He was pleased, however, to read that Lord Lucan and some of the other magistrates of Castlebar had succeeded in having the Liberator's public platform removed on the grounds that it would 'obstruct the public passage'. 'Good for Lucan!' he laughed, 'and too good for O'Connell – "obstruct the public passage" – there's a rub!'

In much better fettle, he returned to the *Mayo Telegraph*. The spirit which a few moments prior had buoyed him up soon evaporated as he read the front page.

> The disease which now so formally threatens our own country last year destroyed three-fourths of the potato crop of the United States of America, as well as a large proportion of those of France, Germany, Belgium and Holland; and whatever be the mysterious origin of the disease, whether it is to be found in fly or fungus, it is but too plain that no effectual remedy against it has thus far been devised in any of the countries which it has afflicted.

'There it is!' he said aloud, in such a manner as to cause an already nervous Bridget Lynch, arriving with His Lordship's tea, to jump back in alarm.

Bridget waited, silver salver at the ready.

'That's what that scoundrel in the Botanic Gardens should be about. Instead of writing impudent letters, he should set to finding a remedy for this blight.'

'Sir, your tea . . .'

'Get out, get out – I don't want tea now!' Pakenham bellowed, waving the girl away.

As she hurriedly closed the door behind her, she heard the sound of a newspaper being torn, and Pakenham shouting, 'Where's my pen? Damned botanist. He'll not have the last word with me!'

Mrs Bottomley, the housekeeper at Tourmakeady Lodge, had heard the commotion from the kitchen. As soon as Bridget arrived below stairs she rounded on her: 'Did you spill the tea, girl?'

'No, ma'am, I did not,' Bridget replied, a hint of defiance in her voice. 'It was some letter he got. He chased me out of the room, not wanting his tea, after all.'

Mrs Bottomley's hard stare remained fixed on the girl, forcing her to explain further.

'He was in one of those "thundering rages", ma'am.'

'Well then, you better tidy yourself up and fix your hair. You know how he gets after he's been in a temper. He'll need you to take his port up to him. Shame such a fine nobleman as him never got married. Get along now, Bridget, see to, and be ready when he sends for you.' It was the housekeeper's duty to see that His Lordship's needs were met, and not to pass any judgements. That's the way things were. Sir Richard had kept all of them in their positions, not least herself, despite mutterings she had heard about large debts mounting on the estate. Where would they be without him? If those lazy tenants of his stirred themselves and produced more, and paid the rents on time, maybe then His Lordship might not be in such dire financial straits.

Sir Richard, having exhausted the newspapers, turned to the two unopened letters before him. Both postage stamps bore the imprint of Victoria, the strong aquiline features of the young monarch gazing out across the white sea of each envelope. Pakenham studied the profile as if he hadn't seen it a dozen times before on letters such as these. Victoria's garlanded hair had been swept back along the royal forehead and then braided into a tight bun at the back of her head. It was a fine representation, capturing her unmistakable nobility. Eventually Pakenham turned his Queen's face downwards and with a slender ivory-handled knife slit open each letter in turn, careful not to render any injury to the ruling monarch of Great Britain and Ireland.

Which to read first? It mattered not a curse, he thought. He knew the contents of each, the gentlemanly yet patronizing tone employed by both Coutts, his bankers, and Crockford's, his club. Knew that the language, however carefully couched, led unerringly to the bottom line: his debts.

He first flicked through the letter from Coutts: *Beg to advise you . . . Your Lordship may have overlooked . . . most earnestly . . . long outstanding . . . early remittance of same . . . sum of twenty-three thousand pounds.*

Pakenham crushed the letter in his fist and tossed it away. He was not too concerned about the bank; such demands were not unusual these days. Why, most of Ireland's landowners were in a state of indebtedness to London banks and living at a level of credit well beyond any viable income-to-debt ratio. Repayment of the loans was therefore impossible – unless, of course, one sold up, or succeeded in extracting further rents from those lazy wretches of tenants.

Like the rest of Ireland's landed gentry, Sir Richard Pakenham was asset-rich but cash-poor, starved of sufficient funds to meet all the demands his lifestyle exacted. 'A temporary liquidity problem,' he had blithely assured Coutts on the one occasion he had bothered to reply to them.

For one brief moment he wondered whether it had been unwise to extend himself so far on the gardens. But the view from his window dismissed all such thoughts from his mind. The croquet lawns; the new sunken gardens with stone-hewn circular seating to accommodate his guests during summer-evening recitals; the bower; the sun-dials set in imported Italian marble; and – his pride and joy – the finest rose gardens in the West of Ireland.

Reluctantly he tore himself away from the window and gave his attention to the second letter. A demand from Crockford's was a serious worry. His losses had mounted in recent years, forcing him to retreat to Tourmakeady for long periods. But he had no wish to become a permanent exile from London, as some of Crockford's members were forced to, being so thoroughly ruined by their gambling debts.

Pakenham had for years been a member of both Crockford's and Boodles, two clubs notorious for their high play. One of his favourite boasts was that, 'apart from alighting my carriage at Drury Lane, my only other exercise of a perambulatory nature in London is to stroll from Boodles to Crockford's, and then back again.'

He liked to gamble. It was a passion with him. He loved it as much for the style, the wit surrounding the tables, and the flamboyant characters who frequented Crockford's, as for the vicarious thrill of watching a thousand-pound wager ride or fall on the turn of a nine or an eight of spades. Then one day, instead of watching others he was watching himself, as if disembodied, bet one thousand pounds against the table at blackjack.

He'd heard the London dandies refer to him as Bog Dicky, and he knew what it was to be singled out by the likes of Sir Reggie Buckingham, whose cutting wit had earned him the nickname 'the Blade'. On his last visit it had been his footwear that provided amusement for Buckingham and his retinue: 'Prithee Pakenham, your boots . . . such style we have not seen here in London for too long now. And the colour – a most unusual hue. Tell me, are they tanned using bog water, or is it with Irish pig manure? Both, I understand, are available in abundance on your estate!' At this the coffee room of Crockford's had erupted into raucous laughter, spiced with Oirish-sounding 'oinks'. His mortification had thankfully been brief; word came through that there was about to be a coup at the tables, and his tormentors disappeared in search of fresh sport.

Now, he would be denied his opportunity to show those London dandies that he was as good as the best of them. His note to the club was for seven thousand pounds. If he were not to pay it soon, his name would appear in the scandal sheets. He might even, God forbid, be caricatured in the *Illustrated London News* or *Punch* – delineated with the simian features so beloved of London cartoonists when they depicted the inhabitants of John Bull's Other Island. His body would be grotesque, distorted, largely made up of two hideously exaggerated riding boots, one sinking into a bog-hole, the other atop a heap of pig manure, squeezing the life out of some hapless tenant whose neck lay between the landlord's heel and the excrement of swine.

If that were to happen – and it could – he would be the laughing stock of London. Eventually the news would travel back here, and those wretched people, those bog-savages who through indolence and idleness were the architects of all his misfortunes would laugh at him in their shifty-eyed way. The very thought of it!

Where was Beecham? It was time that miserable excuse for an agent offered some solution as to how his rents might be increased and the growing list of arrears collected.

Crockford's could not be put off any longer.

He daren't.

The drawing-room call-bell rang in the pantry. God, he's impatient today, Bridget thought, getting slightly flustered as she resettled the starched white bonnet on her raven locks.

Bridget had come to the Lodge six months previously from her home near Partry, the other side of the Mask from Tourmakeady.

At twenty-two years of age she was the eldest of eight children, and so had a responsibility to help support the family. Her bright, perky disposition and ready smile endeared her to all with whom she had dealings. Mrs Bottomley had found Bridget to be an able and willing learner, brisk and businesslike in her doings. 'You'll do well in service,' she told the girl.

The one aspect of 'service' which Bridget Lynch did not take to so readily was the service Mrs Bottomley kept intimating she should provide to help soothe Sir Richard after his rages. Despite her Catholic upbringing, Bridget was as healthy as any young girl her age, and had no lack of admirers amongst the young men of Partry. Indeed, she had on occasion slipped her mother's guard for an hour or two to keep a tryst in one of the many sheltered coves by the lake shore. Meeting with a lusty young fellow whom she had taken a shine to was one thing, but being a landlord's 'tallywoman' was another matter entirely. It was a tricky situation for a young girl to be in. Pakenham was notorious for wenching, and Bridget had once heard him remark that it was a damn shame the right of *primae noctis* had been done away with. This entitled the landlord, in return for granting permission to his tenants to wed, to enjoy the privilege of 'first night' with the new bride.

Bridget thought it must have caused terrible upset, with young husbands, seeing their brides of not yet a day being carried off to the landlord's bed. Any baby born within the first nine months would then have to be scrutinized for fear it was a 'landlord's bastard'.

Pakenham's bell rang again, summoning Bridget. She crossed herself, wondering how much longer she could walk the line between humouring him and angering him. If she angered him, he would cast her out on the roadside. And if she gave in to his advances . . . she would still go the way of the road, like previous servant girls. A mixture of loss of interest tinged with port-induced remorse on Pakenham's part would send her packing. So she was coquettish with him, stringing him along.

Once in a while she would allow him to plant his eager lips on her neck, before dancing away from him. He would pursue her for a while, until, out of breath, he would collapse on the chaise-longue. Then she would mop his brow and cosset him awhile.

'Wait until the next time, you little biddy – you can't escape forever, you know!' he would say between bouts of wheezing.

Bridget knew she couldn't escape forever. But as she entered the drawing room she resolved that today would not be the day.

'M'Lord, you called?'

'Ah, Bridget – tea for myself and Beecham, here,' Pakenham said brusquely.

She left, surprised and relieved to find the agent present, but not at all pleased to see him. Pakenham she could handle – so far – but Beecham was dangerous and cunning – a right *slieveen*. He was always eyeing her when Pakenham's back was turned. It was just like him to slip into the house unnoticed.

'Well, Beecham,' Pakenham resumed the conversation Bridget's entrance had interrupted. 'It seems we have a situation here, if the papers are to be believed. A worrying situation for a landlord whose land will offer up no produce but blighted potatoes, giving yet a further excuse to his tenants to withhold their lawful rents. What are we to do, Beecham?'

Beecham moved to within a few feet of where Pakenham stood looking out at the rose gardens. He clasped his hands in front of him, and paused to check that he had Pakenham's attention.

'It would seem that the blight is uneven in its distribution, and there is no certainty that it will be as melancholy on the potatoes as some reports suggest. Of course, the experts differ, as always.'

'Yes, yes,' Pakenham cut in, 'but what of our own tenantry?'

'Well, Sir Dick – I mean, Sir Richard . . . my apology, Your Lordship,' Beecham said slyly.

Pakenham let that go, maintaining his silence.

'It appears the Catholic Church has done us some favour: the bishops have instructed their flocks to make an early harvest of the potatoes. Most of the peasantry obeyed, and even broke the holy Sabbath to do so. The greater portion of the crop has thus been saved. However –'

'What now?' Pakenham was losing patience. God, Beecham could be so longwinded.

'If Your Lordship will permit . . . ?' Beecham gave an impertinent half-bow.

Pakenham nodded him on.

'I would suggest that, when we summon the tenantry for renewal of their tenure, we make it clear to them that there will be no abatement of rents. Furthermore, we stipulate that arrears of rent will be dealt with by summary eviction, while at the same time impressing on them the need for good husbandry in the coming year.'

Pakenham did not seem impressed, but, undaunted, the agent pressed on, confident that his next proposal would win favour.

'You will remember, sir, the spectacle of the tenantry at Maamtrasna, hooleying and drinking when they should have been tending to their fields. We must outlaw all such folderriderry. The year ahead needs a firm hand.'

At the mention of Maamtrasna, Pakenham's hand involuntarily started to reach for the still-tender spot at the back of his head, but the landlord stopped the movement. Wouldn't do to let Beecham know that a stone-throwing peasant's pot-shot had taken a feather out of him. Beecham, however, had already noted the movement; though sorely tempted to make advantage out of Pakenham's discomfiture, he decided to keep to the business at hand.

'What say you, sir, to my suggestion?' he asked.

'Yes, that's good, Beecham, very good. Call them in and tell them what's what. Damned lucky they'll be if I don't clear the lot of them!'

'Well, sir,' offered Beecham, 'this blight might present you with some opportunity to commence the consolidation of your land into larger, more manageable, holdings.'

Pakenham turned and looked the agent squarely in the eye. Beecham prepared to receive his employer's approbation.

'You know, Beecham, it's a damnable pity that you can be such a disagreeable fellow at times.'

The crooked smile on Beecham's face froze as he waited, not sure of what was to follow.

'You have a good understanding of affairs and a damned good nose for an opportunity to improve your employer's lot.'

Beecham gave as near a full smile as his features and character would allow. Pakenham was being exceptionally genial towards him.

'My Lord, you are too kind, I –'

'However,' his employer interrupted, 'if you don't desist from baiting me, and leering at my personal wench, then I shall have your balls for breakfast – after I have keel-hauled you from one end of the Mask to t'other. Do you have me, sir?' Pakenham snarled, pushing his face towards Beecham's, relishing the sight of the agent squirming away from him.

Before Beecham could reply, if indeed he had a reply to the prospect of being keel-hauled and castrated, Bridget Lynch re-entered the room.

'Bridget,' Pakenham greeted her jovially, 'Mr Beecham will be without tea today. Methinks the Mask air disagrees with him, and he must leave.'

Bridget made to put down the tray so as to see Beecham to the door.

'Oh, Bridget' – Pakenham was enjoying this – 'Mr Beecham is not so poorly that he is in need of your assist.' He turned to the agent then, and in honeyed tones enquired: 'Pray, Beecham, do you require Bridget's assist, or will you escort yourself out? In any event, Bridget must serve my tea before it turns tepid. You know how I abhor tepidity in anything.'

Bridget had a sense that she was caught in the middle of this rather one-sided exchange. Her unease was not assuaged one whit when Beecham, without speaking, pushed past her and stormed out of the room.

Pakenham was cock-a-hoop at Beecham's ignominious exit. 'Now then, Bridget,' he said, 'if that bounder causes you any concern you must inform me at once.'

'Yes, sir. Of course, sir. But Mr Beecham never bothered me none,' she lied. 'He's always been proper and gentlemanly towards me, sir,' she continued, trying to bolster the lie. At the same time she was vividly recalling how, only a week previously, Beecham had come up behind her and, catching her unawares, rumbustled her into the storage pantry, pushing himself against her so that she was 'caught between the ram and the hams', as she put it to one of the kitchen maids later. Though she had managed to joke about it, she was sure Beecham would have undone her had it not been for Mrs Bottomley's footsteps sounding in the corridor outside.

Sir Richard was mightily pleased with himself. He had exposed Beecham in front of the girl, and taught the little upstart a lesson.

The girl's obvious alarm when she walked in on their conversation, and the way her cheeks had flushed when she had lied to him, excited him further. Did she think he didn't know? Pah! Mrs Bottomley missed nothing. Who did she think she was, this Irish peasant girl holding him, Sir Richard Pakenham, on the leash of a promise? Teasing him, and probably Beecham too, with those long black eyelashes and sideways looks? It was time she learned who was master around here.

And there she stood before him – waiting, flushed and unsure, her dark eyes set on him. The blood coursed in him from all the excitement of the hour. Gone were thoughts of the blight, tenants, the rents. All he saw before him was all he desired just then.

'Bridget, now that Mr Beecham has so ungraciously left us, we are one tea too many . . . Would you do me the honour of joining me?' His manner was so uncommonly courteous that all her womanly instincts were alerted. As she walked towards him, balancing the tray with the silver tea service and fine bone-china settings, she prayed she would not reveal her uncertainty to him. But before Bridget Lynch could control it, the tremor in her soul reached her hands and the cups rattled ever so slightly on their saucers. Though she immediately clenched her hands against the silver tray to silence the rattle, she wasn't quick enough. Pakenham had heard it.

He cocked one eyebrow as her eyes darted to him. Heart thumping now, she was only two steps from where he stood. He reached forward. 'Allow me, Bridget,' he said, all helpfulness.

His eyes never left hers. She wanted to dash it all – tray, china, silver, tea, milk – at him and run. But how could she run out of a position which put food into the mouths of her younger siblings through the winter months while her father worked in Lancashire? After all, nothing had happened . . . yet.

Sir Richard Pakenham saw the turmoil in Bridget's face, but he felt no pity for her predicament, only exultation. This servant girl with her spirited ways had dared to challenge him. But now, as she released the tray into his hands, he knew, as she did, that this would be his day.

6

It was now the time of Samhain – the start of the Celtic new year. Patrick and the twins were beside themselves with excitement. Tonight, Halloween, the spirits of the dead would come back to the valley. There would be a bonfire, merriment, singing, dancing and shouting.

Ellen, Michael and the children walked up through the straggling line of cabins. The whole village, save the very old and infirm, had come out into the gathering dusk to make the annual pilgrimage to the bonfire place – a hillock on the high ground, close to the site of the recent *céilí*. Back down the valley in Glenbeg, Ellen could see figures gathering, heading towards the lakeshore where their bonfire would be kindled. From across the lake in Derrypark, unseen, bodiless voices echoed in the night.

The Halloween half-moon was high in the sky, partly shrouded by puffs of mist. Stars sprinkled the heavens above Maamtrasna – one for every soul of the dead, thought Ellen. She imagined the Máistir and Cáit up there, perched on the handle of the great Plough, guiding, lighting, working together in the heavens as they had on earth. Ellen wondered where her own place in the vault of heaven would be. Would Michael be there beside her, her love-star? Would the children know where to look for them on Halloweens to come? And would they, too, claim their place in the firmament – Patrick the dark, strong star; Katie and Mary, the heavenly twins, set close together. Bright flame-stars.

And what of this new star she carried within her?

Where would this miracle-star, not yet of this world, be? Where would it fly across the heavens?

They reached the Crucán. Ellen felt a shiver run through her, and crossed herself. Now, at the place of the bonfire, the children's shrieks of delight drove everything from Ellen's mind save the ceremony of fire about to begin.

Earlier in the day, the village children had scoured the lakeshore for firewood. The men had dragged down from the mountain great pieces of blackened bogwood, the remains of mighty oaks that, thousands of years ago, had stood where today there was only bogland. Now the villagers heaped these pieces of broken wood, along with old rags and bones and straw, on to the misshapen monster that was growing topsy-turvy-like on the hillock above the village. Through the gaps in the wood, Ellen could see shafts of bleak, early winter light, providing an eerie backdrop to this pagan festival.

Then, to a chorus of yells, the great pyramid of wood was kindled. At first the kindling took slowly, with little spurts whenever a lick of flame caught the quick-to-burn straw or rags. Gradually, tongues of flame began to reach up from the lower regions of the pile. The children were mesmerized by the fiery serpents which, every now and then, darted out towards them, to the accompaniment of squeals of excitement and fear. At first they would retreat from the flames, but then, daring the fire-devils, they would edge back to their previous positions, their little faces red and white in the night, the fire dancing in their eyes. The bonfire rapidly grew in intensity and ferocity, sweeping up to the sky. Sparks driven off by the wind illuminating the pale marking stones on the children's burial mound.

Ellen looked out across the Maamtrasna Valley. Everywhere fires roared in the night, ringing the lakeside in a circle of flame, framing the wild gesticulations of the revellers, transforming them into grotesque spectres of shadow and light, more spirit than human. Further back towards Tourmakeady, the great pagan celebration lit up the sky, lifting a downtrodden people into risen people for this night. Ellen knew that Pakenham would see the flames and understand that they were a sign, a symbol of the undying spirit of a culture that had come out of the mists of time and survived for tens of centuries. A culture as old as the bogwood, lying dormant for thousands of years, waiting its turn to be ignited – to crackle and hiss and flame and spark into glorious life again.

Just as the old black wood was liberated by fire, so too this night of celebration freed the people of the valley. A people not yet suffocated by hundreds of years of an alien culture seeking to dominate, to drive out the old ways of this land. A people not yet made joyless by the starched, imposed strictures of the Catholic Church.

'Fire is life.'

Ellen looked for the bright stars that formed the handle of the Plough and smiled, knowing the Máistir was there, wise as ever.

She felt a tug at her elbow. It was Mary, all bright and rosy from the heat of the bonfire.

'Come on, a Mhamaí, give me your hand and we'll do the circle round the fire.'

Ellen, surprised by Mary's initiative – normally Katie was the one doing all the pulling and tugging – bent down and gave her quiet child a hug. Perhaps Mary was at last, getting out of being so backward about coming forward, as Michael put it. It wasn't easy to be the outgoing one, when you had a twin sister who ran at life, day after day, fit for anything – and everything.

'Of course, a stóirín,' she whispered.

Mary grabbed her mother's hand and pulled her towards the ring of people forming around the fire. Someone took Ellen's other hand as it trailed behind her, but she took little notice of this in the general mêlée.

Ellen spotted Katie on the far side of the bonfire, pulling Michael into the ring as Mary had done with her. She could imagine her twins plotting and scheming, the whispered argument: 'I'll get Mammy and you get Daddy.' 'No, I'll get Mammy and you get Daddy.'

Slowly, the ring of fire-dancers, their hands joined, began to move to the right around the fire. Ellen, feeling a cold grip on her left hand, turned to see who it was. With a start she saw Sheela-na-Sheeoga grinning at her, flickers of light darting across her face, giving it a wild look.

'God be with you, Ellen Rua.'

'God and Mary be with you, Sheela,' Ellen returned, alarmed that the old woman should have gotten so close, taken her hand.

'Dance easy round the fire, Ellen Rua. Dance easy tonight.' The old woman's voice rattled out to her through the crackling sound of the bonfire. 'For it's no harm you want to be bringing on yourself this night when the evil ones fly in the air.'

61

Ellen hoped that Sheela would not notice the unsettling effect her presence was having. Why had the old one to be always on her shoulder, appearing out of nowhere, and always with a message that, whilst unclear, was ominous in its delivery? It was as if Sheela had appointed herself both midwife and guardian for this child. Ellen rued the day she had gone over the mountain to see the old *cailleach*.

'Everything is fine, Sheela,' she heard herself saying.

Sheela-na-Sheeoga's eyes glinted back at her, the flickering of the fire adding a demonic intensity to them.

'Let you pick up the burning ember and pass it round yourself to purify your body. Let the fire protect you from the evil ones.'

This advice seemed to Ellen to bring a chilling dimension to the old custom of casting the embers. Glad of the excuse to break off physical contact with the woman, she grasped an ember. Contrary to the old one's admonitions, she did not pass it around her body, but slowly and deliberately made a fiery sign of the cross before casting the ember high into the Halloween night. It turned and twisted as it rose, sizzling and crackling as it cut a path through the air. Starwards it climbed, hanging in the heavens, until at its zenith it flared brightly. Then, like a fallen soul, it dropped. Only a dark, dull redness remained, in stark contrast to its previous showering, sparking glory. Now, thought Ellen, it will burn out alone, hidden in the blackness beyond the Crucán, dying in its own ashes as they returned to the earth.

'Ellen, are you all right?' Michael appeared at her side looking worried.

Since she had told him the news about the baby, Michael had noticed that Ellen frequently seemed preoccupied, as if she had drifted away into some world where he wasn't. He sensed that she was struggling to work something out. He had always been aware that there was a side of Ellen forever beyond his reach, like the dark and mysterious worlds that hung between the stars and beneath the Mask. Sometimes she was like a spirit-woman. Her body was there – you could touch it, feel it, taste it – but her elusive spirit slipped between your fingers.

'Ah, I'm fine, Michael. It's just the night that's in it, and thinking of those who are gone. Nothing ails me. Sure, isn't it the same with everyone else here?'

Katie rushed over to them, her face all alight.

'Did you see that?' she burst out. 'I hit one of them – I hit an evil spirit.'

'Ah! Hush that talk now, Katie,' said Patrick, a little unnerved by the Halloween ceremonies.

'No, but I did – I swear! I threw my lighted stick up in the air, and it went up above the smoke, and then I saw it hit this black thing in the sky, and I heard a sound like a screech. I did! I did! I'm telling you!' Katie stamped her foot in exasperation.

'I believe you, Katie.' Mary's quiet voice penetrated the commotion.

'See!' said Katie, throwing her arms around her sister. 'Twins know these things because they're special. They just know!'

The big bonfire died down, its timbers, weakened by the flames, crumbling and sliding into the pit of glowing ash-whitened wood. Eddies of wind swept in, picking up the ash and floating it into the hills and the valleys in busy flurries of fire-snow. The demons that lurked in the flames continued hissing and spitting, inviting the onlooker in even after their long, ever-beckoning fingers of flame had departed, quenched for another year.

Around the valley, the fires which had roared into the night were now just a row of red, angry eyes dotted along the hillsides. Eyes which by morning would be closed.

The O'Malleys returned to their cabin. Michael took his knife and scooped out a turnip that Roberteen got somewhere, then carved eyes, a nose and a mouth to make a *púca*. Finally, he took a small piece of lighted turf from the fire and placed it inside the turnip. Patrick, who had been clamouring to be allowed to help, positioned the turnip in the window opening. The Halloween *púca* sent out an eerie yellow glow. Its gashed face smiled evilly, the burning innards sending out a sickly wet smell.

The next night – the eve of All Souls – the O'Malleys' cabin was filled with a strange mixture of fear and excitement. The prayers took longer than usual as the family recited the Sorrowful

Mysteries of the Rosary, offering up a decade each for the Máistir, Cáit, Michael's mother and father, and all dead relatives. The dead of the village and all the souls in purgatory, waiting to be released through the prayers of the faithful on earth, were also included.

The Rosary finished without any of the usual 'trimmings', except for the prayer to Mary: '. . . to thee do we cry, poor banished children of Eve, to thee do we send up our sighs, mourning and weeping' – or 'morning and evening' as Katie put it, referring to all the praying that took place at this time of year.

Next came the Litany of the Blessed Virgin, which Ellen gave out in a toneless chant, and the others answered:

'Pray for us!'

'Have mercy on us!'

'Pray for us!'

'Have mercy on us!'

The continuous chanted responses induced a trance-like state in the younger members of the group, providing much-needed release from the pain of kneeling at prolonged prayer.

Afterwards, as the children settled down to sleep, Ellen laid out five settings for food, although they themselves had already eaten. Katie and Mary watched with great interest, but Patrick, showing his disdain for *pisreoga* – superstitions – had turned his face away and gone to sleep. As she set each place, Ellen whispered an explanation to the twins: 'This place is for the Máistir.' They nodded their assent, agog with the mystery of it all. 'And this one is for my mother, Cáit. And this for your other grandfather, Stephen, and beside him Sarah.'

Before Ellen could explain further, Mary, in hushed tones, half-afraid the spirits of the dead would not come if they heard the noise of children, asked: 'And who is the last place for, *a Mhamaí*?'

'Well, *a stóirín*,' Ellen whispered back, 'that place is for any poor wandering soul who has no home to go to, and who would be left beyond on the mountainside, wailing bitterly in the wind and the cold.'

This captured the imagination of the twins, and for a moment there was silence. Then it was Mary again who spoke: '*A Mhamaí*, I'm glad we've set the extra place. It's a kind thing to do for a poor, lonely soul who has no one to welcome it in.'

Now that the place-setting had finished, the twins switched their attention to Michael. Having gathered up some of the almost burnt-out wood from last night's bonfire, he was building a fine welcoming fire in the hearth. Their little minds were alive with hordes of wandering souls filling the night sky over the valley, picking out the welcoming cabins below. Cabins like their own, with glowing fires, doors left unlatched and tables set for the midnight feast.

Finally, Katie and Mary fell into sleep, comforted by the image of the unknown soul slipping in quietly to take its place among their grandparents; having a family, for this night at least.

Ellen lay on her back watching the flames of the fire shadow-dance along the walls and up towards the ceiling. They darted in and out of the loft, burnishing the gold-coloured straw which held their food supply for the year to come. Now and again, the shadow of a flame would seem to pick out the lumpers stored there, casting up grotesque images of stunted men, no arms and legs, only small squat heads set on larger squat bodies.

Ellen wondered whether their little loft would be groaning under the weight of lumpers in the Samhain of the following year. She couldn't quite harness all the feelings of impending catastrophe which seemed to be pressing on her recently – her baby and Sheela-na-Sheeoga; the potato disease; Pakenham singling her out at the *céilí*; Halloween and her thoughts on the stars of the dead. Something was happening. Some force was singling her out, putting her at the centre of things. But why her?

When, eventually, she did succumb to sleep, her dreams were filled with dark and troubling visitations.

She was hurrying down a long, winding road. On every side were people weeping and wailing – calling out to her. She had the children with her – all three of them – and she was carrying a baby.

She had to get to the end of the road, through the hordes standing, sitting, and stretched out all along the way. Way off in the distance, at the end of the road, was a . . . ship. That's where she was running to. She had to reach that ship. She had to get there fast, before the evil following behind caught up with her.

Mary could not keep up. Ellen ran back and grabbed her. She

was losing time – the ship, the tall ship, it would leave without them. She didn't seem to be making any ground at all. The road twisted on, and on, and on, lined with poor, piteous souls calling out to her. She couldn't stop. Their skeleton-like fingers clawed the air, trying to hold her back, to smother her and the children.

Now she couldn't see the ship. Had it sailed already? She hadn't seen it leave. Ahead now was only black. A gaping darkness, waiting to swallow them. The thing that had pursued them was now in front of them, blocking their escape. The blackness seemed to be moving towards them. If they did not move, it would crush them. But the child in her arms was crying; it was heavy, too heavy for her to be carrying.

'Mary, keep up, for God's sake!' She yanked the child's arm, pulling her along.

Then the whole countryside shook as a tremendous booming noise resounded from the road ahead. The vibrations travelled from the ground into her feet, and then up through her whole body, until the sound rang inside her head: boom! boom! boom! The faster she ran the louder it grew. Terrified, she realized she was running towards the booming.

And still no ship to be seen, only a black, black void. The noise was coming from immediately in front of her, advancing on her. She could hardly keep her feet, it shook the ground so.

'Patrick, Katie, not too far ahead now! Wait for us!' she screamed, but the children seemed not to hear her, seemed not to hear the noise of the anvil of hell, booming, threatening, welcoming them into what dark abyss she knew not.

Now heat – gusts of hot steam – enveloped them, drenching them, suffocating them with its stench. The putrid stench of decay that seemed somehow familiar.

And still the white hands clawed at her, the long, curled fingernails tearing into her garments, shredding them. When they reached her skin she knew she would be ripped to pieces. And then who would save the children? She looked for Michael, but he was nowhere to be seen.

Ahead, Katie and Patrick had stopped – their hands thrown up in front of them. They were backing away from something. She tried to close the distance between herself and them. The wailing from the skeletons grew louder, reaching a fearsome crescendo against the booming which was now threatening to explode inside her head. And all the while the vile steam surrounded them, sticking to them, melting their skin.

Without warning, out of the belly of the abyss, a giant horse came charging. A beast so black it shone in the darkness of the pit. Forelegs rippling, it towered over them, pawing the night above their heads. From its nostrils – two great cauldrons – the vapour came beating down on them. From over its fipple there oozed a white froth, threatening to envelop them.

Ellen's eyes followed the run of the reins, trying to identify the rider of this mount from hell. It must be the devil himself, she thought, as she looked up at the hollow red rims of his eyes. He was laughing at her, the laughter burning into her heart. It was Pakenham! But he was not alone. In the air above him floated Sheela-na-Sheeoga, pointing at her, singling her out. 'Ellen . . . Ellen Rua, deliver the child to me,' she wailed.

Ellen clutched the baby to her. 'Michael!' she screamed. 'Michael! Michael! Where are you?'

'Ellen Rua! Ellen Rua!' Sheela-na-Sheeoga mock-echoed Ellen's cry for Michael. 'Hand me back the child I gave you.'

Ellen felt the claws of the multitude grab her, lacerating her skin, drawing blood. She watched, paralysed with fear, as the old woman's arm distended and reached out for her baby. Ellen tried in vain to wrench herself free of the soulless ones, but they pinned her on every side while the arm of the wraith prised the baby from her terrified embrace. 'No! No!' she cried, watching helplessly as her baby was taken back through the veil of steam, back to the evil womb of Sheela-na-Sheeoga.

Ellen bolted upright, panic-stricken, her heart pounding in her brain. She was drenched in perspiration. Frantically she reached out in the dark for Michael, exhaling with relief when her hand found his arm. Michael was there, he was all right – sleeping contentedly. She withdrew her shaking hand for fear of waking him.

And Katie – Mary – Patrick? All safe. All asleep. All here.

She blessed herself thrice and felt for the baby with both hands – gingerly, tenderly, afraid. She felt the inner pulse stroking and caressing this unknown life within her. Finally, she covered her wildly beating heart with both hands, willing them to calm it.

And then she cried. She cried for Michael. She cried for her children. The tears flooded down her face, over the brave, quivering lips, rolling down on to her breasts and over the womb which held her unborn baby. Down along her thighs, it flowed, into the straw of her simple bed, cleansing her body, washing away her fear, releasing her from it.

'Mother of Sorrows, have mercy on me.' Ellen breathed the Litany of Our Lady through her tears. And still the tears came as she sat alone, her knees drawn up, her arms binding them to her, gently rocking herself while all around her slept.

When her tears had subsided, Ellen sat drained, looking into the dying embers of the fire. The settings for the souls of the dead remained undisturbed, the invitations as yet not taken up. She dared not risk sleep lest the nightmare, still vivid in her mind, should return. So she stoked the fire and threw on a few more sods of the black mountain turf. Gradually the heat dried her damp body and restored her. And the smell of the burning turf – the safe world she knew – relaxed her.

She recognized the elements of her dream as grotesque enlargements of her own thoughts and fears. What bothered her most was Michael's absence. Everybody else was there with her: Patrick, Katie, Mary, even the new baby. But where was Michael?

The dream had taken its toll on Ellen. Despite her best efforts to remain awake, exhaustion combined with the warmth of the fire to send her into a fitful slumber.

Once again, nightmarish images began to fill her mind. But before the dream could take hold, Ellen was startled into wakefulness by a high-pitched wailing.

But the wailing did not stop with the dream. This time the keening was real – she was sure of it. She listened, alert, by the fire. There it was again: a single, solitary voice. For a moment she thought it was the high-pitched cry of the fox, but this was longer, more drawn out. The sound had come from down towards the lake. She moved stealthily to the window and removed the burnt-out shell of the *púca*.

The night of All Souls was bright, with a waxing moon riding high across the clouds, seeking openings through which to aim its beams down onto the waters of the Mask. There, they would splash out across the lake's surface – ripples of pale yellow, reflecting back up to the moon its own watery light.

As she listened, Ellen could hear the sounds of the valley – the ever-yelping dogs of Derrypark, the lap of the lake-water. And between these sounds she heard the stillnesses of the night, those silken moments she loved, woven with silence, snatched out of wonder.

For a moment, the moon lost its hide-and-seek game with the clouds, and the lake, deprived of its light, was lost to Ellen's view. But when the Samhain moon reappeared, the sight which met Ellen's eyes chilled her to the very core of her being.

There, hovering over the lake, two or three feet above it, was the outline of a woman, all in white, moving slowly towards her. The woman was not walking, nor was she in flight, nor borne up by anything visible. Instead she glided slowly over the water through the veil of the moonlight, her long white hair tinged by the moon's yellow hue.

Ellen's hand shot to her mouth to stifle the cry. Oh, God – would it never end, this eve of All Souls?

She looked back into the cabin, identifying the sleeping forms of her family. She was, indeed, awake. And if she was awake, then this was a portent more terrible than any dream could bring. She had no doubt as to the identity of her apparition. Hadn't she heard her own father tell how the Banshee – the supernatural death messenger – had appeared to him on the three nights before her mother died.

Ellen was seized by an icy coldness. Whose house was the Banshee visiting this night of souls? She watched the airy figure glide in from the centre of the lake towards the shoreline, her white dress unruffled by the movement, until she reached the place where Ellen had studied her own reflection in the water the day she discovered she was pregnant. Invisible claws tightened on Ellen, cutting off her breathing, constricting the movement of her heart. Then the Banshee floated over the land, the trail of her hemline caressing the stalks above the potato patches. Ellen closed the door, knowing that it went against all the tradition of the night. She would welcome the souls of the dead, but not she who came to call the living. Not the Banshee.

And still the death messenger moved inexorably towards the village. Who did she come for? Ellen racked her brain for households where there was someone old or infirm – these were the houses the Banshee usually visited. Perhaps it was Ann Paddy Andy – she'd been failing with that croupy cough since St Swithin's Day. Or Mary an Táilliúra, the Tailor's wife. Or Peadar Bacach, Old Lame Peter, with that stump of a leg. The long, damp winters were hard on him. It could be any of them. The death messenger, she knew, followed the old Irish families, those whose names began with 'Mac' or 'O', as if she belonged to them.

Then the knowledge hit her as if the whole weight of the world had crashed down on her. She slumped against the window, as if to block the power of the Banshee's death-call from entering the cabin and finding her little family. The old ones said you should never look the death messenger in the face, or she would take you, sucking the soul out of your body through your eyes. But Ellen didn't care. Rather herself than one of the children. Rather herself than Michael.

The Banshee stopped about thirty feet from the cabin. Now Ellen could see her face, beautiful and sad. She saw the tears that welled up and ran down her cheeks – lamenting the one she was about to call.

Then the wraith opened her mouth and emitted a low-pitched, throaty sound that ran through the ground and up into the walls and door of the O'Malleys' cabin. Ellen stood shaking uncontrollably, as the sound raised in pitch and intensity.

It was the death keen, like the noise the old women made at wakes: high, and sorrowful, and lonesome. Yet it surpassed any sound that could ever be made by a human being. The keening of the Banshee found its way into the marrow of Ellen's bones as if her whole body was soaking up the sound, it living in her.

Then, slowly and deliberately, the woman in white drew from her raiment a transparent silver brush. The brush glided effortlessly through her hair, the long strands offering no resistance. As if they required no brushing at all. Again and again, the woman stroked the long tresses, as lovingly as Cáit had stroked

Ellen's own fine tresses, and Ellen in turn had stroked Katie's and Mary's.

Ellen stifled another cry – she must not think of any of her children, nor Michael. She must not be part of whatever death the Banshee would foretell. Ellen tried to will herself into the mind of the apparition, forcing the harbinger of death to choose her instead of them. This she did, but with the sure, sickening knowledge that she was not the one called.

The first pale glow of dawn began to creep in over the mountains, suffusing the wraith with light. As the brightness intensified, the Banshee began to fade away, disappearing again into whatever half-world from whence she came. The keening, too, grew weaker, melting away into the sound of the rising north-easterlies.

Ellen's whole being collapsed. No longer able to support herself, she turned, looking for her small family, afraid for them. As she sank into an unconscious heap below the window, the last act of her conscious mind was to register the two dark heads of Michael and Patrick where they lay sleeping. And the two red heads of Katie and Mary, side by side, arms and legs entangled – trying to be one again.

7

When Michael awoke a few hours later, his first act, as always, was to reach for Ellen. He was unconcerned at finding an empty space beside him, for Ellen was often the first one to be up and about. But when he heard Mary call, '*A Mhamaí, A Mhamaí,* what's wrong?' he leapt up from where he lay immediately.

Ellen was in a crumpled heap beneath the window, her shawl partly covering her. She was deathly pale. He shook her by the shoulders as the children gathered round, sensing that something was amiss.

'Ellen, *a stór,* wake up,' he said, fear in his heart for her and the child she was carrying.

Ellen opened her eyes dazedly, struggling to focus on Michael's face.

'What is it, what ails you?' he asked. 'Why are you here with the shawl over you?'

Ellen made a great effort to see the faces crowding around her – trying to pick them out one by one. When she saw they were all there, she smiled faintly at them.

'See, she's all right!' said Katie.

Now Ellen could see Michael's face. It was strained with worry and the confusion of not knowing what was wrong with his wife. Weakly she reached out one hand to him. 'I'll be all right in a minute. A drink of water from the rock, and I'll be fine,' she said wanly.

Patrick was first up to fetch his mother a cup of spring water. As she sipped it, Ellen felt the cold strength of the water bring her round and fortify her. She put her hand to her stomach, afraid the fall might have done damage, but to her relief everything seemed to be all right.

'The baby is grand – thank God – and so am I,' she said, more strongly now. 'Now, don't be worrying all of you, and making an old woman of me before my time.'

'Did you see something last night, *a Mhamai*?' It was Mary, perceptive as ever. 'Did the wandering soul come into the house?'

'No, of course not, Mary. I just got up a while and I must have dozed off,' Ellen replied, smiling at her child.

Mary was far from satisfied with this response. She looked over at the table settings. Nothing had been moved since last night. Nothing had moved, yet something had come into the house, or tried to come in. It must have been a bad thing. Mary knew her mother didn't frighten easily.

As the day went on, Ellen tried to gather herself back together. Gradually, her physical strength returned. Michael and the children were very attentive, but every time one of them approached or touched her she couldn't help but think: Is this the one marked out by last night's visitor? She studied them anxiously, looking for any sign – a weakness, a dizziness, the start of a fever. But nothing could she discover, no tell-tale sign, no flaw or failing that might prove fatal.

At last, unable to bear it any longer, she went to the lake, declining the children's company when they offered to walk with her.

The late afternoon was crisp and bright. The Mask was calm and peaceful. There was no rising mist, no sign of any occurrence out of the ordinary. No disturbance of the natural order to be seen or sensed anywhere along its shores. Ellen wondered whether the Banshee's visit had been nothing more than a dream. Perhaps she had dozed off by the fire and had dreamed the whole thing, and while in her sleep had been drawn to the window. But surely a dream that terrible would have awoken her, as the earlier nightmare had done?

And what was the connection between the nightmare and the apparition of the keening death messenger? Ellen set about unravelling the dream: Pakenham, she had recognized, and Sheela-na-Sheeoga. The road could be any road, but it must be leading to the sea because of the tall ship at the end of it. But why was getting to the ship so important? She and the children had been fleeing from something, but their escape had been blocked . . . all those ghoulish people trying to stop them, claw them back – why weren't they, too, trying to get away to the ship? And where was Michael?

She had been carrying the baby – a baby too small to walk. Her baby was not due until May, so the dream must be set after May, but sometime within the year . . .

Ellen looked around at the mountain-valley world she lived in. Nothing in this wild and beautiful place was remotely connected to the world she had inhabited in her dream. Yet it was over these waters that the death messenger had floated . . .

She shuddered, recalling her terrifying ordeal. She needed Michael's comforting arms, but how could she tell him what troubled her?

Slowly it dawned on her where her thoughts were leading: the visit of the Banshee; Michael's absence . . . It was Michael the night visitor was crying for, Michael's death she was keening. Michael – her love, her dark-haired boy – was to be taken, and taken before this baby could walk. Oh, God, no – not Michael!

Ellen buried her face in her hands, her grief and tears spilling out into the silent Mask.

Michael could be taken at any time – today, tonight, tomorrow, next week, Christmas . . . It took all the willpower she had to resist the urge to run back to the cabin and throw herself upon Michael and weep into his strong shoulder.

'Heaven guide me,' she prayed. 'I, who should be not seeking consolation but giving it. I should be his shield from whatever dark forces lie in wait. And he such a good man, not deserving of being taken so early, so soon deprived of the love of his children.'

Ellen threw back her head, facing the heavens, storming them with her prayers and grief: 'Oh, God, who sent your only Beloved Son to die on the Cross for us, I implore You, take this cross from us now.' Even as she said the words, she knew in her heart it was wrong to challenge the will of God. Still she could not stop herself.

'Lord, it's little I have in this place, but what little I have is enough if I have him. I ask not that You spare us the time to grow old together, but that even You grant us a few summers more – to walk the valley, to see the dawn rise, to taste the morning dew . . .

'Oh, Blessed Mother, intercede with your Son, I beg you. Protect Michael, just till the children grow. Let him wait a while here with us, and he not yet the age your beloved Son was!'

Yet deep within her she knew there was no hope. God gives life. God takes it away again. She heard again her father's words as he tried to reconcile himself to Cáit's early death: 'Whom the Gods love, die young. They take them back to another place where they are more needed than here.'

But no one could possibly need Michael more than she did.

'Death is ever a moment too soon for those who love.' The Máistir's voice continued to speak to her until at last she was calmed. She asked the Lord to forgive her her sin and give her the strength to do what she must do.

But how was she going to look at Michael? How could she be with him in the night, joined as one with him, concealing her awful secret, knowing that each time they loved could be their last? Somehow she must. She must make these days, however few, the fullest days of their lives. There would be times, she knew, when it would break her very heart; times when she would watch him fall asleep, then lie there warding over him in the dark, fearing lest he be stolen from her in the night. There would be times, too, when he would go with the men to the mountain, leaving her to wait and worry until his safe return.

And she must bear this burden alone. She could not tell the children – their little hearts set on doing things with him at Christmas – that they might never again see their father. She would have to be strong, to bear silently the dashed dreams and bitter tears that soon would be theirs.

She turned from the lake and walked back up to the cabin, and Michael – her darling, lost Michael – keeping all these things in her heart.

As the days shortened into Advent and Christmas, Ellen learned to put the events of All Souls behind her.

Their store of potatoes held fast, as did those of their neighbours. The valley seemed removed from the general fears that stalked the land. Ellen remembered the previous crop failures within her own lifetime. It seemed as if some failing of the harvest was inevitable – a fixed part of living here in the West.

She felt the child within her grow. Untroubled by sickness, or even tiredness, soon she began to feel the kick inside.

The Lessons continued, but now more and more Ellen taught the children in English. If they were going to leave here, then they would be badly served knowing only Irish and a smattering of English. She would see to it that her children were prepared for as many eventualities as she could foresee.

She had managed, somehow, to keep her dark secret from Michael, though it had been difficult. The first nights after All Souls, she could not bear to make love with him; could not bear to have those searching dark eyes so close to hers. So she had him turn to her, burying his head in her breasts. That way he could not see the tears well up in her eyes. Then she would pray over him as he slept – his guardian angel – until sleep claimed her as well.

After those first nights, however, despite the edicts of the Church regarding continence during pregnancy, they made deep and satisfying love that seared her soul and released the great burden of sorrow she was carrying within her.

To wake of a morning and see him there beside her, still alive, was a gift from God. Thankful for this blessing, she embraced life with a spirit and energy that brought joy to all their lives.

Throughout the month of Sundays leading up to Christmas, Ellen settled into a routine of praying which, though outwardly not much different from that of previous Advents, had this year developed a spiritual intensity she had never before experienced. This year, like no other, there would be a real sense of coming at Christmas.

So, day after day, Ellen lived out every moment for Michael and her small family. Mother; wife; teacher; lover; spiritual well; guardian angel.

She loved the long dark wintry nights. Michael was around the house more, the children were out less. To her the short winter days were days of rest and prayer, days of gathering spirit-strength for the miracle of Christmas; days of gathering body-strength for the work of the year ahead.

Often in the dark she would slip away to her place by the lake shore, setting her face to the frothy wind rising off the face of the Mask. She loved how its waters could be. Whipped hither and thither by the wind which came whirling and swirling in from Tourmakeady and Glenbeg before sweeping on down to the unsuspecting Lough Nafooey – the Lake of Hate.

The Mask, too, could be a lake of hate. As it was tonight, seething and spitting at her, trying to beat her away from its shore. The spray stung her face, the winter wind flailing her long mane. Ellen, swept up in the moment, let it take her. She stood, first swaying with the wind then turning and turning like a frenzied dervish spinning between two worlds, the earth elements holding her, the air elements trying to suck her into a whirlwind which would carry her over the land beyond the mountain. If her body did not soar, then her spirit did, deliriously free of mortal toils and worries.

Now she was earth mother, sky dancer, fertile ever-lover – Danu, Mother Goddess of the Celts.

Her hair, sodden with lake-spray, streaked down her face. Slowly she drew both hands through the tangled curls, first combing it with her fingers, then pressing it to her, matting the soaked hair to her neck, shoulders and breasts, feeling its chill sensuality reach for her.

Calmer now, but still breathless, she felt regenerated, at one with the source of wind and rain, mountain and lake, sky and earth. World and otherworld.

Her hands continued their downward journey – seeking assurance that her body was still there, still with her – passing over the swell of her belly to her thighs. Yes, her baby was there, safe within her. And, in this moment, she, Ellen Rua O'Malley was the source of all things. Even life itself.

The wind lifted. The Mask quelled its fury and stillness came on her. Then the shock of her abandonment to the elements struck Ellen Rua. Now filled with remorse at giving way to her sin, she fell to her knees, her hand diving to her pocket, frantically searching out her rosary beads – and forgiveness.

From where he watched behind the hawthorn bush, Roberteen Bawn was terrified at the transformation he saw in his neighbour, Ellen Rua.

Hurriedly he crossed himself and muttered a frantic prayer: 'God between us and all harm, Holy Mother of God between us and all harm.'

Then he tore away into the safety of the deep winter's night.

8

The two acres of land farmed by the O'Malleys were held on a year-to-year basis. They were 'tenants at will' of Pakenham, with no security of tenure. There purely at the will – or whim – of the landlord.

It was Pakenham's practice, before Christmas each year, to issue a notice-to-quit to each of his tenants. The tenant would then be called to account for his stewardship before the landlord or his agent. Provided there were no arrears, the tenant would be granted another year's tenure – at an increased rent. For those unfortunate enough to have fallen into arrears for one reason or another, there was only one outcome: eviction. Most tenants had no choice but to accept the conditions imposed on them by the landlord.

Michael was called to attend Tourmakeady Lodge for a review of his tenantship on 8 December, the feast day of the Immaculate Conception.

A month had passed since the death messenger had manifested herself near their cabin, and yet no one had been taken. This was most unusual. Tradition had it that the Banshee called a night or two before the death would occur. Her visit was a signal for friends and relatives to gather and make their peace with the person whose death was foretold, and then pray over the departing soul. Ellen had never heard tell of an occasion where the death messenger had come and no one had died. The further the days stretched away, the more Ellen's relief grew. Nevertheless, she was always watchful, always on guard.

This trip to Tourmakeady Lodge was Michael's first journey of any length since Samhain. Despite her condition, she resolved to leave the children with Biddy and accompany him, just in case his time would come while he was away from her.

* * *

Ellen and Michael walked up the long approach to Tourmakeady Lodge. The verges of the driveway were lined with rhododendron bushes, which must have been a sight in full bloom.

This was Ellen's first visit and she found it hard to understand how so many areas of good land could have been turned over to useless growth like flowers and shrubs, when it could have been used to grow food for the hungry. How could there be such plenty for one man in the midst of want and scarcity for so many? And why couldn't she and Michael own their pitifully small two-acre patch? God knows, Pakenham didn't need it, and with all the rent down the years they had paid its value many times over. It was wrong, so wrong.

They paused by the gates of a beautiful walled garden. Along its sides, thorny creepers grew; along its pathways were neatly trimmed bushes. Everything was laid out in perfect symmetry. Just like the lazy beds, only here there were no rows of potatoes – no need for that at Tourmakeady Lodge! These were the rose gardens, Pakenham's pride and joy.

'They say Pakenham has a score of men working here – a dozen for the rose gardens alone.' Ellen shook her head in disbelief.

'Aye, and if he does itself he'll have no luck for it,' Michael responded. 'One fine day these fine rose bushes will make a bed of thorns for him.'

''Tis said he guards it as if 'twere the Crown Jewels themselves within.'

'Just as well he does!' Michael laughed. 'It wouldn't take me and Martin Tom Bawn long to make a fine potato patch out of it.'

The image of Pakenham's rose gardens being replaced with lazy beds full of lumpers appealed to Ellen, and she laughed with him.

Bridget Lynch, pretty as a picture, opened the tradesmen's entrance to Ellen and Michael. Ellen was taken by the young girl's beauty and the radiance of her smile.

Bridget leaned towards the visitors and gave the customary Gaelic greeting, but not too loudly. Pakenham would have her flogged if he heard her speaking 'that bog language of the papists', as he called it. It was expressly forbidden to speak Irish in the house or grounds of Tourmakeady Lodge. Ellen, sensing the risk the girl took, laid a hand on Bridget's arm and whispered, '*Dia's Muire dhuit*.'

Bridget took in the woman before her. So this was Ellen Rua O'Malley, the woman whose beauty was spoken of in the four corners of Connacht. It felt strange to be so close to the red-haired woman. It was as if some energy, some spirit-force enveloped her. Yet Bridget was not afraid of it. This woman was not dangerous or evil, like some of the old ones back in the mountains. No, Ellen Rua's spirit was good – and Bridget Lynch liked it.

A whiff of a breeze brushed a strand of Ellen's hair across Bridget's cheek. She felt it fall against her skin – strongly textured, yet fine; the essence of the woman herself. And in the eyes of the red-haired woman, Bridget Lynch saw not only her own reflection, but also the wildness of the green mountain fields, the wide blue of the sky, and the dark brooding of the Mask. Ellen Rua had more than beauty. She was of the land, of history – she was of Ireland. She would never be a landlord's tallywoman. That would be a betrayal not only of body but of soul and country. So Bridget did not fear for Ellen Rua O'Malley. Sir Richard Pakenham would be no match for her. Of that, Bridget Lynch was sure.

The moment between the two women was broken by the arrival of an irate Mrs Bottomley.

'Girl, are you whispering about the place in that foreign tongue again?' she accused Bridget – ignoring Ellen and Michael, as if they weren't there. 'His Lordship will have something to say to you about that.'

Ellen noticed the sadness come into the girl's eyes at the mention of Pakenham.

'Have the peasants cleaned their feet, girl?' Mrs Bottomley harried Bridget, still ignoring them. 'Bring them in, bring them in – the kitchen, mind, no further. And stay with them,' she instructed Bridget, without any hint of subtlety.

'Begging your pardon, ma'am.'

The housekeeper heard herself being addressed. It was with some surprise she registered that it was the tall red-haired woman. Mrs

Bottomley turned, displaying obvious distaste that a peasant should have the audacity to speak to her.

'Begging your pardon, ma'am,' Ellen repeated in as polite but as firm a Queen's English as Mrs Bottomley would have wished to hear in His Lordship's lodge. 'Peasants we may be, but thieves we are not.'

A reply to this insolence was on the tip of Mrs Bottomley's tongue, but something in the manner of the woman affirmed the truth of what she had said. The housekeeper, lost for a response, executed an about-turn and shouted to an as yet invisible figure, 'Mr Beecham! Mr Beecham! The peasants – those people from Maamtrasna are here.'

Bridget, meanwhile, could scarce contain her glee at the routing of Mrs Bottomley by Ellen – something she wouldn't have deemed possible had she not witnessed it with her own eyes. What a story she would have for them back in Partry next time she was home. She hurried to conceal her merriment as Beecham strode into the kitchen.

'Well now, and what do we have here?' the agent asked sardonically. 'Ah, a delegation of the tenantry! What have you to say, O'Malley?' Beecham ignored Ellen and directed the question at Michael.

'His Lordship requested my attendance,' Michael said quietly.

'Yes, O'Malley, precisely – *your* attendance. Albeit a day of religion in the papist Church, it is not a day of family worship here,' Beecham said, looking askance at Ellen. 'Can you not conduct your own business, like a man, without bringing your wife to plead for you?'

'I plead for nothing, Mr Beecham,' Michael said staring down Pakenham's middleman. 'And we have other business in Castlebar.'

'Pah, what business in Castlebar for the likes of you two?' snorted Beecham. 'Business my foot! I know the business you're about: going to "buy the Christmas" – is that what you peasants call it? I knew it! I've told His Lordship time and again, the rent is set too low for you scheming beggars. His Lordship is far too generous, while you filthy idlers spend your time lazing about your lazy beds and begetting children.'

Ellen could feel Michael clench his fists as Beecham continued:

'Well, my Christmas beauties, listen now, and listen well – the rent is to be raised one-twentieth for every child in a house above two children. This will put a halt to your lechery, and overpopulating His Lordship's land. It's time there was an end to the incessant subdividing when these offspring grow up, leaving the land never developed – only with potatoes, potatoes, and more damned potatoes.'

Ellen and Michael listened aghast as the agent outlined the scheme he had hatched with Pakenham.

'Furthermore,' Beecham went on, 'any arrears in rent – any arrears at all, so-called Famine or not – will result in immediate eviction from both dwelling-place and land. There will be no abatements of rent, despite rumours to the contrary being put about by O'Connell and his agitators. Is that quite clear?'

'It is clear that these new rents are unjust and an affront to God for the families he has blessed with children,' Michael began, anger clouding his face. 'It is clear that the potato crop has already failed many people. An increase in rents, facing into a year of shortage, can only drive more of the people to hunger and to the roadside. Is that what His Lordship wants?'

'Yes, that is exactly what His Lordship wants!' barked Pakenham. The landlord had entered the room unnoticed. Now he strode across the room to join Beecham, displeasure written all over his face.

'What is all this noise? I won't have the tenantry raising their voices in my household. Oh, it's you, O'Malley!' Pakenham said, feigning surprise. 'And the pretty red-crested mountain thrush, too.' He paused and looked quizzically at Beecham. 'Is there to be a *céilí* here at the Lodge?' he asked mockingly. Then he rounded on Michael and Ellen: 'Does the law of the Lord not provide for each man to do what he wills with that which is his? And does the Lord not command the servant to increase the profit of his master or be banished forever from his master's sight? Is this not writ in the Holy Books – even of your own papish Church?'

He was like a preacher, Ellen thought, laying out their sins before them.

'It is! It is! It is!' the landlord answered his own question, clapping the fist of one hand into the open palm of the other.

Then he turned on Bridget, who had obviously been as unsettled as they were by his surprise entrance. Ellen was aware of a slight flush on the girl's cheeks, and the nervous clasping and unclasping of her hands.

'Don't fidget, girl! Make yourself useful for once,' Pakenham said gruffly. 'Go bring my port for when I've finished here.'

At this, Ellen noticed that the slight flush on Bridget's face had darkened, becoming a ridge of deep scarlet along each of the girl's cheekbones. She felt sorry for the young servant; Pakenham had obviously set out to demean her in front of them.

'Your Lordship,' said Michael, 'we *Máilleachs* pay our just dues on time, as we have done since my father's day.'

Ellen could see that he was measuring out the words, holding himself back.

'We have used the land well, reclaiming even the marshy land by the lakeshore – to Your Lordship's profit.'

Michael stopped there and Ellen breathed a sigh of relief. He had said it well.

'Show me the book, Beecham!' Pakenham thrust an imperious hand out towards his agent.

Beecham passed over the well-worn rent book, and Pakenham ran his finger down the quill-crafted entries.

'Let me see . . . Yes, O'Malley, Michael. Wife and three children. Maamtrasna. That's you, isn't it?' Pakenham never looked up, never waited for an answer. 'Yes, well everything appears to be in order here, O'Malley.'

The landlord closed the book, ambled to the window, looked out, and then returned across the room to stand directly in front of Ellen and Michael.

'You know, O'Malley,' he said conversationally, 'I'll wager my garden of roses that the marshland which you speak of is not the only land on my property reclaimed by you. What say you to that?'

Pakenham pushed his face closer to Michael's.

Michael, unflinching, stared the landlord straight in the eye. How could Pakenham have known about the lazy beds on top of the mountain? He had his spies about, to be sure, those that would sell out their fellow Irishmen for a shilling. But Michael was certain Pakenham couldn't have known, was only baiting him. He said nothing.

'You see, Beecham? He doesn't answer – I was right! I know these peasant dogs and the way they think. Declare a portion of improved land, pay the extra rent for a quiet life and then rob me blind. Thinking, "Sure, Pakenham will never know, and him beyond in London enjoying hisself,"' Pakenham mimicked the local accent. 'And you – silent woman' – he turned on Ellen – 'You sing, but you can't speak – is that it?' he taunted. 'Speak up, woman! What should I do about fraudsters and tricksters who use my land without fair payment?'

Like Michael, Ellen never flinched from the landlord's onslaught. She waited a beat before replying, 'It's little I know about fraudsters, Your Lordship.'

Was this it? Was this all the songbird was going to sing? Pakenham was angry. She had a nerve, this peasant wench. Well-spoken, too, not like the rest of them. He looked at her intently. She seemed very sure of herself, not attempting to appease him, like many of them did, with their clumsy curtseying.

She was a one, this beauty, with her fine head of hair, fine face, fine . . . Good Lord, the woman was pregnant!

'See here, Beecham – our singing bird will shortly be taking to the nest and we shall have another new tenant! Mark that down in your book, Beecham – mark it down, man. Aye! – this is rum indeed,' Pakenham laughed, enjoying himself. 'Were it not for your visit here, Mrs O'Malley, we would never have known of this happy event . . . and a twentieth on the rent to boot!'

Ellen felt Michael start to move on Pakenham. She reached out, caught his arm, squeezed it.

'A child is a gift from God – as we all are,' she measured out, with not a tinge of irony. 'Now that we have fulfilled our duties, my husband and I must be on our way, and not take up any more of Your Lordship's time.'

She let it rest there. Now was not the time, she thought. But she knew that, before too long a time had passed, they would once again cross paths with the landlord.

Pakenham was intrigued by the redhead's refusal to be goaded into openly insulting him. She had chided him with dignity, adroitly extricating herself, and that husband of hers, from a fraught situation. What features she had! Why, with a decent set of clothes on her, you could parade her up and down Pall Mall all day and every head in London would turn to behold her. She would be a worthy adversary for him, much more so than that flighty, fidgety Bridget, who had just returned with his port. Although the girl had led him a merry dance for quite some time, he had had his way with her in the end. Bridget responded to his look by casting her eyes to the floor. Pakenham could imagine her, running to the priest, looking for forgiveness after sinning against the Sixth Commandment – and with the landlord too! No doubt she'd been given treble the normal penance, for she was thrice-damned, him being also Protestant and still perceived as 'English' by those *sagarts*, even after being here two hundred years!

He would let the O'Malley woman's impudence go for now – wait and see what the lean winter months would bring. This Famine would be of assist to him with this one. Of that he had no doubt.

He turned to Beecham. He had other matters to attend to.

'Yes, well, that's enough for today, Beecham. Mark a further year's holding for O'Malley here, decide on the new rent and . . .' he paused, as if the idea had just come to him, 'I want you yourself to check the extent of land reclamation carried out in the Maamtrasna Valley and report any under-declarations to me.'

'Yes, Your Lordship,' Beecham replied, his lips curling into a smirk.

'O'Malley, ma'am – I bid you the compliments of the season.' Pakenham fixed Ellen with a rather wan smile and then, without looking away from her, commanded: 'Bridget, my port. Fetch it to my study, and wait for me within. I shall be there momentarily, as both Mr Beecham and our other guests are leaving.'

Pakenham knew that the inference would not be lost on Ellen. For the first time, he saw the redhead's eyes flicker as she glanced towards Bridget – now flushed with the humiliation of being publicly shamed.

Bridget nodded and, almost inaudibly, replied, 'Yes, sir,' before hurriedly leaving the room.

Ellen felt much sympathy for the girl. Again Pakenham had used the young servant as a pawn in his game with them. He had made a point in demonstrating to them – and to Ellen in particular – his power over others. Shown how, had he chosen to, he could have used his power to make them suffer by denying them another year's tenancy.

Pakenham, too, had invaded her intimacy. Let her know what was about to happen to the young servant. Let her know that it was she, Ellen Rua, he would be thinking of. She, and not Bridget Lynch. Ellen felt sick. She wanted to get as far away as possible from him.

As if it were not her speaking, she heard herself say, 'Thank you, M'Lord, and may the Christ-Child and His Holy Mother, Mary, Virgin most pure, bless you and keep you free from all sin.'

At this very pointed reference to his intentions towards Bridget, Pakenham gave the merest hint of a smile, but said nothing. Ellen and Michael then left the kitchen, and the landlord's odious presence.

No sooner had they gone than Pakenham, white with rage, picked up the nearest object to him, which happened to be the bone-china teapot, and dashed it against the floor of the kitchen. Bridget rushed back in steadying the glass of port on the silver salver she carried.

Pakenham made a lunge at the girl. Apoplexy contorting his face, he raged: 'Damn them! Damn them to high heaven, these Irish bitches!' That red-haired she-devil had blessed him – her landlord! The gall of her! And not only that, she'd cautioned him not to sin! Not to sin, and she nothing but a whore's melt – born of an unholy union with a disgraced priest. The whole countryside knew of her. How dare she speak to him of sin!

'Damn her!' he roared at Bridget. 'And damn you, too, you little she-witch. You're all hewn from the same tree – sniggering, whispering bog-bitches!'

He made another lunge at Bridget, but succeeded only in grabbing the intaglio-cut Venetian glass, filled to the brim with fine port wine.

'Damn the whole conniving lot of you! Get out of my sight, girl! Go on, get out of here! Go home to that breast-thumping holy mother of yours – or I'll not be responsible for you!'

As Bridget dropped the silver salver and ran, Pakenham hurled the glass past her. Its ruby-red contents, symbol of her downfall, hung for a moment in the air above her before emptying down on her head and shoulders, baptizing her, anointing her with its unholy chrism.

Ellen and Michael heard the crash of the silver and, then, as Pakenham's shouting followed them down the path, the sound of glass smashing into the door. At the rose gardens they stopped, hearing Pakenham's final outburst, followed by the door banging closed and the sound of footsteps running from the house.

Ellen looked at Michael. 'The girl will be all right now – for the Christmas at least!'

As they left Tourmakeady Lodge behind them, Michael was angry. 'Pakenham and his likes should be run out of the country once and for all. O'Connell is wrong: peaceful means will never do it. We have to take back what is rightfully ours – they'll never just hand it over,' he said. 'I think Pakenham would wish the blight to hit us again. If the crop failed and we had no rent for him, he'd have us on the roadside quicker than you could cross yourself. It would suit him to clear the land, and have bigger holdings, with sheep and cattle on them, instead of humans. The people should rise up – it's the only way.'

They decided not to go on to Castlebar. No matter how bad things had been in other years, they had always managed to buy the Christmas. But now, with a rent increase looming over them, they were forced for the first time to break years of tradition.

So they turned and headed back along the road that skirted the western boundary of Lough Mask. It was a December day to the core: bright and frosty and fresh. Along the way they stopped here and there to exchange news and greetings with any they chanced upon. Otherwise, they walked briskly, eager to be back with the children before nightfall, but their hearts heavy that it was disappointment only they brought home with them this year and not the Christmas.

9

They came at first light, Beecham and a trio of the constabulary. Mountain and marshland alike they combed, Beecham writing it all down in his book and drawing lines on some map he had. Roberteen followed them and saw it all.

As they rode off again through the village, Beecham shouted, 'Tell O'Malley that Sir Richard thanks him.'

That evening, after dark, three men called to speak to Michael.

Ellen recognized Johnny Jack Johnny's son from Glenbeg, but the Shanafaraghaun man, as he was referred to, was a stranger to her. She was surprised that Roberteen made up the three.

She put the children to bed, although Patrick wanted to sit up with the men. 'Are they Young Irelanders?' he whispered. She wondered that herself.

They sat with Michael at the hearth for a while, then all four went outside. She noticed that the unnamed Shanafaraghaun man did most of the talking. 'He was in Dublin with O'Connell,' Roberteen had said when he introduced the man to Michael, 'but he broke from O'Connell again.'

An hour or so later, Michael came back alone.

'O'Connell is for repealing the Union with Britain without violence – "Not a single drop of blood," he says – but the Young Irelanders are for the sword, and the Shanafaraghaun man is for the Young Irelanders. He says the sword is a sacred weapon,' Michael told her, his face animated in the firelight, 'and that moral force should be backed by musket force!'

Then he handed her a piece of paper which the Shanafaraghaun man had given him.

> When Grattan rose, none dared oppose;
> The claim he made for freedom;

They knew our swords to back his words;
Were ready, did he need them.

It came as no surprise to Ellen that the gospel of the Young
Irelanders was spreading back here into the valleys and mountains
of the West, where the message of insurrection fell on the fertile
soil of an oppressed people.

'What do you think, Michael?'

'This is not the moment for hasty decisions. We should think
– work out a plan. Without a plan, Pakenham will split us, then
pick us off, one by one, with the backing of the Crown. We need
time. It needs to be the whole country together.'

She listened.

'The Shanafaraghaun man's headed back for Dublin again. He
said the priests and bishops were against any rebellion, but I
think Father O'Brien's a good man – he'll stand behind us against
Pakenham. I'll go to Clonbur tomorrow and let him know what's
happening.'

She read the four lines of the poem again. Swords to back words
– it would have to come to that, she knew.

10

The next morning Michael set off to see the priest. It was a good eight-mile walk to Clonbur, but with luck he'd meet a horse or cart travelling his way. When he reached Béal a tSnámha he would have no choice but to wait for a horse to ford the swirling waters of the Mask. There the lake formed a narrow channel, dividing the road before it opened out again towards America Beag on the Cloughbrack side.

It made him conscious of how cut off by water, how isolated Maamtrasna was from the rest of the Galway–Mayo townlands. Still he wouldn't trade it for anywhere else. Surrounded by mountain and water – sure wasn't that the beauty of it?

Somehow he would get across the Mask, make it to Clonbur, and put it to the priest that something must be done about Pakenham.

He would be home to Ellen and the children by dusk.

Ellen, having seen Michael on his way, sat down with the children for the Lessons.

They said the new learning prayer she had taught them:

> God in my eyes that I might see;
> God in my ears that I might listen;
> God on my lips that they might be closed;
> God in my mind that it might be open;
> God be the hand that guides me;
> God be the footsteps beside me;
> God be the heart of all knowledge.
> Amen.

Ellen could see that Katie was edging for the prayer to finish so she could get in first with whatever was to be today's burning topic.

'Amenarealllandlordsbad, a Mhamaí . . .?' she blurted.

Even Ellen had to draw breath after that. How like Katie it was to get straight to the crux of the matter. She couldn't help but laugh.

Katie sat poised, ready to strike again if Ellen's answer was not to her liking. But before Ellen had time to reply, Patrick cut in: 'Of course they are. Every last single one of them is bad. They say "'tis harder to find a good landlord than it is to find a white blackbird."'

Ellen was taken aback by Patrick's fervour. She wondered who it was her son had been listening to of late. Deciding to let it pass – for now – she got the lesson under way.

'All right, bad landlords it is to be this morning. Now, what do we know about good and bad?'

Katie's hand shot up. 'Well, there's good people and there's bad people, and we're the good people . . . And that's what I asked you: Are the landlords all bad people?' Katie sighed with exasperation. Why couldn't mothers give you a straight answer?

Ellen ignored Katie's impatience. 'And what do you have to say about this, Mary?' she asked her third child.

'Well, I think that nobody is good all the time and nobody is bad all the time . . .'

Ellen nodded at her to go on.

'It's like when Katie does a bold thing . . .'

Katie was up on her knees, ready to defend herself.

'Sit down, Katie!' Ellen paused until she did. 'Continue, Mary.'

'Well, that doesn't mean Katie's a bad person – she's only a little bit bad, and the other times she's good,' Mary explained in her quiet, unerring way.

Katie grimaced and then relaxed. She wasn't sure how to take this, but, on balance, she thought she came out of it all right, so she stayed quiet.

'That's a good answer, Mary,' affirmed Ellen. 'You remember Adam and Eve in the Garden of Eden?'

They nodded.

'When they committed the original sin – the first sin, against God – what did God do?'

'He punished them.' Katie liked this idea. 'And will he punish the landlords too?' she persisted.

'We'll get to that in a minute, Katie. Just be patient,' Ellen admonished. 'The way that God punished Adam and Eve was very wise. He said to them, "Adam and Eve, in spite of all I have given you, you have disappointed Me. You have done the first bad thing, but I will give you another chance. From now on, you will have to choose between good and evil, between right and wrong. When you die, I will judge you. I will add up all the good things and all the bad things you have done. If you have done a lot of good things, you can come back into heaven with Me. If you have done a lot of bad things, then I will send you away from here to hell."'

She paused for a moment to let this sink in. Katie and Mary were agog at the image of God sorting out good and bad sins the way they sorted out good and bad potatoes – the good ones going in the basket, the bad ones thrown away. Even Patrick's attention was caught.

'So, what that tells us is that people themselves are not good or bad, but we can do good or bad things. Now, Katie, to go back to your question, "Are all landlords bad?" The answer is no, but', Ellen moved on quickly, sensing that both Katie and Patrick were itching to put more questions to her, 'some of them do a lot of bad things.'

'Mr Pakenham is one of those, isn't he?' Mary surprised them all by getting the jump on the other two. 'And Lord Leitrim for burning the church?'

'Yes, that's true enough,' said Ellen. 'And they say Lord Lucan beyond in Castlebar is most cruel to his tenants as well. Then again, the landlord at Moore Hall, over beyond Partry, is said to be a very good landlord, what they call an "improving landlord". Instead of wasting money on fancy gardens and going to London parties, he improves the land and the conditions of his tenants.'

'Pakenham isn't like that – he's a bad man, isn't he?' Patrick cut in, wanting her to say it.

'True, Patrick. But one day he'll have to answer to God for the bad things he does.'

'He'll be lucky if the Young Irelanders don't get him first!'

Ellen was alarmed at this kind of talk from Patrick. He must have heard the men talking last night, or maybe young Roberteen had been saying things to impress the boy.

'Now, Patrick, hold your tongue with talk like that,' she remonstrated.

The boy fell silent.

'What about our new baby – will we have to pay extra to the landlord for him too?' Katie was back on target again.

'Well, we don't know if it's a him or a her, yet – do we?' Mary echoed aloud Ellen's thought.

'And it doesn't matter,' Ellen emphasized, 'as long as the baby is healthy and well. Sure, whatever rent Pakenham puts on the baby – the gift of life itself is beyond all price. Somehow your father, with God's help, will manage to provide for the new baby, and the rest of us.'

Ellen, glad that the children's worries and concerns had been given a good airing, wanted to wrap up the lesson on this positive note. But it was not to be.

'When God does the adding up for Mr Pakenham – will He send him to hell?'

As always, Katie had the last word.

Towards dusk Ellen went out of her door many times and looked up towards the Crucán to see if there was any sign of Michael.

With Beecham and his men going about the valleys on the bad business they were on, who knows what might happen if Michael fell amongst them. They would bait and jibe him until he struck one of them.

Or, if the water at Béal a tSnámha was wild and Michael had no horse to take him over, then he could be swept away to drown in the cold and the blackness of the Mask, alone. Without a sinner to say a prayer over him.

It could be at just such a time as this that the Banshee's warning would be fulfilled.

With all these thoughts pressing in on her, Ellen Rua threw her shawl round her shoulders, bade the children to stay indoors until she returned, and set off up the village. She would follow the high road until she came to the crest of the mountain. From there she would be able to look down on the Finny road, watching for a familiar figure winding his way homeward between lake shore and mountain.

The evening was cold, but no matter. Wasn't she better off out here than sitting at home, not being able to settle her mind for thinking about Michael and what might befall him? Anyways, she liked being out under the sky, feeling the cut of the air, having the freedom to go between mountain and valley and lake. Sure, a thousand walled gardens of roses, built by an army of ten thousand gardeners, could never match what was here around her. Unbuilt since time began.

As she passed the Crucán and turned left to ascend the high, mountain path, she remembered her father bringing her to this high place under the stars. Once there, he would say to her, 'Now, find me the North Star.' And she would look up with her little-girl eyes at the vastness of the sky twinkling above her.

'Wonder is a gift,' he'd whisper into her ear. 'Wonder is not lack of knowledge, wonder is not ignorance. No, wonder is a gift – the gift of knowing there are things we cannot know.'

Then the sound of his voice would swirl around inside her head, and she would understand without knowing she understood.

'Never lose wonder,' he used to say, before she even knew she had found it.

'What is it – where does it come from?' she would ask, looking into his wise Máistir's eyes, seeing something there that she now knew was the answer – wonder. A smile would come over his face and he would say, 'Wonder is here now, a stóirín. Wonder is here now.' And then he would say nothing for a while, just letting the wonder flow between them, dance in the air around them, binding them forever.

She never realized – until it was too late, until he was gone – that she was his wonder. Just as Katie, with her wild, generous impetuosity was to her; and Mary, with her quiet ways; and Patrick – dear, concerned, Patrick – struggling to find his feet, caught between boyhood and manhood. They were her three wonders. They wouldn't realize it yet; maybe not until she herself was gone. And the kick inside, slowing her down – that too was her wonder. And Michael, her great love, who she watched for.

She followed the faint line of the Plough to the place where the Plough-maker made a giant leap across the heavens. There, where he landed, high above the mountains of ice, he had cut and chiselled the highest point, shaping it on his star-anvil. Then he blew it aloft, with a puff of his cold breath, to be the brightest, highest star of all – the North Star.

Underneath the North Star sat the North Pole. There, at the far edge of the world, the Máistir had told her, the stars sizzled and flashed, whizzing across the sky, caught in eternal conflict between night and day. The 'Aurora Borealis' was what he called this storm-tossed day-star. The very name rang with wonder: 'Aurora, Aurora Borealis.'

From under that far place, he told her, 'the Northmen came down in their long boats. Fierce warriors they were, coming out of the mists to raid our cattle and our women.'

Nothing much had changed, she thought. Now the invaders came from nearer home, in their fine clothes, speaking the narrow language of the Sasanach, still plundering and raiding our lands, and – she thought of Bridget Lynch – our women. Only now they moved not under stealth of mist, but by stealth of laws made in an English Parliament.

And now the language, too, was being stolen. Language that set the Irish apart, that was the expression of their spirit. English, the tongue of the invader, was now the official language, a barrier to keep out the poor, the peasant, the uneducated. English was the language of politics, of the Established Church; the language of opportunity, and emigration. It was the language of those who held the land. The language of power.

The old language was now a badge of ignorance and backward-ness, the language of the potato people and the landless. It was the voice of the dispossessed.

Now, she too must contribute to the extinction of the language she loved. She must teach her children English. For them English represented escape to a better world somewhere out there under the stars. English was a chance of survival. Without it, they would remain forever impoverished in a landlord-ridden Ireland.

She and Michael still spoke the old language to each other, but to the children they had begun to speak in English. Michael did not like this, she knew. He saw it as a denial of their Irishness. But he accepted that they had no choice. If things got worse they would have to leave – if they could.

When the people left, the language would go with them, and with the language would go the songs, the stories, the *sean-fhocails* – the 'old sayings' – the prayers.

Maybe on the far-off shores of North America and Australia, the exiles would, for a while, speak the old language amongst themselves. But Ellen knew it would be only a matter of time before Gaelic was cast aside as the language of paupers, the language of failure. In time, too, the culture and the spirituality of the people which lived through the old language would be weakened, dispersed to the four corners of the world. Those who stayed behind would also have to adapt to the language and ways of the ruling class – else perish.

The Irish would become English.

A great sadness came on her, and she raised her head to the heavens and prayed.

'Ellen! Ellen, *a stór*!'

Michael's voice cut through her prayer. She jumped up, all vestiges of sorrow lifted from her; no thought save that he was here. He was safe.

And there he was, his silhouetted figure hurrying up the hill towards her.

How could she be so foolish as not to be watching – and that the very reason she was there in the first place! She climbed down from the rock and made her way towards him, not knowing whether the tightness in her stomach was the baby or the love-knot, ever-present when she and Michael were reunited after a separation, however brief.

In a moment she was in his embrace.

'Ellen! Ellen!' he kept saying, as if, having lost her, he had now found her again. 'Ellen, you shouldn't be out here.'

'I came for you,' she said.

'Oh, Ellen, my bright love of the dark night, it is not a time for you to be on the mountain, and you as you are,' he whispered into her hair.

Overflowing with relief at seeing him, she buried her face in his neck. The taste of the sweet salt of his sweat put all else out of her mind. She gathered some on her tongue and swallowed. Then she found his mouth.

'You're home,' she breathed. '*Buíochas le Dia.*'

With Michael's arm still round her, they turned for home, leaving the night and its thousand wonders above and behind them.

The children hung on every word as Michael recounted the details of his journey to Clonbur.

'Things are bad the whole way back,' he said. 'The people are all fearful of the grave times ahead, thinking that God has sent a great calamity to punish them for their sinfulness.'

Ellen thought about this. It was something she had heard said before: that the potato blight and whatever might ensue from it was the Hand of Providence smiting down the lazy, ever-breeding, Irish. Some of this talk was coming from certain of the Catholic bishops, who had not sufficient priests for the population of eight-and-a-half million people. People who, as the Church saw it, had strayed from righteousness. The blight was God's warning to them to observe the laws of the Church and not engage in the old pagan practices, as they did at Halloween, and at wakes and Pattern Days.

London was also quick to see the Hand of Providence at work, as if this absolved the Government from any consequence of the blight. Ellen wondered whether the Government would have stood idly by if the blight had struck with the same severity in England.

Nothing had changed since Ireland had become one with England in the Union of 1800. England, that great all-conquering country, master of the seas, master of distant lands, had left its nearest colony to wither away like a diseased stalk. There had been no reform of land ownership; no schemes to develop an alternative source of food; no laws to hold in check greedy landlords.

Ultimately, Pakenham and his kind would blame the poor, as if they had willingly brought Famine down on themselves. Tenants who could not pay their rents would be evicted to die on the ditches and roadsides.

'I can see it all now, Michael – I can see it all! They're going to blame us for this Famine – they're all going to blame us!' she cried out.

'Who, *a Mhamaí?*' said Patrick, fear in his voice.

'All of them – the Bishops, the landlords, the Government. I see it now. Oh, God, I see it! They're all saying it's the Hand of God moving against us, moving against the poor Irish peasants to punish us for our sins.' She paced up and down the cabin, shaking her head. 'But isn't it the greatest sin of all to be saying that thing? Isn't it a blasphemy to be blaming the Almighty?

'We are the ones going to die – back here in the valleys, with our children – not the Bishops, not the landlords, or the Government safe beyond in London. We're going to be the victims – and they're blaming us already. It's a wicked plan. If they all keep saying it now, it becomes true – it means they don't have to do anything to save us!' she said, anger rising in her voice. 'Oh, I see it all now: the poor, the Irish Catholic poor – England's everlasting problem – wiped off the face of the earth by the Hand of God.'

'Ellen! Ellen!' Michael's arms were cradling her, stopping her.

The children looked at her in disbelief, stunned into shock and silence by what they had heard.

Ellen, seeing them, was overcome with remorse at her outburst. 'Oh, my darlings! I'm sorry! I didn't mean to frighten you so!' she cried, gathering them in her arms. They said nothing, only allowed the comfort of her touch to soothe their silent fears.

Michael had not yet told them what the priest had advised the villagers to do, but Ellen decided he could tell her later, once she had settled the children down for the night.

Then they prayed. Each one, child and adult alike, trying to find a solution to the frightening world outside their small cabin. A world that seemed to be waiting to swallow them up until they were no more.

Ellen looked with tenderness on the bowed heads of her loved ones as they mouthed the Hail Marys in a dying language, seeking relief in the hypnotic chant of prayer.

For her, this knowing what lay ahead was the worst thing of all. As if she were a helpless spectator to their own doom.

'Thy will be done . . . on earth as it is in Heaven . . .' Ellen wrestled with the words as she led her decade of the Rosary. Were blight, famine and eviction the will of God? Were poverty and hopelessness the only road to salvation?

Together they recited the Beatitudes:

Happy are the poor in spirit;
For theirs is the Kingdom of Heaven . . .

Happy are the hungry;
For they shall be satisfied.

At least there was hope beyond the world outside their door, she thought.

When they had finished, Ellen ushered the children to bed. She lay down with them, caressing their foreheads, stroking away the cares her earlier outburst had brought on them.

Tonight, even Patrick did not resist 'being coddled' as he disparagingly called it when Katie and Mary availed of this settling down from their mother of a night.

Gradually, each of them in turn fell away from the world, into a deep and restful sleep. In a final benediction for the night, Ellen placed her hand over the fourth of her children – the child within. Then, with her thumb, she inscribed four tiny crosses on the everstretching skin of her stomach, anointing the growing life-force inside her.

Salvation in the next life or not, she, Ellen Rua O'Malley, would be her children's salvation in this life. The will of God, would, she decided, become one with her own will.

Somehow . . .

11

She nestled in behind Michael, sliding her right hand up over the white nape of his neck, beneath the thick black tangle of his hair, letting it rest there. He was asleep.

Now, she had seen to all of them.

She and Michael would talk again in the morning about the Famine and going to America. Now, she needed time to work things out in her own head – to devise her salvation plan for them.

If, as she foresaw, things were only going to get worse in Ireland, should they just wait here, accepting whatever Providence – and Pakenham – doled out to them? Much depended on whether the blight returned. If it did, then their fate, along with that of half the population of the country, would be sealed.

Of course, it was possible that Her Majesty's ministers in London had drawn up plans to deal with such a disaster . . . But instinct and the lessons of history told her that Ireland and its problems were low on the list of priorities where Queen Victoria and her Government were concerned.

To survive they would have to scrimp and scrape. They must save whatever pennies they could. She was glad they had not gone to Castlebar. Instead, she would go there after the Christmas to sell her silver hairbrush, the one the Máistir had given her. It was no sin, given the circumstances, and her dear mother Cáit in heaven above would forgive her. Anyhow, wasn't it only vanity for herself and her red-haired daughters to be having such fine, silky-brushed hair, and people hungry.

Michael, too, could sell his fiddle, although she would hate to see it go. She loved it when he played for her. Its music lifted her, mellowed her heart when she was troubled. Music was the people's freedom. To sell the fiddle, she decided, would be like selling a birthright.

It would be more than the act itself. It would be an admission of defeat.

She returned to her plan.

Once the baby was born and a bit hardy, she would find work, even if it meant walking all the way to Westport or Castlebar. She'd have to find one of the younger women to take the baby and nurse it for her.

Michael, she thought, would have to find some other place on the mountain, as well as the one discovered by Beecham, on which to plant potatoes. If luck was with them, and the potato harvest was good, they could sell some of the excess by this time next year.

Before Christmas twelve-months, all going well, they should be ready.

There, in the dark of her cabin, as the turf fire slowly died down to a dull glow, Ellen Rua O'Malley resolved that she, Michael, and their family, would not see out another Christmas in Ireland.

It saddened her greatly to think that their fire would be forever gone from the valley. Knowing that once they left, they too would be extinguished from the land not only of their own birth but of their fathers' fathers' birth – and even back beyond then.

Emigration was a death. A double death. It was a death to the one who left, and a death to the ones who stayed behind. Small wonder that the people held wakes for those leaving – the American Wakes, they called them – to keen departing loved ones, to mourn their being torn away from life as they knew it, unlikely ever to return.

In the still of the night the tears welled up in her eyes. She withdrew her hand from Michael's head and wiped them away. She must not weaken now. She had been given gifts to overcome all that lay ahead of them. Gifts of knowledge; of dream; of visitations; of wonder. She must be strong, use her gifts. Else she might lose them.

Somehow the fire in their cabin would be kept alight – she would see to that.

But go they would.

Go they must.

Mhúinfeadh sí Béarla dóibh
She would teach them English.

Rachaidís go Meiriceá
They would go to America.

12

The completed first section of the new curvilinear glasshouses sparkled majestically in the December sunlight, the brightest jewel of the Royal Botanical Gardens. Apart from the Kew glasshouse being built in England, no other gardens in Europe could boast anything to equal Glasnevin. Hopefully the coming year would see the construction of two more glasshouses, the Central Pavilion and the West Wing, which would stand alongside the first in a commanding position near the tree-lined banks of the gurgling River Tolka.

The gardens were rising further into consequence. Yet David Moore looked troubled as he sat contemplating the splendour all around him. Though ample evidence of the advances made under his curatorship could be seen in every direction, his thoughts were preoccupied with what lay beyond the grey wall dividing the gardens from its nearest neighbour: the cemetery at Glasnevin.

Would the coming year see the cemetery filled as a result of the disease afflicting *Solanum tuberosum*? Would the victims of the blighted potatoes which had first come out of the earth on this side of the wall be placed in the cold earth on the far side?

Seeing her husband deep in his musings, Isabella Moore fondly encircled her husband's arm with her own and rested her head against his shoulder.

'Will the construction proceed?' she asked, mistakenly assuming the cause of his concern to be the new glasshouses.

'Of course it will,' her husband replied.

'Will Kew be piqued?' Isabella looked up at him with her bright eyes.

'Who can say?' He smiled. Then returned to his previous train of thought. 'Think you, dear Isabella, that this bounty of happiness can remain?' His free hand made a sweeping gesture which encompassed the whole of the gardens. 'Can all this – our favoured lives – co-exist with the calamity which now faces Ireland?'

Isabella wondered what he was driving at. 'What troubles you, husband?' she asked, concerned. He took so much upon himself.

'It does not rest easy with me that in the midst of want for many, life for the privileged goes on as before. This blight has, in four months, spread to every corner of the country. The food of the masses is destroyed. What are they to live upon but grass and nettles?'

'But Queen Victoria . . . the Government . . .'

'I am afraid, my dear, that there is much talk, but scant action. I see little use of Commissions of Inquiry when it is so obvious that the desolation of the crop is widespread. The Government will use the situation to its own ends. Already there are mutterings of repealing the Corn Laws to feed the starving Irish. This is naked expediency, for, in truth, one has naught to do with t'other.'

'What should London do, David?' Isabella asked.

'The need in Ireland is for a National Calamity Plan to be set in motion. But it is my fear that politics will stay the hand of mercy and compassion for its own sinister ends.'

'And what of the Irish themselves? Can they not do something?' she pressed.

'I fear that, even here, O'Connell and the Irish leadership will become usurers of the situation to press for further gains to repeal the Union.'

'But surely they are right. Little has been done in half a century to develop Ireland's economy,' she said.

'Yes, the Nationalists have a point, I'll grant. The Union has not served Ireland well. But would that they would forgo the making of it at this fearful time.

'Oh, goodness,' Moore exclaimed, withdrawing his pocket-watch from its fob. 'I am afraid I must hasten from you, my dear – young Mr McCallum awaits.'

'Yes, do hurry, David. He's such an eager young man,' Isabella said. 'So intense, the way he arches those dark eyebrows when he questions you on anything. He's from the Isle of Jura, you said?'

'Yes. A very direct people, the islanders. But he's a good student for all that,' the curator said as he took leave of his wife.

As David Moore hastened to his meeting with the student botanist he reflected on the discussion with Isabella. He must indeed find a cure for this blight. But first he must establish its cause. Without a cause there would be no cure.

He regarded it as a duty of the gardens to be a national utility, a practical resource for the good of the nation's agricultural, as well as horticultural, activities. Its function, he believed, should be much more than the collection of rare plants.

'Is the cause of the Calamity yet established?' Stuart Duncan McCallum asked.

'We are divided amongst ourselves it seems,' David Moore replied. 'First there is the "fungalist" school. The fungalists, including the Reverend Berkeley in England, believe the blight is caused by a mould whose growth is promoted by excessive wet.'

The student listened to his mentor's explanation with great attention.

'Second, the "atmospherists". Led by Lindley, who, as you know, is widely regarded as Professor of Botany at the University of London – are of the view that the blight is caused by atmospheric conditions. They admit to the presence of the parasite fungus, but only as a result of the murrain, not its cause. They are in the majority.'

'And you yourself, sir? Which side do you come down on?'

'Well, I am with Lindley . . . at the moment. Furthermore – and I have not yet been proven wrong – if the harvest is carefully housed in dry, airy conditions, it will be safe. Wetness is conducive to spreading the disease. Dryness retreats it. Also, I have discovered that potatoes lifted early, before the atmosphere attacks a particular area, are not so likely to be attacked. People therefore need have no panic to sell early and glut the market,' Moore stated authoritatively.

'Is there any observation of a cure?' the young man asked, raising those dark eyebrows and peering at him intently.

'Well, our experiments continue,' Moore replied. 'But of a cure? None that is empirical. It has been proposed that the tubers be submerged in copper sulphate, a bluestone steep, but it is difficult to proceed to a remedy when we have not as yet identified the cause.' The curator paused. 'And identify it we must.'

* * *

Isabella watched from her window as her husband and his young student made their way to the Octagon House. Her gaze fell on the new state-of-the-art glasshouse. How many thousands of pounds must be found for these, she thought – and at this time?

Isabella Moore, née Morgan, late of Cookstown, County Tyrone, and now of the Botanic Gardens, Glasnevin, Dublin, wondered about it all.

In her small dark cabin in Maamtrasna, Ellen Rua O'Malley huddled the three children to her body, giving them the warmth their fire could not provide. She surveyed the bare walls of the cabin, and she wondered about it all.

Her eyes strayed to the loft. Earlier she had inspected the lumpers lying there. They were cold but dry to the touch, with no sign of disease.

She wondered if somebody somewhere searched for a cure to this blight? What if it struck again next year? Did anyone in London or even Dublin care? Or perhaps there was already a cure – they just hadn't heard tell of it yet, back here in the valleys of the West.

As always in times of worry, she turned to God. To the three children pressed in against her, she said quietly, 'Say with me now, for a very special intention, one Hail Mary in English.' Not knowing for whom it was she prayed; knowing only that it was the right thing to do.

Their teeth still a-chattering from the cold, the children, in an act of faith in the mother who warmed them, prayed with her for this unknown person, and the unknown intention in their mother's heart.

David Moore wrapped his winter cloak tightly about him as he emerged from the tropical heat of the Octagon House into the cold December air. The new hot-air system was working well and the banana plant, a gift from Edinburgh some years ago, continued to thrive.

The chill outside reminded him that Christmas was fast approaching; within the next day or two he would have to make the journey into Dublin to select presents for Isabella and the children. He loved the festive season: the joy on the children's faces; the hymns lifting the rafters; the carolling of the bells; the exchanging of felicitations . . .

These reveries were broken when he saw McArdle, his outdoor foreman, cross the path ahead of him.

'McArdle – just the man I've been looking for! Tell me, do we have any copper sulphate in the stores?'

'I think so, sir,' McArdle replied as the curator fell into step with him.

'In that case, you and I are going to concoct a solution known as "bluestone steep". And then we are going to drown some diseased potatoes in it,' Moore explained without a hint of humour.

McArdle settled the cap on his head and thought about a reply. He had flourished under Moore's tutelage, gaining swift promotion to his current position. The curator usually knew what he was about, but – 'bluestone steep'? Drowning diseased lumpers? He sighed to himself. Never mind, only a week to Christmas . . .

'Of course, sir,' the outdoor foreman replied.

13

Christmas was upon them in no time at all. But unlike any Christmas they had ever experienced. A gloom of foreboding hung over the little cabins of Maamtrasna. Word was filtering through, from all corners of the country, that the effects of the blight were beginning to bite, and bite deeply.

Biddy, Martin Tom Bawn's wife, had dropped by to see how Ellen was keeping, and had told her, ''Tis said, beyond in Westport, that there won't be a potato left in the country for people to eat by the time Saint Brigid's Day comes.'

'How are your own lasting out?' Ellen had asked.

'Faith, we're all right for the moment – making do, sparing them out every day . . . thankful to have them at all,' Biddy replied, before dashing off to see what that *blackguardeen* Roberteen was up to.

Ellen had seen to it that the rationing in their own household was exact and consistent. At times, it was hard for her not to give way and throw some extra potatoes in the pot. But she resisted that temptation, reminding herself of the hard times to come. What she did do, though, was to forgo one potato a day from her own ration, and share it between the rest of the family.

Yet despite the pervading air of gloom in the community at large, she felt good in herself this Christmas. The baby was carrying well – not too lively, just enough to let her know it was there – and growing. The children didn't appear to be too put out about the lack of extras; as their mother suggested, they offered it up as penance for their venial sins and the souls in purgatory. But most of all, Ellen was so happy, as the days shortened into the winter solstice, that no misfortune seemed to be befalling Michael. His time was not yet come. There had been no further supernatural manifestations – no sightings of the Banshee combing her tresses; no prophetic dreams.

All in all, this Christmas promised to be a good one for the O'Malleys.

* * *

On Christmas Eve the night was crisp and clear, and the sky above their cabin was filled with thousands of stars lighting up the valley and the dark surface of Lough Mask.

Before they set out for Finny and the Midnight Mass, the children watched while Ellen lit the candle she had placed in the cabin window. She'd kept it since it had been blessed on Candlemas Day. Even in these inhospitable days, it was still a symbol of welcome for the Holy Family journeying to Bethlehem for the birth of Jesus. It was a sign, too, of hospitality for any poor stranger wandering the roads this Christmas.

As they climbed Bóithrín a tSléibhe, Katie was at them to: 'Hurry up, so we can get near the front to see Baby Jesus!' All three children were excited at the prospect of seeing the Christmas crib with the statues of Mary and Joseph, and the donkey, and the cow. The manger, empty at first of the Baby Jesus, would receive the tiny statue of the new-born Christ-Child at exactly midnight, as Mass began. The twins chattered happily about how, in a few short months, they would 'get a baby of our own', as Mary so maternally put it.

The atmosphere as they approached the little Finny church was one of great joy and mounting expectation at the coming of the Saviour. Neighbours exchanged the traditional Christmas blessings, '*Beannachtaí na Féile*' and Father O'Brien stood at the entrance of the church to welcome his flock.

'Michael, Ellen, and the *gasúrs* – welcome, and may the blessings of the Holy Season be upon all of you,' he benedicted. Then, lowering his voice, he asked Michael, 'Has there been any trouble back in the valley of late?'

'No, Father, nothing at all,' Michael replied. 'Everything's gone quiet. I heard tell Pakenham has gone beyond to London until the Christmas is out.'

'C'mon, *a Dhaidí*!' Katie tugged impatiently at Michael's sleeve, dragging him away from the priest so that they could claim seats at the top of the church where they would better see the proceedings.

Ellen watched as Father O'Brien finished greeting the faithful and prepared to start the service. He seemed to be in good spirits – as well he might, for tonight was one of the high points of the liturgical year. She had often wondered which was the most important – Christmas and the birth of Jesus, or Easter and His death. She herself came down on the side of Christmas. After all, if there was no Christmas, there would have been no redemption on the Cross at Easter. It had to be Christmas – the joy, the hope, the Babe in its crib. Easter was too dark, too much of agony and crucifixion and death. Too much like life as it was experienced in the valleys of Galway and Mayo.

A hush fell over the church as Father O'Brien began his Christmas sermon: 'My dear people, we are gathered here tonight on this joyous occasion to celebrate the birth of a baby . . .'

Ellen was disappointed in the young curate at this opening. Everyone had been hoping that he would denounce Pakenham from the pulpit, but this sounded like the standard Christmas sermon: 'Peace on earth and goodwill to all men'.

The homily went on in the same vein, Ellen growing more impatient with each sentence. She could not believe it: he was going to say nothing. She had thought him to be an independent spirit who would not stand meekly by and toe the Church's line on 'not inciting the people to riotous behaviour', but here he was – ignoring their plight completely. She was growing more angry with him by the minute.

Throughout the sermon she tried to catch his eye, to register her annoyance, but instead he looked at a point in the far corner of the church, above the heads of his congregation.

Pilate! Ellen fumed. 'Pontius Pilate!' she whispered to Patrick beside her. The boy did not understand what his mother meant, but he could tell that she was cross, very cross.

So much for Michael going all the way to Clonbur – and the priest telling him that he would take up their plight with Archbishop MacHale in Tuam. The archbishop had obviously told him to keep the people quiet; the Church wanted no trouble in the West.

But who would defend them, if not the Church? Who would prevent mass starvation or save them from dying on the roadside, their little cabins tumbled down behind them? There was nobody else. Not the shopkeepers, the traders, the *scullogues* with their money-lending, nor the middle-class Catholics in the towns. Not the constabulary, who would be too busy protecting the [...] of the rich. Not a Government beyond in London. Would [...] lift a finger?

When Father O'Brien concluded his sermon with the traditional Christmas blessing, as if this were a year no different from any other, Ellen could contain herself no longer.

Father O'Brien, his back now to the people, had begun to recite the opening words of the Nicene Creed, '*Credo in Unum Deum . . .*' when he sensed a commotion behind him. Casting a quick glance over his left shoulder, he saw Ellen Rua O'Malley – shawl clutched tightly in one hand and her three children trailing from the other – storming for the door, her wild red hair streaming out behind her.

He faltered in the Creed, the Latin words of belief somehow ringing hollow against the sight of this woman leaving the church in anger. A murmur rose from the crowd. Abandoning the service, he turned to face them. Ellen had by now reached the back of the church, whereupon she turned and looked straight at him. He held her stare, though the fire flowing from her eyes ignited the space between them with its intensity. The O'Malley woman was enraged – and with him!

He expected a tirade. What he got was two words – not much above a whisper, but spoken with a vehemence which cut the air – 'Pontius Pilate!'

Then she was gone into the mountains. Into the silent night of Christmas.

Ellen knew he would come. Even before Biddy rushed into her cabin to tell her, 'Ellen, the priest is coming! The priest is coming down the valley!'

Her actions on Christmas Eve had caused quite a stir in the locality. It was unheard of for anyone, let alone a woman, to walk out of the Mass, and at Christmas too! And then to insult the holy priest, and him on the altar of God.

Michael, who had followed her out, supported her actions. 'We can't depend on the Church. The Bishops will always line up with the Crown to get more money for Maynooth, and more power for themselves. And come the day when we're all lying stretched with the hunger, and no one to give us a decent burial, the Church and the Crown will still be saying, "What can *we* do? It's the will of God."'

She nodded. 'We have to leave Ireland, Michael – get to America before it's too late.'

'We will, Ellen. I promise you, we will.'

But now, the priest was coming to see her.

The village would see this as a sign of shame on it, that the priest had to ride out from Clonbur to talk sense to Ellen Rua. But the way Ellen saw it, the priest had more to answer for than she did.

'I'll speak to him alone,' she said to Michael, who wanted to stay. 'Please. You take the children to the Tom Bawns'.'

Michael reluctantly left her, and she could hear him rounding up the children outside as they made a fuss of the horse that had carried her visitor. Then the light from the doorway darkened, signalling the approach of her visitor. She got up from where she tended the fire, and wiped her hands.

'God bless all here,' the figure in the doorway said.

'God bless all who enter,' Ellen responded. 'You're welcome, Father.'

She stretched her hand out towards him, and he took it, exchanging a handshake with the woman. She was not afraid of him, he thought, nor was she overtly deferential, as was common amongst the peasantry. At her invitation he sat across from her at the fire.

'I think we might have a fall of snow yet – the sky has that colour to it,' he began.

She nodded, allowing him to ease into the conversation in this way if he chose. 'Yes, Father, pray that we will. A green Christmas makes a fat churchyard, a white Christmas a green harvest,' she said, quoting one of the many *sean-fhocails* she had learned from the Máistir. The priest, she could see, was uncomfortable at the choice of her words.

Father O'Brien decided he'd waste no more time with preamble. He straightened himself, tore his gaze from the fire, and looked directly at her, this daughter of the Máistir, the disgraced priest.

'The Midnight Mass – it was a wrong thing to do, walking out like that. You caused scandal among the people, and scandal to your children.'

Ellen was prepared for this, but was not prepared to sit meekly through it. 'Well, Father,' she said, 'the Church is always great with condemning people for causing scandal. Sure, isn't it their way of keeping the people down?'

She saw him tense at this.

'Is it not a scandal that the people are going hungry?' she put to him. 'Yet food is being exported to line the pockets of the merchants. Is it not a scandal that there is no work for our menfolk, when the whole country is a disgrace with lack of roads and bridges? Yet Ireland is a part of the great British Empire – the richest power there is?'

Father O'Brien was taken aback by this attack.

'Well?' she challenged him.

'Mrs O'Malley, please –'

'Is it not a scandal that my husband journeyed all the way to Clonbur to tell you how, in the face of Famine, we are being further ground down by Pakenham, for you to say, or do, nothing about it?'

'You're wrong, Mrs O'Malley,' he countered. 'I went to Tuam. I spoke with the archbishop.'

'Then why is the Church silent on this? Why will the Catholic Church not lead us out of our poverty and misery? That is the scandal, Father.'

'Ellen Rua!' The priest raised his voice, demanding her attention. 'Now, you listen to me for a moment. When Michael visited me, I was horrified to hear of Pakenham's doings. Shortly thereafter, I set out for Tuam. Archbishop MacHale, in his wisdom – and he is experienced in these matters – advised that I should neither say nor do anything which might inflame the situation. I am bound by my vow of obedience to obey his Grace in all things.'

'But is nothing to be done, then?' she demanded.

'The Archbishop is doing something: he will consult with the other bishops in General Assembly at Maynooth. They will assess how the Crown is dealing with the present crisis, and if necessary, a deputation will go to Rome to petition the Pope to intercede with Queen Victoria. In the meantime, there should be no disturbances, no riotous behaviour, which might prejudice the position of the Holy Father.'

'This is an old story, Father,' Ellen replied, unappeased. 'Nothing has been done by the bishops to improve the position of the poor since we were joined with England in the Union. And neither Queen Victoria nor her Government will recognize the Church of Rome. All that will happen is that more monies will be sent to Maynooth, and the bishops will fall silent again.'

'It is not right for you to speak this way about Holy Mother Church, who always cares for her flock as Christ did.'

'The Church cares only when it comes to the collection of dues,' she rejoined. 'It is no longer the Church of Christ. It is the Church of businessmen and traders, the Church of towns and cities, not the Church of the hills and valleys. When did the archbishop ever set foot out of Tuam to see how like animals we live, scavenging the bogs and bare rocks for what we can get to keep body and soul together?'

'This is blasphemy you are speaking, Ellen Rua,' the priest retorted, thinking what a mistake he had made in coming here.

'Well, if it is itself then God will strike me down, Father!'

'God forgive you for that, Ellen Rua, for I cannot,' he said, making the Sign of the Cross on himself.

She looked at him across the hearth. 'You are, I believe, a good man,' she said. 'But you have been too long at Maynooth, among the men of power – the priest-politicians.'

Father O'Brien studied her now. How did she know these things? The Máistir must have turned her against the Church, the Church that had turned on him, turned him out. That was it.

'The Church that I, and these villagers, belong to is the Church of no voice, but it is the real Church of Christ. And you and the bishops have forgotten that, Father.'

There, she had said what she meant to say, she would say no more to him. It was not against him she spoke. He had to follow the rules. It was against the system itself that she raged. Layer upon layer of privileged, educated men laying down the law for the uneducated and underprivileged.

She rose as he made to leave. 'God go with you on the road,

Father,' she bade him, no trace in her voice of the anger she had displayed towards his Church.

As he nudged the big grey mare on to the mountain track which would carry him back towards Finny, the young priest's mind was filled with the severity of the woman's attack on the Church he served.

She had a way of hitting the nail right on the head and then driving it home hard. And she had succeeded in forcing him to confront his own set of values.

He had thought for some time that the people felt let down by him, even if he was acting on the archbishop's instructions. And she was right: the bishops had allowed themselves to become removed from the Church on the ground; the Church that had kept the faith alive in the hills and valleys throughout Cromwell's time, and through every kind of oppression. In his heart, he knew that Ellen Rua would have been one of the first in the Penal Days to risk her own life by giving shelter to a priest. She wasn't anti-clergy, nor was she anti-God, but she was anti-Church. A Church that – as she saw it – had gone astray. A strong, devout woman, but she said a thing as she saw it. And she saw a lot that others didn't see, or dared not say out.

And what of her father, the Máistir?

The Máistir, it was said, would have become a bishop, if he had stayed in the priesthood. But he had fallen in love with a woman – Ellen's mother Cáit. She must have been a rare beauty indeed for a man to turn his back on God, Father O'Brien thought. He could never imagine himself in such a situation. A misguided fearlessness, or foolhardiness it must have been, to choose the love of a woman over the love of God. To risk losing one's eternal soul for a woman's touch.

As the grey trotted along, moving faster now that they had reached the road that skirted the lake shore, its rider could not suppress a sense of fascination for the Máistir. Little surprise, then, that the product of that illicit union should possess such beauty, spirit and passion.

When he came to the ford at Béal a tSnámha, the priest thought of Ellen Rua's husband. He remembered how he had ridden out to this point to deliver Michael back across the water, the day he had come to talk about Pakenham. The priest wondered for a moment, as the water swept up around his feet, what it must be like to be the husband of such a woman. Soon he would return to the warmth of his parish house in Clonbur. He would change his wet clothes for dry ones. Yet, back there in the cabin, just himself and the woman across from each other, he had been conscious of something being present. Something that his priest's house in Clonbur, with all its comforts, didn't have. Even while under attack from this woman – her eyes and hair all ablaze in the firelight – he had felt alive, invigorated, unshackled.

When finally he arrived back at his house, he attended to the needs of the mare before tethering her. The long journey had given him much time to think. As he patted the mare's neck, he promised himself that – for the Church's sake – he would not let the red-haired woman down.

14

The snow did come – big soft, downy flakes, dancing earthwards, decorating the valley in white. The children were delighted. Mary and Katie ambushed Patrick and some of the other village boys, who then pelted them with hard, hand-packed snow, sending the young warriors home to Ellen in tears. The tears soon passed, but the snow didn't. It hung on to usher in a white New Year.

Ellen loved the stillness the snow brought. When the first new moon of the New Year came, she went to her place by the lake. She stood and watched the moon's yellow light splash down on to the Mask, whereupon rippling waves carried it to the shore. Unmoving, she listened to the rhythm of the land, the usual night sounds stifled by the blanket of snow. She had been thus occupied for some time when a scratching sound disturbed the tranquillity. It seemed to be coming from the far side of a nearby clump of bushes. Ellen crept up to the bush, expecting to see a fox or some other wild animal. Instead she found Roberteen Bawn.

The boy was bent over the snow-covered ground, apparently burying something. Intent on what he was doing, he had not heard her approach. That *rascaleen*'s up to some mischief again, thought Ellen. Out scratching around in the night, like that. Quietly she plucked a handful of berries from a hollybush, then cast them over the bushes at the crouching boy.

Roberteen Bawn leapt up swearing: 'The divil! God's curse on you – whoever's there!'

He turned this way and that but could see no one. Then he heard her laughter. He knew it instantly: the red-haired woman, making a laugh at him again.

All the same, when Ellen stepped out from the bushes, he was flushed with the gladness of seeing her.

'Well, Roberteen, it's only me,' she greeted him as she approached. 'What was it you were doing?'

'Ah, nothing – nothing at all,' he said, and put his hands behind his back.

'Was it burying something you were – a secret trinket, a message from someone special – burying it under the new moon?' she teased.

'No, not that!' He didn't want her thinking there was someone else, that he had cast off his affections for her now that she was full with the child.

She walked round behind him. He kept turning with her. He had something in his hands. Something he was hiding from her. Something he hadn't yet buried in the hole in the earth . . . Then she knew.

'It's the "Mayo moon" you're doing, isn't it, Roberteen?' she asked, her eyes twinkling in its light. 'Well, well . . . it is.'

Sheepishly the youth looked down at the ground. Then, slowly, he brought his hands to the front and held them out for Ellen to see. They were full of the earth he had taken from the hole in the ground. Only then did he look up at her.

''Tis an old custom,' he began. 'My mother told me . . . for the young men in Mayo and the West . . . the night of the first new moon in the New Year . . . to go and lift the clay out of the ground . . .' he continued haltingly, embarrassed to be telling this to her.

'I know, Roberteen,' she said, helping him out. 'And then, when you say the special words over the handful of earth, you will see your bride-to-be in a dream tonight.'

'Yes, that's it,' he said shyly. 'My mother said I should be thinking now of finding a girl for myself and getting married before the year is out.'

'And you will, Roberteen, you will.' Ellen reached out and gave his arm a squeeze. 'She'll be a fine girl, and a lucky girl too, to get a spirited young fellow like yourself.'

'Well, I hope she'll be half the woman you are, Ellen Rua,' he blurted.

Now it was Ellen who flushed at the passion in his voice.

'C'mon now, I'll say the words with you,' she said breezily, wanting to break off this conversation.

'Does it matter, Ellen Rua, that we're standing here in Galway, when it's under a Mayo moon we're supposed to be?' he enquired with that childlike innocence he sometimes had.

'Not at all, Roberteen,' she assured him. 'Sure, isn't it all the one – Mayo/Galway, Galway/Mayo? The same moon is up over the lot of us. Let's say the words.'

So, in the bright darkness of the Mayo moon, the lake behind them and the white fields before them, they recited the lovers' prayer. He – young, bursting with manhood, holding out his handful of earth, in thrall to her. She, shining in the moonlight before him, all that his young heart desired.

> New moon, new moon, new moon high
> Show to me my true love nigh
> Show her face, her skin so fair
> Show the colour of her hair
>
> Light my dreams this night so she
> May in your light appear to me
> New moon, new moon, let me see
> If one day we will married be

As they said the last two lines, the young man looked at Ellen, and in his eyes she saw the misty look of lost love. The look she had seen there before – the night she had sung at the *céilí*. She felt that the boy wanted to kiss her, but that he would not do so, unless she gave him some indication that it was all right. A tenderness for him swept over her, and for a moment she was tempted to let him. But she mustn't. It would be wrong, and he would interpret it for something else. Instead, she tightened her hold on his arm for a moment and then let go of it.

'There! Now it's done, Roberteen, and tonight you will have sweet dreams of your true love,' she said, trying to dispel the awkwardness. But he didn't answer. 'Promise you'll tell me who she is, Roberteen . . . won't you?' she said then.

At this, he shook himself away from her, and the intensity of his reply startled Ellen: 'I'll not be dreaming tonight, or any night, of some young slip of a girl for me to marry. There's only the one I dream of every night, and the way it is, I'm thinking I never will marry at all.'

He flung the fistful of earth down at her feet, and then he was gone, hurrying, back up towards the village and away from her.

As the new year moved through January, Ellen stuck religiously to her old year resolution of teaching the children English. Each day, excepting Sunday of course, she saw to it that the Lessons, whatever else they covered, contained a large dose of the English language. The children had a good ear for the strange-sounding, narrow language, and so, with a mixture of both pride and regret, Ellen watched them progress.

Michael had decided that they should wait to see what the bishops would do about the landlords before taking action. He had never seemed better in himself, healthy and happy, and things were much as always between them: a mixture of tenderness and caring, and a *frisson* of sexual tension, her condition not dampening their desire for one another's bodies.

All of this gave Ellen a growing reassurance that maybe the events of Samhain had been nothing more than an illusion, a product of the changes taking place in her body, the night itself, and her own fertile imagination.

When the weather permitted, Michael, along with Martin Tom Bawn, had taken to going up the mountain in search of new places where lumpers might be cultivated in secret. This they did under cover of dusk, to avoid the ever-watchful eyes of Pakenham's spies.

In the course of one of these expeditions, the two men came upon a spot overlooking Glenbeg which was inaccessible from the valley below and protected from above by a big overhang of rock.

They stumbled on it by accident after they had startled a hare. The hare, in its flight, seemed to disappear right over the side of the mountain. Turning to Michael, Martin Tom Bawn said, 'Where the hare goes, grass grows, and where grass grows, praties will grow.' So they followed the hare's route to a large outcropping of rock, beyond which they couldn't see. Edging their way along a precariously narrow ledge, they rounded the overhang to find that the mountainside seemed to cut away back into itself, revealing a patch of ground about thirty feet wide and sixty feet long, filled with marshland grasses and boulders and stones of all shapes and sizes.

The two men looked at each other, excited at their find.

'This will do the job rightly!' Martin Tom Bawn exclaimed, bending down to test the soil. 'The lumper will grow well here, Michael.'

'You were right about the hare, Martin,' Michael replied.

'Faith I was! Them's clever fellows. They know every inch of the mountain and it's not too often you see them caught, either. They're even too *glic* for the fox himself!'

With that, the two began the task of clearing their find. Day by day, they started with the small stones, then the bigger rocks, stacking them up around the sides of the Hare's Garden, as they called their secret place. It was backbreaking toil, but if they were to be ready for spring planting, then the work had to be done, and neither man complained. Martin Tom Bawn quoted the old saying:

> No bread without sweat,
> No soil without toil,
> No love without longing.

And together they sweated and toiled to make this soil their own.

'Will we get the dozen beds out of it, Martin?' Michael asked when it was almost cleared, except for three or four of the largest boulders.

The older man straightened up, pushing the cap back off his forehead and, in the same movement, wiping the *soologues* of sweat that had gathered there. He squinted and pondered, and squinted again at the perimeters of the Hare's Garden before he answered: 'Faith, Michael, we'll be doing well if we get the half-score out of it – maybe the one or two extra rows for luck. But I don't think she'll take the dozen, though I could be wrong, mind.'

'Well, whatever,' said Michael, 'it will fill the loft for another few months, or, if we can slip by Tourmakeady without Pakenham knowing, we could sell them in Westport or Castlebar.'

'Aye, the Hare's Garden should see us out most of another year. We could get a blast of spuds out of it.'

On the first of February, St Brigid's Day, Michael and Martin Tom Bawn went to the mountain by spring's first light to tackle the last remaining boulder. They used their *slanes* as levers. It was slow, heavy, and daunting work.

Firstly, they dug under the boulder, then forced the *slanes* as far as they would go into the opening, pushing a smaller rock under each *slane* to provide a fulcrum. Then, together, they bore down on the handles of the *slanes* to dislodge the boulder from the earth and grass which caught at its base. Bit by bit, by *slane* and stone, they managed to hike up one side of the boulder until it came to a point of balance. Now, by getting their hands underneath it and their shoulders against, they were able to move the boulder over on its side. Then they began the dig-prop-lever-lift-shoulder sequence all over again, each time gaining a foot or so of ground.

Michael marvelled at the strength of Martin Tom Bawn. Although he must have been the sixty years out, he was tireless, never asking rest or respite from his labours. When it seemed nigh impossible that further movement could be extracted from the boulder, Martin Tom Bawn would look across at him, their faces inches from each other against the cold, wet, surface of the rock. Then he would nod at Michael to give it another go. Michael would see a purple vein stretching from eyebrow to hairline across the man's forehead. The vein would grow a deeper, darker purple with the older man's exertions, until it protruded angrily. Then, eyes bulging, he would tense himself for a last, mighty heave, and the purple vein would jump and shudder. When it seemed it must burst, Martin Tom Bawn would roar, 'Now!' And the two of them would exert themselves far beyond anything Michael would have thought possible.

By dusk, the boulder had been moved to the far end of the Hare's Garden. The two men stood in the centre of the reclaimed field, arms akimbo, surveying their handiwork.

'It's a grand day's work we've done here, Michael O'Malley,

but we've one more thing to do being the day that's in it.'

'Aye, you're right,' Michael replied. 'The luck sod.'

The two men retrieved their *slanes* and walked back to the centre of the patch. Facing each other they dug down into the cleared ground and out of it lifted a sod of earth each. These they turned upwards on the surface, side by side. These lumps of earth were the 'luck sods', lifted on the first day of Spring each year. An old pagan custom hearkening back to the Celtic festival of Imbolc, the turning of the sod symbolized the true beginning of a new year's work in the fields. An artful Church had christianized the custom, making this, the day of St Brigid, patroness of Catholic Ireland.

The two men rested on the handles of their *slanes*. It had been a long, hard haul this Hare's Garden, but it was worth it. Tomorrow they would begin clearing out the ferns and the low gorse bushes that were dotted here and there, and also the clumps of long-stemmed mountain grass. Finally, they would dig and sieve through the mountain earth, picking out by hand the small stones and the pieces of bog-oak and bog-yew, preserved through the ages in the Hare's Garden.

By planting time, after St Patrick's Day, they would have tossed and turned this earth many times, until it was tilled and ready for its first sowing. With God's blessing on their work, and His hand staying the return of the potato blight, they might be able to pick the first of their new crop in August or September.

Martin Tom Bawn smiled, and drove his *slane* into the waiting earth. Happy with his labours, he spat into his palm, then rubbed his hands together, before stretching out his right palm to Michael.

'Put it there, Michael O'Malley!' he said. 'There's no better man I'd ask to go to the top of the mountain with than yourself.'

The two men pumped hands, lifted the *slanes* over their shoulders, slipped back round the out-hang of rock that protected the Hare's Garden, and headed homewards under the covering mantle of spring's first night.

Down below, Ellen and the children sat awaiting Michael's return for the evening meal. They had just completed fashioning a St

Brigid's Cross from some rushes. As they worked, Ellen told them the story of how St Brigid had tried in vain to explain Christianity to one of the old Celtic warlords as he lay on his deathbed. In desperation, Brigid had gathered a handful of rushes and woven them into the shape of a cross, all the while telling the story of Christ's crucifixion. Before the old pagan chief had died, he had reached for the cross and with his expiring breath, had said, 'My Lord and my God!' thus signifying his conversion to the Christian faith.

Ellen had always loved the story, for the hope it gave. Even in life's last breath, one could, with true faith, be saved by an all-embracing God.

When they had completed the St Brigid's Cross, Ellen moved to place it over the doorway, as tradition decreed. But Mary had said, 'A Mhamaí, this year I think you should put St Brigid's Cross up there with the praties.' And she had pointed a finger to where their dwindling stock of potatoes lay, dark and silent, in the makeshift loft.

Ellen nodded. 'Mary's right – I think that's the place for it.'

The child said no more, but Ellen knew that, behind those few words, Mary was thinking it all out: if the St Brigid's Cross had saved the old pagan chieftain, maybe it would save the potatoes, too. Maybe it would save them.

Though she did not like to single out any of her children above the others, Ellen could not resist the urge to go to Mary and embrace her. God love her, Ellen thought, God love this beautiful child – thinking all the time – worrying about us all. Looking out for us all.

March came in like a lamb and went out like a lion, thus defying the old proverb.

The seventeenth, being the feast of St Patrick, Ireland's other great national saint, was a day of celebration. Some of the villagers made the pilgrimage to 'the Reek', St Patrick's mountain at Murrisk, where they would fast and do penance. This involved walking barefoot up the 2500-foot-high mist-covered mountain, stopping many times on the ascent to do the 'stations'. Plenary indulgences gained for the 'stations' provided a complete expiation of sin and a wiping away of any penitential deficits which might otherwise require the fires of purgatory to balance the books, before the sinner could enter Heaven.

Ellen was too heavy with child to make the arduous journey. Instead, she would 'do the Reek' after the baby was born – probably on Reek Sunday, the last Sunday in Summer.

St Patrick's Day also signalled the start of the sowing season, the villagers considering it unlucky to start earlier. So, it was a time of great prayer, penance, activity and rejoicing.

Michael took down his fiddle for the celebrations on the night. Ellen, too, attended the *céilí*, but she did not sing – it being considered indelicate for a woman in her condition to be too public. Anyway, she decided, she had been public enough already, at Christmas time.

In April, Ellen had a visitor.

The children were out playing and Michael was on the mountain. Ellen was alone in the cabin when she sensed rather than heard a presence in the room with her. It gave her a jolt when she turned to find Sheela-na-Sheeoga there.

'God bless all here, and those who will be here,' Sheela benedicted, putting special emphasis on the latter part of the greeting.

'God and His Holy Mother bless you, Sheela,' Ellen returned guardedly.

'Your time is soon, Ellen Rua. I waited your sending for me, but when I had no word I left it till there was a month yet,' the old woman admonished her.

Ellen had not seen Sheela since Christmas. She had been standing outside the Finny church when Ellen stormed out of Mass with the children in tow. The old one had smiled at her then, in her gap-mouthed way – not without a little pleasure, Ellen thought, at the commotion which her departure from the church had caused. Since then, Sheela had kept very much to herself in her little *bothán*. Ellen had almost forgotten about her, and had been planning to get one of the other women in the village to be her midwife. Now, she was surprised at the boldness of Sheela's turning up like this on her doorstep.

'Well, I've been busy, Sheela, with one thing and another, and I hadn't been thinking much about it lately,' Ellen replied brusquely, needing time to put order on her thoughts.

'Is it how you've been listening to the stories about Sheela-na-Sheeoga?' The old woman seemed to read her thoughts. 'It's only jealousy from them what calls themselves midwives, that's what it is. Why, there isn't a child in this parish that the hand of Sheela-na-Sheeoga first was set upon that didn't grow to be straight and strong in a man, or comely and modest in womanhood. Look to your own three: all fine handsome children, taken from you with these hands.'

The old woman pushed her upturned palms out towards Ellen. 'Look at them!' she commanded.

Ellen, knowing where all this was leading, looked at the outstretched hands, glad not to look into Sheela's eyes.

'Was it not these hands that first foretold this child you carry? Was it not these hands which anointed your womb, Ellen Rua, so that the seed would take in you after six barren years?' The old woman was working herself up. 'This child is a special gift from God. Will you now spurn the hands which were the instruments of the hand of God?' She paused, watching Ellen, waiting for a reply. When none came, she started again: 'I tell you, red-haired wife of Michael O'Malley, the riddle is not yet unravelled. Famine and disease will stalk this land, and you will rue the day you put Sheela-na-Sheeoga from your door. Rue it you will!' she repeated, making for the door.

'Stop it, stop it!' Ellen shouted at her. 'You will deliver me of this child, Sheela-na-Sheeoga, but I want no part of any of your spells or incantations. If this child is harmed or spirited away into a changeling, then I will come for you myself, and you will not see out the full stretch of Summer.'

'There will be no misfortune befall this child, Ellen Rua, no misfortune at all – at my hands.'

'There, it is done, then. Be off with you till the month is out!'

The woman did not move.

'I must see how the child lies,' she said, apparently unruffled by Ellen's dismissal.

'The child lies well,' Ellen retorted angrily. 'I will send for you if needs be.'

'May the Virgin Mary, Mother of all mothers, be with you in her holy month of May.' Sheela gave her parting blessing as if nothing had passed between them.

'I will send for you when the time comes,' Ellen repeated, emphasizing each word.

When Sheela was gone, Ellen had to sit down and drink from the pitcher of well-water. She was in a cold sweat, and the baby seemed heavier than ever before.

How had she let herself get in this position? Sheela-na-Sheeoga, witch-woman, demon of Ellen's worst nightmare, was going to draw the baby from her body. She, riddle-maker, mixer of potions, was going to be the first person to hold the small, pink bundle, the flesh of her womb. Sheela would be the one to snip the cord of life binding the infant to her, its mother. And she, Ellen Rua, had agreed to let her.

What could she do? The old woman was an experienced midwife, and she had implied that something would go wrong if she were not present at the birth. After six years of waiting, and eight months of carrying this child through all the travails of the past year, Ellen could not now take any risk that things might go wrong.

David Moore also went a-visiting in April. He travelled to Leinster House, to report the findings of his experiments to his employers, the Royal Dublin Society.

'Honoured members of the Society, distinguished guests . . .' he began, his strong Dundonian accent tempered only slightly by his years in Ireland. Never before had he seen the assemblage so attentive, so apprehensive.

As the curator of their Botanic Gardens continued, the apprehension of the members of the Royal Dublin Society deepened.

'No storage conditions, no matter how benevolent as to ventilation and dryness, will safeguard the tuber where there is already present some element of the disease,' he warned. 'Likewise, partly diseased tubers soon lead to putrefaction . . .'

The great hall was hushed at his words.

'Badly diseased tubers produce no new growth.'

Now Moore, with each new revelation, heard a collective intake of breath.

'The steeping of seed potatoes in lime and water before planting, as has been suggested, has proven to be of no value . . . Finally, it is with deep dismay and regret that I must inform you of the fact that the murrain has already manifest itself this season.'

15

It was the end of the third week of May when Ellen began to feel differently.

The weight of the child was there as usual. And the feeling of imbalance she had been experiencing recently – the strain on her back, and the pressure bearing down on her lower abdomen. She could feel the child full within her, its beat of life growing stronger and stronger. Katie and Mary had begged to be allowed to cup their ears to the bulge of her stomach, listening for the baby's heartbeat. Both were awed by the pulse of life within their mother's body.

All the usual sensations of quickening were there. But suddenly the movements and the kicks inside were stronger, more insistent than before, keeping her awake at night. If she had counted right from last August then her time was now.

She asked Michael to send for Sheela. He nodded, a flicker of alarm on his face, and hurried off to fetch the midwife. When he had gone, Ellen went to the door. The children were by the lakeside, skimming stones across the flat, still surface of the Mask. Mary looked up from the game and Ellen beckoned her. She could see Mary muster the other two, and all three of them ran back to where their mother stood waiting.

'Now,' she said to her children, seeing the worried looks on their faces, 'there's nothing to worry about, *a stóiríns*. This baby is getting impatient to come out and see what a fine big brother, and two lovely sisters you are. Remember, just as you two' – she nodded to Katie and Mary – 'could hear its heart beating, this little baby can hear, too, and knows all of your voices and would like to see who owns the big deep voice,' she smiled at Patrick, 'and who own the two voices that sound the same – the sound of two little *rascaleens*.'

Ellen tousled the wild hair of her two red-headed daughters, and the three of them laughed together, Patrick making some disgruntled male sound in the background.

'Your father is gone for Sheela, and I want the three of you to go next door and stay with Biddy. You'll be good and help her out with the work, now, won't you?' she asked, fixing her there's-only-one-answer-here eye on them.

'Yes, *a Mhamaí*,' the three answered dutifully.

'Good children! And in no time at all you'll have a little brother or sister, whichever God blesses us with. As soon as it's all over I'll send for the three of you.'

'Can we hold her?' Katie asked, already fixed in her mind that they'd had enough of boys in the house.

The boy they already had wasn't having any of this: 'Who says it's going to be a girl, anyway?' Patrick said, poking his face at Katie.

'Sure, it doesn't matter,' Ellen and Mary found themselves saying together. Mary stopped, allowing her mother to continue. 'Exactly, it doesn't matter – it's whatever God sends. He or she will be part of our family, to be cared for and loved by us all. Isn't that the important thing?'

They nodded in assent.

'Now, come on! Let's go to the Tom Bawns' cabin,' Ellen said, feeling the insistence within her.

Some time later, when Michael returned with Sheela-na-Sheeoga, they found Ellen lying on the straw bed, moaning softly.

Michael ran to her. 'What is it, *a stór*?' he said, worried for her, clasping the hand that lay over her stomach.

'Oh, Michael,' she opened her eyes to his face. 'I'm glad you're here. It's nothing . . . just what you'd expect.'

Her eyes smiled up at him, and he was overcome with love for this remarkable woman. With her free hand she drew his head to her breast.

'I'll be fine. Everything will be all right, but I'm glad you're here, all the same,' she whispered into his dark hair.

'Michael O'Malley, is it that you're going to deliver this baby yourself? Because, faith, if you stay where you are, it's going to be born sitting on its father's knee!' Sheela-na-Sheeoga rattled at him. 'Get me some water off the fire, and some clean cloths, and something to wrap your child in,' Sheela directed, much to Ellen's amusement. 'And then you can leave,' the midwife added. 'There's woman's work to be done!'

Michael, Ellen could see, was glad to get something useful to do, but also, then, to leave.

Sheela waited until he had gone, and then approached Ellen.

'Is it the waters?' she asked, hovering over her.

'No,' Ellen said, the breath going against her. 'I don't think so ... I'm not ready yet ... It's something else. I don't know what it is.'

'All right, *craythur*, let Sheela have a look to see what's going on.'

Ellen tensed as her clothing was loosened. Then she felt the bony hands exploring, probing for a reaction, an intake of breath, a flinch of pain. Sheela was tracing the outline of the child's body with her hands when suddenly she dropped her face against Ellen's stomach to listen. It recalled for Ellen the time Katie and Mary had done the same thing, their faces so still and bright and soft against her. Now she felt only revulsion at the unwashed face of this woman next to her skin. This woman who, she hoped, would deliver her child safely.

Now what was the old *cailleach* doing? Ellen wondered, feeling the vibrations from the low sounds Sheela was making enter the pores of her skin and become part of her.

'Ahh! Mmhh! Mmhh! Aahh!'

It was like the drone of some subliminal chant. The sound entered, not through Ellen's ears, but through her bones and tissue and up into the back of her throat, mixing with her own moans, journeying together with them to some inner ear in her head. The life forces of herself and this old woman were coming together in a way that she could neither understand nor do anything about to stop.

At long last, Sheela lifted her head from Ellen's stomach, and her hands resumed their work. Pushing, prodding, each gnarled finger on Ellen's body like it was some sort of instrument. Drumming and tapping, long notes and short notes, playing and pausing. All the time the eyes watched for telltale, inaudible signs, and the ears listened for what the eye could not hear.

Eventually, the old woman spoke. 'Your time is not yet come, Ellen Rua . . .'

Ellen raised her head and caught the old woman's arm. 'Then what is it, Sheela, what ails me?' she demanded, at once afraid for her child.

'The child has turned. You should have sent for me before.'

'Will it be all right?' she asked, shaking the midwife's arm. Now her life and the life of her unborn child were both completely in the hands of Sheela-na-Sheeoga.

The woman pushed Ellen's hands down, away from her. Ellen searched beyond the cold veils of her eyes for a sign of comfort.

'There is work to be done. Much work. We will see the light go down and rise again before we are finished.'

Ellen's thoughts were in a panic. What was the old woman saying? More double talk – and no talk. More riddles.

She wanted to get rid of the pressure, to push down hard, pull in her pelvic bones, and crush the dam within her. Then the torrent of water could come, could rush uncontrollably, spilling warmly, comfortingly, out of her body, bearing her baby in its wake.

'No, Ellen Rua!' Sheela commanded. 'You must hold back until I tell you. You must wait for my word, if the child is not to be still-born!'

Through the haze of her consciousness, Ellen heard the words. She felt a cold sweat ooze up from within her. Think! Think! her mind told her, as her body wanted to give in, wanting to be rid of the burden it had carried for nine months. Wanting relief.

The child! Think of the child! her mind fought back.

'Think of the child! Think of the child!' Her mind's voice was getting louder, demanding her body's attention – until Ellen realized that it was not her mind which had spoken but Sheela-na-Sheeoga.

'Think of the child! Hold back, Ellen!' the woman repeated.

Ellen could hardly see Sheela's face through the mist of sweat and pain before her own.

She felt the old woman rise and heard her say something. Panicked now, she wondered where Sheela was going? Was the old woman leaving her? Leaving her alone to have her still-born child? Taking revenge for the way Ellen had slighted her?

And what about Michael? Who would watch over him if she were gone? And Mary, and Katie, and Patrick?

From somewhere in the room, Ellen heard a voice say: 'Sheela, don't leave – the child! The child!'

'Sheela-na-Sheeoga has not gone from you, Ellen Rua,' came the reply from the midwife.

Ellen had a sense of something being passed beneath her nostrils. The sweet aroma seemed to seep through her eyes, making her sleepy. Its vapour escaped down the back of her nasal passage, finding the roof of her mouth. There it seemed to crystallize for a moment, like flower-scented dewdrops frosting over her tongue, then melting with its heat, imbedding themselves, sailing into her blood through the pink, fleshy, muscle of her mouth.

'*Méaracán Púca*!' she thought she heard the midwife intone. Ellen was drifting, relaxing, the need to expel this pressure from her body retreating.

'*Méaracán Púca.*'

She tried to focus on the words. *Méaracán Púca* – the finger-covering of the Pooka – the Foxglove. The plant whose purple flowers fit perfectly over little fingers. But fingers which had been dipped in the foxglove must never be placed in your mouth. Ellen was forever warning the children that the beautiful flowers of the *Méaracán Púca* could kill them. They were poisonous.

'Ellen Rua, Ellen Rua . . .' It was the voice of the *Méaracán Púca* that was calling her. 'Don't sleep now . . . There will be time later . . . Not yet . . . Not yet . . . The child, think of the child,' the voice went on, hypnotizing her.

Ellen felt the cold wetness on her belly even before she felt the woman's hands. It wasn't, as she thought at first, perspiration running down her body, cooling it. No, now there was another smell, rising from the lower part of her body, joining with that of the *Méaracán Púca*. This new scent of leaves and bark and flower came from an oily liquid which Sheela was applying to the child-holding area of her body.

'Sheela, what is it you're doing to me?' the words came out dislocatedly.

'You don't worry what it is I'm doing at all, only you be doing what I tell you!' the woman scolded. 'This is nothing but oil of sandalwood and lavender. It will relax the place where you hold the child. Then it will help my hands find the shape of him, and move him back again to where he should be,' she continued. 'After he's settled right, we'll have to move quickly. But that's a while aways yet, so you lie back now and let Sheela do what has to be done.'

Ellen hovered between sleep and consciousness, drifting over the borderline this way then that. And all the while, the old woman worked to save her child.

She felt the midwife's hands massage her stretched body with up-strokes and down-strokes, with strokes which went deep into her aching tissue, relaxing her. Then the hands turned her, first on her right side, then on her left. Using her knuckles, the old woman kneaded the back muscles of Ellen, which had borne so much strain over the past few months. From below the shoulder-blades to the base of the spine and over Ellen's buttocks, the woman worked.

Ellen's original resistance to Sheela's touching her had, over the hours, slowly evaporated. Now she delivered her body to the old woman. Sheela-na-Sheeoga would, after all, be the saviour of her child. Her own saviour.

The old woman worked untiringly, never stopping for food or respite. As evening's shadows crept in, slanting across the cabin, still she worked.

Then the hands stopped, and the midwife examined her, the oils highlighting on Ellen's skin where the head, bottom, arms and legs of this unseen child were positioned. Again Sheela placed her hands on Ellen, and with great care, began working in opposing motions, gradually, painstakingly, turning the baby.

Every so often Ellen was aware of the old woman stopping to put an ear to her stomach, checking that, in the turning, in the life-saving movement, life itself hadn't been extinguished. Hadn't been strangulated by the twisting cord.

The old woman continued to make the low 'aahh! mmhh! aahh! mmhh!' sounds, signifying that she heard a heartbeat. That the child lived. Then she began talking to the child, her face separated from the womb within only by the thickness of Ellen's shining, almost translucent, skin: 'Come on now, *a stóirín*, give Sheela a little *bitteen* of help,' the woman coaxed. 'Just a *bitteen* more now, *a mháinlín,* one little turn more in the womb water . . . Just dip that shoulder, you little *bundleen,* and the rest will follow . . .'

Ellen, more awake now, was aware of every movement within her body as the position of her baby was corrected. There was still pain, but it was a different kind of pain from that she had experienced earlier. This was more like what she remembered feeling when the others were born. Now, she joined with the old woman, willing her child to move, sending the signals down through her body to the blood of her blood, the flesh of her flesh.

The light had long since faded, and now only the lick of the firelight lit the cabin. Somehow, in the midst of everything, the midwife had found time to stoke up the fire, though Ellen couldn't remember Sheela at any time stopping her ministrations. Perhaps Michael had come in and tended to the hearth . . .

Michael and the children would be worried about her by now. It must be midnight, she thought. The old women in the village would be gathering round the fire in Biddy's cabin to see if there was any news, casting things over this way and that, whispering behind their shawls so Michael and the children wouldn't hear them.

'Ah, sure, she couldn't have luck after she insulting the priest. Then driving him out of the house! Ah, no – no luck for that!'

And another would add: 'And wasn't it badly off she was too, bringing Sheela-na-Sheeoga down from the mountain with her spells and potions.'

And the round of the fire would continue until it came back to the first one again: 'Sure, anyway – God between her and all harm, the *craythur.*'

As Sheela toiled, the fire threw licks of light across her face. Ellen saw the beads of perspiration spring from her forehead, the brow furrowed, knitted in concentration, the eyes below never showing a quiver of emotion. No tiredness, no hint of doubt. No possibility of defeat.

She did not mind any more that the old woman's hands were on her, or the closeness of her face, or the sweat from her brow falling on to her, mixing with her own. This woman, this shape in the firelight moulding her body, was giving her all for Ellen's child. She would work as long as it took.

So Ellen prayed in silence for Sheela-na-Sheeoga and the life of her unborn child: 'O Mary, Mother of the Christ-Child, give strength to this woman. Bond us together in our hour of need as Mary of Magdala, reviled by others, knelt – bonded in grief with you – at the foot of your Son's Cross. Holy Mother, by the death of your Child, grant life to mine.'

Now and again the silence broke, the sound rising between them of the breath-chant of the old woman: 'Aahh! Mmhh! Aaah! Mmmh!' as she continued to find life.

When the first light of the sun at last released them from the darkness, Sheela spoke. 'Now, Ellen Rua, my work is done. Your child is ready for deliverance. Now you must deliver it!'

Now it was her time. Ellen drew together all of her bodily strength and power of mind. Focusing the untapped energy of six years of waiting on this moment, she held it poised, contracting her whole being. Then it happened.

First it was a tremor, a rippling, gaining in strength until her whole body shuddered. The force which had been welling up inside her broke its walls and burst forth in one gigantic wash of release. Her cry rang out, rebounding off the mountain walls and around the valley. Anguished, freed, joyful, it echoed into infinity. In Martin Tom Bawn's cabin, the old women heard it and were silent.

'Now, Ellen, push when I tell you – stop when I say,' the voice said. 'Now – breathe in deeply, and push! Again! Good!'

Ellen forced herself to keep in rhythm with the woman's voice, anticipating its command.

'Push!' the voice said. 'Now, stop!'

Ellen resisted the urge to keep pushing. She felt the woman work, freeing the baby's head and neck, positioning its shoulders.

'Now, Ellen Rua. This is it! Soon you will see your baby! Now, Ellen. Now!'

Ellen drew in a deep breath, filling her lungs, and drawing the air down into the pit of her stomach. Then, in one powerful surge, she expelled the air with all the force she could muster. At the same time, she pushed down towards her pelvis. Feeling the initial resistance of the child, she almost gave up, but Sheela shouted at her: 'No, no, Ellen Rua – don't stop! Don't breathe in! Do it! Do it! Push! Push!' and, in one final heave, Ellen did.

From where her strength came she knew not, but she experienced a sense of exhilaration as she felt the baby's shoulders slip from her body. The old woman worked the arms free, touching both child and Ellen. The two women, fused in this moment of sacred intimacy – the one delivering the new life, the other receiving it – looked at each other.

'Now, once more, *a ghrá*,' Sheela said softly. 'Then you can sleep.'

Ellen gathered herself for a final effort to free the baby of her body. When she had done this last thing she would see her child. This miracle child. This child won against the long day into night.

Less exertion was required of her this time before the baby's hips left her body. Then Sheela caught the child, sweeping it out, independent of Ellen, holding it up to the light, as if it were her own.

Ellen was filled with a great emptiness, now that the child had left her, but she was suffused with an even greater, all conquering joy.

Then she heard her baby's first cry in its new world.

She felt Sheela separate the cord between them, the lifeline through which she had nourished and nurtured this child, with her own blood, her own spirit.

As Sheela worked on, silently cleansing the remnants of womblife from the child, Ellen looked at the ceiling of the little cabin. 'Thanks be to God!' she murmured, her words carrying up through the roof to the heavens above. 'Thanks be to God and His Holy Mother.' Her relief at the safe birth of her child was so overwhelming that she was lost for any other words. It had been a difficult birth, harder than any of the others. And there had been times early on when she thought neither she nor the child would come through it.

Now the old woman had finished her work. As she handed the white-shawled bundle of life to Ellen, her lined face glowed with pure tenderness. She looked down at the child who, without her, would have been still-born, a faraway light in her eyes. A sad light, Ellen thought, as if the old woman were pondering the might-have-beens of her own life.

She felt Sheela's hands deliver the baby into her waiting arms. Then, her baby safely cradled into her left shoulder, Ellen clasped the old woman's hand before it was withdrawn. A moment passed between them. Nothing was said. Nothing could have been said. They had worked together to give life. Words would only shatter the sacredness.

Ellen looked into the face of her child. She touched it, anointing its forehead. Then she stroked the streaks of almost jet black hair tinged with an auburn hue, a mixture of her own colour and Michael's, but mostly Michael's. He would be pleased. The eyes, pale blue with a hint of green, looked straight into her own, unseeing as yet, until the thin gossamer of eye skin disappeared. Above the child's eyes were set unusually long, dark lashes and narrow, slightly curved, eyebrows. As the thought hit her, she heard Sheela say, 'It's a girl!'

'My God,' Ellen gasped, her hand flying to her lips, disturbing the baby. 'Oh, I never thought to ask, to look – I was just so thankful it was all over! Oh, she's beautiful, she's so, so, beautiful! It's a girl!' she laughed. 'It's a girl!' she laughed again, as if by repeating it she would quell her own disbelief at not asking before.

'Oh, Mary and Katie will be so pleased to see you, my little dark-haired princess! And Patrick will be too, once he sees you – I know it!'

Ellen ran the tip of her finger along the perfectly formed red-blush lips of the baby, who immediately opened them and sucked on her mother's finger, demanding food after such an incredible journey.

'She'll be hungry, the little mite, after all that shifting around we did of her. But she won't take much. Then she'll sleep, and you can rest too, before we call the others back,' Sheela-na-Sheeoga said, moving to help Ellen.

'I'm grand thanks, Sheela, I think I can manage this,' Ellen said gently, not wishing to offend the woman, but anxious to do something on her own.

She rubbed the surface of her nipple where the milk was. Slowly she drew her infant daughter to her, wanting to prolong the moment, but the dark beauty she held had other ideas, and voraciously clamped those tiny lips on her mother's nipple. Then Ellen felt the warm flow of the interchange between her and her baby, whose eyes, now closed, seemed to be rolling in perfect pleasure with the rhythm of each sucking motion.

Ellen closed her own eyes, enjoying the wonder of the moment – mother and child nourishing each other. She felt Sheela move behind her, still tidying up, making the cabin ready for when Michael and the children and the village would come. Something touched her hair. At first Ellen, her whole being already full with the pleasure of feeding her baby, could not identify this new feeling. Then she realized: Sheela-na-Sheeoga was brushing her hair, gently stroking the matted sweat-sodden mess and untangling the knots in it. Ellen tensed for a moment, but then relaxed, her eyes closed. At last, the brushing stopped, and Ellen could feel the tresses being laid out behind her, a few draped forward over each shoulder, but carefully, so as not to interfere with the nursing.

Now the old woman dampened a cloth, mopping Ellen's face and neck, followed by her shoulders and arms. Then, each hand – not a finger missed – and she continued until Ellen's weary body had been bathed from top to toe. Ellen marvelled at how the old woman kept going, how she attended to every last detail.

'You must be very tired, Sheela. Haven't you done enough for me? You should go home now, and rest.'

'I am nearly through here, Ellen Rua. It's a bad handmaid that leaves unfinished work. See, she sleeps!' the old woman observed, nodding towards the infant. 'Look at her now – as peaceful as the snows of spring, and as beautiful as the bright May morning that's in it. I think she has the look of you, Ellen Rua, although she's dark too, like the father.'

The object of Sheela's observations lay back in the crook of her mother's arm, fast asleep to the world, her rose-petalled lips fuller than before, moist with milk, slightly open. At peace.

'Before I leave you, Ellen Rua, there is one thing I would ask . . . The child – what name will you put upon her?'

Ellen had already decided this. 'I cannot name her in honour of the Mother of God, for my Mary is already named so. Instead, I will call her for the mother of Mary, St Anne.' She paused. 'I will name her Annie O'Malley!'

'Annie,' Sheela whispered quietly to herself as she slipped out of the cabin before Ellen had a chance to say another word.

'Annie,' Ellen murmured to her sleeping baby.

'Annie,' Sheela-na-Sheeoga said to the May-morn, as she hurried for the mountain.

Ellen, as she lay with Annie, nobody in the cabin but themselves, heard another voice. A small, excited, voice.

'Is it sleeping, *a Mhamaí*? Can I come in now?'

Ellen turned her head, a big smile breaking out on her face. There, at the window was Katie, the sun on her hair creating an unkempt halo of red-gold brilliance. Her eyes were wide with delight, and aflame with curiosity.

'Katie, *a stóirín*, of course you can come in!'

Katie didn't need a second bidding; in no time she was beside them, throwing her arms round her mother's neck.

'Oh, *a Mhamaí*! I was worried about you when it took so long. I prayed so hard for you and the baby, I really did!'

Ellen's beautiful, impetuous child poured out her earnest heart, nuzzling into her mother's cheek.

'I know you did,' Ellen said, kissing Katie on the temple. 'I know you did. Thank you.'

'I heard the old women talking,' said Katie, 'and they said it was a bad thing that there was no word after so long. So me and Mary stayed awake all night, and we heard you cry, *a Mhamaí*, and we were worried. So we made a plan.'

'And what was the plan, Katie?' Ellen asked, feeling the excited pant of Katie's breath in her ear, wondering when she would take notice of Annie.

'Well, you know how me and Mary is twins . . . ?'

'Yes?' her mother answered, intrigued.

'That's how we did it. When it was early, before anybody was up, first I stole out for a while and I waited here with you. Then I swapped with Mary, and she came . . . and then she sneaked back into Biddy's house – and then I came again. They never missed one of us at all. They thought the two of us was always there!'

Ellen wasn't quite sure how the twins' plan had worked, but it obviously did. She hugged Katie and said, 'I'm delighted you and Mary did that, Katie – that you were near me. But now, after all that, aren't you going to say "hello" to your new baby sister, Annie?'

'Sister?' echoed Katie, jumping back. 'Oh, I forgot, I forgot, *a Mhamaí*. Let me see her – let me see Annie!'

Now, all of Katie's attention was on the new arrival, the night's adventures forgotten. Her eyes grew even wider than they had been as Ellen turned the baby to face her.

'Oh, she's lovely' – Katie's smile was the width of the valley – 'isn't she, *a Mhamaí*? Will her hair be like mine and Mary's, or like Patrick's? I'm glad Annie's a sister and not a brother. Look at the way she sleeps – are you glad she's a sister, *a Mhamaí*?'

Ellen, faced with such enthusiasm, could only nod her agreement. There was never enough time with Katie to get a word in edgeways.

'If I touch her, will she wake? I washed my hands – I did! Look, they're clean!' Katie proclaimed, as she stuck out a tentative finger towards the baby's cheek.

Ellen couldn't have stopped her, even if she had wanted to. Instead, she just went, 'Sshhh!'

Katie nodded, then drew back her finger momentarily, putting it to her own lips, a serious expression on her little face as she copied her mother: 'Sshhh!'

Slowly, excitedly, Katie inched her finger towards the baby's cheek – not exactly the lily-white finger she had professed a moment ago, her mother noticed. Her lips were pursed tightly together, delight heightening her freckled cheekbones. All the while her unruly mop of hair tumbled about her face.

My hair, my face, thought Ellen. My little wonder. She watched as Katie's finger gave a final lurch forward and indented the soft skin of her new-born sister's cheek. Annie gave a slight stir of recognition, but remained sleeping. Katie, her mouth still tightly closed, made a little exhalation through her nostrils, and arched her eyes to Ellen, scrunching up her face with joy as she did so.

The memory of that first touch between her two children, the sheer magic of that moment of welcome would remain with Ellen all the days of her life. This was wonder indeed. She felt humbled in its presence – as if in the presence of the Divine. The moment proved too much for her. Her body unable, no longer, to hold back its own ablution. Once again the water flowed from her, this time in tears of joy. Katie was looking at her, bewildered. Then, the child saw the light of happiness on her mother's face, and heard the laughter bubbling out through the tears. Great, uncontrollable sobs of laughter.

'*A Mhamaí*, why are you crying when you're laughing?' Katie demanded to know.

'Oh, Katie, you are so beautiful, so precious to me, and I'm just a silly mother!' Ellen said, pulling the child to her.

Katie nestled into her mother's free shoulder, and Ellen leaned her head down so that her mouth was near Katie's ear.

'Katie, *a mháinlín*, do you know what wonder is?' she whispered.

Katie shook her head.

'Well, this is wonder, this special moment with just you and I, and little Annie asleep beside us.'

Katie listened, quiet now.

'When you touched her cheek with your finger for the first time, you felt something strange, didn't you?' Ellen asked.

Katie snuggled into her. 'I was afraid . . . but I was really happy too.'

'Well, that was wonder, what you felt. It was what I felt, too, watching you do it. It can't really be explained, but that's what wonder is. It's a mystery, but it's real,' Ellen whispered to her daughter, passing on to the next generation what her father had made run around the inside of her own head all those years ago.

Katie nodded, trying to sort it all out in her busy mind.

'I think I know it,' she whispered into Ellen's neck. 'Can we make it last, *a Mhamaí*?'

'Yes, Katie, we can.'

And so they lay together, mother, daughter, and new baby. Lay into the gathering dawn – touching, whispering, drifting off – rapt in wonder until the others came.

16

June was warm. Much warmer and drier than usual. This allowed Michael the chance to be at the turf earlier, cutting it, laying it out in rows of sods which he then formed into little stacks. The drying mountain breeze could then waft in and around these *stookeens* until the cut sods were bone-hard and dry as tinder.

After St Patrick's Day, much planting of the potato crop had been undertaken. The people took the view that the blight would, as in previous times, be confined to one bad year alone. The fine days of June saw signs of the first appearances of the green potato stalks above the ground. These were much examined, the lack of blemish or spot lending support to the optimism of the planters that this would be a good crop.

However, after Midsummer's Eve, the weather undertook a dramatic change for the worse. Thunderstorms and deluge after deluge kept the villagers indoors as the rain battered down on their homes, and on the drying turf.

It worried Ellen. 'The seasons are all back to front,' she said to Michael. 'The spring was as severe as winter, with hail, sleet and snow. Now we have this great heat, followed by great *clagars* of rain, and it gone as cold as January!'

Michael knew that with each downpour the turf atop the mountain would be turned back into the sodden peat it was when he had first cut it. Except, now, it didn't have a living, breathing, bog to sustain it, to keep it alive. It would, when it dried again, end up as nothing more than a crumble of turf-mould – useless for burning.

'All ruined – all the work for nothing! There won't be a sod of it left that's fit for burning,' he said.

There would be nothing for it except to go back up the mountain and cut some more. Go through the whole process again, and pray that the weather might be kinder to his labour the next time around.

'It's a hard thing, Ellen,' he said. 'I was hoping I might save some extra of the turf to start the money for America. But all is not lost. We have the harvest ahead of us. God is good, and the summer long.'

Still, all seemed well in the fields. Michael and Martin Tom Bawn, whenever they went to the mountain, would check the Hare's Garden to see if everything was all right in their secret place. And look all right it did. If anything, better than in the low fields.

'Faith, Martin,' he said to his neighbour, 'it was a good day's work you and I did in this spot. I'd swear these lumpers will be twice the size of the ones below.'

'You could be right, Michael,' the older man said cautiously. More summers and winters in the world than Michael had taught him to be cautious. Never to utter a wished-for want, nor foster it too much inside the head either. That way you didn't get disappointed.

'If you're right,' Martin Tom Bawn continued, 'then we have a lot to thank swift Mister Hare for!'

Michael had noticed how the older man always took themselves out of any luck they might have, played down his own and Michael's part.

'So, Martin, whichever way it goes, good or bad, it's not down to us at all – it's a long-legged mountain hare that's responsible?'

'Don't mock me, Michael O'Malley! Things are just so – more than you think! You'll learn yet.'

The weather continued bad into July, and on the fifteenth – St Swithin's Day – Ellen thought that the very heavens themselves had opened, such was the downpour which fell on their valley. If it rained on St Swithin's Day, so the legend went, the rain would continue unabated for forty days thereafter. As it had when the monks of old had tried to exhume the body of their Abbot, Swithin, to bury him in a more exalted place. To punish them for their pride, God had rained down His wrath on them for forty days. Now, thought Ellen, God is again angry with His people.

One evening, at the turn of the month, the sun broke through the clouds in a brief, vain, effort to dry the land. It was the first decent break in the deluge since St Swithin's Day. Ellen, having just bedded Annie down for the night, decided to seize this opportunity to leave the cabin and go out under the valley sky.

How much easier it was for her to walk now. Full for most of the past year with Annie, she had forgotten what it was like not to be carrying the weight of an additional person. Now, she felt light and energetic, with a spring to her step. It was good to be out, too, after the darkness of the cabin.

The sun was warm on her, and on the fields about her. Its heat lifted the moisture from the grass and the potato stalks like a steaming blanket. The lake, too, had a haze of mist just above the waterline. Hither and thither this mist ebbed and flowed as the summer breeze, pushing up the valley, caught it from behind, seeking to bear it up and away.

Soon she had passed the Crucán, the high mound where the valley people buried their children. No mark, no tombstone, only a rock of the mountain to mark their passage from this earth. And, sure, wasn't that as good as any monument? The people who mattered – the grieving mothers – would forever know the rock whereunder their children lay.

The thought crossed Ellen's mind that perhaps she, too, would have had to make the journey here, if it wasn't for Sheela-na-Sheeoga. She crossed herself at the thought, and prayed for the souls of the dead children, and all the souls of the faithful departed.

At last, she breasted the top of Bóithrín a tSléibhe. There she left the well-trodden path to reach her final destination, the *leac* – the large rock where she had sat star-gazing with the Máistir as a child, the place where she had waited for Michael to return from visiting the priest in Clonbur.

The ground was soft indeed. She felt the long blades of wet grass lick at her mud-spattered feet, cooling them, cleansing them. The flat-topped rock with its slightly curved edges resembled a giant grey cradle. She clambered on to it and drew her legs after her, hitching up her skirts so that the sun could dry her feet.

Hot after the walk, she loosened her garment to allow the breeze be at her neck and shoulders. She freed the red plaits of hair which clung to her face, spreading them out, catching the tail of the soft wind. Then she lifted her face to the sun, closed her eyes, and rested.

The sun and the mountain breeze played on her lips and cheeks, warming her, cooling her, cooling her, warming her – in constant rivalry for her attentions. Ellen responded by arching her body to these twin forces of fire and air which vied for her with their teasing dance of touch and whisper.

The breeze ruffled the folds of her skirts, vainly seeking the white skin beneath. Defeated there, it moved down to the exposed flesh of her feet and ankles, busily flicking round them, wanting the inside of her hem.

The sun merely waited, knowing that, in the end, its steady heat would eventually reach through the dark protective folds and find her.

Ellen, suffused by the warmth of the sun, her body bathed as in the afterglow of love-making with Michael, let her spirit soar to where the blue of the sky touched the edge of the earth. That was the place she wanted to be forever, with Michael and the children: beyond the horizon. There they would dance, dance, dance away from the misery of this poverty-ridden life, this uncertain existence where the only certainty was death.

She remembered one of the old mystic poems the Máistir had taught her, and she whispered its words to the sky:

> Over, over I'll take you
> On the Great White Water which swells
> Through the veil of the moon I will sail you
> To the Kingdom of magic and spells
>
> Where the Ages of Man is the blink of an eye
> I will winter and summer with you
> Where the tip of the sea meets the edge of the sky
> And the waves all dance in the blue
> I will dance with the Blue Wave and you

'I will dance with the Blue Wave and you,' she repeated, lost in the moment.

Yes, she wanted to dance, wanted Michael to play for her.

She wanted to swing and swirl in ever-increasing circles, feet barely touching the ground. To be in flight, dancing in the air, whirling in and out of the music as it left the fiddle, until she, the music, and the dance were one. Intertwined, abandoned together. Untouchable . . .

A shiver passed over her body. She sensed a darkness snuff out the light and the warmth. Her eyes flew open.

Above her, where the sun had hung, where sky with only the odd white swish of a horse's tail had been, now there was cloud.

She lay, looking upwards, studying it. Knowing, before her eyes knew, before her mind knew, that this was no ordinary cloud. It was not dark like the thunderous rain clouds she had witnessed of late. It was not white and fluffy like the clouds that brought fleeting showers. This cloud was huge in size, as if the mountains surrounding the valley had been lifted up and brought together overhead to darken the land. Dense and murky of colour, it had drifted slowly in from the north-west, maybe from Sligo or Donegal.

Though the day was remarkably hot and oppressive, she shivered. She got to her feet, pulling her clothes down around her, filled with a feeling of dread.

Underneath the cloud there hung a strange white vapour that trailed earthwards. Some of it fell on her, like mist, softly striking her cheeks and arms. She wiped her face, wanting to be rid of it. But it did not melt to the warm touch of her hand as mist did.

Ellen was held in fascination by this mist which fell out of the heavens, attaching itself to her skin, nestling in her hair. She watched, as the mist settled on the ground near her, covering it like white ash.

What was it? Where did it come from? The questions tumbled inside her head. Never before had she seen the like of it. She turned to look back down into the valley, the truth slowly dawning on her. Below, she saw the fields, green and blooming, the white flower of the new potato harvest fluttering slightly, bending to the breeze. As she watched, she imagined that spores from the vapour cloud descended in their multitudes, like winged messengers from God. Down on to their fields. Down on to their crops.

And then she saw the villagers run wildly out of their cabins looking heavenwards, gesticulating, pointing, following, it seemed, the descent of the little white arrows. Arrows that were poisoned. Poisoned with the blight that would turn the food in the ground into a stinking, inedible mass of corruption.

The fields looked so peaceful, full of the little potato flowers, full of the whitest flower. Ellen needed no reminder of Sheela-na-Sheeoga's riddle to understand what was happening. 'But the whitest flower will become the blackest flower . . .'

And still the mist dropped gently earthwards, silent in its deadliness. A soft white blanket woven by unseen hands, until every stitch, every white-spored thread, was in place, covering the fields like a giant shroud, suffocating all beneath.

Ellen continued to watch helplessly as the fog-cloud passed on its way to the next valley, indiscriminately discharging its death messengers. The sun came out again and shone down on her. But now she felt no warmth from its rays. Despair clutched at her, twisting her within its stranglehold.

In the fields far below she thought she could see Michael and the children rush out, but she wasn't sure.

Ah, Michael, Michael! This would surely be the end of him. First the turf, now the crops.

The nightmare of Halloween came back to her. She, running with the child in her arms, the hands of the dying reaching for her, and no Michael anywhere. The prophesy would, at last, be fulfilled.

And what of the children, and her plans for them? Now there would be no scrimping and saving to put the few shillings aside towards the fare to America. Now, all the English lessons were in vain. She felt so cheated, so helpless, so angry.

As the death cloud darkened the sky over the Lake of Hate, Ellen raised her arms to the Heavens. 'God!' she shouted, 'is this Your vengeance? What have we done except to be poor? And if we have sinned . . . if I have sinned, why punish my children? Why condemn the innocent with the guilty?' She violently hurtled the words at Him. 'Answer me – answer me, if You are up there at all!'

The sinews of Ellen's neck stood out as she flailed her fists after the words, punching them heavenwards, assailing her God, demanding His defence, His reply. Anything but His silence.

She waited. But her God did not answer.

*　　*　　*

Over the days and weeks which followed his address to the Royal Dublin Society, David Moore continued the earlier experiments of steeping the diseased tubers in various copper sulphate solutions.

He had also continued to correspond with the Reverend Miles Berkeley in England as to the cause of the blight. The more he corresponded with Berkeley, the more it led him to question his own evaluation of the blight as being caused by atmospheric conditions.

One afternoon, while Isabella was letter-writing, her husband burst into the house.

'You've found it?' she asked expectantly.

'No, not the cure – the cause! It is now clear to me that, all along, I have been greatly mistaken.'

She listened while he explained.

'Blight which attacked potatoes grown *inside*, in the glasshouses, must have been caused by forces other than the atmosphere. We have all of us – the atmospherists – been greatly, greatly, mistaken,' he said, shaking his head vigorously. 'The fungus is not the result of the blight – it is the cause!'

On 29 July, Moore wrote to Reverend Berkeley – or 'God's Gardener', as he had heard the botanist referred to by young McCallum:

Royal Botanic Gardens
Dublin
29 July 1846
Dear Berkeley,
I cannot longer deny myself the pleasure of congratulating you on the justness of your views . . . Trusting the importance of this matter furnishes me with sufficient apology for thus troubling you.
Moore

17

Overnight, the entire potato crop of the valley was destroyed. Lughnasa, first day of August, feast of Lugh – pagan God of the harvest – saw the harvest devastated. Fields which yesterday were full of hope and promise had withered and decayed, the white-flowered potato plants now black.

For the second year running, the blight had returned to smite the people.

They had laboured on their hands and knees through nightfall into the deep dark. Clawing back the earth in a frenzied search for any lumpers that had escaped the blight. Time after time, hope was dashed from their hands to be replaced by the stinking pulp which waited for them beneath the lazy beds.

'Any that's even part firm – save them!' Michael, in desperation, had shouted. 'We can cut out the bad parts later.'

Everywhere around them the scene was the same. Whole families were sprawled across the landscape, foraging like beasts for whatever morsel of nourishment the unyielding fields might provide. Yet the sound that emitted from them was not the sound of beasts. Nor was it a human sound. It was eerie. Inhuman. Like the keening of banshees it rose up from the fields in a continuous wave, its volume defined only by the level of dismay of those who searched.

At first, the foragers had carried the hope that each next plant might be sound, but as time wore on the dips in the wave of wailing grew less frequent, less distinguishable, signalling that all hope had evaporated. Even the harsh dark moon denied them light in their hour of most need, complicit in their destruction. The unremitting wail of grief echoed and rebounded off the mountains, coming back at them over the lake waters, so that their own sound encircled them, the weight of their grief forcing them lower and lower into the ground, until they sank into the cesspit their fields had become.

*   *   *

Ellen and Michael straggled home after midnight, stinking of disease and decay, with the children – even stout-hearted Patrick – crying.

Back at the cabin, they cleaned and wiped dry the few potatoes they had saved. It wasn't more than a tenth of the crop. Not enough to see them out for even a couple of months.

Michael looked at the exhausted faces of his children, stained with earth and tears. He looked at Ellen, subdued and fearful. Maybe he should have gone from them during the meal months, gone to the picking fields of Scotland, or down into the ground, digging the canals of England, like some of the men did. But it was hard to be away from her. Hard to be away from her laughter in the summer days, her padding over the fields to him with a drink of water. Hard to be away from the smoky smell of her, and the turf fire lighting up demons that danced in her red hair, or in the hollow place of her neck. His need for her had intensified over the past few months, as if they were never going to have enough time together.

She went to him, caught him by the shoulders. 'Michael,' she said, 'you and the children go and sleep – ye had a hard day, and hard days are to come.' She put her finger to his lips to silence his reply. 'I didn't do much: I can sort through the partly good ones, and cut out the rot from them, if ye clear out of my way.'

The children filed towards her to say goodnight, and she gave each of them a longer than usual embrace. Katie waited till last, then reached her lips into Ellen's ear and whispered, 'I'll pray real hard to Holy God tonight that He'll save us all. And if He can't – because it's how He has to take some people from every cabin – that He'll spare little Annie because she hasn't lived as long as we have . . . and that He'll spare you, *a Mhamaí*, and Daddy too, to mind her.'

'Do you know what you are, Katie O'Malley?' Ellen said, holding Katie in front of her, nose to nose. She looked deep into her child's eyes, wondering what was going on in there. It seemed that Katie intuitively knew that this blight and the Famine which would follow would strike at every family, leaving many dead. And there she was, offering herself up – to be taken instead of Annie and themselves.

Katie's nose moved across her own as she shook her head slowly in response to Ellen's question.

'You are a wonder, *a stóirín*!' Ellen said, her breath stroking Katie's cheek. 'A beautiful little wonder!'

Katie, some of her natural animation returning, nodded vigorously. 'Yes, *a Mhamaí*. I remember wonder – it's like the day Annie was born . . . there was just the three of us together, her and you and me, and it was all quiet, and Annie was sleeping . . . and we were kind of asleep too, but not really . . . and you said that that was wonder . . . And now it's the same except this time . . .' Katie giggled, 'it's just you and me. Isn't that it, *a Mhamaí*?'

As always with Katie, answers and questions tumbled out of her head in a string of words.

'Yes, Katie.' Ellen gave her child a long, loving kiss on the forehead. 'Now, off to sleep with you!'

While her family slept Ellen started into the small pile of lumpers they had managed to salvage.

The few good potatoes would be dried and put into the loft. Each one would be carefully inspected to ensure that no infected tubers were allowed in to contaminate the rest. Where part of the potato looked healthy, Ellen took her knife and excised the rot. Many of the potatoes were too far gone to be saved, even though from the outside it looked as if the diseased parts could easily be removed. The rot had a way of insinuating itself into the core of the potato, or coiling round it, like an evil purplish-brown serpent. Sometimes, even as she cut into the surrounding white flesh, it seemed to Ellen as if the rot-serpent moved ahead of her, still destroying, so it might live.

Once, she put down her knife and slowly traced the path of the rot with her finger. Then, with the tip of her finger marking the end of the trail, she had waited, silently fascinated; watching for the rot-serpent to emerge from underneath her fingertip.

Tired, weary, weighed down by it all, she knew she must keep up a brave front for the sake of Michael and the children. It was the only way. Else they might as well barricade the door, block up the window openings, and pull the cabin down over their heads.

Entomb themselves, die together as a family with dignity, before starvation and disease had altered their minds.

But no, that would not happen, she told herself. She might bend with the weight of this calamity, but she would not be broken by it. She had made a plan for survival, for escape to America. It might have to be changed, put back – or brought forward, she had thought grimly – but it would not be put off.

Some had gone to America from around the valleys. No one, yet, from Maamtrasna, but relations of some of the villagers had, and the letters from Boston or New York or Chicago were talked about. And the money, the letters from America always had the money. That was the thing. Everybody knew what 'letters from America' meant: dollars, or this new idea that was starting up – a bank draft. Mici Maol from over beyond Little America had received one from his son who'd gone out to Boston in Big America. It was the talk of the area.

'It wasn't dollars at all, but a bitteen of paper, and *sar* a bit of good it was itself. But you could take it into the bank in Castlebar, and they'd give into your hand whatever amount was written on the paper,' was the explanation Mici Maol gave to all and sundry – without letting out the amount! But the inference was that it was a big heap of dollars that was written on the draft paper. Sure, otherwise wouldn't they fit in with the letter itself, and not be needing the bitteen of paper?

Mici Maol had walked into Clonbur to get Fr O'Brien to read the English writing on the bank draft, the same day Michael had gone to see the priest. They had met and Mici Maol had shown Michael the little printed-up letter that came with the bank draft, with a picture of sailing ships at the top of it. He didn't mind showing this around, seeing as the letter itself said nothing about the dollars.

Michael had described it to her, and only a few days later a widow-woman from Derrypark had come asking her to 'make out the writing' on a similar letter from her daughter in Boston. Boston – that was the place, that was where the dollars were. Ellen had remembered the words, burned them into her mind, as if that would somehow bring her there – be her ticket out.

*   *   *

W. & J. T. Tapscott beg to inform their friends and the
public who wish to send money to any part of the old country
that they draw drafts for large or small amounts – payable
at sight without discount – direct on the National Bank of
Ireland, Dublin, or any of the numerous branches throughout
the country.

W. & J. T. Tapscott
State Street, Boston,
or any of their agents.

It sounded so good, so important. And it was strange, too – for it
was from America that the blight first came. And now the dollars
were coming – sent over by the same people who'd gone to America
to escape the blight! There was no working it out, at all.

Ellen had finished her work, glad to be through with touching
the blighted tubers, as if the disease would spread to her, coiling
itself up from her fingers and into her heart. The fruits of her
labours were meagre indeed. The potatoes, being an early lifting,
had been small to begin with. Now, the small odd-shaped pieces
she had saved bobbed in water; scarcely enough to fill two large
cooking pots and the kettle. It seemed hardly worth the effort. Still,
they would get three, maybe four days' food out of them. The spring
water from the rock would keep them fresh; she would change it
every day, just to make sure.

She gathered the diseased potato cut-offs – eager to be rid of
them, and the smell of them, and the nearness of them – and threw
them into a pit some way from the cabin.

It was just before dawn when she lay down, hoping to get a
few hours' sleep before it was time to go up the mountain with
Michael to the secret potato patch he had told her about. The
Hare's Garden, he had called it. As she drifted into sleep, she
pictured the hare racing over the mountain, always managing to
escape from danger. Maybe the name was a good omen; maybe
the Hare's Garden would escape the worst of the blight.

She estimated that, with the potatoes they had in the cabin loft
and what she had saved last night, they had six to seven weeks'
food. If the Hare's Garden yielded the same again, they would get

through to November. But they would have to divide whatever came from the mountain with Martin Tom Bawn. She'd have to find some way to stretch the food out. One meal a day would do it. If they could keep to that – and she'd see that they did – then they could make it through to Christmas.

In the meantime, they would have to get money to buy food. Maybe she could find some work? Michael had said he'd go to Castlebar or Westport to sign up for one of those new Board of Works schemes the Government had set up. Between them they'd find something . . . anything.

Ellen's eyes could stay open no longer. Sleep, blissful sleep, claimed her, pulling a curtain down on all the troubles of her world.

But as Ellen slipped into sleep, two-month-old Annie was coming out of it. Unaware of anything except her hunger, Annie did as nature had intended. She cried for her mother's milk.

As she nursed Annie, Ellen sensed that Michael, too, was awake. She said nothing for a while. She had watched the resentment building up within him against the landlord. Now this calamity had befallen the family, and he was powerless to prevent it.

'Michael, *a stór*,' she whispered. 'I know how you feel, but you're not responsible for this blight, nor for what Pakenham is doing. You're a fine husband for any woman to have, and you couldn't have done more for me and the children.'

'It's a hard place we're in just now, Ellen,' he said. 'But there's no hard place that doesn't have a road out of it. And even if it's a long road, the longest road will have the turn for home in it.'

'But if the blight . . . if it *is* the Hand of God, as they were saying in the fields . . . ?'

'They're wrong about it being the will of God, Ellen. What god, if he is a right god, would want his people to perish of famine, to fall down with the want of food, and crawl like animals into some hole in the ground to die? They're wrong, and the Church is wrong.'

'Sure, you're right,' she agreed. 'That's only to frighten us poor swarm of peasants into doing what they want. Obeying their laws, grovelling to their cloth and mitre.'

'It's not only the Church that's our enemy – it's the likes of

Pakenham and his black breed, and those beyond in London, who scarcely even know we're here. And probably would prefer that we weren't,' he said, anger rising in his voice.

'Our only hope is to get out of here – to America . . .' How was she going to broach this with him? 'I know we'll never raise the fare in time to take all of us, but we could maybe get the few pounds to get you there, Michael.'

He started to protest. 'I won't go without . . .'

She put her finger to his lips. 'If you stay we'll all starve. If you go we have some chance. It will spread the food out further here, and you'll get work there. Then you can send back the passage money – in one of those new bank drafts from Boston.'

She laughed, and he laughed a little with her. There was some sense in what she said.

'What about you and the children? How will ye manage?'

'We'll manage fine. The baby is getting hardy. After today we'll have in all the potatoes we're going to get. There won't be much to do, and Patrick and the girls will be a great help.'

She was right, he knew. Many's the time on the mountain he had thought it over to himself. Yet the knowing gnawed at the pit of his stomach. He would be separated from her – from the children. Beyond in America, alone.

She was still talking about the passage money: 'If we could scrimp anything together at all . . . I could go to Castlebar and sell my mother's brush and –'

'Ellen, I'd never let you do that! How would you stroke your hair with no brush? I'll sell the fiddle instead. It has a sweet tune and it should fetch well.'

'There's many a *dos* of fine hair beyond in the graveyard,' she said. 'You'll need your fiddle in America.'

It would gain him acceptance more quickly in his new country. She had even heard tell that, in America, people would give you money for making music. What did it matter if her hair went a bit wild for want of the stroking with her mother's brush? Maybe the tradition – the hundred strokes of the silver-handled brush – was all a vanity. A simple comb would do the job just as rightly.

'We'll not say a word to the children yet,' she said to him as she settled Annie down again. 'They can sleep awhile.'

As her parents arose, Mary, who had been awake all through the whispered talk, and followed most of it, closed her eyes and pondered what she had heard.

Armed with *slanes* and *sciathógs*, Michael and Ellen joined Martin Tom Bawn and Roberteen for the climb up the mountain. They went early, and quickly, to avoid notice. When they reached the top, Martin gestured to Roberteen and Ellen to wait.

'Let ye stand here a minute now, and watch!' he commanded.

So they stood, still and silent. Sure enough, within moments, a big grey hare stuck its head up above the scutchy mountain grass and then took off, darting between rocks and bog-holes until it disappeared over the side of the mountain.

'Where did he go to, the divil?' cried Roberteen.

'Follow him now, and ye'll see,' his father replied, giving nothing away.

They quickly followed in the hare's wake, and came to the large slab of rock which blocked the Hare's Garden from casual view. Each of them in turn slipped round the narrow footing of the rock and, in the process, frightened off three or four grey hares, nibbling on the green stalks of the potato plants.

Ellen couldn't get over the rows of lazy beds, sheltered from above and below by the lie of the mountain. She saw the piles of stones that had been cleared to the perimeter of the Hare's Garden, and the big boulders that would have taken so much effort to move. She looked at Michael, pride in her eyes.

'Roberteen,' she said, 'we must be with the two best men to work in all of the West.'

Roberteen, she noticed, was a mite embarrassed that she should address a remark to him in front of his father and her husband. She'd be more careful.

'Didn't I tell you, Michael O'Malley, the day we saw that long-legged grey *buachaill* bounce in here, that it was all for luck, that we'd have a blast of spuds out of this garden?' said Martin Tom Bawn, giving Michael a hard slap on the back.

The four of them then walked up and down between the lazy beds, examining the green stalks and leaves, and the white flowers, searching for the fuzzy white mist that was the first indication of a diseased plant. But they saw no sign of the white mildew that had descended on the valley below, nor any of the sticky brown spots which mottled the leaves, signifying that rot had set in.

'You know,' Michael said, 'I'm thinking they're all free of it. I'll dig one out.'

The others waited while he took his *slane* to the first plant. Carefully he picked his spot and then drove the *slane* into the ground, the weight of his body shifting on to his digging foot. Soon he had levered the first clump of potatoes out of the clay. He picked it up, shook it, and held it for them, while three other anxious pairs of hands cleaned the clay from the tubers. And there they were – the lumpers! Small, but sound: not a sign of the rot anywhere on them.

'Praise be to the good Lord!' Martin Tom Bawn exhaled, dropping to his knees and crossing himself.

They all followed suit, and Ellen, her faith in the goodness of God restored, silently asked for His forgiveness.

Then Martin Tom Bawn and Roberteen started on the next row. The old man put his *slane* gingerly into the ground and slowly, surely, drove it down, afraid of what he might discover. Anxious lest he be the first to break the run of good fortune here in the Hare's Garden.

He bent, he levered, he lifted, leaving it to Roberteen to grab hold of the stalks and then shake the tubers vigorously. 'They're sound!' Roberteen shouted, and did a twirl of a jig. 'They're sound! See, they're sound!' he shouted again, still twirling, still disbelieving what they were discovering.

The two men began to dig faster now, as if the blight, given its rapaciousness, might beat them to it. Might strike at the rest of the patch before they were finished. The boy and the woman worked beside them, bending, shaking, picking, and basketing. The boy working to his father, the woman to her husband. In silence they worked. No one spoke, as clump after clump of lumpers were lifted from the ground, all of them unblemished by the blight that had ravaged the valley below.

Each of the workers was preoccupied with their own thoughts: How did the blight pass these ones by? How many days' extra food would the yield from the Hare's Garden give to them? How would they get the crop down the mountain, avoiding unwanted attention? Any sign of food would attract great notice – and talk. And they could not afford to have word getting back to Beecham or Pakenham. They'd have to chance waiting till nightfall.

Each of them found refuge in these practical considerations, their minds unable to fully cope with the enormity of the moment. That this patch of ground to which they were led by the sheerest of chances, a wild hare, was the difference between life and death for their families. At least for a while longer.

The men, each time they completed the digging of a row, stopped a while to stretch themselves. At one such break, as the diggers leaned on the handles of their *slanes*, Ellen announced that she was going to see to the children below.

'Michael, Ellen – before you go –' Martin Tom Bawn held up a hand, beckoning her to stay. 'What I wanted to say to ye was this,' he started, somewhat awkwardly, 'this place, here, that the hare found for us . . . Well, there's only himself there' – he gave a nod in Roberteen's direction – 'and herself below, and my own self – just the three mouths to feed . . . but there's the six of yourselves in it, counting the little one.'

Ellen sensed what was coming.

'Now, this here garden, and the sight of spuds that's in it . . . well, all we'll be needing is what's come out of those first two rows over there –' he gestured towards the lazy beds – 'and the rest of it I want ye to have.' Having finished his speech, Martin Tom Bawn hunched forward over the spade-handle, looking not at them but at the ripe, upturned earth that had brought such unexpected good fortune to their miserable lot.

'No, Martin!' Ellen got in before Michael. 'You will not do this thing. You and Michael made a bargain: ye would share the work between ye and share the fruits of the work in like manner – equally!'

'Right enough, that was the bargain, Martin,' said Michael. 'And we'll not go back on it now!'

'Well, if it was itself, it was a bad bargain, Michael O'Malley. It's true we broke the ground together, and we broke sweat together, and somehow we saved what shouldn't have been saved. But Martin Tom Bawn – or anyone belonging to him – is not going to take the bit out of the mouths of children because of a bargain between us.'

'No, Martin.' Ellen went up to him. 'Who knows what's going to happen in the times ahead – to any of us? We're thankful to you for your great kindness – you are a true friend and neighbour, but we cannot do this thing – not in these famished times.'

'Well, I'll tell ye what, so!' Martin Tom Bawn said defiantly. 'Roberteen, gather up the lumpers from the first two rows there, and put them in one *stook* over by that big rock. That's what we're taking down the mountain with us.' Then he turned to her. 'Now, Ellen Rua, you and Michael can either leave the rest to rot back into the ground or be picked at by the birds of the air, but neither him, nor me, will carry down one extra lumper above what he'll stack over there. Now, have ye got me?'

This time Martin Tom Bawn looked fully at both of them, lifted his *slane*, and then rammed it back down into the soil, ending all discussion on the matter.

Leaving the Hare's Garden and the men behind her, Ellen hurried back along the mountain to her children. Her conscience was troubled by the old man's offer. Much as she wanted to ensure the survival of her own family, she did not want their future to be secured at the expense of Martin or his wife or young Roberteen – or, the terrible thought struck her, all three of them. She resolved that, while she herself lived, and while they had a bite of food at all in the cabin, the Tom Bawns would not go without. Somehow they'd all manage.

She was so deep in thought that she neither saw nor heard the figure crouched down between the rocks, until she was almost upon it. Nor had the figure been aware of her barefooted and silent approach across the top of the mountain.

One of Pakenham's spies! Who else would be keeping out of sight like that? It had to be a landlord's man. Well, no spy was going to deprive them of the life-saving crop they had just lifted, or have the rent raised further on them because of it. She would protect them – whatever it took.

He still hadn't spotted her. She crouched low, keeping an eye on the landlord's man while running her hands over the uneven surface of the ground. Finally her fingers found what they were looking for: a jagged, fist-sized stone.

She inched forward until she reached the cover of a large rock. Was this close enough? She wondered whether she'd be able to cross the ground between them and bring the stone down on the back of his head before he could stop her. The devil take him anyway! On the mountain spying on them, with Famine staring them in the face. Spying for the sake of a landlord's shilling.

She peered over the top of the rock at the victim of her intended assault. It was hard to make out what he was up to as he crouched, right knee on the ground, left elbow and forearm resting on his other knee. He seemed to be writing something into a notebook. That was it! He was sketching the mountaintop, drawing it all out for Pakenham – marking the spot for him. Marking out the Hare's Garden, the food that would see them through till Christmas.

She made to stand up and rush him, clasping the stone high above her head, ready to crash it down on his.

Whether it was the rush of air or the rustle of her skirts, Ellen never knew. But, as her hand descended to crack his skull, the man turned, dropping his notebook. A strong right hand shot up, grabbing her above the wrist, stopping the death-dealing blow in mid-air.

'Ah, a wild mountain woman!' the stranger laughed. 'Going to split my skull, were we?'

He tightened his grip on her arm, forcing her to drop the stone.

'This is something they don't tell you about in botany school, at least not in Kew, anyway!' he said in a broad accent. 'Maybe Dr Moore should have forewarned me regarding what I might find atop the mountains of the West . . . ?' He seemed amused, despite Ellen's fierce glare as she wrested her arm free of him. 'I suppose you don't understand a word I'm saying, my red-haired beauty?' He tried a few words of Scots Gaelic on her, but she interrupted him.

'*Cogito*,' she said, startling him as much by her mien as by her use of Latin.

He looked at her again, forced to reappraise his initial impression of this beautiful but murderous woman.

'Do you also speak the Queen's English?' he asked.

'Your Queen may hold sovereignty here by virtue of a forced Union, but she holds no sovereignty over the hearts and minds of the Irish people – a people long versed in the use of languages.'

The stranger was taken aback. Here was this peasant woman, wandering barefoot on a mountaintop, not only fluent in the Queen's English but seemingly able to render an account of herself in Latin too. It was extraordinary! Wait until he told them back in Dublin – they would scarce believe him!

'My apologies, ma'am,' he said, inclining his head towards her. 'I did not intend to convey any disrespect, but you must admit the circumstances of our first acquaintance were rather . . . unusual, and somewhat unnerved me. Pray, tell me what action I was engaged in that so incurred your displeasure that you would crack my skull with a rock?' he asked pleasantly.

Ellen was considerably embarrassed by this polite rebuke. 'I, too, am sorry,' she said. 'I intended you no harm.'

He raised his dark eyebrows at her.

'It was a case of mistaken identity – I took you for another.'

'I had better introduce myself, then,' he said with a smile, 'in case you might mistake me again!'

This time she laughed with him.

'Stuart Duncan McCallum, at your service, ma'am. I hail from the Isle of Jura off the west coast of Scotland, and I am a student of botany apprenticed to Dr Moore at the Royal Botanic Gardens in Dublin. You may have heard of him? It was he who, a year ago, first discovered the murrain upon the potatoes.'

Ellen was interested at his mention of Dr Moore. 'And has he yet discovered a remedy?'

'He has pursued many avenues in his efforts to find a cure, but he is at the behest of others. Not many agree with him that the blight is caused by a fungus whose spores are spread on the wind. They would argue that his efforts to find a cure are misdirected, citing other factors as the cause. Factors Dr Moore now believes could not be the cause, *ergo*' – he smiled at her as he slipped in the Latin word – 'precious resources are being dissipated with experiments which Dr Moore deems to be non-scientific twaddle.' The young man shrugged his shoulders, pleased with his explanation.

'With my own eyes I have seen these strange mists,' said Ellen. 'And where they have descended on the fields everything is destroyed. In the plant itself the rot starts first on the leaf and stem, and then goes down into the tuber. Sometimes the tuber is sound even if the leaf and stem is blighted, but never the other way around. *Ergo*,' she emphasized back at him, 'the blight comes from above, not from below. All the people of the valley know this. Yet why do the men of science disagree while we, the people, starve?'

McCallum marvelled at the woman before him. In simple terms she had explained her understanding of the potato murrain exactly as he had heard his mentor, David Moore, explain it. Extraordinary. He couldn't wait to get back to Glasnevin to report on his encounter with this woman whose name he didn't even know.

As if reading his thoughts, she said, 'I am Ellen Rua O'Malley, wife of Michael O'Malley, and we are of the valley below in Maamtrasna. As of now, we do not know how we or our children will survive this winter . . .' She paused. 'And do you, Mr McCallum, rambling the mountains of Ireland – do you search for a cure?'

'No, ma'am.' McCallum gave a nervous cough. 'My work is of a different nature.'

Ellen remained silent, her eyes narrowed against the sun behind him.

'I . . . I am charged with collecting, and documenting, the native flora of the West of Ireland. This past month my occupation has taken me to Connemara, and now along the borders of Mayo and Galway. Some three hundred miles on foot, I have travelled in all.'

'So, you are studying the wild flowers of our mountains and hedgerows?'

'Yes, ma'am, and collecting samples of them, too. In fact, that is what I was engaged upon just now.' He seemed encouraged by her question. 'See here, where I was bending as you approached, this is the *Daboecia cantabrica*, St Daboec's heath, not previously recorded along the Mask.'

Ellen smiled thinly. His was a different world – a world of books and study, a world more interested in new discoveries than old ways. Where plants were more important than people – especially poor, peasant land-occupying people.

He waited for her response, wondering what she was thinking, what lay behind those inscrutable dark-green eyes.

The dark-green eyes studied him, this young man who came from that other Ireland, so far removed from the Ireland in which she, and millions like her, lived on the very margins of existence.

Mistaking her silence for approval, the young botanist ploughed on. 'Ma'am, if I might make so bold as to enlist your assistance in a small matter?'

Ellen was curious.

'I have,' he went on, drawing from his satchel a largish book, 'some other plant specimens that I have gathered in the West.'

The book was divided into sections by thick leaves of paper. Between these were pressed a variety of wildflowers and plants. Ellen found it hard to believe that this could be considered work: putting into a book what grew, free and wild, under God's sky. The young man was speaking to her again.

'I was wondering if you would be so kind as to assist me with their local Gaelic names, for the sake of completeness. The English I have, and, of course, the botanical – the Latin name. We are not required to record our finds in the native tongue, but 'tis an idea I myself have had for some time. They are, after all, native plants . . .'

This foolish young man with his plants and flowers was beginning to irritate Ellen, and she wanted to get back to the children. But he was a stranger – so she would spare him a minute or two.

'I will help you if I can. Then you must answer one question for me in return.'

'But of course, ma'am. Thank you,' he said eagerly. He turned the pages searching for what he wanted. 'This one – "Goldilocks Buttercup". How do you call it?'

How English it sounded, Ellen thought to herself. She looked at the flower, yellow-golden, kissed by heaven's sunlight. 'This is *Gruaig Mhuire*,' she said.

'Would you spell it for me please?'

'Here – let me write it for you,' she said, taking the pencil from his hand.

He, glad not to be embarrassed by his clumsiness with a language which was after all almost sister to his own, proffered the book to her. She inscribed the name *Gruaig Mhuire* beneath the flower.

'Are you not interested in what the name means?' she asked as he made to turn the page.

'Oh, yes, of course.'

'*Gruaig Mhuire* means "the Hair of Mary".'

He looked at her quizzically.

'Mary – the Mother of God . . . Her feast day comes soon – the fifteenth of August. On this day, when she was assumed into heaven, her hair shone like the rays of the sun, brilliant in gold and yellow. So this flower is named for her – *Gruaig Mhuire*.'

'Beautiful,' the young Scot replied, awed by the lyricism of the naming. 'And this one?' he turned the page to reveal the purple-hued foxglove.

'This is the *Méaracán Púca*,' Ellen said as she wrote the words on his page. 'The fingercups of the *púca*, the spirit-man. When he dips his fingers into it, he can drug you with poison. Then the *púca*-horse will carry you away to the spirit world.'

Ellen couldn't resist embellishing her story for the benefit of this avid student, who had taken the book back from her and was now writing feverishly.

'Excellent! Now, just one more – I shan't keep you much longer,' he pleaded, sensing her growing impatience. Ellen relented before his enthusiasm. 'The English name for this one is Chickweed.'

Cluas Luchóige Móinéir, Ellen wrote for him, ' "Ear of the Young Mouse of the Meadow". Now, I must go,' she said firmly. 'But before I do, I have a question for you to take with you on your rambles: In all your travels here, did you not once notice the state of our fields, the blight on our harvest, the plight of our people?

'Did you not see the rags and poverty, hear the keening and wailing, people wondering how will they ever pay the landlord's rent. Then waiting for the moment when the sheriff's knock will come and the crowbar brigade smash down all that they possess?'

The young man recoiled from her attack, clutching his satchel tightly.

'Have you not seen the faces of the people? People with no hope, no future, not knowing if they'll see out another Christmas? Is that not worth writing down in your book to bring back to your masters in Dublin?'

The botanist's face had turned scarlet. 'The potato blight is not to be laid at my door, ma'am, nor at the door of Dr Moore. He merely discovered its first manifestations here. Surely it is as Church and Government have named it: the Visitation of God?'

'How convenient that it should be a visitation of God – now you can all stand idly by saying that nothing can be done. Life must go on, flowers and plants must be collected and new glasshouses built at great expense to house them. Oh, yes, that great news has even reached the West,' she said, noting his surprise. 'Why could that money not have been put to finding a cure for the blight? And you kept in Dublin instead of wandering the mountains, taking even our weeds and nettles from us?'

He stood cowed before her. 'I regret, ma'am, most sincerely, that you think as you do. In truth, it was not something my mind had much turned to, apart from reflecting that perhaps Sir Robert Peel and the Tories might have moved more quickly. I am certain Lord Russell and the new Government will act. You are, after all, Her Majesty's subjects.'

'Peel! Don't talk to me of Peel. "Orange Peel", as he is well named by O'Connell. Peel who sent his hard yellow meal to feed the Catholic Irish. Sure, we're only used to potatoes and shouldn't we be grateful for Peel's Brimstone – hard as the hobs of hell?' she mocked. 'And then the merchants hoarding it, driving up the price till those who needed it most could not afford it.'

'Madam, I beseech you not to speak so desperately of our Government. It will not be as you say. The British Empire is strong throughout the civilized world and beyond. It will not fail its people so close to hand here in Ireland.'

'If you believe that,' she began, her eyes flaming, 'then you know little of the history between our two countries. Ireland is Britain's granary, no more, and Britain cares so little about us we might as well be grain – grains of sand to be scattered from the land of our birth. It happened before – it will happen again. And this Famine, this Hand of God upon us, will be blamed, not Britain.'

'But . . . but . . .' blurted the botanist, unable to come to terms with Ellen's trenchant views.

'You had better stick with your plants, *a bhuachaill,*' Ellen cut him off, 'if that's all you know about the Great British Empire and how it regards the Irish.'

'Well, I . . . do admit to having seen the most unfortunate depictions of your countrymen in the *Illustrated London News* and *Punch* – I cannot say that I agree with the depiction of any human beings as primates,' the Scot offered, hoping that this would end the conversation.

'I'd best be down to my children,' she said curtly. 'And you'd best be back to Dublin and your Royal Botanic Gardens before the men of the valley mistake you for a landlord's spy!'

Stuart Duncan McCallum, apprentice botanist, hurriedly closed his book of pressed flowers, some documented in three languages, some not. He flung the book, and the pencil Ellen had used, into his satchel, and made off at a brisk pace for the comparative safety of the road to Finny.

Ellen watched him go, glad he was gone from her place. Then she hurried down the mountain, following the insistent howl of a small baby, who would settle for nothing less than its mother's full breasts.

'*Daboecia cantabrica*, indeed!' she said to herself as she passed a clump of St Daboec's heath, angry that so small a thing, in the scale of life and death she had to contend with, could occupy some human beings.

'Two Irelands! A curse on them all!' she spat dismissively, as the cry of her hungry infant hurtled her faster down the mountainside towards the cabin below.

When Stuart Duncan McCallum returned to Dublin some days later, Moore was well pleased with his protégé. Some excellent specimens had been acquired by the young botanist while in the West.

McCallum recounted his extraordinary episode with Ellen, and repeated what she had told him.

'She is quite close in her supposition. These small, low-lying clouds carry the spores of *Phytophthora infestans* – invisible to the naked eye, of course. The spores are picked up from the diseased potato plants in their thousands, and transported on the wind.

When the wind ceases to blow, the spores descend earthwards, as poisonous blow-darts, to imbed themselves in whatever healthy leaf, stem, or root they may find.'

'It is a frightening thought,' the young botanist replied, 'that the summer breeze – that gentle breath of the Creator – might carry such silent and unseen evil within its tuck and fold.'

'A frightening thought indeed!' echoed the curator.

18

Over the next few days, under cover of darkness, the potatoes from the Hare's Garden were spirited down from the mountaintop and into the lofts of the two cabins nestling side by side in the valley below.

Sticking by his earlier insistence, Martin Tom Bawn and his son carried away only what the old man's eye told him approximated to one third of the crop. The rest of the potatoes were gathered by Michael, Ellen and Patrick.

All spirits were lifted in the O'Malley cabin as the potatoes were cleaned, inspected, and prepared for storage.

'There's neither blemish nor bruise on any one of them!' said Michael, his dark face lit up with the flush of their good fortune. 'It's a miracle indeed.'

'Praise be to God,' said Ellen. 'I think we should keep them inside. Even if the loft can't take them all, we'll find the room. I wouldn't chance them in the pit – whatever it is that gets at them goes into the earth after them like a great worm or serpent.'

'Yes,' Mary joined in, 'and we should keep these ones away from the ones we lifted from the field, in case they make them rotten.'

'That's a very sound idea, Mary. We'll do that. We'll separate them. What's more, I think we should check them every night just in case. It would be a great shame to lose them now, after our great fortune in finding them.'

So it was settled that all of them would help out with the inspection of the potatoes on a nightly basis. After the Rosary.

A few weeks later, David Moore noticed that his glasshouse plant, *Anthocercis ilicifolia,* from Australia, was in decline. Within days the shrub, with its delicate bell-shaped flowers, was dead.

A member of the *Solanaceae* – the same family as the potato. And its killer: *Phytophthora infestans.*

Shortly thereafter he was asked to visit the Vice Regal Lodge in Dublin's Phoenix Park at the Gardener's request. There, Moore found yet another member of the *Solanaceae* family under attack from the blight. This time it was the tomato plants.

Next the *Gardeners' Chronicle* cited eggplants – cousin to the potato family – as having been attacked by the fungal blight. Even the poisonous Bittersweet could not resist the *Phytophthora* parasite. Soon its vivid purple-and-yellow flower and its bright red berries were no more – turned into the hallmark black mess of decay. Its botanical name: *Solanum dulcamara* – another member of the *Solanaceae* family.

Where was it all going to end? Would the blight, when exhausted of attacking the *Solanaceae*, then adapt and attack other food crops? Would it return again next year – and the year after that?

He wrote to Berkeley, his ally in England:

Our potato crop is lost without exception, I believe, through-out Ireland.

When St Swithin had delivered the promised forty days of rainfall, the weather improved considerably. Michael and Martin Tom Bawn went to the mountain to take a second cutting of turf. This time the weather held and the cut turf dried into hard black-brown sods that would be slow burning throughout the cold winter.

During the days, Ellen continued the Lessons – now the English Lessons – with the children. They were making good progress, and she prevented herself from thinking that her efforts might be in vain, that they might never get the chance to use this narrow language.

Each day she rationed out the portion of potatoes for the family. Before the blight, they would have eaten three meals a day; now they had to make do with one. At noon-time she would put three dozen potatoes in the large black pot and place it over the fire. A dozen for Michael; two dozen to be divided between the children and herself: seven for Patrick, five each for Katie and Mary. As to her own share, she had thought to take the same as the twins, but, worried that this might affect her milk for Annie, she had increased her share to seven. The same as the boy.

'It's better we feel the small pangs of a little hunger now than the big pangs of a great hunger later,' she told them, and they accepted the rationing without protest.

A month later, as conditions around them grew worse, she had reduced the number of potatoes in the pot to 'a score and a half, plus one for luck' – thirty-one in all, each person's ration being reduced by one.

She brushed it off by saying to them: 'Sure, you'll never miss the one if you don't count!'

Canon Prufrock was happy as he toddled along through the Royal Botanic Gardens: '*Alphabetagammadelta* . . . beautiful flower . . . late this year . . . *epsilonzetaeta* . . . fine specimen . . . *iotakappa* . . . diseased . . . never see the Christmas . . . *pirhosigmatauupsilon* . . . good morning doctor . . . *phichipsiomegaamen*.' His alphabet complete he stopped now to look at these new, strangely-shaped Curvilinear glasshouses.

What was Moore about these days? It was a pitiful shame that his experiments to find a cure for the blight were unsuccessful. The country at large had lain its hopes at the gates of the Royal Botanic Gardens. It was a melancholy state of affairs, thought the canon.

He remembered well the day Moore had first discovered the blight here in the gardens. The date, 20 August 1845, was indelibly etched on the canon's mind. Over a year had gone by without a cure, and the country was in a grievous state; particularly in the West and South, where the populations of peasantry were greatest. Of late he had heard worrying reports of diseases related to the deprivation of the rural poor attacking the middle classes in the city. And there had been riots as starving paupers from the surrounding districts had invaded the streets of Dublin. Bakers, going about their daily rounds, had been waylaid, and whole cartloads of bread stolen from them. Perilous times, perilous times, thought the canon.

In his own parish he had actively promoted almsgiving for the relief of suffering. His flock – devout and decent Protestants – had responded most generously. The monies collected he had sent to MacHale, the Catholic Archbishop at Tuam, a diocese in the heart of much suffering and want.

Still in his musings, Prufrock came upon the curator and a team of men, building something or other over the potato patch. They had erected wooden poles, about twice the height of a man, the circo-distance between them some thirty to forty feet.

His curiosity further heightened, Canon Prufrock moved closer. From this nearer vantage point he could see that down the side of each wooden pole ran a length of copper wire which disappeared beneath the earth's surface. This wire also protruded above the top of each pole, and the extensions were joined by a large circular band of copper wire which ran the complete circumference of the copper tent. Some form of experimentation to do with the potato blight, no doubt, thought the canon.

'God bless the good work!' he saluted.

'Reverend Canon, how nice to see you!' Moore said, not at all sure how the canon would react towards these new experiments.

'I see copper, I see rods pointing towards the heavens and, yet, earthed into the ground . . . And I see potato beds . . . ?' Prufrock arched a questioning eyebrow at the curator.

'Quite right, Canon. What you see before you are giant lightning rods which, when connected, form tractors of electricity . . .'

The canon's quizzical eyebrow was busy again at 'tractors'.

'Or, if you prefer,' the curator elucidated, 'conductors of electricity.'

The canon's eyebrow resumed its waiting position.

'If, as the atmospherists believe, that the heavens deliver excessive electrical discharge thereby causing the disease . . .' Moore immediately regretted blaming 'the heavens'. And hurried on with his explanation. 'Then these conductors – on the one hand, by attracting greater electricity to the ground where the tubers grow, and, on the other hand, by diverting the electricity away from the tubers into ground where they do not grow – will scientifically test their theory. It will be proven or disproven, as the case may be.' Moore found it hard to sustain even a semblance of conviction in the case he posited to the canon. It was, however, the will of his employers, the Royal Dublin Society, that the theory be tested, and he must obey that will.

But official will or no, in plain Dundonian it was daft. Moore knew it, and he knew the canon would know it. But he was not prepared for what was to come next.

'The heavens!' the canon exploded. 'Sir, how many seasons has it now been bestowed on me by the All Powerful Creator, the pleasure of perambulating in these gardens?'

The canon held up a bony finger to silence any answer.

'How often, sir, have I had occasion to compliment you, since your arrival here, on the manner in which you have seen fit to carry on the great work of the Creator?'

As in all his best Sunday sermons, Canon Prufrock, having first posed the question, now paused before pouncing on the assemblage.

'Now, after all those hours, those days, those seasons, those years, in which the gracious and good God hath blessed these gardens and the work of His labourers herein, I now fear the hand of another to be at work in this Garden of Eden. It is the hand of Satan I speak of!' the canon pronounced, punching his finger through the air at the tractors.

'Now, really, Canon!' the curator broke in. 'This is work which may result in the earthly salvation of many of God's children.'

'Earthly salvation is it that concerns you, sir?' the canon interrupted. 'Well, well, well! How far we have strayed from the path of righteousness with new-fangled tractor contraptions seeking to confound the heavens – undo the work of the Creator.' The canon's face was white, his lips trembling. 'And now, good sir, you speak of earthly salvation! Show me the psalm, show me the verse, show me the word even, whether in New Testament or Old, which speaks of earthly salvation? It is not there – you will not find it!'

The canon rose to the occasion, further regaling his now swelling congregation.

'There is no salvation save Heaven. It is a blasphemy to speak of earthly salvation! I see no salvation in . . . in this –' and he beat the air with his cane at the tractors. 'Only the pride of man!' he thundered at them, and then reduced his voice, bringing his congregation with him, hanging them onto his every word.

> Blessed are the poor in spirit;
> They shall see Heaven . . .
> Blessed are those who hunger and thirst for what is right;
> They shall be satisfied . . .

He quoted at Moore from the Beatitudes, each beatitude a winged arrow, transfixing the hapless curator.

'These "tractors", as you call them, are tractors of sin, monuments to man's pride. This will bring no cure for the pestilence – it will redouble pestilence! You have been led astray in this aberration by the nincompoops of Leinster House! But tell me, Moore – is there anything, anything at all, in this endeavour which is worthy of pursuit?'

Moore, stoically, remained silent.

'It is a farce, is it not? Is it not a waste of your talents to be so occupied, a squanderment of the finite time, which the Creator hath bestowed on us? Time better spent pursuing other avenues for a remedy to the murrain which afflicts the potato crop?'

Moore's annoyance at Prufrock's questions was directed both at the canon and at himself. For his own views were aligned with the canon's: it was a farce, a waste of his time and talent. He knew it, Isabella knew it, and now the canon knew it.

'My private views, Reverend,' Moore found himself saying, 'are not for public consumption until proven – or not, as the case may be – by scientific experiment.'

The canon 'hmmphed', glared at Moore, and turned on his heel to leave. 'Beware of the wrath of God on this evil work – no good will come of it,' he warned, then strode off through the crowd muttering to himself as he went.

He would not speak of it again to the curator.

On 1 November, the Feast of All Saints, Ellen reduced their daily rations further, down to two dozen potatoes, plus one for luck. Michael's portion had shrunk to nine potatoes, the twins got three and a half each, while Patrick had four and a half. Ellen, too, got four and a half potatoes, out of which portion she mashed a bit for Annie.

Once or twice Michael caught an injured hare, and Roberteen brought her one of a brace of birds he had trapped using a basket. But it was getting harder. All the men, women and children of the village scavenged for food. Any wildlife that remained seemed to have taken to high ground.

Ellen herself had combed the few bushes and trees there were, but the valley between mountainside and lakeside was barren, providing few berries or nuts that were edible.

The Mask had fish – she had seen them herself – but Pakenham owned the fishing rights, and the poaching laws were more strictly enforced than ever. Already Johnny Jack Johnny had been caught by Pakenham's bailiff, and now languished in Westport Gaol, fortunate not to have been hanged. Michael, against her wishes, had chanced it a few times, but as he himself said: ''Tis no use. Even the fish are fearful, the people are so famished with hunger.'

Now Ellen looked around at her family as they thanked the Lord for the diminishing helpings on their plates. They were healthy still, thank God, but they had all lost weight. Michael's eyes had sunk into their hollows, hardened with bitterness at 'the Dublin and London set – ignoring the cries of the poor, whose sweat on the land allows the likes o' them to live their high lives.' Patrick was getting taller, more like a man every day in spite of the deprivation. Mary's cheekbones were now more pronounced than ever, the freckled bloom gone from her face. Katie, beside her, was as animated as ever – even one less than adequate meal a day couldn't knock that out of her. But her arms were painfully thin.

As for Annie, now six months old, she was thriving. She fed well at her mother's breast, blissfully unaware of the privations that all around her suffered. Mercifully, Ellen's milk supply remained good, though she had long since lost the fulsomeness of figure brought on by Annie's birth.

As an antidote to eating insufficient food, they had taken to sleeping later in the mornings and going to bed earlier at night to conserve their energy.

The previous night had been an exception. They had gathered at the bonfire near the Crucán as in Halloweens gone by, and Ellen had scanned the shores of the Mask, looking for the bonfires of the other lakeside clachans. But where there had once been a ring of fire, this Halloween the circle was scarred by dark gaps, filled only by the spirits of those who had left, or died.

Michael had taken down his fiddle and rosined his bow, but there wasn't any real lustre in his playing and few were of a heart for dancing. Instead, people sang laments and recounted stories of famines past, comparing them to this *Aimsir an Drochshaoil* – the

Time of the Bad Times – as the current famine was called. Ellen had sung *Ochón an Gorta Mór* – the Lament the Great Hunger – unaccompanied, in the old style.

> *Ochón, ochón,*
> *Ochón Aimsir an Drochshaoil,*
> *Ochón, ochón,*
> *Ochón an Gorta Mór.*
>
> The people are broken, devastated,
> Scattered to the wind.
> And our children littered
> On the side of the road.
>
> There is no harvest to divide,
> No potatoes to save.
> Only the long wild grass
> Waiting to be over us.
>
> Alas, alas,
> Lament the time of the Famine,
> Alas, alas,
> Lament the Great Hunger.

Her song with its harsh beauty silenced the listeners, each one recognizing in it the fate of a loved one, a child, a sister, a husband, a mother. Each of them recognizing their own probable fate.

But if the dark night of Halloween was the harbinger of grief and darkness to come, then the approach of Christmas – season of light and glad tidings – seemed to mock them even more, sealing the black year with even grimmer forebodings.

On 8 December, the feast of the Immaculate Conception, Michael set out on the long walk to Tourmakeady Lodge. It was a strange day for Pakenham to be summoning him to discuss renewal of their tenancy. The landlord had done this to them last year, too. And Pakenham well knew it was a special holy day for his Catholic tenants. Michael sensed some badness in it.

This time he was alone. Ellen had stayed behind to look after Annie.

'You're the lesser of no man, Michael O'Malley!' she had whispered as she embraced him at the cabin door. 'Hold your tongue and hold your dignity.'

'Pakenham won't rattle me,' he reassured her. 'Anyway, he's at no advantage, for who else would take our land? No one around here!'

She bid him *bóthar slán* – a safe road. She always worried when he was away from her. Afraid that the death the Banshee had lamented the previous All Souls would come to pass, and she wouldn't be there to comfort him in his last moments. It made matters worse that he was so strained of late, ready to snap at any moment. His hatred of 'the landlord class that cripples this country' was further fuelled by their deteriorating situation as the store of lumpers in the loft dwindled away to nothing.

As soon as he was gone, she summoned the children to kneel and pray with her. The Mother of God would keep him safe, even if she couldn't.

Later in the day, as Ellen stood outside and looked across the lake towards Derrypark and the road which would carry Michael home, a shiver passed over her. A shiver that had nothing to do with the mid-winter chill coming off the Mask. Instinctively she crossed herself, and then ran back into the cabin.

Once inside, she went to the hearth and rubbed her arms and shoulders to get rid of the cold feeling.

The shiver – the one a person got when someone walked over your grave – did not repeat itself.

19

Michael, his eyes ablaze, his fist clenching the paper, stopped for a moment as he left Tourmakeady Lodge.

How could he go back to her? How could he show her the piece of paper he held in his hand?

He looked at the crumpled Notice of Distraint which informed them that whatever goods they had would be seized in lieu of the outstanding rent. Goods! Sure, they had nothing, nothing except the roof over their heads, and whatever was on their backs.

He thought of the potatoes in the loft. He'd have to save the last few lumpers they had left – he couldn't let Pakenham take the last bite out of their mouths. Not that what they had left would see them much past Christmas, anyway. But over his dead body would Pakenham seize them.

'God's curse on him, the black devil!' he said, ramming his fist into the Notice. And Beecham, too, all the time sloping around behind Pakenham. The agent would be a lucky man not to end up in the Mask with a big lump of rock tied to his ankles. And he, Michael O'Malley, would be the first one to tie it.

Pakenham had toyed with him, making a pretence of trying to help them.

'Now, O'Malley, let's see what we can do here!' the landlord had started. 'I am aware, as any man must be, of the distress upon the nation caused by this . . . this . . . blight. And being mindful of the season, and all that . . .'

Michael knew better than to trust him. Pakenham wouldn't have forgotten the last time he and Ellen had been there, or the incident following the break-up of the *céilí* below the Crucán. Wouldn't have forgotten a bit of it.

'I suppose, O'Malley, this time you have no surprises up your sleeve, so to speak . . .' the landlord went on, his words laced with sarcasm.

Beecham, observing the ragged state of Michael's clothes, smirked at this.

'No more secret hoards of potatoes, eh?' He paused for a moment, raising a questioning finger at Michael. 'And what of that fiddle – been playing it for that pretty red-haired wife of yours lately?'

Beecham smirked again.

'A boy or a girl, was it, O'Malley? Well, last year . . . when she was here with you . . .' the landlord went on, feigning coyness.

'A girl,' Michael answered him quietly.

'A girl. Well, well, Beecham, isn't this news to be welcomed? Congratulate the fellow!'

Beecham offered his congratulations with a simpering smile.

'And tell me, O'Malley, does she take after you, or is she pretty like her mother?'

Michael ignored the landlord's remark.

Then Pakenham got down to the real purpose of this meeting: 'Now that Mrs O'Malley has returned to her . . . normal condition, by coincidence, Mrs Bottomley tells me that things have become a mite slovenly downstairs. We could do with some help here at the Lodge. What say you, O'Malley?'

Michael, who had contained himself up to now, saw red. 'My wife is no man's *tallywoman*! I would rather die at the side of the road like dogs than allow any wife of mine be a landlord's whore!'

Pakenham's face was white with rage. 'And so you shall, O'Malley – so you shall! Beecham, give him the Notice!'

At the landlord's signal, Beecham thrust the Notice of Distraint into Michael's hand and began pushing him towards the door.

'You're just like the rest, O'Malley: always whingeing, turning on the hand that feeds you. Now, see how you and your high and mighty wife likes this for a Christmas present!'

They had made such a fool of him, baiting him for their sport, intending all along to issue him with the Notice.

He couldn't bring it home to Ellen. Not now, not two weeks before Christmas. He slipped into the walled rose gardens, bereft of colour now, except for one bush which defied the hardships of the season and stood lonely but majestic in its winter beauty: *Rosa chinensis* – the last rose of summer.

Michael took in the *terrazzo*, the bower, the pergola, the pathways, the walls. The stone in them would have built twenty cabins such as his, and now they were going to be left with no cabin at all! The roses grew on land which, if planted with lumpers, could have fed a family for a year.

Outraged at the injustice of it all, Michael approached the flowering rose bush. He bent to its base, intending to tear it out of the ground with his bare hands and then trample it – let Pakenham know he wasn't beaten yet. But the last rose of summer, having wintered out the seasons of many a harsh year would not now give itself up easily to man. Its thorns lacerated the side of Michael's neck and dug into the palms of his hands, darting sharp pains up through his arms.

Bloodied and defeated by the rose bush, Michael was forced to stop. In his frustration he began to pull off the heads of the flowers, flinging them as far away from him as he could. Then he stopped, and began to gather them up again . . . This was not the way.

'*Tiocfaidh ár lá!*' he said in a whisper to the crumpled petals in his hand. 'Our day will come!'

Before he left, he impaled Pakenham's Notice of Distraint on the highest point of the bush of the *Rosa chinensis*, the white paper fluttering above the red flowers, the black print of its death-dealing message reefed and ripped by the thorny beauty on every side.

Michael tried to make a brave face of it for Ellen.

She ran to him the moment she spotted him from the door, glad to see him back – to see him alive. Katie and Mary ran at him too, almost pulling his arms out of their sockets. Even little Annie did the best she could to welcome him home, flashing her dark eyes and making happy gurgling sounds when he entered the cabin.

Though he had washed his face and hands in the Owenbrin River on the way back, Ellen saw the telltale marks on his neck where the skin had been pierced by Pakenham's roses.

He caught her looking at them and plunged his hand into his pocket, pulling forth the rose-heads.

'I brought you these, Ellen,' he said, handing the broken flowers to her. 'For the Christmas.'

'Oh Michael, they're so beautiful. *Mo bhuíochas dhuit*,' she said, slipping back into the Irish to thank him, ignoring the scars on his upturned palms.

'And one for Katie,' he said, hurrying on, wanting to distract her, not wanting space so she could look at him, see it all in his face, 'And one for Mary.'

'What sort of a flower is it?' Katie broke in, never having seen a rose before.

'And Patrick – I brought you one, too. It's little I have to give you all this Christmas,' he said, wondering when Pakenham's men would come.

The boy took the flower awkwardly, shyly, and thanked his father, knowing somehow the gift was more than it was.

Moore's private views on the experiments, and the canon's public denunciation of their uselessness, were both found to be correct. 'The tractors,' the curator reported to the 'nincompoops' – Moore liked the canon's word – of the Royal Dublin Society, 'have not had the slightest effect, one way or another, on the contamination of the potato.'

Now, as 1846 drew to a close, the country was in a state of mass poverty, mass emigration, mass starvation and mass death.

Isabella Moore was sorely troubled. 'The reports from every corner make sorry reading,' she said to her husband. 'Whole families wiped away in the most inhuman conditions: typhus, cholera and famine fever racking their bodies alongside starvation. It is too appalling.'

'Yes,' he replied, 'and Government seems incapable of dealing with it. I cannot believe that there is unwillingness in London. Disbelief at the scale of it, incompetence in handling it, perhaps, but not disregard for duty.'

Isabella shook her head trying to come to grips with it all. 'Our good and Sovereign Majesty, Queen Victoria, whose thoughts are surely with her suffering subjects in Ireland, would surely not stand by if greasy politics were to stay the hand of mercy and compassion?'

Even as she spoke, her husband's thoughts had moved on to pressing matters nearer to hand. 'Now that we have terminated with the electro-culture experiments, or, as your friend Canon Prufrock is wont to call them, "Beelzebub's tractors", the gardens' coffers are too depleted for the carrying out of any further experiments. We are rendered somewhat impecunious. What is more, there are many who are still arraigned against my views that the blight is fungal in origin, and this is unhelpful to my plea to the Committee of Botany for extra resources.'

'Does this mean the experiments to find a cure for the disease are ended?' Isabella asked in disbelief.

'I regret to tell you, my dearest, that without more finances, it means just that.'

'It makes not a whit of sense!' Isabella said angrily. 'At a time when millions are starving to death, there is no money for research to save them. That these' – she pointed towards the Curvilinear glasshouses – 'should be built in such times of hunger and destitution, while paltry amounts cannot be given you to continue your experiments. Ohh, it makes me not myself to think of it!'

'Isabella,' he said tenderly, 'rarely have I seen you moved to such strong feelings, for you are indeed the gentlest of souls. I have today again composed a letter to the committee. I pointed out, most clearly, my deep unhappiness at being unable to carry out any further experiments into the cause of the potato failure, due to the financial strictures placed upon me. Finally, I requested an increase in financial support so that the gardens, in consequence, be rendered more useful to the country than hitherto.'

Moore's letter to the Royal Dublin Society's Committee of Botany did not bring the required benefits to the gardens. No further monies were extended for experiments into the cause of the blight.

There were to be no more bluestone steeps for the diseased tubers.

20

On Christmas Eve they came: Beecham, the crowbar brigade, the militia.

Ellen was readying herself and the children for Midnight Mass. A year to the day since she had stormed out of Finny church over Father O'Brien's failure to speak out against Pakenham and the landlords. Almost a year since the priest had come to her cabin and she'd flung bitter words at him. In the interim, an uneasy truce had developed between her and the young clergyman, aided, in part by Annie's arrival and the necessity for the child to be baptized. But events had proven her right – the situation with the landlords had deteriorated steadily. Lord Lucan was already evicting in Mayo, while hundreds had marched on Lord Sligo's house in Westport as early as August. Word had it since that the landlord, hitherto lenient, was to commence evictions, saying he was under the necessity of 'ejecting or being himself ejected'.

Pakenham himself had already started back around Partry, and had tumbled a few cabins in Derrypark as well – targeting the outlying districts, not wanting, at this stage, to take the risk of stirring up the tenants in the vicinity of Tourmakeady Lodge. At least he had let those evicted take the thatch with them. That way they could lean it over a ditch somewhere for shelter, make a *scailpeen* over their heads.

There was talk among the women in the valley that Pakenham owed a big sight of money in London and that he had unpaid dues to the Westport Union as well. But Ellen could feel no pity for him. She had got it out of Michael about Pakenham's intention to evict them, and was beside herself with worry. There was nowhere for them to go except the roadside, and the children wouldn't last long out in the extremes of winter – even if Pakenham did let them keep the bit of thatch for shelter – and as for Annie . . .

Michael had taken the few potatoes they had left and hidden

them in the ground in the driest place he could find, bedding them well with straw. Each day they would go to the pit and take only the handful that made up their daily ration. That way Pakenham's men, when they came, wouldn't seize the last of their food. Then, after their turn came to be evicted, Michael could creep back under cover of darkness from whatever *scailpeen* they were in and get the remainder of the buried potatoes.

Ellen had made up her mind that straight after the Christmas – the day after St Stephen's Day – she herself would go to Pakenham. Whatever had to be done to save them, she would do it. But for now they would go to Finny and pray that God would somehow deliver them.

In the event, the O'Malleys were not to get the opportunity to see one last Christmas out in their home.

Ellen was just finishing with Katie's hair. The child, as usual, was full of questions.

'*A Mhamaí,* can we sit near the back this year?'

'No, Katie . . . why?'

'In case we have to leave early like last year and walk all the way down the church and everybody looking at us!'

'Oh, Katie, shush for once!' Ellen said to her, turning over in her mind her idea of going to Pakenham.

The first she knew anything was amiss was a raised voice outside the door.

'I, Richard Albright Pakenham, do hereby give notice to Michael O'Malley, Maamtrasna, in the County of Galway, and all thereof unto him, to forthwith quit the tenure which he holds from me. Furthermore all goods –'

'Beecham!' Michael had rushed past her to confront them. 'It's Christmas Eve, man. For God's sake!' he shouted at the agent.

Ellen ran to the door behind him. What she saw facing their cabin was the end of her world as she had known it.

Beecham was accompanied by four men, each armed with a long black crowbar. She thought she recognized one of them. But the crowbar men kept their eyes to the ground, awaiting the order to go to work, levering out the stones which would tumble the cabin to the ground. Behind the crowbar brigade, on horseback, were six militia men, muskets with bayonets attached at the ready.

'It matters not what day it be, O'Malley,' said Beecham, glancing back at the militia men. 'What matters is your failure to pay due rent to His Lordship, and your subsequent refusal of his suggestion as to how you might overcome the default.'

'Damn His Lordship's suggestions and damn you, Beecham!' Michael cried, rushing at the agent.

The six horsemen moved forward as one, their bayonets levelled at Michael's throat.

'Resist at your peril, O'Malley!' Beecham shouted, visibly shaken by Michael's attempted attack on him.

'Michael,' Ellen said calmly, 'leave it be.'

He looked at her, ready to argue. But she was right. He would not lose his dignity in front of that *slieveen,* Beecham, or let hers be undermined by arguing with her.

By now the other villagers had gathered, with Roberteen Bawn to the fore.

'Cowards – are ye Christians at all to be putting them out this night?' Roberteen yelled, his face wild. 'She has a child to care for, bastards!'

Ellen heard the commotion outside as she gathered up Annie, wrapping her in as many layers of clothing as she could. Then she said to the children, 'Now, we are going to leave our home together, and together we will go over the mountain and down to Finny to Mass. We will not fight nor beg. Neither will we take the few things we have, to have them taken from us again.'

They listened, each of them knowing that for Ellen Rua O'Malley there could be no other way.

'We have each other, we have what they can't take from us, or pull down, and we have our faith,' she reassured them, confirming that what they were about to do was the correct thing.

'Your mother is right,' said Michael. 'We are *Máilleachs* and neither landlord nor Crown will break us.'

Outside, Beecham was getting agitated – he could see that the crowd was becoming more and more angry. He had been right in convincing Pakenham to enlist the militia's help for this particular ejectment. He wanted to get on with it, to get out of there. 'Come on out, O'Malley, or we'll torch the roof over your heads,' he shouted. And when there was no sign of them, he gave the order: 'All right, men, move in! Tumble it and torch the thatch – they'll not have it!'

The crowbar brigade moved forward. The militia men edged their horses towards the crowd, forcing the people back, threatening them with the sharp steel knives on the ends of their muskets.

Then, Ellen emerged with Annie in her arms. Tall, straight, she was. From between the hands that carried the child hung a rosary. From between her lips fell the sound of the third Joyful Mystery – the Nativity.

Behind her followed Katie, she, too in prayer, afraid but reverent for once. Then Mary. Then Patrick. And, lastly, Michael.

Ellen led her family into the circle of the men who had come to evict them and knelt down in their midst, followed by the others. The men with the crowbars stopped advancing. The militia men reined in their horses, and the people of the village fell to their knees solid in prayer with those being evicted.

For a moment, Beecham was rendered speechless – stunned by the dignity of this woman kneeling not an arm's length away, oblivious to him and the destruction he was about to visit on her and her family. They had no home, no food, these people, and they weren't fighting back. They weren't beseeching him not to do it – begging him to let them take away the miserable thatch on their backs. He had always thought the red-haired woman dangerous. Now here she was, getting them all to kneel and follow her. This was her way, her message to Pakenham, and to him, that she couldn't be broken. She was trouble all right, the redheaded bitch.

'Tumble it! You heard me! Tumble it!' he shouted at the men, shaking them out of their trance-like state.

They set to, glad to be at it, dealing with what they were sure of, the thud of their crowbars in stark contrast to the murmured prayers rising to Heaven around them. One of them, the one Ellen thought she recognized, got a purchase high up with his crowbar and levered on it. The cornerstone budged and tumbled inwards, sinking the thatch with it. Next the far corner went, and then the other two corners, until the roof caved in completely.

> 'Hail Mary full of grace,
> the Lord is with thee,
> Blessed art thou amongst women . . .'

Ellen, the sound of her home being battered down behind her, continued the Rosary.

Next the lintel stones above the window openings were levered out, causing the walls over them to collapse.

'Glory be to the Father, and to the Son . . .' Ellen prayed the *Gloria* which concluded the decade, undeflected by the clank of the crowbars, or thoughts of what their noise signified.

Now, robbed of support, the larger stones round the doorway posed no problem for the sweating men who prised them away, causing further collapse.

'Oh, my Jesus, forgive us our sins, save us from the fires of hell, and lead all souls to heaven, especially those who have most need of your mercy . . .'

The people, with Michael and Ellen and family, prayed.

The battering crew ran the crowbar handles against the side of their breeches, clearing the sweat away, before attacking those parts of the walls which had not yet fallen.

Against this, Michael led them into the 'Our Father' of the next Joyful Mystery. Ellen, the children, and the valley people raised their voices to Heaven in response.

> 'Give us this day our daily bread,
> And forgive us our trespasses,
> As we forgive those who trespass against us . . .'

And then, not even bothering to execute the Distraining Order and seize the few earthly goods of the evicted, those whose trespasses were forgiven torched the roof of the cabin of those who forgave them.

The flames of their wicked doings lit the Christmas sky, giving heat and warmth to those who knelt and prayed. The last they would get that winter.

21

Father O'Brien took them in. Took them back to Clonbur with him, after the Christmas Mass.

Ellen was grateful to the young priest, who said they could stay 'for as long as the Archbishop doesn't find out I'm keeping lodgers'.

Michael told him they would stay only till the Women's Christmas – the feast of the Purification of Mary on 6 January.

They were better fed than they had been for months. But even in the two weeks they were there, Ellen felt the constrictions of presbytery life. Moreover, she missed the Mask and the mountains and the valley people. After Christmas, there was a surge in the number of supplicants coming to the presbytery gate 'looking for a bitteen of help', and as a result the priest had to cut back on his own rations. The extra demands on his charity made Ellen and Michael feel all the more uncomfortable staying there, getting preferential treatment.

At night, when the children slept, the three adults talked.

'I am afraid that the year ahead will be the blackest yet,' the priest gravely predicted for 1847. 'Many will perish. Even if the blight should not strike for a third year running, so few seedlings have been sown it will make no difference. Everywhere the people have been driven off the land, or left it, drifting to the towns in search of food.'

'The people should rise up,' said Michael. 'They should take back from the landlords and the Crown what is rightfully theirs. The food is leaving the country for England while we starve!'

'This is true, Michael,' the priest said. 'And many now feel that O'Connell's "not a single drop of blood" policy plays into the hands of the oppressor. In dogma there is such a thing as "a just war". Maybe that time is approaching, but I would be slow to advocate violence, whether against oppressor or no.'

Nevertheless, Ellen could see that the idea was taking root in Michael's mind.

When they moved out of the priest's house and back into the mountains, Michael became more and more obsessed with the thought of 'striking a blow'.

They had built their *scailpeen* up in the Hare's Garden, under the outcropping of rock. Martin Tom Bawn and Roberteen had brought them some straw and sticks, and what they could salvage of the singed thatch from their tumbled cabin. The few lumpers that they had buried in the pit had miraculously survived, and the villagers gave them whatever scraps and fuel they could. But as times hardened for the village, the scraps stopped, along with the few sods of turf which they had chanced only to burn on especially cold nights, for fear Pakenham would get word of their presence.

Michael got a job on the Relief Works out Maam way. Ten miles a day he walked to break stones for a 'famine road' that led nowhere. Then he walked the ten miles back. For this he was paid six pence a day. Meanwhile the merchants of the West held fast their stores of potatoes, waiting till they made 'a penny a piece'. Thus Michael, with his labour of six pence a day, could buy only six potatoes – one for each of them. The work and the walking were killing him, but he insisted on going. 'It's one potato or none,' he told Ellen.

From their *scailpeen* high above the valley, Ellen could see down over her own place and Glenbeg and across the Mask towards Derrypark, and back along the Tourmakeady road. At night while the others slept she would count all the little cabins, identifying them by the dim glow of their fires or the wisp of white smoke, like an untied ribbon above them.

'Where there's fire there's life,' she would say to herself, echoing the Máistir's words.

Then one night, she noticed that where the previous night there had been the glow of a fire, now there was none. The next night another fire had gone out. The following night two more cabins were dark – no white ribbon of smoke above them. All along the far shore of the Mask, where once there had been a chain of glowing fires, was now only a long dark line.

'Michael!' she called, shaking him awake, panicking at what she was witnessing. 'Look – the fires are gone! Every night there's more going. Pakenham is tumbling them – he's tumbling the cabins one by one along the road! That's why there's no fires – because there's no people! Where there's fire there's life; where there's no fire there's no life . . .' her voice trailed off.

The people were systematically being driven out, their lives extinguished. It was too terrible to contemplate.

Roberteen came to visit them the next night, whether by design or accident, and she overheard Michael ask: 'Is there any word of the Shanafaraghaun man?'

In the mornings she kept the children asleep later and later to conserve their energy. She let them up for a while, then made them lie down again in the afternoon. At night they went earlier to bed than ever before. There was nothing else to do.

She watched them fade before her very eyes, bit by bit, day by day. They were dying around her in stages, sleeping more and more. More sleeping than living. Soon she thought they would not wake up at all – sleep would become death. Still she did not give up hope.

Somehow she managed to have milk for Annie, though her breasts had lost their roundness, the skin more loose on them, the ripe colour of her nipples faded.

But Michael had work, though he was foundered by it and the twenty-mile walk every day. He had become more like a walking skeleton than the fine body of a man she married.

They never made love any more. Their bodies were not able. Survival now was their greatest need. Their only need. At night he would hold on to her, but not like before; it was as if she were the reed of life and he must cling to her or drown. In the hollow of his eyes the light of passion, once always there for her, no longer burned. Only the dull glint of desperation.

'I'll have to do something, Ellen, when the Shanafaraghaun man comes,' he would tell her, and she would nod and put her hand to his forehead and say, 'You are, Michael, *a stór* – you're keeping us alive,' and she would sing him the old love songs, and hold him until he slept.

She was losing him, she knew, losing all of them. Losing them by inches and minutes, almost beneath her notice.

If they could only hold out until the finer weather came it would give them some respite. She could take Annie with her – take them all – comb the hedges for berries. There wouldn't be much, she knew, but she knew what was safe to eat, and which roots to dig. And she could glean here in the Hare's Garden, or in their old field below, for any odd potato that might still be there, missed by the other women. Get Biddy to boil up some of the nettles, if they weren't all taken. Whatever.

She did not think beyond the spring. She could not.

One night Michael did not come back.

She knew he had finally broken.

The cracks had started to show a fortnight ago. Two days running he had walked the ten miles to break the rocks for the 'Famine road'. Two days running he had come back again. The Relief Works had stopped – waiting on some letter from Trevelyan, 'the Government man in charge of the Famine', before any more work could be done. Eventually the letter came and work resumed, but the following week the Clerk of Works had no money to pay them. They would have to wait for payment until Trevelyan himself gave Treasury approval for the funds to be released.

The past week, waiting on the Treasury, had been the hardest yet. Ellen wondered whether they would survive to see the money. If it did not come soon, death would bring an end to their suffering.

Roberteen, hearing of their plight, had climbed the mountain to bring them one potato – all the Tom Bawns could spare. She mashed it with water – skin and all – into a kind of thin, gruelly paste so as to spread it out.

Then Roberteen came a second day. This time he brought a small tin. When he offered it to her, she saw it had blood in it. She pushed it back at him.

'It's all right, Ellen – it's fresh from last night,' he told her, and he put the container to his lips and sipped from it, then he handed it back to her, a red smear staining his mouth. 'We go over the next valley at night, and puncture a hole in the neck of a cow and suck out a *dropeen* of the blood.' He didn't tell her it was the landlord's cow, for fear she wouldn't drink it. 'Go on, take it! It'll stand to you!'

She closed her eyes and raised the container to her lips tasting the cold mucous of the thickened blood, no longer warm and fresh from the beast's neck. Quickly, she gulped it down before she could think any more about it, tilting the tin so her tongue could find every last salty clot of blood.

She held it down as Roberteen carried on with his explanations. 'It don't kill the cow,' he said, wanting her to know that they had done no grievous harm to the animal, 'and we patch up the wound again so no one can tell.'

Later, as she sat waiting for Michael, with Annie at her breast and the other children, ragged and listless, lying against her, Ellen felt stronger in herself. The blood must have worked, she thought.

She looked down at her little ones, distraught with helplessness. They'd never get out now. Never see Boston, or anywhere. Her great plans for teaching them English, saving some money, getting them to America had been shattered. Tumbled in a heap like the cabins below her. They were going to die here on the top of the mountain. Die like wild things – their flesh to wither away, their bones to be cleaned by the birds of the air. The thought terrified her: the children coffinless, picked and clawed at, their flesh being fought for. She shuddered and tried to get the children closer to her.

It had all started with Sheela-na-Sheeoga and her riddles. It was a bad day she had ever gone over the mountain to the old woman. The prophecy had been fulfilled: the whitest flower had become the blackest flower. But how was she to crush its petals, as the riddle said, lying up here on the side of a mountain with four starving children? How was she to overcome the suffering that had been visited on them? It tormented her that the thing she was meant to do, the thing that would save them, was not being revealed to her.

She saw now that it wasn't just Michael's death the Banshee had foretold. It was all of their deaths. She looked at them all half in death already. She looked down at the valley. The death messenger could have stood on top of this mountain and keened for all the people in the valley below, and beyond that into the next valley, and the next, so many would be taken by this Famine.

What lay in store for them if Michael again returned empty-handed? It didn't bear thinking about, she knew. They could go to the workhouse . . . All of them would have to go in, including Michael. At least they'd get shelter and some food for as long as they were in there. Michael would be put to work breaking stones for more 'famine roads', but this time with no pay. Maybe Patrick too. And they'd be separated – Michael and Patrick in the men's quarters, herself and the three girls in the female side. And then there were the diseases . . . She remembered Biddy telling her: 'When you go in the door at Castlebar or Westport, you only come out again by the window' – meaning the gable-end windows from which the bodies of those who died were slid on a board into the lime-pit beneath. But at least they'd be buried, not left exposed on a mountaintop for their bones to be picked clean. And they might even survive it – if they could survive till they got in.

To do that, they had to survive today.

She had to look at it like that, not too far ahead, or she'd give up. Just today.

She put Annie, partly fed, down at her side, and pulled Katie to her. Katie was so light, like a bony feather. The child was half-asleep, her once beautiful red hair now unkempt, falling about a face devoid of all devilment and mischief.

She cupped Katie's chin in her hand and drew the child's face to her still-exposed breast. Gently she placed the nipple between Katie's lips, and held the child's head to her.

'Now, Katie, *a stóirín*,' she whispered, looking out over the valley. 'Don't think of anything – anything at all.'

She caressed the back of the child's neck, *cronauning* softly into her hair. She felt Katie waken and stiffen, trying to draw back. But the child was weak and Ellen was able to force the little head to stay against her, until she felt the first involuntary tug. Then, she relaxed her hold on Katie, as some long-forgotten instinct within the child took over. After a while, she laid Katie down, closing the child's eyes as they separated so that they wouldn't have to look at each other.

Then she fed Mary.

When she had finished with Mary and was laying her down, the child momentarily opened her eyes and looked questioningly at Ellen. Then smiled before going back to sleep again.

Now it was Patrick's turn. Nervously Ellen drew the boy to her. Patrick was two years older than the twins, quite a bit taller, and more difficult for her to manoeuvre. She felt awkward, embarrassed. The girls had been one thing, difficult enough, but they had always been physically close to her. Patrick, in the last year or so, had not been close to her in that way, had begun to shy away from physical intimacy. She had understood his reluctance to be hugged or kissed, had put aside the little hurts it brought. Now, she was about to suckle him at her breast. Her eldest child. Her son. Tampering with old taboos, that – even in the primitive, confined conditions in which they lived – had always been observed. She had no choice. She had to keep him alive, whatever the cost to them both.

But what if she woke him and he resisted her? His emerging manhood would be unable to bear the shame. He would never forgive her.

It was a struggle for her to pull him towards her. She prepared her breast for him, and, when finally she felt his face against her flesh, she closed her eyes, saying to herself: 'Jesus, have mercy on me. Mary, Mother of all mothers, help me.'

And then he awoke.

At first she felt him tense, uncertain what it was she was doing. Then he jerked his head back against her arm, almost forcing her to let go of him. But she didn't.

'Patrick, Patrick, don't fight me – it's all I can do for you, *a stóirín*!' she whispered to him, trying to keep her voice down.

Still he pulled against her.

'No! No, I don't want to!' he said, twisting his head away from her breast.

'Patrick, you'll die if you don't!' she said, forcing him back in against her.

He shook his head violently from side to side, keeping his mouth closed, refusing to engage with her.

'Patrick, don't make me force you,' she said, praying that the others wouldn't wake up. 'Don't fight me – I don't want to lose you.'

Still, his dark head resisted her. Still, she held him.

Somehow, with her other hand, she clamped her thumb and forefinger over his nose, cutting off his breath, forcing his mouth to open, to gasp for air. He tried to get free of her, sensing what she was at. But she was determined not to let go of him. She thrust her breast forward into his open mouth, felt him try to close his teeth against her, and then the sharp stab of pain as they caught the side of her nipple, drawing blood. She fought back the urge to withdraw from his mouth, to see to the cut, and continued to talk to him, to try and soothe his anguish: 'Patrick, shssh now, *a stóirín* . . . shssh . . . I only want to save you – you're my child and I love you. I don't want you to die . . . shssh now!'

Slowly, she felt him respond to her, and this time, when he unclenched his mouth for air, he resisted her no more. Still, she spoke softly to him and stroked the back of his head, dark and curly like Michael's, in the place she had so often stroked his father.

A shudder went through Patrick's body as the life-fluid passed between them.

She spoke to him again, soft and loving as before, feeling for him, for what she had forced him to endure. 'It's all right, Patrick . . . it's all right. It's not a wrong thing when there's nothing else. It's all right, *a stóirín.*'

And she felt the hot tears run down over his lips and on to her breast.

And fall.

22

They brought Michael up the mountain to her on a makeshift stretcher, Martin Tom Bawn and Roberteen.

The previous evening Michael, with Roberteen, had waited in the woods below Tourmakeady.

'Will the Shanafaraghaun man himself come?' Roberteen asked him, nervous with excitement at what they were about to do.

'*Éist do bhéal*, Roberteen, and listen.'

Michael could make out the sound of someone approaching. He recognized the tall figure of the Shanafaraghaun man and the equally tall but much gaunter figure of Johnny Jack Johnny's son. But he did not know the other two men with them.

'*Tiocfaidh ár lá!*' the Shanafaraghaun man greeted them.

'*Saoirse*,' Roberteen said back. 'Did ye bring the musket – "the landlord doctor" – ?'

The Shanafaraghaun man brushed aside the question and spoke instead to Michael: 'Dublin knows – the leadership supports the plan.'

Whereas Johnny Jack Johnny's son and the other two men looked nervous, the Shanafaraghaun man did not. It seemed to Michael that he had done this kind of thing before. For his own part, Michael just wanted to get on with it.

'The only good landlord is a dead landlord – isn't that right, Michael?' Roberteen contributed, eager to prove himself.

The Shanafaraghaun man glared him into silence. 'The time for revolution is upon us. Violence is justified if it is defensive, and it is justified here, where the people are ground down. O'Connell has at his disposal a force larger than the three armies at Waterloo, but use it he will not. So it is left to us, the Young Irelanders, to strike the first blows.'

Then, imbued with the spirit of revolution, they had worked

themselves up into a near-frenzy, chanting the slogans of rebellion: '*Saoirse!*' Freedom! and '*Tiocfaidh ár lá!*' Our day will come!

Brandishing some makeshift weapons, and with only one musket between them, Michael and the Young Irelanders had then mounted a raid on Pakenham's house.

The plan was that Michael would pin a 'notice to quit' on the landlord's door while the others hid. When Pakenham appeared, the Shanafaraghaun man would shoot him. But the alarm was raised too early, and – the element of surprise having deserted them – they had no choice but to flee. Michael, however, could not bear to see the landlord go unpunished. In a last-ditch attempt to inflict some damage, he tried to knock down one of the rose garden walls with a *slane*. The others shouted at him to come on, but he had promised Ellen he would do something and he could not let her down. He attacked the wall with the *slane*, striking it again and again, at last damaging it. Intent on its destruction, he no longer heard the warning cries of his comrades, or the noise of Pakenham's musket before the ball pierced his side.

They waited till morning to bring him to her. Thankfully he was not dead.

'We would have kept him longer below in the cabin with us, Ellen, only . . .' Martin Tom Bawn said apologetically.

'I know, Martin. I know,' she said.

Soon the constabulary summoned from Westport by Pakenham would be in the villages, searching out those who had committed the outrage against the landlord. To harbour a rebel who had committed such an outrage would invite terrible retribution from the authorities.

'Michael, Michael, can you hear me?' she called anxiously.

He opened his eyes. He was weak and, though they had patched him up as best they could, he had lost a lot of blood.

The children gathered round, frightened, crying. His eyes took them in – feebly he reached a hand towards them.

'Ellen . . . I did it . . . I did something about it all. The roses!' he said, scarce able to get the words out.

'You did, Michael, *a stór,* of course you did!' She knelt down beside him, her hand on his forehead, eyes brimming with love and pride. Inside she was deeply worried.

'Roberteen, you'd better go for the priest,' Martin Tom Bawn said to his son. The frightened young rebel scampered away over the mountain, glad this time to be gone from her, for fear she might think he had let her husband be shot.

She and Martin brought Michael in under the shelter of the Hare's Garden, and she lit a small fire with the few pieces of turf they had brought to her, to keep him warm.

Martin Tom Bawn also produced some boiled potatoes in a cloth. 'The pay came from London. Michael bought these and left them below with us, before they left for Tourmakeady. Biddy boiled them up. I'll bring the rest tomorrow – here's the few pence left over,' he said, handing her the money.

It was morning when Father O'Brien came with Roberteen. Michael had rested well, and the food and her care had given him some courage. He seemed a bit stronger. She was pleased with this, but still anxious about him.

Father O'Brien gave him Extreme Unction, anointing him with oils. Then the priest helped Ellen to bandage Michael using a length of white gauze cloth which he had brought for the purpose.

'He needs care, Ellen – medical care, or he'll die up here,' the priest said. 'Even if the constabulary don't find him.'

'What can we do?' she pleaded.

Father O'Brien thought for a moment. 'I could probably get him into Westport, into the workhouse hospital, without too many questions. The parish priest there is known to me and sits on the Board of Guardians. Michael would get the medical care he needs, and chances are the constabulary will be too busy looking for him back here to think to look in there for him.'

He saw the look cross Ellen's face. The workhouse was anathema to these people, a place of shame, a last resort.

'I know. I understand your reluctance . . . and there are risks. But it's his best chance, Ellen.'

She watched from above as Roberteen and his father lifted Michael off the stretcher they had used to carry him back down the mountain, and set him up on the big grey horse behind the priest.

Michael turned his head and looked up to the place where she might be. She raised her hand to wish him God's speed, though she didn't know if he could see her – half-conscious as he was.

It was the last time she ever saw him alive.

23

That same evening Ellen had a visitor: Sheela-na-Sheeoga.

'I heard you was back on the mountain, Ellen Rua,' said the old woman.

Ellen wondered how she did hear, how she knew where they were.

'I heard of your misfortunes, too. And about himself,' she continued. 'How is the little one-een?' she asked more brightly, looking at Annie.

She had brought them some food in a kind of a *tooreen* with a handle. A mix of herbs and water, it looked like. Like a thick soup.

'That'll do them a power of good,' Sheela-na-Sheeoga said, seeing Ellen eye the soup-like mixture.

Whatever it was, they would eat it. It gave them another day. It was generous of Sheela, who couldn't have had much herself. Ellen thanked her.

'For nothing – an old woman doesn't need much to keep body and soul together! What little I take wouldn't feed a sparrow,' the old woman replied, as if knowing her thoughts.

As always, Ellen had the feeling that Sheela had sought her out, had come to her with something on her mind. She wasn't wrong.

'Where is himself gone with the priest?' Sheela ventured.

'To Westport,' Ellen told her.

'The workhouse, is it?'

'Yes.'

'Mmmh . . .' The older woman pondered this for a moment. ''Tis not a good place to be in, Ellen Rua,' she said. 'Not a good place at all.'

'I know,' Ellen replied, her voice filled with worry.

'Walk to the edge of the garden with me, Ellen.'

Ellen went with her, telling the children to wait behind in the shelter.

The old woman took her arm, and they both stood looking down over the valley and the lake.

After a while the old woman spoke. 'He can be saved . . .' She had turned her face towards the valley, not looking at Ellen at all.

Ellen said nothing, waited. That was the way with the old woman – you waited.

'The *Slám*,' Sheela-na-Sheeoga let the words out softly, so none but Ellen would hear her secret. 'Some have the gift you know.'

Now it was the old woman's turn to wait, letting the words seep into Ellen's mind.

The *Slám*. Ellen had heard her mother mention it once or twice – not to herself but to the Máistir, in a whisper. When she had asked about it, she was told, 'Some things are best left alone.'

Years later, Biddy had used the expression, walking home after a wake. It had to do with passing death from one person to another, she said. Some special mixture of herbs and water was made, and thrown in the face of whoever it was first entered the room of the dying person. The one recovered, the other died. The conduit was a woman. It was said only the women of the far valley had 'the gift', or curse, of the *Slám*.

Could it be that this was what Sheela was putting to her: another's life instead of Michael's? The horror of the thought seized her mind. The old woman had said it out as easily as you might talk about replacing a diseased potato with a good one. At the same time she had managed to allow much to remain unsaid, leaving it to Ellen to work out. To decide.

She turned her head to look at Sheela-na-Sheeoga, who stood impassive beside her, looking far out over the Partrys to where the Reek was. The old woman's lips moved.

'Westport's a long way off, *craythur*. A long way.'

Ellen was in a panic, her mind riven by grief over Michael and her starving children. Michael was dying – the old woman seemed to know it. She knew he would never come out of the workhouse alive. Ellen knew it too. Deep down she knew, even while she had agreed to let Father O'Brien take him to Westport.

She should have kept Michael here, with her and the children, for his last days; nursed him, comforted him, prayed with him. Given him that, even if he wouldn't know them half the time. She had been wrong to let him go. Then, when the end came, she could have used the stones that he and Martin had cleared to make the lazy beds for a tomb for them all, here in the Hare's Garden. The *Máilleachs* would have been together in the end.

If only she'd thought it out right – she would never have agreed with the priest. If only she had another chance ∴ . .

Now the old woman was offering her another chance. Michael could live, be restored to health. He could work again. Then, they all would live: Patrick, Katie, Mary, Annie . . . even herself. All she had to do was go the road to Westport with the old woman. Agree to the *Slám*.

Ellen had no doubt that the old woman was serious. No doubt at all that she had 'the gift'.

And the other person? He'd be some stranger in the workhouse. Maybe already dying with the famine fever? Maybe glad to be taken out of his misery . . . And she'd have Michael back.

She stared at the side of the old woman's face – grey, wrinkled, pinched in silence. Ellen wanted her to say something. The woman must know the turmoil she was going through. Why didn't she speak?

Ellen looked back at the *scailpeen* where her children lay.

Patrick was stirring. The boy sat up and rubbed the sleep from his eyes, then looked out and saw her there with Sheela. He waited a moment, thinking of something. Then he stood up and came towards her. He was so like Michael, the way he walked. Deep like him, too, she thought. He stood near her, saying nothing, looking from her to the other woman, then back at her again. Then he took another step closer to her and slowly slid his arm round the small of her back, his head against her shoulder.

Together they stood, mother and son, silent, looking out over the valley to where the mountains hid the seaport town where her husband, his father, was.

When finally the boy's mother spoke, it wasn't much.

'It's alone I'll go to Westport, Sheela,' she said softly, as if breathing out a prayer.

The old woman said nothing. Only nodded down into the valley below them, before disappearing across the mountain.

24

Ellen left at daybreak. She took the children to Biddy's cabin, then set off on the long walk to Westport. Every mile along the road there were people. Standing, sitting, sleeping, wandering. Trying to get to somewhere where there might be food. Many were in a worse state than she was: nearer death than life.

Westport itself was teeming with the destitute, scattered like leaves about the place, wherever they might fall. The scale of the desolation frightened her, robbed her of hope that they themselves could survive it. But she pressed on. She had to find Michael. Get him out of this place. Back to the mountains. If she was with him, he'd be all right. Hadn't she watched over him up to now?

She had to push her way through the crowd milling around the workhouse, and brazen her way in past the guard.

'It's not signing myself in I am, it's to take someone out of here – give you one less mouth to feed,' she said, an air of conviction about her. She mentioned the name of the priest Father O'Brien had said was one of the workhouse Board of Guardians. It worked; she was allowed inside.

If the state of affairs outside the workhouse had been grim, inside was a thousand times worse, heightening Ellen's fears for Michael. Those who were immured there were the most wretched creatures she had ever seen. The clothes fell from them through raggedness and the inability of their shrunken and deformed bodies to fill garments made in better times. Skin hung paper-thin from bones. All eyes – some unable to see, caked with cataracts as they were, or gangrenous – followed her. Mouths gaped, no sound escaping them. Some dragged themselves, one-armed, along the ground towards her, their flesh showing signs of mange, their heads infested with lice.

And the children . . . Everywhere on the filthy ground, their heads too large, grotesque atop their skeletal frames, their little bodies translucent, skin so stretched that the daylight shone through it. Children whose only instinct now was to stay close to those who had brought them into this famished world – if they could find them. She saw one poor mother, with barely the energy to do so, take the skin of her child and wrap it round the girl's arm, so loose it was.

Few spoke or made any sound. As though the grief of the people here was so great as to be beyond the power of words. One woman, her own age, exemplified this hopelessness by stretching out a hand to her, then withdrawing it, recognizing the uselessness of her gesture. The woman then pressed the back of her hand against her forehead in abject despair. Ellen, anguished beyond anything she had yet experienced, ran to the fever wards. Here the stricken people lay on single beds, two and three diseased bodies on top of each other, the pus from their sores, the droolings from their mouths, the excrement from their bodies, coagulating in one putrid mess.

Desperate now, she ran between the rows of beds, trying to find him amid the mass of bodies. Ran until she reached the open window at the end of the ward. There was no sign of him.

She looked out of the window. She saw the wooden chute, polished to a shine by the passage of diseased bodies, sliding down in endless procession to be burned in the lime-pit below.

The smell came up to her. It burned her nostrils, burned her eyes, stopped her from seeing the faces and hands half-eaten by the quick-lime. Stopped her from noticing the large blackened section against the gable wall, rising like a giant black sun. Here the lime had done its macabre work, imprinting forever on the bricks the shape of the great mound of corpses it had disposed of. She thought she would faint with the stench, with the horror of the place.

This was no refuge for the poor and the hungry. This was a graveyard with walls. All inside it were already entombed, ultimately doomed.

Frantically she ran back along the ward to search the work-house yards. Perhaps Michael wasn't here at all, perhaps Father O'Brien had taken him somewhere else . . . Castlebar, Ballinrobe. Anywhere, she prayed, except here.

Then, in the yard, she saw him.

Slung on the back of a cart, his black head rolling from side to side, as the cart was pulled along by a bent old man.

She tore across the yard, knowing she was too late yet hoping she wasn't. Through the crowds of the near-dead, impervious to one more death among them, she jostled her way to him.

'Michael! Michael, *a stór*,' she cried, throwing herself on him, forcing the bent old man to stop the cart.

'He's gone, woman,' the man said, showing no interest, not even pausing to set down the cart handles.

'No – he's not!' she cried. 'No, he's not gone – he can't be!' She cradled Michael's head against her, the tears streaming down her face when she felt no beat of life in him.

'Oh, Michael, Michael, what have I done?' she sobbed into his dark head, kissing his cold white forehead. 'I should never have let you go . . . *Tá d'éadan ciúin, mo bhuachaill bán, mo ghrása!*' Broken-hearted, she whispered her love to her 'fair-haired boy'. 'I should have known! Oh God, I should have known!'

'Woman, I can't stand here all day while you *ullagone*. I've work to do and there's more after this one,' said the old man, no hint of callousness in his voice.

'Where are you taking him?' she demanded, without raising her head from Michael.

'Don't worry, he'll be buried proper . . . without the walls, not in the pit. He had no fever, he died natural – from the wound.' The old man, deformed from pulling the carts of the dead, nodded towards the workhouse gate. 'Out there – without the walls.'

She went with him, walking alongside the cart, her hand on Michael's chest, the heart torn inside her.

At the cemetery there was a queue of handcarts with bodies ahead of them. And ahead of that were rows of bodies stacked at the sides of big open graves.

What Ellen saw then horrified her more than anything she had witnessed so far in that day of horrors.

'Buried proper', the old man had called it. First the clothes were removed from the dead and laid to one side for re-use. Then, each naked corpse was placed in a coffin, which was then borne to the graveside. The pall-bearers positioned the coffin over the open grave and held it poised there for a moment while one of them pulled a lever; suddenly, the floor of the coffin fell away, and the corpse tumbled out through the bottom, down into the waiting grave. The men then snapped the hinged base of the coffin back into the closed position and returned to collect the next corpse.

Ellen was aghast, but this procedure did not seem to bother anyone else present. Not the priest who chanted prayers for the repose of the departed soul, not the pall-bearers, not the men with the corpse-laden carts who waited in line to deposit their load.

Ellen, crushed with sorrow and guilt at Michael's death, was panic-stricken at the thought of what lay ahead as the queue inched forward. This was not a right thing. She didn't want this for Michael. But what was she to do? Soon it would be Michael's turn, and they would strip the clothes from him, and go through this mockery of giving him a decent burial by putting him in the one side of a coffin and out the other.

She saw her chance when the priest and the gravedigger stopped. The old man at last dropped the handles of the cart and gruffly ordered her: 'Wait there, woman. I'll be back in a minute. Don't lose place!'

She watched his bent back, his broad shoulders, shamble away from her, back towards the workhouse. Then she quickly stepped into his place between the arms of the cart, lifted it, taking the weight first. Somehow she found the strength to tug the cart out of the queue and turn it round. She was gone with Michael before the old man returned.

The gap they left in the burial line closed behind them as if they had never been there.

Once she had broken its initial inertia, the cart with her dead husband was not too difficult for her to manage. The biggest problem was avoiding the bodies of the poor strewn at every side, and the stopping and starting that this entailed.

She was nervous until she reached the outskirts of Westport lest the constabulary or militia should stop her, but her spirit was buoyed up by the knowledge that she had reclaimed her Michael. Now she'd bring him home to their own place, bury him properly, with her and the children gathered round to pray over him. Up there on the Crucán, in the midst of their mountains and the Mask and Lough Nafooey.

'God give me the strength for the journey!' she asked, looking up at the Reek, knowing that what she was about to undergo would demand infinitely more of her than the barefooted climb to the summit of the holy mountain.

So she started – not too fast, somewhere between a walk and a gait – for the long road ahead of her. She carried on going until her arms ached and she could hold up the cart no longer. Then she rested, and talked to him, settling his hair back from where it had fallen over his eyes; whispering a prayer or two in his ear. And then she set off again, the next rest needing to be sooner – the aches now pains, her arms almost out of their sockets, her back breaking under the strain of the death-cart.

The rivers without bridges were the worst. The stones on the river bed would block the wheels from turning and she would have to reach down into the water and loose them one by one.

Now and again some of the helpless wretches she passed would try to lend a hand, but their weak attempts would only hinder her the more.

At one place, a woman, hardly a stitch to her back, offered her some milk, and a meagre-looking boy gave her half a crust of hard bread. Like her, they had nothing. But, deeming her to be worse off than they were, they wanted to share their nothing with her. It was the way of the poor, Ellen thought.

She would rest again before she reached Tourmakeady. There was something to do there for Michael, and she wanted to make sure she still had the strength.

She pulled the cart in off the road and concealed it as best she could amongst the trees at the start of the long driveway. Michael would be all right there, and she wouldn't be too long.

What she was about to do would be a sign between them that she understood his need 'to do something'; that she honoured and respected the sacrifice he had made. It would be a sign, too, to a trodden-down people. A symbol of her defiance of Pakenham and Beecham and their crowbar brigade – a rallying call.

Pakenham would understand it too when he heard about it. And he would, soon enough.

* * *

No one was about.

She stooped, selecting the reddest rose on the solitary bush of the *Rosa chinensis* that remained in flower within Pakenham's walled gardens.

She cut the stem, puncturing it with her fingernail, careful not to damage the bloom.

Then she left, as quickly and as quietly as she had come, pausing just a moment at the wall where the fresh damage was.

The damage that had cost Michael his life.

The sight of the Mask – and beyond it the valley where her children waited with Biddy – gave her fresh courage. Though great water-blisters rose on her hands adding to the pain she already endured, she did not stop again until she reached the foot of the Crucán.

There she left his body, and stumbled down the *bóithrín* to Biddy's house.

Her face said it all to Biddy and the children.

When it was time she led them up to the cart where his body lay.

Biddy and Roberteen and Martin Tom Bawn came with them, and those of the village who had the strength to walk.

The men lifted Michael's body from the cart and bore it up the hill ahead of the women. At the top, before they set it on the ground, she instructed them: 'Let him see it the once more.' So Martin and Roberteen held him aloft on the highest point of the Crucán. First they faced him towards Finny and Lough Nafooey, and Glentrague, almost hidden in the far mountains beyond the lake. Then, reverently, they wheeled about with him towards Derrypark, and the lofty peaks of the Partrys, and the Tourmakeady townland. Finally, they faced him to the Mask, with its multitude of islands, to Glenbeg, and, below him, his own valley – Maamtrasna, where his tumbled cabin lay in ruins. Finally the two men turned their eyes upwards to the Hare's Garden, the place where they had sweated and dug with him in the empty hope of salvation from the blight.

Ellen followed them, wanting to share these last moments with him. Be his eyes, see for him what his own dead eyes couldn't see.

On the near hill, some distance from the rest of them, she recognized the bent figure of Sheela-na-Sheeoga. The old woman just watched. Made no attempt to approach them.

Ellen then turned her eyes to the field below. The raised mounds of the lazy beds just sat there, staring remorselessly back at her. She thought of the good times they had had in that field, bending together, laughing, gathering in their harvest for the year ahead, the children playing. The time, when she was pregnant with Annie, he said that the sun danced around her – and the whitest flower dancing on every side of them. The whitest flower of Sheela-na-Sheeoga's riddle. She looked up, but the old woman was gone again.

Death was in the whitest flower. They were cursed by it, cursed by the vengeful God who sent it. And now it had led to this.

'Ellen, it's the time,' Biddy whispered, taking her gently by the arm.

The men stood waiting – still bearing Michael's body on their shoulders.

She walked to them, held up his face in her hands and kissed him for the last time.

Then they buried him.

As he walked in his gardens it seemed to David Moore that scant attention had been paid by the authorities to his warnings. There was little sign of any plan to stave off the continuing and worsening effects of the Great Hunger, as it was now being called. All Government activity was at best, reactive, interventionist.

Nearer the Gate Lodge, the curator stopped awhile at the Jenkinstown Rose – *Rosa chinensis*. The flower was so named, one story went, because the composer-poet, on seeing this rose at Jenkinstown Castle, had been inspired by its beauty to pen the immortal words of 'The Last Rose of Summer' to an old Irish melody 'The Groves of Blarney'. This spot, this rose, was much loved by Isabella. Moore remembered how, when first married, they had stood here and Isabella had softly hummed the words of the song to him. He had been deeply moved by her rendition.

'Tis The Last Rose of Summer,
Left blooming alone,
All her lovely companions,
Are faded and gone . . .

It worried him now to see Isabella over-reaching herself. She had taken to heart the Committee of Botany's refusal to grant him the funds for continued research. And she complained bitterly about the insanitary conditions in which they lived – the Society having allowed the Gate Lodge to fall into a state of disrepair.

But most of all it was the suffering of the people that affected her, driving her to take an ever-increasing role in Canon Prufrock's fund-raising committee, working tirelessly to improve the lot of the poor.

Moore resolved to have a quiet word with the canon. Perhaps he could persuade Isabella that she was doing too much.

25

Ellen remained on alone after the others had left, Biddy taking the children home with her.

It was hard to pray. Hard because she couldn't think of him being dead, now that he was back here, with her, in the valley.

So she talked to him, the way she used to talk to him – before the last month or so, before she had started to lose him, before his mind was altered.

And she cried a little and softly sang to him of her love and she whispered to him of how she would place on his grave not the whitest flower but the reddest rose. Then she kissed the petals of the flower and laid down the red rose: *Rosa chinensis*, the last rose, symbol of her love for him; symbol of his blood spilt for her; symbol of her defiance of him in whose garden it had grown.

The next day Roberteen scrambled up to the *scailpeen*.

'Ellen! Ellen! – Pakenham's sister has sent word for you to go to her at Tourmakeady. She says it's important for you and the children!' he panted, all a-fluster.

So word had gotten around already about Michael, and her taking his body all the way back to the mountains. She had known the rose would do it, that its meaning would not be lost on them.

'Where's Pakenham?' she asked, angered by the message the boy had brought.

'They say he went to London after . . . That the sister will stay at the Lodge while he's gone,' he answered, adding, 'Don't go, Ellen! 'Tis a trick, I'll warrant – though she said no harm would come to you, that it would be to all ye're advantage. But I wouldn't trust her. Isn't she the one breed with Pakenham?'

She thought about it. She had nothing to be afraid of from either Pakenham or his sister. What more could they do to her, that they hadn't already done? There was nothing left to take away from her. Her home was gone. Her husband was gone. All she had left were the children.

She would go, she decided. See what the woman wanted. Anything that might help the children.

Edith Pakenham was plain but well-preserved, showing none of the signs of dissolution so physically apparent on her brother. Her hair, neat and brown with the glimpse of grey, was braided and pulled back into a bun, giving her the look of a middle-aged schoolmistress.

She hid her disdain at the tattered state of the peasant woman shown in to her by Bridget.

'Thank you for coming, Mrs O'Malley . . . at such a time. Bridget, fetch something from the kitchen. Mrs O'Malley must be thirsty after her journey.'

Ellen studied her. She had never heard tell of Pakenham having a sister. But then, she wouldn't have if the woman lived beyond in London.

As if reading Ellen's thoughts, the woman said, 'I have come to Tourmakeady to see to things while Sir Richard is on business in London. I shall probably remain here in Ireland for some time to assist him in straightening out the affairs of the estate.'

Ellen wondered as to where all this was leading.

'Now then, Mrs O'Malley,' she went on in the same matter-of-fact way, 'far be it from me to criticize my brother's actions, but certain . . . practices seemed to have crept into the running of Tourmakeady Lodge. These practices were prompted in part by other persons, and the pressures under which Sir Richard has laboured of late . . .' She paused, studying Ellen, picturing how the tall red-haired woman might look if she were properly nourished and suitably outfitted. Striking, Edith Pakenham thought.

Ellen waited for her to continue.

'The times are indeed severe for all of us, landlord and tenant alike,' the landlord's sister said. 'The London press lays the blame for the "calamity" in Ireland squarely, but unjustly, at our feet. Our Government in Westminster decrees that "Irish property must pay for Irish poverty", when Irish poverty is, in fact, impoverishing Irish property. However, be that as it may . . . I have asked you here, Mrs O'Malley, because I propose making reparation to you for the wrongs visited on you and your family by my brother.

'What I propose is as follows: that you leave Ireland forthwith for Australia – your passage to be paid for by the estate.'

Ellen was stunned at Edith Pakenham's proposal. It was the last thing she had expected to hear.

Could it be, could it possibly be, that at last she would see freedom for herself and her family? Freedom from the tyranny of living on the edge of poverty? Freedom from the almost certain death facing them?

'Once in Australia you will be taken into employment by a Mr Coombes – an old friend of the Pakenham family, and the proprietor of Crockford's, a large holding in the Barossa region of South Australia.'

Edith Pakenham paused to let it all sink in.

'What say you to this, Mrs O'Malley?'

Ellen steadied herself before replying.

'Why, thank you, Miss Pakenham. Thank you kindly indeed,' she said, trying not to show too much delight; still cautious, given the most unexpected nature of this development.

A smile creased the edges of Edith Pakenham's schoolmistress's mouth.

'It is indeed a great opportunity, Mrs O'Malley,' she said. 'A few small conditions attach, of course.'

Ellen knew it. There had to be a catch, a price to pay. Her body stiffened, her mind alert, waiting for the 'few small conditions'.

'Firstly, you must leave without undue delay,' Edith Pakenham began.

That was all right, Ellen thought. Easy comes first.

'Secondly you must not induce the people – these Young Irelander persons – to any more riotous behaviour, or incite them to further outrages against my brother or the Pakenham estate. I will be clear with you: it is said the people would rally behind you if you were to align yourself with the rebels.' The landlord's sister hurried on, not wanting to give Ellen a chance to interrupt until she had finished. 'Thirdly: that you do not return to Ireland within a period less than three years. That is what I seek in return, Mrs O'Malley.'

Ellen couldn't believe it – Pakenham was afraid of her, wanted her out of the way. It had never occurred to her to lead an insurrection, or rally the tenantry to her cause – but clearly the Pakenhams had convinced themselves that this was a real possibility. And they were worried. So worried that the landlord had taken refuge in London, leaving his sister to attend to the security of the estate.

She was relieved too. They would escape! She knew little about Australia, except that it was far away, much further than America. But did it matter? It would give them a new start, fresh hope.

'I agree to your conditions,' she said.

'Good. But I am afraid, O'Malley, I require somewhat more than your mere agreement. I require that our position is protected. You could, prior to leaving, instigate an attack on my brother's life – as your late husband did – whenever Sir Richard returns. And even if you personally did not initiate reprisals, there are those known to you – the Young Irelanders, I believe – who would seek revenge on your behalf. Indeed, you might orchestrate vengeance even from Australia.'

'But what can I –'

'You must speak with them. Exact an undertaking from them.'

'They would take no heed of me –'

'But they will, Mrs O'Malley,' Edith Pakenham interrupted, 'if I have a bond of good faith from you.'

'I've given my word I'll do what I can. But I cannot speak for others.'

'I require a bond greater than your word.'

Ellen looked at the woman.

'I require a bond of good faith from you which cannot be broken – your children.'

The words jarred Ellen to the core. She could scarce comprehend what Edith Pakenham had said. But her body knew – every fibre and tissue knew. She was unable to speak.

'The three older ones must remain behind,' the woman continued, as if she were giving instruction to a classroom of children.

'The infant you can take with you. They will be looked after well, given enough to eat, schooled – and you have the word of a Pakenham that they will not be proselytized to the Established Church. When you return in three years, with some means at your disposal, you can reclaim them. They will be kept safe for you.'

Ellen could not believe what she was hearing. Leave her three darlings behind and go to Australia for three years? Desert them! Betray them!

Her voice at last found the words her body was screaming to get out. 'No! No! No! – I won't do it! I won't leave them!' she railed at the woman, fire and tears at once in her eyes. 'How could you – a woman – ask such a thing? How could I agree to this? Never! I'd die first!'

'Well, you may get your wish, Mrs O'Malley. The choice is yours,' Edith Pakenham said, unperturbed by Ellen's outburst. 'How will your children survive on the side of a mountain with no food to eat? You are, regrettably, widowed, with no husband to earn you substance. How will you yourself survive to provide for them now that you are destitute? There is always the workhouse . . .' she added, without emotion, merely laying out the logical option.

Ellen was frantic. She wanted to get out of there, run from Edith Pakenham and her scheme, so full of guile and wickedness. Run back to her children. Not listen as this woman reminded her of the grim realities of their lives now. A life without Michael, a life without hope.

She made for the door, her thoughts tormenting her.

But then what? She herself was weakened by lack of food. The long journey to Westport and the physical and mental agony of the journey back to bury Michael's body had taken its toll on her. As well as this journey to Tourmakeady today.

How long could they last? How long could she last? Without her, all of them would be doomed. Biddy would try to mind the children for a while. But how much longer would the Tom Bawns survive if they had to share their limited supplies with four other mouths? She couldn't expect that of them, to take the bit out of their own mouths for her children.

She and the children would hardly see the spring out and the way things looked, would hardly see it in. She had the balance of Michael's last two weeks' pay, but after that . . . ? Her mind revolted at the very notion of the workhouse. If she hadn't known, hadn't gone in there, maybe she would have considered it. But she had gone in and she did know. Knew that before too long they would all end up in the lime-pit, or stacked up naked, the clothes ripped from their bodies before they were dropped into eternity through the false bottom of a hinged coffin. The thought made her skin crawl.

'I'll leave you alone for a moment to ponder it,' Edith Pakenham said.

As the landlord's sister left the room, Bridget entered it carrying a tray and tea. When she saw how distraught Ellen was, she immediately put the tray down and went to her, taking Ellen's hands in her own.

'It's sorry I am, Ellen Rua, to hear of your bad news,' she said gently.

Ellen looked at her. Was the girl in on it too?

Bridget interpreted the quizzical look to mean that the woman was too upset to know what it was she was talking about. 'Your husband . . .' she said.

'Oh!' Ellen was relieved that the girl didn't know, wasn't part of it. 'Thank you, Bridget. It's another thing entirely that troubles me. Another terrible thing,' she blurted out. She hesitated for a moment, but then, instinctively trusting the girl, unburdened herself of the impossible choice she faced.

Bridget was shocked and for a while said nothing. Then, her pretty face furrowed, she said, ''Tis a terrible thing you have before you, but if the children of Ellen Rua O'Malley cross the doorstep of this house then Bridget Lynch will see to it that not a hair of their heads will ever be harmed. You can count on that, if it gives you any small comfort . . .'

Ellen looked at the girl. She was good-hearted and spirited. She would set out to do as she had said. But what could she, a servant, do to protect them if harm was at hand?

'Thank you, Bridget. I know you'd do your best for them, but how could I leave them? Leave three and take one?'

'I know it's a cruel thing, but what else is open to you, Ellen

217

Rua? If you stay, you'll all perish – like half the countryside already has.'

Ellen tried to think calmly, logically, but the questions kept crowding in on her. What if anything happened to her on the voyage, or in Australia? Then Pakenham would have no reason to continue keeping the children. Where would they end up then? And what if anything happened to any of them – or all of them – while she was gone? They could be dead and buried unbeknownst to her! Oh God, she should stay. Then she could pull in the *scailpeen* over themselves. At least they'd all die together then, close to each other.

'What can I do, what can I do?' she cried out. 'Holy Mother of God, spare me! Sweet Crucified Jesus on the Cross, take away this moment from me!'

How could she tell them, with their father not cold in his grave, that she was now deserting them? Leaving them with the man who had caused them so much hardship and suffering? Leaving them with their enemy – he who had murdered their father. How could she ever look at them and tell them?

'I can't do it, Bridget – I just can't!' Ellen shook her head violently, moving to break away from the girl and go.

'Don't be afeared of Sir – of Pakenham,' the girl tightened her grip on Ellen's wrist. 'I'll see to him!' she said, looking Ellen straight in the eyes. She was so pretty, thought Ellen – her hair, her face, her eyes, her lips like a bright red rosebud. So full of life and youth.

Ellen knew the girl was saying something to her, something which she didn't fully understand.

'It's the only choice you have, Ellen,' Bridget said, a little more quietly. 'Sometimes we all have to make hard choices for the sake of others.'

Ellen knew the girl was right. There was only one choice for her – a choice she never thought she'd have to make. One between living and dying.

A terrible choice – to desert her children in order to save them. How would they ever understand – or forgive her?

She had wiped the tears from her eyes before Edith Pakenham returned.

The sister of Sir Richard Pakenham did not even have to ask the woman her answer. She knew it by the way the woman stood, the uncharacteristic droop of her head, the slope of her shoulders.

The road back to Maamtrasna was the longest Ellen had ever known it.

26

She didn't say anything to Biddy.

And Biddy didn't ask her. Biddy Martin Tom Bawn knew that Ellen would tell her in her own good time. She also knew that, whatever Ellen's news from Tourmakeady was, it was bad news: something was disturbing her neighbour greatly.

Biddy didn't even question the food which Ellen pressed on her. 'Food,' Edith Pakenham had insisted Ellen take, 'to restore you for your travels.' Already broken, this final humiliation had scarcely registered with her.

Ellen waited to be on her own with the children.

When they reached the *scailpeen,* she gave them some of the food, a little bread and some milk, and a small piece of the sweetcake, and settled them down for the night. They said the Rosary and the night prayers: 'O Angel of God, my guardian dear . . . ever this night be at my side to light, to guard, to rule and guide me . . .' Offering them all up, along with their tears, for their dead father.

That night, she couldn't bring herself to tell them that she was leaving them – and so suddenly. But the quicker she went, the better chance they had.

Instead, she comforted them, watched over them till each one was asleep. Then agonized until at last she, too, was asleep.

In the morning she again portioned out some of the food to them.

Mary wanted them to go to Michael's grave, so Ellen took them.

It was there, on the Crucán, that she told them.

Already torn with grief at the sight of their father's grave, they watched her silently, as she tried to form the words, to somehow make it sound less awful than it was.

'Mammy is going to have to go away for a while,' she began, as if she was talking about someone other than herself, removed from it all, as if it was one of the Lessons.

They listened through it all, not fully comprehending what she was telling them, but implicitly trusting her that when she said they'd be all right, they would be.

'You will come back for us, *a Mhamaí*,' Katie stated rather than asked, the tears held back in her eyes.

'Yes, Katie, I will, you know I will. The minute I can.'

'Promise?' Katie asked, uncertain of what it meant for them.

'I promise. And then we'll all be together forever and ever.'

'But how will you find us?' Katie, needing further reassurance, asked.

'Of course I'll find you – you'll be at Miss Pakenham's house,' she said, giving Katie a hug.

'But if Miss Pakenham doesn't like us and we're not there?' Katie persisted, touching a fear which already held her mother.

'That won't happen, Katie,' Ellen said with as much conviction as she could muster. 'But even if I had to comb the length and breadth of Ireland, you know I'd find you, my little *stóiríns.*'

'Is Pakenham a good landlord now?' it was Patrick.

She thought about that for a moment. She didn't want to tell him a lie, but she didn't want him going over to Tourmakeady in any sort of rebellious mood.

'Let's just say he knows Ellen Rua O'Malley will be back. And us *Máilleach* women, or men,' she added for his benefit, 'are not to be trifled with.'

'Or the Young Irelanders either,' Patrick added. But he seemed happy enough with her response, indicating as it did, some retribution hanging over the head of Pakenham if he didn't remain 'good'!

Ellen was glad they hadn't stayed silent, for all that they were unable to do anything to change things, no matter what they thought, no matter how much they wanted to – the poor little darlings.

But it wouldn't be until she was going that it would really hit them. And her.

'Is Australia far away?' It was Mary, who hadn't yet spoken.

She had been listening, thinking, working it all out in her own way, trying to fill in all the missing pieces.

'It is, Mary – it's a long way,' Ellen said, unsure herself just how far away Australia was.

'Is it a longer way than Boston?' her child asked.

'It is, and I wish it was to Boston I was going,' Ellen answered.

'What age will we be when you come back?' it was Katie again.

The question of time was one Ellen didn't want to get into too deeply. To say too short a time would build up false hopes in them. When she hadn't come back by that time, the waiting would be terrible and they would feel further betrayed by her. Yet, to tell them she would be gone for three years, as Edith Pakenham had said she must, would seem like forever to them.

'Whatever age you'll be, Katie, you'll still all only be little *rascaleens!*' Ellen said, with a laugh, trying to deflect the question. 'But what I want you all to do is to say your prayers every morning and night so that your Guardian Angel, and Holy Mary, and the Baby Jesus will mind you. And pray for your father – he'll be there, too, in Heaven looking down on you, watching you for me till I come back. And,' she went on, trying to be brave, not to let her voice crack.

'And, another thing, you're to look after each other. No one of you is in charge while I'm gone, but each of you is to look out for the other like true *Máilleachs.*'

'Yes, *a Mhamaí,*' they all said quietly.

Then, she told them about Bridget: 'There's a woman, a good woman where you're going, named Bridget. She's my friend and you can trust her – she knows you're coming. So do whatever little jobs you're given to do by Miss Pakenham, and don't be cheeky or *drochbhéasach* to anybody. But if you do get into trouble, tell Bridget.'

She wanted to finish it then – get them to rest so as to build up their strength for the journey, and for when she was gone.

'Is Australia a good or a bad place, *a Mhamaí?*' it was Mary still pursuing whatever line of thought it was she was on.

'Well, it's not really the place, Mary,' Ellen replied, realizing how little she knew herself about where she was bound for. 'It's the people. And there are good and bad people everywhere. Don't worry, *a stóirín* – I'll be fine. I'll stick with the good ones!' she said, hoping her answer would satisfy Mary.

'Can we keep Annie with us?' Katie wanted to know.

'We'll look after her until you come back – won't we, Mary?' she said, full of the idea.

'Now, Katie,' Ellen said, always forced to smile at Katie's ideas, 'you'll have enough to do looking after yourselves. I'll take good care of Annie and bring her back safe and sound to you, if that's what you're worried about.'

'Now, home to the *leaba* – or, I should say, the "bed",' she said, whooshing them on ahead of her.

Over the next few days she talked with them again and again in between the sadnesses.

Each day they visited the Crucán.

The day they left for Tourmakeady, they first stopped at Biddy's to tell her. Biddy was grievously sad at their going.

'But it's the best thing, Ellen – there's nothing left here only grass, and it's soon we'll be feeding the grass ourselves. God speed ye,' she said making the sign of the cross over them.

Roberteen came as far as the Crucán with her.

'I'm sorry, fearful sorry, Ellen Rua, for all your troubles . . .' he paused, looking down at the ground between them. 'And it's sorry I am to see yourself going from . . . us.'

'I know, Roberteen,' she said, touching his arm. 'Now, I want you to do something very, very important for me.' He looked up into her face, glad to be of service to her one last time. 'You must tell the Shanafaraghaun man: "Ellen Rua is gone, but her children are with Pakenham." He will understand what that means.'

'I'll have him told what you said, Ellen Rua, before the day is dark,' he pledged.

She knew he would keep his promise. Her mind settled that her bond with Edith Pakenham was now secured, and that there would be no reprisals by the Young Irelanders, she said goodbye to the fair-haired boy-man who worshipped her. 'Look after your mother and father, and take care of yourself too, Roberteen. *Slán go fóill.*'

'I'll miss . . .' he started to say, then hastily blurted, 'ye all.'

Then he waited at the foot of the Crucán, leaving them to make their final good-byes to Michael. Before he set out for Shanafaraghaun, he watched the ragged little group of them – the three children hanging on to her tattered skirts; she, tall above them, the child in her arms – thinking it was how he might never see her again. He watched them until they vanished out of sight.

Vanished into the dip of the bend for Tourmakeady.

At the entrance to the grounds of Tourmakeady Lodge she stopped, and gathered them around her. The walk had been hard on them. They were physically weak, but weaker still in spirit at the thought of what lay ahead, of her going from them.

'My heart is heavy, *stóiríns* – I want to hold each of you one more time before we say good-bye. But I want you to be brave up there at the Lodge, in front of Miss Pakenham – brave like your father was. Let her see what we *Máilleachs* are made of.'

She handed Annie to Katie.

'Now, Patrick . . . son . . .'

He came to her and she embraced him tenderly, holding her first-born till she could bear it no longer. He said nothing, but the bones of his fingers dug into her back as she gave him the parting kiss.

'And Mary . . . dear Mary . . .'

Her quiet, lovely Mary clung to her neck, tightly, silently, until Ellen thought her own heart would break, so great was the weight of sorrow that was on her. As they broke their embrace, the child said to her, 'I'll mind Katie and Patrick . . . like you asked, *a Mhamaí* . . . until you come home again.'

Ellen kissed her on the lips, aware of how pinched the poor child's lips had become.

'And now, Katie . . . *mo mháinlín* . . .' she said, a lump in her throat at the words.

Katie precariously passed Annie over to Mary, and rushed to her mother, flinging herself into Ellen's arms.

'*A Mhamaí! A Mhamaí!*' she called, her little heart beating wildly. 'I'll miss you – I will. I love you, *a Mhamaí*!' she said, as if her life depended on it. 'Say it again – say you'll be back!'

'Oh, Katie . . . I promise . . . I promise you, I will.'

Ellen fought hard to keep her composure in front of them. If she broke down now she knew she would turn back, not go through with it. She squeezed Katie so tightly, closing her own eyes to keep back the pressure within from bursting through.

Eventually, she spoke to them – like the mother they had always known – determined, resolute, knowing what the right thing was.

'*Muintir Uí Mháille,*' she said, as if summoning the great clans of the O'Malleys. 'Let us go to Miss Pakenham!'

And she lifted Annie from Mary, and led them up the long carriageway to the house where she would surrender them.

BOOK TWO

AUSTRALIA

27

'Welcome to Australia!' Kitty O'Halloran dug her elbow into Ellen's side, mimicking the words of Captain Ebenezer Penneman Marble, Master of the *Eliza Jane,* who now addressed the passengers from the ship's quarterdeck. The *Eliza Jane*, having carried them across the wide ocean, was now aground on a sandbar, unable to reach its destination – McLaren's Wharf in Port Adelaide (or 'Port Misery', as some of the sailors referred to it).

It had been a nightmare voyage, so it was with some surprise that Ellen now heard the captain describe their passage as: 'A healthy trip, with deaths other than infants amounting to only fifteen souls, most of whom were maladied when boarding.' Ellen thought of the sounds at night, the weighted sacks splashing into the water, sinking to the bottom of the great ocean – the sounds of a burial at sea.

She held Annie closer to her. The child had done well, proved to be a hardy traveller. Ellen had lost count of how long they had been cooped up in the forever dark of the steerage section with Kitty and the other girls. Marble, not wanting to be labelled a 'slowcoach' in the Adelaide newspapers, had driven his crew to exhaustion to save a few days on the journey. More to do with saving on provisions, Ellen thought. Under Marble's 'rough but honest' captaincy, as he liked to call it, the withholding of provisions was not the only problem the emigrants faced: assaults on young women by the crew were commonplace.

No wonder, then, that the women in steerage had greeted the first shouts of 'Land ahoy!' with such joy. They had wanted to get up to see this new land, this '*Terra Australis*', as Marble called it, but he'd kept them below for a few hours longer, some poor wretches calling out the name to the battened hatches, 'Australia! . . . Australia!' Like the Westport woman beside Ellen: at the start of the voyage she, with her lustrous hair and eyes, black as night, had been the object of general admiration and had sung for them; yesterday, Ellen had tried to talk to her, but the Westport woman only stared through her, seeing nothing, fixed on some place far beyond this life. Now she wailed for 'Oss-tray-lee-ah', her hand reaching out towards the upper deck and the land she would never see. Ellen breathed a prayer for her.

Thank God she and Annie had made it.

'Marble by name, and Marble by nature – a healthy trip, how do!' Kitty O'Halloran said quite loudly, to Ellen. Sarah Joyce and Nora Burke laughed at their younger companion's brazenness. Kitty, a nineteen-year-old native of Louisburgh, Co. Mayo, would say anything to anybody – and get away with it. It was the way she had of flicking back her head of nut-brown hair and laughing at you when she spoke.

Sarah and Nora were pretty too: dark-haired, more comely than Kitty, but not as bright and breezy. The few years they had on Kitty probably gave them a bit of sense, Ellen thought – though not much, the way they giggled and laughed at everything, almost like twins.

The three girls were part of a group of young Irish women sent out to South Australia as part of an official Government scheme to 'populate the Colonies'. Or, as Marble had referred to them: 'Famine-starved Irish wenches happy to be brood mares on the stud farms of Australia.'

When they had at last been allowed on deck, Ellen's first views of South Australia filled her with apprehension. She'd expected green majestic shores, like those of the Mask, or a blue inlet like the one at Leenane, cut from the mountains by the giant glaciers gliding ever seawards from the land. Instead, the banks of Misery Creek where they were foundered, looked like a large festering sore of mud banks and tangled mangroves, and tea trees – identified for them by Fletcher, one of the few crew members to treat the women with respect.

Her fears were compounded when Captain Marble informed them that McLaren's Wharf – constructed by the South Australia Company to capitalize on the increase in traffic to the province and shake off the old Port Misery tag – was fully berthed. 'Since we cannot dock there,' said Marble, 'we must disembark you here, on to the boats.'

*   *   *

It was mid-afternoon when Ellen's turn to be handed down into one of the boats ferrying the passengers up Misery Creek finally came. She had watched others being bundled unceremoniously into the boats below, their trunks, parcels, band-boxes and carpet-bags thrown in on top of them. The waters around the *Eliza Jane* were strewn with a flotilla of boxes, some of which had spilled their contents so that hats, dresses, stockings, shoes, and a whole colourful array of outer- and under-clothing now swirled in the Creek – much to the dismay of their lady owners.

The boat, when it filled, was like a floating general store piled in on top of Ellen and Annie and the three other Irish girls: Kitty, Sarah and Nora. At least, Ellen noted with relief, the kindly Fletcher was to be their boatman. On either side, his passengers could see the sandy bottom of the Creek. The old sailor rowed as far as he could, but it wasn't long before he exclaimed, 'Devil take it, we're grounded!' and the gentle forward motion of the boat gave way to the arresting bump of the keel striking sand.

While the women sat wondering, 'What next?', Fletcher peered out on every side. Clearly less than pleased with what he saw, he turned to them and said, 'Well, ladies, looks as if instead of being your boatman today, I'll have to be your dray-horse.'

Ellen did not understand what he meant by this, and neither did her grounded companions, who all looked at each other quizzically. With a laugh, Fletcher jumped over the side carrying a length of strong hawser rope which he looped round the prow of the boat. Then, with the other end over his shoulder, he proceeded to pull them along the Creek towards Adelaide – the Land of Promise.

Without Fletcher's weight aboard, the boat lifted, and the ladies sat, four modern-day Cleopatras of the Nile, being tugged up Misery Creek by their manservant, who sweated and strained and stumbled through the mud-stained waters. The young girls tittered and giggled at the good of it all, but Ellen found it embarrassing. She couldn't help but pity Fletcher as he good-naturedly soldiered – or sailored – onwards.

For a while, progress in this manner was satisfactory, if slow, but the tide and the sands of Port Misery were yet to prove their undoing. Again the boat was sand-wedged. And this time, despite

Fletcher's Herculean efforts, it simply would not budge.

'Well, missies,' he said, panting for breath, 'that's it – journey's end!'

The giggling of the young girls stopped. What were they to do now?

'Nothing else for it, I'm afraid: you can either sit it out until the tide changes again – which could take a few hours . . .' The look on the young girls' faces turned to one of dismay. 'Or . . .' Fletcher paused, looking at Ellen with a mischievous twinkle in his eye. 'You can hoist your mainsails!'

'What does he mean?' Kitty asked Ellen.

'He means, Kitty, that unless we want to sit here half the night, we'll have to lift our hemlines . . .' And she grabbed the side of her dress, yanking it up over her ankles to illustrate the point.

At this, Kitty and the others let out a horrified, 'Oh!' and then started 'tee-heeing' again, hands over their mouths.

'. . . and walk the rest of the distance through that –' Ellen released her skirts and pointed to the swampy, mangrove-infested shoreline.

'Oh!' they exclaimed, even louder than the first time.

'Them's the choices, ladies, I'm afraid,' Fletcher chipped in, not without some merriment.

'I'll stick with you and do what I can until you're on dry land.'

It was decided that Fletcher would lead the way, to try and find a safe path through the treacherous shallows. It was also decided, after much giggling and blushing, that he would carry Kitty, the youngest, on his back. The others would maintain single file behind Fletcher: Sarah first, then Ellen – carrying Annie – with Nora bringing up the rear, ready to support Ellen if she stumbled.

And so they struggled up the Creek, inching towards their destination. A destination which seemed always that tantalizing and wearisome few extra steps ahead. All except Ellen 'hoisted their mainsails'; with both arms clutching Annie to her, Ellen had no choice but to let the water soak the hemline of her dress, driving it against her legs and making her progress even more unsteady as she gingerly moved forward. When the dress did free itself, it floated out ahead of her, obscuring her view of the bottom.

Behind them in the boat they had left most of their belongings, apart from what they wore and what little they could carry, thrown over their arms and shoulders.

On they edged, Fletcher calling out, warning, encouraging them, with Kitty clinging to him for dear life, trying not to press too hard against his Adam's apple, which she could feel against her forearm.

Suddenly, Fletcher stumbled and disappeared from view. At first the screaming Kitty appeared to sit on top of the water, her dress billowing out from her like a canopy. The others froze, watching the water bubble up over the sides of her dress, as she began to submerge into the canopy, and then down into the Creek. But, miraculously, she began to slowly rise again, borne up out of the water like some sea-goddess, as Fletcher found his footing and regained the shallow ground. Apart from swallowing some creek water, he appeared none the worse for wear. Kitty, however, refused to straddle him again – something which, Ellen thought, Fletcher might be grateful for at this stage.

Eventually they reached an accessible part of the shore and Fletcher bade them farewell: 'Missies, I hate to leave you, but I'd best be back to the *Eliza Jane* presently, else old thunder guts will have my hide on the rigging! You should be all right from here on. Just hug the shoreline and use the mangroves for support, and you'll reach McLaren's Wharf. So, stick together, and Godspeed!'

He turned to go.

'Mr Fletcher!' Ellen called to him.

'Thank you for your great kindness in bringing us safely ashore, and for your assistance throughout the passage to Australia.' She smiled at him, and he hoped she'd be all right out here in this wild, untamed country. She was a fine woman, this redhead – a fine woman indeed.

'May God take you in His care, and keep you there,' she said, giving the sailor her blessing.

'Thank you, miss. Likewise, to you in your new country – may the Lord keep you all safe. It was a pleasure to be of service to you.'

He bowed towards them and, with slight heaviness of heart,

set off once more, wading into the waters of Misery Creek, back towards the rowing boat and the *Eliza Jane*.

Ellen and the others, meanwhile, carried on with their journey towards the port of Adelaide. If traversing the Creek had been bad, this was a thousand times worse. With each footstep, their feet sank, sucked downwards into the mud in which the mangroves flourished. It was torturously slow progress. Ellen used the trunks of the swamp trees, as best she could, for support. But the gnarled roots of the mangroves tripped and thwarted them in their progress – each root curling up out of the water towards the life-sustaining air, the root-tips like giant fish-hooks, waiting to impale the unwary walker – so that shins and legs were scored and bruised over and over again.

Mosquito-bitten and bloodied, soaked to the skin, and weak from the hellish conditions of the long voyage, each step they took into the slimy muck beneath them seemed to strip away the last vestiges of human dignity. With each exhausting minute that passed, Ellen grew more and more dispirited about this Australia, with its bloodthirsty insects and its hostile and forbidding landscape.

What must Jasper Coombes be like? A man who had come to this wild land and tamed it, made good for himself. Try as she might, she could form no mental picture of him – but his name sounded narrow and mean, and grasping.

28

'Welcome to Australia!'

Ellen awoke from her fatigued sleep on McLaren's Wharf, to find a tall, well-built man standing over her. He smiled at her as she blinked up at him.

'Mrs O'Malley?' he enquired.

She nodded. Was this Jasper Coombes? This clean-shaven, sandy-haired man, roughly of an age with herself, looking down on her with twinkling eyes. Surely not. He was dressed fine enough: wide-brimmed hat, neckerchief knotted above a partly unbuttoned white shirt, brown trousers tucked into leather boots. Still, he didn't look like one of Pakenham's clique, and, sure, wasn't he too young anyhow.

The man reached out a hand to help her up. '*Dia dhuit, 's tá fáilte romhat go dtí an Astráil,*' he said, extending to her the traditional Irish greeting, and again welcoming her to Australia.

Ellen almost fell backwards with the shock of these words, spoken with the West of Ireland *blas* with which she was so familiar. He was Irish – and from the West! The greeting was music to her ears.

She gripped his hand tightly, and Kevin Lavelle, from Achill Island, County Mayo, saw the biggest smile he had seen since leaving Ireland's shores.

'*Ó, Dia's Muire dhuit, Dia's Muire dhuit,*' she repeated, returning the greeting.

Lavelle took her in. He had barely recognized her from the description given him by Coombes: 'A tall, red-haired woman with a young child.' All afternoon he had scoured the port looking for her, anxious for sight of this woman from the West, this Ellen Rua. He had almost given up hope of finding her when he overheard two port scavengers talking about a shipload of women from Ireland being disembarked up the Creek, leaving their fineries behind them.

Lavelle had then walked the length of the wharf, almost passing by the dishevelled heap of rags that was Ellen, asleep on the dockside. Only when he noticed the child beside her did he realize that it must be she.

Now, as she stood up and smiled, lighting up with the joy of seeing one of her own, Lavelle was impressed by the beauty of this woman. Covered as she was with grime and slime, her hair tangled and knotted like the mangrove roots, Ellen Rua O'Malley's spirit nevertheless shone out at him.

Ellen, for her part, was conscious only of how bedraggled she must look to this young stranger from her homeland.

'Mr Coombes is waiting for you, ma'am, at the Halfway House Inn.' He pointed back towards the sprawling port town. 'We won't travel to the Barossa today – it will soon be nightfall – so I suggest we go to the inn. You and the baby can get cleaned up, and get some food into the two of you.'

By now the other three were awake, and Lavelle saluted them in Irish. They were mightily brightened up by this, and when he enquired, 'Is one of you, by any chance, a Kitty O'Halloran from Louisburgh, County Mayo?'

Kitty leaped up with a 'Yes, that's me, sir – Kitty O'Halloran!' while Sarah and Nora giggled.

'Well, then, you'll be making the journey with us,' Lavelle told Kitty, much to her delight.

'And what about you two?' he asked of the others.

'We're bound into the service of a Mrs Hopskitch, of Adelaide,' answered Sarah importantly.

'Yes, we're to be indentured to her,' said Nora, with a giggle, adding: 'Whatever that means!' And the two of them set off laughing again.

'Well, I doubt Mrs Hopskitch of Adelaide will be too pleased with the sight of –' Lavelle stopped himself, realizing that they looked no worse than Ellen and Kitty. 'What I mean is . . . I'd better bring you two, as well . . . to the inn . . . first of all,' he stammered out.

As he turned away, Ellen saw a wash of scarlet flood his tanned face. Not wishing to increase his embarrassment, she made no comment as she fell in step behind him. But she thought again how harsh the country must be if the sun out here could burn his face that colour brown. She'd never seen the like of it before.

There was no sign of Jasper Coombes at the Halfway House Inn, so Ellen first washed and changed Annie, and then tended to herself. Lastly she washed the clothes they had been wearing, which were stained and torn from the journey.

Lavelle called for food for all of them. The inn with its weather-board exterior was crowded and bustling with all sorts: sailors, stockmen, merchants, with an Irish accent or two thrown in here and there.

Ellen noticed how quickly night fell like a blanket over every-thing. No beautiful, lingering twilight of imagining, with spirits moving hither and thither. No slow dimming of day's light into the soft darkening, no lazy broom sweeping in the colours of the two lights. Just day. Then night. Would she ever get used to this strange, strange, land?

That first night in Australia, as she lay in exhausted sleep, the bed pitched and rolled with the mountainous swells beneath her; the cries of the dying, and the mad, filling the room about her. Behind these sounds came a deathly chorus, hushed by hunger: the fearful mouthings of her famished people. Stricken by the desolation on every side of them, they walked, spectre-like, through the dead villages with their torn-down shacks. They picked their way – these grey, dancing skeletons – between the arms and legs of those strewn before them, who would dance no more.

Her own village was deserted, tumbled to the ground. Not even a wisp of smoke – a wisp of life – rose up to the stars. Above stood Crucán na bPáiste, stone-sepulchred against the hill. She saw Michael's fine face, starched by death, looking up at her. She threw the tufts of grass and the cold clay down on him, wanting to be rid of the sight of him staring at her, willing her to be with him. He remained silent as the clay covered his pink-blue lips, and the grass tufts covered his eyes with their green blindness. Then she cast a fistful of mountain pebbles on his black Spanish locks, battening them down, turning them grey – prematurely ageing him in death. Around the graveside were shapes – the shapes of his children, and hers. Lengthened by shadow, silently watching her entomb their father. They raised not a hand to stop her, or to assist her. Just stood there, motionless shapes diffused by the light. Witnesses.

Were they all there? She couldn't tell – couldn't count them properly, with the rolling and pitching of the ship. She started to soft-call them into their real shapes, but they wouldn't materialize, wouldn't answer her.

'Katie, *mo mháinlín* . . .Mary, *a stór* . . . Patrick, *a chroí geal*,' she whispered to them in the old tongue across their dead father's body.

Desperately, with both hands, she shovelled in the earth and the scraws over Michael.

Why couldn't she cover him and be finished with it? And why weren't they helping her, instead of standing, sentinel-like, in judgement on her? Blaming her for burying him – she who loved him. Why wouldn't they answer her? Come and be with her, instead of over there, across the grave?

At last she was finished. She searched for a *leac* to mark his resting place. A stone she would recognize again. She found one, but couldn't move it. She begged the children to help her in this final act.

'We must mark your father's grave, else we will never find it again.'

They listened not.

In anger she bent to the *leac* again. This time it budged. She crouched and slowly rolled the gravestone ahead of her, hunched over it, legs apart, her bare feet clenching the earth. The stone, balled within her body space, seemed to come from her as she delivered it to the grave, inch by inch, straining and convulsing with the effort of its birthing.

This was its purpose. This was what she had formed it for, brought it forth with her own body. To forever mark his death, and life.

But what had happened to the rose, the brightest flower? She scrabbled in the dark, searching, until it, finding her, drew the blood of her palm. She held the rose to the light, looking for where her own dark-red stain had smeared its green stem. Then, she drew its petals to her lips, before placing it on the grave.

From the grave mound she took the handful of earth she would carry with her. As she scooped up the soil, something caught her eye. She bent to examine it: a piece of cloth – maybe a shawl or a blanket. It was not hers. One of the children must have dropped it – left it there. She called again to them as she lifted it. '*Cé leis é*' – Whose is it?

And still they answered her not.

29

The instant Ellen saw Jasper Coombes she knew him.

He was arrogant, condescending – everything she didn't like. She wondered if it came with being British.

An hour earlier, she had been released from her nightmare by the sound of Lavelle rapping on her door. But though the dream ended, the children's silent faces and the image of Michael's dead body lingered on. As she washed and dressed – her clothes having dried overnight on the inn's balcony – her mind was tortured by thoughts of her children: was the dream some terrible omen, like the one she'd had that All Souls night in Maamtrasna? She tried to concentrate on getting herself ready, determined to present herself with some semblance of decency to her employer. Her hair, though, would not be tamed, defying her best efforts to put a shape on it. It remained lank and unkempt, no body to it, giving her a *streelish* look.

'Good day, Mrs O'Malley. Welcome to the Promised Land!' He stuck out his hand to her. 'I'm Jasper Coombes.'

She held out her hand and he grasped it tightly for a brief moment, then let it go.

'You've had a long and arduous journey from Ireland to South Australia, and, I believe, further tribulations since you've arrived here?'

Ellen nodded, but remained silent.

'I trust you rested well, for we now have another journey, of some forty to fifty miles, to the Barossa. There, you can have some respite at last. Pakenham – Edith, that is – has charged me with looking after you well, and I have assured her that we will most certainly do our best.'

He beamed at her, his thin lips drawn back over gleaming white teeth.

'Thank you, Mr Coombes.' Ellen broke her silence.

Coombes nodded in acknowledgement, and continued: 'I am sorry, too, to learn from my old friends of the misfortunes which have beset your troubled land . . . and of your own great misfortune in losing your dear husband.'

Ellen nodded, liking him even less for mentioning Michael. Then she found herself saying, 'Many thousands – many tens of thousands have died.'

She stopped herself there. No point in making an enemy of this thin man who was a friend to her mortal enemy, Pakenham.

Coombes was speaking again, but not to her.

'Lavelle!'

She brightened to see the young Irishman again, and he darted her a quick look and a 'Good morning, ma'am.'

'Are we ready to depart yet? And where are the other three?' Coombes snapped.

'They're on their way, and the spring-cart is waiting outside,' Lavelle answered him.

'I knew it! I should not have deviated from our plan by listening to you, Lavelle, and agreeing to carry those other two to Adelaide. Now, see how they delay us?'

Coombes cut short his remarks as Sarah and Nora bounded into view, followed by a bright-faced Kitty.

'Which one of you three is Kathleen O'Halloran?' Coombes asked, rather tartly. He was clearly not amused by their late, if breezy, entrance into his presence.

Silence greeted his question.

Both Ellen and Lavelle looked at Kitty, who had her lips firmly pressed together, brazen-like, staring straight ahead of her.

'Did you not hear me?' Coombes rasped out more loudly. 'Which of you three . . . *ladies* is Kathleen O'Halloran of Louis . . . Dammit, Lavelle, what's the name of that confounded . . . ? – Of County Mayo.' Coombes blurted, having found a way out without having to be told by Lavelle.

Yet, again, he got no answer. Now Sarah and Nora turned to look at Kitty, who was still trying to keep a straight face.

'Is it you, girl?' Coombes spoke directly to Kitty.

Kitty just looked at him.

'Answer me, damn you!' he swore at her.

'No, sir!' said Kitty.

The other two put their hands to their mouths, horrified at Kitty's reply.

'No, I'm not Kathleen . . .' Kitty gave a little laugh. 'I'm Kitty O'Halloran, and it's Louisburgh, sir!' she said, emphasizing the 'sir'. Then she burst out laughing – joined, somewhat nervously, by the other two.

Ellen caught Lavelle, who stood slightly behind Coombes, smirking at Kitty's cheek towards his employer. She noted, too, Jasper Coombes' clenched knuckles, and hoped Kitty would not pay for her sport with him at a later date.

The flash of anger, however, seemed to leave Coombes as quickly as it had arisen. His only comment was: 'I see we have a bright spark coming to join us.' Then he turned to Lavelle – now straight-faced once more – and said, 'Well, it's a tough life in the bush, and a sprinkling of fun is to be welcomed. I'm sure Mrs Baker will be delighted with our new arrivals.' Leaving the girls wondering who this Mrs Baker was.

Ellen watched the way Coombes, from under his narrow brows, studied Kitty as they filed out to their transport. She knew he would be looking her up and down in the same way as she passed him.

And Jasper Coombes, gambler, overlander, colonist, smiled. He liked what he saw.

Outside, they boarded the spring-cart, to which two hefty bullocks, a black and a brown, were harnessed. Lavelle took the reins and Coombes sat up front with him. Ellen, Annie, and the three younger women, sat bundled in the rear along with the remnants of their belongings.

Ellen was eager for a sight of this unknown land. Maybe the night's rest, food, and the new day's light, would give her a different perspective of her surroundings.

Although it was yet early, Port Adelaide was bustling. Men on horseback, sailors in twos and threes, looking the worse for the previous night's wear, filled the morning. Dogs yelped in the road; large drays trundled along behind teams of bullocks. One dray in particular had them all agape – it was being drawn not by beasts of the fields but human beings! Harnessed to a cart containing two large wooden churns, were four flaxen-haired young women, all straining to take the load.

'Those girls . . . ?' Ellen began incredulously.

'Lutherans!' Coombes replied as if that explained everything.

'But . . .' Ellen started again, unable to take her eyes from the four neatly-bonneted beasts of burden.

'Lutherans, from Prussia,' Coombes volunteered. 'New migrants – persecuted at home, fled here for their religious freedom.'

Ellen felt that, for some reason, Coombes did not want to discuss the Lutherans further. So she persisted.

'Yes, but why do they do the work of animals?'

'Well, ma'am,' – it was Lavelle who replied this time – 'they came here with nothing. In their own lands they were fined for their beliefs, and their goods seized. Anything they had left, they sold for the passage money to South Australia. Once here . . .' Lavelle hesitated. '. . .they borrowed money to buy land.'

Ellen saw Coombes give Lavelle a sharp look, but the man from Achill Island continued: 'So, they work and pray, and pray and work, to develop the land, and no work is beneath them – or their womenfolk . . .'

'Lavelle!' Coombes cut across the younger man, and then turned back to Ellen. 'You'll learn plenty of the Lutherans, in due course. Where we're headed, the place is overrun with them.'

Coombes faced forward again, giving Lavelle a stern look in the process. Then he said, 'Are we to grind, at snail's pace, the whole route to Adelaide?'

A question, Ellen knew, which had nothing whatsoever to do with the speed, or lack of it, of their journey.

She twisted in her seat for one last look at the strong, serious-faced young women, seemingly undaunted and unashamed at their lowly task. She remembered her own journey, from Westport back into the mountains, drawing behind her a much lighter cart than these girls strained at. The weight, then, was not in the cart, but in her own heart, for the cargo she drew – her poor, wasted, lovely Michael. She crossed herself at the memory of that terrible journey.

'*Ar dheis Dé go raibh a anam,*' she whispered, asking into the great vastness of South Australia that his soul be at God's right hand.

Her mind returned to these Lutherans – driven from their own land, persecuted for their beliefs. Was it the same, in every country, as it was in Ireland? It made no sense to her. Wasn't it all the one God – the Lutheran God, the Church of England God, the Catholic God – her God?

She wondered about the God of this untamed land, this place at the bottom of the world. Which God ruled here, over men like Jasper Coombes? If any.

And why did Coombes not want to talk about the Lutherans? Was he a landlord, in this place of never-ending land? With tenants as poor, dependant, and exploited as she and Michael had been? And what of the islandman – Lavelle: what was his relationship with Coombes? They seemed as unalike as night and day. Probably Coombes had some sort of hold over him. Already she could see her new employer was that kind of man.

On they travelled over the *bockedy* road – if indeed it could even be called a road – towards Adelaide. Though the dirt-track, for that was all it was, was unmade, it attracted a reasonable amount of traffic. Some travellers were on horseback; some walking, looking weary and footsore; some resting by the dusty roadside. Then there were the carts with bullocks. Even a coach – imported from Hobart in Tasmania, as Lavelle told them when it approached.

The coach had big round wheels, the spokes showing signs of damage from the hard roads. The passengers' faces, too, bore signs of wear and tear as they journeyed past them, jolted this way and that. The coach driver, a sombre-looking fellow, being both black-coated and black-hatted, spurred on his charges with the frequent touch of a long whip. Impervious to the terror he caused his passengers, he charioteered them onwards, maintaining a kind of stoic indifference all the while.

The sky went on forever here, thought Ellen, and it needed to, to cover such a country. Yet this was only the Southland of Australia. Beyond this province was the northern region, and there must, by rights, also be a western and an eastern part. Her mind, accustomed to mountain, lake, and valley, could not encompass what she saw. This land seemed un-valleyed, unbounden, infinite. Scrub and gum trees, as Lavelle called them, stretched for miles and miles, broken only by the semblance of a village here and there. Now, and again, a farmhouse appeared on the horizon, solitary, except for a few cattle dotted around it. There were a number of wayside halting places along the route where they stopped – primarily, it seemed to Ellen, for the benefit of the bullocks. Whatever the reason, the women, numbed and bone-shaken, were only too glad to alight.

'I've never done as much buck-leppin in me life!' was Kitty's way of describing the journey. ''Twas better than any *céilí* at the crossroads, and not a note of music!'

Kitty was good company and helped keep all their spirits up.

Ellen took advantage of the stops to feed and bathe Annie. The journey had made the child hot, but she was a surprisingly good traveller.

After miles of emptiness, they passed Hindmarsh – named, Coombes told them, after South Australia's first Governor, John Hindmarsh. Ellen noted a flurry of growth: a flour mill, a tannery, and a brewery. But not until they had been on the road ten hours did they reach their final destination: Adelaide. Only when they crossed the River Torrens and entered the city itself did Ellen feel she had truly arrived in Australia.

Adelaide, named for the consort of Queen Victoria's predecessor, King William IV, had a name which seemed to fit this British colony. Ellen wondered how Barossa, where Coombes' estate was, had come by its name. It didn't sound at all English.

Coombes, who had been remarkably quiet since the Lutheran episode, was now as gracious as could be.

'Of course we could not have left the young ladies' – he gestured towards Nora and Sarah – 'to fall prey to malevolent influences in Port Adelaide. Nor can we now throw them upon the mercy of a strange city. I shall go and seek out this Mrs . . . ?'

'Hopskitch!' interjected Kitty, rather pertly.

'Yes – Mrs Hopskitch. And when everything is in order we will deliver Miss Sarah and Miss Nora safely to her. Then, in the morning, when we are all well rested, we will escort Mrs O'Malley and Miss Kath– I mean, Miss Kitty, to the Barossa.'

Everything having been settled to his satisfaction, Coombes dropped them off at a boarding house in Morphett Street and then departed in search of Mrs Hopskitch – leaving them in no doubt that he would succeed in his errand.

On his return, however, he announced: 'I am afraid there is bad news!'

They waited anxiously as he paced in front of them, hands behind his back.

'I did, indeed, find the said Mrs Hopskitch, after much searching – although it seems she is known well in some quarters of the town,' he added.

Ellen wondered what Coombes was hinting at.

'What did she say?' Sarah Joyce asked, apprehension in her voice.

'She said . . .' Coombes bit his thin upper lip, as if not wanting to repeat Mrs Hopskitch's news. But he did: '. . . that, having waited a number of days for news of your arrival, and hearing none, she had feared the worst. Either you had not travelled, or you had been . . . You had not completed the journey.'

'Oh!' the girls exclaimed, looking at each other.

'What was she to do, being understaffed? I am afraid – there being many Irish girls arriving under this Orphans and Paupers Scheme instituted by Westminster . . .' Before he said it, Ellen knew – they all knew – what it was, he would say: '. . . Reluctantly, Mrs Hopskitch was forced to hire two other Irish girls.'

'Oh!' went Nora, again, hands to her face, aghast at the news.

'What are we to do now, with no work, and nowhere to live, and no money to support ourselves?' Sarah said, frightened, looking from one to the other of them.

Ellen turned to Coombes, hoping for an answer to the plight of her two young travelling companions. He had one.

'The news is not all melancholy . . .' He gave the women a watery smile. 'Mrs Hopskitch, in great distress at this situation, prevailed upon me to take you into my service, and transferred your indentureship to me.'

The two girls burst into gasps of delight at this news, and Ellen watched Coombes' smile widen at their show of gratitude.

'Adelaide is not a goodly place for homeless young girls to wander about in – not a goodly place at all!' he said. 'But, no need to worry about that now!'

When Coombes left them, Sarah and Nora were beside themselves with joy.

'Now, we'll all be together!' said Sarah.

'Isn't it a great thing, surely?' Nora chipped in.

'Isn't it a great fortune that we met with Mr Coombes?' Sarah laughed, hugging Ellen.

Ellen was not so sure. She waited until Annie was tucked up in her bed, asleep, then returned downstairs in search of Lavelle. There were answers she needed. Many answers – and she felt Lavelle held the key to them, if only he would tell her.

She found him in the saloon, alone. He seemed glad to see her, and asked for news of Ireland and the Famine. And how she came to be here. On her telling of Michael's death, and her children left behind in Tourmakeady, he offered his sympathies to her in a very heartfelt way, the sweep of his hair falling over his brow as he leaned forward, close to her. Unlike Coombes, he appeared to be completely sincere, interested in her story.

For his part, Lavelle was fascinated by Ellen. Her obvious beauty aside, he detected a strength of character in her, an instinct for survival – something she would need in abundance if she was to last three years in this harsh, unyielding, country. He loved hearing her speak. Her voice had cadences to it – like music. It rose and fell, undulating with the telling of her story, yet it was always soft and clear: as easy on the ear as she was on the eye. He wanted her to go on talking all night.

Ellen was more interested in getting him to do the talking.

'How did you come to be here?' she asked.

'Well, I got in a spot of bother back home and they moved me out here – courtesy of Her Majesty's Government.'

'What happened?'

Lavelle smiled, amused at her. Insistence fell so gently from those lips.

'It was the proselytizers,' he replied. 'They came to Achill from England, wanting to save our souls with soup and sermons. To save the poor papish Irish from themselves and the wiles of the unholy Roman Catholic Church.'

'And what was wrong with that?'

'Nothing at all, but they divided the people on Achill. You were given food if you went over to their Church. Then, "the soupers" – the ones who changed over – took their children out of the

Catholic schools and put them instead to be raised as Protestants. This caused much bitterness, and the local clergy were up in arms. "Soup for souls", they called it, and soon half the island was against the other half. 'Twas a bad business indeed, this "taking the soup".'

'I can guess what side you were on!' said Ellen, laughing.

'Well, I wasn't much for *souperism* or its doings. So, a few of us decided it would be a good idea to brighten things up a little on the island, and we lit a tinder to the soupers' church at night. Oh, it made a great bonfire, entirely!'

Lavelle chuckled, seeming to enjoy the re-telling of his church-burning story.

'Then, the Peelers came, and caught a few of us. They didn't try us in Westport or Castlebar but shipped us off to London. Less chance of stirring up a riot over there, I suppose. The Magistrate said he wouldn't return us to Ireland "for fear of inciting riotous behaviour among the local populace, permanently disposed, it seems, towards violence." So New South Wales got us instead. Three more Irish rebels shipped out of harm's way to Australia.'

Lavelle was proud to be part of the 'ship 'em or swing 'em' tradition by which the Crown dealt with the 'Troubles', and troublemakers, in Ireland.

'It seems to me,' said Ellen, 'that religion is at the root of a lot of problems, wherever you go. What the people back home need is food, not foolishness. The Church is too busy saving souls instead of bodies. The bodies of old people, dying from the want of someone to wet their tongues. The bodies of children, stricken with every disease under God's sun, and their poor mothers, dragging themselves along the ditches, trying to gather a few nettles here and there . . .'

Lavelle looked at her. She was a firebrand, this woman. No wonder the landlord had wanted her out of Ireland. She'd torch a church, all right – or a landlord's house, at that – if she was put to it.

'You must have seen the worst of it.'

'I didn't see the half of it,' she said, the anger rising in her. But she didn't try to suppress it. She needed to speak out after so long cooped up with the thought of it in the foul hold of the *Eliza Jane*.

'And I saw the wasted bodies of the fathers, too, tramping ten or twenty miles a day to food depots closed against them, only to be sent home, empty-handed and broken-hearted, to their families. Like as not, passed on the road by carts three times the size of the one you drive, bursting at the seams with every kind of food, all of it heading for ships to take it over to England.

'Oh, yes – England sups while Ireland starves. And most of the priests and the bishops, of every persuasion – they sup too. While their flocks starve away on the roadsides!'

'Take it easy, ma'am.' Lavelle reached over and caught her by the arm, and she realized she was trembling with the enormity of it all. Always in the background, the thought of Michael, and her own flight. Like the bishops and the priests, she, too, had turned her back on her flock – her own children. Oh, God, how could she live with it? Out here, a world away from her three darlings, Patrick, Katie and Mary.

'I should never have left them, never . . .' Ellen's voice trailed off in despair, and Lavelle caught her by the other arm.

'Listen to me,' he said firmly. 'If you had stayed, you'd all be dead by now. This way, at least there's some chance for you and the child . . . and some chance for you to return for the others.'

At this, she turned away from him – tried to break his hold. She didn't want to listen. But he continued, forcing her to hear him out.

'From the story you tell, those Pakenhams just wanted you out of the way for a few years, until things settle back again. They won't let anything happen to your children – they wouldn't dare. They'll be looking over their shoulder for this Shanafaraghaun man, afeared of what he'll do if they break their word to you. And of what you might do to them on your return!'

She looked into his eyes – blue and intense. He meant what he said.

'No, what you had to do, Ellen Rua, was a hard thing, but it was the best thing – the only thing.' His voice was comforting, assuring, trying to set her troubled mind at rest.

She wasn't shaking so much now. Lavelle's words struck a chord: whatever she had done – stayed or left – she stood to lose her children. It was the devil's choice for her, damned if she did and damned if she didn't. She needed God, not the devil, on her side. But not the God of divisions, not the God who had the Catholics and Protestants at each other's throats, and the Lutherans at their own. She needed a new God, a different God. The God of Australia.

If there was one.

They talked for hours, interrupted only when she slipped upstairs every so often to check on Annie. The child slept solidly. She was easy minding – her new country not seeming to knock a *faic* out of her.

Lavelle, recognizing a kindred spirit, opened up to her. Both were strangers in this strange land, bound together by a common language and history, and an uncertain future.

He told her how, on arriving in Botany Bay along with the other deportees, he had been put to work clearing bushland just north of Sydney, on property owned by Coombes and a consortium of others. Coombes, it seemed, had been well-connected in London, frequenting the Covent Garden tea-gardens, and the gaming clubs – Crockford's, his estate in the Barossa, was named after one of them.

As Ellen listened, the links between Coombes and Pakenham began to emerge: the landlord's 'sojourns' in London, the rumours of his debts to the banks and gaming clubs.

Lavelle continued his story: 'It seems that Coombes fell foul of the cards. Disgraced, and with huge debts, he fled to Australia, funded by some of his friends – including Sir Richard Pakenham.'

It all fell into place for Ellen now. Coombes was not only a friend of Pakenham's, but indebted to him. Pakenham, therefore, was calling in the debt by getting Coombes to take her into his charge, out here – out of the way – probably reluctantly.

So, she could expect little favour from Jasper Coombes. She returned her attention to Lavelle as he described how his employer had realized that, with European immigrants pouring into Sydney, a killing could be made on the vast tracts of undeveloped land there held by the Aborigines.

'Coombes and his associates swindled the local tribes out of thousands of acres. All for the price of a month's supply of tobacco, trinkets, knives – and alcohol. Officially, the Crown, which itself seizes the land, doesn't approve of that sort of thing, but generally turns a blind eye. The rights of the Aborigines – their traditional hunting grounds and sacred places – don't count, even though they've lived here for tens of thousands of years. It all goes back to Captain Cook, the one who "discovered" Australia. He declared that the only inhabitants here were 'flora and fauna'. They call it the "Captain Cook lie",' he told her.

Ellen, shocked and fascinated by Lavelle's story, encouraged him to continue.

'The Aborigines soon found out what it meant to have their land taken by this new "whitefella" tribe – fencing. They got driven deeper into the wasteland, with more and more of their hunting grounds cut off from them. At first, they tried to carry on hunting. But Coombes, and other whites, considered the land theirs. So the Aborigines were accused of trespassing on their own lands. Trespassers could be shot – and they were.'

'But what about the constabulary?' she asked.

'This was out in the bush – there were no police. Once in a while the Aborigines would retaliate – like when Coombes' men captured a dozen or so Aboriginal women, and kept them penned up, to be used by them. There was a bloody battle – but the Aborigines, with their spears and knives, were no match for Europeans on horseback, armed with guns. Those who weren't massacred were taken prisoner.'

Lavelle spared her the detail of what had happened to the captives – how the Europeans, avowed Christians to a man, had vied with each other in their desecration of human life and dignity to teach these 'black heathens' a lesson. The depths of depravity to which they had sunk was evidenced by an ultimate act of savagery, in which they had hacked off the penis of one of the Aboriginal leaders. To shouts and howls of drunken laughter, they had sat and watched as the man, bleeding and in agony, had stumbled and pirouetted within the flickering light of their campfire. In this horrific death dance, he had sought the help, the mercy, of his murderers, spattering them and the land they had taken from him with his life-blood. Finally tiring of this display, Coombes had decapitated the man to 'deliver him from his agonies'.

Coombes then had the man's head pickled and sent in a hat-box to London as proof of how 'we Europeans are winning the war against the savages'.

No white man was ever prosecuted, despite an inquiry conducted by the constabulary. Coombes had distanced himself from 'any acts of savagery committed by the scum I am forced to employ, to develop the Crown's Colony.' He portrayed himself to the constabulary as an angel of mercy arriving on the scene 'too late to intervene, except to put the heathen out of his final misery.' Moreover, he called on the British Government to send more missionaries 'to Christianize and civilize the heathen blacks' – a call which corresponded with the Government's own view as to how Australia's first inhabitants should be dealt with.

Lavelle picked up the story: 'Eventually the Aborigines – pushed further and further to the outer limits of their traditional hunting lands, their women stolen and held caged as prostitutes – had had enough. When Governor Gipps in Sydney got word that a multi-tribal army was massing, intent on wreaking vengeance on Coombes, he put pressure on Coombes to leave the colony. The Aborigines were told that Coombes had returned to England. In return for a few empty promises, they made peace with the Government.

'Coombes, in the meantime, had blackmailed his partners into buying him out of the company by threatening that he wouldn't leave New South Wales without his share. They knew that if he didn't leave, they'd all go down. So they coughed up.

'He needed some men to go with him, men who hadn't been mixed up in the massacre. I was working at a camp a hundred miles north with another transportee, a young lad from County Monaghan called McGorry. Coombes sent for us – he wanted Irishmen for some reason, said we might be thick but we weren't scum like the English convicts. We didn't want to go – we'd heard the stories about what Jasper Coombes had done – but he told us: "If you come with me, you'll be free men. South Australia is a free colony, no convicts are allowed there. If, on the other hand, you elect to stay here . . . It's said that the Governor will be looking for scapegoats to assuage the 'Abos' – and the Cockney rabble who were involved in this lapse plan to finger the two of you rather than face the consequences themselves."'

'But surely, if you were a hundred miles away –' said Ellen.

'The Crown didn't want to put the blame on their own – they'd have been only too happy to have two Irish transportees delivered up to them. Coombes had us, and he knew it. Though we were ticket-of-leave men, bound not to move outside the area, nevertheless we set off overland for South Australia, along what they call the Murray–Darling route. First, you follow the banks of the River Darling from New South Wales, then join up with the River Murray in South Australia. Coombes had heard there was land going cheap there. He planned to use the money he got when he cashed in his share of the company, to buy up land and sell it on, at a handsome profit, to German immigrants.'

Ellen had never heard such a story.

'It was a tough trek, and Coombes didn't talk to us much, but McGorry was great company, kept me going with that sharp Monaghan wit of his – when I could understand him.

'Then disaster struck. McGorry's horse must have disturbed a nest of snakes. Next thing the horse panicked, baulked backwards and lost its footing on the riverbank. Itself, with McGorry still astride, went into the swirling waters of the Darling. Coombes was thrown from his horse too. I didn't know which one to go for, Coombes or McGorry. Coombes had got hold of the bank below, but McGorry and the horse were both being swept away.'

'What did you do?' Ellen couldn't bear it.

'I turned and tried to get downriver of McGorry, but I couldn't make it. I saw the current take him out into the middle, and even the horse couldn't go against it. I had to let them go – I couldn't save him.'

'And what about Coombes?' Ellen asked.

'He was still hanging on. The snakes had gone back into the bushland, so I left the horse on the bank and clambered down, holding on to the reins. I thought the horse would never hold me. Then I got onto a rock where I could reach Coombes. You know, Ellen, I was tempted to leave him there. I had a hold of him and his face wasn't an arm's length from mine. He must have seen what I was thinking. But it was the strangest thing ever. Never once did he beg me. Never once did even a flicker of fear come into his eyes.'

The moment had stuck vividly in Lavelle's memory. Jasper Coombes cared not much for life – neither anyone else's, nor indeed his own. It had struck a chill in Lavelle – this man, hollowed of all emotions, even self-preservation. A human shell without a soul.

'But I couldn't do it. I couldn't let the river take him, no matter what he'd done.'

Ellen was filled with admiration for Lavelle. She could see he blamed himself for not saving the young Monaghan lad, but he had done the right thing in saving Coombes – more's the pity.

'Eventually we made it to Adelaide. Coombes didn't waste any time in finding out who held the power here. He made contacts in the South Australia Company, which was set up to develop the colony, and soon had the inside track on land surveys. He bagged three thousand acres at a pound an acre, and, within nine months, he'd sold two thousand of it on to the Lutherans at ten pounds an acre. Having been dispossessed of land in their own country, they were intent on holding it here where they could build their German hamlets and live according to the Bible. They were so desperate, they'd pay almost any price. And Coombes made sure they got land – at his price.'

Lavelle stopped and looked at Ellen, her eyes wide at his story.

'Will I carry on?' he asked, knowing her answer.

'Coombes looked down on the Germans,' Lavelle explained to her. 'He used to say that the Lutherans' bullocks had more wit than their owners. But he wasn't above watching what the Lutherans did with the land, seeing how they tilled and cultivated it – cared for it. He watched what they planted, and what grew well.

'A few years earlier, a Lutheran called Johannes Menge had carried out a survey for the South Australia Company. Menge had said that the land would support vineyards and orchards and great fields – there was no better soil in all the colony. So, Coombes started ploughing some of his profits into hiring labour and developing the thousand acres he had left. He planted almond, and peach and plum trees. But most of all, he planted vines. He knew he would be able to sell the wine to the European immigrants flooding into South Australia. And what he couldn't sell here he could export, shipping it out of Port Adelaide.'

Ellen was so enthralled by Lavelle's description of his adventures in Ireland and Australia, and Coombes' villainy, that she almost forgot the time. The islandman was a natural storyteller. But she couldn't help feeling that he had skirted around some of the things she really wanted to know about – and now it was too late.

Still, as she retired for the night, she had much food for thought. One thing she was sure of: Jasper Coombes was not a man to be trifled with. Nor underestimated.

30

The next morning they set off for the Barossa. It would take them two days over the broken and treacherous road. Ellen was feeling surprisingly refreshed, considering how little sleep she'd had, though her head was still buzzing with all that Lavelle had told her the previous night.

Coombes was in a talkative mood, explaining to them that a Colonel William Light, South Australia's first Surveyor General, had surveyed the area not many years previously. He had mapped the hills, where the valley swept eastwards, as the Barossa range – in honour of his friend, Lord Lynedoch, who defeated the French at Barrossa in Spain, during the Peninsular War. *Barrossa* – hill of roses. What a beautiful name, thought Ellen, whispering it to herself. It rolled off the tongue like soft rain on summer flowers.

But she couldn't take her eyes off Coombes. How could he sit there, so calmly, and talk to them like this, after all he'd been a party to?

'It's as hot as August,' Ellen said. And Lavelle laughed.

'You should have been here at Christmas.' He let them wait for a moment before explaining, 'Christmas is summertime down here – it's autumn now.'

Ellen couldn't get over this – they had seen no rain since they came, only hour after hour of sunshine. The seasons were all upside down here.

With each mile they travelled, the beauty of the countryside was revealed to Ellen, and she put all thoughts of the previous night out of her head. Opening out before her was a land of flat plains of open grasslands and gently rolling hills that couldn't have been more different than the mangrove swamps close to the Port of Adelaide. Coombes pointed out to them the various eucalyptus trees native to Australia – blue gums, river red gums, white ghost gums. A kookaburra startled the newcomers, the bird hidden safely somewhere in the trees, sending out his strange jack-ass's laugh at them.

True, the land did not have the stark mountain-valley beauty of Maamtrasna. But it was striking nonetheless with its vast blue sky, and its blue-greens set against the red-brown of the soil. And it looked cared for.

'Who owns all this land?' Ellen ventured, remembering Lavelle's story.

'Nobody – it's just there. Crown land, or maybe the South Australia Company. Nobody yet,' Coombes answered her, sure of his answer.

'But what about the Australian people who live here?' Ellen persisted. 'Don't they own it?'

'Hah! My dear, there are no Australians,' Coombes cut in quickly. 'Only British and Germans and' – he nodded back at them – 'Irish, if you like. We are the Australians, and this' – Coombes pointed to each side of them – 'all this, was a barren wasteland before Captain Cook. Before we came and developed it!'

Ellen wouldn't give in to him. 'But the land looks ordered, tended to. See – there are the grasses, and there are the trees and the shrubs, but each has its own place. Was this from God's time?'

It just didn't make sense. Land, in much smaller parcels than these vast ranges, had always been important in Ireland – for survival, for handing down. Somebody always owned it. Could it be any different here in Australia?

She could see Coombes was becoming irritated by her questioning. Kitty, beside her, dug an elbow into Ellen's ribs, to silence her. After all Coombes was their master, their lifeline in this new land.

'The Peramangk Aborigines live here: they formed the shapes you see around you – the park lands and the woodlands – through their practice of burning-off,' said Lavelle.

'Burning-off?' Ellen echoed Lavelle's words.

'The fire burns up the scrub, and clears the land. The mallee, mulga and other acacias come back stronger, with more seed and fruit. Then the animals return for the seed and fruit, and the Peramangk come for the animals. It's quite simple really – it's the circle of life.'

'But what if the fire was to keep spreading?' Kitty was interested in possible disaster.

'It never does,' answered Lavelle. 'Except when white settlers try it!' And he shot a glance at Coombes.

'Fires – hmph! That's all they're good for!' It was Coombes. 'These savages! Black savages, wandering the land, bone idle, not a grain of wheat have they grown, not a potato planted – only practising their heathen ways!'

Coombes' attack on the Aborigines reminded Ellen of how she had heard her own people described: lazy, indolent, good-for-nothing, priest-ridden Irish. She had already begun to empathize with the indigenous people of Australia, without yet having seen one of them.

She had not long to wait.

'The gun!' Coombes shouted. 'Lavelle – give me the gun!'

Lavelle made no move, only tightened his grip on the reins.

'Goddammit, man, I'll have you flogged for this! Get out of my way!' Coombes shouted, as he jostled Lavelle aside to get at the firearm under the driver's seat.

Ellen and the others wondered what was going on as Coombes grabbed the gun and brought it to his shoulder. Were they under threat from some quarter, or had Coombes spotted some animal he just wanted to shoot?

The latter proved to be the case. But it was not an animal – it was a man.

In the fraction of a second it took Ellen to follow Coombes' line of vision along the shiny black metal of the gun's barrel to the quarry in his sights, Ellen moved.

She thrust Annie into the arms of a bewildered Kitty, and lunged at Coombes, who was on his feet, slowly squeezing the trigger of the gun. Both Coombes and the gun were toppled out of the cart by the suddenness of Ellen's action, the gun exploding, harmlessly, into a nearby bush. Ellen stood, defiant, waiting for Coombes to speak as he got up, dusting himself off. But he said nothing, merely glowered as he retrieved his gun and clambered back aboard.

'Drive on!' he ordered Lavelle.

She could see that Coombes was angry, very angry at what she had done. She just couldn't believe that he would shoot down another human being in cold blood.

The man whose life she had saved had emerged from the bush where he had crouched for cover at the sound of the gunshot. Now he drew himself up to his full height – unafraid – the point of his long spear in the earth beside him. He was tall and broad-shouldered, with black curly hair and a beard to match. He was the first black man Ellen Rua O'Malley had ever seen. And he was almost naked, a fact which drew gasps and gapes from her three younger companions, his only covering being around his lower abdomen.

'A class of a small grass skirt!' Kitty took delight in recounting to them later, again and again. They were at a distance that prevented them noting fine detail, but they did notice one thing: his face, upper body, and arms, were covered with wide white lines of paint.

'That was a mistake, Mrs O'Malley.'

Coombes' ice-cold tones spun Ellen round to face him.

'You were going to shoot him!' she challenged, just as coldly.

'Yes, I was!' he retorted. 'That savage is dressed for war, and some poor settler's family will rue your action before the night is out. If I'm not mistaken, it was Samarara, one of their chiefs. He's been leading raiding parties on the farms around here and running off livestock into the bush.'

'Is it any surprise if you take their land, and push them further away from their hunting grounds and their sources of food?'

The red-haired woman was putting it up to Coombes, Lavelle thought, enjoying this.

'There's plenty of land left for them,' said Coombes. 'And what do they do with it? Nothing! It just lies there. Those blackfellas won't lift a finger, never mind do an honest day's work at tillage, or at improving the land. They only want to be dancing, pagan-naked in the moonlight, clacking their spears and their boomerangs, and blowing animal noises into those hollow tree-logs – what do they call them, Lavelle?' he snapped impatiently.

'Didgeridoos,' Lavelle supplied, adding: 'And, by the way, I think that's where that fellow was off to – a *corroboree*. He wasn't painted for fighting, but for a celebration.'

'Celebration, war, dancing, fighting – it's all the same to those heathens, they can't tell the difference.' Coombes was dismissive of Lavelle's correction.

'And we can?' Lavelle threw back.

Coombes let it rest at that, falling into a morose silence again.

The rest of that day's travels passed without incident. That night they reached Gawler, a pretty, well-planned, country town, nestled under the Mount Lofty Ranges, between the North and South Para Rivers. Colonel Light, he of the Barossa Surveys, had located it there in 1839, Coombes broke silence to tell them. She noted how interested he was in anything to do with land or its surveys.

After dinner, Ellen made a point of seeking out Lavelle. There were still many questions she wanted answered from yesterday, and now there were more – from today.

She found him almost immediately.

'I knew you'd come,' he said.

She tilted her head quizzically.

'Well, any time I looked at you all day, I could see the questions racking up in that head of yours.'

She laughed. 'Was it that obvious?'

'Yes,' he joined her laugh. 'It was.'

Lavelle was glad that Ellen had come. He was truly fascinated by her. She read things so quickly, and having sized up a situation she was not afraid to act. He could scarce believe that a woman whose life depended on Coombes, should be so un-afeared that, when it came to it, she had physically upended the man out of his own carriage.

She was completely different from the others. Girls, that's all they were. Girls who were in a state of trembling over Ellen's action. She was older, true – maybe late twenties, Lavelle put her at – but that wasn't the only distinction. This woman would master her own destiny, the others would not.

He liked talking to her. She pushed and probed with those straight questions. Then, she pinned you with those eyes of hers, while you answered – or sought not to.

Ellen did not feel as relaxed in his company. Lavelle sensed this. She drew comfort in talking to somebody from home, but he did not fool himself. He was merely a link into the past – a reminder of what she had come from and what she must go back to. And he was also a link for her into the future. She had a mission to complete in Australia: to gather sufficient funds to leave here in three years and redeem her children. He was part of her mission, necessary to her because of his knowledge of the environment and the people – who might be her friends and, more importantly, her enemies.

'The Aborigines . . . ?' She formed the first part of the question with such simplicity. He waited for the second part to be sprung: '. . . and Mr Coombes?'

The previous night he had glossed over the grisly details which had led Coombes and himself here to South Australia. She had known there was more, and now she wanted to hear it.

'I thought you were very brave today, saving that Aborigine – Samarara's – life,' he answered her.

'Why did I have to?'

'It's just like back home,' Lavelle explained. 'Here in Australia, the Aborigines are regarded by those who take their land as savages – not much above the level of the kangaroos they hunt. No one in authority is going to raise more than a token hand of restraint if you shoot them, or drive them further into the wasteland of the interior.'

'It's "to hell or to Connacht" in Australia,' she interrupted.

'Exactly,' Lavelle agreed. 'The Aborigines don't have any bits of paper proving ownership of the land, so the South Australia Company commissions what it calls "special surveys", and then declares that the Crown owns the land covered by the survey. It then buys the land from the Crown, cheaply, and sells it to the likes of Coombes, who's usually in on what's going on. He, in turn, sells it on to new arrivals like the Germans, and reaps vast profits. Speculators like Coombes don't want the Aborigines returning to their hunting grounds – now German farms – and frightening the women. So, they look for any excuse to shoot the Aborigines, and drive them away.'

'What about the Germans – I thought they were God-fearing people?' Ellen asked, wondering if they, too, hunted the black people.

'They are,' Lavelle replied. 'They only want to work their farms and pay back the big debts they incurred in the first place. They don't really understand the natives, and are probably a bit scared of them. But, in truth, they don't raise a musket against any man, be he black or white.'

'And the missionaries?'

'It's the same old story,' Lavelle said rather resignedly. 'None of them countenance violence against the Aborigines, but they won't speak out too much when it occurs. The missionaries just want to Christianize them – it's "take the soup and give us your souls" all over again. And, sure, it doesn't make a blind bit of sense to the Aborigines, who were here long before Christ anyway – God forgive me! Their Ancestors created the very ground that the missionaries stand on. Then, throw in the Lutherans, as well, and the blackfellas must be having the last laugh on us.'

'Except they're not laughing,' Ellen interjected. 'They're dying, and it sounds like their culture and way of life is dying. The same, shameful thing is happening here, done by the same people, and for the same reasons. Power, and greed for land.'

'How's that?' Lavelle asked her.

'Didn't you know that we, too, were called heathens and savages?' she said, as if it were something he should have known. 'In the London newspapers, the Irish are drawn with baboon's faces. I saw it myself – the Shanafaraghaun man brought the picture to . . . to Michael . . . before . . .' she faltered for a moment. 'There was no food, no work, no money – only the land being cleared of millions of dying baboons. It makes it all so easy when people are only baboons, or savages. Oh, it's so inhuman – so unchristian – and yet it all gets passed off. It makes me that upset – sorry it is that I didn't grab the gun from Coombes, and shoot him with it myself!' she said, feeling the anger rise in her. She fought against the bitter frustration welling up inside her. Dammit! She was not going to cry in front of this Lavelle, with the strange name, from Achill Island. No, she was not.

'Oh, God!' she swore. 'One day, some way or another, if it kills me, I'll change the way things are. It's so . . . so wrong. So very wrong!'

Then the tears came. An unending, violently shaking wall of tears. Tears for the Aborigines. Tears for the famished and wasted back home. Tears for twisted children, yellowed and putrefied with disease, shovelled into workhouse lime-pits. Tears for the young, mad women who travelled to Australia with her, consigned by night to a watery grave. Tears for her dark-haired, lovely Michael – taken from her, after so little time, so little love together. And tears for the children she had given up – deserted.

She was shaking uncontrollably with the held-back tears of years of being strong, being the survivor. And for what? For this – all the same evils, same injustices. Swap Coombes for Pakenham, it was all the same. It was hopeless! She'd never get out of this God-forsaken land to save her children.

'Oh, sweet Jesus, what a mistake I made!'

She turned her head away from Lavelle, hating herself for this, her hair falling about her in a red and tangled shield, hiding her, protecting her.

Lavelle had seen her anger mount, sensed the struggle going on within her to hold these emotions in check. But, when they did burst forth, he was not ready for the ferocity with which they came, and the pride with which she fought to keep them from him. He moved towards her, encircling her shoulders with his arms. So distressed was she that, for a moment, she didn't realize they were there. But when she did, she shook her head violently.

'No, no! I don't want –' and beat at him with her arms.

He resisted her blows and, without forcing her to rise and face him, he pulled her to him. Her head lay turned against his stomach, and through it he could feel the sobbing and shuddering, as if it were leaving her body and entering his. He held her there till she no longer resisted. Still her arms lay crossed above her knees – a last barrier between her and the man. A mute refusal to surrender completely.

Gradually, the spasms of grief which racked her grew less frequent. At last, her body, broken by this huge outpouring of pain and anger, subsided into small, irregular tremors and, then, into sheer, silent exhaustion.

Lavelle let her rest there a while without speaking. Then he unlocked her slowly, letting her sit upright again. Unsure of what to say to her, he said nothing. Ellen straightened herself, and then forced herself to pull back her hair so that her face was no longer shielded. Lavelle could see the tracks of her tears where they stained her face, and the blue-green eyes now specked with red. Unflinching, she held his eyes, her two hands holding back the red mane on either side of her forehead. When she spoke, her voice was soft and clear, without a hint of a tremor.

'Thank you, Mr Lavelle, for your kindness and compassion.'

Before he could formulate a reply, she had stood up, still looking at him, one hand only now holding the hair back off her face.

'*Oíche mhaith*.' She wished him a good night with the merest flicker of a smile.

'*Oíche mhaith, leat fhéin,*' he called after her as she mounted the stairs. For a moment, Lavelle thought she was going to stop, to turn, and acknowledge his words.

Then both the moment, and Ellen Rua, were gone.

31

The autumn air was crisp the next morning when Coombes and Lavelle, and their five female passengers, set off with renewed spirits. The events of the previous day had been put to one side by all. Today was the day they would reach their final destination in South Australia – the Barossa.

Ellen saw it first. Never had she seen land to compare with that spread out before her now. Her eyes opened wide with delight, as they looked over the valley of the hill of roses – the Barossa. Here were green, grassy plains, stretching out as far as the eye could see, topped with a canopy of blue and red eucalyptus trees. Apart from these gum trees presiding over the vast meadowlands, the land had been cleared of shrub and scrub and planted with fields of wheat and barley. Stock grazed the hillside: cattle, sheep, pigs, and goats, shepherded by a herdsman with staff and horn. This was the Common, Lavelle told them.

Already, along the way, Ellen had seen flocks of white cockatoos, so dense they darkened the sky. The area, not surprisingly, was called Cockatoo Valley. Now, Lavelle pointed out the strange and fantastical creatures native to the Barossa: emus – long-necked birds as tall as a man; giant red kangaroos that bounded away soundlessly on their strong hind legs, covering vast distances. Mesmerized, the newcomers watched as the big reds fled from them, scattering turkey, duck, and other wild fowl, to the safety of the nearest creek.

Ellen's mind could not fully comprehend all that her eyes saw. 'It's . . . it's like some place out of the Bible. The Garden of Eden . . . Noah's Ark . . . with all the animals and birds. It's just wonderful!' she burbled, almost unable to fit it into words.

'Oh, it's like a dream,' Kitty exclaimed, her young face shining with the wonder of it all.

Sarah and Nora, too, were overcome with excitement. Never in their wildest dreams had they imagined a place like this. Nothing could have prepared them for the treasure nestled here in this paradise of Barossa.

'Ahead lies Bethany – or Bethanien, as the Lutherans call it,' Coombes told them. 'Crockford's, my estate, is just a few miles beyond. There we shall rest at last.'

This announcement provoked a sense of anticipation, of having travelled hopefully finally to arrive, all of which added to the heady mix of excitement and wonder at the Barossa.

Bethany – dwelling place – was named for the town of Judaea where Jesus resurrected Lazarus. It was unlike any village Ellen had ever seen. And certainly, a far cry from the one she had left behind at Maamtrasna. Coombes explained that it was typical of the forest-farm villages of Silesia in Germany: 'The Germans call it a *waldhufendorf* – quite a mouthful.'

The houses, some with two chimneys, were much taller than the *botháns* of Maamtrasna, and sturdier. Built of stone and wood, and topped with a fine thatched roof, most of them stood 400 links apart. According to Coombes, this was something less than 300 feet. Behind each house was a long strip of land known as a *hufen,* of about ten times the width of the plot – making 4000 links, or almost 3000 feet. Each *hufen* was bordered by rough wooden fences.

Behind the Bethany houses, before the farmlets began, were the gardens – each one a beauty to the eye. It was as if they picked up the colours of the blue and purple Barossa Hills and then washed them into the soft and dark shades of peach and plum, hanging heavy on Bethany's boughs. Flowers of earthen red and cerulean blue scattered themselves as they pleased, it seemed. But, no, it was all part of the order that was the hallmark of Bethany. Each garden had a large gum tree, the dark resinous leaves and oozing trunk giving out a medicinal scent. Ellen liked the smell: it had a cleansing, purifying note to it. Here and there, a pussy willow with its furry catkins broke the monotony of the eucalyptus-dominated landscape.

'See there!' Coombes' excited voice cut across her thoughts.

Ellen looked up.

'Just below the gardens, before the farm commences – there is the future!' Coombes proclaimed. 'And mark my words, one day this Barossa Valley will be renowned the world over for these . . .'

Ellen strained her eyes to see what Coombes was getting so excited about. She could see no animals, no crops, no flowers, no fruit trees – only some neat rows of small, stunted, trees.

'Yes, there, Mrs O'Malley!' Coombes had seen Ellen's quizzical stare. 'What Mrs O'Malley now sees, and wonders at, is something none of you will have seen in Ireland. Nor indeed, are we fortunate enough to see them in Mother England – those parts of the Empire being too intemperate for their nourishment. But here' – Coombes swept his arm round in a semi-circle – 'here, on every side the climate is most conducive to their flourishment.'

'But what are they?' broke in Kitty, frustrated with his melo-dramatic build-up.

Coombes made a sucking-in sound of exasperation between his tongue and his teeth, and ignored Kitty. 'These are vines!' he announced with a flourish. Ellen and the girls looked non-plussed.

'Vines?' Kitty voiced for the three of them.

'Vines!' Coombes repeated, more loudly. Silly Irish potato-peasants, he thought to himself. 'Ah, but what would you ladies know of vines? Well, let me tell you: vines produce grapes. Just as your own countrymen sometimes produce a brew,' he wrinkled his nose in disgust, 'from the humble potato, so is it possible not only to eat the fruit of the vine – but also to derive from the noble grape . . .' – he paused for effect before imparting the information which he had been building up to – 'the nectar of the gods – wine!'

Coombes was pleased with having finally delivered himself of this. He drew a breath, and carried on: 'This place – the Valley of the Barossa will, one day, become the Vineyard of the Empire. And those of us who are now its pioneers, its first vignerons . . .' Coombes seemed to like this word, he lingered over it, pouted it out through his narrow lips. 'Vignerons, or wine growers, will become the masters of the Vineyard of the Empire. The first will be first as always, not last – no matter what the Bible tells!' he laughed. 'Mind, there is much work to be done.' Coombes shook his head seriously. 'But there are those, here, who should know better . . .'

Ellen knew that he had the Germans in mind.

'Who make out of this noble grape nothing more than pig's swill – little better than what you might make out of your potatoes.'

Coombes was in his element, enjoying his authority on the subject. He wouldn't have his wine, his Crockford's label, derided as mere 'grocer's claret', as other produce of the valley was called by London. No, he'd see to it that London would fork out a pretty penny for his limited vintage claret, Crockford's Reserve, or for the Shiraz, Crockford's Gold. They'd see the sting in it all, those who drove him out over miserly debts of a few thousand pounds. Oh, yes, when they lifted their hand-cut glasses and saw the fine, ruby-dark tincture of the Barossa glistening in the crystal light – having paid for it twice over, the dimwits. Once with his unpaid debts, and now again, when they drank to his wealth. The best of it was that they would know he had survived their niggardliness, outwitted them. He would be the toast of London society, though he dare not go back to enjoy it.

Jasper Coombes, would-be master of the Vineyard of the Empire, luxuriated in the glow these thoughts brought him.

As for Pakenham, the old scoundrel could keep his rose gardens – if this wild redhead didn't go back and run him through or put a musket ball through his gut. And she just might, too – she was fiery!

He would have to watch that – and watch it himself, personally. He couldn't trust Lavelle with this one. He saw the way the Irishman looked at her. Maybe he could foist one of the others on Lavelle. That Kitty – the brazen one – she was sprightly, but not a threat like the O'Malley woman. If the redhead had been English instead of Irish, she might, with a bit of work on his part, have made a fine mistress or even a wife. She was exactly the kind of woman this place needed, tough and spirited, and afraid of naught, save the Almighty – if she was at that. He'd need sons too, and soon, to take on Crockford's. Sons to leave it to. She'd give a man such pleasure conceiving sons, with that long sinuous body of hers. Not wanting it, but feeling it to be her duty. Coombes dwelt for a moment on this thought, then, quickly, banished it from his mind.

He had enough to be doing just now, without complications.

And anything to do with women, beyond ordinary honest-to-God-whoring, always brought complications.

As they passed through the village, the well-kept main street of Bethany was empty, save for a few goats and some fresh-complexioned Lutheran girls, like the ones Ellen had seen in Adelaide. They wore white aprons over blue skirts, white blouses, and red waistcoats. All were busy carrying pails, pitchers, or baskets, their white sleeves rolled up to the elbows in the style of women at work. Women who were happy at work in this new motherland, as their wide smiles bore witness.

Ellen smiled back at them. How well their brightness and colour seemed to capture the spirit of the place, she thought.

'"Faith, vision, trust, and hope," that's their motto,' Coombes said cynically, coming out of his reverie as one of the girls pleasantly acknowledged them. 'All they had when they arrived here were their Bibles, braces and beer-steins! *Stein* – that's a German drinking mug,' he explained for their benefit. 'Now look at them – half the valley's been taken over by them, on borrowed money. We let it go too cheaply. They're like flies on a dunghill, swarming all over the place, calling it New Silesia, trying to change things, bringing their German ways with these *hufen* and *hufendorfs* and *waldhufendorfs*. How's a person to know what they're about?'

'How is that, Mr Coombes?' Ellen interrupted him. 'It seems to me that, like the Aborigines, the Germans have done much good for this land.'

Ellen had decided she was not going to let Coombes get away with anything from now on. She did not like him, and the more she saw of him and his prejudices, the more her dislike grew.

'I'll tell you what they've done,' he responded tartly. 'The Lutherans fled here because they could not tolerate their own country, and it was British capital that provided passage for them to this country. Upon taking the Oath of Allegiance to Her Majesty, they have been allowed, without let or hindrance, to build their Lutheran churches and found their Lutheran schools. And how do they repay this?' he posed to Ellen, and then went on. 'Well, I'll set it out for you. They agitate for change in Her Majesty's laws. They even wish to subvert the role of the Royal Police and the judiciary by themselves conducting public punishment such as bodily chastisements and pillory for those resisting their Lutheran laws!'

Ellen was taken aback – was there any group of people for whom Coombes had anything but contempt?

She said nothing, and he continued: 'Their priests – "pastors and elders" they call them – having come here fleeing tyranny, they now wish to impose their own tyranny on those who fled with them. Sheer hypocrisy, all this religion! Those in power serve neither God nor the people.'

'All true people of God are not like that!' Ellen challenged him.

'Those I've seen are,' said Coombes. 'And the greatest example must be in your own blighted country.'

Ellen was not going to stand for this. 'My country is blighted not because of the priests, but because of union with the Crown. A Crown that took, and took, until the very marrow was sucked from the bones of the people.' Ellen's anger rose. 'And what is more, Mr Coombes, I see the same bloodied hand of the Crown, here, in this new land. This time, supported by land-grabbers with grand ideas about estates and wine, but evicting people off lands which have been theirs for centuries past!'

The others remained silent, aghast at Ellen's attack.

'Now, you listen here –' Coombes had turned on her, fury in his face at her insult.

'No, Mister Coombes, I will not!' She wouldn't have him talk her down. 'It was a mistake I made ever to agree to come here! Even in my blackest grief I should have known better. You, Pakenham – you're of the same ilk, and God help this South Australia if the likes of you ever get a grip on it. It will surely flounder.'

The air between them rife with tension, Coombes looked at the woman. Pakenham had indeed done well to be rid of her. He drew a long, deep breath, keeping his fury in check.

'Mrs O'Malley,' he said, coldly but evenly, 'being that you are recommended by a family long befriended by my own, and being that you are tired from your long journey, I will overlook your actions up to now, and these most intemperate remarks of yours, concerning my own personage, and that of our gracious Queen. However, I caution you to temper your tongue whilst you are in my employ. You will find in me a fair and even-minded employer, but I will brook no more of your insubordinate manners. Do you have me?' Without waiting for Ellen's reply, he turned to the others.

'And, do you girls understand me clearly, as well?' he said in the same tone.

Kitty was the first to respond. Giving a disdainful, sidelong look at Ellen, she said, 'Yes, Mr Coombes, sir, we do!'

Sarah and Nora nudged each other nervously, looked at Ellen, looked at Coombes, looked back at each other, and then, in tandem, nodded their assent.

Coombes looked then to Ellen, who met his gaze. She let him wait. She would let it rest, for now. She would not confront him further, but neither would she bend to him.

Lavelle broke the silence. 'Crockford's is ahead!'

Coombes, tired of waiting for Ellen to end the deadlock, turned to face forward and, as magnanimously as he could manage in the circumstances, announced: 'Welcome to Crockford's, my home – and yours.'

32

Jasper Coombes' Crockford's Estate was huge. Its scale such that Ellen, even on seeing it, could scarcely comprehend. One thousand acres. You could put all of the smallholdings in Maamtrasna together with all of those from across the mountain at Finny, and you still wouldn't have the fill of a thousand acres, Ellen thought.

As they drove under a large sign spanning the entrance which proudly proclaimed, THE CROCKFORD ESTATE – PROP. J. M. COOMBES ESQ., Ellen's eyes widened even further. On one side, she saw paddocks of fine-looking horses, while on the other side were great pasturelands of cattle and sheep – 'Merinos from Van Diemen's Land,' Coombes offered proudly. As they wound their way up the driveway, beautifully cultivated on either side with shrubbery, Ellen could see acre upon acre of well-husbanded fields that with the Australian spring would be brimming with crops of every kind – wheat, barley, rye and oats. Oh, if only the ravaged land she had left behind her had a tenth of this bounty, what a difference it would have made to all of their lives.

Beyond those fields were the vineyards. In the gardens of Bethany, the vines had grown in small, straight rows running parallel to each other. Here, row after row of the ugly, little stunted trees stretched out before them on either side as far as the eye could see – each one of them individually staked.

'This is the future!' Coombes said excitedly. 'The future for the Barossa, the future for the province and the future for Crockford's and Jasper Coombes.'

He went on: 'It's a gamble, but, then, so is life itself, and Jasper Coombes never faced away from a risk. The rest of them here only play at this grape-growing – it's just another fruit to them. Maybe they make a few bottles to lay by – to remind them of back home in Prussia, or wherever it was they were run out of. They don't see it – these Gottlobs, Gottliebs and Gottfrieds. They don't see the potential at all – too busy bible-bashing and complaining to the Governor.'

'Isn't it that they don't have the money? What with every penny they earn going back to pay interest on the high borrowings they made to buy the land in the first place?' said Lavelle cuttingly.

'Nonsense, Lavelle! Land values are rising all the time. It's simple economics. More people are coming here, so demand increases and prices rise accordingly. The Lutherans paid market value, no more – no less.'

'Certainly not less!' Lavelle rejoined. 'And it will be decades before they can pay off the debts they incurred.'

Ellen admired Lavelle's *sponc* in confronting Coombes.

Coombes, however, decided not to pick up the gauntlet. 'Well, either way, they'll not make the investment necessary over the number of years which viticulture requires. I expect to be keeping this vineyard for many years yet, before it starts keeping me. It will be the British here, the pastoralists, who will develop all this into an industry and make wine-producing commercial. You just can't grow grapes in your backyard and expect to make a success of it. It has to be a business.'

'Oh, look! Sarah, Nora, will you look at that . . . that mansion!' Kitty shrieked with delight.

'And are we going to live there?' Sarah shrieked back.

'Yes, indeed you are, ladies.' Jasper Coombes flashed his thin smile at them.

What Ellen saw made Pakenham's Tourmakeady Lodge pale into insignificance. It was how she imagined the lords and ladies of England lived on their big country estates.

First there were the lawns. Big rolling lawns, furlongs of green turf dipping down from the elevation on which the house stood.

'You could race a horse on that!' said Kitty.

'Indeed, and we do – this is the Great Ride of Crockford's.' Coombes spoke with obvious pride.

Beyond the lawns were the front gardens, within which were enclosed a number of smaller lawns whose centrepieces were rockeries decked with the most exotic flower and plant life imaginable.

'Crockford's enjoys a good relationship with the Botanic Gardens in Sydney, and we import specimens, as well as vine cuttings, into the valley,' Coombes continued his narrative. 'The fruit gardens – run for commercial advantage, of course – are situated to the rear of the house. Also to the rear of the house, you will find the herb garden. Over to the far right is the maze, which, if you are fortunate enough to negotiate, you will be rewarded by arriving at the lily pond and the Chinese tea-house. To the left are the rose gardens, bower, and water grottoes. Again, to the rear of the house you will find the creamery. We churn every other day, and produce a thousand pounds of butter per week from a herd of four thousand cattle. We also produce a rather fine cheese. The butter and cheese we sell at the Adelaide market, as well as exporting it – there is demand from such a far-flung location as Mauritius in the Caribbean.'

Ellen was stunned by the scale of operations at Crockford's, but most of all by Coombes' description of it. As if this sumptuous living were the norm.

She was distracted by Sarah and Nora, in chorus again, shrieking with delight: 'Oh, look at the house! Just look at it!'

'It has ten chimney stacks!' Kitty chimed in.

Ellen said nothing, and Coombes turned to her.

'Well, Mrs O'Malley, what say you to Crockford's?'

'What I say, Mr Coombes, is what does any man need with ten chimney stacks when only the one fire at a time can warm him?'

Coombes' smile froze on his face. This was not the reply he had sought, nor expected, from her.

'So,' he said icily. 'Mrs O'Malley is not afraid of the cold . . . Hmmm, we'll see.'

Ellen tried to bite back her reply but couldn't. 'I'd rather freeze to death in this life than be roasted on the coals of hell in the next!'

Coombes' face blanched even further as the true thrust of Ellen's remark hit home.

'Well, maybe after we teach you some manners here, Mrs O'Malley, you'll experience both!' he snapped back at her. Then he ordered Lavelle to stop the cart, and with that, Jasper Coombes, country squire, leapt from the spring-cart and headed towards the house.

Kitty turned on Ellen. 'Ellen Rua, what do you think you're at? You haven't stopped at Mr Coombes since we arrived. This is the best chance any of us has ever had, and your speechifying is going to ruin everything!'

'Yes, Kitty's right!' the other two chorused.

'I'm sure you're right, Kitty. I'm sure all of you are right,' Ellen said. 'But don't you see it's all wrong, all of this. This land belonged to others. It's no different to back home.'

'Mrs O'Malley, ladies!' Lavelle played peace-maker. 'I think we should say no more about this now, only get you all settled in after the long journey here.'

People had started to gather around the cart to gawk at the new arrivals. Mostly men, some young, some grizzled, but all staring at the new female arrivals with great intent, and not a few leers. It struck Ellen that there must not be too many women about here. Not too many at all.

Then, a female voice rang out. 'OK, boys – you've seen enough! Now, back to work the lot of you, or you'll get no tucker this evening – lazy bastards!'

And into view strode Mary Magdalen Baker, housekeeper at Crockford's, known affectionately, but with some trepidation, as 'Ma-Ma'.

As the men scattered out of her way back to work, Ma-Ma Baker barrelled over to the new arrivals. Her big frame filled out a black-pleated pinafore, which was overlaid with a generous-size white apron with lace edging.

'Why, look at the state of these poor wretches! Mr Lavelle, they look famished – skin and bone!' she admonished.

Ellen took in the woman. She was what, in the West of Ireland, they'd call 'a ball of a woman', with a big florid face, and two arms on her like rolling pins that could knock the head off you with one clatter. She had a sunny enough disposition now, but Ellen sensed that, if crossed, this woman would instantly change into something quite different.

'And look at that poor child, too!' the housekeeper said, pointing at Annie. 'Why did you and Mr Coombes not look after them and give them aught to eat?

'Ladies, welcome to Crockford's – I am Mrs Baker, Mr Coombes' housekeeper, which means I run the house . . .' She paused to let this sink in. 'Now, let's get you inside and sitting down for a nice cup of tea and some hot bread – and a drop of fresh milk for that poor child. Come along, now.' Then she commenced to herd them up the steps, through the pillared porch, and into the grand homestead that was Crockford's.

Once inside the house, as Ma-Ma Baker flurried on ahead of them, Ellen felt a tug at her sleeve. It was Lavelle. Catching her arm, he pulled her aside into the open doorway of a book-lined room. He put his finger to his lips, signifying for her to be quiet.

'Look, I agree with everything you said back there – I'm on your side in this, but there's more you should know. I need to talk to you, later, alone. Can you slip out for a half an hour when Annie's asleep?'

Ellen nodded.

'Do you remember the maze?' he asked her.

Ellen did.

'No one goes there after dark, so we'll meet by the entrance at nine.'

She agreed and he pressed her arm, and drew her back into the hallway just in time to hear Ma-Ma Baker's voice call out: 'Now, where have Lavelle and that other woman got to? I do hope she's not going to be troublesome – a red-haired woman on a farmful of men – not a good idea!'

Ma-Ma Baker could sense trouble when it came her way.

Lavelle looked at Ellen, and they both laughed – quietly.

Later, Ellen made sure that Annie was snuggled down comfortably for the night in their bedroom. A bedroom far bigger than the cabin she, Michael, and their four children had lived in. She was about to steal away to meet Lavelle, when a large upright clock in the hall began to chime the house. Quickly, she pulled the door behind her, for fear the noise would waken Annie. She'd have to be sure to be back before the clock struck ten.

The realization that she was late, coupled with the sudden fright of the clock's loud chimes, caused Ellen's heart to beat faster. There, in the silence of the long wooden-panelled corridor, it seemed as if the pounding of her heart was so loud as to bounce off the walls, alerting the whole household to her mission. She was sure, too, that she was bound to bump into someone – there were so many doors leading on to the corridor. She didn't care if she got caught, so long as it wasn't by Coombes or that Mrs Baker.

In the event, she managed to reach the front door without being accosted and, with a little sigh of relief, slipped outside. She left the door unlatched, thankful that there was nothing more than a slight breeze – not enough to blow it open.

It took her a moment to get her bearings, coming from the well-lit house into the night gloom. She veered left, and knew if she kept a straight path she would, soon enough, strike the maze.

She thought she heard talk, somewhere towards the side or back of the house – she couldn't quite pinpoint it. So she proceeded cautiously, crouched and barefoot, testing the ground ahead of her, coiled for escape. The moon was low, misted over, and the four-starred Southern Cross, normally so prominent in the night sky, was likewise muted.

After what seemed an age, Ellen saw the outline of the maze rise up ahead of her. Tall and still, its dense dark-green walls of foliage close-cropped, it was far more daunting by night than in daylight. A shiver ran over Ellen. A cockatoo shrieked, causing a sharp intake of breath into her tightening chest.

Where was Lavelle? He was late . . . No, she was late! Maybe he'd left already? Maybe Coombes had collared him to do something or other? She didn't like this place.

The voices she had heard earlier seemed closer than ever. She would have to hide – steel herself, wait it out. Now the tightness had moved down from her chest into the pit of her stomach – pulsing out from there all over her body.

She moved into the dark awning of the maze. What if she got lost? She might never get out again. And what about Annie and the loud upright clock? God, this was a bad idea, to agree to meet Lavelle out here! What was it that was so important that it couldn't wait for another time?

Ellen edged further into the maze, the voices seeming to trail after her. The path went left and right. She decided to keep to the left, that way it would be easy to remember. Left going in, right coming out. Yes, that was it. That was her plan.

She hadn't taken two steps when it happened. She felt the swish of air first, then a hand grabbed her arm, and another shot over her mouth, stifling her cry. She couldn't see her assailant – but somewhere she still heard the voices. Whoever had hold of her had been hiding where she could have turned right. He was strong, and now dragged her back into the dark corner from whence he had sprung. Once there, he spun her round. Only then, their faces just inches apart, was his identity revealed: it was Lavelle!

She was furious, but Lavelle pressed her tighter in against himself, knocking the breath out of her, so that she could neither speak nor resist him. Then she felt his lips at her ear, his breath moistening its inner folds. She was angry at him, yet she did not fear him.

'*Ciúnas, Ellen! Tá siad ag teacht*,' he whispered to her: 'Be quiet – someone's coming.'

Now, she could hear the voices more plainly. It was Coombes and another man.

'You haven't seen the maze?' Coombes' voice enquired of his companion.

'No, but I've heard talk of it – that you have it designed around some card game?' The other man raised the question in an accent which reminded Ellen of the young botanist she had met on the mountain. Only this voice was older.

'Yes, George! The maze is designed, not in the usual circular or rectangular shape, but in the shape of a king-sized heart. Hearts, of course, being my favourite suit at the tables. There are twenty-one bluffs, or dummy paths, in the maze after –'

'Of course, Coombes – I've got it!' the older man interrupted. 'After "vingt-et-un": twenty-one – the prince of gambling games.'

'Very good, George, very good,' Coombes complimented his companion. 'At twenty-one you must make quick and correct decisions. The flick of a card can make or break you. Likewise here – one wrong move and you are lost. A right move – many right moves – and you win the prize: the Queen of Hearts, who presides over the maze's only exit.'

Ellen was finding it difficult to follow Coombes' explanation, but 'George', whoever he might be, was much amused by it.

'Come, George – I'll show you. I promise I won't lose you, and we can talk – heart to heart – so to speak.'

At this, both men laughed, and Ellen heard them enter the maze opening, where she had been just a few moments ago.

Lavelle now released her, only to grab her hand and pull her deeper into the maze in an effort to escape Coombes. She followed him blindly. He must have some idea of the path through this horrible place, she thought, as they tumbled on, as silently as they could. Suddenly, they came to an abrupt halt. Lavelle leaned closer to her, and she saw his face tight and drawn.

'We're trapped,' he whispered. 'There's no way out.'

They were in a dead end – the high hedge of the maze ahead of them, and on either side of them too. One of the twenty-one bluffs of Coombes' maze had ensnared them.

'We have to go back!' Ellen said anxiously.

'No, wait!' Lavelle whispered back. 'If we go back, we'll meet them and be caught. Let's stay here – Coombes knows the way through, he won't come into one of these dead ends. Let's just sit tight and wait.'

Ellen agreed that this seemed the best plan, so they both fell silent and waited, pressed into a corner of the impenetrable maze wall. If Coombes did take a wrong turn, then they were finished. They would be discovered.

Ellen and Lavelle barely breathed as they heard the two voices move unerringly closer to where they hid. At one stage the two men were so close – in the next section right behind their backs – that she could hear the inhalation and exhalation of breath as they spoke.

'But, George, dear chap – it is imperative you talk to the Governor. And if he won't deign to listen, you must do it via London!' Coombes sounded concerned. 'It is essential, if the industry is to flourish here in the province. I mean, either way, it will have no material effect on *my* business, but the smaller growers need the benefit of it, and it will impact strongly on the business of the South Australia Company – your company. If viticulture flourishes, then more people of means will be tempted to migrate here. More land will be sold – and at better prices. More development will take place, more goods and services will be required. All our ships will rise, George.'

Ellen and Lavelle were intrigued, but both held their breath in panic when they realized that the two men had stopped walking and now stood within a few feet of them. If they could hear the breathing of Coombes and the Scot, then so, too, could their own breathing be heard.

'Well, Jasper, I'll do what I can, you know that. My word will carry weight. But – and it is a big but – there is a strong mood abroad among the legislators to repeal Governor Grey's Distillation Act of 1842. And you know rightly why that is, Jasper?'

Ellen, intrigued, listened for Coombes' reply.

'Yes, yes, yes! Of course, George, of course.' Coombes was attempting to be dismissive. 'I know that the Act has been abused by some, that they are flooding the market with illicitly distilled spirits and brandy made from vineyard refuse, and unhealthy wines. But, nevertheless, George, the Act achieved its primary objective. It staved off the need for the industry to import the brandy and spirit necessary to prevent fermentation. We are not yet ready for sulphur, and these new-fangled methods which Dr Kelly is promoting.'

'Yes, Jasper, I –' the other man tried to intervene, but Coombes would not be stopped.

'Furthermore – and you know this, George, only too well – we need the spirit for sterilization purposes: the casks, vats . . . even the corks.'

'Yes, yes, I know all that, Coombes,' the Scot said, sounding a little impatient.

Ellen wondered what Coombes was after. She sensed that he wasn't telling his companion the whole story – something in his voice struck a false note.

Coombes continued: 'You have to understand, George, that us colonial wine-makers are a new breed of pioneer. We need the support of Government, we need the right to distil. This Act must not be repealed, George. No repeal – else there will be trouble. And how will that sit with the image the South Australia Company is trying to promote back home of everything in the Garden of Eden being rosy? Eh?'

Lavelle looked at Ellen – Coombes was running true to form.

'All right, Coombes, don't over-labour it. I've got the point. I'll do what I can,' the other man said, traces of exasperation in his voice.

'Good, George! Well, let me show you the way home – the way to the Queen of Hearts.'

The voices trailed off for a while, then Ellen heard a roar of laughter, followed by the Scot exclaiming: 'By gosh, Coombes, I see her – the Queen of Hearts! Well, there she is, the royal lady. Oh, it's a rub, right enough. You're a damnable rogue, Coombes – a damnable rogue! Wait till I tell them in London! When Crockford's hear of it, the tables will be closed for a month!'

More guffaws of laughter split the night air, this time led by Coombes.

'Jasper, you know this is the only place on earth fit for you – you scoundrel. This Southland needs villains like you!'

Then more laughter.

Ellen and Lavelle waited until the laughter faded into the distance.

'They've gone,' Lavelle said, still in hushed tones.

'Let's get out of here, if we can,' Ellen replied.

Lavelle nodded in assent.

'What was all that about?' she asked.

'Illicit brandy and spirit. Coombes distils hundreds of hogsheads of it here, then exports it to the Swan River Colony and the other provinces. Makes a right killing out of it. He doesn't want the Act changed. It would ruin him before he gets on his feet with his own premium wines. So he's been lobbying like hell. I'm not sure who the Scotsman is, but he's obviously powerful enough to try and prevent any move to repeal the Act.'

'But why should he do anything for Coombes?'

Lavelle laughed. 'Coombes has probably done some deal with him: land, labour – whatever. It's called blackmail. You'll learn, Ellen Rua O'Malley. You'll learn all about Jasper Coombes and the way he works.'

But Ellen didn't have time to learn anything more just then.

Clear as a thunderclap it rang out. Ten times in all, each 'dong' sounding progressively heavier in her heart.

'Oh, my God, Lavelle! It's ten o'clock, and that racket will surely wake Annie. We've got to get out of here! I've got to get back to her!'

With Ellen leading, they tried to find their way back. Every route seemed to be the right one, the way they had come. But every route they took was wrong. One after the other, finding them in a dead end.

Ellen was frantic by now. 'There must be some way, some trick for getting out of here, Lavelle – there has to be!' she pleaded.

'I have it!' he said. 'We've been going about it the wrong way. We've been trying to find our way around this blasted puzzle, instead of finding our way over it.'

Ellen looked up at the high hedge of the maze. Was Lavelle mad?

'Come here,' he instructed her, 'and climb on to my shoulders. From there, you should be able to pull yourself on to the top and crawl along it. That way, you can guide me through and we'll be out of here in no time.'

They weren't. But Lavelle's idea did work – albeit more slowly and painfully than she would have wished. First Ellen had to crawl on her stomach along the top, identify the exit from the maze, and then follow the route of the path all the way back from the exit to Lavelle. By the time she had done this, her dress was in ribbons, her body cut and torn by the hedge-top branches, which were too far apart to allow her to walk. She could kneel, from time to time, to get her bearings, but she could only make progress by inching forward while stretched out flat, the hedge-tops punishing her breasts and lower body at every move.

Eventually, they made it. Ellen let herself down into Lavelle's arms. He was shocked at the damage her urgency to get back to Annie had inflicted on her.

After she had taken a moment to recover, she and Lavelle left Crockford's maze, passing under the large and incongruous effigy of a laughing Queen of Hearts which straddled the exit. This required those who successfully negotiated the maze to get down on their hands and knees, and crawl out from underneath the Queen's gaily painted dress. One final indignity.

When Ellen, half running, half stumbling, got back to the front door – it was closed against her. She raised the heavy black Jack-of-Spades knocker, but, thinking better of it, gently lowered it again.

It seemed to take her forever to make her way round to the back of the house. Thank God! She found a rear door was only closed – not locked. Quickly, she let herself in, and raced into the kitchen, half-expecting to find Mrs Baker awaiting her.

Her luck was in. Nobody was there.

She dashed along the hallway to her room. There was no sound from Annie, she must have slept through. It looked as though Ellen had gotten back just in time – it was nearly eleven, and the next set of chimes must surely awaken Annie. Her guardian angel, Michael, Cáit or the Máistir – somebody was looking down on her. She would clean herself up, creep into bed, and sleep, sleep, sleep until morning.

Tomorrow, she would get hold of Lavelle and make him tell her whatever it was he had intended to tell her tonight.

Careful not to make a sound, Ellen turned the knob, pushed the door in gently, then slipped inside, turning quickly again to close it. When she faced back into the room, she got the shock of her life. There, silhouetted in the dark, sat the large frame of Ma-Ma Baker, an empty food bowl on her lap and, in her arms, being rocked to sleep, a drowsy Annie.

Without saying a word, the housekeeper arose, put the bowl on the bed, and walked towards Ellen, handing the child to her.

Ellen was so stunned by this turn of events she could only whisper, 'Thank you!'

The housekeeper looked at Ellen – her hair entangled with twigs and leaves, her face and hands bloodied, her dress torn, almost shredded from her body.

'Well, Mrs O'Malley!' Ma-Ma Baker started. 'You look as if you've been dragged through a hedge backwards by a team of horses all going different ways. Though, I daresay, two-legged animals have more to do with your state than four-legged ones.'

Ellen remained silent.

'I knew you was trouble the moment I clapped eyes on you. I

said to myself, I did: "Ma-Ma Baker, watch this one closely. Watch this red-headed Irish!"'

The woman drew her face back from Ellen's, and made her way to the door. Ellen watched her go, cradling Annie against her cut and bruised breasts.

On reaching the door, Ma-Ma Baker turned and raised a warning finger to Ellen.

'I knew you was trouble, Irish!'

33

If Ellen expected some retribution from Coombes or Mrs Baker for her night escapade, there was none from either. Coombes seemed not to be about much – probably off somewhere up to his shenanigans, Ellen thought. And the housekeeper, while she was civil enough to her, appeared to be biting her tongue, biding her time. Lavelle wasn't much to be seen either – probably off with Coombes.

A week at Crockford's had made a big improvement in Ellen. Her injuries from both the mangroves and the maze, even if they hadn't disappeared, had all but healed – aided by various lotions, ointments and poultices from Ma-Ma Baker's medicine chest.

Best of all, she had time to herself. Time for herself and Annie, who was flourishing in the new environment. The child was going to be very beautiful, Ellen thought. The early promise of this at birth, stunted by the deprivations of the Famine, was now beginning to show through again. She had grown dark, like Michael, with black-as-the-night ringlets of hair hanging down from her head like strings of black pearls. Her eyelashes were the longest Ellen had ever seen – even longer than her own – and sat curving heavenwards above a pair of blue-green sparkling eyes.

Yes, Annie would be beautiful.

Kitty, Sarah and Nora had also responded well to their new surroundings. Ellen was amazed at how pretty they were now Ma-Ma's cooking had put a little flesh on their bones, and how lively. She was glad that things had been patched up between them all since the journey to the Barossa and her attacks on Coombes. After all, they had more in common than they had differences. And the girls were great with Annie, each of them wanting to take her for a while, help with her walking, even feed and change her. Annie, in turn, proved quite happy to be the centre of attention, and the smile never left her bright little face when in their company.

The four women were happy to have time to recuperate from their travels, and to indulge in the luxury of Crockford's, but they knew this life of leisure could not last. As yet, though, they had no idea what kind of work Coombes had in mind for them. Attempts to elicit information from Mrs Baker proved fruitless, and were met with: 'Well, Mister Coombes wants you all to be at your best before you start work. Told me I wasn't to let any of you so much as lift a hand, he did. I'm sure he has something in mind for you all, and no doubt he'll tell you, in his own good time.' Then Ma-Ma would wipe her hands as if to say, 'That's that' – signifying the end of all conversation on the matter.

The others seemed to accept this explanation, but something about it didn't ring quite true to Ellen. Coombes was no lover of humankind, and it was costing him good money to keep them there, for no return – as yet. Unless she was mistaken, Jasper Coombes had some plot afoot concerning the women.

On his return to Crockford's, Coombes summoned the four of them to his study. Lavelle was not in attendance, though Ellen had earlier seen him riding up the long driveway with Coombes.

'Well, now . . . let me see,' he began, eyeing them up and down. 'Ladies, you have, in my absence, been transformed, or should I say, restored to your former glories. What a picture you all look! Yes, Mrs Baker, you've done well with your charges, very well indeed!' Coombes continued, pleased at what he saw.

'Thank you, sir.' Ma-Ma Baker slightly raised the edges of her apron and curtsied, somehow managing to put one hefty ankle behind the other.

'Now, it's time we placed all you young ladies in profitable employment. It's a busy time for us here at Crockford's, what with the grape harvest,' said Coombes. 'Mrs Baker, I believe you require some assistance in the kitchen?'

Ma-Ma nodded.

'Well, how about young Sarah here? She looks as if she could find her way about a kitchen – couldn't you, Sarah?' he prompted, his mind already made up.

Sarah blushed at being singled out and gave a nervous, 'Yes, sir, Mister Coombes.'

'Capital! Now you, Nora – how would you like to work in the dairy, making the cheese and the butter and all that?'

'Oh, yes, thank you, sir. I'd like that very much.' Nora, like Sarah, was blushing – but more from the excitement of it all than from embarrassment.

Kitty could scarcely contain herself as Coombes turned to address her.

'Kitty, what I originally had in mind for you was to work in the dairy. But, as we have acquired Nora, who will now fill that need, I thought that working in the vineyard might be agreeable to you?'

Ellen could see that the girl was filled with anticipation at this; delighted, no doubt, to have something that was different from the kitchen, or working with the cows. She wondered what surprise Coombes would have in store for her. She would soon find out. He turned to her, hand to his chin, index-finger rubbing his nether lip.

'Now, Mrs O'Malley – our Irish rebel – I've put some thought into finding something appropriate for your particular talents. Can you read and write the Queen's English?' He couldn't resist the rub.

'Yes, I can, Mr Coombes, and the Queen's Irish too!' Ellen replied, tongue in cheek. The others found it hard to keep straight faces.

'Such insolence, Mrs O'Malley – tut-tut . . .' Coombes feigned offence. 'And such disrespect for our Sovereign! I think I shall need to keep you close at hand. I have therefore decided that you will assist me in the vineyards. Mrs Baker and Sarah will tend to the child during the day, when you are otherwise occupied.'

Ellen was dumbfounded at this. She was not one bit happy at having to work so closely with Coombes, whom she increasingly despised. Why couldn't he have put her with Kitty, or placed her somewhere else altogether? Preferably somewhere away from himself.

Coombes saw the consternation on Ellen's face.

'Don't worry your pretty head one whit – I personally shall teach you everything you need to know about the job. There, it's all settled then – everybody gainfully employed.'

'Isn't it wonderful?' Sarah enthused.

'Sure, we're going to have such a time of it here, I just know it! Who could have imagined it?' chirped Kitty.

'Oh, yes, Mr Coombes is a grandly man – a real gentleman. What fortune he found us, and that Mrs Hopskitch in Adelaide had no need of us!' exclaimed Nora.

As one, they turned to Ellen, sensing she did not share their excitement.

'Yes, of course it is all good news, and I'm very happy for all of you, but we should be cautious. We are strangers in a strange land – a very strange land!' she said, watching them listen without hearing her.

For the second time since she had come to Australia, Ellen hoisted her skirts. Kitty did the same. Beneath their bare feet the pulp of Crockford's harvest of white grapes kept them cool while they worked. 'Green grapes', Ellen had called them on her first day. 'We prefer the term "white", Mrs O'Malley,' Coombes had corrected her, 'after the wine.'

To begin with, he had put them with the pickers. They worked between the long straight rows, carefully cutting the fruit from the vine. The grapes, luscious and full after the hot summer, were placed into wicker baskets which were then emptied into a dray and transported for wine-making. Ellen marvelled at how heavy the bunches were, and how strong and hardy the little vine trees must be to bear them. Yet the grapes were soft to the touch and rolled pleasurably over your palm. Ellen tried the various varieties as they worked. They were both sweet and sour to the taste and everything in between.

Here and there, they came across vines planted further apart than the others, or in circular rows. When Coombes came by on one of his inspection rounds, Ellen asked to know the reason for this.

'More experimentation is needed with both space and soil,' he explained. 'The Lutherans plant too close. Everything needs space – the vine to grow, the soil so it is not depleted in feeding the vine. I want Crockford's to be a model for all future vineyards in the Province.'

Mostly the vineyard labour was carried out by men, and those women who were there seemed to be their wives. Ellen didn't give it much thought as the work and Kitty kept her occupied. And then they were taken off harvesting the grapes and given the task of treading them.

Ellen observed that only the white grapes were pressed into the 'must' with bare feet; the black grapes went into wooden wine presses. (Black grapes that, Kitty insisted, should be called red: 'If green becomes white for white wine, then red should remain red for red wine, not black – they just make it up to sound interesting,' she reasoned.) They learned that white grapes required gentler treatment to avoid the skins being bruised, which would give the wine a bad colour. Also, with pressing by foot, the seeds were not crushed – which would give the wine a harsh flavour. The seeds, or 'stones', could then be removed before fermentation began.

Coombes' wine-making building was constructed into the side of a hill and on a sloping site so that at every stage of the process – pressing, fermentation, blending – everything moved downwards towards the cellar. The Great Cellar, as Coombes rather grandly referred to it, was a split-level building constructed of stone hewn out of Bethany rock for coolness, with access from either the hill or at ground-level.

It soon became Ellen's favourite place. There she could think – when the wine-maker, a Frenchman named Chevalier, whom Coombes had brought in from Bordeaux, was not annoying her. There, in the silence, among the casks of sturdy French oak which housed Crockford's wines, she could reflect on all that had happened, sift her thoughts, and pray.

Each cask or hogshead – Ellen preferred 'cask', not liking hogshead, for some reason – had a tin label which gave the vintage quality and the quantity of the wine within: fifty gallons. Coombes had explained: 'A hogshead is fifty-two and a half imperial gallons. We ship fifty. I'm endeavouring to have sixty-gallon hogsheads made, to make life simpler and more cost-efficient.'

Coombes kept Ellen busy, and she had to admit to herself that she found this new learning very interesting. He was a good teacher, and behaved like the perfect gentleman. He never once referred to their previous skirmishes, or to the night of the maze, which Ellen was sure Mrs Baker had told him about.

Yet, there was something about Coombes, about Crockford's, that didn't fit, that didn't sit comfortably with her. The more time she spent with him, the more Ellen began to appreciate just how clever Jasper Coombes was. Cunning and ruthless, she knew him to be, but he was also very clever. *Glic* but *cliste*, she thought.

She needed to talk to Lavelle, but try as she might, there never seemed to be an opportunity to see him alone. She sensed that Coombes was deliberately keeping the two of them so busy that there was no chance of a meeting by day. And in the evenings, she needed time to be with Annie, and to read. Coombes had given her a publication – the first in the Barossa, he had boasted – called *The South Australian Vigneron and Gardener's Manual* by George McEwin. She wondered if this was the George she had heard in the maze that night.

Meanwhile, she continued to learn about the Barossa and wine-making. How the mild, dry climate of the valley, and the cooling gully winds, provided a perfect combination of climatic conditions for viticulture. How variations in the soil favoured different vines. Alluvial sandy loam was ideal for producing the yellow-white Riesling. Darker, heavier soils, like those found back towards the hills, tinctured the red Grenache. Soils laced with ironstone spiced the black-red Shiraz with a distinctive pepper flavour.

One day on their rounds, they came upon some white grapes rotting on the vine. Ellen, startled, pointed it out to Coombes.

'Look, they're rotting! It's like the blight on the potatoes – there will be nothing left of them!'

But Coombes only laughed. 'No, no, no, my dear. We actually encourage some of the grapes to rot. *Botrytis,* or "noble rot", produces a particularly sweet flavour in the wine – the Auslese quality styles.'

Ellen, having seen the devastation caused by fields of rotting lumpers, could not imagine anybody drinking the produce of rotting grapes. But Coombes assured her that: 'Those of us with a cultivated sense of taste imbibe it. Moreover, we have, of late, con-signed a case of it to Her Majesty Queen Victoria. We understand it to have been well received by the royal palate,' he gloated.

His boast brought home to Ellen, yet again, the inequality of the world. Queens and their wines, peasants and their potatoes. For the former, a luxury, for the latter, an absolute necessity of life.

Coombes was passionate about his vineyard, referring to it as 'the pride of the province' whilst dismissing the other English wine-growers like Gilbert, just commenced at Pewsey Vale, or Evans at Lindsay Park, 'where it is yet only a subject for dinner conversation', as being 'so small in their thinking, they will scarcely see the decade out, never mind the century. As for the Germans, they are consigned to their station – the Bible, and the grapes of wrath. Hymns and hock, in that order.'

He gave her more reading: *Letters on the Culture of the Vine* by William MacArthur. And he sent her to Chevalier. The Frenchman would sit too close to her and teach her to taste the wines. She didn't like their taste – any of them – at first.

'Monsieur Coombes, he tries hard, Hélène . . .' He always called her by the French version of her name. It sounded strange, but she liked it. 'But this place, it will never be France – the land is harsh, the *vin* is too raw,' he told her. 'See, Hélène, you do not like it – it has no *raffinessement*. Your people, the *Irlandais* were clever. The Wine Geese, when they fled your country, did not come to Australia to grow wine. They came to Bordeaux, to Champagne. The Hennessys and the Lynches, the Bartons – they knew, Hélène, they knew.'

'Why?' she asked.

'I told you why, Hélène: the soil. I am the best, the *barriques* of French oak are the best – everything with Mr Coombes is the best. But why always do I have to put so much unrectified spirit in the *vin*? It is the soil, I tell you. The soil – the *Irlandais* knew.'

Ellen was fascinated by it all – a new land, the petty rivalries, the ambitions, the endless possibilities. How long would it take her to succeed in this great Southland? How long to gather together her passage home? And maybe a little extra besides, so that she wouldn't go back as she came – a pauper.

Coombes, for his part, was pleased with Ellen's application to learning the secrets of the vine. He had seen it in her from the start. That questioning of everything, her mind working all the time, taking in information, sifting it, reacting to it.

Pakenham was right to be rid of her, though – wily old badger that he was. She could be a barrel of trouble, what with that resoluteness of purpose, coupled with the anger, the passion for righting things. She was a woman men would die for – either following her, or fighting for her. Those deep, dark, mysterious eyes and the wide mouth – all challenging a mere mortal to win her, or take her. She probably isn't even aware of it herself, Coombes thought, and that is her power, her strength.

He would not try to take her. No, that was for others. It would be fun watching them try – and fail.

He thought of the upcoming Crockford's tastings, and his guests from Adelaide, and her, and it amused him. He had been holding tastings the past few years to mark the end of the harvest. Guests would be wined and dined, entertained, and educated: Chevalier was always on hand to advise his guests and instil in them an appreciation of the *vin*. Jasper Coombes would do his bit for his guests, but he couldn't conjure her into their beds. No, he could only present them with the opportunity to try their seduction techniques on the red-haired woman. And yes, they would fail, of that he was sure!

The others, they were mere girls, playthings. They would succumb easily enough. Keep his guests happy, for the evening, maybe many such evenings. Eventually, he would toss them back to that abominable Mrs Hopskitch in Adelaide, where they would probably end up on the streets. Like all the others sent out from that blighted country only to end up blighted in the whorehouses of the colony. Coombes laughed to himself; 'twas oft repeated that over half of the whores in Adelaide were Catholic girls from the West of Ireland.

The twist in it was, the big-wigs in Westminster were aiding and abetting the problem with their half-baked schemes. Sending out orphaned and pauperized young girls into service in South Australia. Service, indeed – aye, the oldest service in the world! Most of them could hardly write their names in English. And as for 'domestic skills', that was a misnomer if ever there was one. And impudent as bedamned, to boot, like that Kitty. No wonder they couldn't hold down steady work. There was scarcely one decent set of girls amongst all the shiploads that poured into Port Adelaide.

Still, the Colony needed women. Men would only stay for so long working in the harsh conditions, far out from Adelaide, if they had women – any women! If it wasn't for the black *lubras* his men netted from time to time, or their own men handed over for tobacco and whisky, there would be endless fighting and drinking, and desertion. How, then, would the province be developed? Women were good for men – and for the province, Jasper Coombes thought.

'Look after the girls, Mrs Baker. Rest them, feed them, dress them up. Get them used to the easy life.'

That was the way Ma-Ma Baker knew not to push the girls too hard. Her job was to keep an eye on them, make sure they stayed out of any mischief and followed the three Cs: care, cleanliness and Crockford's. Then, they would be brought out to meet Craigie and Kendall and the others when the time came.

Crockford's, he knew, was beginning to become known in Adelaide for its *soirées*. Good food and wine, followed by some horse-racing on the Great Ride, and then for the select few the real Barossa Races: the maze chases, with the girls running barefoot, and the male guests bare-backed on Coombes' stallions riding them down.

Oh, yes, Jasper Coombes caused many an eye to be closed to his business dealings, and many a tongue to be loosened to his advantage, as a result of tastings and racings at Crockford's. He had to be careful, though, to keep the likes of Lavelle from finding out. The girls, too, had to be changed every so often – couldn't have one of those old geezers catching anything. That would bring the shutters down fast. By that time, the girls would not want to leave. Some, their services no longer required, would settle down with his hired hands. That was good – it kept the men happy, and, more importantly, it kept them at Crockford's. The rest of the girls he spirited away to Mrs Hopskitch.

In the meantime, he was looking forward to seeing how Craigie, the crusty old Scots Presbyterian, would react when he propositioned the red-haired woman, only to have her reject his advances. Probably relish it, Coombes thought. Craigie hadn't been to the tastings before this year, but Coombes was aware of the man's predilections from previous experience in Adelaide. Now Coombes was anxious to guarantee Craigie's support in the battle against repeal of the Distillation Act. The old blackguard liked nothing better than a bit of spirit in a woman. He had once told Coombes that the Catholic Church's greatest gift to Irish womenfolk was to: 'Put a bit of spunk into them. All that repression and saying "no" – good for a woman, makes 'em feisty.' And how George Alderton Craigie liked the undoing of feisty women – especially feisty Catholic women! Coombes was sure it had something to do with the missionary zeal with which Presbyterians, particularly Scots Presbyterians, seemed to be endowed.

It would be quite a contest, the fiery redhead against the forceful Scot. And he wouldn't have long to wait to find out the outcome.

The day of the tasting arrived and Crockford's was bedecked on all sides with bunting and decorations. Ma-Ma Baker had surpassed herself, and every type of delicacy was laid before those assembled.

Ellen, resplendent in a new emerald-green dress with matching ribbons for her hair, baulked at the idea of kangaroo-tail soup and hard-boiled platypus eggs. Yet, despite strong misgivings about attending a public and festive gathering within a year of Michael's death, she enjoyed the afternoon.

Lavelle, as soon as he saw her, seized the opportunity for a few words. A few words was all he had time for, however. No sooner had he complimented her on how well she looked, than Coombes arrived on the scene, accompanied by another man. Lavelle, recognizing his cue to depart, hurriedly whispered: 'You'll be at the barn dance later in the Great Cellar?'

'It's not a right thing for me . . .' Ellen started to protest.

'I know, but, please be there,' he insisted.

She hesitated.

'Say you will!'

'All right, I will,' Ellen conceded, still uneasy about breaking the old code of mourning: 'the widow's year'.

'Mrs O'Malley,' Coombes and the other man were upon her. 'I'd like you to meet one of the province's most distinguished servants, and a dear, dear, friend to Crockford's. May I present Mr George Alderton Craigie.'

The other man swept off his tall grey hat and bowed to her.

'George, this is Mrs O'Malley, recently from Ireland. Mrs O'Malley is deserving of our condolences, having, within the year, been bereaved of her dear husband.'

Ellen was discomfited both by Coombes' reference to Michael and the reminder that, here she was, not in deep mourning, as she should have been, but all dressed up and meeting people.

As soon as he spoke, Ellen knew George Alderton Craigie was the man in the maze.

Craigie was courteous to a fault in his commiserations on her loss, and his felicitations on her appearance. She studied him: tall and big-boned, with a slight forward stoop, he looked to be in his late fifties. He had a handsome face, if somewhat furrowed by time; though to Ellen's mind the effect was ruined by a nose which would have had a fine line, had it been straight instead of exaggeratedly hooked.

Coombes excused himself, leaving Ellen alone with the Scot. She felt uncomfortable, being unused to this kind of company and only too conscious of the unsettling aura of power which surrounded Craigie. It was clear to her that she was dealing with a keen, perceptive intelligence – and a man accustomed to getting his own way. He was, he told her, 'one of the visionaries who would shape and mould this untamed Southland into a model province.' And Ellen well believed him.

'What is needed in South Australia, Mrs O'Malley, are men of vision, risk-takers, entrepreneurs like Coombes here. And, of course, the women to go with them. Women of spirit, women who can help their menfolk forge this new country. Women like yourself!'

As Craigie spoke, Ellen thought of the strong women of her valley, women who had kept the body and soul of all around them together, even when all seemed lost. How well they'd prosper out here, if only given the chance. Like her.

Coombes returned presently and, taking Craigie by the arm, excused them both. Ellen scanned the crowd for a sight of Lavelle, but, again, he was nowhere to be seen. She noticed that, of the women present, none seemed to attract the attention of male admirers both young and old as did Kitty, Sarah and Nora. Kitty was rapt in conversation with a rather glossy-looking gentleman in his thirties. Another of Coombes' guests from Adelaide, no doubt.

As evening fell, the festivities moved to the Great Cellar. Ellen, rather reluctantly, joined them once she had finished settling Annie for the night. Mrs Baker had given her an assurance that she would keep an ear out for Annie, in case she awoke. But, just to be on the safe side, Ellen herself would slip away and check on the child periodically.

The Great Cellar looked transformed. Ellen was used to seeing it in darkness, but now the area was flooded with light. Lanterns had been hung from the hogsheads to create a rectangle of illumination in the centre of the cellar – the place of the dance.

In the far corner, where the Shiraz slept – deepening, darkening, cocooned within the oak-panelled casks – the musicians sat. To Ellen's surprise, Lavelle was among them, and to her further surprise he was armed for playing with, of all instruments, a fiddle and bow.

As the musicians played, she thought of Michael. How sweetly he played, his fingers dancing on the strings, his dark eyes dancing with delight at the music he made for her. Fingers and fiddle fusing into one, always connected with something deep within him for which he could never find words, except through his music.

She remembered the *céilís* at the three roads above Maamtrasna, and how, in the dance, when you spun around one way, you saw the little cabins, the smoke swirling heavenwards from them. Then, when you spun the other way, you would see the far shore, towards Tourmakeady, ever-shadowed by the Partrys. Finally, the dance would come full circle, bringing you to face the Crucán, high on its hill, overlooking both valleys and Lough Nafooey.

There, now, his grave marked only by a rock, lay Michael. Looking down on the place where his music once caused many a heel to click high in the air in a merry dance. Here, now, as the musicians struck up a set of lively reels, Ellen remembered him. Remembered how, without saying a word to her, he had walked the long miles to Castlebar to sell his beloved fiddle so that she would not have to sell her silver brush. The previous night, he had played for her, and she had sung for him – spinning out their love for each other by the glow of the hearth. Encircling each other with the words and music, until, at last, it drew them to each other in the love-dance they always knew it would.

That was the last reel Michael had played for her before they had been evicted, before Pakenham's bullet had shattered his side. Before his young body danced in the delirium of fever until it could dance no more, and she laid him down on the Crucán, silent, still, and in final rest.

She smiled sadly, recalling how she had asked him why he'd sold his fiddle, his pride and joy. His face had lit up with one of those big, bright smiles he had.

'It was for a selfish reason.'

'What do you mean?' she asked, cross with him for having done this thing without first discussing it with her.

'Well . . .' He had continued to smile at her, his eyes sparkling. 'If I hadn't sold the fiddle, then you would have had to sell your silver brush. And there's more music in watching you stroke your hair of a morning with that brush, than all the jigs and reels that old fiddle could ever play!' And then he had laughed.

She had laughed too, disarmed by the great joy of his love for her – unable to tell him, then, that she had already sold the very thing he spoke of, the thing which brought him so much joy. Sold it, so that he wouldn't have to sell his fiddle.

When he found out, he was furious with her. They had both laughed, then cried, and finally consoled each other in deep, nurturing love-making.

'Ellen . . . ?'

Lavelle was standing in front of her. She hadn't noticed that the music had stopped. She looked up from her thoughts.

'You were so far away – are you all right?'

'Yes, I'm fine – the music just reminded me of . . . well . . .'

'I know,' he said, saving her from explaining.

'Thanks, Lavelle.' She smiled at him.

'What do you think of the orchestra?'

'Good. I thought I recognized some of the tunes, but they sound a bit different,' she replied, glad to be on a different topic.

'Yes, the music gets mixed up together a bit out here. It was mainly brought out by the Scots and Irish, with a few English tunes thrown in – though *they* don't have much music,' he laughed. 'The Germans have their own music – a lot of it religious organ music – but beautiful. And their *lieder*, and their *Deutsches marches* – their "oompah music", we call it. But they mainly keep that to themselves – thankfully!'

Ellen liked him. He knew things and could talk about them in an interesting way. And his humour perked her up.

'It's a good thing if people's music is kept alive in a new country, even if it is watered down a bit,' she said. 'In Ireland now, it's in the Famine graveyards that the best music is and the best Irish is spoken.'

'Well, that should please both Church and Crown,' he responded. ''Tis long enough the both of them have been trying to beat the music and the language, and the sporting, out of us!'

How much like herself he was, Ellen thought.

'I'd ask you to dance if I wasn't playing, but I suppose you couldn't . . . ?' Lavelle was more tentative now.

'No – I couldn't. It's too soon,' she said politely, not wanting him to take offence.

'All right,' he said. 'But would you sing one of the old songs? I've heard you have a fine way with a song.'

Ellen started to refuse but, this time, Lavelle pressed her. 'Go on,' he said gently. 'A slow air, something he liked.'

Ellen looked at him.

'*As Gaeilge*, maybe?' He smiled at her. 'I'll play for you – I'd like to!'

'All right,' she said, finding it hard to refuse him. 'But just the one, mind!'

He was pleased at this and rejoined the band, announcing: '*Ciúnas anois* – one of our new South Australians – Ellen Rua O'Malley from the County Galway will now entertain us with a song.' At which announcement, there was a polite burst of applause.

Ellen remained where she was, seated on one of the large casks which had been rolled back to make a centre clearing in the Great Cellar. There, half in the light of the overhanging lantern, she sang. She sang in the old tongue to the strange gathering – the colonists of English would-be gentry, Scots Presbyterians, a German Lutheran or two. But mainly she sang for her own people. '*Ochón an Gorta Mór*' – Lament the Great Hunger.

> *Ochón, ochón*
> *Ochón, Aimsir an Drochshaoil*
> *Ochón, ochón*
> *Ochón an Gorta Mór*

> Alas, alas
> Lament the time of the Famine
> Alas, alas
> Lament the Great Hunger

She sang to them all, her voice resounding off wine-filled casks, creating an eerie, polyphonic sound as it echoed and re-echoed. From the oaken *barriques* the notes sprang, running along the timber frames which supported them; the words ringing from the heavy wooden rafters, rebounding from the Bethany stone, surrounding and mesmerizing, all who listened.

Lavelle played with her, below her, underscoring her soaring voice. Following her, as she weaved in and out of her lament for their generation. The notes from his fiddle spun across the space of the Great Cellar, meeting her song in the air, twisting around it, melting down into one sound within her.

He was a fine player, though not so sweet on the bow as Michael. He was more aggressive, earthy – but a fine player nevertheless. So fine, she thought, that but for the once she was not aware of his playing, only that it was there, in a one-ness with her.

All were hushed as she sang. Some understood her Gaelic lament. Others, not understanding the language, were moved by the sound of the words and the cry of grief in her voice.

She hadn't sung for an age, not since long before Michael had died and the bad times had come. Now she was torn with it all coming back to her: the stench of rotting potatoes, her people devoid of hope – death their only saviour.

When the song came to an end, it took her a moment to return from that place where she had been, back into her body.

Not a soul in the cellar stirred. They, too, were held suspended in the moment. What they had experienced was more than a song, beautifully, heart-rendingly sung; it was a transcendence, a going beyond the song to the thing of which the song spoke.

Only when Ellen exhaled did the moment break. Then there exploded a spontaneous release of tension from all present, glad to have been taken with her, glad to be back.

'Ellen!' Lavelle was in front of her again. 'That was . . . I just forgot where I was . . . forgot what I was playing. You were beautiful, Ellen.'

'Your playing was beautiful,' she returned. 'You were with me all the way.'

'It was easy to follow – you have a voice like nothing on earth, nothing I've ever heard!'

As they talked, others approached to congratulate both singer and musician. Ellen caught sight of Coombes and Craigie – heads close together, talking – some distance off. More conspiracies, no doubt.

But it was of her they spoke.

'By God, Coombes! That girl – woman can sing. What's her name again? Ah, yes, Ellen Rua – Ellen of the red hair. Where did you get her from?' George Alderton Craigie was excited.

'Pakenham sent her over – to get her out of *his* hair. She's a bit of a rebel,' Coombes replied.

'Pakenham . . . yes, I remember: the Irish landlord, late of Boodles, Crockford's and other gaming establishments. Like yourself, Coombes!' The Scot poked an irritating finger into Coombes' chest. 'Well, Pakenham must have no ear for music, or he'd have held on to her!'

'I'm not one bit surprised he didn't,' Coombes retorted. 'Knowing her, if she had sung for Pakenham, she'd probably have sung something lampooning him straight to his face. Even that' – he nodded back towards where Ellen was – 'was probably advocating sedition against the Crown in that peasant language, and the fools here were applauding her! Well, was she, George? That's your native language too, isn't it – Gaélic?' Coombes couldn't resist the rub.

'Well, Jasper, if she was indeed singing sedition against the

Crown, then I have heard sedition no sweeter sung. She sang it like an angel!'

'Or a she-devil!' was Coombes' riposte.

'Quite. Angels I sometimes have trouble with, Jasper – unless they are the fallen kind! She-devils are much more fun!' Damned if he wasn't going to break this red-haired she-devil. 'Stop dallying, Coombes! Get her over here – unless, of course, you want her for yourself?' Craigie demanded, impatiently tapping the cellar floor with his walking cane.

'Good God, no, man!' Coombes spluttered. 'I have enough problems without her, though I will say, she is of excellent application in her industry. Damn near knows more about vines and wines than I do. We'll go to her – it will be better.'

They sauntered over to where Ellen and Lavelle remained, now with only Nora and Sarah in attendance, Kitty being nowhere to be seen. As Coombes and Craigie approached, Nora and Sarah made away. Lavelle, though, waited with her.

'Well, well, Mrs O'Malley! What a talent we are fortunate enough to have in our midst,' Coombes said loudly. 'What a talent indeed – eh, George?'

'Yes, indeed. My compliments to you, Mrs O'Malley, on such a fine instrument as you possess in your voice. And also for the skill you bring to bear in knowing how to use it! And you too, Mr Lavelle,' Craigie added by the way.

'Thank you, sir,' Ellen said, not wanting all this attention.

'No, no, Mrs O'Malley – you must call me George. This is Australia, not Ireland. May I call you Ellen, or do you prefer Ellen Rua?'

'No, just Ellen,' she said, slightly flustered by this man, who said everything right.

Coombes, with a word of apology to Craigie and Ellen for deserting them, turned to Lavelle and said, 'You'd best come too, Lavelle. I'll be requiring your assistance.' And with that both men left.

'If I'm not mistaken,' the Scot continued, barely noticing their leaving, 'that song of yours was a lament?'

'Yes, a lament,' confirmed Ellen.

'About the Famine in Ireland?' he asked again.

'Yes, *an Gorta Mór* – the Great Hunger, we call it.'

'And, dare I say it, being in the old style – the *sean-nós* style – it should really have been sung unaccompanied, to allow maximum freedom of expression?'

Ellen was intrigued by this George Alderton Craigie. She had not expected interest in the old songs from such as he. But then, he seemed to know a lot about everything, did this man.

'Well, he is a fine fiddle player,' she responded, on Lavelle's behalf.

'True, and a fine young man, too!' Craigie's eyes searched hers for any tell-tale signs. He smiled when he found none. 'But your voice, Mrs O'Malley – Ellen – needs no embellishment of any kind – none whatsoever!'

Ellen had been a bit taken aback at the departure of Lavelle and Coombes. Now, as the last stragglers left, she discovered that she was alone in the cellar with Craigie. It would certainly not have been the thing in Ireland, but then, she was never much of a one for convention. Everything did seem much freer, more relaxed here, which was a good thing. And this Craigie, with his burr of a brogue, and charming manners, was behaving like a perfect gentleman towards her.

Still, she wouldn't stay too long. Didn't want the others talking. Didn't want a repeat of the night she had almost encountered Craigie in the maze and got back to find Mrs Baker sitting up with Annie.

'Could I ask a great favour of you, Ellen?' Taking her silence for assent, Craigie continued: 'Coombes was telling me you have the makings of a fine vigneron; that you possess remarkable aptitude for matters of the vine . . .'

'Yes, I enjoy my position here very much. I have learned a lot, and Mr Coombes is a good teacher,' Ellen responded, wondering where this was leading.

'Good, good. I'm glad you like it out here,' he replied warmly. 'As well as a ball of malt from the Highlands – when we can get any – I have quite an interest in wine myself. Drinking it, mind – not growing it. I wondered if, perhaps, you might grant me a quick tour of Coombes' cellar so I might be acquainted with what varieties he carries. Then, next time at his table, I shall astound him by calling for some of his Special Reserve, that he knows not I know of.'

Craigie's enthusiasm had Ellen agreeing before she realized she had.

'I know some of the smaller vignerons,' he told her. 'One, a friend near Moorooroo – or Jacob's Creek, as it's getting to be called – tells me he produces three thousand gallons annually out of twenty-five acres of the vine. That seems high. What does Coombes have planted here . . . two hundred acres? He must have eight to ten times as much under vine as at Jacob's Creek . . .'

Ellen nodded, impressed at how well-informed Craigie was. 'Just over two hundred acres – some vines younger than others, not yet mature enough to bear the grape.'

'Ah, so I was right – Coombes has done remarkably well. Remarkably well indeed. And how much wine does Crockford's produce?'

'Seventeen thousand gallons per year,' Ellen volunteered, as warning bells began to sound in her head.

'Seventeen thousand gallons!' Craigie exclaimed. 'But Crockford's should be producing almost half as much again for the acreage here against my friend's three thousand gallons out of a mere twenty-five acres!'

Ellen didn't like the turn this conversation was taking. She wished Coombes would return.

'Well, as I explained, Mr Craigie –'

'George,' he interrupted her.

'Some of our plantation is of very young vintage, and grapes like the Shiraz, which is one of Crockford's specialities, give a very low yield: barely a tonne per acre.'

'I see,' he said.

'And,' she added, 'Mr Coombes sets his vines at a greater distance from each other than do the rest.'

Ellen could see that Craigie was not convinced by her reply, and she felt she was being walked into something which would backfire on her with Coombes. She wouldn't have been worried at all by Craigie's innocent-sounding questions if she hadn't overheard Coombes and himself talking that night in the maze.

Was this what Craigie was getting at – illicit liquor? The Scot was trying to get something on Coombes. Maybe trying to even things up, for something which Coombes had on him. But where did Coombes keep the stuff? She had never come across it. It had to be here, in one of the hogsheads – unless there was a secret cellar somewhere else. She wondered if Chevalier knew. For all his chatter, he was secretive enough about some things.

Craigie didn't have much to say as she showed him the large wooden storage casks, each dated, each with the wine type, each holding fifty gallons of maturing wine.

'The reds are casked at this end of the cellar. The Grenache, Crockford's Claret and the Shiraz – Crockford's Gold, which will be held for some time yet. The whites – the Hock, the Blanche, the Rieslings, and the Verdelho –'

'Verdelho – what is that?' Craigie appeared genuinely interested.

'It's a dessert wine – sweet and fortified,' Ellen replied.

'Fortified? Fortified with spirit?'

'Yes,' said Ellen, tapping the cask. 'With brandy spirit.'

'I see,' Craigie said slowly. 'Interesting – very interesting, thank you. I see what Coombes means about you: in no time at all you'll be a sommelier, I'm sure.'

Craigie moved closer, reaching over her shoulder to tap the cask behind her.

'Verdelho, you said?'

'Yes.'

'What an unusual sounding name it has, Ellen.'

Now he had moved in front of her and put his arm over her other shoulder and she smelled the staleness which rose from his coat. Ellen did not like his staleness, his closeness, this being caught between him and the cask of Verdelho.

All the while, Craigie continued to make polite conversation. But she was tense, her body alert for fight or flight. Then, still chatting to her in a friendly, non-threatening way, he suddenly dropped his right hand and caught a fistful of her hair.

'Ellen Rua, how well named you are – and such a remarkable woman. Beautiful, talented, adaptable to new surroundings . . . a survivor,' he said, his brogue caressing the words, his stale hand now moiling her red locks, soiling them.

She held her nerve. She would not fight him – yet. Calmly but forcefully she said, 'Mr Craigie, I'd ask you not to do that – it's time we were leaving.'

'Och, we have no hurry! Coombes will be back for us shortly . . . You don't like him much do you?'

This surprised Ellen, but she said nothing. Still Craigie had not moved.

'I don't blame you,' he continued, as if nothing had passed between them. 'He's a nasty sort – holds a grudge. Why don't you come down to Adelaide and work for me? I'll see you're well looked-after, and paid decently. I bet you haven't seen a penny out of Coombes yet – nor will you – and they say us Scots are mean-fisted!' he said, his fist pulling down on her hair, forcing her face up to him.

Ellen was beginning to panic. In this corner of the Great Cellar it was quite dark. There was no one about, no sign of Coombes returning, and Craigie was strong – too strong for her. He was still talking with his honeyed tongue, smiling at her, the low rhythmic pattern of his speech seeking to entrance her until he was ready.

This was a dangerous man. The realization steeped her in fear. Craigie's arm was now round her neck, the strong fingers drawing her head towards his great craggy face. She put her hands up against his chest to push him back, but he only laughed in her face. She could do nothing to prevent him as he pressed himself against her, whispering, mocking at her: '*Ochón*, Ellen Rua! *Ochón! Ochón!*'

She could feel his hot breath on her lips as, spread-eagled, he crushed her body. Escape was impossible – there was no way she could push him back or slip out from under his arms. Her protestations, her cries for help, which now rebounded off the cellar walls and oak casks as the strains of her song had earlier, only served to arouse him the more.

But Ellen Rua had not come twelve thousand miles to be debauched by a stale-smelling Scotsman, no matter how powerful he was. Or what he meant to Jasper Coombes. She summoned all the energy she could and, while Craigie pushed to find those flared lips he desired so much, she drove her knee up into his groin with such speed and ferocity that even she wasn't prepared for the result, much less the Scot.

Craigie's face, inches from her own, twisted into a paroxysm of pain as his body was driven backwards by the sheer force of the blow. His neck muscles bulged as he struggled to regain his breath. Then he let out a scream of pain that almost deafened her. Such was its intensity, she thought it must split asunder every cask in the cellar.

Seizing her moment, she ducked out from under Craigie.

'Jeeesusss Kerrroist!' he swore in Scots-English, and lunged forward to grab her, only to fall heavily against the Verdelho. In his fury, he smashed the trestle supporting the hogshead. The fifty-gallon cask was sent crashing to the ground, narrowly missing him. The French oak timbers creaked at the impact and, for a moment, held their breach. But the pressure from without and the pressure from within was too great: in a mighty sundering of wood, the side of the cask burst open, and fifty gallons of fortified dessert wine, labelled Verdelho, cascaded over Craigie.

Ellen watched, awe-struck by the spectacle – the damage she had caused. Then the fumes of the spilling wine rose to her nostrils. Only this was not the honey-sweet bouquet of Verdelho.

Before she could gather her senses sufficiently to identify the smell, she heard Craigie, still gasping with pain, shout: 'I knew it! I knew it! I'll have that bastard Coombes now! Him and his Irish whores – I'll fix him for good! By God I will! There'll be no more Distillation Acts in this province – George Alderton Craigie will see to that!'

She turned to go. But before leaving the cellar, she bent down and stuck a finger in the sticky liquid at her feet. Then she raised the finger to her lips.

It was not Verdelho. It was pure spirit, distilled for illicit sale.

It was Brandy.

34

Ellen awoke next morning to the sound of loud banging on her door. Coombes, she thought. Well, she was ready for him, no matter what the consequences. Craigie had obviously been led to expect a more compliant response from her. The reaction he got must have come as quite a surprise; she recalled with some satisfaction the look of disbelief on the Scot's face as he picked himself up off the floor, drenched in Coombes' illicit brandy. At least he'd smell better now.

Coombes would have hell to pay now. Her set-to with Craigie would put paid to any political lobbying in return for sexual favours. Worse still, from Coombes' point of view, Craigie now had the goods on him! The Scot knew where the produce of the unaccounted-for acreage had gone: into illegal liquor stored in mis-labelled casks. And Ellen Rua O'Malley was the one Coombes would blame for this reversal of fortune.

She took a moment to compose herself before opening the door, preparing for the onslaught. But instead of an irate Jasper Coombes, she was confronted with Sarah and Nora, in tears. Ellen's first thought was that they had been subjected to an ordeal like her own. These thoughts were quickly dispelled.

'It's Kitty!' they both sobbed, rushing into her room.

'She's missing – she didn't come home at all!' Sarah said, frantic with worry.

'Something awful has happened – I just know it!' Nora joined in.

Ellen closed the door behind them and sat them down on the bed.

'All right, now, tell me what happened, from the start,' she said, her arms round them, consoling them.

In fits and starts, each one taking over from the other, they told how Coombes had introduced them to three of his friends from

Adelaide. Despite close attention from two of the men, Nora and Sarah had stuck together, and eventually managed to shake off their admirers.

But Kitty had remained deep in conversation with the glossy dark-haired man to whom Ellen had noticed her talking. When everyone else headed for the Great Cellar, she had told Nora that she and Mr Kendall – for that was his name – were going to the maze.

Ellen remembered, right enough, looking for a sight of Kitty in the cellar – and you couldn't help but notice her, the way her personality bubbled and spilled over – but seeing no sign of her. Nora and Sarah had not been too worried that Kitty had still not returned by the time they retired. They'd passed it off with a joke or two about where it might all lead, 'such a fine gentleman from Adelaide showing an interest in our Kitty.' When morning came, however, and Kitty still hadn't returned they became worried. The news that Mr Kendall had left and gone back to Adelaide late last night had thrown them into a complete panic.

Ellen didn't share their view of Kendall as a fine gentleman. Like many of the men she had seen about the place yesterday, he had a practised way about him and she didn't care for it one bit. But that was neither here nor there. She suspected that, just as Craigie had tried to manoeuvre her into a position from which there would be no escape, so Kendall had ensnared Kitty. Then he had simply returned to Adelaide without a qualm, leaving Kitty too ashamed to face the others. She was probably hiding somewhere, not knowing what to do next.

'Right, let's start by searching the maze,' she said, rising. 'She might have been lost in there all night with all those dead ends.'

So Ellen and Sarah left for the maze, while Nora stayed behind to mind Annie.

By day, the maze looked nowhere near as forbidding as it had the night she had gone in, looking for Lavelle. Yet, as she and Sarah passed through the entrance, Ellen felt the hairs on the back of her neck stand on end. There was something eerie about the place. She noticed that Sarah reacted in the same way, huddling close in behind her.

'Kitty! Kitty! Are you here?' Ellen called out.

But the only sound was the echo of her own voice. She tried to remember which path she had followed on the previous occasion, but all paths looked the same. She noticed too, that the ground underfoot had been well trampled. Must have been the partygoers, yesterday, she thought.

Each time they drew a dead end, Sarah became more agitated. 'She's not here, Ellen – let's go back! I don't like it in here – we could get lost,' she said in a frightened whisper, tugging at Ellen's arm.

'No, Sarah, we won't,' Ellen said firmly. 'We may as well see this through now. Think how frightened Kitty must be if she's been in here alone all night. She could be lying in a faint, not hearing us shouting. We have to make sure she's not here before we leave.'

Eventually, after they had covered what seemed like the length and breadth of the maze, calling Kitty's name at every turn, and looking into any nook or cranny big enough to hide her, they saw, to their great relief, the large effigy of the Queen of Hearts ahead of them.

'We're there,' Ellen said. 'That's the exit ahead!'

At this, Sarah brightened up. 'Oh, good. Am I glad to be leaving this fearful place!'

'First we have to crawl under the skirts of the Queen of Hearts to get out,' Ellen said.

The two women got down on all fours as the Queen of Hearts laughed at them, mocking their efforts, enjoying their indignity at being on their knees in the muck beneath her. Sarah, not wanting to remain behind, had pulled level with Ellen so they could crawl side by side through the darkness underneath the Queen's skirts.

'Is it far?' she whispered.

'No, not really,' Ellen replied. 'You'll be all right here beside me. Or do you want to go first, and I'll be right behind you? We'll be out in no time!'

'Yes, that might be better,' Sarah said, edging in front. 'Where d'you suppose Kitty can have got to?' she whispered back to Ellen.

'Well, she's not here, or we'd have seen her. She is a terror, staying out like that, and not telling a soul where she'd be,' Ellen said, a bit annoyed at Kitty, but not too surprised.

'Do you think she's all right?' Sarah turned her head, seeking out Ellen's reassuring presence in the darkness, while still crawling in the direction of the exit.

'Yes, I'm sure she –' Ellen hadn't finished the sentence when the air was rent by a terrified scream. Sarah appeared to have stumbled on something, and fallen on to her face.

Ellen scrabbled forward as fast as she could, to reach the screaming girl. Then she, too, stumbled – against Sarah, she thought – and fell face-down into something soft and cold and sticky. She pushed herself up off the ground, petrified by the thought that was framing in her mind, her hands and fingers now covered in the stickiness. She wanted to throw up, her whole body convulsing with fear and horror.

'No! Oh, God, no! It can't be! It can't be! Oh, Jesus, Mary and Joseph – no!'

Ellen steeled herself to look at what she had stumbled over. Her eyes now accustomed to the darkness, she could distinguish what was stretched out on the ground before them, blocking their exit. In her new dress – the white cloth now patterned with seams of dried blood, trying to hold together the gashes where the knife had entered – lay the mutilated body of a young girl.

Back at the house, rocking a wide-awake Annie on her knee, Nora knew in her heart of hearts that their friend – their young, bouncy, laughter-friend, was dead.

She knew it, even before Sarah lifted her head from the wet, sticky breast where it had rested, and rent the heavens over Crockford's with the cry: 'Kitty – Kitty's murdered!'

In the morning room, Jasper Coombes – like everyone else at Crockford's – heard Sarah Joyce's cry of terror as it knifed through the calm of the Barossa morning.

'What now?' he said angrily to himself as he dashed out of the house.

First Craigie had stormed off in a temper because the O'Malley woman had got the better of him. Then fifty gallons of his best brandy distil had somehow ended up on the floor of the Great Cellar. Damn! If he'd been there himself he would have put a lantern to the spirit and sent it, Craigie, and the red-haired woman to high heaven!

Now this – Kendall misbehaving himself again, no doubt. He had warned the young politician before about his treatment of the girls. A bit of rough stuff was all right – some of them even liked it. But the screams coming from the maze told him that, this time, Kendall had gone too far. This time, even he wouldn't be able to cover it up.

When he reached them, Ellen and Sarah were almost beside themselves with terror – their hands and faces smeared with Kitty O'Halloran's blood.

Coombes looked at Kitty's body. God, what a mess! It was worse than he'd thought. There would be a big hullabaloo over this one. He would be ostracized, and Crockford's cut adrift. Think, man, think, he told himself. He was not about to lose everything because one slip of an Irish girl, who would have died anyway had she stayed in her own country, was dead in a maze. His maze.

As others approached, he shouted: 'Quick, get these women to the safety of the house. It's the natives – they've cut her up pretty badly, the bastards! Hurry! There could be more attacks. There are reports from Bethany of them terrorizing the womenfolk there as well.'

Lavelle appeared and, seeing the blood, ran to Ellen, thinking she and Sarah were wounded.

'What is it, Ellen? What's happened – are you all right?'

'Yes, we're fine,' Ellen sobbed. 'But poor Kitty – she's in there – dead . . .'

'Oh, my God!' Lavelle said, his face ashen.

'Lavelle – get the horses, break out the guns – we're going after those natives! I should have shot that chieftain of theirs when I had the chance.' At this, Coombes looked scathingly at Ellen, before turning away to issue more orders: 'You men! Cover the body and take it below – we can't leave it lying there – those scavengers could come back for it.'

Ellen only half-registered the gist of what he was saying. Even in her state of shock she knew that something was wrong, but everybody was running to Coombes' orders, fired up by the awful deed, and filled with desire for revenge. She couldn't think. She wanted to call Lavelle and tell him, make him understand there was something wrong, but she couldn't focus. Then Lavelle was gone and Mrs Baker was cradling her. Through a fog she heard Coombes say, 'Get them back to the house, and keep them out of harm's way. You know what I mean, Mrs Baker.'

It was near evening when Ellen awoke. After sleeping for most of the day she was still drowsy and confused. Still unable to escape the horrible image of Kitty's body, lying there bloodied, under the gaudy skirts of the Queen of Hearts. Ellen just couldn't come to grips with it all. She had seen death before – death all around her, wasteful pitiless death. But never before had she confronted violent death inflicted so hideously, and on such a young and radiant body as Kitty's.

Ellen's insides began to churn as she remembered. Coombes mustering his men to wreak revenge on the Aborigines. It didn't fit. She didn't believe that Samarara, the proud-looking Aborigine whose life she had saved, could lead his men in an attack on a lone defenceless woman. And how, with so many people attending the tasting, could they have slipped in undetected? Then, having entered the grounds, why didn't they attack anyone else? Coombes had it all wrong.

Then the thought struck her: Coombes deliberately had it wrong. Kendall – Kendall, he was the missing link – that's what she couldn't think of. It had to be Kendall. Coombes was protecting him, covering for him, even if it meant more lives would be lost – Aboriginal lives. Oh, my God, what sort of a monster was she working for?

She must tell Lavelle, get to him, make him stop it! She dressed, and ran to the front of the house. She thought she heard men shouting. But maybe that was all part of the confusion in her head, for when she reached the door there was no one in sight.

She ran towards the maze. It was deserted. Then, towards the side of the house and the back gardens. Nothing, nobody – where was everybody?

She ran to the Great Cellar, heart thumping, exhausted, frightened, driven by the fear that she was too late. She threw open the cellar door, and her knees crumpled at the sight that met her eyes.

There, hanging at the end of a rope slung over the rafters, was the body of Samarara. Cut and bruised, the corpse swung in a slow circle of death, over the self-same spot she had, the night before, been raising her voice in song.

She walked towards Coombes, her eyes fixed on him. He returned her gaze – ice cold, unmoved – and something snapped in her. She lunged at him, her nails reaching for his face, screaming: 'No! No – you bastard! You murdered him!'

'Grab her!' Coombes barked out, and two men stepped from the shadows and caught her. 'You saved this black heathen once before – and look what he did to your friend in return. But you can't save him now, nor the ones we already accounted for – you Irish *boong*-lover,' Coombes spat out at her.

'You're wrong, Coombes,' she shouted at him. 'This man didn't kill Kitty. And you know who did,' she screamed. 'It was your friend, Kendall!'

Then, as she struggled with the two men who held her, she saw Lavelle for the first time. He was stripped to the waist, stretched and tied over one of the casks, a gag in his mouth.

'You've just arrived in time, Mrs O'Malley!' Coombes said sarcastically, ignoring her accusation. 'Your fellow musician, Lavelle, refused my order to hang this Abo found guilty of murder. He got a fair trial – didn't he, men?'

Coombes' henchmen chorused their approval.

'But our Mr Lavelle thought differently. So now we're going to teach *him* a little lesson in Australian justice.'

And, with that, Coombes grabbed a large flailed whip – the ends of which were tipped with some kind of metal pieces. Ellen tried to break free, but she was no match for the arms that restrained her.

'Bring her forward, men, so she can see how Crockford's treats traitors!' Coombes ordered.

They dragged Ellen to within a few feet of Lavelle. One of them, despite her best efforts, forced her head round so that she would have to look into Lavelle's eyes as he suffered.

Coombes stood back. He raised his right arm above his head and smiled, looking at Ellen, before bringing the lash down hard on Lavelle's bare back.

Ellen flinched at the sound as the metal-tipped whip bit into flesh. Lavelle did not flinch, though Ellen could see his eyes racked with pain as he fixed on her face. He remained unflinching as again and again, unceasingly, Coombes wielded the lash.

Ellen fought, and kicked, and bit, to try and get away from her captors, desperate to get at the one who took pleasure in inflicting such cruel punishment, but it was no use. She tried to avert her eyes – as if, in forcing her to watch, Coombes had made her a part of his evil. But then it struck her that Lavelle might gain some strength from her. She deliberately stopped fighting and fixed her eyes on him, willing him that strength and solace, until his whole body shuddered once, and he slipped into the blessed release of unconsciousness.

Only then did Jasper Coombes stop flogging the broken body strapped to the cask marked Verdelho.

He turned to Ellen, and in tones devoid of all emotion said: 'You can have your fiddle-player, Ellen Rua O'Malley – for all the jigs and reels he'll play you now!'

35

After Coombes, cold-sweated from his exertions, left the Great Cellar, they let her go. Most of the men slunk off too. A few hung around, looking sheepish and unsure of themselves, as if waiting to see what would happen next.

'Untie him from the cask!' Ellen shouted at two of them, and they leapt to, stung by the ferocity in her voice. 'And you! Take down that man from the rafters,' she ordered another two.

'Mr Coombes said we was to leave him hang until morning time, ma'am!' one of them said.

'Take him down, now – or I'll take this whip to you. Do you hear me?' she threatened, reaching for Coombes' whip.

This had the desired effect, and the two men moved to carry out her orders. Lavelle, cut free of the ropes that bound him, lay draped over the wine cask, motionless.

Ellen was fearful of moving him, lest he be damaged further. So she sent one of the men to fetch Mrs Baker and her medicine chest, while she remained with him.

Ma-Ma Baker soon arrived, her big frame panting with the effort of her haste. When she entered the Great Cellar, she stopped short at the doorway, shocked at what she saw. One lifeless corpse of an Aborigine and one flayed body of a white man slumped over a cask.

'Oh, my God! Oh, my good God!' she exclaimed, looking at Ellen. 'Are they both . . . dead?' she managed to get out.

'That poor soul is, I'm afraid,' Ellen said, inclining her head towards the body of Samarara. 'Lavelle is still alive, but barely, I'd say. Coombes whipped him to within an inch of his life.'

'Did Lavelle kill the native?' Ma-Ma Baker asked.

'No,' Ellen said. 'Coombes had him hung – for Kitty's murder. Lavelle tried to stop it, so Coombes flogged him.'

Mary Magdalen Baker moved to Lavelle, handing one jar of ointment to Ellen, holding another for herself.

'This was savage,' she said, as she gently applied the balm to the lacerations on Lavelle's back. 'There was bad work done here tonight. Any fool would know it wasn't the Aborigines. I warned Mr Coombes about having that Kendall about the place, but he wouldn't listen to me.' The housekeeper shook her head ruefully.

'So you think it was Kendall too?' Ellen asked, surprised at the woman's forthrightness.

'Of course I do, girl! There was an incident here last time Kendall came – not as bad as what happened in the maze, but bad enough. It all got hushed up, though. Mr Coombes sent the girl away. Irish, she was, too,' the housekeeper whispered to Ellen.

The two women worked side by side, mostly in silence, anointing, as if in the Sacrament of the Dying, the bloodied body of Lavelle. Not once did he stir, nor utter a sound, in response to their ministrations.

'We'd better get him into the house now,' Ma-Ma Baker said, taking charge. 'You there – Bodkins! Stop skulking about and help us carry him . . . that is, if you want any victuals in that greasy belly of yours for the next month,' the housekeeper of Crockford's rasped into the shadows.

The shadows responded, and produced Bodkins, a hapless-looking creature if ever there was one, thought Ellen. However, he proved reliable enough, and helped them peel Lavelle from off the wine cask. Mrs Baker then covered his torn skin with a light gauze dressing she had fetched from the house. They then carried Lavelle face downwards, Bodkins supporting his legs, wheelbarrow-style, with Ellen and Mrs Baker linking arms under his chest. Eventually, they got him to a guest room and laid him face-down on the bed.

Ellen sat with him, dabbing a wet cloth to his neck and temples, trying to cool the temperature that raged in him. Mrs Baker checked on Annie. Then, Ellen left, and the housekeeper remained. During Ellen's second vigil with Lavelle his head moved, ever so slightly, to her touch. More worried about him with every passing moment, she put her mouth to his ear and softly called to him: 'Lavelle! Lavelle! Wake up – you're going to be fine, thank God. It's me, Ellen. I'm here with you. Wake up – please, wake up!'

She waited at his ear, listening, the skin of her lips on his skin, knowing that if he moved, however slightly, the sensation would be carried to her.

Nothing.

She called to him again – this time more strongly.

Again, there was no response.

But she would not give up. She tried again, and this time, as soon as she called his name, she heard him say in a barely distinguishable whisper: 'You're here . . . Stay.'

'Yes, Lavelle,' she said. 'Of course I'll stay. I'll stay until you're mended again. Don't worry; I'll stay!' Uncertain whether her words were registering with him.

Lavelle spoke again, struggling to form the words: 'Get away, Ellen . . . Danger . . . Coombes . . . Got to get . . . I . . . help . . . you!' Then he fell back into unconsciousness.

Ellen set to thinking as she nursed him. She had already decided, after finding Kitty, that she must get away from this awful place. No wonder Coombes looked after them well, didn't work them too hard, and, in her case, educated her so that she might mix more easily with his gentlemen friends. *Striapachs* – prostitutes – that's what Coombes wanted them for. Well, she wasn't going to be anybody's whore, more education or not. But where would she go? She could hardly run to Adelaide, she would be discovered straight away. And who knew what Coombes might do? If anything happened to her, Annie would perish too. Then, once Pakenham found out she wasn't returning, he might cast out Patrick and Mary and Katie.

She had to stay alive. And to do that, she had to escape from South Australia and Jasper Coombes.

By morning, Lavelle was moving his head and moaning. Even if he was still in delirium, thought Ellen, it was a welcome sign.

Mrs Baker did everything that could be done. She brought more liniment for his wounds. She forced a sponge soaked in quinine between his teeth, so that he could suck the pain-killing liquor into his agonized body. She spoon-fed him morsels of bread steeped in milk, gently prising the spoon through the corner of his lips.

Ellen went to see how Nora and Sarah were. She wanted to tell them that she had decided to flee Crockford's and to ask if they wanted to escape with her. They weren't in the servants quarters, so she didn't persist. There wasn't time to go to the dairy or the vineyard – she had to get back to Lavelle.

As the day wore on, Lavelle's spells of consciousness grew longer. In between he fell into what were now bouts of sleep rather than unconsciousness. Despite his ordeal and the pain he must have been suffering, even with Mrs Baker's quinine, he managed to speak to her.

'Thank you for saving my life, Ellen . . . And for being there – it helped.'

'You're a very brave man, Lavelle, to stand up to Coombes,' she told him. 'And obviously tougher than you look, too!'

Her remark drew a short laugh from him, and she was pleased at this.

There was still no sign of either Sarah or Nora later that day. Ellen, beginning to fear for their safety, asked Mrs Baker if she knew where they were.

'Well, he didn't tell me, as he should have, but it seems Mr Coombes took them off to Adelaide to that Mrs Hopskitch friend of his. Bodkins readied the cart for them.'

Ellen's ears pricked up.

'Mrs Hopskitch is a friend of Coombes?'

'Oh, yes – they go back years!' the housekeeper answered. 'He always calls on her when he visits Adelaide, though he's never had her up here. Why – what do you know of her sort?' she turned the question back on Ellen.

'Only that Sarah and Nora were bound for her as indentured servants, but Coombes brought them here, instead. What's strange is that he made a great showing of how he had gone to a lot of trouble to find out where Mrs Hopskitch lived. He said he had talked her into letting the girls come here with us,' Ellen said, an uneasy feeling growing inside her.

'Indentured servants – hah! The service Mrs Hopskitch runs is the oldest in the world, and you don't need no indentureship to take to it! Didn't you know, Mrs O'Malley? Mrs Hopskitch is a madam – the biggest in Adelaide. And that's where those two girls are bound for. Coombes and her is as thick as thieves. It's a shame!'

Ellen was shocked. First Kitty, now Nora and Sarah gone. The two young innocents wouldn't last long on the streets of Adelaide. She felt helpless, as if events were moving all around her – and she was powerless to change things. But change things was exactly what she had to do.

If Coombes was getting rid of Sarah and Nora in this way, then what were his plans for her? She knew far more than them about the goings on at Crockford's. She had to leave, and leave now. Where she went, what she did, was secondary. She just had to be gone from Crockford's before Coombes returned. It was her only chance.

Later that night, when the house was quiet, she went to Lavelle. He was sleeping, so she woke him, motioning to him to be silent. She could see the pain shoot across his face as he turned towards her.

'I've come to tell you that Annie and I are leaving this place,' she whispered close to his ear. 'Nora and Sarah are now spirited to Adelaide by Coombes, and I fear for my life, and Annie's life, if I am here when he returns.'

Lavelle's face twisted with the comprehension of what she was saying. 'Ellen, you can't go alone . . . Where will you go to? You'll never survive – it's wild land out there, and you with a small child!'

'I have to go, Lavelle. I've made up my mind!' she said, hating telling him when he was like this.

'What if Coombes contacts Pakenham – your children?' he gasped.

'I know – he might. But I don't think Pakenham will harm them,' she said, remembering the Shanafaraghaun man.

'Let me help you – come with you. I know the bush!'

'Lavelle, no! You can't move – those wounds will take time to heal. No, I'll make it on my own – but thank you!'

'Ellen, listen to me,' he argued. 'I can't stay here either, I've had enough. Coombes will be gone for three more days. Give me time to recover . . . time for us to plan it properly.'

Ellen reflected on what Lavelle had said. It would be difficult on her own with Annie. She didn't know this land, the conditions, the distances. Also, whereas a lone woman might travel safely in

Ireland, here she was unlikely to have safe passage. And he was right – what would Coombes do to him if, on returning, he found her gone?

'All right,' she said, making her mind up. 'We'll go together.'

'Good,' Lavelle replied. 'We can talk more tomorrow.' He smiled at her as best he could.

She smiled back, and noiselessly slipped through the dark house to her own room and Annie. The child was still sleeping. This time without the strong, rocking arm of Ma-Ma Baker.

The next morning, to avoid arousing suspicions, Ellen went to work as normal. Chevalier, when he had stopped complaining about the state in which his cellar had been left by the friends of Monsieur Coombes, wanted to teach her some old picking *chanson* from the Champagne district. He made no mention of the awful happenings at Crockford's of only a few days ago.

Later she went to see Lavelle again. He seemed much stronger and greeted her with, 'I think I have it!'

Ellen listened as Lavelle explained his plan to her. The three of them would leave the Barossa, taking with them four of Coombes' horses – two to carry them, and two to carry water and provisions. They would head south-easterly down towards Hahndorf. Then to Mount Barker and on to the mouth of the Murray River at Encounter Bay.

'Will that way keep us well clear of Adelaide?' Ellen asked him.

'Yes,' he replied. 'My guess is, Coombes will work out that we'll avoid Adelaide, and will think we've headed overland along the Murray–Darling route for Sydney, which is the route by which he and I came here. Then again . . .'

It wasn't easy to second guess what Coombes would do, and harder still to figure out a way to stay one step ahead of him.

'But where are we going to?' Ellen asked.

'We're going to go along the coast to Melbourne. It's not the most direct route, but we're less likely to meet overlanders coming against us, who would carry word back here. And then, once we get there, we should be able to find some work in Melbourne, if I'm not spotted by the law.'

It sounded to Ellen as though Lavelle had thought it out well. She knew little of the terrain or the distances they must travel, but it made sense to avoid any route which Coombes might suspect they would take.

And Melbourne was a port. Once she had raised the passage money, they could get a ship to America – to Boston, where the Irish went. She thought of Mici Maol and the woman who had come to her about the money draft. Once there, getting home would be easier. A lot easier.

'How long will it take us to get to Melbourne?' she asked.

Lavelle thought for a while, working it out, before he answered. 'Well, Goolwa and the Lower Murray would be over a hundred miles. With a bit of luck, we should hit the coast in five to six days. Then, we have to cross the Coorong. It depends, too, on how the Aboriginal tribes are. If they've had trouble from any white overlanders, then we could be in for a rough time. I suppose, to get to Mount Gambier, near the border, would be another three hundred miles.'

'What?' Ellen said in disbelief. 'That's more than the length of all of Ireland, from Malin to Mizen, and we won't even be gone from South Australia?'

'This is a big country you came to, Ellen Rua,' he said, choosing his words carefully. He could see that she was losing courage. 'We'll just have to see how we go.'

She wondered about Lavelle's fitness for such a trip. And Annie's – how would the child survive such an arduous journey? She would just have to ensure that Annie got enough nourishment and rest. She would protect her, see to it that the two of them made it to Melbourne.

But as soon as she eased one doubt from her mind, another arrived to replace it. Could she rely on Lavelle? She hardly knew him, had no way of knowing what his motives were in volunteering to join them on this long, difficult journey.

She decided to put aside all these questions. Her choice was stark, and simple: go or stay.

She had to go. And since she couldn't make it alone, it had to be with Lavelle.

*   *   *

She saw Lavelle again the following day. Ma-Ma Baker had dressed his wounds and he was up and moving about, though still in pain. They made their final arrangements for that night.

The Crockford's clock rang out the midnight hour.

That was their signal. Ellen hurriedly gathered up the rest of her own and Annie's belongings, and stuffed them into a holdall. Then she swaddled Annie into a blanket. The child was awake, so she whispered to her to be very quiet.

As she left the room, carrying her child, Ellen closed the door behind them with a finality that made it seem she was shutting out of her life all the bad experiences of Crockford's. She crept along the hallway to the kitchen, where she was to meet Lavelle.

The kitchen was in darkness, but she could make out his silhouette. Together they filled two sackfuls of food from Ma-Ma Baker's well-stocked pantry. Ellen also helped herself to some potions and salves from the medicine chest for Lavelle's back. When they had as much as they could carry, they slipped out through the back door.

They had just reached the paddocks, when Lavelle laid a hand on her arm and whispered urgently: 'The fiddle, Ellen – I've forgotten the fiddle. I've got to go back for it.'

It seemed an eternity before he returned, she worrying all the while lest he had been discovered and their plans thwarted. Annie, too, seemed restless, and Ellen was terrified that she might begin to cry. The relief she felt when she saw him coming towards her, the house and the maze rising out of the dark behind him, was indescribable.

With a soft whistle, he called the horses to him. The animals waited patiently while he loaded two of them with their provisions. She had had some chance on the horses during her time at Crockford's and liked the animals, wasn't frightened of them. All the same she was glad when Lavelle reassured her with the words, 'I picked a quiet mare for you, Ellen. I'll lead it on the rein a while till you get used to her.'

So, mounted on two horses, with Lavelle leading hers and the other two, they rode out, gently at first, putting the low, Barossa moon between themselves and Crockford's.

Neither looked back once.

36

Once out of Crockford's, they skirted around Bethany and rode southward, keeping Jacob's Creek to their right and the *Kaiserstuhl* – the Emperor's Seat, highest point in the Barossa – to their left.

Neither spoke. Lavelle, having complimented Ellen at the start of the journey that her healing hands had worked miracles – now felt as if every wound on his back was opening up again. Ellen, herself, was preoccupied with recurring doubts as to whether she was doing the right thing, whether the small child strapped to her back would survive the journey that lay ahead of them. Her mind raced back and forth, trying to make sense of it all.

After some hours riding, they stopped and Lavelle built a small fire to heat a billycan of tea.

'We won't wait long here – better we ride through the night,' he said to her over the flames.

'Yes,' she agreed. 'Yes, we should.' She wanted to put as much distance as possible between herself and the place they had left.

'Lavelle,' she asked when they were back on the horses. 'What will happen back there?'

'Coombes has probably taken Samarara's body to Adelaide, as proof that he caught and hanged Kitty's murderer – after a fair trial, of course! Then the Peelers need not be beating about up at Crockford's looking for the killer.'

'Surely they won't believe him?' she said incredulously.

'Oh, but they will! Especially when Kendall, and some of Coombes' other guests – though maybe not Craigie' – He gave a little smile at the mention of the Scotsman's name – 'throw their weight behind Coombes' version. After all, we're not talking about human beings. Nobody in Adelaide is going to get too excited about one less black savage roaming the bush frightening the white womenfolk. That's the way it is!'

'It's white savagery – what's going on out here – and Coombes is the devil himself!' Ellen said angrily. 'And what about the girls?'

'Coombes always made sure of keeping me well away from all that – would send me to Adelaide or out Bush. I had my suspicions, but he always covered up everything so well. Said he was giving the girls a new chance in life and if they were flattered by the attention and became infatuated with some of his friends, what was wrong with that?'

'And Mrs Hopskitch in Adelaide?' she pressed. 'Coombes pretending he didn't know her . . . ?'

'I had no idea Coombes was connected to her. He always had a story to explain why any of the girls went back to Adelaide – like they found Crockford's too isolated, or that they'd run off to one of his men-friends there.'

'Do you think Mrs Baker knows what's been going on?'

'Ma-Ma isn't a bad sort – bark worse than her bite, but she wouldn't let out anything on Coombes. He's got some hold over her, though she'd never say.'

Ellen felt that many of her questions were now laid to rest. Coombes was too cunning to let Lavelle, or anyone else, in on his secrets. She believed that the Achill Island man was innocent of any involvement. He had shown great courage in standing up to Coombes, trying to save Samarara's life – and had paid a savage price for it.

They continued to make good ground, following the Onkaparinga River, keeping the Chain of Ponds and Kangaroo Creek to their right, until they reached the German village of Hahndorf. They were now, Lavelle informed her, about halfway to Goolwa and the southern coast.

He decided they would stop at Hahndorf for a while. They could rest themselves and the horses, and replenish their food supply out of some money Lavelle had. Ellen was glad of the break: Annie was becoming increasingly fretful and restless, and she herself was saddle-sore. Lavelle was getting stronger, but still needed Ellen to apply fresh liniment to his wounds at regular intervals.

After Hahndorf, they continued southwards, taking more frequent breaks now that they were further away from Crockford's. The Mount Lofty Ranges, to their left, provided a regular point of reference for them, until, close to Dingabledinga, the gently rolling hills before them unfolded away into vast flat plains stretching down to the waterlands of the Lower Murray Basin.

On and on they rode until they saw the great expanse of Lake Alexandrina, named for the young princess who had since become Queen Victoria and Encounter Bay. Beyond was Encounter Bay and the Southern Ocean on which Ellen had sailed into Australia.

'Another day without mishap should see us in Goolwa. Then, when we cross the Coorong, we'll be well on our way!' Lavelle said enthusiastically.

Ellen, too, was happy with their progress, feeling that Lavelle had done well by them.

However, she was anything but happy about Annie. The child was not sleeping well and had become uncharacteristically crotchety. Ellen had hoped that, sooner rather than later, Annie would settle into the travelling. Otherwise, they would make very slow progress indeed.

That night, Ellen lay down beside her and *cronauned* to her the old lullabies – the *suantraithe* – all the while caressing Annie's forehead as she sang. This seemed to settle her. After a while of looking wide-eyed at Ellen and then reaching up tiny white fingers into her mother's mouth as if trying to catch the notes, Annie fell into a sound sleep. Ellen watched her for a while, thinking that perhaps she ought to put her own tiredness aside, and give more time to Annie.

The following day Ellen was reckoning that they mustn't be too far from Goolwa, when she became aware of two, not unconnected, sensations. The first was a sense of some energy or force being present. She couldn't explain it, but she recognized it. She had been aware of it once before – the night of All Souls – when she had witnessed the presence of the Banshee. A glance at Lavelle was enough to tell her that he was not experiencing it. The force came from without, but something within her was receptive to it. She opened herself to it, not trying to resist.

The second sensation was that they were being watched by unseen eyes; eyes in the she-oaks and eucalyptus trees; eyes in the acacia shrubs; eyes in the banks of the creeks.

She didn't need to be told that this was a sacred place – a place out of the old, like the mist-shrouded Reek. But as she was later to learn, this was not the place of a Christian saint. Goolwa – the Elbow – had a history beginning long before that of the 'Island of Saints and Scholars' which she had left. Goolwa was long before Christianity.

'*Kringkri!*'

'*Kringkri!*'

The shouts ripped through Ellen's consciousness.

'*Kringkri! Kringkri!*'

At once, Ellen and Lavelle were surrounded by a band of excited Aborigines yelling and pointing at them. In their hands were boomerangs and hunting spears.

'Just stay calm – they mean no harm,' said Lavelle. Then, holding his outstretched palms towards the Aborigines, he said, '*Yant, yant el our ou*' – Peace, peace with you.

The Aborigines quietened, but still nervous, moved in closer. They took a particular interest in Ellen, shuffling around her, staring at her face, fingering the long tresses of her hair, all the time whispering in awe: '*Kringkri! Kringkri!*' – The Dead! The Dead!

Lavelle told her, 'They think we're back from the dead. They've probably never seen a white woman before, let alone one with a head of red hair like yours – they'll probably keep you!'

Ellen was about to react to this when she saw that Lavelle was laughing.

Now the Aborigines gathered around Annie, who awoke and looked back at them, her eyes following them as they moved about her.

'*Tyinyeri! Tyinyeri!*' they said, excitedly, pointing at the child, and again looking at Ellen with a mixture of awe and respect. Then it was Lavelle's turn. They tugged at his clothes, fingered his unbearded chin, and tugged at his sandy-coloured hair. Ellen noticed Lavelle's discomfiture with this inspection, and, when he looked over at her, it was her turn to laugh as she said, 'I think you're the one they want to keep!'

The Aborigines, picking up the intent of Ellen's jibe, also began to laugh at Lavelle, calling something out to him.

'*Mimini! Mimini!*' they pointed.

'*Korni! Korni!*' others laughed.

'*Mimini! Mimini!*' the first, bigger group, chorused back, much to Lavelle's chagrin.

Ellen was not to know the meaning of these words until later. Nor, indeed, did Lavelle fully understand them. If he had, he might not have gone so willingly with these people of the Lower Murray River.

When they reached the outskirts of the Ngarrindjeri encampment they were met by a group of the women. Like their menfolk, the women took a great interest in Ellen, but also, in Annie. Ellen felt comfortable about letting the women, who were very excited and friendly towards them, touch, and even lift Annie from her arms.

However, it was when the women inspected Lavelle, who had dismounted, that the fun began.

Ellen again heard the words '*mimini*' and '*korni*' being bandied about among the women. It seemed to her that they were in dispute about something that had to do with Lavelle.

All was soon to be revealed. The bare-breasted Aboriginal women were clearly fascinated by the colour of Lavelle's hair and his clean-shaven face. It puzzled them that he looked so different from their own heavily bearded men. Now they came closer, dancing against him all the while, still laughing, till he found himself ensnared in a circle of almost naked black bodies. Then one of the women, who they later learned was called Kalinga, held up her hand and the dancing and laughter stopped.

Kalinga now looked into Lavelle's face and posed the question: '*Mimini?*'

There was a titter of laughter from the others.

Not receiving an answer to her first question, she now asked: '*Korni?*'

This was followed by more laughter. Ellen had guessed what it was the women were at. Kalinga was asking if he were '*mimini*' – a girl, or '*korni*' – a man. With no answer forthcoming from Lavelle, the women set about finding out for themselves.

At a nod from Kalinga, a few of the stouter women grabbed his arms and pinioned them behind him. Then the others caught his legs and hoisted him off the ground. As the full realization of what the women were about to do hit him, Lavelle bucked and twisted, but to no avail. First, they undid his boots and removed them, then unbelted his trousers and removed those. All that then remained were his long johns – within which lay the answer to their question. Lavelle struggled to get his hands round to the front of his body, but the Ngarrindjeri women were not, at this stage, going to be denied; they held him fast.

Then it was too late. With a great tug, Kalinga and another woman whipped off the long johns, revealing the manhood of a mortified Lavelle.

Kalinga first looked, then pointed to the proof, finally shouting it out, *'menane! menane!'* At this, a great crackle of noise and laughter went up from the rest of the women. *'Korni! Korni! Korni!'* settling it, once and for all, that Lavelle was indeed a man.

Lavelle's misadventures at the hands of the Ngarrindjeri women did not, however, end there. He had to suffer the further indignity of being carried, trouserless, into the village, while each of the women satisfied herself, by individual inspection, as to the legitimacy of his credentials – his *menane*. Eventually, he was set down in the midst of all and his clothing returned. He dressed himself to much good-natured bantering.

Ellen, for her part, couldn't but help feel a pang of pity for him. He had taken it in good part, she thought, even if he had been embarrassed by the women's actions.

He approached her, still flushed, and she tried to keep the smile from her face. Then she could hold it in no longer. For a moment Lavelle was taken aback, but, her laughter being contagious, he too began to see the humour of it all and joined in with her.

'All right! All right! – I was fair game this time, Ellen Rua,' he conceded.

'You enjoyed it, Lavelle – all that attention from those women,' she said, trying to embarrass him further.

The Ngarrindjeri studied them both – the *kringkri* with no hair on his chin, but his *menane* intact, and her, the *kringkri mimini* with the *thuwi* of fire on her head. And the *tyinyeri* –

the girl-child, in her arms. The men and women encircled Ellen, touching her white skin, and handling her hair – *thuwi*, as they called it. Around her they spoke to one another in hushed tones, *prolin . . . kene* – red . . . fire. Ellen found herself amused by all the attention, and surprisingly unflustered by it, given that before this she had only seen one Aborigine. Now she was surrounded by dozens of them.

Kalinga approached, pointing to herself and saying, 'Kalinga'. Then, pointing at Ellen, she asked: '*Yare mai ru?*'

'My name is Ellen. This is Annie.'

'You – Annie*anikke*?' Kalinga pointed at Ellen in surprise.

'Yes,' Ellen replied, rightly assuming that Kalinga asked if she was Annie's mother.

'*Thuwi? Thuwi?*' Kalinga said, pointing at Annie's dark hair and Ellen's red mane, not understanding how she could be the child's mother. Ellen noticed that all the Aborigines were of a similar hair colouring.

'*Alinta,*' Kalinga said, pointing at Ellen. '*Alinta.*'

'*Alinta,*' they all said. The woman of fire.

A tall man approached her. Ellen was struck by how noble and graceful he seemed – as indeed did many of these people.

The others fell silent as Rupulle, leader of the *Tendi*, the council of elders spoke: 'You *Alinta*, Fire Ancestor, come among Ngarrindjeri again,' he said in broken English. 'You have come as a *kringkri*, but you have come. This *napelle* – *Alinta* husband?' he asked, pointing his spear at Lavelle.

'Oh, no!' said Ellen. 'My husband is dead. He is my friend, he helps me.'

'Ngarrindjeri peoples are your friend, *Alinta,* Annie*anikke*,' Rupulle said. 'This place here, where *Murrundi* flows to great ocean, this your place, *Alinta* – many long time of the Dreaming. This your *Ruwi,*' he said, pointing to both land and water on every side.

Ellen realized that, despite her white features, these people took her to be a reincarnation of one of their gods or Ancestors. Somehow, in their eyes, she was one of the Aboriginal spirit people – like the spirit people of her own Celtic race, the *Tuatha Dé Danann*, those shape-changers and dream-chasers who could go between worlds.

That she could cope with. Given her own experience with the Banshee, the idea was not alien to her. But did this mean the Ngarrindjeri would expect her to stay here? She decided to say nothing; to take things as they came for the moment and accept the hospitality of these people.

Later, that evening, the Ngarrindjeri held a feast in honour of their visitors. Even in Crockford's, had Ellen never seen such an array of food.

There was the *pinyali*, which she understood to be emu – run down by the Ngarrindjeri hunters, driven into their waiting nets – and cuts of *wangami,* the kangaroo, neither of which she liked. These were roasted on hot slabs of stone in holes dug out of the ground, over which grass was laid. Hot stones and coals were also placed inside the animal to ensure it was cooked throughout.

Then there was every kind of *mami* netted from the Coorong's waters: the *pondi,* the large Murray cod, and *thukeri* and callop. These were placed into the oven hole wrapped in wet grass and surrounded by earth. The fish were then steamed by pouring water down three or four hollow reeds pushed through the earth to the oven below. Ellen found the steamed fish to be delicious, as she did the *kuti* – cockles – and other shellfish.

Then, but not for Ellen, there was *pellati*, an edible grub found in the banksia trees. And after this came *muntharri*, made from the berry-like wild Coorong apples, dried and crushed into a cake. And roots and fruits – *kongi* and *kuntyaring* – whose kernels would later be mashed into an oily paste to be applied for head or back aches. For drink, there was the opaque nectar of *kurku,* taken from small insects which lived in the branches of the mulga tree.

Ellen was amazed at how advanced the Ngarrindjeri were, how they made use of all that was about them – huts built of bent tree branches, covered with nets and reeds woven in basketry style. One hut, she noted, was made of giant curved bones. 'Whale bones,' Lavelle told her. These were nothing like the black heathen savages depicted by Coombes.

Rupulle sat with them, and another who seemed to command great respect: Wiwirremalde – the *kulduke*, the tribe's medicine man.

The women, she noticed, were not in any sense subservient

to the men. There were no servants in this society. Instead, a dignified courtesy was observed all round. In fact, some of the older women seemed to be accorded a special respect. Like the *sean-daoine,* she thought, remembering how it was at home with the old ones who handed on wisdom and learning and custom. This Coorong of South Australia was not so very different to her valley in Maamtrasna. Only here the people had food – and plenty of it.

They talked – the Ngarrindjeri and *Alinta,* the Fire Ancestor. They came to touch her again, the women, and the young men, initiates painted in red ochre, flush from their new-found manhood. Rupulle and Wiwirremalde touched the face, the hair of this *kringkri* ghost-woman many times, as if making sure she would not fade away again before their eyes. Be sung back into the rocks and lakes – into the Dreaming. Or, like Ngurunderi – the great Creator-Ancestor, law-maker, land-shaper – descend to the depths of the sea before rising to the Milky Way to eternally light their passage.

The Máistir and Ngurunderi, she thought – both ancestral seers, shapers of things.

She told them her own story of the far-away land beyond the great ocean, of the people, other *kringkri* who came to take that land, pushing back the native peoples. She told them about the Great Hunger, and the people being again driven off the land. Spoke to them of her own ancestors, the Celts, the magical *Tuatha Dé Danann,* the Máistir. Finally, she told them of her three children abandoned in the far-away land that she had to get back to.

In turn, the Ngarrindjeri spoke of the whitefellas who had come, taking first their land and then their women, repaying them only with the whitefella sicknesses – venereal disease and smallpox – unknown to them before the coming of the Europeans.

Rupulle spoke: 'Once Ngarrindjeri nation strong. Many tribes, many *lakalinyerar* all along Coorong and *Murrundi.* Now we are few. Even children gone, taken by *kringkri* holy men to mission schools, teachem whitefella ways and whitefella God. It's all broken now. All broken,' he said despondently.

'It's proselytizing all over again – just like back in Achill,' Lavelle said to Ellen.

She felt a sadness in her heart for Rupulle, leader of a disappearing race – a race many thousands of years older than her own.

'You must hold on,' she said. 'You must not let go of the old ways, your customs and traditions. You must get your children back, teach them yourselves, as you always have.'

'It is the law of the *kringkri* Queen,' he replied. 'She send holy men and soldiers together to take our children. And we have no guns, only *plongge* and *yande*.' He picked up the lump-ended fighting club and the long, barbed throwing-spear. 'To kill the *wangami* – yes, good! To fight Peramangk tribe – yes! To fight whitefella – no good!'

Rupulle shook his head and continued. 'When children return, they question *raukkan* – the ancient way, the way Ancestors teach us. Whitefella world come to Ngarrindjeri world. We cannot stop it . . . must let our children go . . . must learn whitefella talk, *kringkri* ways. Only way now for Ngarrindjeri people to live on. Too much bad thing already done, too much bad thing . . .'

As she listened, Ellen thought how familiar the story sounded. She'd not had to 'take the soup' or send her children to a proselytizing mission school – at least she'd some choice about that. But she, herself, had taught them English. And she had known that once she'd gone down that road with them, she'd never get them back to the old language, the old ways – the *sean-nósanna* . . . the *raukkan*.

Wiwirremalde spoke to her, his dark eyes shining: 'Now, *Alinta*, Annie*anikke*, you will see the story of Ngurunderi – long time ago Dreaming Ancestor.'

Ellen watched as the actors gathered for the *ringbalin*. Red-ochred, feather-plumed, white-splashed, they first danced the ceremonial *palti* to bird sound and dingo howl. Shuffling dust devils they were – hunter and hunted – hopping, swimming, flying on the ground. The men made a clacking noise with their spears and *woomera* – the spear-throwing holder – their boomerangs clapping in rhythm. The women beat their digging sticks, on the stretched possum-skin drum. This *plangkumballin* rumbled underneath all the other sounds rolling into the night across the wetlands and gibber plains of the Murray Basin. The didgeridoo, not common to the Coorong, droned its circular bush rhythms in the hands of a visitor from a northern *lakalinyeri*.

As the story of Ngurunderi unfolded, Ellen and Lavelle watched, entranced, swept along by the dance.

The Dreaming Ancestor's two wives had stolen away from him. He pursued them down along the Murray in a canoe made from the bark of the river red gum. *Pondi*, the giant cod, went before him, widening *Murrundi* with its tail. With Ngurunderi's permission, his brother-in-law Nepele speared *Pondi* and together they divided the cod into every different species of fish now known, both freshwater and sea water. Then Ngurunderi, by the smell of the cooking of *thukeri* – the bony bream, a fish forbidden to women – found his wives, but they escaped him again, heading southwards along the Coorong to Kangaroo Island. There, in a voice of thunder, Ngurunderi called up the mountainous waters of the sea to drown his treacherous wives, whose bodies became the Pages Islands.

The frenzied dancers twirled to the ever-increasing rhythm of stick and bone. Their stage the Never-Never Land of *Murrundi*, above them, *Prolggi* – the one-star galaxy of the Clouds of Magellan.

Soon Ngurunderi began to mourn his wives and it was time for him to enter into *Waieruwar* – the spirit world. To prepare his spirit, he dived into the depths of the ocean at the far end of Kangaroo Island – *Karta*, the Island of the Dead. Out of the depths, he arose again, flashing fierily through the southern sky, homewards to the firmament from whence he had come. Then was Ngurunderi at peace, whitest and brightest star within the Milky Way.

The dancers stopped, the music stopped, as heavenwards every eye was cast to where Ngurunderi sailed in the great waters of the night sky.

Ellen, too, carried along by the music and dance, had floated away, borne upwards and outwards in the Dreaming, absent to herself but present in some other-world where she wanted to stay.

'Annie*anikke*, come quickly!' Kalinga tugged at her arm.

It took Ellen a moment to recover herself. The next words Kalinga uttered made her forget all the mystery that a moment previously had been hers – frightened her to the quick of her being.

'Come! Annie *wiwim* – sickness!' Kalinga, too, was frightened as she pulled at Ellen. 'Wiwirremalde come too!' Kalinga summoned the tribal doctor.

Ellen then knew in her heart that she would not yet leave this place. The spirit of Ngurunderi filled her senses wanting to tell her something, but she pushed it away, unwilling to listen, closing herself to everything as she rushed to her sick child.

37

For three days and three nights, Ellen and Wiwirremalde sat with Annie. Ellen watched helplessly as her child, her special, long-awaited child, drifted in and out of consciousness, the fever taking her to places where neither Ellen's love and comforting, nor all the ancient skills of Wiwirremalde, could reach her.

Annie, her black curls limp with fever-sweat, her beautiful, dark eyes glassed over, just lay there. Sometimes she whimpered and responded to the cooling touch as Ellen mopped her brow, trying to dampen the heat of her child's rising temperature.

'*A Mhamaí . . . a Mhamaí . . .*' she would say faintly, and Ellen would bend even closer to her face.

'Ssshhh, *a stóirín*, I'm here beside you. Ssshhh now . . . Sleep, my little one!'

And sometimes, for a moment, the glassy look in Annie's eyes would retreat, to be replaced by the tiniest spark of a smile. Then hope would rise in Ellen, and she would fight the tiredness and the heaviness, and *cronaun* to her sick child in low soothing sounds. As she did this, on the edge between speaking and singing, Ellen unconsciously rocked forwards and backwards over Annie, as if her own body's life-energy sought to transfer itself once again to the child which had been delivered of it not two years ago.

Into the night she would sit, and gently rock, and sing, like the Ancestral Beings who sang shape into life, forming the rocks and the lakes and the sacred places. Or knelt, singing to her dying child – some force within compelling her song to bridge the chasm between life and death; to reach the fading life-spark, and sustain it; to re-ignite it.

Lavelle came and went silently, bringing fresh water to replenish the two limestone bowls. The larger one was for dipping the cloth with which Ellen mopped Annie's brow. From the other bowl, Ellen would sip the cold water and then tenderly, slowly let it spill from her own lips into the child's parched mouth.

As the night closed in and the camp fires were lit around them, Ellen's mind went back to the night Annie was born, and the fire flickering on the wall of the cabin while Sheela-na-Sheeoga worked tirelessly to bring Annie into the world. Annie the child of whom she had foretold, 'When the whitest flower blooms, so too will you bloom, Ellen Rua.' The old woman had anointed her tongue and womb with herbs when she had made that prophecy. Sheela had again used the extracts of plants to mould her body into shape for Annie's delivery, probably saving both her own life and Annie's in the process.

Now Wiwirremalde, black old man of an ancient race, made his potions from the plants and berries of this exotic land brought to him by Kalinga. He administered them, sometimes anointing – *tyetyin* – sometimes in a poultice to Annie's body, all the time chanting, as Sheela-na-Sheeoga had done. Now, he with hands and herbs and sounds of healing, was trying to preserve the life that, twelve thousand miles away, the old woman had brought into the world with the same ancient skills. He rarely looked at Annie*anikke*; all his energy and spirit-force being concentrated on Annie herself. As Ellen watched him work she wondered whether Sheela-na-Sheeoga, were she here, would be able to save the child.

A dark thought entered Ellen's mind. The *Slám*! The life-swapping ritual of herb casting. She looked at Wiwirremalde leaning over Annie, not a foot or two away from her. Did he know of the *Slám*? Not that these people would call it by that name. They would have their own word for the sorcery.

She recalled how she had agonized over the decision before finally rejecting Sheela-na-Sheeoga's offer to make a *Slám* for Michael – to let Death claim some other poor soul in his stead. She couldn't bring herself to do it then. No, not even for Michael, her dark, lovely Michael. But now – here – for Annie?

Why should yet another of her loved ones be taken from her? Hadn't she suffered enough already? Now the one she thought she was sure of, thought she had saved by bringing to Australia, was slipping away from her, and she couldn't stop it. She should have known that Annie wouldn't have been able to make this long, hard journey – shouldn't have let Lavelle and her own foolishness talk her into it.

She reached out, fingers trembling, and touched the shoulder of Wiwirremalde. The doctor of the Ngarrindjeri turned and looked at her, momentarily stopping his ministrations.

'Wiwirremalde . . . ?' she began. His impassive eyes looked directly into her, seeing the terrible thought she held there. 'Is there . . . is there anybody here . . .' the words came out slowly, tortured between grief and guilt at the thing they asked, '. . .who is very old, very sick?'

'Ngarrindjeri people plenty *wiwim*. Whitefella bring white queen *wiwim* allem time blackfella die,' Wiwirremalde said, his eyes not moving from hers.

'I . . . I know, Wiwirremalde.' Ellen forced herself to go on. 'But now . . . tonight, in the *lakalinyeri*, is there anybody . . . ?' She stopped and looked down at the child lying between them, washed paler in the moonlight, her eyes now closed. 'I don't want Annie to die! She hasn't even lived. Wiwirremalde, help me, help me!' She grabbed the medicine man by both shoulders.

'*Alinta*, Annie*anikke*!' the old man addressed her, a sad look coming into his eyes. 'Ngurunderi takem Annie child in *yuke* canoe sailem down *Murrundi* to Karta.' He looked far out beyond the peninsula of the Coorong to where the mighty river opened into the sea, and Karta, the Land of the Dead. 'Listen, Annie*anikke* . . .' Wiwirremalde broke off his story of Annie's spirit journey with Ngurunderi. 'Listen!'

Ellen listened, her senses alert. From far away across the wetlands of *Murrundi*'s lower lakes it came. It was not the same sounds of the Coorong she had heard earlier as the night world of the bushland came to life. This sound was different – this cut through it all. With a start she looked at the old Aborigine. It couldn't be, she thought – not out here, in this wild place! 'No! No! No!' she shrieked. She wouldn't listen to it! She drew back her hands from Wiwirremalde's shoulders and clasped them to her ears in an effort to keep out the sound. But it was useless.

The noise grew louder and louder – high-pitched, intense in its beckoning – until her head felt as if it would burst. At last she dared to look towards its source, expecting to see the translucent form of the Banshee floating over the Coorong's flat, marshy lands towards her. But she saw nothing. No form from which the sound emitted.

Terrified, she looked again at the tribal medicine man. What had she started? Had he read her thoughts? Was it that her asking for the *Slám* had conjured up what she recognized as the death-warning?

Wiwirremalde spoke: 'It is the cry of the Mingka bird, Annie-*anikke*. Him first to know allem time. Mingka bird live in big cave holy place Mount Barker. Only leavem sacred mountain before Ngarrindjeri make spirit journey with Ngurunderi. Mingka fly in sky make big cry. Tell Ngarrindjeri people be ready.' He stopped and looked down at Annie. Slowly, sadly, he said, 'Tell Annie*anikke* be ready.'

'No, Wiwirremalde, no!' She didn't want to hear this as if it were all over for Annie – she didn't want to hear this mumbo jumbo talk of Mingka birds and Ngurunderi. Annie was still alive, still breathing. She could see the soft puff of her little rounded cheeks rise and fall.

'No, she's not going to die – I want you to save her!' Ellen beat the old man's shoulders with her fists. 'I don't care! The Mingka can cry for someone else, not her – not her. I know you can do it – I can tell!' she screamed at Wiwirremalde. 'Do it – do the *Slám!*'

The old man caught her flailing fists.

'*Alinta*, Annie*anikke* – do not ask me do this thing – Ngarrindjeri will be finished – all brokem up – very bad!'

She fought against him.

'I don't care!' she spat in his face. 'Christ or the devil – I don't care!'

By now Lavelle had run to them. He wrapped his arms round Ellen, holding her together, saying over and over: 'Ellen, Ellen – don't!'

When she had subsided apart from the sobbing, the old Aborigine put one of his hands against her stomach. Through her grief she heard him say from somewhere far off, from wherever the cave of the Mingka bird was: 'Annie*anikke*, you have good *mewe*. Other thing you ask bad *mewe*. Not askem Wiwirremalde,' he said gently, pressing her womb, as Sheela-na-Sheeoga had done.

The sound of the old man's voice had a relaxing effect on Ellen. Her body, deprived of sleep and nourishment, could endure no more. She was defeated – wanting to sink into her sorrow, to let herself collapse within the tight comfort of Lavelle's hold on her. All she had to do was allow herself to drift off as the *kulduke* spoke to her of Annie sailing with Ngurunderi across the skies to his home in the Milky Way.

No. She wouldn't give in – be comforted out of what she had to do while Annie was still alive. Annie was the one needing to be comforted.

'Let me go,' she said quietly to Lavelle. 'I'm all right now.'

She reached down and, with exquisite tenderness, gently encircled Annie within her arms, drawing the child to her bosom. As she snuggled Annie within the white swaddling cloth, the child's eyes flickered for a moment, then opened, and looked up into her own.

Ellen heard the faintest little whisper.

'*A Mhamai!*'

It said everything to her.

She walked away from the two men, walked out into the wilderness with her child. Then she sat under a giant she-oak tree, its leaves drooping downwards – the tears of Ngurunderi. There, in a final act of love and intimacy, she bared both her breasts and cradled Annie against them; talking to her, singing the old *suantraithe*, caressing the soft rise of her baby's cheek with her fingers.

The sun began to break over the Coorong. The new dawn unveiling the middens – giant stores of fish shells accumulated by the Ngarrindjeri over many centuries. Middens which were now places of mystery and sacredness.

With the rise of the new day, Annie opened her eyes, making a small murmuring sound. Ellen felt her forehead – it wasn't hot. Her eyes were brighter too – gone the glasslike look. For a moment Ellen's heart surged. Then she realized that, instead of a raging temperature, Annie's forehead was cold and clammy. The bright look in those dark and beautiful Spanish eyes with the hint of green, was not the sparkle of life, but the cold hard glint of a battle lost. It was the sign of a little body no longer able to hold back the ravages of a consumptive fever.

The tiny hand somehow reached up to Ellen's lips, and Ellen took the fingers between them, blowing gently, giving them some warmth. Annie always liked this little touch game they had. Now the child lifted her head a mite and made a small broken sound instead of her usual gurgle of laughter. '*A Mhamaí . . . a Mhamaí,*' she whispered weakly. 'Annie cold.'

As Ellen bent now to kiss once more her darling child – she noticed how the colour of Annie's lips had changed. Where once there was rosebud red, now a blue whiteness had appeared around the edges pushing back the bright colours of life.

How unusually cold to the kiss they were too.

At the touch of her mother's lips, Annie closed her eyes against the cold that was enveloping her.

Ellen, filled with inestimable grief, knew her child would never open them again.

38

Out of the morning she came: wild-headed, her face gaunt and streaked, bare-breasted, unashamed of her nakedness. But she walked, head high, carrying her dead child. Lavelle ran to her, but she did not see him. Then Kalinga and the women came. Then the men, and what few children there were left in the *lakalinyeri*, then Wiwirremalde and Rupulle. The cry went up: 'Annie *meralde!* Annie *meralde!*' – Annie is dead! And the wailing and *ochóning* of the women of the Ngarrindjeri filled the air.

Ellen walked, as if unseeing, unhearing, until she reached Wiwirremalde and Rupulle. She stood before them.

'I am sorry,' she said in a vacant voice to the medicine man. 'I ask your forgiveness and that of your people.'

Then the women came around her, embracing her, keening the great loss of *Alinta*, Annie*anikke* – Ellen, the mother of Annie.

Later that day, Kalinga and the women took Ellen with them to the sacred place where women's business was conducted, to which no man could go.

Many hours later, when Lavelle saw Ellen again, he could scarce believe his eyes. Had she not been the centre of attention of the women who returned with her, and taller than the rest, he would not have recognized her at all.

The women, he knew, had taken her to prepare for mourning. Now he stared in disbelief at the transition. Naked to the waist, Ellen's bare body was covered with the white paste of *bulpuli* – pipeclay paint. On her breasts, finger-painted with great precision, were close concentric circles. Her arms too were adorned with the white Aboriginal mourning colour.

And on her shoulders . . . Lavelle tried to make out what it was. The colour was something like the red ochre paint the young men – initiates of the tribe – wore. But as she passed him, flanked by the women, he could see it was not paint but blood. Congealed blood, on wounds about three inches long, running from the top of Ellen's shoulders to her upper arms.

Lavelle was shocked beyond belief. He knew the Ngarrindjeri women would not have taken it on themselves to do this to her. Ellen must have decided to mutilate herself.

With a quartzite knife-blade, she had inflicted on herself the traditional 'sorry cuts' of the Ngarrindjeri. She had sliced into her own flesh to give physical expression to the agony of her great loss.

But the greatest shock was yet to come for Lavelle. Ellen's face, except her eyes and lips, was completely covered in white, and on her head was a casing of thicker, heavier white paste. He tried to see how they had managed to fit all that wild red tangle of hair he'd seen on her this morning under the shell of paste on her head. It was impossible.

Lavelle strained to get nearer, to see her better. He got behind the group of women. He could see the back of her head. The wisps of rich red hair running down the nape of her neck that he loved to look at when she pulled her hair forward of a morning – where were they? As he jostled to get closer to her, he stumbled and fell against Kalinga, knocking from her hands the large covered bowl she carried. As he steadied himself, he saw her grab for it, but she was too late – the contents spilled out. Lavelle reeled back from the sight. Strewn over the ground before him were long rich tresses of human hair. Ellen's hair. All of her hair, Lavelle realized, as she turned at the commotion behind her.

The wild mane of red hair that had earned her the name Ellen Rua, was gone, completely shaven off.

Ellen Rua was *kunkundi* – bald.

Earlier, when Annie had so gently gone into the new morning of the Coorong, Ellen had sat a while in the shade of the giant she-oak. On the ground, amidst the fallen apples of the she-oak, she sat nestling her dead child to the breasts that not so long ago had nourished her.

She reached down, finding her nipple, rolling it between her fingers until it hardened. Then she pressed it against the blue-white lips, and bruised it between them. She waited for the warming tug, but there was none. No pleasuring, comforting flow of life-juice between them. Then, rocking gently, holding her unhungry child's head against her, Annie*anikke*, sang to and for her dead child. As she sang, the tears of Ngurunderi tumbled down about her from the drooping branches of the she-oak. And in the nearby billabong, she saw the bark canoe held by the beak of the giant Mingka bird. Boat and bird waited to receive Annie, waited to sail away with her across the heavens to live forever with Ngurunderi in the Dreaming.

She had risen then and, still singing, danced with Annie. Danced around the base of the she-oak; danced to the edge of the Billabong; danced until her body was numb.

Danced because she couldn't cry.

When exhaustion set in and she could dance no more, she left, leaving behind her Ngurunderi's canoe, and the Mingka bird, still awaiting their *kringkri* passenger.

Now she must bury Annie. She would bury her according to the customs of these people. She had offended them deeply by asking what she had asked of Wiwirremalde. She must seek their forgiveness, by accepting their ancient ways. Hadn't they lost enough already? Yet these people had such dignity, such spirit. She would respect that. It had been wrong of her to seek to interfere, breaking their laws, no matter how desperate her own needs were.

When later Kalinga had handed her the razor-sharp quartzite knife, she had not flinched. The women had prepared her for mourning with great concern and tenderness. Now it was her turn. She had felt the cold edge of the blade bite into her, the jagged quartz serrating her flesh. Three times she had done it on each shoulder: making the incisions, running the blade down over her shoulder to the fleshy part of her upper arm. The pain was excruciating, her determination unflinching as the women talked to her, touched her, supported her. But the pain brought with it release from her anguish for the uncried-for Annie, and from her shame at what she had asked.

When she had finished the *munggaiynwun* – the cutting of the body – she was tempted to draw the knife down twice more, not on her arms, but on her breasts in a final act of grief. Kalinga, sensing her intention, stayed her hand and took the bloodied blade from her.

'No, *Alinta!* No cut! All finished now!'

Now, the *munggaiynwun* complete, the sorry cuts daubed with steamed leaves of the stinging nettle, her body painted, her hair shorn in mourning, Ellen felt liberated, inured against further pain.

Now, she was ready to bury Annie.

First, according to custom, an inquest was held. Annie's corpse was carried aloft on a wooden *birri* of rushes and soft leafy branches. The *birri* bearers halted outside each shelter in the campsite until Wiwirremalde's hand signalled them to move on, satisfied that he had detected no sign of any sorcery or evil-doing. Only when the old man was satisfied that no one present was responsible for the death of Annie, could the ceremony proceed.

Annie's remains were placed on a burial platform and covered with rushes and netting. The raft-like platform was arranged so it faced towards Kangaroo Island, to make it easier for Annie's spirit to follow the Dreaming path of Ngurunderi and be cleansed by the sea before ascending to *Waieruwar*. The keening and mourning continued until finally Annie was taken down and placed in a small, beautifully woven sedge encasement – her coffin.

Ellen spoke to Kalinga. 'Kalinga – soon I must go from the Coorong and from you, my friends. I must leave Annie here among your people . . .' She looked to the myriad of stars in the heavens above Kangaroo Island. 'But her spirit will always be above me with Ngurunderi, so I will not grieve.'

'Yes, *Alinta* Annie*anikke*,' Kalinga replied. 'Annie all finished now below here.'

'I want her to rest under the big she-oak by the billabong – underneath the tears of Ngurunderi,' Ellen said.

And so it was arranged. The grave was dug within the embrace of the she-oak under which Annie had breathed her last. It was dressed with leaves and boughs. Ellen gently laid the coffin-basket into the grave, removing and keeping Annie's shawl. Now Annie, born in the green mountainous valley of Maamtrasna, was laid to final rest in the flat grey wetlands of the Coorong. Ellen reverently gathered up a handful of earth from Annie's grave and passed it to Lavelle. Then she untied the piece of cloth in which, all this time, she had kept the handful of earth from Michael's grave. Slowly, she let it fall over Annie, the earth from Crucán na bPáiste replacing the earth from the Coorong, which would now go with her.

Then the women keened for the last time – the same keening as the women of her valley, and Ellen sang a lullaby of the Dreaming, swaying, holding the lifeless shawl against her, dancing as she had danced with Annie so short a time ago. Slowly the women beat their digging sticks, the men joining in with their spears and *woomeras*. Lavelle took up his fiddle and with it grieved for her, and the visiting didgeridoo-player from the north cast his own hollow sound into the ground until it ran up again into her feet and bones.

As the rhythms became more insistent, Ellen moved to them, encircling the she-oak. The Ngarrindjeri danced – sailing Annie's body to the Island of the Dead, paddling Ngurunderi's canoe until it surged from the ocean and shot across the sky to *Waieruwar* – the spirit world.

Now Ellen/*Alinta, kringkri* fire-woman, was at one with her people, stomping the ground in the *konkonbah* – the hunt for the giant kangaroo. Then the dance of *pinyali,* the emu, running from the hunters, but running into their net-traps. As the pace of the hunt increased, the women's *plangkumballin* started up, pounding them onwards. Soon the dance had taken over Ellen's body. She gave herself to its short staccato rhythms, and its thumping rolling crescendos. White against the red-ochred bodies of the young initiates, she danced, her mind altered by the great grief she bore.

Ellen wasn't aware of feeling anything: no pain, no joy, no tiredness. She was bodiless, floating into the spirit-world with Annie, and *Pondi* and the Mingka bird, rising with Ngurunderi to be with her child in the white wasteland of the Milky Way.

Lavelle watched her, troubled. He knew her grief over Annie's death was immense. Too much for one person to bear with what she had already been through.

He had respected her sorrow, what she felt she must do, her feeling of kinship with the Ngarrindjeri, her wanting to right the wrong she had done them. He had said nothing, stood back up to now, stood by her. Now he must stop her – she had gone too far.

He moved towards her. The music stopped at his intrusion. She, trance-like, her arms thrashing wildly, never even noticed, but carried on dancing like some white demonic dust devil, lost to everything but her own insistent rhythm.

He ran to catch her, to save her before she went beyond the point of no return. He was only a few steps from her when the shots rang out.

Cries of *'pandappure'* – guns – erupted from the Ngarrindjeri. As Lavelle reached Ellen, two of the dancers beside her twisted and fell in a final death reel, blood reddening the ochre which adorned their bodies. Pandemonium broke out. There were shouts of *'Kringkri! Kringkri!'* as the tribesmen dispersed, running, fleeing from the shots that cut them down.

The gunshots, the noise, Lavelle grabbing her, brought Ellen back. As Lavelle pulled her along, behind her she heard a voice – an Irish voice: 'Stop the bloody *boongs* from escaping! Get the *lubras* and the *piccaninnies*! Net them – don't harm them!'

She turned, trying to see the owner of the voice – to tell him to stop it all, that it was the burial of her child, that these people were her friends. To tell him that she was Irish – like him.

'C'mon, Ellen! Don't stop – they'll kill us! Run for it!' Lavelle yelled at her, trying to yank her away to safety.

Before she could respond, the big bay galloped up behind her, the horseman swung his arm and then, like *pinyali,* the emu, she was netted, unable to claw her way out. She fell, dragged to the ground, as the net-thrower rode by her, pulling her in his wake. In front of her she heard a thud as Lavelle hit the ground, ridden down by the horseman.

Then the Irish voice, mocking her. 'What have we got here – a white *lubra*? *Anam an diabhail!*' the voice added in Gaelic, invoking the devil as its owner looked down at Ellen with her body painted in the mourning custom of the Ngarrindjeri.

The owner of the Irish voice aimed a boot at her, sending Ellen over on to her back, still entangled in the net. Like a wild animal she was, arms and legs splayed, her fury visible even through her white face-mask. The hunter, all six foot of him, stood over her, watching his captive struggle, enjoying her frenzy.

'A *bhastaird*, get me out of this!' she spat at the overlander.

'Ah, a fellow countrywoman, so to speak,' the Irish voice said, poking at her through the loops of the net with his whip-handle. She twisted away from him, thinking that at least he wasn't a Westerner, didn't speak like her, or Lavelle. 'Shame, shame, shame – didn't get time to get dressed, did we not? And what's your name, Irish *lubra*?'

For a moment she studied this Irishman with the smooth voice. He was in his thirties, maybe the two score. It was hard to tell by a face hardened beyond its years from overlanding Australia's great bush territory.

'My name is Ellen Rua O'Malley, and this is the burial of my child –'

He cut her off. 'Ellen Rua, is it? Red-haired Ellen? And where is this crowning glory you were named after, or is it hidden somewhere else?' he mocked, his whip-handle prodding her thighs. She tried to kick against him, to roll away, but the net prevented her.

'A *bhastaird*!' she swore at him again.

'A burial, you say?' he continued, ignoring her. 'Isn't it a fine way for you to be disporting yourself in front of all these *boongs* – you an Irishwoman and your child buried? Gone native I suppose? Was it a *piccaninny* child?' he taunted her.

'McGrath!' another voice shouted. 'Some of them got away – we'll never catch them now.'

'OK,' the man called McGrath, who stood over her, shouted back. 'Let them go. Besides, we have an interesting catch or two here.' With that, he reached down and yanked Ellen, net and all, to her feet. 'C'mon you *boong's* whore – *striapach!*' And he spat on the ground beside her.

Ellen was brought back to the Ngarrindjeri camp. There, McGrath's men had herded the women and children into a circle in the middle. The men, Wiwirremalde in their midst, were kept under guard by overlanders armed with muskets.

Ellen could neither see Kalinga nor Rupulle anywhere. Either they had escaped or were dead. She reckoned that about half of the women and children had fled to the bush, but that only about a third of the Ngarrindjeri men had succeeded in getting away.

'Someone get me a shirt to cover this white *lubra*,' McGrath barked. 'It's disgraceful what they get up to out here – whoring on the streets of Adelaide and, worse yet, dancing naked in the moonlight with these black savages.'

'Shut your filthy mouth,' she heard Lavelle shout at McGrath before being silenced by the blow of a gun-butt to his head.

Overnight they were held thus while McGrath's men pillaged the Ngarrindjeri village. They took what weapons they could find. They took the possum-skin coats, the intricately woven baskets, the hunting and fishing nets. And they took the Ngarrindjeri women. When one of McGrath's men dragged out from the group a young girl, the tattoo on her chest signifying she was barely past pubescence, Ellen tried to stop him but was knocked to the ground.

The women who were taken, Ellen never saw again. Lavelle, from where he was held, knew only too well what 'sport' the Aboriginal women were used for, and with what barbarous cruelty they met their end.

The next morning they were all herded down to the place where the tidal sea water met the land water of the River Murray. This place, Ellen had learned, held great spiritual significance for the Ngarrindjeri, who regarded it as having a special life-force, fed as it was by the two waters.

Here, McGrath had Ellen and Lavelle bound close together, separate from the rest. The tribesmen and women were crushed into tighter groups, and the actions of the guards became even more intimidatory. The Ngarrindjeri women had become very agitated, as if they knew what was about to happen, and they pulled their children closer to themselves.

Cries of *'pulyugge'*, which neither Ellen, nor Lavelle understood, went up from the women. At this, the men too, started to make noises and show signs of disturbance. One young man, his thighs well-marked from *lagellin* – punishment spearings – managed to break through the cordon of guards, but he was shot unceremoniously at point-blank range. In the back.

Then McGrath strode to the women and children's group and pulled out six kicking and screaming children of both sexes aged between about seven and ten years. The guards battered back their mothers, who fought to hold on to a leg or an arm of their little ones. The intermittent cries of the women had now turned into continuous wailing, punctuated still by the word '*pulyugge*'.

'What is it? What's happening?' Ellen asked Lavelle.

'I don't know – they're going to do something to the children – but what I don't know.'

'McGrath!' Ellen called out. 'McGrath, stop this, whatever it is. No true Irishman would harm children. Let them go!' she shouted at him.

He walked over and stood in front of her. Then slowly and deliberately he drew back his arm and backhanded her, his knuckles splitting her lip, the salt of blood in her mouth, its red trickle running down her white pipe-clayed face.

'Let them go!' He pushed his stubbled face against hers, and she saw the hardness in it. 'Listen, Irish *lubra*, these heathens are not human. They're hardly above the animals they hunt, and they've held back this country for too long now,' he said viciously. Then he left her, her mouth throbbing with pain, her heart torn by the evil intent on his face and the knowledge that she could not save the children.

McGrath turned back to her. For a brief moment she thought he had relented, thought that her words might have stung his humanity, thought he might let the children go.

'What you're going to witness, *boong* whore, is what the British Government started here years ago – population control!'

'Begin the digging!' he shouted at his men.

Ellen watched as the overlanders beat and forced six of the male Aborigines to scrape out holes in the flat hard sand of this holy place. The men were then musket-whipped back into their group.

Then, one by one, the frightened, crying children of the Ngarrindjeri were crammed down into each sand-hole. The sand was shovelled in on top of them until only their heads remained above the sacred ground of their homeland. The holes were in a straight line about four feet apart from each other, the heads of the children all set looking out to sea, towards Kangaroo Island, the Island of the Dead. Terrified, the children tried to turn their heads to look at each other. To seek even the tiniest comfort from the faces of their friends.

Ellen shouted and screamed at McGrath. 'You bastard, may you rot in hell for this! For the crucified Christ's sake – let them go! Don't let them drown.'

McGrath smiled at her in his strange, hard way.

Would they even survive that long, she wondered, until the river and sea swelled to cover them? Would their small bodies be able to withstand the weight of the close-packed sand crushing in on their lungs, bruising the few short years of life they'd had out of them? She struggled at her ropes, until her arms were bloodied. Lavelle, too, strained and fought to get free, but it was no good. The two of them were forced to watch helplessly, shamed by their colour and race.

'McGrath!' cried Lavelle. 'For pity's sake, let them go. Take me instead – I'm wanted for horse-stealing back in the Barossa. You'll get a reward!'

McGrath came over to them, his interest aroused.

'Horse-stealing, is it? You spoke too soon, *buachaill* – now we get paid for handing you over, and we still get rid of the *piccaninnies*!'

Then he grabbed a musket from one of the others and viciously cracked it against Lavelle's already injured jaw.

'That'll teach you to keep your mouth shut!' McGrath sneered.

Meanwhile the wailing and keening of the Ngarrindjeri women rose to a crescendo of grief as they watched the faces of their little ones grow pale with terror. Helpless, the mothers listened to the pitiful crying sounds rising from the mouths of their children.

Ellen searched frantically for sign of the rising waters. The children would never last, she thought. Thankfully they would fall unconscious before long, be spared the agony of waiting, wondering, seeing the water seep towards them, then feeling it lap at their lips, rise above their noses, until there was no air to breathe any more. Only water, the drowning killing waters of the Coorong.

Still the cries, the sobs of '*pulyugge*' rose, renting the air with grief. There was something about the way with which the Ngarrindjeri women screamed this word that cut into Ellen's nerves. It was as if the quartzite knife of the *munggaiynwun* had screamed again into the raw tissue of her shoulders. It was as if the screams signified something beyond the impending deaths of their children, something more horrific.

McGrath's brogue, now more clipped, cut through the din and a great fearful hush arose from the people.

'All right! All right!' he called, and again Ellen's hopes were raised. '*Pulyugge* is it? *Pulyugge* you want?' the Irishman taunted the Ngarrindjeri. Something about the way McGrath said the words plunged Ellen's soul into despairing blackness.

'All right then, boys – let's show them how good we whitefellas are at *pulyugge*. Winner gets the white woman. Furthest wins – first bounce. Let's play *pulyugge*!' And he waved his arm above his head as a signal.

Before Ellen could comprehend what was happening, six of McGrath's overlanders lined up about thirty running paces behind each of the Aboriginal children, their eyes fixed on each *pulyugge* – each ball – ahead of them.

McGrath raised his pistol in the air.

'Steady, boys – no going before the gun!'

Then the shot rang out, and Ellen saw the men start to run, their heavy boots crunching into the sand. They ran straight, picking up speed, altering their stride, measuring, adjusting their approach to the targets ahead of them. Terrified, the children tried to turn their heads to see what caused these tremors in the sand, the shuddering impact of boots that, in seconds, would thud into the backs of their necks severing sinew and spinal column, spinning them through the air towards the ocean, kicking them – for the prize of the white woman – into eternity.

Ellen closed her eyes against the absolute horror of it all, her body retching, convulsing, her lungs refusing at first to function before they forced out the throat-tearing non-human sound she made – 'Nooooooooo!' – as one by one the heads of the Ngarrindjeri children sailed towards the Island of the Dead, their bodies remaining behind in the sand, life seeping out of them into the sacred place of their Ancestral Fathers.

Ellen was saved from unconsciousness only by a great shout going up from every place around her. This was not the death-wailing of the women, nor the screams of terror which accompanied the grisly 'game' of the overlanders. This was a mighty shout of liberation. She opened her eyes, still dazed, to see the six 'footballers' dead on the sand, the barbed death-spears of the Ngarrindjeri transfixing them. Almost simultaneously she felt someone behind her, at her hands. It was Kalinga.

As soon as she was freed, Ellen – maddened with the horror of it all, her whole body shaking – grabbed the knife from Kalinga, and looked for McGrath. She saw him down on one knee, his back to her, shooting at the Ngarrindjeri who had gathered reinforcements and returned, but too late to save their children. Now they were being shot down, butchered, the element of surprise gone, their wooden, quartz-tipped spears no match for the guns of the overlanders.

Her heart pounding, she started to run towards McGrath, possessed with a hatred that consumed her. She ran, unmindful of any danger, wanting only vengeance for the children, wanting to rid the world of this evil. This evil the same colour as her, the same creed as her, the same Irish blood as her, and who had offered her as the prize for the lives of six innocents. She ran, her lips drawn back, her teeth bared like fangs, her nostrils flared.

McGrath turned, sensing the danger, and raised his pistol arm to shoot her. But he was not quick enough and the ferocity of her attack sent him hurtling backwards. Suddenly, she was astride him, white, fearsome, savage. He started to shout at her: '*Striapach!* Fucking *boong* whore!' Until she drove the jagged quartzite blade deep into his throat, severing his jugular – silencing his smooth-lipped Irish brogue forever.

39

The next day amidst the devastation and grieving in the camp of the Ngarrindjeri, Rupulle advised Ellen and Lavelle to be on their way.

'Whitefella killem Ngarrindjeri – no one come to *Kurangk*. Ngarrindjeri killem whitefella – many people come to *Kurangk* catchem Ngarrindjeri,' the leader of the *Tendi* said, knowing from bitter experience the way things were in the colony.

The Ngarrindjeri would move, Rupulle told them. They would bury their children, search out the bodies of their women discarded after use in the billabongs, or half-buried in the middens. Then they would remake and refashion the items stolen by the overlanders who had escaped on horseback. Just as they had been doing since the white man first came sixty years ago.

Ellen was sickened to her soul by the events of the previous day. Sundered with grief at Annie's death, the desecration of her burial had been a further blow. Then the horrific murders of the Aboriginal children, followed by her murder of McGrath, had kept her deeply traumatized. Lavelle had tried to comfort her, but she was beyond comfort. She just kept going between the she-oak tree where Annie was buried and the place of *pulyugge*. There she sat on the sand, hoping forlornly against all hope that some holy force would rise out of this sacred place and purge her soul of its darkness.

And she wondered how long the Ngarrindjeri could survive under continuous onslaught from the settlers with their diseases, their murderous attacks, their enslaving religions.

Rupulle had seen to it that they were given sufficient food for the journey. Fortunately, the horses had come through the onslaught of McGrath's Overlanders unscathed, so they would have transport and a means of carrying their provisions. A tracker would lead them safely east to the boundaries of the land of the Meintangk – also part of the Ngarrindjeri nation – near Kingston. The tracker, Piltayinde, would then hand them over, using the passage rituals required by each of the *lakalinyerar*. European Overlanders, Lavelle later told her, had in the past forced Aboriginal guides to break these rules to gain clearance to cross boundaries. To their cost.

Then Rupulle said to Ellen: '*Alinta,* you are fierce warrior, killem enemy of Ngarrindjeri, Rupulle give you this.' And with that, the leader of the *Tendi* presented Ellen with a lustrous nugget, which radiated a kind of dull sunlight.

'It's gold!' Lavelle exclaimed beside her.

She didn't want to take it.

'*Pondi* swim long time to mouth of *Murrundi* bring this for you *Alinta*,' Rupulle said, pressing it on her.

Then the grieving Ngarrindjeri gathered to say good-bye.

'*Nugune ngoppun*,' Kalinga and those staying behind said.

'*Slán agus beannacht*,' Ellen replied in her own language. Then, '*An ungune*,' she added in theirs, throwing her clasped hands away from her stomach the way she had seen Kalinga expressing thanks.

Finally, as they mounted their horses, Wiwirremalde – doctor, sorcerer, priest – stepped forward and raised his hand in blessing over them.

'*Kau-kau Alinta*,' he benedicted.

Alinta, Ellen Rua, Fire Ancestor, spirit-sister to the Ngarrindjeri, returned the blessing. '*Kau-kau*.'

40

Ellen did not speak for the first two days of the journey. She was hardly present to them at all. Just a shrouded shape on horseback, whose spirit was absent, somewhere back there in the place they had left.

She had washed the grease and pipeclay from her body and head, ridding herself of McGrath's bloodstains at the same time. Her naked head she had wrapped with a cloth tied tightly at the back of her neck. This she then covered with a sedge cloak given her by one of the Ngarrindjeri women. As she rode, she clutched to her breast Annie's swaddling shawl and the cloth with the handful of Coorong earth from Annie's grave.

Wiwirremalde had treated Lavelle's face, and Kalinga had attended to Ellen's shoulders and her wrists where they had been chafed by the rope.

Now they rode in silence, each with their own thoughts, thankful to have survived, but burdened with all that had taken place.

Piltayinde was an experienced guide and their journey out of the Coorong towards Kingston, was uneventful. At times he would seek the higher ground to look backwards for any signs of pursuit. There were none.

They were herded safely from *lakalinyeri* to *lakalinyeri*. And they made good time by horseback and boat until they had left the peninsula. Day after day they journeyed dawn to dusk, close to the coast, heading towards Mount Gambier. Nineteen days in all it took them.

At the Blue Lake they rested for two days, recuperating in both mind and spirit.

'Another two weeks, at this rate, should see us in Melbourne,' Lavelle said.

'It's Boston I've decided on,' she said in reply. 'It's the near side of America. I could get something started there – something me and the children could come back to.'

She had begun to converse with him more and more. But their talk was of the countryside, its changing nature, and how she would get from Melbourne to America. Never once did she allude to the death of Annie. Never once did she speak of McGrath or how she had gone for him like some avenging angel. The most she would say, and more to herself than him, was, 'We are all savages beneath the skin – all of us,' and that would be it.

It seemed to Lavelle that she saw Boston as her – and the children's – salvation. A place to make her mark and then go back home strong, and reclaim her children from Pakenham. Boston, because she had some idea that it was an Irish place, full of people like herself, and because it was near – 'The last parish of Ireland,' she called it.

He didn't mind himself. Boston was as good as New York or Chicago, or anywhere. He wanted to be with her, wherever she was. He wondered what she thought of him.

Ellen did not think much on Lavelle at all. Her thoughts were of Annie: her long hard coming, her quick going. An angel, if ever there was one. Now she was back there in the Coorong, under that she-oak tree. There would be no mother's tears to be shed over her, only the tears of Ngurunderi, Dreaming Ancestor of the Ngarrindjeri. Ellen realized that she would probably never again see the place where Annie rested. But, if she looked skywards, she would see her at night, up there in the spirit world. Up there with the Máistir and Cáit, as she had always imagined it would be. She clutched Annie's shawl tightly to her breast. God, it was a cruel thing – first Michael, then Annie. How was she ever to fulfil Sheela-na-Sheeoga's riddle, to crush the petals of the blackest flower, when she was the one being crushed, ground down by grief and loss?

Now she had murdered a man as well. Sat across his chest, looked into his eyes, and then taken his life in a savage act of violence which she felt compelled to do, even wanted to do.

She crossed herself. 'God forgive me, for such a grievous sin,' she whispered into the confines of her sedge cloak. The Ngarrindjeri, or Lavelle even, would probably have killed McGrath anyway, but – and this is what horrified her – *she* had to do it. *She* had to avenge the deaths of those children, had to put it right. McGrath, one of her own, had done a terrible, terrible, thing to the children of the people who had taken her and her child in. These people had tried so hard to save Annie's life, and then failing had laid her to rest with such ceremony and dignity – and love.

McGrath wasn't like the men of the valley back home. How could such evil get inside the heart of a human being? Was it this lawless, wild land, with no priest or bishop to be looking over your shoulder? Was it having no village to come home to, where the old ones sitting around the fire would smell out the wrong, see it in a look, or an uneasy way of standing, and then fix it to you? It was a man's thing though, she thought. No woman would ever do what McGrath had done to those children – couldn't. No woman would ever be like a Pakenham, or a Coombes. Men had to do things to other men, and to women and even children – it didn't seem to matter – as if some bad seed was in them. Michael wasn't like that; never was, nor could be. And she didn't think Lavelle was like that. He had been good back there with the Ngarrindjeri – attended on her while she sat with Annie. She knew he had been shocked when she came back with the women – painted and cut and shorn. But he understood that she had to go through with it, stood by her. Then offered himself up to McGrath instead of the children.

She stole a glance at him out of the corner of her cloak. He looked ahead, not noticing her. He had a kind face, she thought, hadn't been turned by this harsh land, yet.

Calling themselves Mr and Mrs Coogan as a precaution against any pursuit, they took separate rooms at the Eagle Tavern at the corner of Little Bourke and Queen Street, next to Melbourne's Theatre Royal.

Lavelle had cut loose the four horses with their telltale Crockford's brand – three Cs on each off-shoulder – at the outskirts of the frontier town, and driven them back towards the bush.

She slept the first day – the whole twenty-four hours of it. The second day she soaked her body for hours in the large tub provided by the Eagle Tavern for the ablutions of its clientele. Food they took in their rooms.

Lavelle's savings had fortunately not been located by McGrath's men. An old habit, he had buried them near the encampment. Now Ellen used some of the money to purchase some medication for their wounds, a few toiletries for herself, and a newspaper. Both she and Lavelle still had the clothing they had brought with them. It had not been ransacked by McGrath's men for fear that the possession of white people's clothes, amongst what they had stolen from the Ngarrindjeri, might cause questions to be asked. Ellen felt that they looked presentable enough for the Eagle Tavern, but not for Melbourne's leading banks. They needed to be dressed 'right' when they went to sell the nugget to buy their passage to America.

It took a fortnight to bring about the transformation Ellen had in mind. They needed that time to recover, and the healing process could not be rushed. Some scars, she knew, would never heal, but having survived such an ordeal had, if anything, made her even stronger than before.

So, after two weeks' rest, Mr and Mrs Coogan in their new clothes looked every inch the respectable couple – the sort of people any bank would be glad to do business with.

As they left the hotel, Ellen caught sight of their reflection in a window. They looked the part, all right. And they were ready.

William Ferintosh McKillop – named for both William of Orange, scourge of Catholics, and the Ferintosh Distillery, makers of fine Scotch whisky since 1690 – the Battle of the Boyne – peered over the rim of his pince-nez at the well-dressed couple seated before him. Irish, without a doubt. Could be Protestant or Catholic, but probably the latter.

The Coogans, however, were of less interest to the banker than the item Mr Coogan had just placed on his mahogany desk. McKillop adjusted his pince-nez, delicately, almost imperceptibly, controlling the movement of his fingers, masking the rush of excitement he felt. 'Be sober, be vigilant, do thy self no harm,' – the motto of the Australia Felix Total Abstinence Society, of which he was a leading light, ran through his mind. Vigilant he now required himself to be, as never before.

He said nothing, letting his eyes fall away from the couple and back down to the perfectly formed nugget on the desk. He wanted to reach out and touch it again. Pick it up, feel its texture, hold it so the light could fire up its yellow dullness.

But he would not. William Ferintosh McKillop knew when to be patient. Knew when opportunity smiled on him. And right now, it was positively beaming. These Coogans almost certainly had no idea of the nugget's value, and he was not going to alert them to it by exhibiting any haste or unseemly eagerness. No, 'do thy self no harm'.

'Have you resided long in our town?' the banker asked, a pleasant burr in his voice.

'My wife and I are taking some travels,' the sandy-haired man answered, not giving anything away.

He tried again. 'Where is it you are domiciled – if I may ask?'

'Well, we haven't decided yet,' the man replied evasively.

Nothing. William Ferintosh McKillop hid his annoyance.

'This nugget – have you shown it to your own bankers yet, or an assayer?'

'No . . .' a pause from the Coogan man and then: 'We wanted a bank we could trust – like yours, Mr McKillop.'

This was going nowhere, the banker thought. His pince-nez slipped down again, this time helped by the slight clamminess developing on the bridge of his nose.

'Yes, of course, Mr Coogan – the Bank of Australasia does indeed have that reputation.'

The Bank of Australasia's man in Melbourne realized that he was now answering questions instead of asking them. He was not being vigilant.

He wanted to ask these Coogans – these close-by-the-wall, canny Catholics – where they had gotten the nugget. There had been rumours for some time of gold in the vicinity of the Port Phillip Community. Nothing substantial mind, but one heard these things if one was vigilant. Could this nugget be the first manifestation of what would become a gold rush? This backwater frontier town would overtake Sydney in importance if there was gold to be had in the region.

McKillop had had his fill of graziers, and the stench of tallow from the boiling down of their sheep. Melbourne was turning into a quagmire. Three million sheep and half a million head of cattle its pasturelands held. And the squatters who tended these beasts had brought with them a moral quagmire. Night after night, drinking their sly-grog and poteen. Then roistering in low public houses like the Lamb Inn in Collins Street, until they were 'lambed down' and fleeced of their cash.

Whilst a gold rush would attract yet more roughnecks, it would also underpin the city's financial stability. Perhaps Melbourne would at last cease to be governed by those noxious northerners in Sydney and become capital of its own colonial state.

But back to the business at hand.

'Begging your pardon, Mr Coogan,' he began, 'but could I enquire as to how you came into possession of the nugget? Mind, I am not implying any wrongdoing on your part – absolutely not,' he hastened to add.

The pince-nez had slipped again – it was beginning to irritate him.

'Mr McKillop!' The tall woman spoke for the first time, and in such an imperious way that his finger, so gingerly edging the pince-nez back to its position, had jolted forward, ramming the spectacles back against his eyes, and unsettling him.

'Ma'am!' he said, startled.

'Mr McKillop,' Ellen repeated, her patience with this little banker at an end. As much for the way he had ignored her, addressing all his *slieveen* questions to Lavelle, as for anything else. 'We are busy people. Now, do you wish to purchase this valuable nugget or not? We can always take it to the other side of Queen Street . . .'

McKillop did not like this, did not like it at all, the Irish woman addressing him thus. But she knew her business – the stress she put on the word 'valuable', the oblique reference to the Port Phillip Savings Bank on the other side of Queen Street. He thought of his counterpart at the Port Phillip, a tight-fisted accountant named Smith, who was into everything where there was a shilling to be turned. It was unthinkable that he would ever let Smith get his grasping hands on this nugget.

No, he couldn't lose it now – the chance to be the first, to prove his mettle to the higher-ups in Sydney. If it got out that the Coogans had been here and left, his life would be a misery. Why, he might even be deployed to some place worse than Melbourne. Maybe even to Adelaide – heaven forbid! No, he could not let them leave with the nugget.

'Do thy self no harm,' he muttered to himself, without realizing it.

'Pardon me, Mr McKillop?' he heard the woman say in that voice of hers.

'Well, ah, yes, Mrs Coogan,' he started, recovering himself. 'If you wish, you may go across the street. But I guarantee that you will get no better offer than the one I will make you on behalf of the Bank of Australasia.'

He stopped.

Ellen waited too. Her time with Coombes was paying off.

'I will offer you three hundred sovereigns for the nugget, Mrs Coogan.' King Billy's banker opened out his hands expansively.

Ellen said nothing, only reached her hand across Mr McKillop's mahogany desk and closed it over the nugget, standing up as she did so.

Lavelle looked at her. What was she doing? Three hundred sovereigns! Why, that would not only see them to Boston, but comfortably allow them to start up a business there too!

But Ellen was already heading for the door of the Bank of Australasia, McKillop in her wake, his pince-nez now dashed to the desktop. He looked forlorn without them, and his nugget.

'Five hundred sovereigns then!' his voice caught up with her.

She never looked backwards, only turned the big brass handle.

'Six hundred! That's the best I can do, Mrs Coogan – the very best!'

She yanked the door half open, then turned.

'Eight hundred, Mr McKillop – that's the best I can do!'

The banker was frantic. He was sure he'd get a thousand sovereigns for it: the nugget was almost flawless, pure carat through and through. But this woman, this Irish woman – she was squeezing him, squeezing the life out of him. She knew what she had, and now here she was halfway out his door, headed for the enemy: the Port Phillip Savings Bank and that skinflint Smith. What was he to do?

As the door of the Bank of Australasia swung behind Ellen, it cut off the perspiring banker in mid-sentence: 'Seven hundred and –'

But it was enough.

Ellen let the door close all the way behind her and breathed a sigh of relief. She thought she had pushed him too hard. Now she would agree at whatever figure he'd offered, not push it to the eight – let him win a little. The fifty sovereigns could be her 'luck penny' to McKillop and the Bank of Australasia.

She composed herself, waiting until the door would be pulled open behind her. It was.

'Mrs Coogan, did you hear me? I said seven hundred and fifty sovereigns!' The little banker was now panting as well as perspiring.

'I said eight hundred guineas,' she countered, without the hint of a smile. She saw the look on his face – maybe she miscalculated, so she added quickly: 'But we won't fall out over fifty sovereigns, Mr McKillop. I think you've made a fair offer. Don't you agree, Mr Coogan?'

She had difficulty suppressing a laugh at the white look of disbelief on Lavelle's face. But he recovered quickly enough.

'Yes, I think it's a fair offer, Mrs Coogan,' he replied, as if it was what they had expected all along.

The banker's face at last creased into a smile and he dabbed at his brow, his handkerchief already damp.

'Do please sit down again, Mrs Coogan – and of course, Mr Coogan – and we will complete the formalities.'

The 'formalities' having been completed – seven hundred and fifty sovereigns bright now being the property of Mr and Mrs Coogan, and one gold nugget being the property of the Bank of Australasia, McKillop locked his door, wiped the moisture from his pince-nez, and sat back in his leather-upholstered armchair.

Oh, he hated bargaining with the Irish. Where did they get it from? Always pushing you to the edge, the Catholics. His father and King Billy were right about them: 'Never trust a *Taig*.'

But he had the nugget – at last.

For a few moments he feasted his eyes on his golden prize. Sydney would be proud of him. He was the first, the very first – and yes, there would be a gold rush, of that he was sure. But he had almost lost it – she had pushed him hard. The thought of it sent a shiver through his body. He bent to unlock the bottom drawer of his desk, in the same movement wiping away with his sleeve some droplets of perspiration he had missed with the handkerchief.

William Ferintosh McKillop, leading light of the Australia Felix Abstinence Society, carefully wrapped the gold nugget of the Ngarrindjeri in a soft chamois cloth and placed it into a corner of the drawer. Then he took out the bottle of single malt Scotch whisky he kept for times like this, and dispensed himself a 'stiff wee dram' of the pure gold liquid. 'Fit for a laird,' the banker named for a distillery, proclaimed with satisfaction.

Later that evening, Ellen looked out of her window at the Eagle Tavern and saw the banker race past the corner of Little Bourke and Queen Streets. She wondered where he was off to. Home, she supposed, anxious to tell his wife about the gold nugget he had bought from them and the hard bargain he'd had to get it.

Thanks to the *Taigs* and their damned nugget, William Ferintosh McKillop was late for his meeting at Melbourne's Orange Association, of which he was Grand Master.

He hoped the Association's upcoming celebration of King William's victory over the Irish at Aughrim would not attract the unpleasantness of last year. It was, after all, a long time ago. True, it was unfortunate that amongst the seven thousand put to the sword were women and children – he could not condone that. Nevertheless, 1691 was a significant date in the history of the Orange Association, and they should be allowed to celebrate it as they wished. He couldn't understand why last year Dr Palmer, the Mayor, had had the Riot Act read to him and his loyal brethren, followed by the ignominy of being faced down by the bayonets of Her Majesty's militia. And now the authorities had passed the Party Processions Act, prohibiting 'the exhibition of party symbols and to prevent the further public procession of antagonistic political societies.' He would call for its repeal tonight. They would not be denied the right to march freely where they willed.

Then his mind strayed to the Coogans and their gold nugget. Strange he hadn't seen them before. And the man was very secretive . . . McKillop had heard about the trouble brewing in Ireland – those Young Irelanders and the like stirring up trouble because of the so-called Famine. Could it be . . . No, it was too much to think they would be sent to ferment trouble in the colonies, or . . . to raise funds.

Two hours later, as he stood to prolonged applause, and pledged 'God and King William', William Ferintosh McKillop, King Billy's banker, wondered how much Irish insurrection the Bank of Australasia's seven hundred and fifty sovereigns would fund.

'I think we'll have to travel further, Ellen. To Sydney, maybe.' Lavelle looked up from the *Melbourne Argus*. 'There are no sailings from here to America. Look –'

She perched beside him on the chair as he pointed out a column headed 'Cleared out'.

Ellen ran her eye down the column:

Flying Fish, schooner, 122 tons, Clinch, master, for Hobart town.
Swan, brig, 149 tons, Carder, master, for Launceston.
Diana, brig, 103 tons, Lawrence, master, for Sydney.

She looked then at the 'sailed' section. It was more of the same – Hobart, Launceston, Sydney. There were no direct sailings from Melbourne to America.

'Maybe you should go back to Ireland now, Ellen – take a ship to England and go over from there,' Lavelle put to her, mirroring her own thoughts.

She grimaced at the idea of going anywhere near England.

'Oh, I dearly want to go home, Lavelle – the first moment I can, I want to,' she answered. 'But what if word gets out about . . .' she didn't want to say McGrath's name '. . . that man, and Coombes hears of it? He'll send word to Pakenham, thinking I've gone back there. I might be arrested, sent back out to Australia. I could lose the children altogether,' she said, clearly worried at the thought.

'But Coombes probably won't hear about it – the Overlanders will want to keep it quiet this time because whites were involved. Our story might be believed in court, whereas normally the Aborigines wouldn't.'

She wasn't convinced. Better to let things rest, settle down. If Coombes did hear and contacted Pakenham, now would be the wrong time to go. Next year some time would be better. It would all have blown over by then. No, she couldn't go back yet. Besides, she wanted to have something for them to come out of Ireland to – a new life in America. That would need time to build.

She resisted dwelling any further on the notion. She would stick to her plan – maybe not the full three years of Edith Pakenham's bond, but until next year, anyway.

Still, they shouldn't remain too long in Melbourne either, just in case word did get out about the Coorong business. Best out of Australia, but not back in Ireland yet.

Lavelle scoured the papers, particularly the columns headed 'Domestic intelligence', for any sign of 'intelligence' from Adelaide of their flight, or the Coorong affair. His heart missed a beat when he spotted the headline: 'Daring case of horse-stealing'. But it was a false alarm. The 'strayed stock' listing, while giving a description of six horses found straying, did not list the horses he had cut loose.

For Ellen, it was another insufferable delay. So much had befallen her since she set foot in Australia Felix – Australia the Happy – as the newspapers referred to this land, that all she wanted was to be out of it. She felt that once she set sail from Australia she would be homeward bound – even if she was taking the least direct route. Once in Boston, she and Lavelle – purely on a business footing – would establish a base there. Then she could return to Ireland and collect the children, knowing she had somewhere to take them, and the means to feed them. Like the ones who left America Beag, she would establish herself in Boston and tow her children after her, like links in a chain.

She never considered the possibility of bringing her children to Australia. And certainly not to Melbourne. She didn't like the bustling, brawling town, spreading out by the minute, topsy-turvy-like. It was full of squatters and Vandiemonians – convicts on ticket-of-leave, brought in from Van Diemen's Land as cheap labour for the squatters. And then there were the Pentonvillains, from the Pentonville Gaol in what the newspapers referred to as 'the mother country'. It was clear from the papers that some in

Melbourne were opposed to convict labour, fearing that the quality of society would suffer. But others didn't care, as long as there was a profit to be made.

And, she could see, it was all run from London, as Ireland was, the only difference being that here there was plenty for everybody. Why couldn't they ship more people out from starving Ireland, if they needed labour so badly?

Her eye caught two items in the newspapers Lavelle had been reading for word of ships. The first appeared under the heading 'Irish Relief Fund'. She read it aloud:

> . . . but little interest appears to be taken in the Fund; indeed, it must be admitted that the pockets of the Port Phillipians have already been pretty considerably drained for charitable purposes. On Wednesday last, the day appointed for the weekly meeting of the Committee, there were only four members in attendance, consequently no business was transacted.

'Can you believe it?' she said to him. 'Thousand upon thousands, dying in Ireland, and here every type of wealth and growth, and only four people try to do something.'

She read Lavelle the second piece – a letter:

> We have surely a right to some voice in the selection of the people to be sent out to us . . . swamping us with a purely Irish population. I do not object to such a population . . . only let them come in due proportion; let us not have them exclusively, so as to have our noble colony transformed into another Tipperary.

'Another Tipperary?' Lavelle said. 'More like another Van Diemen's Land . . . that's what they should be worried about.'

'It's like we're lepers,' she said, dismayed, 'everywhere we go.'

'Some of our own are the worst. There's enough Irish here to make that Relief Fund work. On Elizabeth Street today, I saw a couple of priests – Irish they were too. They should be leading the Relief Fund for their own country.'

'If we were staying in Melbourne, I'd help,' Ellen said, thinking out loud. But what she was thinking about most of all she did not say aloud.

She would have to seek out one of those Catholic priests and confess the grievous mortal sin she had committed against the Fifth Commandment – 'Thou Shalt Not Kill'.

Ellen was nervous as she walked towards St Francis Catholic Church on the corner of Elizabeth and Lonsdale Streets. What if the priest refused her absolution? Then her soul would remain blackened by mortal sin. The only thing that would be between her and everlasting damnation would be life itself.

The street was wide, brimming with life – men on horseback, carriages, bullocks hefting heavy drays, people everywhere. She passed the corner of Collins Street. On her left was Harris and Marks, with their London Mart and Liverpool Mart. Victoria House was on her right. Everywhere it seemed as if the colonists were trying to recreate their own little England, out here in this land as different from her own as it must be from England.

When Ellen knocked on the presbytery door it was opened by Father Patrick Ignatius Boylan, previously of Adam and Eve's Church, Dublin, and the first Catholic priest of Melbourne.

Ellen took in the round-framed glasses, high balding forehead and the bushy hair that curled over his ears. He didn't look too severe, she thought. He smiled at her, easing the knot in her stomach.

'Can I help you?' he asked genially.

'Father, I need to confess . . .'

'Confessions are this evening, my child.'

'I am in grievous sin, Father.'

Five minutes later, Ellen knelt in the small dark cubicle of the confessional, her eyes fixed on the side of the priest's face as he listened expressionless.

'Bless me, Father, for I have sinned . . . failed to observe mourning period . . . guilty of stealing horses . . . guilty of travelling alone with a man . . . neglect of my children . . . inflicted damage on my body, the temple of the Holy Ghost . . . engaged in pagan dancing and immodestly exhibited my body . . .' she drew a deep breath. 'And, Father, I killed a man in a savage rage. For these and all my sins, I am heartily sorry,' she rushed on, wanting to get it all out, finished with.

The priest turned and looked at her, his face only a few inches away.

'The man you killed – was it in defence of your person?'

'No, Father. He was an Irishman. He caused six of the Aboriginal children to be murdered, and some of their parents too. I don't know what came over me . . . I realize it is a terrible sin.'

'And the pagan dancing – you disported your body in front of the natives?'

'It was the death of my child!' she whispered in the dark.

'And you engaged in heathen burial practices?'

'It wasn't . . .' she hesitated. 'There was no Catholic priest.'

'Is there anything else?' he asked.

'What, Father?' Ellen was on tenterhooks, wondering what the priest was getting at.

'Anything else, my child?'

Could he sense she was holding something back, hadn't told him it all? It was the taking of human life that she had to get rid of, get forgiveness for. Not all this other business that the priest seemed to be more interested in. She hadn't wanted to tell him about Wiwirremalde, but it was as if he knew there was more.

'Well . . .' she began hesitantly.

'Go on,' he said.

'It was when my baby was dying . . . I . . . I asked Wiwirremalde – the medicine man of the Ngarrindjeri people . . .'

'What did you ask him?' the priest pressed, his breath pushing through the aperture between them.

'The *Slám*!'

There, she'd said it.

'The *Slám*?' he repeated, nonplussed. In his eight years in Melbourne, Father Boylan had heard of most every sin on God's earth. But not this one.

Ellen had thought that the priest, being Irish, would know what she meant, that she would be spared having to explain it further. But it was not to be. When she had finished, the priest sat in silence. Even in the dim light of the confessional, she could tell that the colour had drained from his face. She waited – was he going to refuse absolution to her? Was she going to have to leave the confessional, still in a state of mortal sin?

She was conscious of her knees starting to hurt her; of how cramped the cubicle seemed, the priest's face so close to hers. After what seemed an eternity he said, 'How long have you been in this fair land, my child?'

'Not a year yet, Father,' she replied.

'Not a year yet,' he repeated, and then paused. 'And in that period of time you have broken almost all of God's Commandments, and in a most grievous manner?'

'Yes, Father.'

'And have you not considered the scandal you give to others, as an Irish Catholic woman, by this . . . behaviour? To others of your gender, to your own race and creed, and to even the pagans with whom you consorted?'

'But –' she began, attempting to explain to him the spirituality of the Ngarrindjeri, the circumstances.

'There are no "buts" at the Last Judgement,' he cut across her chillingly. 'You are not contrite in heart!'

'But I am, Father,' she protested. 'I am heartily sorry for the life I took.'

'But not for these other transgressions. Without true contrition, I cannot dispense absolution. Return in a month when you are in a more contrite state.'

And with that he withdrew his face from the aperture and tugged the purple curtain across, cutting her off from him, darkening her to the Church and its sacraments. Stunned, she knelt in the darkness hearing the flap of his vestments pass outside her door. She listened as his footsteps hurried along the aisle – away from her – until they, and he, passed out of the church and out of her hearing.

Trembling all over she placed her hands down on either side of the space where, but a few moments previously, her confessor's face had been. Her face dropped on to the small lip of the aperture, disconsolate that her God had disowned her.

After a little while, she lifted her head to the cross in the corner of the confessional. Then turning to the crucified Saviour she prayed: 'Oh, Jesus, even if your priest has not, I ask You to forgive me, as You forgave the thief on the Cross next to You.'

Then she made an Act of Perfect Contrition: 'Oh, my God, I am heartily sorry for having offended Thee, and I detest my sins . . . because they displease Thee . . . I firmly resolve never more to offend Thee and to amend my life. Amen.'

She crossed herself and then left the church of St Francis.

'Listen to this,' Lavelle said to her, and he began reading aloud from the *Port Phillip Herald*:

The Irish horse Matthew, in a field of twenty-six starters, emerged victorious in the first ever Grand National Handicap Steeplechase at Aintree, Liverpool.

In the greatest test of mount and man yet designed, Matthew, a nine-year-old gelding, confounded critics of the opinion that the Irish are incapable of racing horses, by finishing ahead of England's pride, St Leger, to lift the purse of twenty-three gold sovereigns.

The attendance was put at over fifty thousand and so many had sailed from the Emerald Isle, and such was the amount in wagers riding on Matthew, that should he have lost 'tis said half the population would have had to flee that country.

'I'll wager the English didn't like that result,' Lavelle said. 'Maybe things are getting better back home.'

Ellen doubted that things could have improved that much – it didn't make sense. Lavelle continued reading from the 'Liverpool News' section:

Riots in City

The citizens of the mother country's second city, having suffered in three months alone the arrival of fifteen thousand paupers from Ireland, have said enough is enough. They have revolted and attacked the wretched hordes who swarm their streets and clog up their hospitals. Now the Guardians of Liverpool have invoked the provisions of the Settlement Act, and a sum of four thousand pounds has been collected – not to feed the hungry masses, but to send them home again . . .

Lavelle stopped reading. 'Nothing has changed, nothing at all,' he said, aghast at the news.

'Two Irelands,' was all she said.

The following morning, she and Lavelle decided they could delay in Melbourne no longer. With each passing day, they expected word to come from Adelaide, and awaited the constabulary's knock on the door.

Since the newspapers had not proved fruitful, they decided to go directly to the docks and enquire there.

They were in luck. At first it was the same old story – plenty of ships for Hobart, Launceston or Sydney, but for Boston they would first have to sail to Sydney.

He came to them, and Ellen liked him immediately. Captain Nathaniel West, master of the *Enterprise*, was middle-aged and of impressive height and build. A shock of white wavy hair, brushed back off the forehead, was linked to a short white beard which ran round the rim of the man's genial features. All of this set off by a pair of bright blue eyes.

He introduced himself and smiled. 'Mr and Mrs Coogan, I presume? I hear you are looking for a ship.'

Lavelle answered him. 'Are you sailing for Boston?'

'No, not precisely,' West answered, dashing Ellen's hopes momentarily, '. . .but I am sailing for Québec, not far north of Boston, and at first tide in the morning. I can accommodate two more fare-paying passengers.'

'How would we get to Boston?' Ellen enquired.

'Without mishap, the *Enterprise* should anchor in Québec well before the ice sets in. You could then quite readily sail from there to Boston, or, if you willed, travel overland from Québec.'

'We'll go with you.' She looked at Lavelle, her mind already made up.

So it was that Mr and Mrs Coogan took their leave of Australia for Québec City on the banks of Canada's St Lawrence River.

But Boston bound.

BOOK THREE

GROSSE ÎLE

41

Conditions aboard the *Enterprise* proved infinitely more pleasant than those on the *Eliza Jane*. Captain West was at all times solicitous; their quarters, though cramped, were the height of luxury compared to Ellen's previous experience; and the provisions were ample and varied.

Ellen had been concerned at the prospect of sharing married quarters with 'Mr Coogan' on such a long voyage, but Captain West had unwittingly come to her rescue. Welcoming them on board at first light, he had been most apologetic: 'I ought to have told you, Mr and Mrs Coogan, but the *Enterprise*, being a cargo vessel, has but limited space for passengers. I regret that the larger staterooms have all been taken; the two remaining will only accommodate one person – but they are adjoining. I trust this will not discommode you . . .'

'No, that is fine, Captain,' Ellen said, trying to keep the relief out of her voice.

There were six other passengers on the *Enterprise* apart from the young 'Mr and Mrs Coogan'. A French couple, Edouard and Marie-Claire Chabot, and their six-year-old son Phillipe, bound for Montréal. A prim, self-possessed little surveyor with the odd name of Thimble, who would remain with them as far as Valparaiso in Chile. A large, moustachioed gentleman named Mr Knatchbull, whom they gathered was a servant of the Crown. And then there was the Reverend James Bonney, an Anglican missionary from Somerset. He had been stationed in the Port Phillip District these past few years, but was now posted to Grosse Île, a small island thirty miles downstream from Québec City which had been used as a quarantine station for European immigrants since 1832.

Ellen took an immediate liking to the Reverend, a quietly pleasant man in his mid-thirties, and they whiled away many an hour in conversation. He knew much more than she did about their destination, and was only too happy to share his knowledge.

'Many of your countrymen,' he told her, 'fleeing the pestilence in Ireland, are perishing on the journey to Canada or on Grosse Île itself. While most are Roman Catholics, amongst them are scattered members of the Established Church who also suffer. Often they are deprived of our solace in their dying moments, because there are so few clergy and it is difficult to detect the members of our faith amongst the inhabitants of the fever sheds.'

'But does it matter, Reverend, who ministers to whom, when all the dying need is a comforting hand?'

'My dear lady, would that it were so simple. Each soul seeks to enter the Kingdom of Heaven by his own gate, lest he approach by the gate of another and it be closed against him. It matters indeed.'

'But don't all the gates lead to the same place, once you've passed through them?' she posed, a hint of mischief in her voice.

Reverend Bonney reflected for a moment, then asked her: 'Where is it in Ireland that you hail from, originally?'

Puzzled, she replied: 'Maamtrasna.'

'And is this a village or a town?'

'It is a village, Reverend.'

'And in what county does Maamtrasna reside?'

'In the county of Galway, near the border with County Mayo,' she told him, wondering where all this was leading.

'Precisely!' he said. 'See how, in a simple way, you have answered your own question?'

Ellen was perplexed. 'How?'

'Because, when I enquired as to from whence you came, you did not say County Galway, but Maamtrasna – your own individual place in the county of Galway. Then, you were quick to explain what Maamtrasna was not: that it was not in County Mayo. Yet, before everything, you are Irish, only then of County Galway. So, why is it that you define yourself first by village – the smallest unit?'

She thought about this for a moment, getting the drift of his argument. Somehow it didn't seem the same as the point she was making.

'It is because you, like all of us, prefer particularity,' he continued. 'We each need our own smaller identity, even though we belong to a larger grouping. The same applies in how we, His creatures, worship our Creator – each to his own beliefs. Each believing we are right, and that He has called us to be different.'

The pleasant and neat-haired Reverend Bonney was pleased with how he had made the point to her, and she let it go at that.

When the *Enterprise* hove-to at Valparaiso to disembark Thimble, Ellen and Lavelle took the opportunity to go ashore.

Never before had she seen mountains so high as those in the distance behind the Chilean port. The Andes, it seemed, reached through the outer skin of the earth and tipped beyond the blue edge of the sky into the very heavens themselves.

The people here spoke Spanish and were coloured – not the black black of the Aborigines, but an attractive hazelnut brown. They were beautiful to behold. Despite their obvious poverty, they displayed such infectious good-humour that Ellen would have liked to remain amongst them a little longer. The *ranchos* they lived in reminded Ellen of the *scailpeens* back home: a few sticks in the ground with some pieces of wood for a roof, topped off with a layer of grass and straw.

Fowl ran riot all over the place, and the streets were thronged with donkeys slung with *kishogues* similar to those used for carrying the turf in Ireland. At the roadside were bamboo stalls selling exotic fruits and dubious-looking cuts of meat, the stallholders seemingly unworried by the multitude of strange flying insects which landed on their wares and, once replenished, took off again, buzzing and whirring their noisy approbation. And amidst the hustle and bustle, oblivious to it all, children ran naked as the day they were born – free spirits.

Drawn by the sound of music, Ellen and Lavelle came upon a procession of people who appeared to be celebrating something – perhaps the feast day of a local saint. Then she noticed a group at the head of the procession, bearing aloft a wooden board on which reposed the body of a beautiful young girl, no more than six or seven years old. The child was dressed all in white, as if for a wedding, her hair garlanded with white flowers. At her head and feet, two large candles burned. Ellen watched, entranced. This, she learned, was an *angelito* – a little angel. White and pure, untainted by sin, the girl's direct passage to heaven was here being celebrated on earth with music and dance.

Lavelle, when he realized the nature of the procession, kept an anxious eye on Ellen. He knew that it would act as a poignant reminder of the passing of her own *angelito*, Annie, into the Aboriginal spirit world.

But Ellen was captivated by the beauty and the joy of the occasion, and returned to the *Enterprise* uplifted by what she had witnessed.

On leaving Valparaiso, the captain informed them that they would tack southwards along the coast of Chile to 'round the Horn'.

'This side, the weather will be even enough, but once we turn eastwards to round the Horn expect anything,' he warned.

Later, trying to assuage her fears, he told her, 'Mrs Coogan, the art of captaining a Cape-Horner such as the *Enterprise* is in knowing, not how to extricate oneself from troublesome situations, but how to avoid them in the first instance. You need have no worries – trouble, I avoid like the plague.'

He was true to his word. The *Enterprise* was a frenzy of activity in preparation for its voyage through the Straits of Magellan, and past Tierra del Fuego – the southernmost tip of the continent of South America.

The shipwright, a friendly young fellow known as 'Chippy', fixed what seemed only minor damage to her cabin door by putting in a whole new panel. 'For the next few days I won't have a minute to spare, miss! Doors, hatches, spars – everything that moves and doesn't move – I have to make it right for the captain. And caulk the decks an' all!' he said cheerily.

And every time she stepped on deck, she'd find the sail-maker busy with his needle and twine. 'Stops me stitches from rotting – beeswax it is, miss,' he explained when she stopped, inquisitive about his work. 'If I don't smother 'em in it, those westerlies would shred me sails in five minutes – and might do anyway!'

The ship's farmyard – the stalls and pens where the livestock were kept – was lashed down even more securely than before.

Lifelines were rigged along the deck for the crew to hang on to while working. Safety nets were rigged above the bulwarks to catch any crewman washed overboard by one of the giant waves they were likely to encounter.

But some excitement was to ensue before they ever reached Cape Horn.

The *Enterprise* had been making good progress against the Humboldt Current. In readiness for the westerlies ahead, the best sails had been broken out of the locker and a new mainsail had been set. The old sails, which would not now be used again until more clement weather was reached on the far, eastern coast of the continent, were being furled away.

Ellen watched, marvelling at the men as they hauled in the giant sails, singing their sea shanties, and heaving in unison to the rhythm of the songs, some of them swinging aloft on the ropes.

'"Norwegian steam", Mrs Coogan!' the captain said. Then, seeing her puzzled expression, he explained: 'It's a seafarer's joke. "Norwegian steam" is plain old-fashioned muscle-power, that's all. Though it won't be long, I'd wager, until all of this is no more –' He made a sweeping gesture that took in all the hauling and setting of the sails. 'Another five or ten years, and these beautiful old Cape-Horners will be replaced by steam-ships. Can you imagine it, Mrs Coogan?' he asked, a hint of something in his voice. 'Instead of seeing the great white sails of the tall ships rise on the horizon, all you will see is ugly black smoke darkening the skies.'

Suddenly the lookout on the fo'c'sle-head rang out his bell, once, twice, thrice.

'Three bells!' said Captain West, excusing himself. 'Something straight ahead. Probably whalers!'

He was right. Soon Ellen could see three large windjammer whaling ships.

'Thar she blows! Thar she blows!' the lookout shouted. Then, from out of the water halfway between the *Enterprise* and the whalers, Ellen saw a giant block-headed sperm whale surface, madly spouting water from his blow-hole as he did so.

'It's a bull, by the size of him!' Captain West ventured, having returned to her side. 'Now you'll see something. He must be worth forty barrels if he's worth a one!' he said, excitement in his voice.

The whale, all forty feet of him, thundered on ahead of them surrounded by blackfish. Now, in his wake, Ellen could see another, slightly smaller whale and just behind this one a very small whale indeed.

'The cow and her calf following the bull,' said the captain.

As the *Enterprise* neared the whalers, Ellen could make out the crewmen hard at work. The four boats slung to the starboard of the windjammers were quickly lowered into the water, each carrying six to eight men, some of whom rowed, while others sat clutching long steel poles.

'At the prow is the boat-steerer, or harpooner,' the captain pointed out. 'Watch him.'

The boats made straight for the on-coming whales, which were being herded towards them by the *Enterprise*. To Ellen, the boats looked like tiny pieces of flotsam pitted against the giants of the deep.

Two of the boats made for the great black bull, two for the cow, it seemed. But to her horror, Ellen saw these two boats bypass the cow, heading instead for the calf who trailed in its mother's wake.

'What are they doing?' she demanded of the captain, sensing something awful was about to happen.

'Perhaps you had better retire to your cabin, Mrs Coogan?' he replied, dodging her question.

She held firm, waiting for a proper explanation.

'When the hunt is over, you can return on deck, and perhaps we can engage in some gamming with the whalers – they're sure to be out of New England,' he said, still avoiding her question.

That was it.

'No, I'm staying here,' she said defiantly.

'Ma'am – as you wish!' The captain gave a quick bow, and then went astern.

Ellen watched as the man steering the leading boat of the second pair stood upright on its prow. He then drew back his arm and, in one swift throwing movement, cast his harpoon into the sleek back of the baby whale. Its cries cut across the ocean towards her, sickening her. The harpooner made no attempt to further harpoon the calf, and then Ellen realized what plan it was the whale-hunters had.

The mother, who had swum beyond the boats, now turned, summoned by the cries and thrashings of her calf. She would not leave while her harpooned baby lived. Back towards death the loyal mother came, an easy target now for the second of the two boats. The boatmen waited the certain enactment of the cow's fate.

Soon the harpoons bit deep into her, until she too cried and thrashed like her baby. She died, the trap sprung by love's fatal flaw. Only when the mother's death-throes were in their final convulsions did the harpooner in the first boat deliver the *coup-de-grâce* to the crying calf.

Meanwhile, cries of a different kind were emerging from the other two boats. The great bull had been speared thrice. But he battled wildly, his body and huge tail turning the waters about him into a seething mass of foam. Now, at the death-cries of his young, the giant leviathan turned and made directly for the killing boat. As he neared it, the massive jaws opened wide, revealing his awesome weaponry. Before the boat could take evasive action, the rows of fierce pointed teeth crunched down on its prow. It was splintered into firewood, the harpooner severed at midriff as if he had been no more than fowl meat. The severity of the attack catapulted the other members of the crew, more fortunate than their harpooner, into the water from which they were eventually rescued.

But the drama was far from over.

Ellen saw the mighty sperm whale, not yet finished with his attackers, roll in the water as if trying to rid himself of the harpoons. The ropes with which his tormentors had made him fast now became twisted. When he swam out to sea, the two boats were towed crosswise behind him in what she later learned whalers whimsically called the 'Nantucket sleigh-ride'.

'Jump! Jump! The bastard's going to sound!' the gallied sailors shouted, terrified of the watery grave that would be their lot if the whale sounded for the depths of the ocean.

As the men plunged overboard, Ellen saw the bull, black skin glistening, arch out of the water in all his power. Then he plunged downwards into the dark lairs of the sea, pulling behind him the two empty boats. She was greatly pleased at this, feeling some justice had been done.

'Floating palaces of sin!'

She gave a start at the sound of Reverend Bonney's voice. She'd been so engrossed in the battle between whalers and whale that she had not been aware that the Reverend and Mr Knatchbull had joined her. The Reverend was obviously not enamoured of whaling ships – or those aboard them.

'When those men leave shore on one of these expeditions, they leave their wives behind them – and, I am afraid to say, their souls too!' he gave her by way of explanation.

'Aye, Reverend, they've turned the Pacific Islands into a tropical whorehouse! Begging your pardon, Ma'am,' said Mr Knatchbull. 'More of your lot needed out here to put a halt to their gallop, Reverend. Mostly New Englanders, of course – not Her Majesty's subjects!'

Both Ellen and Reverend Bonney were surprised by this most unusual lack of reticence on Knatchbull's part.

'Indeed, Mr Knatchbull!' was all the Reverend would add.

The *Enterprise* and the nearest of the three whalers, the *Lucy Goodnight* of New Bedford, flagged each other, sending their communications over the bloodied brine of the Pacific that was between them.

Captain West approached Ellen, in obvious good spirits. 'Mrs Coogan, I am pleased to tell you that the *Lucy Goodnight* carries a woman aboard. Captain Brock's wife would be pleased to gam with you and Madame Chabot!'

Ellen looked at him askance.

'"Gamming" – it's what the ladies do out here!' he teased, before explaining: 'Visiting, talking. Originally it referred to a group of whales socializing together – no offence intended to the ladies, of course,' he laughed.

'I see.'

'Not many of the whalers carry wives . . . For various reasons,' the captain said, unaware of the discussion that had just taken place in her presence. 'But of late the ladies seem more determined to be with their men, gaining for the ships they travel on the name "petticoat whalers"!'

So it was that Mrs Almira Brock came and gammed with the ladies of the *Enterprise*, while Captain West and Lavelle gammed aboard the *Lucy Goodnight* with Captain Shubael Brock. Monsieur Chabot remained behind to watch over Phillipe. The Reverend Bonney and Mr Knatchbull declined the invitation to board the whaler, for different reasons. The clergyman again invoked 'Floating palaces of sin!' while Knatchbull cited 'the God-awful stench!'

Almira Brock of New Bedford was a handsome, dark-haired Quaker lady. Ellen estimated her to be somewhere in her midthirties. She was clearly delighted to see not one, but two other white women. The greatest surprise, however, was what she carried on board in her arms: a baby, not yet two months old, bright and beautiful as could be.

'She weighs all of fifteen barrels!' Almira Brock gushed at them delightedly – fifteen barrels of sperm oil being not an unworthy weight for a two-month-old!

'What have you named her?' Ellen asked, eager to hold the child, thinking of how such a short while it had been since she had cradled Annie in her arms.

'No name yet,' Almira Brock replied. 'The *Lucy Goodnight* had, until today, failed to raise a whale since the day she was born. It invites misfortune to name a child born on a whaler until such an event. Now, thanks to your captain, I can name her. I think it will have to be Patience – don't you?' she beamed at them.

So they gammed, and gammed, and gammed some more. Ellen learned how the whaling wives put in their time crocheting, and scrimshawing whalebones into clothes pegs and decorative ornaments. And she learned of New England, and Boston.

'Having regard both to learning and commerce, I would place no city in the New World higher,' the *Lucy Goodnight*'s petticoat whaler enthused.

'And the Irish in Boston?' Ellen ventured.

'The Irish . . . Indeed, Mrs Coogan, the wretches – begging your pardon – have landed in their thousands there, pauperized and diseased. And I am sorry to relate there has been much rioting and resistance to their arrival in Boston. But I am sure you will not encounter such difficulties, dear Mrs Coogan,' she hastened to reassure Ellen. 'Bostonians are, at the heart, warm, hospitable people.'

Reverend Bonney sat with them, and when, finally, Mrs Brock and her newly named fifteen-barrel baby were ready to leave, he presented her with two bibles.

'For the salvation of the men,' he explained.

'Reverend,' Almira Brock said to him in her pleasant, no-nonsense way, 'while Almira Brock, and Patience here, are aboard the *Lucy Goodnight*, no "wahine" will stand on her timbers. I'll warrant you that not a man aboard her will get the "ladies fever" before we dock again in New Bedford!'

Ellen was sure Almira Brock would have her way.

The captain's wife refused the two bibles, causing much fluster to the mild-mannered Reverend. Ellen fought hard to keep back a smile at this interchange between them.

She had a sense that, with women like Almira Brock setting an example for the wives of New England, it would not be too far a day before the South Seas were awash with whole flotillas of sin-empty 'petticoat whalers'.

Lavelle returned from the *Lucy Goodnight*, wrinkling his nose. 'Such a stench!' he complained. 'They were flensing the whale. Do you know, Ellen . . .' he asked mischievously, sensing her distaste at what he was telling her, 'in the tryworks – this big brick furnace – they have huge cauldrons for turning the blubber into oil – "the stink" they call it, and it is well named! Anyway,' he continued as she moved away from him, 'as I was leaving there was a celebration going on – it being some months since they decked a whale . . .' Lavelle paused and she moved even further away from him. He was enjoying doing this to her, she knew. 'And the men were actually throwing dough into these trypots. Can you believe it? They were deep-frying doughnuts in the "stink"!'

Before she could tell him she didn't want to hear any more, he threw something towards her.

'Here, I brought you this!' he laughed.

Involuntarily, her hands went out and caught the soft, greasy object.

Realizing at once what it was, and disgusted by his description of it, she dropped the offending doughnut and chased after Lavelle to reprimand him. But he had anticipated her and was too quick. She arrived just in time to see the door of his cabin close smartly behind him.

Later he came and apologized to her. She was more relaxed about it then, even laughed at the idea of it, though wrinkling up her nose. He sat with her a while, seeing how she had come back into herself since the terrible events of the Coorong. As they chatted, he had to fight back the urge to put his arm round her shoulders. But he knew she would resist, stiffen up and retreat from him. So instead he just continued to talk to her, content, from now on, with her nearness.

He talked of the sea, of the strange sights and places they had seen. She talked of America, telling him what she had learned from Almira Brock about Boston.

And, as they rounded the Horn at the other end of the world, away from its mountains and green valleys, they talked of home.

42

Ellen felt a great surge of excitement rise in her when, finally – having rounded the Horn without event, and pausing for only the briefest of stops at Buenos Aires, Rio de Janeiro and the West Indies – the *Enterprise* sailed into the northern Atlantic Ocean.

Now, at last, America was within her reach.

Once she got there, her children would be within touching distance, she felt. Never a day on the long voyage did she forget them. Never a night did she lay down to rest without counting every hair on their heads, every freckle on their faces, every goodnight kiss she had missed. Oh, how much they would have changed! Patrick would be taller, more grown-up, more like Michael. The twins, Katie and Mary – would they have grown more alike or more unalike? She hoped that Mary would fulfil the promise she had shown of coming out of herself more, and, who knows, maybe Katie would have settled down a bit.

She wondered if they were thinking of her. They must be, every day, just as she was of them. For the thousandth time she agonized over the decision she had made, wondering whether they would resent her for deserting them. Pray God nothing had happened to any of them – she'd never forgive herself.

And Annie – how would she tell them of Annie?

Lavelle had been a great source of strength to her. They had discussed the various things they might embark upon in Boston. His ability for looking beyond the immediate, which he had demonstrated previously in planning their escape from Australia, was even further evidenced in these talks. She sensed his growing affection for her, and his attentions, she had to admit, partly pleased her. But his behaviour towards her, if at times a little playful, was always respectful, and he never imposed himself on her. Thrown together in such close proximity, and given his obvious feelings towards her, the temptation to act upon his desires must have been great.

But he showed restraint, and, as a result, grew in stature in her eyes.

Her talks with Reverend Bonney had been another source of strength to her. While not revealing the reason why to him, she had, on many instances, brought up the subject of sin and forgiveness. As a result of these discussions she had decided what she must do. But she would not broach it with the Reverend just yet!

Ellen's recovery had been helped by the other company on board, also. Madame Chabot – petite, refined, demure – often sought Ellen's companionship, and from her, Ellen learned much about French Canada, its fur and timber trade, and its history. Captain West was always happy to answer her questions, whether they be about Boston and New England, or anything else, from his voluminous knowledge of the world and its ways.

Only Knatchbull remained distanced from them, though he was always polite to her in that superior way of his. The most they could glean from him was that his business in Québec had to do with the resettlement of Her Majesty's subjects.

So, before she ever reached the shores of North America, Ellen felt prepared. As if the names and places she had learned about were already known to her.

Yes, she was ready: her mind and body healed. She put her hand to her hair. Nowhere near as long as it had been – yet. But thicker, she thought, more life to it, and attracting much notice from the other passengers because of its colour. Even Reverend Bonney, to her surprise, had remarked: 'If I may, Mrs Coogan, I must compliment you on your hair – it is indeed your crowning glory!'

She had thanked him, pleased that he had noticed – and that he had not been too retiring to have made the comment.

Yes, she was ready.

43

The Canadian coastline in sight, and just a few days out of Québec, disaster struck.

The *Enterprise*, having safely negotiated the hazards of the South Seas, the Horn, the coast of South America, and now almost in its home waters in the Gulf of St Lawrence, was blown on to the rocks of Cape Breton Island, and foundered there.

Ellen was in her cabin at the moment of impact, having been driven below by a sudden North Atlantic squall. The force of the collision between the *Enterprise* and the east coast of Canada knocked her off balance. She heard the crunching sound as the rocks of Cape Breton held their ground, reefing the *Enterprise* below its waterline.

The next thing she knew her cabin door had crashed open and Lavelle was at her side.

'Ellen, quick!' he shouted, alarm all over his face. 'We're on the rocks!' Then he grabbed hold of her, pulling her after him out of the cabin.

'The sovereigns! I've got to get the sovereigns!' she shouted, trying to break free. Without the sovereigns she was at nothing.

She wrenched free of him as the *Enterprise* shuddered to a halt. Outside, she heard the bells, and the running, and the shouting, as panic set in. She steadied herself, and grabbed the heavy bag of coins, wrapping its strings about her wrist. If it was going to be lost, then she would be lost with it – but let go of it she would not!

Lavelle ran back and grabbed her again, dragging her up on deck. It was pandemonium: men ran here and there, some trying to lower the sails, Chippy, and a team, vainly trying to plug the great gaping holes in the ship's hull. Others bailed out the sea-water. Hen-coops and animal pens had sundered their fastings, crashing into the bulwarks and releasing the last of the pigs and chickens to career wildly, adding to the chaos. Only the *Enterprise*, with the wind still catching its white sails, was static.

Captain West looked panicked, for once, his credo of 'avoiding troublesome situations' in shreds about him on the Cape Breton rocks.

'The boats – lower the boats!' he ordered. 'Passengers first!'

'Ellen, a ship! There's a ship coming!' Lavelle shouted. 'It's English! It carries the Union Jack!'

As the saving ship approached their boat from downwind, Ellen and Lavelle were hit by the most nauseating of smells emanating from it.

'It must be a whaler,' Lavelle called to her. 'Nothing else could smell so foul!'

But it was not the carcasses of whales that the *Dove*, out of Liverpool, via Cork, carried. It was human carcasses – over four hundred of them – locked into a hold designed for the transportation of great swards of Canadian wood to a timber-starved Britain, but now carrying fare-paying passengers as ballast on its outward journey. In short, the *Dove* was a coffin ship.

They were winched aboard, their senses assaulted by the overpowering smell and the wailing, crying, grief and despair rising up to them from the steerage. This was accompanied by a deafening banging, as those still alive sought to escape from the dead and diseased beside them in the crude bunks, or littered on the floor beneath their feet.

The Reverend Bonney went straight to the *Dove*'s master, Captain McNab. 'These unfortunates below, Captain – they are in distress.'

'Well, Reverend,' the cross-faced captain replied, 'it's not of my making. The Colonial Office in London has decreed that "no ship should leave Great Britain empty, with so much surplus population". So, when we'd dropped our cargo at Liverpool, we were instructed to take on board these starving wretches at Cork for the return journey. But we took on board more than we bargained for, Reverend. We took on typhus as well – and that's what's down there!'

'And have you lost many souls en route, Captain?' Reverend Bonney enquired, visibly concerned.

'Ninety, at least, Reverend, with probably the same again diseased,' the captain replied matter-of-factly, adding, 'It's a miracle we haven't all been fevered!'

'The situation in Ireland . . . ?' Ellen interrupted, almost afraid to ask. 'What way is it this year?'

'The worst yet, ma'am,' McNab said bluntly. 'The blight itself didn't strike, but the peasants had no money for seedlings. And for fear of blight, others didn't plant. Disease now kills the Irish as much as starvation. "Black Forty-Seven" they call it,' the captain explained, confirming her worst fears.

'And have you members of the Established Church amongst your passengers, Captain?' Reverend Bonney then enquired anxiously.

'There could be, Reverend – I don't know. I expect they're mostly Roman Catholics.'

'Well, then,' the clergyman said, starting to move away, 'I must go below and find out. My ministry is now with the sick and the dying.'

'I'm sorry, Reverend, I can't let you do that,' the captain said, raising his voice. 'Those hatches will not be opened until we reach quarantine at Grosse Île. The crew wouldn't have it. I've lost two already to the disease. The last thing I want now is a mutiny!'

'At least let some fresh air in to them,' Ellen implored him.

'Not a chance, ma'am.' McNab was unshaken by her appeal. 'The very fumes carry the malady. I'll not risk it – they stay below!'

And that was it. The *Dove,* with its live cargo of contagion, drew anchor off Cape Breton Island and set sail for the quarantine station at Grosse Île.

While still in open seas, and before they had reached the mouth of the St Lawrence and Grosse Île, a further four hundred miles upriver, Ellen and Lavelle noticed McNab in a huddle with some of the crew. They watched, knowing there was something afoot. When the group finally dispersed, McNab approached them.

'Everybody aft for now,' he ordered. 'Manoeuvres on ship. Don't want accidents, do we?' he explained. Then he herded them ahead of him to the stern.

Once he'd ushered them as far astern as they could go, they turned just in time to see one of the hatches to the steerage as it was being opened. Putrid yellow fumes billowed up from below: a steam of excrement, urine and vomit which had, until now, been trapped below decks with its owners. Next, there emerged a noise like the din of the damned, clamouring to get out of their sulphurous hell. Then a gunshot sounded, warning the damned to stay below.

Reverend Bonney made to go to the helpless souls, but McNab who had pulled the pistol, pointed it at him. 'I'll shoot the first of you what makes a move: man, woman, child – or Reverend!' he threatened.

And so they stood, helpless bystanders, as those below handed their dead up through the hatch. The crew, without touching the corpses, attached grappling hooks to clothing or limbs and hauled the lifeless bodies along the deck, then hoisted them over the side, into the deeps of the ocean. Ellen's heart was wrenched at the sight, the indignity of it. No coffin, not even a shroud.

Beside her, Reverend Bonney commenced prayers for those so 'ignominiously departing their mortal coil'. As Ellen watched horror-stricken, one young girl was winched up, held aloft over the side, the movement freeing her hair. The sea breeze caught it for a moment. It was red and rich and long, like Ellen's, but not yet the growth of fourteen summers. As Ellen looked at her, she thought she saw the girl's head move, turn towards her.

'She's alive! Stop! Stop!' she shouted at the men.

But it was too late. Before the words were out of Ellen's mouth, the girl was released and went to her watery grave, her red hair like ribbons of sunlight streaming in her wake.

'The redhead was dead!' was the captain's only comment at Ellen's cry of horror at what she had witnessed.

'You could have held the winch,' Lavelle accused him.

In all, twenty-one bodies were buried at sea. The sheer callousness of it was worse than anything Ellen had experienced on her outward voyage to Australia.

How many of those poor twenty-one souls had been buried alive in the North Atlantic Ocean? One, at least, she was sure.

44

The St Lawrence River was unlike anything Ellen had ever seen. Even the mighty Murray was dwarfed by comparison. Now, as they neared Grosse Île, on the southern banks she saw the muddy beaches of the town of Montmagny. While to the north, Cap Tourmente looked down from high amidst the Laurentian Hills. The St Lawrence, being the main artery not only for the Province of Québec – or Canada East, as Knatchbull referred to it – but for the entire Canadian interior, was a-bustle with ships of every type. There were sailing ships, converted hulks like themselves, and steamships working the shorter runs along the North American coast. And dotted amongst them, row-boats and scows going back and forth between the islands of Île Aux Coudres and Île Aux Oies, and the shoreline.

The *Dove*, as required of a ship in contact with contagion, hoisted a blue flag at the fore masthead. She would not be allowed to proceed upriver to timber country until the authorities issued a Certificate of Health and gave permission for her to fly the red flag of clearance. Thus her first port of call was the tiny quarantine island of Grosse Île – only one and a half miles long, half a mile wide – in the middle of the channel.

'Dammit! We'll be here for bloody weeks! Just look at that –' shouted McNab, pointing upriver.

Ellen looked and saw about thirty to forty ships moored in the channel ahead of them.

'Every one of them has the blue flag, waiting on inspection and clearance. And every God-blasted one of them is ahead of us!' the captain fumed.

Ellen wondered if all the ships queuing up ahead of them were carrying people from Ireland. If, like the *Dove*, they all carried the dead and the diseased.

'Lavelle, it can't be this bad, can it? There must be thousands on those ships, and this is only one day – one day of "Black Forty-Seven"?' she asked, willing him not to give the answer he gave.

'I think we're only seeing the tip of it,' he replied. 'What must it be like back home for them?' he added, his voice trailing off.

McNab would have chanced bypassing the queue of waiting ships and heading straight for Québec, had he not noticed the cannon on the high ground of the quarantine island, and the redcoats who manned it. He had no choice but to drop anchor and wait in line.

As the *Dove* held position, Ellen decided the time had come to broach with the Reverend Bonney the subject she had been thinking about for some time now. It would delay her getting to Boston, maybe getting back to the children. But the needs of these people, her people, were grievous indeed. And she had sinned, sinned against life itself.

'Reverend, I want to ask something of you – a favour . . .'

'Yes, of course, dear Mrs Coogan – anything. Please ask!'

'I would like to remain on Grosse Île for a while – to work with the sick and the dying. It seems from what you have told me that there is a shortage of people to help, and I could be of some use.'

He looked at her, seeing she was serious, that this was no idle request.

'You have thought about this, I can tell,' he said. 'And it is a noble and generous thing which you propose. But in doing so, you expose yourself to great peril. You may contract typhus, or any of the other dread diseases in such a place. You may even die, Mrs Coogan.'

'And so might you, Reverend – and so we all will one day. That's no argument.'

'And what of Mr Coogan?'

'Leave Mr Coogan to me,' she told him. 'He may be of use also!' she quipped, wondering how she might present this to Lavelle. Maybe he would want to go on ahead to Boston.

'One final question, Mrs Coogan. May I ask what it was that motivated you to take such a step – to make this sacrifice?'

'You did, Reverend!' She smiled at him.

He seemed genuinely taken aback at this and flushed, a mite embarrassed by her directness.

Then, cutting off all further discussion as to her reasons, she said: 'Let's say that this is now between me and my Maker. The favour I ask of you, Reverend,' – she saw his eyebrows go up, wondering what this red-haired woman would come out with next – 'is that I would like to assist you in your work.'

'But you are not of the faith!'

'But I am, Reverend,' Ellen protested. 'As you are. And I promise not to confine my good works solely to those who are Anglicans, but to assist Roman Catholics also, and all who are needy!' she riposted, with a certain element of tongue-in-cheek.

The Reverend knew she was returning to their old argument about all Christians being Christians first, despite their differences. He could not gainsay her generosity, her ecumenism, so he said nothing.

'And I trust you will follow my lead in this, Reverend?' she couldn't resist adding.

Reverend Bonney realized then that, in the end, you always lost to this woman. This Ellen Rua.

'David, it all seems so hopeless, so utterly hopeless . . . Two successive years of blight, followed by a year of respite – yet no respite, the poor being afraid to plant or having no money for seed. What is to be done for them?'

Isabella Moore was exhausted. As conditions for the poor had worsened with Black Forty-Seven she had redoubled her own efforts to improve their lot, throwing herself into relief work with one of Canon Prufrock's many committees. Her husband, anxious that she was overtaxing her strength, had suggested a stroll in the gardens so he might broach the subject. Now he took her arm and led her gently under the sheltering canopy of the hundred-year-old yew trees which lined Addison Walk.

'You must not over-reach yourself, Isabella,' he said caringly.

'But what can I do to desist?' she responded. 'When the poor creatures are not dying of starvation in the most abject manner, then they are stricken with cholera, typhus, dysentery, scurvy, road fever, famine fever – there is no end to their suffering. There is neither work nor food for them, yet food leaves the country in great amounts. When they seek refuge, the workhouses are full.

No hospital in the country can cope with the number of the diseased and the dying. There are none even to bury the dead with respect and dignity. They lie in the ditches and on the roadsides ...' Isabella broke off, weeping. 'Oh, David, it upsets me so to speak of it – life is become without any dignity ... any dignity at all!' she sobbed.

'There, my dear ... you can do no more than you do,' Moore said, cradling his wife in his arms.

He held her a while, until the tears abated, then they resumed their walk through the gardens, him picking out for her this plant and that. The tall, willowy Pampas Grass from Argentina. The Irish plants, some of which he had brought to the gardens himself: the Killarney fern, the romantically named Blue-eyed grass.

Eventually, and as always, they ended up beside the Last Rose of Summer – *Rosa chinensis*. Isabella reached over and touched the full-faced flower of the single rose. Its satin-softness soothed the weariness that had grown over her these past few months. The pink petals of the rose ran in places to a red blush, and her fingers followed the changing hue.

'What a gift,' she said, in awed, hushed tones, 'to be able to stand in the presence of beauty – to see it, smell it, touch it, be one with it ...'

How many of those who had so horribly died in the last few years had ever seen a rose, or had time to stop and look? To escape, for one awful moment, from the incessant tramping of the roads looking for a single scrap of food. The thought entered her head for a moment of the woman McCallum had met in the mountains. The woman had denounced the Government, yet she had helped him with naming the wildflowers. Isabella wondered if the woman was still alive. She must ask David if he remembered the woman's name. Ireland was full of such women; believing in the same Christian God, yet bearing their children to milk-dried breasts, carrying the older ones on their backs. Good, strong, noble women, of a noble race. But poor. And doomed.

She felt the overwhelming sadness come over her again and, as her fingers slowly caressed the rose petals, Moore heard his wife, his beautiful Isabella, haltingly, movingly sing:

'Tis The Last Rose Of Summer,
Left blooming alone;
All her lovely companions
Are faded and gone . . .

So soon may I follow . . .

Later it seemed to him that she had sung as if she knew.

45

Four days they waited, moored in Quarantine Pass off Grosse Île with the dead and the dying, as the forty ships before the *Dove* underwent inspection.

At last, the doctor, the priests and the soldiers came on board.

'Quarantine until further notice,' ordered George Mellis Douglas, Medical Superintendent of Grosse Île. 'And all passengers to be transported on to the island for observation and treatment.'

The new dead amongst those providing ballast for the *Dove* were winched out of the ship's hold and unloaded by the priests and the military, and Reverend Bonney. They were placed into the flat-bottomed scows and ferried to land for burial. As before, the crew would not touch the bodies and used hooks to drag them along the deck.

After the dead had been dealt with, the yellow, vacant-looking spectres of the living were taken off. With their expressionless faces, they seemed to Ellen somehow more lifeless than the dead that had gone before them. But the foul stench that came off these walking dead was so repellent in itself as to almost drive pity and charity away.

'Some won't see the day out!' she said to Lavelle. 'Isn't the state of them just pitiful? How could they send people out here like this? It's a death sentence!' She turned away, finding the sight of her people too harrowing to bear.

'Death if you stay, death if you go – what a choice!' Lavelle said, numbed by the horror of it all. He wondered whether she would reconsider her decision to remain on the island and work with the dying. Whatever happened, he would stay with her.

Then the 'healthy' were disembarked.

The difference between the healthy and the diseased was barely discernible. Almost forty days between decks in a space designed for carrying timber had seen to that. Decks which had no light-giving portholes, no air-giving ventilation save for a few hatches, which, for the latter part of the voyage, had remained battened down. Thus had the 'paying ballast' been entombed in the floating coffin that was the *Dove*.

'Lord God, have pity on those suffering, and have mercy on those who caused it!' the Reverend Bonney said, in front of McNab, stricken at what he was witnessing.

They travelled to the quarantine island with Dr Douglas, who left McNab with orders to disinfect the *Dove* with lime.

'I am delighted you are joining us, Reverend. And Mrs Coogan, too. Any help is most welcome,' the doctor said to them. Then he told them about the island itself.

'Grosse Île was first opened to prevent a cholera epidemic which had swept the world from sweeping Canada. It has remained open since. After cholera, it was smallpox. Now it's typhus. So far this year, we have already lain some five thousand souls to rest, many fallen with typhus. Our role is to prevent the disease from reaching upriver to Québec and Montréal. Clergymen and nurses are also afflicted by the contagion. You must exercise extreme caution whilst on the island,' he warned them.

They landed at the quay on the western section of the island. Close by was the police station, Mr Bradford's store, and the angular-shaped buildings which provided shelter for the immigrants. Further back, at a distance removed from the hospitals, and shelters of those who could afford no better, were houses for 'respectable families'. Nearby were the Catholic chapel and presbytery. To the far south of this western sector was Grosse Île's highest point, Telegraph Hill. Here, from what looked to Ellen like a large wooden cross, signals were sent by semaphore across the St Lawrence to the mainland, and from there through other relay stations onwards to Québec.

Towards Back Bay were the Protestant and Catholic cemeteries.

The landing place was shallow, only suitable for the row-boats that now carried them to shore. Along the spine of the island, dividing it in two, was a high rocky ridge which confined all of the island's activities to this, the near shore. But Ellen could see that the island itself was quite well wooded. Above all, the flag of the Union Jack floated high, Grosse Île being under the command of the military.

Nurses were in severe shortage, Ellen learned. Many feared to work on the island. Those who did come, and who were then forced to leave – through fatigue or illness, or who just died – were even more difficult to replace. The medical staff and the clergy worked round the clock, there seeming to be an endless line of ships in Quarantine Pass, queuing up to disgorge yet ever more diseased Irish immigrants on to the island. It was estimated that "Black Forty-Seven" would see some ninety thousand arrive on Grosse Île, three times the number for the whole of the previous year. Fifty thousand directly from Ireland, the remainder Irish migrants from Liverpool and the other English ports.

Ellen was dismayed, almost rendered useless, by the sheer magnitude of the numbers.

'What must it be like at home?' she said to Lavelle after her first day in the fever sheds, shocked by what she had seen there. Made of boards, the fever sheds or 'Lazarettos' had been prefabricated in Québec during the summer and erected on the island in August. Ellen wondered what on earth it could have been like before there were sheds to house the sick.

She worked, and she worked, and she worked, trying to stem the tide of human misery. Some food here, a drop of water there, a few words of comfort and hope in another place. Not much time for anything save, 'What's your name?' and 'Where do you come from?'

And despite all her efforts, they died around her, by day and by night, and the next day, and the next night, until their faces and names were all just a blur to her.

Lavelle and the men ferried the dead from the fever sheds to the Dead House in wheelbarrows, then buried them so quick and so shallow that downwind you could smell the decomposing bodies, even though they were in coffins.

One evening, Ellen went to what some called the 'Irish' Cemetery. Ringed by trees and small bushes, and the waters of Cholera Bay, it was a peaceful bower away from the yellow madness of the fever sheds. Beneath here lay the remains of five thousand of her people.

'Five thousand!' she whispered into the breezes that blew up along the St Lawrence. Unmarked and unmourned for, God help them! One shallow mass grave in a green field across the ocean.

She knelt in the wet grass to pray over them. Only then did she notice the eerie contours of the 'Irish' Cemetery.

'Oh, God! Lazy beds – lazy beds!' she said aloud as her eyes picked up the narrow ridges in the ground, running parallel to one another. For a moment she half-expected to see the green stalks with their white flowers sprouting out of the ridges of graves. But here were no life-giving lumpers awaiting harvest. Here lay instead the final remains of those who had fled the blight on the lumpers, and the inept response of a hostile government.

She waited a while in silence, deep in her thoughts. The words of Dr Douglas burned in her mind: 'In this secluded spot lie the mortal remains of over five thousand persons who, flying from pestilence and famine in Ireland, found, in America, but a grave.'

And he had told her of those who tried to save them, like the young doctor from Dublin who had arrived on Grosse Île earlier that year, on 19 May. Only in his twenties, Dr Benson had, like herself, decided to stay and help. Eight days later he was dead from the disease.

What would be her own fate? She had been careful – as far as she could be. Washed daily and checked her hair and body for the lice which carried the typhus. Perhaps she would have been better off without her hair, she thought ruefully.

Ellen worked wherever she was needed. Despite her earlier plan, she seldom met with Reverend Bonney in the course of her work, and when they did come into contact for a fleeting moment both were too busy to indulge in the long leisurely discussions she had enjoyed so much on the voyage there.

With frightening regularity, the ships came and went, disembarking their deadly cargo. The death registers of both Catholic and Anglican chapels added daily to the litany of those lost to typhus. The fever sheds grew so overcrowded that the overflow had to be housed in tents.

Those released from quarantine were taken upriver by steamship to Québec. For 'healthy' immigrants a quarantine period of six days was considered adequate. The error proved fatal, it later being learned that the disease could have an incubation period of up to twenty-one days. Some, initially showing no sign of the disease, carried it into the citadel, some carried it further – to Montréal. In both cities thousands died.

As a result, some began to fear the immigrants. Two thousand rioters attacked the immigrant hospital in Québec, believing it to be the source of cholera in the citadel. But such attacks were the exception rather than the rule. In general, Ellen marvelled at the French Canadians. Threatened with disease, over-run by destitute immigrants, they displayed extraordinary generosity. Bishops and clergymen of every denomination came to the island from Québec, Montréal, and elsewhere, and worked to exhaustion, some even offering the ultimate sacrifice of their lives. The doctors and nurses too, did not spare themselves in their service to the sick and dying. But it was the stories that came back to her of ordinary citizens, and the organizations and societies they set up to assist the tens of thousands who arrived pauperized from Ireland, which most impressed Ellen.

One day in the fever sheds she had come upon a woman called Mary O'Donnell from Scramogue in County Roscommon. Mary's husband had not survived the voyage, and her two boys had died on the island. Broken-hearted and riddled with typhus, Mary O'Donnell had at last left behind the sorrow of the world she knew. She had been the same age as Ellen. Beside Mary's corpse sat her three-year-old daughter, Ellen. Unaware that her mother had died, the child still played with her mother's hand, still talked to her mother's prostrate body.

Ellen took the child up into her arms. 'What's going to become of you at all, *a Ellen bheag*?' she said, cradling the child to her. 'You poor little thing, nobody left at all in the world to you!'

'God will provide for her, Ellen,' said a voice from behind her. It was the young Catholic priest, Father McGauran. The priest, only a year out of the seminary in Québec, had already contracted typhus on his first visit to the island in May. Upon his recovery he had insisted on returning again. He looked tired now, grossly overworked. She knew that the young County Sligo man would often go three, four, or five nights without any sleep, so great was the demand upon his time. So great his commitment.

'But who'll take her? She can't stay here with no one to mind her.'

'The good families of Québec will take her. They have already taken hundreds like her through the parishes,' said Father McGauran. Then he told her how the French Canadians, and the settled Irish, had opened their hearts and their homes to the orphans of Grosse Île.

News of this goodness lifted Ellen's spirits, kept her going, when she, like Father McGauran, foundered on her feet. There was hope after all.

She didn't see much of Lavelle, given the long hours she worked. When she did meet him he was shocked at how she looked.

'Ellen, are you all right?' he asked, taking her by the shoulders, worry written all over his face.

'Yes, I'm fine, just tired, that's all,' she replied.

'You've done enough. We should leave,' he said. 'Get to Boston before the ice comes and freezes the river.'

'I can't leave just yet. They're dying in there, Lavelle, day and night – children being turned into orphans every day,' she said, fighting him.

'You can't save them all, Ellen. Think of yourself, and your own children!'

She looked at him. He was right. 'I'll give it two more weeks,' she said, feeling the tiredness descend on her. 'The numbers will be easing off now until the island shuts down in November. We'll go before the ice comes.'

She smiled at him, thankful for his concern.

'I'll be ready,' he said, returning her smile. 'But in the meantime, get some rest.'

She didn't. For the next two weeks she would give her all – then her month's penance would be done. Then would she go to the young priest from Sligo and ask forgiveness for her sin.

It happened during the third week of her time on Grosse Île.

It was evening-time. Having already worked elsewhere throughout the day, she was tired when she reached the Lazaretto. Too tired to read the register – who had come, who had left, who had died.

She walked between the rows of bunk-beds. The smell was foul.

They had washed the bedding and put it out to air, but then the rains had come. Now, some had no bedding, only the thinness of a blanket between their naked bones and the hardness of the wooden bunks. As ever, the moans of the sick and dying, and the grief and *ullagoning* of those bereaved, filled the Lazaretto. Yet – and it seemed a miracle to her – still they bore their suffering with great dignity and forbearance. She had witnessed the same thing at home, among the famished and the starving. As if this earth had nothing more to offer them, nothing worse it could do to them. And death and heaven was their only hope.

She heard someone retch at the far end of the Lazaretto and grabbed a water can and a cloth. If it was in a top bunk, then the vomit would drip through the boards, or slide down the sides of the bunk on to the unfortunate person below. Not an uncommon problem for her to deal with. With the advances of the disease some of its victims seemed to lose all control over bodily functions. At first she had found this work nauseating and had to turn away, couldn't look at what she was doing – and so didn't do it properly. 'It's not meant to be easy,' she had told herself. And, inspired by the devotion of others, she had trained herself to control the impulse to look away. Now this work bothered her not. Weren't they a lot worse off than she was?

She was returning the water can to its place, having finished her chore, when first she heard it through the din that always filled the fever sheds. Then the sound stopped. She couldn't identify it, but there was something familiar about it. Then the doctor called her to the other end, and she hurried away, forgetting the sound she had heard. Later she heard the sound again. She stood alert, listening. To begin with it was almost a whispering, then a low murmuring, not strung together as it should be. Then, as it grew in strength, the other noise subsided, as those suffering seemed comforted by the sound, soothed by it. Ellen traced it to one of the bunks in the far corner. Slowly she walked towards it, disbelieving what she was hearing. She stepped closer. The sound stopped for a moment as if sensing her closeness. When she moved again, it restarted.

> Oh my fair-haired boy, no more I'll see
> You walk the meadows green . . .

It was her song – and sung in her way!

She moved forward quickly now, sure of the sound, sure of where it was coming from.

She moved out of the light into the shadow of the corner where the sound was coming from and approached the bunks. It was the top one.

> '. . . my fair-haired boy to see . . .'

She felt the hair rise at the back of her neck. It was like a signal from the past, a message from the dead. It was her song for Michael. But who was the singer?

'Roberteen? Roberteen Bawn! What . . .'

The words flew out of her mouth. Confused, stunned, she could only gape as the pale yellow hair and the pale yellow face of the boy-man who had been singing turned fully to her.

'Ellen! Ellen Rua! I knew I'd find you!'

She clasped his hand in hers. Its flesh was shrivelled and shrunken – cold to the touch.

'Roberteen! Oh, Roberteen! I'm so glad to see you, *a stór*!' she tumbled out the words. 'So glad!'

He smiled back, the light for her in his eyes, brighter than ever she had seen it before. Brightened by the sickness.

'How . . . how did you get here?' she gasped, settling the blanket around him. 'Here, let me get you some water first,' she broke off.

When she returned, she held the water to him and he reached for the touch of her hands.

'Oh, Ellen,' he said, brokenly, 'it's all gone back home, all gone!'

'What's gone? Roberteen, tell me!'

'The houses are all thrown down, the people destroyed with the hunger . . .' he told her, a far-away look in his eyes. 'Things was that bad we even had to keep in the dog for fear he'd be eaten!' He gave a little laugh.

'And the people?' she pressed him, hoping for something, some little *bitteen* of news of life in her valley.

He looked at her, and slowly shook his head. 'No, Ellen, not a fire, not a wisp of smoke. Them that's not lying dead up on the Crucán is in the workhouse, as good as dead – or like me.'

'How did you get away, Roberteen?'

'Pakenham and that divil's melt Beecham evicted whoever they could and the crowbar brigade battered down the houses. They even went after the *scailpeens* on the side of the mountains, and drove the people off Pakenham's land and back along the road towards Westport and Castlebar. But the workhouses couldn't take them all – these days, they're closed, more often than not, for want of money. Then Pakenham said he'd put the rest of us on a ship, if we left peaceably . . . and, sure, what could we do? We had no choice, Ellen . . .' The tears filled his eyes.

'I know, Roberteen, I know. You didn't run away – none of us did – we were forced out!' she said, trying to console him. 'And Martin and Biddy?'

His grip on her hands tightened.

'They wouldn't come with me, Ellen – said they was too old to be uprooting themselves. I didn't want to go then either . . .' He started to cry again with the memory.

'Sshh now, Roberteen. They were right to make you go. And, sure, maybe things have improved for them since,' she said, knowing in her heart that this was not the case.

At last the question she had put off asking him – dreading what the answer might be – came out. 'Roberteen, the children . . . ?' she asked, trying to steady her hands.

'I told the Shanafaraghaun man what you told me, Ellen – I did,' he replied, his mind set off by her question.

'Yes, Roberteen, but Patrick and Katie and Mary – is there . . . is there any news of them?'

'We put him in the lake – me and the Shanafaraghaun man . . . We put Beecham in a big sack with stones – dropped him into Lough Nafooey . . .' He laughed. 'And he yelling and kicking to get out.'

His mind was altered, she knew. She waited till he was finished, then asked him again. He looked at her. Her heart sank as he shook his head.

'I didn't hear no news, Ellen – only that you went off on them to Australia . . . Where's Annie?' he asked of a sudden, as if his memory had been shaken.

Ellen didn't know what to think. He had told her nothing . . . That was probably good. If anything had happened to them, then Bridget would somehow have got news back to the valley . . . But he was rambling . . . mightn't know . . .

She answered his question about Annie. 'No, Roberteen. Annie is in Australia – a fever . . .'

'A fever,' he repeated. 'And what happened to your fine *dos* of red hair?' His fevered mind leapt on to the next question, not grasping what she was telling him.

'Oh' – she put her hand back to the red tresses that hung just below her neck – 'I lost that, too, in Australia,' she said, not thinking of it, only wondering whether her children were still with Pakenham. Whether they were still alive . . .

'And O'Connell is lost too. The Liberator is dead,' Roberteen was on to something else again. 'The Shanafaraghaun man'll be busy now.'

She thought of the man who had been with Michael when he was shot – the shadowy figure who was the only guarantee of her children's safety. What would happen now, with O'Connell dead? Would the Shanafaraghaun man and his Young Irelanders cause a revolution?

Roberteen's hand twitched in hers. She looked at him closely. He was very ill. Dying. No sign of the intensity he always had when he talked to her. She put her hand to his forehead, and he moved into her touch.

'Ellen, d'you remember the summer mornings, before the hunger came? You'd be at the lake . . . And I'd . . . I'd be watching you . . .' he asked, his face brightening.

She smiled down at him, brought back to the needs of the moment.

'Yes, Roberteen, indeed I do – you *rascaleen*!' She brushed back his hair with her hand.

'And the day the lumpers were lifted, you bolted the door on me?' He gave a little laugh, his mind focused now for a moment – on her.

'Yes,' she said, letting his memories bring back her own. Wasn't she badly off that day doing that on him, and he only a love-struck *gasúr*.

'And the *céilí* and Pakenham,' he went on – all the memories he had stored of her coming out now in a torrent. 'I near knocked him sideways off the horse.' He stopped, as if wondering whether to go on.

'Yes, Roberteen, I do. You were very brave that day – for me.'

'Oh, I was . . . I was. I wouldn't let Pakenham or no man put upon you. And . . .' he paused again, and she wondered what it was he wanted to get out. 'And . . . you sang the song for me, Ellen.'

For a moment it almost escaped her. Then she realized – remembered the evening. The priest, Father O'Brien, had wanted her to dance, but she wouldn't. Then he had laid it on her to sing instead, and to keep him from asking questions about her condition, she had agreed. She had sung 'The Fair-Haired Boy' for Michael, but remembered seeing Roberteen's face through the crowd as she sang. The boy had thought she was singing it for him – Roberteen Bawn. Fair-haired Roberteen! Oh, the poor *gasúr* . . . She was so stupid. He had kept the song with him all this time.

'I did, Roberteen,' she lied, as his features crinkled with delight. 'Would you like me to sing it for you again, *a stóirín*?' she asked him, softly, in the voice she would have used to one of the children.

'I would, faith, Ellen!' he said, all excited. 'But first, do the Mayo Moon with me . . . And put me sitting up here till I see out the window!' he went on, pleased with himself that she was taking notice of him, treating him like a man.

She had to smile at him. However far gone he was, he didn't forget anything – not a thing that had happened between them. She propped him up against the wall of the Lazaretto. God, he was no heavier than a child, all skin and bone!

'Roberteen, will I get the priest for you?' she asked, thinking he wouldn't last long now. 'There's a nice young priest here from the County Sligo.'

'No! No!' he said, shaking his head emphatically. 'No priest!

Don't go away, I want you to stay with me, Ellen. I'll be all right – no priest!'

And, sure, he'll be all right, she thought. Wasn't he, this boy-man, not yet twenty-one years, only a *duine le Dhia*, an *angelito*. 'Twas few and far between his simple sins were.

'I won't go,' she assured him.

He peered out of the window. 'Is there a moon at all in this place?' he asked, emboldened by all that had passed between them.

'Look out there, across the river,' she directed him. 'See the lights? That's Montmagny. Now, look up over Montmagny . . . See it?'

'I do! I do!' he said, excitedly. 'But it can't be a Montma . . .' he stumbled over the strange-sounding word. 'It has to be a Mayo Moon or it won't work!'

And so, the two of them transformed the Québec moon over Montmagny into the Mayo Moon over Maamtrasna. The mighty St Lawrence river became Lough Mask, as together, they recited the old lovers' folk-rhyme:

> New moon, new moon, new moon high
> Show to me my true love nigh
> Show her face, her skin so fair
> Show the colour of her hair
>
> Light my dreams this night so she
> May in your light appear to me
> New moon, new moon, let me see
> If one day we will married be.

When they had finished, both fell into silence. Each with their own memories of that night of the Mayo moon when she had crept up on him, caught him with the handful of earth behind his back – part of the ritual of making the wish come true.

'She's here now,' he said, looking straight at her.

'I know, Roberteen, I know,' she smiled at him, squeezing his hand. Remembering, from before, this exact moment – the awful awkwardness of it. He had wanted to kiss her, but she had broken the moment. 'The last time, Ellen, I . . . I wanted to . . .' he faltered, not so sure of himself now.

She kept looking at him, her heart going out to this fair-haired boy who loved her with unswerving loyalty and devotion. She knew he was about to speak, about to ask her. But she would not let him, would not cause him to do it – to beg. Instead she reached her fingers to his lips. 'Sshh,' she said. 'You'll break the spell.' And then she leaned over him, drawing her fingers away, replacing them with her lips. And she kissed him tenderly on his almost lifeless mouth. As she let her lips linger there for a moment, she felt his arm reach up past her shoulder – to her hair.

'Ellen . . . Ellen Rua,' he said, his fingers feeling out the redness of it. '*Buíochas*,' he thanked her. '*Buíochas do phóg an dorais.*'

She drew back from him. What was he saying? Thanking her for 'the kiss for the road' – a kiss for dying.

'Ah, shush now, Roberteen – no talking like that. You're not ready to go yet – you have to wait here a little while with me,' she said, knowing his moment was soon.

He looked at her – the old smile on his face – serenely happy to be with his Ellen Rua.

'Now sing the song, Ellen,' he asked of her, all the awkwardness gone out of his voice, all the boyishness vanished. Ready to go now – like a man. Everything he had always wanted, settled at last. It was beyond words between them, so she took his hand and sang for him.

There, in the fever sheds of Grosse Île, the woman and the man were framed in the window of the Lazaretto. He looking out across the wide Saint Lawrence, at the moon hung low over Montmagny; she singing out of the shadows, out of the darkness of death all around her, singing him into the light.

> 'Oh my fair-haired boy, no more I'll see
> You walk the meadows green . . .
>
> Your ship waits on the western shore
> To bear you o'er from me
> But wait I will e'en to heaven's door
> My fair-haired boy to see.'

She felt the squeeze on her hand – knew he was gone then – but never opened her eyes; sang out the song to the end. When she did open them, his were closed.

Roberteen Bawn, the fair-haired boy, was at last at peace.

46

A week later she fell ill.

At first it seemed as if she had simply been overtaken by lassitude, she was so weak, so listless. But Dr Douglas' examination confirmed the worst: 'She is stricken with the fever.'

Ellen could hear them talking about her.

'Rest, fresh water, plenty of food – gruel or soup,' the doctor ordered. 'And change the straw on her bedding. It's probably from that source the contagion came!'

Her own view as to the source of the contagion was different, but she was not saying.

'She was so desirous to help the afflicted that she put herself at risk,' said Reverend Bonney.

Lavelle was angry. 'She can't be left here, in the fever sheds,' he challenged them. 'The place is foul and reeking with disease. She'll not survive in these circumstances – she'll have to be moved!'

'Mr Coogan is correct.' It was the young priest from Sligo. 'When I was so afflicted, it was only my removal away from here to Québec that allowed my recovery. We must do no less for Mrs Coogan – she deserves better than we can offer here,' Fr McGauran said.

'I emphatically concur!' the Reverend Bonney chimed in.

Dr Douglas therefore arranged for Ellen to be transferred to the Hôtel-Dieu Hospital, 32 Rue Charlevoix – the place where Father McGauran himself had been sent to recover from his bout of what was variously known as *an fiabhras dubh,* ship fever, the malignant fever, and the Irish ague: typhus.

'Will she come out of it, Doctor?' Lavelle pressed the Medical Superintendent, worried for her.

'If we have caught it early enough, then ... with the more individual attention she will get in Hôtel-Dieu, she may well be saved. But if the ague persists, then I am afraid, Mr Coogan, that her heart, weakened so, will fail.'

Within days, her lassitude had turned into fever. Ellen's chest and abdomen had also begun to exhibit the spotted rash characteristic of typhus. As the fever mounted, her mind began to wander where it would, beyond her control. Spectres from the past rose up before her: Pakenham; Sheela-na-Sheeoga; Annie – her tiny hands reaching out, the small voice calling – '*a Mhamaí, a Mhamaí!*' Then Ellen had a knife in her hand – she was painted and wild, running towards somebody. Somebody who had his back to her. As she raised her hand to deliver the death-blow, he turned, arm raised in protection, terrified, calling on her to stop.

It was Michael! She tried to stop herself but it was too late – the knife sank deep into his neck. She had murdered Michael!

Sometimes, she was aware of the comings and goings of people as they tended to her, trying to force food and water into her unwilling mouth. She fought them, believing they were poisoning her, punishing her for Michael's death.

Someone sat beside her most of the time – she wasn't sure who. But in the in-between moments of non-delirium, she was aware of a presence.

Then, somebody was burying her. Praying over her. Putting the sign of the cross on her forehead and on her eyes and mouth. Anointing her with the oils of the dead.

Only she wasn't dead.

But the voice continued to mumble over her, consigning her to Lavelle's wheelbarrow, to be transported to the Dead House. There, she was put into a wooden box. She shouted at them, but they couldn't hear her. The Reverend Bonney and Father McGauran looked solemn and mumbled faster and faster in the strange tongues. Then they whispered to each other about her, as if she were already in the ground, saying things like, 'Mrs Coogan . . . dedicated woman . . . So sad for poor Mr Coogan. *Requiescat in pace.*'

They stopped mumbling then, and there was silence and she felt herself being lifted. She was going to be buried under the shallow earth of the lazy beds in the Irish Cemetery!

'No! No! No!' she banged and kicked at the sides and top of the wooden box.

They didn't hear her!

Out through the slatted timber, she could see the Canadian sky. She could see arms – strong hairy arms, the arms that lifted her, covering part of the slats at each side, blocking out the light. The movement stopped and she felt herself being lowered, heard the thud of timber on timber, as her box was placed on the one beneath it. She tried to raise herself up, put an eye to the slat above her. If they couldn't hear her, then perhaps somebody would see her looking out at them – and stop it all!

She could only raise herself a bit. There were people outside – she could see their feet. She made one great effort to lift herself.

Yes – she made it!

Now she could see. The feet with the black shoes had white stockings and long black skirts above them. The hands of those in the skirts were holding prayer books. Their faces still hidden from her.

The other feet, the ones with boots, had rough trousers tied up with pieces of string. The hands of the boot-people had spades in them.

The owners of the small bare feet were more difficult to see because they were over to the side. She strained her neck. Children! Children, their hands joined in front of them, praying, crying. Now she could see their faces and she realized that the children who prayed for the repose of her soul, their faces reddened with tears, were her own.

She shouted out their names:

'Patrick!'

'Katie!'

'Mary!'

They kept on praying and crying. They had not heard her. She shouted their names again and again. Still they did not hear her.

Then, with a soft clatter, the clay sprinkled over the wood on top of her. It darkened the sky, cutting off the faces of her children. Then, the choking taste of it was in her mouth. She spat it out.

If she shouted louder they had to hear her.

She did, driving out the screams of desperation, trying to compete

413

with the incessant sound of the clay falling, darkening her space, blanketing her in. Again she banged frantically with her hands and feet against the walls of her coffin. Then lifted herself up to bang against its roof with her head.

Anything, anything to make more noise, to make them hear her.

But something was holding her back, keeping her pinned to the floor. She struggled and struggled, but she could make no ground against the force which held her.

Then voices.

'Reverend, I think she's coming out of it!' an Irish voice said.

'Yes, Father, thanks be to the Good Lord!' an English voice said. 'But hold her yet, lest she harm herself.'

Then, a third voice: 'Ellen, Ellen – it's me, it's me!'

She stopped screaming. She tried to focus on this third voice. The pinioning hands relaxed their hold on her. Now she could sit up, start the banging again. But no wooden coffin confined her movement.

And the sound of the clay falling – it too had stopped.

Had she gone beyond this life? Or somehow escaped?

She opened her eyes fearfully, the perspiration stinging them as she did. Her whole body was drenched in it. She blinked to clear them, to identify the shapes that still spoke to her.

Lavelle! Lavelle was beside her. She felt his hand on her own.

She was alive!

She tried to manage a smile at him. And the others – Reverend Bonney and Father McGauran – who stood by her bed, beaming at her.

'Ellen, you've come out of it!' The young priest looked gaunt and tired, yet his face was lit with joy.

'Yes indeed, Mrs Coogan, a remarkable recovery by a remarkable woman!' his Anglican counterpart added. 'How fortunate that we were here, that Father and I had just come to visit and pray with you a while. The Lord is all powerful!'

Lavelle, overwhelmed with happiness, embraced her. The two clergymen continued to beam with delight at the husband and wife, reunited in life.

'I'll be fine now, Lavelle,' she said – the confusion of the moment making her forget who she was supposed to be. The two reverend gentlemen looked at each other, bewildered.

Lavelle saved the day. 'It is a name by which Mrs Coogan calls me in our private moments!' he said, without a hint of a smile.

The two priests looked at each other and nodded almost in unison. 'Oh, yes . . . of course,' they said, slightly embarrassed. Thereafter the beaming resumed.

'Eight days now you have been in the grip of the fever, Mrs Coogan,' the Reverend Bonney informed her.

'Yes, Ellen, and now you must rest here in Hôtel-Dieu for a while longer,' his Catholic counterpart added. 'Maybe then, when you have recovered sufficiently, we will remove you to the Blue Store for a period of recuperation.'

'The Blue Store?' Lavelle asked.

'Yes, Mr Coogan,' the priest answered. 'The Blue Store is a large warehouse here in Québec where healthy relatives of those who remain on Grosse Île await their safe release.'

'Grosse Île . . . ?' Ellen asked, latching on to the words, slowly remembering.

'The situation is still serious there, Mrs Coogan. The ships continue to come, but not so many now. The timber season draws to an end,' said Reverend Bonney.

'We still do what we can to ease their suffering, but it is a daunting task,' Father McGauran added. 'One wonders if they are better to be kept at home to die, instead of on a foreign shore, or in the foul hold of a coffin ship. It is a cruel choice, indeed. Anyway, you must not worry about that. Reverend Bonney and I will leave you now with our blessings and see you in a week or so,' the priest concluded, brightening at the prospect of her recovery.

And so, in the Hôtel-Dieu of Québec, Ellen Rua O'Malley joined her hands and closed her eyes to receive the joint blessings of the Church of Rome and the Church of England.

A week later, when Father McGauran returned, she was much stronger. Immediately she saw the priest's troubled face she knew something was wrong.

'It's good to see you, Father. *Dia dhuit!*' she greeted him.

'*Dia's Muire dhuit*, Ellen,' he returned. 'I'm afraid I have sad news,' he added, coming closer to her.

'What is it, Father?'

'It's the Reverend Bonney . . . I am sorry to relate that he contracted the illness and could not be saved.'

'Oh, no,' she said, unable to take the news. 'Oh, no . . . Will it never end, these afflictions?'

Father McGauran took her hands. 'He was truly a most holy person, Ellen. He is gone to his Maker. He is at peace.'

'Oh, Father, he was . . . He was so kind to me, though we did not agree on everything,' she said, thinking of the long hours of conversation they had had. Thinking of how he had worked among the sick and dying, until he almost keeled over from exhaustion. Now, his devotion had brought upon himself the thing he had sought to warn her of.

'Yes, I know. He told me of your "theological" talks.' Father McGauran gave a little smile. 'I think you had a great influence on him, Ellen. Throughout his illness, he often spoke your name, enquiring as to how you were.' The priest paused, remembering their mutual friend. 'He asked me to give you this . . .' He handed her the well-worn leather-bound copy of the Old Testament that she had seen the Reverend Bonney use so lovingly.

She clasped it to her, and said, 'Thoughtful of others even in his own suffering. I will treasure this all my life. *Ar dheis Dé go raibh a anam.*' She smiled to herself, certain that the soul of the Anglican clergyman would be at the right hand of God, but wondering by which gate it was that he had entered God's Kingdom.

They talked a while of Ireland. News from there continued to be dire. Thousands upon thousands still died. The hospitals were unable to cope. The workhouses were bankrupt, and the people continued to be cleared from the land – to die, or take the boat. Often it was one and the same thing.

'The land is now labourless,' Father McGauran told her, 'and the production of food decreased. The Crown, instead of sending relief, sends more forces to protect the traders and merchants, and to quell riotous behaviour at the ports as food leaves the country.'

'The country will be brought to its knees before it will be let stand again! And is the Church doing anything?'

'Well, at last the bishops are moving,' he answered. 'Archbishop

MacHale of Tuam seems to be the driving force. But their hands are tied. What can they do except write to Her Majesty and the Government demanding aid and reform?'

'First, they could stop blaming the people for what has befallen them,' she answered. 'It is not the Hand of God but the hand of man, in London, which has brought this horror down upon Ireland.'

She stated this with such conviction that Father McGauran knew she was well on the way to recovery.

'I see you are getting stronger, Ellen!' he said, with a smile. 'I will arrange for you and Mr Coogan to have accommodation at the Blue Store for a week or so. But if you are to see Boston this year, you must go quickly before ice closes the St Lawrence. You are in no condition to travel overland,' he advised.

'Father, there is something I would ask of you . . .' she broached.

'Ask,' he said.

'That you would hear my confession.'

He looked at her, wondering what it was that troubled this woman who had all but sacrificed her life for others.

'Of course, Ellen!' He bowed his head beside her face, his ear close to her lips.

There, in the Hôtel-Dieu – the House of God – she whispered her sins into his ear.

She held nothing back, told him her whole story: Michael, the children, Sheela-na-Sheeoga – the *Slám* – Pakenham, Coombes, Annie, Wiwirremalde, Lavelle, and McGrath. It seemed to her that she traced out all her recent life to the young priest.

He listened attentively, silently, never once lifting his head. When she had finished, he waited a few moments and then said to her: 'You have made a good confession, Ellen. God has forgiven you your sins, and, in His name, so do I . . . As for your penance, this you have already done by your work amongst the dying and through your own suffering. I only ask that you pray for the happy repose of Reverend Bonney's soul . . . and that, also in your prayers, you remember your confessor.

'And now I absolve you. *Ego te absolvo peccatus tuus . . .*' And he made the sign of forgiveness over her.

She lowered her head to accept it. Freed at last of her burden.

417

BOOK FOUR

BOSTON

47

Boston did not like the Irish. Especially if they were Catholic, and poor.

In fact, Boston hated them with a bitterness and revulsion that was evangelical in its zeal. The very day she and Lavelle disembarked on Boston's Long Wharf, they overheard the remark: 'St Patrick's Vermin bringing with them the twin scourges of pestilence and Popery.' The man who made it, probably a merchant, seemed not to care who overheard him. His was a view that was widely held in the New England capital. The Puritanical Bostonians, staunchly Anglo-Saxon, despised the Irish for threatening their well-ordered society – and they were not slow to say so.

But Boston was also booming. It had the best of all worlds. The city – gateway to America – took on the learning and wisdom of the Old World, yet had the enterprise and spirit of the New: travel, communication, invention. The New England city was at the forefront of the railroad industry, developing routes throughout America, whilst new shipping routes were the avenues to increased trade and commerce with the rest of the world.

Boston's education system, she learned, was the most advanced in the new continent. Here Patrick and the twins could study anything they wanted: history, philosophy, finance, business – anything. The city was moving towards a free school system so that its citizens could develop the mental disciplines and economic skills to see Boston into a prosperous, well-ordered future.

For all its bigotry and hatred of things Irish, Boston was still the place for her. If she could make something of herself here – break through that barrier – then Boston, she knew, would hold no limit of opportunity for her and her children.

They had left Mr and Mrs Coogan behind when they left Grosse Île, and both felt much more comfortable having reverted to their own identity. Smartly dressed and having money at their disposal, they managed to acquire comfortable but separate lodgings at opposite sides of the street from each other in Boston's South End, despite the proliferation of signs stating: 'No Blacks, No Dogs, No Irish'. It was a lesson for Ellen. 'Few will bite the hand that feeds them,' she remarked to Lavelle. Money, if you had enough of it, would overcome most prejudices. Which left them with only two such prejudices to surmount in Boston: poor, they apparently were not – Irish and Catholic they would always be.

Boston was about three to four times the size of Melbourne. Of a population which the newspapers put at 120,000, a quarter were Irish. The women went to the clothing factories, working all the hours God sent for five dollars a week. But five dollars a week was better than 'five potatoes a week or none', and the women were luckier than the men.

Many of the Irish men were forced to head west to find work on the railroads. Building America with shovel and pick, and sweat and blood, moving wherever the work and the railroads went.

Those who came to Boston with nothing had to work hard, or be inventive. She noticed how plentiful Irish pedlars were, their stock on their backs needing little money to start up.

'Everything is dollars,' she said to Lavelle. 'That's the way it is here.'

Dollars and business and busy-ness. Everybody bustled and hustled, scrabbling and scraping for the next dollar.

It was good and it was bad. It gave you a chance, a start at life. But it left you with no time for each other – not like it was back home. No time to stand and talk, or just look at a thing. No time for anything, only dollars. And surviving.

It wasn't so, she knew, for the 'Scotch-Irish' or the 'Ulster-Americans', as they liked to call themselves. Ellen thought that strange: they didn't want to be labelled as Irish, yet they didn't want to be Americans. They wanted to stand apart, be neither one nor the other, but above both. They were the chosen ones, but she – like the rest of the Irish Irish – knew them for what they were: 'Cromwell's children'. The ones who sold out their own for land in Ireland. Then later sold out their country for union with Britain so they could hold on to that land – and get more of it.

It was the same here in Boston. They were a close-knit bunch, who mixed only with each other. Along with the 'purer-than-pure' English-Americans, they handed down the laws of the land, and the laws of God. As Lavelle said of them, 'The Ulster-Americans speak only to God, and then only to speak down to Him!'

She would have to deal with them, these people who spoke down to God, and the old-line English. Knew she would come into conflict with them if she and Lavelle became too visible – too successful. It would be a battle, like her and Michael against Pakenham all over again – only this time the enemy would be even more powerful.

Only this time, there would be no Michael.

Her first experience of Boston's Ulster-Americans came sooner than expected.

On 5 November, Guy Fawkes' Night, it being a Friday, the gathering for the annual celebration and fireworks was bigger than usual. Ellen was not inclined to go, and only relented after Lavelle talked her into it, saying it would be a good opportunity to 'see what they get up to here'.

But in Boston the celebration of Guy Fawkes' attempt to blow up the English Parliament had, for large sections of the population, turned into something quite different: 'Pope's Night'.

The parade, a colourful and noisy spectacle, wound its way down King Street led by fife and drum, marching to the tune of 'The Battle of the Boyne'. The banners of the Protestant Associations of Boston unfurled alongside those of King William of Orange. The King was depicted on his steed, sword aloft, smiting the reviled Catholic Jacobean army. Now, a hundred and fifty years later and in a different land, the victory at the Boyne was still cherished and celebrated as if it were yesterday.

'It's even worse than Melbourne,' she whispered to Lavelle.

'Much worse,' he replied.

Other banners – the slogans stitched in orange thread from Boston's clothing factories – proclaimed: 'King Billy was right! King Billy for Boston!'

Ellen and Lavelle were further shocked when the band struck up 'Thank God I am no Papist', and the marchers yelled and jeered and chanted:

> The Pope's a whore!
> The Pope's a whore!
> Lays down with the biddies
> On St Patrick's shore!

Then a large banner titled 'the Whore of Babylon' appeared, held aloft by two of the marchers. It portrayed the naked breasts and heavily-rouged nipples of a harlot. Printed in large letters above one of the nipples was 'Rome', while above the other the word 'Ireland' was emblazoned. The face of this Whore of Babylon was a caricature of the new Pope, Pius IX, enthroned the previous year. On his head sat a green pontifical hat; in his hand was a green mitre, pointed like a spear, on which was impaled an orange-coloured serpent – obviously implying papish regard for anything of Protestant lineage!

Other banners with 'Anti-Christ' slogans showed the Pope with satanic horns and cloven feet. And the phrase which Ellen had first heard on the Long Wharf was now proclaimed on a banner headed 'Saint Patrick's Vermin'. It presented the Pied Piper of Boston all regaled in orange colours and playing an orange flute, leading scores of green-coloured rats past a sign which said, 'Long Wharf rat drowning – this way.'

The crowds loved it. The more they were taunted by the parading Orangemen and Nativists, the more they loved it. The more they were incited by the Know Nothings' chanting of:

> 'From Ulster-Scot
> To Yankee Brahmin
> Boston says "No"
> To Saint Patrick's Vermin.'

Next, the 'Whore of Babylon' banner was wedged between the topmost timbers of the traditional Guy Fawkes' bonfire, to shouts of 'Burn the whore! Burn the whore!'

Lavelle turned to her, his face tense and angry at what they were witnessing. 'We should leave here, Ellen,' he said.

He was right. The last thing they wanted was trouble. And what she was now seeing, what disgusted and horrified her, was trouble.

This was Boston's 'Orange welcome' that she had been warned about in Québec.

As they turned to make their way out of the crowd, they heard other, different music. For a moment the mob fell silent, their only voice the crackling of the avenging flames which licked at the breasts of the Whore of Babylon.

'It's the Irish!' Ellen said to Lavelle as the whistles and fiddles of the approaching group broke into a rollicking reel.

'It's the Irish!' the crowd shouted, echoing Ellen's words.

As cobblestones and bricks rained down on them, the Orange band started up again. Then, on the streets of Boston the music of the two rival cultures played it out. Note for note they traded with each other, as their supporters traded blow for blow – re-enacting, it seemed to Ellen, the bloody battle of a century and a half ago.

'*Sinn féin, sinn féin*,' she said to Lavelle as they made away from the mêlée. 'Ourselves are ourselves,' she repeated in English. 'We love a good fight.'

'It seems it's the only way we'll get anywhere,' he replied. 'There may be more of us, but somehow we're always at the bottom of the heap – both here and at home.'

'Do you think it will ever change?'

'Only if we change.'

'What do you mean by that?' she asked.

'We have to adopt new ways, forget about the old language, the old tunes and stories of the old country. The Irish need to stick together, help each other and get into positions of power – into politics.'

'The French-Canadians in Québec didn't give up their language and culture, and they've survived. Why should we?' she challenged him.

'But Québec is Catholic – that's the difference!' he said. 'The Catholics have the power there – not the English Protestants.'

'Why is it always down to religion? If you scrape away everything else – it's always religion!'

'Yes,' he said, 'God doesn't rule the world – religion does!'

And she remembered a saying the Máistir had when he spoke of such things: *Is olc an iomarca creidimh!* – 'Too much religion is a bad thing' – and she wondered about the wisdom of bringing the children here.

There must have been over a hundred newspapers and periodicals printed regularly in Boston. In the early winter days, Ellen devoured as many as she could lay hands on, wanting to learn as much as she could about the city – past and future.

She learned how the Bostonians had built up their seaboard city trading with far-away places. How its whaling fleet combed the waters of the world for the great leviathans of the deep. How the rapidly expanding clothing industry would be revolutionized by the invention of Howe's sewing machine in the adjoining town, Cambridge, the previous year.

She gleaned every scrap of information the newspapers could provide about this New England where she would raise her children.

Yes, she would still bring them here, but she would shelter them, educate them, lift them above all of the horrors of Pope's Night and for what it stood.

Wine!

She had discussed the idea many times with Lavelle during the long journey from Australia and while she recuperated at the Hôtel-Dieu in Québec.

At first he was slow to warm to the idea, thinking the importing of wine to be too sedate a business for him. But in Québec, while she was ill, he had taken the trouble to wander the city. He was surprised to find the stores so well-stocked with a variety of French wines.

When he then saw the size of Boston and its wealth, this convinced him further. Besides, the idea of laying railroad tracks – hammering steel in the mid-Western sun – did not appeal to him greatly. He knew something about wine from his time at Crockford's, and so did she. It would be interesting, he thought, to pit themselves against Boston's business brethren.

'Wine is the only thing I know anything about,' she said, 'apart from picking praties and gathering turf, and I don't see too many lazy beds, or bogs either, around Beacon Hill!'

'No,' Lavelle replied, 'and no grapes are grown on Beacon Hill either.'

Previously she had told him that the proceeds from the sale of the Ngarrindjeri gold were 'as much yours as mine'. He had resisted, saying she should take the money and go back to Ireland.

'I can't go as yet, Lavelle. It's too soon, I must first establish something here that I can bring the children back to, else there's no point me going to Ireland,' she had answered him. 'For what would I do if we stayed in Ireland? Become a trader making profit out of those starving? Buy a parcel of land and have to keep the dying out of it? Ireland has no future for me – only to take my children and get out of it. I've decided on Boston.'

Now they had to get busy.

'We will get French wine from Québec to start with. Then maybe from France itself, when we are established. The Irish Earls fled there after the Battle of Kinsale, and set up in Bordeaux. Chevalier told me about them – he used to call them "the Wine Geese"!'

'Well, if all else fails, we could always import some of Crockford's Gold!' he said, laughing.

'It's a warehouse not a whorehouse we're letting!' Ellen was told when she first set about trying to secure premises for their wine business.

Lavelle was faring no better: 'Can't you Irish read? "Positively no Irish need apply". "Positively" means "at all, at all" in your manner of speaking!'

But eventually, after countless refusals, they found a small warehouse to rent not far off the Long Wharf. It was expensive, being so close to the waterfront – and, being Irish, they had to pay an additional bond above the asking price – but they thought it the place to be.

They cleaned out the disused warehouse. Lavelle started making trestles and shelving. She hired a tradesman to put up the name outside in bold lettering: THE NEW ENGLAND WINE COMPANY – IMPORTERS OF FINE WINES, PORTS AND LIQUEURS. Ellen was pleased with that. She would play them at their own game. Think like them. Be one of them.

* * *

One day she came into the building, all excited, waving a letter at him, her hair streaming behind her.

'Lavelle! Lavelle! Look – it's from Father McGauran. He has found us a supplier in Québec: Frontignac, Père et Fils, importers from Burgundy and Bordeaux. Isn't it great news? Now Boston will drink our wine!'

So thrilled was she, that before either of them knew it, she had thrown her arms round his neck.

It was the first time they had touched since he had sat beside her bed in the Hôtel-Dieu, trying to soothe her as she wrestled with the torments of the fever. Now, he could smell her sweetness, feel the flush of her cheeks against his, her hair straying into his nose and mouth.

'I'm so happy for you, Ellen. You go at life so hard.'

He held her there, a little longer than the moment required. She felt him against her breast, the slight insistence in his arms, knew she had to break this, regretted that her spontaneity had placed them both in this situation.

'Thanks, Lavelle,' she said, lifting her head away from him. 'I knew we'd succeed – now all we have to do is get it here and sell it. And we will!' she said, more flushed than she had been before.

He let go of her slowly. Fighting the urge to pull her back to him, tell her how much he admired her, wanted it all to work out for her . . . To hell with it! Just to tell her he loved her.

She must have sensed something in him, because she looked away, then started reading Father McGauran's letter out loud:

'Grosse Île is now closed for the winter. Over ninety thousand came in all this summer, the highest number of any year yet. Many did not survive the crossing. Many more found their last resting place in the "Irish" Cemetery. Dr Douglas and his staff have saved many too, who otherwise, would have perished. The orphans also prosper with their new families . . .'

She was pleased with news of the orphans.

On 7 November 1847, Isabella Morgan Moore, caring Christian, loving wife, and mother of two young children, died of typhus.

Moore was devastated. Isabella had been his strength, his confidante after the untimely death of his first wife, Hannah, seven years ago. Isabella had regard for the two children of his marriage to Hannah as if they were her own, with an especial affection for her namesake, little Isabella. Like Hannah, she had borne him two children, and, like Hannah, Isabella had had an enriching and nurturing effect on him.

He had been twice blest in the fairest of creatures in God's dominion. Yet twice the Lord had taken away what he had bestowed, after less than five years of happiness in each case. Stricken them both with typhus.

Always crossings between lives ... connections ... Moore thought sadly.

Three weeks later, the New England Wine Company received their first consignment of *vin supérieur de France* from Frontignac, Père et Fils, Québec.

'The Christmas should give us a good start,' Ellen said to Lavelle.

She had been excited when the crates arrived: checking them off against the consignment notice, seeing the words for the first time – saying them aloud: 'Twelve crates of Burgundy, twelve crates of Bordeaux, two of Hennessy.'

Selling them was a different matter, though.

There was a strong temperance movement in Boston, and the Catholic Church had spoken out against 'the fruit of the bewitching glass'. About the only thing it and the Protestant Church held in common was a denouncement of the demon drink.

Drink, intemperance, intoxication were all evils Bostonians associated with the Irish. It was said that Boston had a thousand groggeries, pubs, and bars – a good proportion of which resided in the Irish neighbourhoods of Fort Hill and the North End. The Irish groggeries, however, were not the intended market for Ellen and Lavelle's fine wines.

Armed with samples of their newly arrived merchandise, and in positive spirits at the thought of making their first sales, Ellen left the Long Wharf and walked up State Street with its banks and large trading houses. Tapscott's was here – 'Mici Maol's Bank', as she called it. To the left then was the Merchants Exchange with its high Grecian pilasters. Ahead, with the British unicorn atop it, was the Old State Meeting House where the Declaration of Independence was first read aloud to Bostonians.

This area would be their market. This was where the money was.

During their first few days in Boston, she and Lavelle had scouted the area and decided that Pendleton's, on the corner of Washington Street, looked promising. The exterior walls were painted with signs proclaiming: 'Gourmet Foods. Tobacco. Liquors. Wines.'

Tall, angular and anxious, Ezra Pendleton took in the handsome well-dressed woman who entered his emporium. With a quick glance at his reflection in the side window on to Washington Street, he moved towards her in greeting. Business had been good of late and Pendleton looked forward to a continuation of that state of affairs, especially when he saw customers with such potential as this one had.

Pleasantries having been exchanged, Pendleton was less sure of his new customer. She was Irish, obviously, although not from the lowest orders of that race which afflicted his city in their thousands. His taxes had been increased to fund hospitals and asylums for them, and – even more unpalatable to him – schools in which to educate their filthy offspring. However, none of these thoughts seeped through the quiet effusiveness of Ezra Pendleton.

'What service can the house of Pendleton be to madam today?'

Ellen noticed how sallow of complexion the man was; waxen, like his moustache. The thumb of his right hand found the inside of the revers of his dark coat. Ezra Pendleton seemed to be glad he had something to hold on to.

'Would the house of Pendleton be interested in purchasing some fine imported French wines and brandies?' Ellen asked pleasantly.

This seemed to surprise the man. She watched his other hand find and finger his top buttonhole.

'We are importers – the New England Wine Company.' It made her nervous to say out the name like that for the first time.

'Oh, yes. Quite!' the merchant said, still completely taken aback by Ellen's question. 'But you are . . . Irish,' he said, his comprehension fumbling along with his fingers, trying to make some sense out of this ridiculous situation.

'Yes,' Ellen said, raising her eyebrows to him. 'Irish.'

'But how . . . I mean, where . . . ?'

'From our suppliers. We have a licence to trade,' Ellen answered the unformed question.

Jumped-up Irish are almost worse than the ones who have nothing, Pendleton thought to himself. There should be laws confining them to the factories and the railroads. Selling wine, indeed! He would give her short enough shrift, with her wine.

'I am sorry, madam, but we have our regular suppliers – proven quality and delivery. In any event, we are completely over-stocked for the Yuletide!'

Though his true thoughts remained unspoken, Ellen could read them in Pendleton's eyes. The disdain at having to deal with her, even to talk to her.

'At least look at the samples I have with me,' she said, sorry almost immediately to have given him another opportunity for refusal.

'I see no point, madam. Good day to you.'

Without removing his hands, both now firmly clasped below the lapels of his coat, Pendleton ushered her back out on to the street.

And so it was at Endecott's, and at Sheldon & Seaward's on Faneuil Hall Square. At least Mr Sheldon, with some semblance of humanity, had explained to her: 'Were my clientele to become aware that I was buying from Irish Catholics, they would boycott us, take all their business to Pendleton's or Endecott's. I just could not risk it, madam – for the sake of the business. I do hope you understand.'

Ellen did understand. There was an in-built distrust of her because she was Irish. What she had to sell was tainted by this distrust – they seemed to think that if the Irish were involved it had to be illicit!

But there had to be somebody in Boston who'd buy her wines and brandies. She would just have to find that person – and she would.

*   *   *

431

The minute she saw him, Ellen knew that Jacob Peabody was both a skinflint and a lecher – and their best hope yet.

Peabody's was on South Market Street across from Quincy Market. The Market itself was constructed in a nouveau-Grecian style of architecture out of granite. A covered walkway connected the upper floors of Quincy Market and Faneuil Hall. Above this on the Hall's domed cupola perched Boston's famous weather-vane – the copper grasshopper which Jacob Peabody liked to keep an eye on when business was slow enough to permit it.

The proprietor of Peabody's did not walk to meet his most recent customer, Ellen noticed. He glided towards her, hand outstretched, white hair down to his collar, white eyebrows raised. Below the eyebrows, his canny eyes glinted as he studied the red-haired woman. He held her hand, lingering over it, rubbing his index finger along the soft flesh of her Mount of Venus.

'Delighted, delighted, Mrs O'Malley!' he said with relish when she introduced herself.

'Mr Peabody!' she said, withdrawing her hand. The old *buachaill* didn't even try to hide it – wasn't afraid of himself like Pendleton.

'Mr Peabody,' she stated matter-of-factly, 'I am Irish, a Catholic . . .'

Peabody listened, his eyes not straying from her mouth, watching her lips form the words.

'The wine and the brandy, is French, superior, absolutely legal . . .' she paused, and decided to say it anyway. 'Yes, despite being papists, my partner and I managed to get a licence.'

She had decided to be blunt with this Mr Peabody, put it up to him.

'The price, Mrs O'Malley – the price?' Jacob Peabody pushed his lips out.

His equally blunt reaction caught her off guard. There was no polite side-shunting with Mr Peabody. Profit not Popes was what Jacob Peabody was interested in, and younger women.

She hesitated momentarily in her reply.

'Why should I buy from you?' he went on, watching her hawk-like. 'Untried, untrusted, unorthodox of your gender. You may not survive in the tough world of business, and then where is Jacob Peabody?' He watched her response, but she kept his gaze, unwavering, waiting until he was finished. 'My friends would say

I ruined myself for the smile of an Irish beauty. Laugh me out of the Market they would!' He laughed himself at the idea of this. 'The price, Mrs O'Malley – the price?'

She liked him, this Peabody. He didn't put a tooth in anything. An idea was beginning to form in her head – but could she trust him? Her instinct said yes. She would have to keep an eye on him, and keep his hands off of her, but yes, she could handle him.

'I'll tell you what, Mr Peabody,' she began. 'I'll make a bargain with you on which you can't lose.'

'Oh, ho!' he laughed, his eyes lighting up even more. 'I've heard all that before – "Beware of Greeks bearing gifts," Old Papa Peabody used to say. I suspect it applies to the Irish as well, but I'm listening, Mrs O'Malley. Jacob Peabody is listening.'

'This is my offer,' she started: 'I will supply you, Mr Peabody, with the finest of French wines and brandy at cost price, taking no profit. And you will not have to pay me until you have sold them.'

Peabody's eyes narrowed, watching her, waiting for the sting.

'But when you have sold them,' Ellen continued, 'you must split the profit with me. Then I will immediately replace the items sold.'

Jacob Peabody laughed. 'I've never heard the likes of it! Are you sure, Mrs O'Malley, you're not Jewish instead of Irish? Old Papa Peabody would have been proud of you!'

She was a risk-taker this Irish woman – like himself. You had to be if you were an outsider in Boston. He was still an outsider, he knew, even though he was now second-generation Bostonian. Even after his smart old papa had changed the family name to Peabody.

She would be out of money until he sold her wines. If he failed to sell them, it would break her. It was unlikely she was benefiting from the same credit terms that she was now offering to him.

'But fifty per cent of the profit, Mrs O'Malley? That's high, very high.'

He wondered how she would react to this. She was new in Boston, he reckoned. Probably having difficulty in getting started, wherever it was she was getting the wine from. But he liked her, and if he could beat her down some on the profit, then . . .

'But you have no risk, Mr Peabody, none at all. I stand to lose everything, acting both as your supplier and your banker!' she protested. Then added: 'I'm afraid I'll have to approach Endecott's or Pendleton's.'

Oh, she was a right vixen, this Irish redhead. A right smart vixen – good to be in business with. Endecott's? Pendleton's? Why, she'd be lucky to get past the doorway with either of them – if they hadn't already shown her the door! But she had some nerve all the same, for a woman and an outsider.

'Done!' he said, and grabbed her hand again. 'Done. It's a bargain, Mrs O'Malley!'

'One other thing . . .' she said, and he stopped pumping her hand.

'What?'

'You agree to pay me on a weekly basis for wine sold.'

He nodded.

'And,' she went on, hardly acknowledging his agreement, 'you agree to display my wines separate from the rest, in the entrance, on a special shelf-rack. My partner, Mr Lavelle, will come and construct it for you.'

'That is two other things, Mrs O'Malley,' he said, still holding her hand. It was soft, but firm-formed, especially her Mount of Venus.

'No, Mr Peabody, it is one,' she said, ignoring that he was again rubbing her hand. 'The second thing I do for you, at no charge!'

Jacob Peabody laughed. She was hard-nosed too, this fine-looking woman! But she had style and he wasn't going to argue with her. After all, he had nothing to lose. His eyes twinkled.

'Seeing as we are asking things of each other, I have one small request to ask of you, Mrs O'Malley . . .'

'And what might that be, Mr Peabody?' she asked, knowing that he was up to some mischief, some trick.

'Only that you yourself – and not this partner of yours, this Lavelle – come weekly to see how sales of your wine are.'

'Oh, I will, Mr Peabody! Don't worry, I will!'

48

Ellen learned a lot from Jacob Peabody. He was as good as his word: the wines of the New England Wine Company were prominently displayed, and instead of going for a low profit margin he marked up the prices.

'Those who will buy these wines have money a-plenty, and if we set them too cheaply they'll not buy them,' he explained to her. 'They equate price with value.'

By Christmas Eve, Peabody's had sold seven and a half of the twelve crates of Bordeaux wines and five crates of the Burgundy. All but four bottles of the Hennessy Cognac had been sold. Peabody was pleased, as were Ellen and Lavelle.

Lavelle's shelves at Peabody's had been replenished and Ellen had re-ordered more stock from Frontignac, Père et Fils. But the racks at the New England Wine Company were empty, and now they must wait until the heavy snows and the ice cleared to get more stock.

Part of her hoped that the sales at Peabody's would slow down after Christmas, as she did not want to fail to supply him so soon. The other part wanted the sales to keep up as the warehouse rent was a constant cost and did not reduce in line with a reduction in sales.

Lavelle accompanied her to Midnight Mass. She couldn't help but think that it was only last Christmas Eve when Pakenham had evicted them and tumbled their *bothán* to the ground. In one short, terrible year she had lost almost everything: Michael, Annie, her home, her children gone from her. And she had almost lost her own life. Now it looked as if things were beginning to turn for her at last.

What did the year ahead hold? This night next year, if God spared her, what would her thoughts be of? God willing, Patrick and Katie and Mary would be with her to share them. She had decided she would go in the early summer for them, come what may. She would have to take the risk – she just couldn't bear the thought of being away from them any longer than that. But summer was the earliest she could go. Things here would take a few more months to settle down, and both she and Lavelle needed to be here to work at it. Maybe they could, after a while, import directly from France – but she'd wait and see.

She prepared a meal for Lavelle and herself on Christmas Day, and he arrived looking pleased with himself about something. He couldn't wait until they'd completed the meal.

'Ellen, I've brought something for you!' he said, producing a package wrapped in pretty Christmas paper, tied with a golden string.

She, too, was excited, her interest aroused.

'Open it – go on, open it!' he urged her.

She did.

'Oh, Lavelle – it's beautiful, so beautiful!' she said, as she dropped the wrapping to the ground, and threw back her hair so as to take the silken scarf he had gifted her. Like running water it was in her hands, it was so sheer. Shimmering golden water, shot through with shafts of emerald green.

'The Mask in August!' she said, in wonderment at its colours. 'Thank you, Lavelle – you picked it with such care!' Her hands fumbled with the excitement, trying to make the knot under her chin.

'Here, let me!' he offered, stepping forward, happy at her pleasure with his gift.

She stood still. His fingers grazed the line of her neck. Instinctively she raised her head clear of them, not looking at him.

'There,' he said. 'It's fixed!'

She smiled at him, in thanks.

'*Nollaig shona dhuit a Ellen!*' he said quietly, wishing her a happy Christmas.

She opened her mouth to return the greeting, but, if she did, no words came out. Instead Lavelle's mouth was against hers, swallowing her words, kissing her with all the pent-up emotion of months.

She felt the bruise of his lips against hers, pushing them back, keeping them open, breathing into her.

It took her a moment to recover, such was the hunger with which he sought her.

'No, Lavelle! No, don't!' she said, breaking away.

He stood back from her, shaking, and she saw something in his eyes which made her afraid.

'D'you think I'm not human, Ellen? To be with you all this time and –'

'Don't say it, Lavelle!' she interrupted him, her body unsure of its reaction. 'It'll be easier if we don't say anything!'

He looked at her. Was she made of stone instead of flesh and blood, this woman before him?

He started to say, 'I'm sorry . . .' then changed his mind, because it wasn't true. 'I'm not sorry, Ellen. Not one bit sorry,' he told her, his eyes flashing, and he turned and left, going out in the Christmas snows to his own place.

Slowly, she undid the scarf, feeling Lavelle's knot come away easily in her fingers. She looked at the scarf – its colours bringing her back across the ocean. It was beautiful indeed.

She crushed it into one hand and put its silkiness against her cheek.

'Oh, Michael, *a stór*,' she whispered into its green and gold folds. 'Help me.'

Slowly, as he walked round the gardens, deep in December, David Moore thought that it was indeed the dimming of a black, black year.

Black for the country of Ireland.

Black for its dead, its starving, its diseased, its homeless.

Black for him – no cure found – only his love lost.

Black for his dear, dear, Isabella.

As he walked the route he and Isabella had walked for the last time some months previously, he heard footsteps fall in with his own.

Canon Prufrock said nothing for a while, and the curator was really not of a humour to be welcoming company. So they walked awhile in silence, each with his own thoughts.

Eventually the canon spoke, gently, a slight awkwardness in his voice: 'David, dear, dear friend . . .'

Moore kept his eyes on the path. During Isabella's last weeks the canon had visited her bedside every day, showing no fear of catching the dreaded typhus himself. The old man would just sit and be silent with her. She, even when falling in and out of the clutches of the fever, seemed to know when he was there, and her face would take on a glow of serenity. The curator knew Isabella had an unfailing admiration, even a tenderness, for her pastor. She understood and accepted the old cleric in a way Moore never could. 'He is not of this world. He is a true man of God, David,' she would say.

'I had a great tenderness for dear Isabella,' the canon's words broke in on Moore's thoughts. 'In the darkest of hours, with the poor and the needy, she was as a beacon of light . . . smiling, uncomplaining, no thought for herself . . . only for those more wanting,' the canon said haltingly.

Moore nodded, lost in the images dragged up by the old man's words.

'Many is the time I was obliged, reluctantly, to send her away, or she would have striven in good deeds from dawn to dusk. And she would remonstrate with me' – his voice picked up some of Isabella's spiritedness – '"Canon," she would say, "Canon, will this sick child rest while I rest? Will this mother, who has lost two of her children, sleep while I sleep? Will these two orphaned urchins eat while I eat? The answer, in each occasion, is no! How then can my soul be at peace, if I leave them not eased in their suffering?"'

The old man looked at Moore.

'This was your Isabella, dear friend, moved by the spirit – tireless in God's work.'

'Thank you, Canon, thank you most kindly,' Moore whispered in reply.

'The wisteria climbs to the heavens above the Chain Tent? The stridulation of the *Sigara dorsalis* rises from beneath the water of the Pond? These are His mysterious ways. We know not the answers. Know not why, sometimes, He picks His fairest flowers the first – gathering them homewards, to Himself, for All Eternity . . .'

Moore was grateful for the canon's words, and spoke for the

first time of his feelings for Isabella: 'She was a saint in all things – a source of wonder. Always within her only sunny humours, and a heart unquenching in its affection . . . I am sorely grieved to be without her.'

They had come to the Jenkinstown Rose and the curator stopped walking.

'Of all, this was her favourite spot in the gardens.' Moore pointed to the lone rose ahead.

'Ah, yes, *Rosa chinensis*,' said the canon. 'Oft I heard her sing that sweet tune, "The Last Rose of Summer", to the dead and the dying . . .' Again, the old man's voice trailed off, remembering.

They stood in front of the rose, still alive, still lingering, long past summer. Head more bent now, petals more faded, browning towards the edges. Tired of the long, hard year. No soft hand now to bring back the blush of summer.

The curator and the canon stood silently in its presence, each remembering her who once sang its beauty. Each remembering the last, sweet rose of Black Forty-Seven.

The curator's thoughts were broken by a low sound from beside him. He listened. The canon was intoning something – probably the *De Profundis*, or some other prayer for the dead. A shiver passed over Moore, as he realized what it was Prufrock was saying . . . singing:

> 'Tis The Last Rose of Summer,
> Left blooming alone;
> All her lovely companions
> Are faded and gone . . .

The phrasing was the same. The canon must have learned it from listening to Isabella. The old man talk-whispered the song through:

> . . . Since the lovely are sleeping,
> Go, sleep thou with them . . .

The curator stole a look at him. He detected a quiver in the clergyman's lips. He looked again. This time, a tear descended the old man's cheek. Prufrock was weeping as he sang his song for the curator's dead wife. Moore was deeply moved – it was probably the nearest the canon had ever let himself come to feelings of love.

Canon Prufrock continued his love song, the words now becoming more broken:

> When true hearts lie wither'd,
> And fond ones are flown,
> Oh! . . . Who . . . would . . . inhabit . . .
> This . . . bleak . . . world . . . alone?

Moore was overcome by a genuine depth of feeling for the old man. He waited until the last traces of Prufrock's song had faded into the early eventide of the gardens. Then, without looking up, he gently said, 'Canon, thank you for that – it brings such fond, fond, memories.'

Prufrock merely nodded, keeping his gaze fixed on the rose – Isabella's rose.

The curator waited a moment before tentatively, and with great kindness, enquiring, 'And . . . Canon, would you do me the great honour in continuing the tradition dear Isabella commenced, and joining us . . . I mean, me . . . over the Christmas . . . for a glass of port?'

The canon, too, waited a moment before replying. 'Thank you, my dear friend . . . most kind of you . . . but I think not . . . not without, eh . . .' he corrected himself: 'not this Christmas.'

49

Over the next few months Ellen and Lavelle worked hard and late, side by side, building up the New England Wine Importing Company. Neither mentioned the events of Christmas Eve.

While Lavelle looked after the shipping, warehousing and deliveries, she looked after the ordering and her one customer, Jacob Peabody, who had now opened a second store. And what a job that was – on every front!

As she had suspected, trade quietened somewhat for the few weeks after Christmas. But after *Lá Bríde* in February, it began to pick up again.

Peabody was demanding. He wanted replacement stock immediately; harangued her over the prices she was paying to Frontignac, Père et Fils arguing that she should be receiving a discounted price from them because of the growing volume of business; and wanted to hold her hand at every opportunity. Neither was he as old as his white hair implied, nor as he liked to pretend. She put him at 'not yet the three score', and a lively fifty-something he was too! She imagined he was probably flirtatious with all women of his acquaintance – as long as they were young and pretty – but she suspected that he had a real notion of her, as well.

Peabody often asked after Lavelle, calling him 'that young helper of yours' to annoy her though he knew perfectly well that Lavelle was her partner in the business. 'He'll never amount to anything, that young helper of yours. Too busy making doe's eyes at the boss,' he said to her one day.

Most of the time she ignored him, laughed it off, but once in a while she would rise to him, retorting: 'Mr Lavelle is not my helper, nor am I his boss.'

Then Peabody would catch hold of her hand and clasp it mockingly over his heart, saying, 'Better to be an old man's sweetheart than a young man's slave. Marry me, Ellen!'

'Ah, get away with you, Jacob, and stop that old molly-coddling talk. You wouldn't share your fortune with any woman. Pay up what you owe me!'

And he did. He always paid her on time.

As the flow of cash improved, so were they now able to bring in some ports and a selection of the better finer from Burgundy. It was better this way: the gold of the Ngarrindjeri had been put to good use. Now, even though she had little left of the original money, at least she had something that was starting to build up, slow and all as it was. She didn't want them to do it too fast. But when she came back she would have to try and get new customers. Supplying Peabody's two stores was fine, and he was a good customer, but . . .

'France will have to wait until I get back from Ireland,' she said to Lavelle, thinking that was another thing to be done. 'And as for the Barossa wines . . .' she looked at him. 'Well, that's a further while off.'

These days her heart was beating faster at the prospect of going home, and seeing her beloved children at last. Sometimes, an irrational fear would grip her that maybe, with all she had been through, they would not recognize her. Or worse still, be alienated from her, unable to forgive her for abandoning them.

She rehearsed it all in her mind. Once there she'd slip in quietly, visit the Crucán, find Michael's *leac* and pray a while over it. Then she'd go by Maamtrasna, stand on the hearth in Biddy's house, if they were still in it, and tell them of Roberteen. They'd be consoled to know that she had sat with him at the last – that he had been with one of their own – and that he got a decent burial, in a proper graveyard. She wouldn't tell them that it was a *bás gan sagart* – a death without a priest.

And Sheela-na-Sheeoga – was she still alive? She'd have to see her, tell her about Annie. Ask her about the riddle of 'the whitest flower'. She needed to know if her going back to Ireland would be the solving of it at last – the crushing of 'the blackest flower', whatever the old woman had meant by that.

She wondered too about Father O'Brien. Still beyond in Clonbur, coming out to Finny on his horse? Or, like Reverend Bonney, maybe

442

taken with one of the famine diseases. She had forgiven him for bringing Michael to the Westport Workhouse. The priest had done what he thought was right. Once or twice she had been tempted to write to him, to ask about the children. But she had been afraid to, in case it got out by accident where she was. It was unlikely she'd see him when she went back – it would delay her too much.

She'd do all of that first, before she went to Tourmakeady for the children. That way, once she had them, she could flee Ireland quickly in case there was trouble with Pakenham, or, even worse, with the constabulary.

She squeezed the outside of her handbag. There she felt the small hard object that Jacob Peabody had drawn from under the counter one day and slipped into her bag. He had stood close to her, as he always did, and taken her hand.

'I want you to come back safely to old Jacob,' he had said, smiling at her – for a change, there was no hint of lechery. 'Take "Dr Peabody" with you, and you'll have good health in the old country!'

Now, through the cloth of her bag she could make out the short, slender barrel and the pearled handle of 'Dr Peabody', just the right size for her hand.

'A lady's handgun,' Lavelle had called it.

At first she had been tempted to return it to Peabody. What truck did she have with a gun? But Lavelle talked her out of it.

'Listen, Ellen,' he said. 'You don't know what awaits you back there. What if Pakenham tries to prevent you getting your children?'

'Even if he did, Lavelle, I couldn't shoot him. I couldn't kill a person. Not after . . .' She didn't complete the sentence.

'I wouldn't worry about it. You'll probably never have to unwrap it. But carry it, just in case.'

Reluctantly she had agreed.

'Maybe I should go with you – in case you do have problems.'

'No, Lavelle, thank you,' she replied, having expected this moment. 'This is something I have to do myself. And, anyhow, you're needed here. Who would look after things?'

'Well, it would only be a few months, and we could talk old Peabody into taking extra stock for the time . . .' said Lavelle.

But she was ready for this, too, very clear as to how it should be. 'We've put too much into making this work,' she told him. 'We can't risk losing it now. What if there were any problems to be sorted out? I'll be fine – you'll see.'

She couldn't agree to him going with her. It would start up things between them, let him across that line she was determined not to let him cross – or herself either!

It just couldn't be.

The evening before she was to set sail, Lavelle came to see her.

'I came to wish you well, Ellen, to say God speed . . . and hurry back.'

She was glad to see him, *streelish* and all as she thought she looked with last-minute readying.

She would miss him, had grown used to his being around. But she was going to keep the good-byes between them light and breezy.

'Lavelle! Come to help me pack, have you?' she mocked. 'Here!' and she threw a dress at him.

Blushing as he caught the dress, Lavelle responded playfully: 'Don't give me any bad manners now, Ellen, or it's yourself you'll find bundled into that suitcase!'

She shot a quick glance at him as she leaned over the suitcase. He seemed *sonasach* enough, she thought. Light-hearted was the way to keep it all right!

She snatched the dress back out of his hands and folded it into the case. He watched her as she leaned over.

'You know,' he said, as she pushed down, trying to make more space for the children's clothes she had bought, 'it's a prettier sight than Clew Bay ever was!'

'What is, Lavelle?' she responded automatically, her mind not on what he was saying, until she heard him laughing.

Then she realized with some embarrassment to what he was referring. She should have been more careful – was getting too used to him being around her. And he was getting too smart, too pass-remarkable. Too easy with her. She'd teach him a lesson!

She grabbed her bag and pulled out the pistol, turning it on him.

'Now, Mr Lavelle, what remark did you make about my person?'

'Ellen! For God's sake put that thing down – it could go off!' He waved his hands at her, backing away.

'You were the one who said I'd never have to use it!' she challenged him, not even the flicker of a smile on her. 'Well, now I've found a reason – to defend my honour! You can't go around insulting a woman like you did and expect to get away with it. Clew Bay, is it? Apologize, or you'll never see it again,' she demanded of him, fighting to keep a straight face.

Lavelle couldn't tell if she was serious or play-acting. You never knew with her.

'I'll be damned if I'm going to apologize for a compliment to your person,' he said.

She had thought he'd back down, thought she could pull it off, give him a fright. He had been getting exceedingly cheeky in his remarks to her of late, but she enjoyed the banter, was well able for him. Now he had called her bluff. What was her next move to be?

Too late.

Lavelle saw her waver for just that moment. His arm shot out and caught her wrist forcing the gun up and away from him. He tightened his grip on her until she dropped it.

She knew, by the look that was on him – the one she saw there at Christmas – knew what he would do next.

This time she did not resist him.

50

Never, in all the voyages she had undertaken, had Ellen experienced such a mix of emotions as she felt on sailing out of Boston. Her mind was in turmoil, full of hope and fears, excitement and dread. This was the moment she had looked forward to ever since she had agreed to Edith Pakenham's conditions.

She was coming home again.

This would be her final test. But what would be the outcome?, she wondered, as she saw the queue of ships waiting off Deer Island – Boston's quarantine station. Was it already pre-ordained whether she would succeed or fail? Something, someone was putting her through all this. She hadn't chosen the sequence of events. Maybe the Church was right all along: the Famine was the Hand of Providence. Maybe that same Hand of Providence which had shaped her, had not yet finished shaping her.

She was imperfect. Filled with pride. Thought that on her own she could save Michael, save the children, hold back the ravages of famine – succeed where Government and Church had failed. In her eyes, even God had been wrong, and she had railed at Him in His heaven, trying to make Him see it her way. Accusing God of failing her.

But it was she who had failed. First she had failed Michael, then Annie. She had failed her other children, too, leaving them behind. And she had failed her God: killed another human being, broken His most sacred Commandment – 'Thou shalt not kill'!

She herself would have been dead if it hadn't been for the help of others. But this was more pride. Why should she be so important? Her one little life worthy of all this attention? Was she any different from the mad vacant wretches on the *Eliza Jane*? Any better than the Aboriginal women used by the white settlers, their bodies then stuffed into the middens of the Coorong? Was she any different from the red-haired girl taken from the hold of the *Dove*, and buried alive in the depths of the North Atlantic Ocean? What was her special right to life, to anything?

And what of Lavelle – and Michael?

This thing with Lavelle, she hadn't counted on. She had thought she had the situation with him well judged. That she was in control of it. They had been through a lot together and she liked him. He was respectful but good-humoured and, yes, she admitted to herself, he was a fine handsome cut of a man. But that was it, nothing more.

Certainly, she had known he was attracted to her. At first she laughed it off, thinking that in Boston he'd meet someone else. But he hadn't looked. For a while she had denied this to herself, putting it down to everything and anything, except what it was. Then Christmas Day, when he had kissed her . . . Although she had pushed him away from her, something had happened. At first she had put the feeling down to her own high spirits; the day that was in it; the success with Peabody's; the surprise of the silken scarf. Anything but what it was, she now thought. More denial.

But her reaction to him had niggled at her. It was something she had been unable to package away.

Michael was her love, her one and only love. She would be faithful to him to the grave. She had prayed to him, asked for his love to strengthen her, but . . .

It was all pride, she now knew, more pride. Thinking she could control Lavelle's emotions as well as her own. Thinking she could go to the grave without the touch of another man. She was stupid, so stupid.

Lavelle had taken her by surprise last night. But he must have sensed something. It must have been written on her face. Maybe the thing with the gun was a last-ditch attempt to deny the trembling inside her? Maybe it had been a device to assuage her guilt, so she could tell herself it wasn't her fault that she'd betrayed Michael. After all, she had held Lavelle off at gunpoint, and he had overpowered her. Or, was the gun her provocation? Knowing that he wouldn't give in to her game, knowing that the gun wasn't loaded. Had she initiated it all?

Dammit! She thought, was it ever possible to get to the bottom of a thing, to stop thinking once you had started?

Lavelle had declared his love for her, said he wanted to marry her when she returned from Ireland. This morning he had come to the Long Wharf to see her off. He had wanted to kiss her too, but she would only allow an embrace. Neither did she wear his scarf. But he hadn't commented on this. That morning she had decided not to – and had stuffed it into the case between the two print dresses for Katie and Mary. It was a distancing. She was not ready.

Lavelle, and her feelings for him, were a complication she could do without.

Pakenham . . . her children . . . These were the things she had to deal with. The only things.

And, besides, the earth had hardly yet settled on Michael's grave. His body was hardly even cold.

There could be no other man for her.

BOOK FIVE

IRELAND

51

It was the early dawn of the thirty-ninth day at sea when she saw Ireland.

The bright August sun rose in the east ahead of them. It flickered out over the green fields and the Western seas, lighting all in its path. Welcoming them home. Ellen's heart leapt for joy at the sight. Passengers familiar with the area called out the names of the islands as they sighted them: Inishark; Inishbofin; Inishturk; Clare Island – stronghold of her ancestor, Grace O'Malley; Achill Island, home to Lavelle.

Then, they tacked in for Clew Bay with its three hundred and sixty-five islands, it was said – one for every day. On past Louisburgh, and the Old Head. Towering above everything, the Reek with its crown of mist. Although she recalled all too well the severity of the barefoot ascent to the summit, the sight of the Reek was somehow comforting, reminding her of a time when life was simpler for her. All those Reek Sundays of years gone by: the long walk from Maamtrasna over the mountains to Murrisk. Then the climb up the Reek, gaining indulgences as you went, which, in the next life, would lessen the fires of purgatory, or shorten your stay there. Then the walk home again. It was hard, and it was faith alone that kept you going. The faith of St Patrick's Vermin. If only Boston's bully-boys and bigots could have seen them, she thought, scurrying down the Reek through the mist, like rats blinded by faith.

At Westport Quay, as they disembarked, there was a riot to welcome her home. Hundreds of people, their clothes in tatters, some with gnarl-topped blackthorn sticks, were trying to prevent food being loaded on to a cargo ship, the *Lady of Plymouth*. But, determined as the crowd were, a large force of the constabulary kept them back from the convoy of food.

Ellen watched in horror as a young man broke through the cordon and jumped on one of the crates, shouting, 'Food for England while Ireland starves!' to great cheers, until he was clubbed to the ground and cast back into the crowd.

Then a constable of some rank mounted the same crate and unfurled a large notice which he proceeded to read to the seething mob: 'On the authority vested in me by Her Gracious Majesty, Victoria, Queen of these Islands, I hereby read to you the Riot Act of the Parliament of Great Britain and Ireland, and caution all forthwith as to the gravity of its provisions . . .'

Nothing had changed, except for the worse. The reading of the Riot Act was met with booing and jeering, accompanied by any missiles to hand, and shouts of: 'Famine Queen!' 'Give us food, not Riot Acts!' 'Irish food for Irish bellies!' 'Attack the Peelers!' And at this there was a great surge forward which broke through the ranks of Peelers. Starving people swarmed over the boxes of food. Even as they were rounded on and beaten by the truncheons of the policemen, they tried to tear open the boxes. The young man she had seen clubbed to the ground was up again, in the thick of it. With his strong blackthorn stick he managed to lever open one of the crates. Then, with a shout, he heaved the crate on its side so that its contents spilled out. As if by signal, the other rioters stopped and the Peelers too desisted, all mute witnesses to the scene: rounded, unblemished, perfectly formed potatoes tumbled out of the crate, hopped this way and that, the sunlight picking them out as they bobbled along the quayside.

Potatoes being taken out of Ireland – it couldn't be!

She remembered what they had had to endure. How she had laboured, cutting out the good bits from rotting potatoes, saving any shred of skin she could. How she had doled out the under-sized lumpers to Michael and the children, week by week reducing the amount she gave to each of them. Sacrificing one at each meal from her own ration, until there wasn't even one left to sacrifice.

Now, with the people still starving, potatoes were being sent out of the country! It was unthinkable. The worst insult to the poor.

Angrily she stormed over to the constable in charge. Some in the crowd jeered as she passed them: 'Merchant's tallywoman!' 'Look at her! She never knew want!' She was tempted to retort, annoyed at being challenged thus. But these were her people – had probably come in from the valleys looking for work or a handful of grain. The realization shocked her.

'Who is the owner of this produce?' she asked the constable in charge. He, seeing her fine clothes, took her to be someone of importance and directed her to a well-heeled man with hat and cane.

'Sir,' she asked, 'are these your potatoes?'

He doffed his hat to her, and in a West of Ireland accent said, 'Yes, madam – for whatever good they are now, scattered on the quayside by these ruffians.'

'A shame on you – why don't you let these poor starving people have them, then?' she challenged him.

'Why, madam,' he started, flustered by her directness, 'I'd rather see them in the bay than let these wretches have them now!'

'No need to, sir. I'll buy them from you with good Yankee dollars.' And with that she pulled out her purse.

The merchant was flabbergasted – didn't know what to make of this finely dressed woman from America.

'Ten dollars seems a fair price for damaged goods,' she said, pushing the money into his hands.

'Well, yes, I suppose so, madam. Yes, take them away,' the merchant blurted, embarrassed by it all, but glad to have recouped some of his losses.

So, in her first moments back in Ireland, Ellen Rua O'Malley hiked up her skirts, knelt on the Quay of Westport and gathered up potatoes, returning them to the crate from which they had spilled.

They were round and smooth, no eyes or dark marks on them. Definitely not the ugly, misshapen potatoes the poor knew. Only the best class of potato would do for the tables of England!

As she gathered them, the *Lady of Plymouth* continued to be loaded. She heard the ship's captain check off his bill of entry to Liverpool port: 'Pigs – one hundred and one; Cows – fifty-four; Sheep – three score and ten; Fowl – six boxes; Calves – seven . . .'

When she had finished, she approached the ranking Peeler again. 'Now, Constable,' she addressed him firmly. 'Since I am the new owner of these potatoes, I wish them distributed to the needy here, without violence to their persons.'

'Oats – fifteen barrels,' the captain's voice called out in the background. 'Wheat – forty-four bags; Oatmeal – one hundred and eighteen bags; Coarse meat – nineteen barrels; Bacon – a dozen pounds . . .'

The constable, thinking her to be the wife of some official, acceded to her directions without demur. 'Yes, madam. As you wish, madam,' he said. 'Men – set up an orderly line. Any person being disorderly will be disqualified from relief.'

As she left the scene, Ellen was horrified to see that as soon as the famished people received their paltry lot of potatoes, they devoured them raw, so great was their distress.

Behind her, the checking of the cargo continued: 'Butter – three hundred and fifty firkins; Lard – two terces; Tongues – ten firkins; Ale – four hogsheads; Whiskey – twenty-four puns; Potatoes – delete the potatoes . . .'

Ellen instructed the driver of her carriage to take her to Maamtrasna via the coast road through Louisburgh and Leenane. That way she would come by the Crucán and Maamtrasna first before going on to Tourmakeady. Once she had the children there would be no stopping, they would go straight from Tourmakeady to Westport – a much shorter route.

The driver, Faherty, a thin, talkative fellow from Westport, at first refused.

'Begging your pardon, ma'am – but I daren't go back the valleys,' he said.

When she pressed him, saying no harm would come to him, he replied, 'Begging your pardon again, ma'am – it's not my own person I'm afeared for but old Nell here. 'Pon my oath, they'd eat her for sure, things is that bad back there!' And he patted the horse's neck.

Eventually she convinced him, saying she would hire him for the return journey to Westport, 'with something extra for yourself.'

Faherty's description of how bad things were in the valleys sent a shiver through her. Despite all she'd heard in Grosse Île and Boston about the state of Ireland, nothing could have prepared her for the riot on the quayside. Ragged wretches so desperate for food they risked being clubbed to death rather than starve.

Now, around the outskirts of the town she saw hordes of the poor roaming aimlessly, while others sat passively, staring at nothing, waiting for the release that death would bring.

'Why are so many in Westport?' she asked him.

'Well, ma'am,' he told her, 'they swarm in from the countryside looking for any relief. Walk miles and miles in all weather. There's nothing else left for them to do. They're mostly evicted. No homes, no places to sleep, no work, no potatoes. They might as well walk the roads – it gives them something to do. They walk here, then they walk back again, or walk on to Castlebar, mostly saying nothing to no one.'

She noticed he spoke in English all the time to her.

'What about the workhouses – can't they take them in?' she asked, knowing the reply.

'The workhouses is all filled to overflowing. For every corpse they slide out the window at the back, there's another ten banging on the front door to get in. 'Pon my oath, it's harder for the poor to get into the poorhouse, than it is for the rich to get into heaven. Asides, those that's supposed to pay money to keep them open won't pay it. Whether they have it or not is another thing. So the Guardians close the workhouses and put everybody inside out on the street. It's a terrible thing, ma'am – a terrible thing.'

Ellen sat back, stunned into silence by what she had already witnessed and heard in her first hour here.

Dear God, it was worse than when she left – a thousand times worse! And had nothing been done for the people? No relief, no food, no work, no shelter? She couldn't believe things had been let go so far. This was the fourth year of Famine. Surely there had been enough time for the Government to do something?

'They say, ma'am, a million is in the ground, and another million is beyond in America – if it's a thing it's true,' Faherty said, as if reading her thoughts.

A million of her people dead – could it be? Maybe Roberteen wasn't wandering in his head, after all, about how bad things were. She could well believe that a million had gone out of Ireland. Weren't the seas themselves black with the coffin ships and the tens and tens of thousands pouring into Grosse Île and Boston alone!

'Well, ma'am, they got what they wanted, 'pon my soul, they did.'

'Who did?'

'Russell and Trevelyan and them all beyond in Westminster,' he replied. 'Kill us all off, clear the land, and make Ireland like England. Make all big farms of land instead of the little stripes we have back here in the West. That's what it is, ma'am, 'pon my oath it is!'

'What about the soup kitchens?' She had heard great talk of the soup kitchens in Grosse Île.

'Soup kitchens, is it!' he exclaimed. 'I'll tell you what about the soup kitchens, ma'am. They brought over a famous chef from some big hotel in London – Soyer he was – a Frenchman to make the soup! And 'tis said at one stage they were giving that old pea-water to three million people a day. It could be done, all right, my oath it could be done. But what did Trevelyan do then?' He gave her a moment, and then told her: 'They tumbled all the soup kitchens down because they was keeping the people alive – that's what! Anyway, it was the Quakers that mostly kept them going – not the Government.'

He kept talking, half turning his head to her now and again, making a little nervous wink with his eye when he said, 'I'll tell you what' or, 'my oath it is!' or ''pon my soul'. He took her silence for agreement with this analysis of the situation, and continued: 'But they don't hate us all the same, the English. 'Tis afraid of us they are, my oath it is. Sure, don't I see it with my own two eyes?'

Ellen listened as the coach-driver continued his dissertation on the English.

'The way it was heading in Ireland, there was going to be more of us than them – until the blight came. We was heading for the nine million, they had only the fifteen or sixteen. They was dead afraid we'd go beyond to London and places, and take the work off of them. But that's not even the most thing they was frightened of. No, I'll tell you what – and I have the proof of it too,' he went on. 'They was afraid with all of us going beyond that England would turn Catholic – that's what!' And he turned his head to see her reaction.

She was fascinated by him, how he kept firing out his opinions, and with such certainty too. She nodded at him. She was sure he was right – that somewhere at the bottom of it all was religion.

'*Is olc an iomarca creidimh,*' she said to him, and he looked at her oddly. 'Too much religion is a bad thing!'

'You're right, ma'am,' he replied, and he was off again: 'Sure, didn't they pull down Peel when he gave the money to Maynooth – and he their Prime Minister. 'Tisn't too long since they gave the vote to us Catholics – only for Daniel O'Connell, God rest him, we'd never have got it. And now the latest. The whole West of Ireland is crawling with these proslatators. Plenty of food with them and they proslatating the people out of being Catholics into Protestants. Then blaming the poor people for the Famine on account of them being papists and not being true believers. You're right, ma'am, religion is at the bottom of the whole thing – my oath it is, like it always was!'

Faherty rested his case – for a while.

Ellen was inclined to believe that Faherty, in his own simple way, had arrived close to her own truth. History told her it was so – and she had seen it with the Aborigines: 'Christianize and colonize them,' was the cry. In Boston she had experienced naked sectarian hatred, so vicious in its expression it was scarcely believable. But it was there – and not hidden either.

Yet how could a Government behave like that towards its own people? Stand by and see whole sections of them wiped out like vermin – Saint Patrick's Vermin. It was too awful to consider.

They were on higher ground now, back a few miles past the Reek, heading towards Kilsallagh. To the right, she could see the beauty of the bay she had first sailed into with all its islands. How different the landscape here was to anywhere else she'd seen. There was no place like it – if it didn't have the Famine. No place in the whole wide world.

'Look at her, now, ma'am!' Faherty interrupted her thoughts.

Ellen looked to the other side of the carriage. There, running barefoot alongside them, ragged, unkempt, was a waif of a girl. Probably only twelve or thirteen.

The girl, not looking at Ellen, seeing nothing only some space far beyond where they were, just ran, silently keeping time with Nell. She did not stretch out her palm to them, as many whom they had passed had done. It seemed as if the girl sought nothing – only wanted to be with them. To step for a moment, out of her poverty and misery and hopelessness, and run beside a carriage with a fine lady.

Ellen was transfixed. The girl's legs and arms sliced the air in rhythm with Nell's canter. The silent up and down of her arms was only interrupted when the few threads, which barely held the front and back of her garment together, slipped down over her shoulder. Without breaking stride, her hand would shoot across and hoist up the fallen fabric, covering again bones from which hung the merest filament of skin.

Still she made no sound.

'Go on, get up there, Nell!' Faherty flicked his whip at Nell's broad rump, wanting to leave the girl behind in case his passenger might be offended. The carriage drew away from the girl. Ellen was about to tell Faherty to stop, when the girl reappeared, having increased the tempo of her running so as not to be outpaced. Still she neither looked at them nor made any sound. It was as if she were some expressionless puppet attached to the side of the carriage. Ellen knew that no matter how fast they went, she would be there. Like the wandering hordes of the poor, she had nothing else to be doing.

'Stop the carriage at once, Mr Faherty!' Ellen ordered, ashamed that she had been so mesmerized by the girl as to allow this macabre race to continue.

The carriage stopped.

The girl stopped.

She did not seem to be out of breath, or in any distress. As if her spirit had been the runner, and not her body. She stood at the side of the carriage, still looking ahead, looking into some future which only she could see.

She was only a child, Ellen thought, as she opened the door and got out. An underdeveloped, emaciated child. Lank brown hair brushed the top of her shoulders. Her pert little nose was pinched back with the hunger, her dark eyes, expressionless, locked on her vision.

Ellen touched her on the shoulder. It was cold, despite the girl's exertions.

'What's your name?' Ellen asked her softly, but there was no flicker of a response. '*Cad is ainm duit?*' She tried the same question in Irish. Still the girl did not speak.

'We have to get her some food, Mr Faherty. I'm bringing her with me to Louisburgh!' she said.

The coachman started to say something but thought the better of it.

Ellen gently shepherded the girl into the carriage, talking to her soothingly. The girl moved with her. Apart from that, Ellen may as well have not been there for all the response she got from her.

'She's probably an orphan,' Faherty ventured at last. 'Family all taken with the hunger – there's hundreds of them everywhere.'

And so they travelled the further few miles on to Louisburgh. It was from there that Kitty had hailed. Louisburgh. The name had stuck in Ellen's mind: it was near Louisbourg on Cape Breton Island they had been rescued by the *Dove*. When she asked Faherty about it, he knew – as she had known he would. ''Pon my oath, you are right, ma'am – it's named for some place out foreign – some battle Lord Sligo's people was at way back.'

Ellen was tempted to ask about Kitty's family, but she decided against it. There wasn't enough time, and she couldn't afford to have word get back to Pakenham. Besides, Kitty was beyond any human help now.

In the Octagon that was the town square of Louisburgh, the general store was barricaded against attacks by starving peasants. But most of the people were listless, incapable of breaking in anywhere. Waiting only for death's door to open to them. When Faherty had raised the store-keeper and convinced him to open, Ellen purchased food and milk for the girl, who took not the slightest interest in it.

'It's no use, ma'am – she's gone. Her mind is altered!'

'Oh, God, Mr Faherty, what am I to do?'

Ellen was torn in two. How could she leave this girl, not much older than her own two, helpless here on the roadside? On the other hand, how could she keep her, take care of her, if she wouldn't eat or even drink a drop of anything? She'd have to leave her in Louisburgh. They could take her to the priest's house.

Ellen dashed back to the carriage and opened her case. She

returned carrying one of the dresses she had brought with her for Katie and Mary.

'I can't leave her like this, the rags falling off her body. This'll fit her, cover her for a while, at least.'

Faherty shook his head. The woman from America could make up her own mind.

Ellen, telling him to turn away, slipped the soft new dress of New England print over the girl's head, throwing away the threadbare shift she'd had on.

The dress fitted the girl easily, fell down over her bones, making her shine like any of the young ladies who, on Sundays, strolled Boston Common with their parents.

The August sun picked up the bright blues and pinks, as Ellen settled the ruffled collar of the dress. Then she loosely tied back the white lace strings in a little bow behind the girl's waist. The dress seemed to light up the girl's face, catching something in her eyes and bringing her to life. Yet she neither moved nor spoke while Ellen tended to her.

Ellen stood back from her now, admiring the transformation in her, and wondering what she should do. Her heart reached out to the girl: abandoned, locked in silence into some other world. As she stood there, Ellen had a sense that the girl was about to speak.

She was almost right.

First, a solitary tear rolled from the girl's eye and fell, staining the bright fabric of the dress. Then, another single tear formed, and another, and another, as if the child could only cry in single tears, so great was her trauma. Until, from both her eyes, the tears began to come in a steady stream.

Ellen threw her arms round the child and held her. Soon she could feel the wet flow from the girl's eyes seep through her own clothes, and on to her skin, so great was the torrent of tears.

'I'm taking her with me, Faherty! Whatever – I'm taking her with me!' she said, confirmed in her decision.

They left Louisburgh, turning inland, the silent girl within the comfort of Ellen's arm, her stare now fixed not ahead, but on some spot on the Boston dress.

Faherty wasn't sure how much longer the journey would take

them. 'Delphi must be the ten miles from here, and Leenane another seven or eight . . . Beyond that I don't know – that's your country . . .' He put it over on her without actually asking her.

Finny, she knew, was about twelve miles on from Leenane, and she told him this. She had been in luck that her ship had landed so early in the morning. It gave her a good start. And the day would be bright late into evening.

'Would we be back in Westport by nightfall?'

'That depends as much on you, ma'am, as anybody. If your business gets done quickly . . . And it's down to Nell, here. She's a sturdy horse, strong as an ox, but she'll need resting and watering, and time for grass.'

Ellen thought for a moment. She wouldn't spend long at Maamtrasna – just enough to 'stand on the hearth' to Biddy and Martin, wait on the Crucán a while with Michael. But she couldn't delay for fear word would go back to Pakenham. She wanted to surprise him, give him no time for anything. Once she had the children, then she would get away, back to Westport, and take the first ship they could out of Ireland.

'I'd be grateful if you'd try, Mr Faherty,' she said. 'Very grateful.'

Her thoughts returned to the girl, silent as ever beside her in her bright new dress.

Ellen supposed that the girl, aimlessly drifting towards Westport from back in the valleys somewhere, had never owned a proper dress. Had probably never even seen a dress such as this with its bright New World colours. Yet something within the girl knew the dress was special, not a thing ordinarily meant for her. Now its pretty pinks and blues had become her new fixation.

Ellen hoped the girl would sleep awhile. Then maybe she might eat or drink something.

Ahead of them, to the left, were the Sheefry Hills, and to the right the high peak of Mweelrea. Between the interlocking spurs of the two sets of mountains was Doo Lough, the Black Lake, and the Pass Road that would take them to Delphi and round the mouth of the Killary, to Leenane. They would not have much further to go then.

But she had not reckoned on something like this. The girl was another thing for her to contend with. Yet she couldn't have left her to die, as she surely would have – and still might, Ellen thought, if she was beyond eating.

She wondered about the girl's parents and family. Faherty was most likely right: if they weren't dead, they soon would be. Stricken bodies lined the roadside. There seemed to be no hope for the people. Times had been bad, very bad, when she left Ireland, but she couldn't believe how much things had deteriorated.

And the silence . . . As they headed towards Doo Lough, she heard no living thing – no sheep, cows, pigs. Not even a dog.

'Faherty . . . ?'

'I know, ma'am,' he said, reading her thoughts. 'Everything is sold for rent or eaten – even the dogs.'

The further back into the mountains they went, the more distressed Ellen became at the sight of the people. They seemed to make an unending line of misery along the roadside. Ragged, diseased and starving, they made no sound. Some put out a hand towards them, but they were so weak that their hands could only stay outstretched for a few moments. It wasn't that they were begging – they were beyond that. It was more a gesture of utter hopelessness; as if trying to reach out towards something that lived. For they were not alive.

They were the dead walking. Their purgatory was now, here along the Doolough Pass Road in the corridor between the shadow of the two mountains and the black edge of the lake. The road wound downwards beside the long narrow lake, then curved away into nothing where it snaked through the pass between the two spurs of Ben Creggan and Mweelrea. It was beautiful, so coldly beautiful, this country, presiding over all the horrors along its valleys and roads. Not that those who lined the roads saw any beauty in it. Even those that were still able to lift their heads.

The wind whipped up a bit, blowing little white edges on to the water's ridges.

'It does that back here, ma'am. It whips up when you least expect it to. Look –' he gesticulated.

There, ahead of them, as the wind in the narrow valley blew up suddenly, Ellen saw first one, then two more of the phantom-like figures who had been teetering along the road, weightless with

462

starvation, caught by the wind and swept into the dark waters of Doo Lough as if they were wisps of straw.

The phantoms made no sound as the black water received them. The others in the line made no sound, gave no recognition that anything out of the ordinary had happened, but just kept on walking to where they probably knew not.

'The walking dead, ma'am!' Faherty whispered out her earlier thought, making the sign of the cross as he did so.

The whole countryside was a graveyard, peopled with these grey hollow corpses. Whether they died in the lake or on the roadside seemed not to matter to them.

'Why do they keep just walking and walking?' she said, more to herself than Faherty.

But he answered her. 'Well, if they reach the workhouse – and it's open, and they can get in – then, at least, they'll be put in a grave when they die. They know that. They just want to die decent. There's nothing else in life for them. They just want to die decent.'

Back deeper they went, past Delphi Lodge, home to Pakenham's cousin. Hundreds of the poor were silently milling around the entrance. Faherty asked one of them, strong enough to speak, as to the reason. It seemed that five or six hundred starving people had descended on Louisburgh looking for any morsel of food or a ticket to the Westport Workhouse. The Relieving Officer, washing his hands of the problem, had sent them to walk the ten or eleven miles to Delphi Lodge, where two of the Guardians of the workhouse would dispense relief.

By the time those who hadn't died on the way reached Delphi, the two Guardians were at lunch. When they finally appeared, no relief – not a scrap of food, not even one ticket for the workhouse – was given out. Many had then left to walk back to Louisburgh, and then on to Westport. These must have been the line of people she had seen along the way, so weakened, so defeated, waiting for death to take them any way it chose.

The others, the hundreds she now saw, had remained, sitting among the trees at Delphi, hoping against hope that, if they remained long enough, something would happen to improve their lot.

They pressed on, leaving behind them the starving hundreds. Ellen was consumed with guilt and grief. How much worse could it get?

'There's not a thing you, nor I, nor anybody can do, ma'am,' Faherty said. 'It's the identical same all over the country.'

Ellen said nothing, growing more silent, like the girl. Understanding that no words could convey the horrors, heaped one on top of the other, that she was witnessing. Understanding how the weight of it all could silence you – strike you dumb.

The Bundorragha River bounced and bubbled beside them as once more they left the low ground. She and the girl had sat on one of the many large rocks whitened by the sun while Faherty watered Nell and let the horse graze a while on the river's banks. She took some food herself and tried the girl again, but to no avail. Then up and on they went, over the brow of the land, while below them the Killary spread out. And as they followed the sinuous road, trapped between mountainside and sea, far beneath them she could see the low-water mud flats and sand bars, and far above, towering over them and the harbour, the peak of the Devilsmother.

Before the town they stopped by the Erriff River, she wanting to look a while at the low waterfall of Aasleagh. Here the Máistir had taken her as a child to 'see the water dance over the rocks'. Beautiful then, it was still beautiful now. Even in this wasteland. Even in the midst of so much desolation.

Now she was home, in familiar territory. Just ahead was Leenane, where once she had come for the Pattern Days. Where she had first set eyes on Michael – and, she thought darkly, Pakenham.

Soon she would have to face him, stand up to him, and take her children away from him. She consoled herself with the thought that, until that moment, the children would at least be safe at Tourmakeady, sheltered from all that she had seen on this terrible, terrible journey. She looked for a moment at the girl, still vacant, beside her. At least at Tourmakeady her children would be spared the fate of this poor child, and thousands like her.

After Leenane, Faherty drove on through the valley, then before Maam turned left bringing them high into the mountains of Joyce's country. Soon they reached the gap that led to the next valley and

Currarevagh. Then they would swing down by the *Trá Bán*, the silver strand near Shanafaraghaun, and on past Lough Nafooey until they forked off before Finny on to the rough track that would take them to Crucán na bPáiste.

There would be her valley: Maamtrasna.

Then she would be home.

52

She was by then excited, nervous, fearful, and excited again, as they breasted the hill below the Crucán that would allow her her first view of home in almost two years.

Then she saw it!

She made Faherty stop the carriage. Below was her valley. To the left, under the Partry Mountains, the ribbon of road that would take her past Derrypark then on to Tourmakeady and her children. Ahead was Lough Mask, sparkling in the sun as it had that August morning three years ago when she had looked into its waters and known she was carrying Annie. She thought of her child for a moment – far away in Australia, laid down beside different waters. Now, here, all the little green islands that she remembered were still there, catching the glint of sun and water.

Her eye drew back along the road from Glenbeg, then up along the side of 'the mountain', as they always called it, giving it no other name. Up there, hidden away somewhere, lay the Hare's Garden, where Michael and Martin Tom Bawn, and Roberteen, had left their sweat in the rocky ground to take from it the life-saving lumpers.

Life-saving? With Michael gone, Roberteen gone, Annie gone? And what of Martin Tom Bawn and Biddy?

She would see them later.

Now she must go to the Crucán.

She walked up the hill of the burial place of the children, to look for the *leac* with which she had marked his grave. First, she removed her shoes and stockings. Never before had she walked this place anything other than barefooted. Now she wanted to feel its grass welcome her, to clench its earth with her feet. Be part of it again.

She entered the burial area. Everywhere there were *leacs* and mounds of earth. This wasn't how she'd remembered it. She stumbled, reached out a hand to save herself, then recoiled when it touched something that was neither rock nor grass. Something that lay partly uncovered by the thinnest layer of earth. The remains of a human hand.

With a shock she realized that all these mounds were graves, all these stones were markings. Some of the newer graves were barely covered. Time and the elements would soon expose them. Those who had made them must have been too weak to dig. Too weak to cover in properly the bodies of their loved ones. The memory of Grosse Île flashed across her mind, the mass unmarked graves. At least there they had coffins, and a priest, or a minister.

At last finding the large rock which stood over Michael's grave, she fell to her knees and began to pray.

Her prayer was a remembrance. A remembrance of their life and their love; of days in the fields working together; of days on the mountain when the blue and the brightness were almost blinding. She remembered Sundays going with him over the high road of Bóithrín a tSléibhe to the small church at Finny, Katie running to the edge to bring her a fist of wildflowers. All those miles they'd walked – she happy just to be by his side. Evenings by the hearth, watching the flames rise, thinking of nothing, but thinking of everything too, stealing a glance at him – her dark 'Fair-haired Boy'. And the nights when all these other joys seemed to come together, to be expressed in the deep joining of themselves as man and woman. When even the act of love itself was transcended, left far behind them, as their beings sang to each other.

She told him then of all that had befallen her since she left him, asked his forgiveness for the times she had let him slip her mind.

Told him about Annie. Felt his stillness, his sadness, as he listened to how his last-born had died in the strange far-off land.

She had so much to tell him. There was no knowing when or if she would come back again. Maybe it would be years until they were all settled in America and she could return to kneel here, talk with him again.

She told him about Lavelle. No angry words crossed his lips. She wanted him to reproach her, to say it wasn't a right thing what she felt, to say it wasn't yet time – that he wasn't yet cold in the grave. But he said nothing, nothing at all to her.

As he did in life, so in death, she thought. He was leaving it to her, trusting her to work it out for herself. But she didn't want to.

Finally, she asked him for the strength to do what she must do for their children. To rescue them. To bring them all safely out of this blighted land. She crossed herself in concluding rite and stood up, startled by the presence of the girl behind her.

She had left her in Faherty's care at the carriage, wanting to be alone with her thoughts on the Crucán. She wondered when the girl had joined her. And what was going on behind that vacant stare of hers, as she stood in some kind of mute testament, halfway between the living and the dead all around them?

Below, Faherty looked up at them.

'What a strange sight they are, the two of them,' he whispered to Nell. 'Standing on top of that hill: the red-haired fancy woman from America, in her finery and bare feet, with that waif of a girl – not saying a word to a soul, all dressed up out in this wild place, and she herself barely in it at all.'

The girl shadowed Ellen as she walked to the large *leac*, down a bit from the Crucán, on the Finny side. It was here, sitting on the cradle of rock, that Ellen had waited for Michael the day he went to Clonbur to see Father O'Brien. Here, she had felt the chill of the blight-cloud as it had rained down its death on her valley.

What a place of unnatural beauty it was. She looked at the girl. Did she see any of it? The grandeur of the place was in stark contrast to the girl's own emaciated condition. If she couldn't get her to eat soon, the girl would die. The bright Boston dress would be her shroud.

Ellen looked across the mountain path. Was old Sheela still stuck away up there in her hidden corner of the mountain? Was she even alive? And what of the riddle – was it answered now? Needing to know, Ellen decided that she would cross the threshold of the old woman's hut. She'd bring the girl with her – not that she'd have any choice, for the girl was sticking to her like a second skin.

The door of Sheela-na-Sheeoga's hut was ajar. Nevertheless Ellen knocked on it.

Receiving no reply she entered, the girl in her wake. 'God bless all here!' she called out in English into the darkness.

Silence.

'*Sheela, an bhfuil tú ann?*' she asked, enquiring if the old woman was there. Movement in the far corner caught her attention.

'Ellen, Ellen Rua,' a weak voice said. 'I knew you'd come . . .'

'Sheela!' Ellen said, beginning to move towards the sound.

'Keep back! Keep back!' the voice struggled to raise itself. 'The *fiabhras dubh* is on me!'

Ellen strained her eyes to see the old woman. So she had contracted the dreaded typhus. 'Sheela, can I help you? Get you anything?'

'Not a thing, *craythur* . . . not a thing. 'Tisn't long more Sheela-na-Sheeoga will be in it at all.'

'Don't say that, Sheela.'

'Ellen Rua, don't talk *ráiméis*! Remember who it is you're speaking to. What of the child?'

Ellen knew the old midwife would want to know. 'Annie is dead, Sheela. Beyond in Australia . . .' Ellen said, her heart heavy with the saying of it.

The old woman fell silent.

'Last year?' she asked presently.

'Yes, last year,' Ellen replied, in a low voice.

'I should have known it. A strange thing came over me a while last year,' the old woman began to tell her. 'First it was a cry in the night like the Banshee, but not the Banshee. Then I was floating, and there was strange music drumming all around me, and voices speaking to me in a foreign tongue . . .'

'Yes, Sheela, that's how it was,' Ellen said gently, remembering the cry of the Mingka Bird and Wiwirremalde, and Annie's spirit rising with Ngurunderi to the white wasteland of the Milky Way.

'Oh, Annie, *mo stóirín*,' Sheela-na-Sheeoga said, and Ellen could hear the sadness in the old woman's voice. 'She's at rest now in the stars with the Máistir and your dear mother Cáit,' she added, her voice fading.

'Sheela, I have something to ask you . . .' Ellen began, wanting to ask about the girl.

But the old woman stopped her. 'I know, Ellen Rua,' she said weakly. 'I know . . . She who is with you will speak at the moment of silence. Her voice will be great in the far-off land, and she will be silenced no more!'

Ellen was startled by this and looked at the girl beside her. The girl, as ever, showed no reaction, no movement, only stared into the dark corner where the old woman was.

How could Sheela have known what she, Ellen, was going to ask her? How could she have known about Annie and the Mingka Bird and the Ngarrindjeri? And what was she saying now about this girl beside her? Ellen hadn't yet fully understood the first riddle about the whitest flower; now she had given her another one.

'Speak at the moment of silence.' What did that mean? The girl was already silent. 'The far-off land' ... was that Australia, Canada, America – or somewhere else? 'She will be silenced no more.' Was the old woman predicting conflict or greatness for this waif of a girl who had no family, no speech, not even a name?

'You have another question, Ellen Rua?' came the almost inaudible voice from the corner. 'Ask before it is too late.'

'Sheela . . .' Ellen took a step forward into the gloom '. . . the riddle you made me – the whitest flower becoming the blackest flower, and me to crush it. Is it finished now when I get my children back? Will that be the end of it all, Sheela?'

Ellen waited, bent forward, listening intently. She heard the starting of a sound as if the old woman was ready to answer her.

She waited, but there was nothing.

'Is it finished, Sheela?'

Ellen moved forward again, as if to physically will the answer from her.

The old woman never answered her before she died.

53

Ellen came back down the mountain, back past the Crucán. She had been afraid to touch the old woman for fear of getting the typhus again, so instead she blocked up the doorway with stones, making the cabin her burial place. Her grim task complete, she turned right on to the path that would take her down the valley to the village. So intent was she on trying to make sense of what had passed between Sheela and herself that, at first, she didn't notice it.

The valley was silent. Nothing stirred except the puff of a breeze over the Mask. No bird sang. No sound of the dogs of Derrypark yelping carried across the lake to her. No sound of men calling in the fields, or the high, bright sound of children. Nothing. It chilled her blood.

In silence she and the girl picked their way down into the village. First one cabin, then the next, and the next, and the one after that again. All of them silent.

'Where there's fire there's life.' She looked above the village seeking the tell-tale sign of life. Now, she saw nothing – not even a wisp of smoke from any of the cabins. All of the fires of the valley had gone out. There were no fires because there were no people. They, like the fires, had been extinguished by *An Gorta Mór*.

It was as if they had never been.

Where had they gone to? The extra stones she saw on the Crucán – some of her people were there, she knew. Some would be amongst the long thin line of road people they had passed along by Doo Lough. Or those at Delphi, hoping for food from the big house, then, in desperation trying to make the workhouse at Westport. She felt ashamed that she had not recognized them – her own neighbours.

Some, like Roberteen, would have gone to Canada or America. The New World or the next world, their only choice.

She stood by their own cabin. All that was left in place were a few corner-stones, and a scattering of other stones, the grass licking up around the sides of them.

This was all that remained of their lives. All the days and nights of them. This place where prayers were said. Where she had sat and held the Lessons with the children. Where the children were born. This was the place where laughter and love – and tears – had been. Now it was only a few stones, a few blades of grass. Pakenham would move sheep in here when the time was right.

She looked at where the door had been. Her eye then followed the line from it up to the spring-well, where she would stand calling Katie and Mary down from drawing the water, they spilling the half of it on the way. The same door she had looked out of, watching for Michael and Martin Tom Bawn and Roberteen to come back down the mountain with the turf, or the hidden lumpers.

And what of Martin Tom Bawn, and Biddy? Slowly, she went to the cabin of their nearest neighbours. It was still standing. But the roof was pulled in and the doors and windows blocked up.

What had happened to Biddy and Martin? Was there any possibility that they, too, like Sheela-na-Sheeoga had been, were still alive?

She pulled at the stones blocking the door.

'Here, help me!' she called to the girl.

But the girl just stood there as before.

Ellen tore back the stones to make a big enough hole for herself to clamber through. The stench which met her nostrils was nauseating, forcing her to retreat and gasp for air.

Covering her nose, she called into the hole, 'Martin! Biddy! Are ye in there? It's me, Ellen!'

She got no answer.

She put her head further in through the opening, hauling herself up on the stones.

'Martin! Biddy!' She broke off, sensing some movement, hearing a sound.

She pulled herself over the stones until she was more in than out of the cabin. Inside, it was dark, like Sheela's, and she couldn't see that well. Gingerly she set her feet down on the cabin floor.

'Biddy!' she called out again, the awful putrid stench going down her throat, almost having a taste to it. She swallowed hard, trying not to retch.

There was a movement – they were alive!

She moved forward, stumbling over a large stone. She fell, her hands outstretched. As she did she heard the sound of a low growl. She looked up alarmed. There, a few feet from her face, eyes shining, lips pulled back over its teeth, stood the Tom Bawns' dog.

The dog snarled, forcing her to retreat. But not before she had seen what was behind it. What it was guarding. What she had disturbed it from. There, huddled together in the corner, lay the lifeless bodies of her neighbours, Martin's arms around Biddy in a final embrace. But that was not all.

She had seen, too, the shirt reefed from the man's arm and shoulder where he had sought to protect his wife from the starving animal. She had seen the flesh torn from his bones.

Outside, Ellen threw herself against the wall of the house, sobbing, gasping for breath, praying that death had claimed Martin and Biddy before their dog had.

Oh, Sweet Jesus on the Cross, it was horrible! Horrible!

Her two dear friends had tried to entomb themselves, wanting to die together. Not out on some road where they would lie unburied. The dog must have slipped in somehow. They surely would never have kept it with them, she thought, although they loved the mangy thing.

What was happening in the world when this could happen? Her people, her friends, all gone. Every single last cabin empty, levelled or pulled in on top of themselves while people still had the strength. The whole village deserted. In the name of all that was holy or even unholy, how could anybody who had witnessed any of this – seen even one hundredth of the suffering and agony she had witnessed, stand by and do nothing?

Had any of those in power ever set foot in the place? And, if they had, how in God's name could they not do something? How could they close the soup kitchens, the workhouses, the Relief Works – speeding up starvation and death? Unless that was the result they had wanted all along.

Maybe Faherty was right. Maybe it was fear. Old, deep-rooted, and unspoken, fear.

*   *   *

473

Still shaking, Ellen searched until she found a length of wood. Then she re-entered the tomb of the Tom Bawns. She could not leave until she had done this last thing for them. The dog growled at her again and, when she did not retreat this time, crouched with its belly to the ground and bared its teeth at her. She edged forward, the wood between her and the dog. It sprang at the wood, viciously snapping at it. She pulled the wood back to draw the dog to her. Again it slunk to its belly, ready to attack. Ready to defend its food.

She whipped her free hand forward. Instinctively, the animal went for it. Too late, the dog turned as the blow from the wood cracked its skull. Ellen, sickened by what she had to do, quickly covered its twitching body with stones.

Once outside she blocked up the door, entombing her friends once more as they had wished.

Martin Tom Bawn and Biddy would now rest together in peace.

The girl, who had stood watching the whole time, accompanied Ellen back up to where Faherty and the carriage awaited them.

As they walked, her mind full of the awfulness of what she had been part of, something caught Ellen's eye. There, below the road, in the fields, was the flower – the whitest flower of the potato plant. Pristine, radiant, beautiful.

Down to the field she ran, falling to her knees, wildly scrabbling away the earth. She pulled up the plant, shaking the clay from it. There wasn't a speck of the blight anywhere to be seen on it.

She turned to the girl. 'Look there's no blight! It's gone! Praise be to God – it's gone! The blight is gone!' she cried out, her mind overcome by all she had been through.

The girl, unmoved, looked somewhere over Ellen's shoulder into the high peaks of the Partry Mountains.

Ellen ran up to where Faherty was, the girl trailing behind her.

'Look!' she said, pushing the potato plant at him, the lumpers small but perfect. 'It's good! No blight – look!'

Faherty looked at her. 'It don't matter now, ma'am, if it is or not. There's no one left to dig them.'

She looked at the plant in her hand, then back towards the field. Faherty was right. Even if the lumpers stayed sound – and she'd seen before how overnight this whitest flower could turn black and rotten – there was nobody left to dig them out of the lazy beds.

She plucked the flower from the plant.

Back in the carriage, her spirit beaten, the flower in her hand, she remembered something.

'Mr Faherty, what date is it today?'

'It's the twentieth, ma'am,' he replied, not understanding the import of her question. 'It's the twentieth day of August in the year of Our Lord eighteen hundred and forty-eight, so it is,' he said jauntily, adding: 'Why do you want to know, ma'am?'

She didn't tell him.

54

Before they set off for Tourmakeady Lodge, she asked Faherty to pull down off the road a bit and to look at the lake while she changed her clothes.

She was going to confront Pakenham as she was now, not as she had been when she had left here. The landlord would be taken aback to see her, 'that peasant O'Malley woman', in shoes and stockings. To see her once wild hair pulled back and tied, the emerald-green dress, finely pin-tucked from shoulder to waist with discreet white frills at the neck and cuffs. Yes, Pakenham was in for a shock. She felt her handbag, making sure, yet again, that Dr Peabody was at home. She wondered again, too, if she had the nerve to use it? She hoped she wouldn't have to.

When she returned to the carriage, the tiny white flower was lying where she had left it. She picked it up, remembering when she had first begun to unravel Sheela-na-Sheeoga's riddle.

'When the whitest flower blooms, so too you will bloom . . .'

It had started this very day three years ago. When the whitest flowers of the new harvest had danced in the morning sun.

'But the whitest flower will become the blackest flower . . .'

How could the old woman have known the blight was about to strike? That the white mist, eerie and beautiful, would descend on the potatoes, coating their leaves with a terrible whiteness, before destroying them.

And the last part of the riddle: 'And you, red-haired Ellen, must crush its petals in your hand.'

Ellen understood now what that meant. But had it been achieved?

Sheela-na-Sheeoga was telling her that she must overcome all that the blackest flower would bring – hunger, eviction, separation, death – and that the power to do so was in Ellen's own hands.

That she had done. Every tragedy, every grief, every trial –

476

somehow she had come through them all, survived. And now her quest was over.

Or was it?

This was what Ellen had been trying to get from the old woman before she died. Strange how Sheela-na-Sheeoga had out-stayed and out-lived the rest of the valley people – waiting until she came . . . But then died before answering the very question Ellen needed answered most.

Faherty knew she was upset – the Crucán, her village thrown down – the dog. He tried to comfort her.

'It's a sorry thing what the English have reduced us to – either eating the dogs, or them eating us.'

Ellen shuddered with horror at the picture Faherty had just painted for her.

'I didn't want to be saying any of these things to you, ma'am . . . before . . . But it is a common enough thing. I heard tell of a man and his wife, back a ways over in Connemara, that was dead a few days with no one to bury them. When they found them – and there's not the word of a lie in this, ma'am – their own pig had eaten the legs off the poor woman up to the knees. And worse, the people what found them had to beat the pig away from the man's body with sticks.'

'Faherty, that can't be true!' she reacted, but now not so sure.

''Pon my oath, it is, ma'am,' the coachman said. 'The pig was driven to it by the hunger – and that's not the worst that I heard . . . But I don't know if telling it is a right thing.'

Ellen, horrified, listened to his story, her eyes transfixed on the back of his head as it rolled from side to side while he recounted to her the unspeakable.

'They say the children were worse than the pig. They fought that hard not to be pulled off the dead bodies of their parents. Back Clifden way, it was – but it's true enough, all right! God bless and save us all!' he said, crossing himself. 'But that's the way they have us gone now.'

The thought of the scene Faherty had just described to her almost caused Ellen to be sick. It was beyond belief. Here in Ireland, back here in the West! She thought of her own children. She looked at the child beside her. She looked at the children along the roadside. Children were . . . just that: children. They were all the same. There was nothing different between any of them and the ones Faherty spoke of.

Could this girl with the stilled tongue and the vacant look – could she do what Faherty had described? Had she already . . . in order to survive?

Ellen stared at the girl, looking for some sign, as if there would be some outward mark of the child's great sin against nature. The girl's dress caught her eye. Could Katie, or Mary – no matter how desperate, how separated from sense by hunger – could they, her own flesh and blood, do such a thing to her? The thought was too awful to imagine.

'God forgive those little ones,' she said aloud. 'God, and His Blessed Mother, forgive them.' Then, with a strange twist in her voice, she ordered the coachman: 'Faherty, drive – just drive. Get me to Tourmakeady!'

She did not speak again until they came to the long driveway.

'Wait here, Faherty, and keep the girl with you.'

She gripped the girl by the shoulders. 'You're to stay here until I return. You'll be safe with Mr Faherty, and I will be back shortly. Do you hear me?'

The girl gave no sign if she did, so Ellen repeated herself, shaking the girl to try and get it through to her.

Ellen hurried to the Lodge. The girl was getting under her skin. Would she ever speak? And was the old woman's riddle about her connected with the first riddle – the fulfilment of which now filled Ellen with fear?

She was tense with dread and anxiety. She scarcely noticed how the rose gardens had decayed: the walls broken, the roses themselves now faded-looking, their leaves blotched with disease.

The house itself didn't look nearly as impressive as she had remembered it. By comparison with Crockford's it was small. And there was an untidiness to it. Little things, nothing that she could put her finger on. But it unsettled her.

Nervously she waited at the main entrance.

It was Bridget who answered the door. Ellen didn't know why, but somehow she had expected the girl not to be here – to have fled from Pakenham's service.

The girl, once so dark and pretty, had aged. She was slightly more plump, her hair straggly – like the Lodge itself she had an untidiness about her, a sense of carelessness creeping in. But it was in Bridget Lynch's eyes that Ellen noticed it most: a tiredness, the sparkle gone.

'*Dia dhuit a Bhríd!*' Ellen addressed her.

The girl, not recognizing Ellen, looked surprised that the elegant lady in the green dress knew her, and would address her in Irish.

'I'm sorry, ma'am,' she replied, 'but we are forbidden to speak the native tongue.'

Ellen thought she could get the hint of alcohol from the girl when she spoke.

'*Bríd, is mise atá ann – Ellen Rua!*' Ellen said, identifying herself.

The girl's eyes brightened in recognition and she looked Ellen up and down before throwing her arms round her and drawing her into the house.

'Oh, Ellen – it's glad I am to see you!' she said, and then whispered: 'He's gone very strict against the use of Irish.'

Now Ellen was certain of the smell of alcohol: the girl had been drinking port.

'Bridget – what's happened to you?'

Bridget looked away, not wanting to meet Ellen's gaze. 'Oh, nothing. It's just the times that's in it – that's all. But Mr Pakenham's been very good to me . . . kept me on. A lot of the men have gone. And he's fallen on hard times himself,' she added hurriedly.

'I want to see Pakenham,' Ellen said. 'My children – where are they?'

Before Bridget could answer, Ellen heard Pakenham's big boom of a voice ring out. 'Bridget – who is it, for Heaven's sake? What's taking you so long?'

At the sound of that voice, all her previous misfortunes at the hands of its owner re-surfaced in Ellen's mind. She brushed past Bridget into the entrance hall, and then on into the study where the landlord stood at his desk, his back to her.

'Sir Richard!' she called out.

Pakenham swung round, a look of astonishment on his face, unaware until now that it was anyone other than Bridget entering the room.

'What the blazes! Who are you?' he thundered at her.

'I've come for my children!' replied the fashionably dressed woman before him.

'What?' Pakenham started, and then he began to see: the red hair, the fire in the dark-green eyes. 'My God! It's you – the O'Malley woman,' he said, astounded.

'My children, Sir Richard – where are they?'

He flinched slightly, taking her in, the change in her, her clothes, her assurance.

'You have the devil of a cheek bursting in on me in this manner!' he said loudly, dismissing her question, seeking to redress the advantage she had gained on him.

Despite this Ellen noticed that he wasn't at all the same Pakenham as of old. Yes, he was still a big build of a man. But he had gone soft, unhealthy-looking, his eyes not as clear. Most of all, she noticed, the voice had changed. The 'I'm to be obeyed', order-giving quality was still in it. The loudness was still in it. But there was something else in it, something Ellen had never noticed before – a hesitancy. It was slight, but it was there.

She remembered Bridget's reference to him 'falling on bad times himself'.

He kept talking at her: 'Look at you! Thinking that a dress and a pair of shoes would make a lady out of you. It takes more than fine feathers –'

She put up her hand to stop him. 'Sir Richard, I am no longer your tenant. I am not here to be lectured at by you – I am here for my children. Your sister Edith and I had an agreement –'

'Agreement is it!' he cut across her. 'Well, Mrs O'Malley, you've broken any agreement a thousand times over. You have caused nothing but bother for Coombes, an old friend, and now you are back here before time – agitating again . . . Agreement!' he added, waving his finger at her.

'Pakenham!' she shouted at him, dropping the 'Sir Richard'. 'If you do not hand over my children at once, I will drag you through every court here and in England too!'

He was momentarily taken aback by her threat. London . . . the courts . . . the banks . . . his debts.

'Courts be damned!' he cursed, recovering himself. 'Who the hell do you think you are? You jumped up bog-peasant! How dare you threaten me!'

The landlord was purple with rage, shouting at the top of his voice. More like she remembered him. Now she was frightened. Suddenly, he was beyond control, unable to speak. He struck out at her. She felt the back of his hand strike her cheekbone. Then he hit her again. This time she tasted the blood in her mouth.

'I'll teach you – you priest's bastard!'

Ellen, her vision blurred by the blows, felt weak, ready to fall. The children . . . the children . . . she had to get them. Peabody's gun . . . her handbag . . . somehow she had managed to hold on to it. In desperation she tugged at the bag . . . got her hand inside . . . felt the cold pearly handle . . .

Before she knew it, she had pulled out the gun. She pointed it at Pakenham as he came at her again.

Ellen felt the kick, heard the clap of the explosion, without even realizing she had pulled the trigger. Pakenham reeled backwards from the impact of the bullet at such close range, then took one step towards her. Finally he fell forward, the crash of his body shaking the floor beneath her.

She stood there, dazed, gun in hand, looking at him stretched at her feet.

The next she knew there was commotion everywhere. People running into the room, and screaming: 'She's killed Sir Richard! Oh! She's killed him!'

Bridget ran by her to get to Pakenham, flinging herself on his body. 'Sir Richard! Oh, Sir Richard!' she called to him, shaking him, the tears rolling down her cheeks.

It was only when Bridget looked up at her that Ellen understood the change she had seen in the girl.

'You shot him, Ellen Rua! You shot him! You came here to shoot him!' Bridget accused her.

Before she had time to reply, Edith Pakenham strode into the room.

'You!' she said, shocked at seeing Ellen with the gun in her hand.

'What have you done?' she cried, looking at Pakenham, motionless on the floor, Bridget over him. 'I knew it from the start – you were always trouble, no better than that murdering husband of yours.'

'Well, if I am then I may as well be hung for two Pakenhams as one!' Ellen threw back at her, turning the gun on the woman. 'Where are my children?'

Inside she was quaking. This had gone all wrong for her, terribly wrong – but she couldn't weaken now, no matter what the consequences.

Edith Pakenham's face turned white. The O'Malley woman was dangerous, unbalanced. 'Bring the boy!' she commanded, to no one in particular.

'I want all three of them!' said Ellen, advancing on the landlord's sister.

'The other two – the girls – are not here. They are at Delphi Lodge in the care of my cousin,' Edith Pakenham said nervously – not knowing what the O'Malley woman would do next.

When Ellen heard the words 'Delphi Lodge', a cold clammy feeling clawed at her insides. Her whole plan was unravelling. What had happened to Katie and Mary? She couldn't think straight any more. She just had to get Patrick and then get out of here, rescue the girls.

'Bring Patrick, then. Now!' she ordered.

More quickly then she expected, the housekeeper, Mrs Bottomley, and one of the men returned, with Patrick between them.

Ellen's heart sighed with relief on seeing her first-born. He had grown so tall, so strong-looking. Thanks be to God. Now she had him back at last.

'Let him go!' she shook Jacob Peabody's gun at them, giving emphasis to her words.

Patrick was looking at her, taking her in: the mother who had abandoned him, now back . . . different, her face bruised and cut . . . and Pakenham lying on the ground.

'Patrick, come here, *a stór*,' she called to him.

Slowly the boy came to her side, saying nothing.

'We're leaving now, Miss Pakenham,' Ellen said. 'But if anything has happened to my children, if a hair of their heads has been harmed . . .'

She said no more, the woman understood her.

With that, Ellen propelled Patrick ahead of her, out of the house. She wanted to hold him to say she missed him, but there was no time for that. She had to get to Delphi to free Katie and Mary, then chase back to Westport and out of Ireland before the constabulary could be after them.

'Patrick,' she gasped, as they ran down the driveway, 'I'm so happy to see you again! Thank God, you're all right.'

He said nothing.

'What happened to Katie and Mary?' she asked, her breath heaving.

This time he answered her. 'Pakenham put them to Delphi before the Christmas. Too many of us together,' he said. Then, to her surprise, he added, 'But he wasn't that bad to us . . . And Bridget looked out for us, like you said.'

That was it. Bridget had become Pakenham's tallywoman. The landlord must have softened towards her, as she obviously had towards him. Was that what the girl was trying to tell her, Ellen wondered, the time she went to meet with Edith Pakenham? Now Patrick was telling her that Bridget had held sway with Pakenham, saw to it that they came to no harm. The girl had been true to her word.

Now, as they ran back towards the road, Ellen could see that Faherty had the carriage ready, facing the shorter route back to Westport. This time the girl had waited with him.

She shouted at Faherty: 'Turn it around, Mr Faherty, turn it around – we must go back to Delphi!'

Faherty was worried.

The woman from America with the red hair was trouble. When she told him what had happened, he knew no good would come of it. He was all for shooting landlords – taking the 'landlord doctor' out to them – if you could get away with it. But soon the constabulary would be out looking for them. He stole a look back at her, the marks on her face, the boy in one arm, the girl in another. She had spark all right, the redhead. She'd been right to do what she'd done – he'd back her on that. The landlord had no right to mark her like he did.

Worried as he was, Faherty was more worried about Nell. He had grazed the horse, wiped her down with a cloth while she was up at the house shooting them. Now they had to go back the long way to Westport. Mind, there'd be light for a good few hours yet, but it was warm – hard on Nell. He'd have to stop more often, give her plenty to drink. What with two extra on board as well . . . They might have to stop the night at Louisburgh if she got too tired, but by then it'd hardly be worth it. He'd see after Delphi.

Ellen knew Faherty was thinking. He had had little to say since she had asked him to turn the carriage round, and he had protested: 'Delphi? It's backways we're going, ma'am . . . it's a pity you didn't know it earlier . . .' He had stopped then, when he saw the look on her face. How could she have known it earlier – if only she had?

She wondered if the horse would make it – if they'd have to put up somewhere for the night, at Maam or at Leenane. But they couldn't – word would get back to Delphi ahead of them and she'd be stopped from getting the children. She looked at Patrick. He hadn't said much at all to her, had seemed taken aback by the presence of the silent girl. Ellen thought he was glad to see herself, but she wasn't sure. Didn't know what he was thinking.

Patrick sneaked a look up at the woman whose arm was round him. She looked like he remembered her, but different. All the hair that used to fall down around her face when she tucked him in was tied up now; cut short, he thought. And her voice sounded different, the way she wasn't afraid of Pakenham. She smelled different too, not like she used to when she'd shown him how to stack the fire of a morning. Now she smelled all fancy, like Miss Pakenham.

At first they used to look out for her every night once the summer was over, thinking it was a long time since she had gone. Although Mary kept saying it was too soon. Then the Christmas, then the next summer was in. And there was no sign of her. Before they were taken away, Mary still got them all to pray for her. But he began to think she was never coming back, that it was all a trick of some kind. Now she was here all dressed up like a fancy woman, and he wondered did she have a fancy man beyond in wherever she was? And the girl in the fancy dress that said nothing – was she going to be one of them now? And Annie – little Annie – had she left Annie behind with the fancy man?

He had started to like it at Tourmakeady Lodge after a while. He liked working with the men, out in the yards, or the fields, carrying things for them, listening to their talk. He didn't like Beecham – he remembered the agent from the night their house was thrown down. He'd been glad when Beecham was put into Lough Nafooey. Heard some of the men whisper that it was young Roberteen and the Shanafaraghaun man that did it. He remembered the two of them coming to the house to his father. And when he was older he had decided he'd run away and join up with the Shanafaraghaun man and the Young Irelanders. But what would happen now, if she took him back with her to America? They'd have to get Katie and Mary first – he'd help her with that. He felt her arm squeeze him and it gave him a funny feeling, like it was long ago again, back in the valley, before she went.

Ellen turned to her son and took him by the shoulders.

'Let me look at you, Patrick,' she said, filled with happiness at having him back. 'What a man you've grown into. Your father would be proud of you – as I am.'

She threw her arms round him, but he stiffened, not wanting her embrace.

She let go of him, hurting at his rejection. It would take time. Who could tell what stories he had been filled with about her, what tricks his mind had been playing on him all those long nights.

'You look different,' he said accusingly. And then, looking at the girl in the bright dress, he asked, 'Where's Annie?'

She hesitated before answering him. 'Annie died, Patrick, of disease . . . in Australia,' she said quietly, putting her hand on his sleeve.

She could see that this took him aback, affected him, but he said nothing, only his father's eyes hardening at her.

'This girl was abandoned' – Ellen flinched as she said the words – 'I brought her with me . . .' Realizing how it must sound to his

485

ears. That after leaving behind him and her other children, she had first rescued someone else's child, and not her own.

For the rest of the trip to Delphi, Patrick did not speak to her. He was as silent as the silent girl.

55

Faherty and Nell did well and they reached Delphi Lodge before the light failed them. Apart from a brief pause by the river so that Ellen could clean her wounds, they had travelled without stopping.

Along the way, Ellen tried to tell Patrick about her life. Tried to ask him about himself, and the last two years. Tried to ask him about Mary and Katie, and whether he had heard any word of them since they were sent to Delphi.

She got nowhere.

It grieved her deeply, the more so because she had been living for the moment she would see him again ever since they parted.

But when they arrived at Delphi and she told him to stay with Faherty and the girl, he wouldn't. He insisted on coming with her. So she agreed, thinking it would help ease things between them.

She untied her hair as she approached Delphi Lodge – worrying in case Katie and Mary wouldn't recognize her. Patrick's 'you look different' had taken her aback. She knew he had meant more than what was said.

They kept to the perimeter of the gardens, using the shrubbery for cover. She hoped that maybe she would see Mary or Katie in the kitchen or one of the rooms and attract their attention without raising the alarm.

They were in luck. Patrick spotted one of the twins in a room towards the back of the house. Ellen's heart pounded madly, the instinct to call out, almost unbearable.

For a moment she wasn't sure which one of them it was.

She told Patrick to wait in the trees that surrounded the Lodge. Then she crept closer to the window, trying to control her feelings, afraid that if she made a sound it could ruin everything after all this time wanting to get them back.

It was Mary!

Ellen felt as if her heart would burst with the feelings of relief and joy she experienced on seeing her child again.

She tapped at the window.

Mary, startled, looked up from sorting out the linen in the laundry-room.

Ellen saw her daughter's eyes open wide with disbelief. Then Mary ran to the window, her face breaking into the widest of smiles. Like Patrick, she had grown taller, but she was thin and tired-looking. Under her fine head of red hair, Mary's face looked pasty and drawn.

Now she pressed her face against the window, her fingers reaching up to where Ellen's face was. Then Mary faltered, her expression changing to one of concern as she saw the marks Pakenham had made on her mother.

Ellen, her eyes alight, her whole body trembling, beckoned Mary to come outside.

'At last I have them safe, thanks be to God and His Holy Mother,' Ellen whispered, waiting for her children, breathing up a prayer to Heaven.

In a few moments Mary flew straight into her arms, no reticence, no holding back. Nothing had changed between them.

'*A Mhamaí, a Mhamaí*!' the child called to her, having no words that could say more.

Ellen clasped Mary tightly to her, keeping an eye over her shoulder for Katie.

But there was no Katie.

In her arms Ellen felt Mary's happiness change with a shudder into big, uncontrollable sobs of grief.

And she felt the knot of fear rise in the pit of her own stomach again. Something was wrong, awfully wrong.

'Where's Katie?' she said, terrified to let the words come out of her – once they were said needing an answer.

Mary raised her tear-stained face from her mother's embrace. 'Katie's gone, *a Mhamaí* – Katie's gone!'

56

Would it never end? Every time she seemed to be on the point of at last getting out from under the curse of the old woman's riddle, it was snatched away from her in some cruel and vicious twist. Now this!

Mary had told her and Patrick what had happened, sobbing out her little heart as she did so.

She and Katie had been very frightened when they had first been separated from Patrick and taken to Delphi – not knowing what would happen to them, or if they would ever see Patrick again. They were also afraid that, having been moved, Ellen would not be able to find them when she came back for them.

The work was hard at Delphi Lodge, but the twins were together, and they were fed regularly. Daily they watched from inside the Big House as the poor came looking for any scraps, any leavings at all – even from the animals.

Mary described how one day, a girl came begging for food round the back of the house and appeared at the laundry window as Ellen had done.

'*A Mhamaí*, she was so hungry, and her clothes all torn . . . I ran into the pantry and took a *bulóg* of bread and ran out to her with it. She bit into it there and then, she was that starved.'

But when Mary had come back into the house, the housekeeper, Mrs Joyce – a harsh mistress from back the Killary way – was waiting for her.

'Well if it isn't her ladyship of the house, giving out bread to beggars,' the Killary woman had greeted Mary with. 'We'll see about this when the Master returns.'

Katie had leapt to her twin's defence: 'Mary was right to do it.'

The Killary woman had then turned on Katie. 'Oh, was she, you impudent little *dalteen*? Well, we'll see about you too!'

489

It was left at that until a few days later. Then the woman had come to them and said, 'The Master has decided that as *your* punishment, Lady Mary, for stealing bread, your sister will be sent to the Westport workhouse. There she will remain for four weeks. If, during that time, your behaviour is beyond reproach in every respect, then Katie will be returned here to you.'

'I told her, *a Mhamaí*, that it wasn't Katie's fault – to take me, that it was *me* who stole the bread, not her!' Mary said to her mother, the cruel memory of it causing her to break out in great wrenching sobs again.

Ellen took the child up in her arms.

'It wasn't your fault, Mary – it was a bad thing for those people to do – you couldn't have stopped it, *a stóirín!*' she said, her heart bleeding for the suffering her child had been caused. 'Go on, tell me the rest, Mary. It's all right – we'll get Katie back.'

Mary went on to describe how the twins had clung to each other, frightened but defiant. Despite Mary's pleas to take the two of them, the woman had separated them and dragged Katie away, saying, 'Maybe the workhouse will teach this other *cailín* a mouthful of manners as well!'

The last thing Mary could tell her was that, before she was taken away, Katie had shouted to her, 'Tell *Mamaí* where I am if she comes!'

That was over two weeks ago now.

Mary had worked and worked, worrying in case anything she might or might not do would be further used to punish her – to keep Katie away from her. Never before separated from her twin sister, each night she cried herself to sleep, praying that Ellen would return and rescue them.

No wonder the child looked so thin, so haunted – bearing the guilt of Katie being punished for her wrongdoing. Working herself to the bone to get Katie back.

What a cruel, cruel punishment to visit on the children, Ellen thought. The crueller the fact that they were twins. Then her thoughts raced on to Westport Workhouse. Pray God they weren't too late!

A shiver ran through her as she remembered the time she had gone there for Michael. The misery in the place – the hopelessness, the overcrowded conditions, people sleeping on top of each other. The diseases.

The black, black wall, where the lime would burn and corrode away the typhus, or the dysentery, or the cholera. Corrode everything that went into it.

Her insides churning, she shouted at Faherty: 'Westport – the workhouse! Quick, Mr Faherty, quick, before we're too late!'

As they headed the last twenty-five miles for Westport, back along the road they had come in the early morning, Ellen knew that they would not make the town before nightfall. She explained to Faherty what she had learned from Mary, but Nell, tired after a long day, now had to haul five of them. And even if the three children between them didn't weigh much, it was still extra.

Faherty was deeply concerned about Nell. They must have been a good fourteen hours on the road by now, he thought. He rested the horse every few miles, made them get out 'to take the weight off her back'. Ellen was anxious, impatient to be on the road. Every hour mattered for Katie. She thought of Michael. She had been too late with him. She couldn't fail Katie.

Faherty encouraged Nell: 'Come on, Nell! Come on, girl – don't let us down now!' hoping that it was not all going to be a wasted journey.

'More comes out dead than comes out alive out of them places!' he whispered under his breath so she wouldn't hear him.

He'd bring them as far as Louisburgh and decide then. Nell couldn't take much more. And if anything happened to the horse, he'd be finished.

Patrick was genuinely delighted to see Mary, and didn't try to hide it. He was also very upset, Ellen could see, as Mary whispered to him about Katie.

Ellen had decided not to tell Mary about Annie until they rescued Katie. The child already had too much to cope with. But the first thing Mary asked when she got into the carriage and saw the silent girl was, 'Where's Annie?' As if, somehow, the silent girl had something to do with Annie not being present.

So Ellen had to tell her, and hold her, and explain that Annie would want them to be strong and brave and get Katie.

Mary didn't say much except, 'Yes, *a Mhamaí*.' Then she cried all the more.

On past Doo Lough they went again; as before, the wasted bodies of the dead in ditch and drain, a grim reminder of what might lie awaiting them in Westport.

'I'll get out and walk a while, Mr Faherty,' Ellen said. 'It'll make it easier on Nell.'

So she took off her fancy shoes and stockings and threw them on the floor of the carriage. The silent girl made to come with her, but Ellen pushed her back down into the seat again. But she remained close to the carriage on the side the girl sat.

Her feet, softened by Boston's streets, were no match for the Pass Road of Doo Lough. Soon, like her face, they were bloodied and bruised. But her not being in the carriage had made a difference to Nell, who picked up somewhat from the laggardly pace to which she had fallen – thus causing even further problems for Ellen.

When eventually they reached Louisburgh, darkness was in on them.

Ellen begged Faherty to take them on to Westport. 'If not, I'll walk it myself with the children,' she said, meaning it. How could she sleep even the few hours to dawn, and Katie only fifteen miles down the road from them – in the workhouse?

Faherty had to admire her. She'd do it too – she'd neither give up nor give in, this woman from America, not while there was breath left in her body. He agreed to bring them the rest of the way. Now that night had come it would be cooler – easier on Nell. And, at any rate, if he himself wasn't back at all tonight, Herself at home would only be worrying about him.

The Reek pushed itself up out of the night as if searching out some higher light.

Faherty urged Nell onward. 'We're nearly there, girl – the last few miles and then a long rest and a nosebag of hay for you,' he coaxed.

Westport was thronged with the poor. Ragged and wretched they were, wandering, wandering, ever wandering, hoping for something, they knew not what, to happen. Some miracle that would descend on them and relieve them of their woe, and the slow, slow death by starvation.

But Westport had no miracles for them. Many lay huddled within its streets, waiting, sleeping, dying.

'It's closed, ma'am. It's closed again!' Faherty's words cut into her.

The doors of Westport Workhouse were closed, not to keep its inmates in, but to keep them out. All around the entrance, the people for whom it was a last refuge, even a place to die, clamoured and wailed. Keening their own deaths, it seemed, that must surely result from them being ejected on to the streets of Westport. Without food, without anywhere to go, they would join the other hordes wandering aimlessly until Death saved them further misery and took them.

Ellen was frantic. How would she find Katie amidst all the masses of starving people?

She asked Faherty to take the girl for an hour or two, till they found Katie. He agreed, if she'd come. Ellen then spoke to the girl, telling her to go with Faherty, that she'd be back for her. She went easily enough.

'Patrick, Mary, come with me – and stay by me!'

Ellen knew they didn't have much time, but that weight she bore herself. She did not tell them her fears.

They worked their way around the walls of the workhouse, hoping that Katie might have stayed close by. The destitute in their ragged clothes eyed Ellen with suspicion, nervous of this handsome, well-dressed woman who was not one of them. Who had somehow escaped the clutches of Famine. Yet they did not insult or assail her as she moved amongst them, searching for Katie. 'Lost a child, poor woman,' they said. 'Lost a child!'

But there was no sight of Katie at the workhouse.

Then they searched the streets, calling out her name softly into the huddles of people, aware of the plight of those who looked vacantly at them. Trying not to disturb them, to step round those who lay on the ground in small heaps of two or three.

They searched, and called, calling and searching well past the hour of midnight, the three of them tired and fatigued, with hope fading of ever finding Katie. But still not wanting to give up.

Faherty and the girl, after feeding and bedding down Nell, had come back to look for them.

Now they all stood disconsolate, wondering where next to look in the town. Faherty ran through the names of the streets and lanes, making sure they had missed none of them.

Then, out of the darkness, the call came: '*A Mhamaí, a Mhamaí!*'

Ellen's blood almost froze with the sound she knew so well, the way they always called her in Irish.

'Katie!' She spun round to see the child coming towards her in the dark, arms outstretched for its mother.

Ellen ran to her and swept up the ragged little bundle into her arms.

'Oh, Katie! Katie, *a stóirín*, you're safe! You're safe!' she cried, holding the child into her shoulder, kissing, and kissing again the matted red hair against her face.

'Mary! Patrick!' she shouted. 'She's safe! Katie is safe! Thanks be to God! She's safe!'

Mary and Patrick ran over to where their mother stood with Katie in her arms. The child, obviously very weak and in distress, just acknowledged all this fuss by repeating, '*A Mhamaí, a Mhamaí!*'

Ellen held Katie out from herself to let Mary see her twin sister.

'Now, Mary, I told you, everything's all right – we're all together again, and Katie . . .'

She stopped – seeing the look on Mary's face.

'*A Mhamaí . . .!*' Mary was looking at her twin sister. Her face was stricken with sheer terror, her speech falling back into her first tongue with the shock of what she was seeing.

'*Ó, a Mhamaí,*' she cried. '*Ní hí sin Katie!*'

57

'*Ní hí sin Katie!*' – She's not Katie!

The words struck Ellen like a thunderbolt.

'Of course she is, Mary! Look, she's . . .' Then she stopped, peering at the child, who only said, '*A Mhamaí, a Mhamaí!*' to her.

'Oh, God! Oh, God!' Ellen's hand flew to her mouth as if wanting to block the words coming out, wanting to stop them, so that what was happening would stop. 'Oh, no! It isn't . . . it isn't her!' Ellen cried out, not believing what she was saying, looking from one to the other of them, seeking some explanation.

How could she have made such a mistake? And she, Katie's mother? The one who had brought her into the world.

The child looked at Ellen, looked at Mary and Patrick, looked at Faherty and the silent girl, forlorn, lost in the middle of all of them. Only wanting to find her mother. Any mother. '*A Mhamaí, a Mhamaí!*' she cried, frightened now. Hopelessly, she reached out for Ellen, tears filling her eyes, wanting desperately to be the child wanted by this woman who had held and kissed her.

Wanting desperately to be Katie.

Ellen felt so dashed down, so guilty. Yet again, her hopes had been raised. Yet again, they had been shattered, smashed to nothing. Now what was she to do about this child, who, with her tousled red hair, she had thought was Katie? She couldn't just leave her here, let her go back into the night to keep searching for her mother – a mother who in all likelihood would be unable to care for her anyway. Maybe even was dead by now. But she couldn't keep collecting every child she happened upon. She still had to find Katie.

In desperation she turned to Faherty. 'Mr Faherty, what am I to do with this poor child?' she asked, hoping, by some miracle, that the coachman had the answer. It was too much. This Famine was too big for any one person to do anything about it. There were thousands like the child, God love her. She was so like Katie. Ellen looked at her again. So like her.

'I'll tell you what, ma'am,' he said. 'I'll take her back to the house, to Herself. She can have a bed there with us for the night. Tomorrow, we'll have a search for the parents, and if we can't find them, or they don't want her – and they mightn't . . . Well, then, the nuns won't turn her out.'

'Thank you, Mr Faherty!' Ellen said, much relieved at the solution that he had come up with.

He took the child, who went willingly enough, but still calling, '*A Mhamaí!*' to Ellen as she left.

Ellen found the whole episode very upsetting. Not only was there nothing she could do, but in a way she felt outside all the desolation that was about her. She was here for one purpose only and that was to get her children – to get Katie. Then she would be gone, out of Ireland, leaving it all behind her. Leaving *them* her own people, all behind her. She realized she hadn't asked the child her name. Nor did she know the name of the silent girl. That was it – victims became nameless in the midst of such horrors. Like the thousands in the unmarked graves at Grosse Île, or the thousands who went into the lime-pit here. But each of those people's deaths was a tragedy in itself, as awful as any other. As awful as Michael or Annie, or the silent girl, or the crying child. It was all lost when it was in thousands or tens of thousands. When they couldn't be named. But each one – each person – was a heartbreaking story. An individual nameless tragedy.

Faherty returned shortly. He was excited, having rushed back to them with his news.

'The road to Castlebar, ma'am,' he said to her, all of a fluster, as if she would know at once what he meant. 'They're on the road to Castlebar – the childer!'

Tired Nell was hauled back into service again and harnessed to Faherty's carriage, and with Faherty's 'gee-up there, Nell' they headed down the town, across the Carrowbeg River, and up where the hill rose out of Westport, and on to the road to Castlebar.

Everywhere were the never-ending fearful sights of people along the roadside, lying down in sleep or in death, or somewhere between the two. They slowed, calling out her name into the midst of each group.

'Katie! Katie! Katie!' But they got no response. Nothing.

The huddles of people along the ditches were now fewer in number, and they were at less frequent intervals. The journey to Castlebar exacting its toll on them, selecting the weak and the near-dead.

Ellen looked back. 'All those people! All those poor people!'

It was Mary who saw her first.

'Katie! Katie! Katie!' her twin shouted wildly.

Mary had leapt out of the carriage before Ellen had fully grasped what was happening. Now she, too, jumped out after Mary, who ran back behind the carriage and over to the roadside grass.

'It's her! It's her, *a Mhamaí!*' Mary shouted, delirious with joy. 'Patrick, it's Katie – I found her!'

Mary was first to Katie, repeating her name, over and over again. She threw herself on her twin sister, who lay on the ground, and hugged her.

'Katie! Katie! Katie! It's me, Mary!' she said excitedly, shaking her twin.

But Katie, weakened, hungry, only looked back at her. In vain, her lips tried to get out the sound of the word 'Mary'.

Ellen reached them.

'Mary, let her up – you'll smother her!' she said, concerned.

Mary scampered up, but it made no difference to Katie. She just lay there.

Ellen knelt down beside her. 'Katie, *a stóirín*, it's me – I've come back for you!'

The child scarcely moved.

Ellen put her hand to Katie's forehead – it was hot to the touch. Gently she brushed back the curls and knotted strands of hair that fell about the child's face.

'Come on now, *a stóirín!*' she said, bending close to her child, her arms underneath the wasted body, cradling her.

As she bent over Katie, Ellen heard, in a voice so weak, so whispered, that she could scarcely pick out the words: '*A Mhamaí, a Mhamaí – tá tú ar ais . . .!*'

'Yes, Katie, dear, I'm back. I came back for you,' she said tenderly, her voice breaking with grief.

She lifted her daughter – skin and bones was all Katie was – and saw the sunken cheekbones of that once-bright face, the hollow look in those once mischievous eyes.

Ellen knew Katie wouldn't last long, even before she saw the dark brown blotch on her tongue.

An fiabhras dubh. Katie had typhus.

In the lightening dark of the August morning, Ellen held her darling child in her arms. From the height above the town where they stood she could see the Reek. The high mountain of St Patrick towered over them, dwarfing them, magnifying her grief.

She looked down at Katie.

'Will she be all right?' Mary asked her, putting her hand up to Katie.

Ellen hadn't the heart to answer her.

'She'll be all right now,' Mary said, not asking any more, just wanting to believe it. 'Now that we have her back . . . Won't she, Patrick?'

Like his mother, the boy did not answer her.

Ellen was heartbroken. She'd come back – she'd kept her word to them! God, what more could she have done? But it all was at nothing now. She was too late for Katie.

She'd seen it so many times before in the fever sheds – her child was too far gone, too weak to fight the fever.

Ellen started walking back towards Westport, carrying Katie in her arms, ignoring the carriage.

They had just crossed the dip of the road back down into Westport when they came for her.

She had walked, unaware of anything, only the child in her arms, Mary at one elbow, Patrick at the other. Behind them Nell and Faherty, with the silent girl in the back, made up the procession.

Silent as the darkest hour before dawn was, and locked in her grief, Ellen never heard them, never saw them approach until she felt the hand come down on her shoulder.

She offered no resistance, even before Sergeant Moriarty asked: 'Now will you accompany us quietly, Ma'am?'

It was all so unreal. There they were, on the road between Westport and Castlebar, people strewn all around them, like rags on the roadside. Faherty and the silent girl. Patrick rescued. Mary rescued. Katie dying in her arms. The holy mountain staring down at her, judging her. And the hand of the law, heavy on her shoulder, arresting her.

'Let her go! Let her go!' shouted Faherty, breaking through to her. 'Can't you see her child is dying? Let her go!'

'Faherty, I know you,' Sergeant Moriarty of the Irish Constabulary said threateningly. 'This woman has committed a most serious crime. She'll get a fair trial.'

'Fair trial, *mo thóin*!' Faherty swore at the sergeant. 'Look at her face, look what he done to her – she was right to shoot him! If it was an Irishman she shot, there'd be no trial at all! Who's going to be tried for all these?' he demanded, pointing back along the roadside, littered with bodies which the Peelers must have passed. 'Fair trial be damned!' he cursed at them again.

'Faherty,' Sergeant Moriarty warned, 'you're asking for me to feel your collar, too. Maybe a night or two in the gaolhouse would do you no harm – at least keep that old nag of yours from fouling the street!' he added, drawing guffaws from his men.

Ellen ignored them. It was all part of the unreal dream. The only reality was Katie in her arms.

Dying.

Later, she barely noticed the clank of the key as it locked her and Katie into the cell of the Westport gaolhouse. The sergeant had allowed her to keep Katie with her, and had put them into a cell on their own. Faherty had taken the others.

They gave her some water and threw in a crust of stale bread. She soaked it in the water, mashing it in her fingers, then forced it into Katie's mouth. She held Katie's nose, making the sick child swallow it.

Ellen then tore off a piece of her underskirt, dipped it into the water, and washed the grime and dirt from the child's face –

uncovering the old Katie, as it were. Bit by bit, the white and freckled skin of her child was revealed to Ellen.

Katie seemed to like this, and made some low murmuring sounds. Ellen talked to her, tried to soothe her fever, all the while *cronauning* to her, as she had done with Annie.

Maybe there was a chance yet – maybe Katie would come out of it. In the end she had known Annie wouldn't, but Katie was older, stronger, and with the bit of food in her . . . Maybe this once, God would favour her and not take the child. After all she had been through, maybe He would spare her this. No, she decided, not for herself. She wasn't going to ask for anything for herself any more. No, it was for Katie, to spare her, to let her live and see the New World. And give her the chance of a new life there beyond in Boston.

'It can't all end like this, Katie,' Ellen whispered in the cell, gazing on the freshly cleaned face of her child, half-expecting a cheeky back-answer. But there was none.

Ellen forced some more of the mashed bread between Katie's lips.

She'd seen people come out of the typhus before. Hadn't she come out of it herself?

She wondered about Patrick and Mary. Thank God she'd got them safe. Now that she had, that didn't seem to matter so much, only that she hadn't saved Katie.

For her child to die in her arms, in a gaol in her own Ireland would be too much for her to bear. It would finally break her. What use would Boston be to her now – without Katie? What use anything?

On the second day in Westport Gaol Ellen had a visitor. Immediately she saw the long black cassock swirl at the door of the cell she knew who its owner was. Father O'Brien!

She was stunned and genuinely glad to see him. But how did he know?

The young priest looked tired, had aged more than he should have. 'God be with you, Ellen Rua. I'm here in Westport now – Mr Faherty came to me.'

'*Dia's Muire dhuit*,' she said back to him in Irish.

'You never changed, I see,' he said, good-humouredly, acknowledging how she hadn't let it go that he had addressed her in English. 'You *look* different, Ellen, but you never changed.'

How wrong he was – if only he knew, she thought.

'Your face – what happened to your face?'

When she told him, he insisted on bringing in Sergeant Moriarty to be a witness to her injuries. 'It could stand well to you in the court, Ellen,' the priest told her. 'Mitigating circumstances – self-defence,' he explained.

After Faherty had told him her story, and about the child, Father O'Brien had come prepared. He had with him the *Oleum Infirmorum* – the oil of the sick – blessed by the bishop on Holy Thursday. And a small crucifix. The gaoler procured for him two candles, blessed on Candlemas Day, and the priest lit them either side of Ellen as she held the child.

'*In nomine Patris et Filii . . .*'

She blessed herself with him.

Then he began the Sacrament of Extreme Unction. The Last Sacrament, she thought to herself. It was good she had washed Katie before he came.

'One of the effects of the Sacrament, Ellen,' he gently explained, 'is the restoration of bodily health . . . if this is for the good of Katie's soul.' She prayed fervently it might be. The reason for the other effect he didn't tell her – that as Katie crossed the threshold of death the devil would make his final attack to win the child's soul. The Sacrament of Extreme Unction would ward off such dangers.

She listened, offering her own prayers for Katie, as he anointed her with the consecrated oil of olives. '*Per istam sanctam unctionem et suam piissimam misericordiam indulgeat tibi Dominus quidquid per . . . Visum*' – Through this Holy unction, and through His most sweet mercy may the Lord forgive thee whatever sins thou hast committed by . . . sight.

She watched as he signed each of Katie's closed eyelids. As he made the tiny crosses with his thumb, first on the right eye then on the left, Ellen wondered what sin of sight it was the child could have committed that needed such forgiveness?

Then *Auditum* – the sense of hearing – he anointed her ears.

Odoratum – the sense of smell – Katie's nostrils.

Gustum et locutionem – her mouth – always full of questions, interruptions, Ellen remembered, a great sadness coming down on her.

Tactum – touch – the palms of Katie's hands.

At *Gressum* the priest gently raised each of Katie's feet – the feet that so often landed her in mischief. Tenderly he anointed each instep in turn. '*Per istam sanctam unctionem . . . Gressum,*' laying them down again against the folds of Ellen's dress. Then he put holy water on both mother and child, sprinkling it over them with the sprig of a small-leafed plant.

Father O'Brien concluded the ceremony by giving Katie the Last Blessing.

Then it was done. Her *angelito* was now ready.

He stayed with her a while, comforting her, talking to her. He was now the curate in Westport. The Archbishop had moved him – thought he could go places if he kept his nose clean and out of politics.

He had been grief-stricken when he had heard about Michael, blaming himself for having brought him to the workhouse. By the time he knew, it was too late – she had left for Australia.

She didn't comment, made it easy on him. Then she told him her story, cutting back about Australia and what she had already confessed, but mentioning Roberteen and Martin and Biddy.

He said he would visit her before the trial and speak on her behalf at the assizes.

She thanked him for everything and he left.

Father O'Brien came every day for the next three days, seeing how they were, praying over them, sneaking in tiny parcels of food. 'For you and Katie,' he said.

Katie had not gotten any worse. Maybe the Sacrament, the *oleum infirmorum* had restored her as Father O'Brien had said. Ellen herself thought she saw signs of improvement, and kept whispering and singing to her. She felt that the child heard her, and sometimes Katie would respond, mumbling a few words.

* * *

The night before the trial she sat up with Katie as usual, telling her stories of Ngurunderi, and *Pondi*, the giant Murray Cod, and how Annie was in the starry Milky Way, sailing through the skies in Ngurunderi's canoe.

Ellen asked for her suitcase. Reluctantly the gaoler agreed, having first searched it for any concealed weapons.

She washed Katie from head to toe, and patiently brushed out her hair, giving it one hundred strokes of the brush as she used to before, when preparing her for Sunday Mass. Then, Ellen took out the dress, a matching one to the silent girl's, bright with its pinks and blues and its white collar and cuffs.

The dress looked wonderful on Katie, as Ellen had imagined it would. Full of life and colour, as Katie once was. She talked to her beautiful *máinlín* as she dressed her: 'This is the dress I brought you from Boston, *a stóirín*. One for you, one for Mary, for going to America in . . .'

Ellen fought to keep back her tears. America – would any of them see it now, let alone Katie?

It had all gone wrong for her – even the dresses. She had been imagining how the two would look, all dressed up identically, and like American girls. Now one of the dresses was on the silent girl, the other on Katie – she almost silent too.

Ellen smartened herself up in readiness for the morning. She was tired, not up to it. But she had to defend herself. Had to get free, see to Katie, get them all out of here to America. She couldn't fail now at what surely must be the final obstacle to being fully and completely rejoined with her children. It would be difficult. Pakenham wasn't dead, she knew. Father O'Brien told her she had only wounded him, shot him in the shoulder. So the landlord would be in court, facing her. Would the court ever take her side against him, believe her story? She doubted it.

When she had finished with herself, she cradled Katie in her arms again. What a little mischief she had been before. Always in trouble, always testing to see how far she could go with people.

Ellen looked down at her child, remembering the fights at the Rosary, the interminable questions from her at the Lessons. But Katie had great nature in her too. Like the Sunday morning going to Finny when she had dashed to the side of the mountain, and brought back a fistful of wildflowers for Ellen. And how she was always protective of Mary, her twin – the two of them sharing that special world where other, single children could not go.

And now that special bond, that twin-ness, had been turned against them, used to separate and break them. Katie was now paying the ultimate price for the twin sister she loved.

She was dying for her.

Ellen lovingly rubbed her daughter's forehead, clearing a space on it amongst Katie's mass of red hair. She made a small cross on the spot, leaning forward to kiss where she had crossed, her lips tasting the hot salty moisture of the fever as she did so. Then, she sang to Katie a *suantraí* – lullabying her – still caressing her forehead. Katie always liked that.

When she had finished the lullaby, Ellen heard Katie make a sound. She put her ear to the child's lips.

'What is it, *a stóirín?* I'm here with you!' she whispered.

She felt the feverish lips move against her ear. At first no sound came. Ellen, motionless, held back her own breathing, to try and catch whatever it was Katie was trying to say to her.

Again she felt the lips move against her ear, the way the Máistir used to whisper to her about wonder. The way she herself whispered to Katie the morning Annie was born, when the three of them lay together in absolute silence, in absolute wonder.

This time the sound came, whispered, but clearer than Ellen had expected: '*A Mhamaí . . . a Mhamaí, tháinig tú ar ais chugainn!*' Ellen almost choked at the words: '*A Mhamaí,* you came back to us!' was what Katie had been trying so hard to say to her.

'Oh, my God – my poor child!' Ellen said, kissing her on the cheek, overcome with emotion.

Then, with her task completed, the words at last transmitted between them, Katie expired. Her tired little heart gave up, no longer able to meet the demands that the fever which racked her body had made on it.

Ellen knew she was gone. Knew that Katie had summoned up all her last resources of strength to tell her how happy she was she'd come back for them. That that was all that mattered.

That she had forgiven her for ever going.

'*Tháinig tú ar ais chugainn* – you came back to us,' Ellen repeated, whispering it into the stony walls of the Westport Gaol.

58

Through the night into the morning, Ellen sat with Katie, talking and singing to her as if she was still alive.

When they came for her at about ten o'clock, Ellen pretended nothing was wrong. Katie was just sleeping.

If they knew, they would take Katie's body away from her. Throw it into a grave somewhere. She didn't want that.

She would have to win this trial. Be freed.

Then, together with the others, she would get Faherty to bring them back to the mountains. Back to Maamtrasna. Back to Crucán na bPáiste.

There was no other place Katie could be buried.

That was her place. High up in the mountains, overlooking the Mask and Lough Nafooey.

Back there with Michael.

59

Ellen was nervous as she was led into the court and told to stand in the dock while the charges of Malicious Injury and Attempted Murder were read out against her. What chance did she have? Pakenham would have them all lined up against her with their big words. She glanced at the judge, bewigged and in his black garb, sternly looking down on all of them – especially her, she thought.

Father O'Brien was as good as his word. He had been there when she arrived and had smiled at her. She was glad to see him.

Patrick and Mary were there too, and they looked nervously at her, fearful for her, and wondering about Katie, Ellen guessed. The silent girl sat between them and Faherty, who was with a soft-faced, good-hearted looking woman. This must be 'Herself', Ellen thought, Mrs Faherty.

Sir Richard and Edith Pakenham both appeared. The landlord's arm was supported by a sling bandage. Ellen was relieved she hadn't killed him, the more so when she saw Bridget there behind him. The girl sat with her eyes cast downwards throughout, never once meeting Ellen's gaze. On one occasion when Ellen glanced over, she caught Bridget looking at Pakenham. It suddenly dawned on her that Bridget – in spite of everything the landlord was, in spite of their strange, unequal relationship – had grown to like, maybe even, love Pakenham. She dismissed the idea from her mind, almost as quickly, thinking it too improbable.

Pakenham gave evidence. He traced the history of his 'O'Malley tenants' going back to Michael's attack on him, the disappearance of his agent, Mr Beecham, and 'Mrs O'Malley's most recent assault on my person with a firearm.'

Father O'Brien cross-examined the landlord, informing the court that he had witnessed with his own eyes the harassment visited by Sir Richard on his tenants. He then questioned the landlord about the immoral raising of rents in the face of Famine, citing Pakenham's sur-tax on the children of his tenants. When he asked Sir Richard if he had 'occasioned the eviction of Mrs O'Malley and her family on the eve of Christmas', a gasp went up from the courtroom.

The priest then began his defence of Ellen, stoutly attesting to her good character and extraordinary courage.

'Why, even now,' he told the packed courtroom, 'while she stands here before you falsely accused, her child lies within the gaolhouse, grievously stricken.'

Again, this drew exclamations from those present.

Then he asked Ellen to turn first one side of her face to the Bench, then the other.

'Sir Richard,' he asked deliberately, 'bearing in mind that you are under oath, please tell the court: did you inflict these wounds on Mrs O'Malley?'

Pakenham hesitated, flustered.

'You did, I saw her cut and bleeding!'

It was Patrick, standing up in the courtroom, shouting at Pakenham.

Ellen couldn't believe her ears. Her heart, filled with sorrow and apprehension, now lifted at her son's intervention. Patrick, whom she had thought was lost to her, was now returned – true to his nature – standing there defiant, defending her. Like Michael would.

When the court had settled again, the judge issued a warning against further interruptions, then addressed Pakenham: 'You must answer the question, Sir Richard.'

Ellen watched Pakenham. He looked at the judge, looked at the priest . . . started to say something – then changed his mind.

'I – dammit, I was afeared for my life with the woman!'

'Did you strike her before she presented the weapon?'

'Yes, Goddammit! Yes, I did – the woman has caused me such trouble . . .'

The judge called the court to order again.

After some more questioning of Pakenham, other witnesses were called. Then it was Ellen's turn.

Ellen, when called, gave her evidence calmly, trying not to think of Katie lying back there in the cell, bedecked in bright colours. Her beautiful, beautiful, Katie.

Somehow, she got through it, somehow remaining dignified and restrained on the outside.

After Pakenham's evidence the judge seemed not to be as stern. Father O'Brien had further discredited Pakenham by revealing that the landlord owed almost two thousand pounds to the Westport Union, charged with running the workhouse. By failing in his civil duty, the priest reminded the court, Pakenham amongst others had caused the workhouse to close and its inhabitants to be evicted, including Mrs O'Malley's child – who had been entrusted into the Pakenhams' care on the promise that she would be kept safe.

Then the judge addressed the jury: 'The accused, by her bearing and demeanour, is no ordinary peasant bent solely on wronging her landlord,' he began. 'But she and her children have been subjected to much oppression by a superior power, who also inflicted wounds on her person. You must decide if the sum of these events, culminating in the final assault, constituted sufficient grounds for possessing a firearm, and for using it in self-defence – as she claims – on Sir Richard. You may retire to your deliberations.'

Eventually, the jury returned. It seemed a lifetime to Ellen, another lifetime before the verdict was read. She stood up, her body tense, afraid to look at the children.

'Not guilty!'

'Not guilty'! She could scarce believe it – they hadn't gone against her. She looked for her children. Patrick and Mary cheered and clapped. Faherty threw his cap in the air, then threw his arms round Herself as far as they would go.

Father O'Brien took her hand in both of his and said: 'God is good, justice has been given to you at last, Ellen Rua.'

She thanked him. 'Without you, Father . . .'

He silenced her. But it was not over yet. The judge, having granted her freedom, addressed Pakenham: 'You, sir, have, by deceit, caused this woman to be separated from her children for your own ends. You then assaulted her in a most cowardly and ungentlemanly manner when she came to retrieve her children. You are a disgrace to your breed, and your position as a gentleman! The constabulary may well wish to speak further with you,' he added.

The judge departed the courtroom. And Sergeant Moriarty approached her.

She looked at her children, thought of all the suffering inflicted on her family over the years by Pakenham.

She looked at Bridget. The girl's face had gone pallid at this unexpected turn of events.

She looked at Pakenham, the man who had battered them out of their home. The man who had shot her husband, and who had tricked her into leaving behind three of her children and going to Australia. And then separated her children. This man who had beaten her, as if she were a dog at his heels.

He had been shamed now, called for what he was. The newspapers would carry word of it to any who were left to read them. And to London and Australia. His house was fallen, he was a ruined man.

She looked again at Bridget. This time the girl's eyes met hers, frightened, imploring. If Pakenham was arrested, imprisoned, she would have no job, no means of supporting her mother and family. But there was more in her eyes than just that.

Sergeant Moriarty waited. Did Mrs O'Malley wish to press charges?

'No,' Ellen said quietly. 'No charges.'

60

There was a great mêlée about Ellen, Mary hugged her delightedly, and Patrick after his outburst seemed to have thawed a bit, but still she had to hug him.

She got Faherty on his own for a minute. 'Mr Faherty, thank you for everything.' Embarrassed by this, he stood fidgeting with his cap. 'There is one more thing I have to ask of you – an important thing.'

'Ma'am?' the driver said willingly.

'I need you to bring us to Maamtrasna, one more time, and thence back to Westport for a ship to America,' she said.

'Yes, ma'am, of course I will, and delighted too. 'Pon my oath, you stitched Pakenham up rightly, I'll have a word with Herself first,' he replied.

Then it was settled.

She made her good-byes to Father O'Brien, thanking him again, promising to write to him from Boston.

Once in the carriage, Mary was all concerned about Katie, but excited by the new dress on her, the same as the one on the silent girl. Mary never referred to the fact that the girl's dress was obviously meant for her.

'*A Mhamaí*, Katie looks beautiful,' Mary said, reaching her hand over to Katie's face. 'Will she be all right? Her face is very cold, not hot like before . . .'

Mary looked at her mother, the searching eyes knowing before Ellen spoke that Katie, her sister, her twin, was dead.

'Katie isn't with us any more, *a Mhamaí*, is she?' Mary asked, very quietly now.

Ellen shook her head, not able to say it. Then she reached out her arms to this other, most beautiful child.

The two of them, then, mother and child, were locked in each other's arms, silent tears for Katie streaming down their faces, when Ellen felt a pressure at her side. She turned. It was Patrick, his eyes filled with great big tears – unable to speak his grief, to ask for her comfort. She reached for him, encompassing him in the circle of the family once more.

They passed the Reek, ever present it seemed, ever over them, witness to all they suffered. She, with the dead child across her lap, her two other children half-stretched across Katie's body. She, the mother of the living and the dead, somehow binding them all in together at last.

The silent girl looked out along the road ahead, unmoved by the grief beside her. Like a living part of the holy mountain she was. Impervious to everything.

Faherty doffed his cap, put it beside him on the seat. Not saying anything. Understanding it all.

61

Up they went.

Up the Crucán in single file.

She at the front, still cradling Katie, refusing to let Faherty help her carry the body.

Gently she laid Katie beside the *leac* which marked Michael's grave.

It was a wonderful, sunlit day, the waters of the Mask and Lough Nafooey glistening, the grass green beneath their feet, the mountains tall and grand all around them.

The breeze, attracted by the bright colours of Katie's dress, picked at it, ruffling its hem. Then it caught her hair, holding strands of it aloft for a moment like fine, golden-red gossamer.

No one spoke. Nor was there any other sound in the valley, only the sound they made with their hands pulling back the grass and the clay to make a space for Katie next to Michael.

Faherty and the girl stood back, while the woman and the boy and his sister worked.

Soon, the shallow grave was ready. Shallow, but deep enough so that the dogs, whenever they came back to the valley, would not get at it. Nor hungry ravens.

Together they laid Katie into the cold clay. Solemnly, lovingly, not wanting to let go of her.

The children waited, watching their mother.

She knelt.

They knelt.

Faherty knelt.

The girl just stood there.

Ellen, all her grief, all her energies fixed on the face of her dead child, and putting off the final act of covering Katie's body, did not feel the girl approach them. Did not see her until she was in front of them, beside Mary.

The girl looked down at Mary, and then slowly, deliberately untied the bow at the back of her dress, and undid the buttons. Then, before their amazed eyes, she lifted the dress over her head, and took it off.

Ellen was too dumbstruck to move, to stop her. The girl, up to now, had shown no sign of movement other than to walk, shadow-like, beside her. She had never appeared to hear anything, to understand anything, to be able to do anything.

And now this.

They watched, as in a trance, as the girl reached out the dress, offering it to Mary.

And then she spoke: *'Ní liomsa é seo . . . is leatsa é.'* In beautiful, perfect Irish, the girl was telling Mary that the dress she had been wearing did not belong to her, that it was Mary's. But she was saying something beyond that, Ellen knew. She was returning the dress to Mary, at this precise moment, for a reason. She wanted Mary to wear the dress, the same dress that Ellen had bought for her and her twin sister Katie, lying there before them.

She wanted Mary to wear it before Katie was closed in.

'Go on, Mary,' Ellen said gently. 'She wants you to wear it . . . and I think Katie would like to see you in it, too.'

Mary slowly put on the dress, fixing it, tying it back, taking her hair out from inside the collar.

She stood facing them.

Ellen looked from one to the other of her twin daughters. How alike they were. How beautifully alike.

She watched as Mary knelt again beside the grave. The child put her hand down into it and took Katie's.

'Twins,' Mary said, holding her sister's hand for the last time. 'We'll always be twins, Katie.'

Then they prayed the Rosary in Irish – the Joyful Mysteries. Faherty and the girl joined in. 'Hail Mary . . . Holy Mary . . . Now and at the hour of our death . . .'

Before they covered her in, Ellen took a lock from Katie's hair, so golden-red, it could have been her own.

Then she laid into the grave with Katie the shawl she had kept with her all the time since Australia.

'This is Annie's shawl,' she said to the others.

Slowly, then, handful by handful, gently, lovingly, their tears mixing with it, they put back the clay. Then the small stones to hold it together. Then the tufts of grass.

Carefully, tenderly, each small thing was laid over Katie, as if not to hurt her, to bruise the soft, unripened skin of their little *angelito*.

When they had finished, they prayed again into the soft green mound. Katie's lazy bed.

Then, Ellen, remembering something, her mind only half-connecting it all together, got up, saying to the others, 'Wait here a moment!'

Barefoot, she ran down the Crucán, down the *bóithrín*, down into what was once their small field.

There, on the lazy beds she saw them. Still there – as yet unblighted, dancing in the sun, waiting for her.

'The Whitest Flower!' she said as she picked a handful of them.

She hurried back up to the spot where they waited, and, one by one, set the tiny, white flowers of the potato plant into the crevices between the tufts of grass they had replaced.

They watched her, not understanding what it was she did. But knowing it was the end of something.

AUTHOR'S NOTE

IRELAND

The Census of 1841 gives Ireland's population as 8.2 million. By 1845, at the onset of the Famine, the population is variously estimated to have grown to between eight-and-a-half and nine million – over half the combined population of England and Wales. As an immediate result of the Great Hunger, over a million people died and over another million fled Ireland. In Connacht alone, one in four of the people perished. By 1900, more than four million Irish had gone to the 'New World or the Next', a legacy which has left Ireland as the only country in Europe whose population has decreased rather than increased since the 1840s.

Tourmakeady Lodge, during the time of the Great Hunger, was in fact owned by Bishop Plunkett, the Protestant Bishop of Tuam. The local landlord, he later was responsible for the infamous 'Partry Evictions' of Catholics who refused to convert to his religion.

Delphi Lodge, formerly owned by the Marquess of Sligo, is now a fishing retreat. In 1850, The Lodge, including fishing rights, was leased to the Honourable and Reverend William C. Plunkett, a brother of Bishop Plunkett of Tourmakeady Lodge. The Delphi or Doo Lough Tragedy, as described in the story, occurred in March, 1849. Two monuments now stand at either end of the Doolough Pass Road in memory of those who died en route to the Lodge; some being swept into Doo Lough's black waters. A walk commemorating the 'Death March' from Louisburg to Doo Lough takes place annually in May.

Crucán na bPáiste [sic], the burial place of the children, restored by the local community in 1996, remains overlooking Maamtrasna and Lough Nafooey. Béal a tSnámha – the Mouth of the Swimming Place – is today known as the Ferry Bridge. Bóithrín a tSléibhe, 'the little road over the mountain', still links Maamtrasna with Finny. To the right of the Bóithrín on the way to Finny is a large rock split in two – the *leac* which was Ellen's rock.

The Finny church has also been restored, and now has its own priest. Lord Leitrim, who owned the church and had its roof burned a number of times during the Famine years, was assassinated in 1878. He was a cousin of Lord Lucan.

References to 'the *Slám*' are based on people's experiences as recounted to me.

Visitors to Dublin's Botanic Gardens today can see *Rosa chinensis*, the Jenkinstown Rose – sometimes called 'Old Blush' or 'The Thomas Moore Rose' after the composer-poet who immortalized it as 'The Last Rose of Summer' (*Irish Melodies*, 1813). The rose bush from the original was presented to the Gardens by the Thomas Moore Society in 1950. The potato patch with the original lumper variety, where curator David Moore – no relation to Thomas Moore – first discovered the blight, still remains. Moore became Director of the Gardens in 1869, and remained so until his death in 1879. The story of his search for a cure is based on fact.

No cure was found in David Moore's lifetime; it was not until 1885 that a French scientist named Millardet, seeking to eradicate *Peronospora*, a fungal blight on the vineyards of Bordeaux, developed a solution of copper sulphate and hydrated lime. This 'Bordeaux Mixture', as it came to be known, not only saved the vineyards but proved effective in treating potato crops blighted with *Phytophthora infestans*. Ironically, it was not dissimilar to the 'Bluestone steeps' David Moore had experimented with some forty years earlier in the Botanic Gardens, the key difference being that Millardet sprayed the leaves with the solution rather than steeping the diseased tubers in it.

AUSTRALIA

Under the British Government's 'Orphans and Paupers Scheme', between 1845 and 1849 over four thousand young girls aged 14–18 were sent from the workhouses of Ireland to Australia. Untrained and unsuited to the work to which they were assigned, many of these girls ended up on the streets. One contemporary source estimated 50 per cent of Adelaide's prostitutes, at the time, to be from the West of Ireland, leading to the accusation that the Irish girls were 'Tipperarifying the moral atmosphere' of South Australia.

From when the first vines were planted there in 1838, the Barossa Valley has now become one of the great wine-producing regions of the world. While Jasper Coombes and his Crockford's Estate are fictitious, details of the development of the Barossa and the early winemakers are based on fact. This includes references to some of today's most successful Barossan brand names. Bethany remains a beautiful and flourishing village at the heart of the Barossa, where many of the old German names and traditions still survive. A monument to those early Lutheran pioneers who '*um des*

Glaubens willen nach Australien' – to Australia for the sake of their faith – stands atop nearby Mengler's Hill.

The Ngarrindjeri people still live along the Coorong. At Camp Coorong, near Meningie, George Trevorrow, with others, provides an educational facility for those who wish to learn about the customs and culture of the Ngarrindjeri.

The outrages against the Aboriginal people described in the book are based on recorded fact or as handed down by oral tradition, and recounted to me.

The terms *boong*, *lubra*, natives, *piccaninny*, used in the mouths of some characters in the story, are all offensive to Aboriginal people.

GROSSE ÎLE

Accounts of conditions on Grosse Île, the adoption of orphans by the French-Canadian people, and the numbers who perished there, are all based on fact. Father McGauran was a Sligo-born priest who, after successfully combating typhus contracted on Grosse Île in 1847, returned again to serve there a few months later.

At the cemetery, the monument put there in 1848 by Dr George Mellis Douglas, Grosse Île's medical superintendent, still stands: 'In this secluded spot lie the mortal remains of 5,424 persons who, flying from pestilence and famine in Ireland, in the year 1847, found in America but a grave.' More recently, the large Celtic Cross, on Telegraph Hill, erected in 1909 by The Ancient Order of Hibernians, also commemorates those who perished. One of the fever sheds built in 1847 still remains, as does the cannon which guarded 'Quarantine Pass'. Grosse Île and the Irish Memorial were declared a National Historic Site in 1984 and opened to the public. The Site is now run by Parcs Canada and is open from 1 May to 31 October each year.

BOSTON

Deer Island, Boston's Quarantine Station in 1847, is today the site of the city's waste-water treatment plant operated by the Massachusetts Water Resources Authority. The cemetery, which holds the remains of 852 Irish immigrants who died during the Famine, is currently being restored, and a memorial will be erected in 1999. In June 1998 the Irish Famine Memorial Park was unveiled in downtown Boston at the corner of School and Washington streets. It features twin sculptures by artist Robert Shure, and eight narrative plaques, text by Professor Thomas O'Connor, describing the odyssey of the Irish immigrant from tragedy to triumph in America. The memorial is located along Boston's Freedom Trail.

GLOSSARY OF IRISH AND
ANGLO-IRISH WORDS/SAYINGS

A bhastaird! You bastard!
A chroí geal! Bright heart! [lit.]/love!
A Ellen bheag! Little Ellen! (addressing her)
Anam an diabhail! In the name of the devil!
An bhfuil tú ann? Are you there? Are you in it?
Ar dheis Dé go raibh a anam! At the right hand of God may his
  soul be!

Bás gan sagart Death without a priest (no last rites)
Beannachtaí na Féile Blessings of the Feast (to you) [lit.]/Happy
  Christmas
Bitteen (Anglo-Irish) A small piece
Blas Accent (e.g. Irish accent)
Bockedy (Anglo-Irish) Broken, lame
Bóithrín Little road/dirt track
Bothán Hut/cabin
Bóthar slán! A safe road! A safe journey!
Buachaill (A Bhuachaill!) Boy/Boy!
Buíochas (. . . le Dia!) Thanks (. . . be to God!)
Buíochas do phog an dorais Thanks for the kiss for the door
  [lit.]/the kiss before death
Bulóg Loaf (of bread)
Bundleen (Anglo-Irish) Small bundle

Cad is ainm duit? What is your name?
Cailín Girl
Cailleach Hag/crone
Céilí Irish dance gathering
Cé leis é? Whose is it?
Ciúnas, Ellen, tá siad ag teacht! Quiet Ellen, they're coming!
Clachan (Anglo-Irish)/*Clachán* Cluster of cabins
Clagars (Anglo-Irish) Heavy showers of rain
Cliste Clever

Craythur! (Anglo-Irish)   'Poor thing!'/Creature
Cronauning (Anglo-Irish)   Humming, talk-singing
Cúpláin   Little twins

Daidí (A Dhaidí!)   Daddy/Daddy!
Dalteen (Anglo-Irish)/*Dailtín*   Brat/impudent pup
Dar Dia!   By God!
Dia dhuit!   God be with you!/Hello!
Dia's Muire dhuit!   God and Mary be with you!
Dos   Bush/Mop . . . of hair
Drochbhéasach   Bad mannered
Dropeen (Anglo-Irish)   A little drop
Duine le Dia   A person with God, a simple soul

Éist do bhéal!   Listen!

Faic   Nothing
Fáilte romhat go dtí an Astráil!   Welcome to Australia!
Fiabhras Dubh   The Black Fever [lit.]/Typhus

Gasúr   Child/Young Person
Glic   Clever (in a sly way)
Goltraí   Crying song [lit.]/Sad song
Grá (A ghrá!)   Love/Love!

Is mise atá ann!   It's me who's here/It's me who's in it!

Kishogue (Anglo-Irish)/*Ciseog*   Basket for carrying turf or potatoes

Leaba   Bed
Loy (Anglo-Irish)   Narrow-bladed spade

Mamaí (A Mhamaí!)   Mammy/Mammy!
Máinlín (A mháinlín!)   Angel/Darling! (of a child)
M'anam/M'anamse!   My soul!
Meannán aerach   Goat of the air [lit.]/Snipe
Mo bhuíochas dhuit!   My thanks to you!
Mo thóin!   My backside!/Me arse!
Moladh le Dia!   Praise to God!

Ní liomsa é seo . . . is leatsa é!   This is not mine . . . it's yours!
Nollaig shona dhuit!   A Happy Christmas to you!

Ochóning (Anglo-Irish)   Lamenting/keening
Oíche mhaith (. . . leat fhéin!)   Good night (. . . to yourself!)
One-een (Anglo-Irish)   Small one

Pisreoga/Piseoga   Superstitions
Púca   Pooka (Halloween superstition/evil spirit)

Ráiméis   Nonsense
Rascaleen (Anglo-Irish)   Little rascal
Rí-rá   Commotion/noise

Sagart   Priest
Saoirse   Freedom
Sar (Anglo-Irish)   The devil a one/ne'er a one
Sasanach   English person
Scailpeen (Anglo-Irish)   Small shelter/Lean-to, with roof of
   grass/straw
Sciathóg   Shallow oval basket of sally rods/straw
Scullogue (Anglo-Irish)   Pejorative term for money lender
Sean-daoine   Old people
Sean-fhocail(s) (Anglo-Irish)/*Sean fhoclaí* (pl.)   Old saying(s)
Sean-nós/Sean-nósanna (pl.)   Old way(s)/custom(s)/old style of singing
Sinn féin sinn féin!   Ourselves are ourselves!
Slane (Anglo-Irish)   Narrow digging spade
Slán agus beannacht!   Go safe and bless you! [lit.]/Goodbye!
Slán go fóill!   Goodbye for now!/Goodbye for a little while!
Slieveen (Anglo-Irish)   A sly one
(The) *Slám*   A handful [lit.]/Death Curse
Sonasach   Happy disposition
Soologues (Anglo-Irish)   Beads . . . of sweat
Sponc   Spirit/spunk
Spraoi agus ceol   Fun and music
Stór   Dear/Love/Darling (of an adult)
Stóirín   Dear/Darling (of a child)
Stookeens (Anglo-Irish)   Little stacks . . . of turf
Streelish (Anglo-Irish)   Slovenly/Bedraggled
Striapach   Whore/Prostitute
Suantraí/Suantraithe (pl.)   Lullaby/sleep-song(s)

Taig (Anglo-Irish)   Papist/Catholic (pejorative term)
Tallywoman (Anglo-Irish)   Kept woman
Tamailleen (Anglo-Irish)/*Tamaillín*   A little while
Tá d'eadan ciuín mo bhuachaill bán, mo ghrása!   Your forehead is
   quiet my fair-haired boy, my love!

Tá tú ar ais!   You are back!
Tiocfaidh ár lá!   Our day will come!
Tooreen (Anglo-Irish)   Tureen, a dish for soup
Traithneens (Anglo-Irish)   Straws/lots

Ullagone (Anglo-Irish)   Cry/Wail/Lament

Note: Irish words and phrases directly translated in the text have been omitted from the above.

Acknowledgements

De Bhaldraithe, Tomás (ed) – *English-Irish Dictionary* – An Gúm, An Roinn Oideachais, Dublin 1992.
Ó Dónaill, Niall – *Foclóir Gaeilge-Béarla* – [Eagarthóir Comhairleach – Tomás De Bhaldraithe] – An Gúm, An Roinn Oideachais, Dublin 1992.
Ó Muirithe, Diarmaid – *A Dictionary of Anglo-Irish Words and Phrases from Gaelic in the English of Ireland* – Four Courts Press, Dublin, 1996.
Sandra Ní Gharbháin
Mary Tom Ó Liam

QUOTATIONS

The following quotations come in the main part, from the Famine years 1845–52. The rest are identified by year. Those persons quoted frequently are listed below.

Sir Robert Peel – British Prime Minister, Tory Government, to June 1846.

Lord John Russell – British Prime Minister, Whig Government, June 1846–52.

Lord Clarendon – Lord Lieutenant of Ireland, from June 1847 (on the death of the previous Lord Lieutenant, Lord Bessborough).

Charles E. Trevelyan – Permanent Assistant Secretary at the British Treasury with prime responsibility for Famine relief in Ireland.

John Mitchel – Author; Young Ireland leader; transported to Van Diemen's Land in 1848.

IRELAND

The Irish

You see more ratted and wretched people here than I ever saw anywhere else. **Queen Victoria**

The strongest men and the most beautiful women perhaps in the British dominions, are said to be, the greater part of them, from the lowest rank of people in Ireland, who are generally fed from this root. **Adam Smith, 18th century economist**

The wretched people seem to be human potatoes a sort of emanation from 'the root' – they have lived by it and will die with it. **Clarendon**

Quite obvious, that the Irish people are giving their children classical educations on smaller means than would be thought sufficient. **Thomas Colville Scott, Scottish surveyor, Connemara, 1853**

Slothful, improvident and reckless. *The Liverpool Mercury*

Whenever ten square yards of soil can be found between the rocks, it is scraped up with exemplary industry into 'lazy beds' for potatoes. **Colville Scott**

I am haunted by the human chimpanzees I saw ... To see white chimpanzees is dreadful; if they were black, one would not feel it so much, but their skins, except where tanned by exposure, are as white as ours. **Charles Kingsley, English clergyman, 1860**

One would think that starving men would become violent. But such was by no means the case ... The fault of the people was apathy.

The Irish press is not proverbial for a strict adherence to unadorned truth. **Anthony Trollope, English novelist**

The real question at issue is the improvement of the social and moral condition of the masses of the population. **Peel**

We have granted, lent, subscribed, worked, visited, clothed the Irish, millions of money, years of debate ... the only return is calumny and rebellion – let us not grant, clothe ... any more and see what that will do. **Russell**

Disgust ... at the state of Ireland and the incurable madness of the people. **Charles Greville, English diarist**

The missing link between the gorilla and the Negro. *Punch* – **London Magazine**

Alas the Irish peasant had tasted of Famine and found that it was good ... For our parts, we regard the potato blight as a blessing. *The Times*, **London**

Blight/Hunger

What may be the result of this is too fearful to contemplate. **David Moore, Curator, Botanic Gardens, Dublin**

Some days before the disease appeared ... a dense cloud resembling a thick fog, overspread the entire country, but differing from a common fog, being dry instead of moist and in having in almost every instance, a disagreeable odour. **Canon John O'Rourke, Catholic clergyman and author, 1874**

27th [July] this doomed plant bloomed in all the luxuriance of an abundant harvest. Returning on 3rd inst. [August] I beheld with sorrow one wide waste of putrefying vegetation. **Father Mathew, Temperance Movement leader to Trevelyan**

They picked over and picked out their blackened potatoes, and even ate the decayed ones. **Asenath Nicholson, American author**

Irishmen could live on anything . . . there was plenty of grass in the fields even though the potato crop should fail. **Duke of Cambridge**

In this fairest and richest of countries, men are suffering and starving by the million. **William Makepeace Thackeray, English novelist; *Punch* satirist**

I saw a bunch of withered nettles there which I was told to be intended for breakfast. **Lynch, Constabulary, Co. Clare**

A government ship sailing into any harbour with Indian corn was . . . sure to meet half a dozen sailing out with Irish wheat and cattle. **Mitchel**

He . . . was hoarse from roaring with thirst. I procured some drink for him. As I passed next morning, he was relieved of his suffering. His corpse and that of his wife were borne to the grave. **Fr. Quaide, Co. Limerick**

Distance from the workhouses . . . being in part about twenty-six miles . . . some unfortunate fathers and mothers, each carrying a child or two, had in the depth of winter to attend three reviews lest they should be too heavy in flesh for outdoor relief. **Fr. O'Reilly, Co. Mayo**

It was enough to have broken the stoutest heart to have seen the poor little children in the union workhouse yesterday – their flesh hanging so loose from their little bones, that the physician took it in his hand and wrapped it around their legs.

All the sheep were gone; all the cows, all the poultry killed; not one pig left; the very dogs which had barked at me before had disappeared; no potatoes. **William E. Forster, Quaker, Co. Galway**

Even their bed-clothes and fishing nets had gone for one object; the supply of food. **Society of Friends Report, Co. Donegal**

It is not a very unusual thing for men . . . to work all day without eating one morsel but during the hours for breakfast and dinner, lie down behind a fence, unwilling to be seen by those who have something to eat. **Public Works Engineer, Queen's County (now Co. Laois)**

The town of Westport ... its streets crowded with gaunt wanderers sauntering to and fro with hopeless air and hunger-struck look. **Forster**

In many districts their only food is the potato, their only beverage water ... worst-fed, worst-housed, and worst-clothed peasantry in the world. **The Devon Commission Report**

The exact corresponding event to an Englishman's Sunday dinner was a Coroner's Inquest in Ireland. **Mitchel**

Though we met multitudes in the last stages of suffering, yet not one through that day asked charity and in one case the common hospitality showed itself by offering us milk when we asked for water. This day I saw enough, and my heart was sick-sick. **Nicholson**

A girl of about twelve years of age ... ran beside our car ... we told her again and again, we would give her nothing ... my companion gave way ... he gave her a fourpenny; I confess I forgave him – it was hard-earned, though by a bad sort of industry. **Sidney Godolphin Osborne, clergyman (on a journey from Leenane to Westport)**

Be quiet, be peaceable, be patient. Believe me that in a Christian country no man will be allowed to die of hunger. **Reverend Duncan, Co. Galway**

Death

The custom when all hope was extinguished was to get into the darkest corner and die, where passers-by could not see them. **Nicholson, Co. Mayo**

Out of a population of two-hundred-and-forty, I found thirteen already dead from want. The survivors were like walking skeletons; the men stamped with the livid mark of hunger. **Forster, Bundorragha (near Delphi), Co. Mayo**

Families found ... in one putrid mass, where, in many cases, the cabin was tumbled upon them to give them decent burial. **Nicholson, Co. Mayo**

Both the legs as far as the buttocks, appeared to be eaten off . . . Those who saw the body were of the opinion, from the agonised expression on M'Manus's countenance, that he was alive when the pig attacked him. *The Vindicator*, Belfast

Shocking to relate that the unfortunate victim, the deceased, cut off the feet from the ankles of one of the children and eat of them. **Kerrigan, Constabulary, Co. Galway**

Entire villages prostrate in sickness, or almost hushed in the last sleep. *Banner of Ulster*

'How can the dogs look so fat and shining here, where there is no food for the people?'
   'Shall I tell her?' said the pilot to Mr Griffith, not supposing that I heard him. **Nicholson, Co. Donegal**

Landlords/Evictions

The landlords exterminate right and left. **Fr. Brady, Co. Cavan**

A Tenant, 'Pat Heffernon', who had actually improved a few acres of hill land . . . was afraid his rent was about to be raised when he saw us. **Colville Scott**

Shortly before Christmas Day, William Heffron . . . came into the house and told us to leave – that he might throw it down. We all went out . . . The house was thrown down the moment we quitted it. We returned to the ruins and lived in a corner of it, having made a sort of tent there. The tent was thrown down by Heffron shortly after Christmas. **Catherine Coyle, evicted tenant, Co. Mayo**

The tenants and labourers of Mr Gerrard from another part of his property were obliged to attend there (very much against their will) in order to assist in levelling those houses. **Cummins, Constabulary, Co. Galway**

My fine virtuous, holy people have been starved to death. The landlords of all sects and creed have conspired for their destruction – the Catholic landlords the most cruelly disposed. **Fr. Browne, Co. Mayo**

A good landlord is as rare as a white blackbird. **James Daly, Editor, *The Connaught Telegraph*, 1879–92**

Religion

I attribute many of Ireland's misfortunes to the principles of her dominant Church. **Colville Scott**

We rise at four o'clock . . . and . . . hold . . . confession for the convenience of the poor country people, who . . . flock in thousands . . . to prepare themselves for the death they look to as inevitable. **Fr. Quigley, Co. Clare**

The sufferings of the present time bear no proportion to the glory to come. **Archbishop Murray, Dublin**

The Catholic and Protestant clergymen vie with one another in acts of benevolence. *The Freeman's Journal* **(Nationalist newspaper)**

How ungrateful of the Catholics of Ireland not to pour forth canticles of gratitude to the ministers who promised that none of them should perish and then suffered two million to starve. **Archbishop MacHale, Tuam, Co. Galway**

A network of well-intentioned Protestant associations spread over the poorer parts of the country, which in return for soup endeavoured to gather the people into their churches, really believing that masses of our people wished to abandon Catholicism. **Alfred Webb, Quaker**

Divine Providence has again poured out upon us the vial of its wrath. **Fr. Mathew to Trevelyan**

If ever there was a time for England to make a great effort for the evangelization of Ireland it is the present; the poor are ready; the great distress has softened the hearts of the poor. **General Irish Reformation Society Report**

Language and Culture

Hang the harpers wherever found. **Queen Elizabeth of England, 1603**

The Irish-speaking people have songs by the thousands. **Thomas Davis, poet, Protestant nationalist, co-founder of** *The Nation*

Dancing is so universal among them. **Arthur Young, English author and political commentator, 1777**

The Irish language, although evidently on the decline is still the vernacular tongue of about two millions of the population . . . the best Irish is spoken in Connaught . . . the language . . . is almost unknown in the King and Queen's counties. **Mr and Mrs S. C. Hall, Travel Writers, 1840**

That children of the Popish and other poor natives in Ireland might be instructed 'gratis' in the English tongue. **British Parliament Select Committee on Education in Ireland, 1835**

The 'land of song' was no longer tuneful; or, if a human sound met the traveller's ear, it was only that of the feeble and despairing wail for the dead. **George Petrie, author, musicologist, 1855**

Keens are also a medium through which the disaffected circulate their mischievous principles . . . the Irish Language being a sufficient cloak for the expression of seditious sentiments. **T. Crofton Croker, English author, 1824**

Poetry, music and dancing stopped . . . The Famine killed everything. **Máire Ní Grianna, Co. Donegal**

AUSTRALIA

I will, in confidence, venture to assure you that this country will never answer to settle in. **Lieutenant Governor Major Ross, 1788**

The province of South Australia is a delightfully fertile and salubrious country, in every respect well adapted to the Constitution of English men, and is one of the most flourishing of all our colonies. **Shipping Poster, Truro, England, 1839**

An equal number of free female emigrants to be sent out at the charge of the British Treasury . . . as an equivalent to the Exiles already introduced. **Charles La Trobe, Superintendent of Port Phillip/later Lieutenant Governor of Victoria**

Blacksmiths, tanners, fellmongers, house and ship builders, sail makers, masons, &c., not to forget confectioners, saddlers, gun-makers, milliners, tobacconists and hairdressers! **George Arden, Melbourne, 1840**

The Barossa/Lutherans/Wine-making

A considerable proportion of the inhabitants of South Australia . . . are

Germans . . . We may safely add, that they form a highly valuable class of our colonists, being exceedingly industrious, sober, and persevering people . . . the Germans have built their village of Bethany; their land being divided into long strips. *The Southern Australian,* 1843

So-called Old Lutherans . . . a German breed of people, the like of which I had never known at home, who seemed to originate from the 14th century, and over whom all tremendous progress and a lack of culture had lightly passed. **Carl Muecke, Lutheran Minister**

We the undersigned . . . requesting in favour of the maintenance of good civil order Your Excellencies most affectionate approbation for introducing of small correctives in Bethany, for example, bodily chastisements and pillory for those resisting the . . . power of God. **Mayor and Elders of the Parish of Bethany,** 1843

I am satisfied that New Silesia [i.e. The Barossa] will furnish the province with such a quantity of wine that we shall drink it as cheap as in Cape Town. **Johannes Menge, Land Surveyor, Barossa Valley,** 1840

Aborigines

Black men. We wish to make you happy. But you cannot be happy unless you imitate white men . . . you cannot be happy unless you love God . . . learn to speak English. **Governor Gawler, Adelaide,** 1835

That permanent benefit . . . from attempts to Christianize the natives can only be expected by separation of the children from their parents and the evil influences of the tribe to which they belong. **Report of British Parliament Select Committee on Aborigines,** 1860

I have heard again and again people say that they were nothing better than dogs, and that it was no more harm to shoot them than it would be to shoot a dog. **Reverend Yate,** 1835

Many of the middle-aged and young [Ngarrindjeri] men have quite a dignified bearing, with an air of freedom altogether different from low-class Europeans. **Reverend George Taplin, Anglican Missionary,** 1873

The Aborigines were in good physical condition at the beginning of colonisation, but that their health had been declining ever since that time.

I do not think it unadvisable to Christianize them; for I would rather they died as Christians than drag out a miserable existence as heathens. I believe that the race will disappear either way. **Select Committee Report**

Ireland/The Irish

Our Natives commonly attach some idea of inferiority to what is Irish. **Reverend Gunther, Anglican Missionary, 1837**

A set of ignorant creatures whose whole knowledge of household duties barely reaches to distinguishing the inside from the outside of a potato. *The Melbourne Argus*

Pure, innocent, Irish country girls are being placed in the closest contact, such as sleeping in the same berth, with English Protestants of the lowest class. **Fr. Dunne to Cardinal Cullen, 1859**

These London people . . . swamping us with a purely Irish population. I do not object to such a population as free emigrants . . . only . . . let us not have them exclusively, so as to have our noble Colony transformed into another Tipperary.

Whilst Famine is making damning strides in the United Kingdom, Port Phillip is, from the scarcity of labor, compelled annually to destroy vast quantities of human food. *The Melbourne Argus*

The Police force . . . is with one exception exclusively composed of Irish [i.e. Northern Protestants] and could not be prevailed upon to . . . prohibit the exhibition of party symbols and to prevent the further public procession of antagonistic political societies. **Dr. Palmer, Mayor of Melbourne**

Irish Relief Fund – But little interest appears to be taken in the Fund; indeed it must be admitted that the pockets of the Port Phillippians have already been pretty considerably drained for charitable purposes. *The Melbourne Argus*

We have no further intelligence of the potato disease, except of a negative character. *Port Phillip Herald*

CANADA

We cannot turn those people away famished like the Eastern United States and Liverpool did. **John E. Mills, Mayor of Montreal**

It would be better to simply send a battery of artillery from Québec City to sink these ships to the bottom, than to let all these poor people suffer such a slow, agonizing death. **Fr. E. A. Taschereau, Catholic Missionary, Grosse Île**

They come out ignorant of everything beyond the use of the spade.

From the North of Ireland . . . as a class these people are much superior in intelligence to their countrymen from the South and West. **Dr. George Mellis Douglas, Medical Superintendent, Grosse Île**

It is of great importance that the Emigrant should be greeted, upon his landing, by the voice of the Church, whether a soothing or a warning voice. **Reverend G. J. Mountain, Anglican Bishop of Montreal**

The excrements arising from the dysentery of the sick frequently descend from the upper tier on the unfortunates in the lower tier. **Fr. O'Reilly, Catholic Missionary, Grosse Île**

The number of orphans is very great . . . Most will die . . . happy not to have known their misfortune here. **Taschereau**

Nearly all the nurses from Québec have sickened, and the emigrants furnish but few from their own body. **'Dan Drake', Emigrant's letter**

I have not gone to bed for five nights . . . it is impossible that two priests will do, my legs are beginning to bother me. **Fr. McGauran to Archbishop Signay, Québec**

The government cannot undertake to convey emigrants to Canada . . . some £150,000 would have to be spent in doing that which if we do not interfere with will be done for nothing. **Lord Grey, Colonial Secretary, London**

There is a large British force in Ireland, larger than the whole army and navy of the United States including the armies of Mexico. *Québec Mercury*

Sailors took ashore a child who had died the day before; they brought a bit of snow with them when they returned. **John Roberts, emigrant aboard the *Clio***

UNITED STATES OF AMERICA

The Irishman looks upon America as the refuge of his race . . . The Shores of England are farther off, in his heart's geography, than those of New York or Massachusetts. **Thomas Colley Grattan, author, 1859**

That inefficiency of the pure Celtic race furnishes the answer to the question: How much use are the Irish to us in America? The native American answer is: 'None at all'. **Edward Everett Hale, American clergyman and author**

The increase in foreign-born pauperism in our midst is an evil. *Boston Daily Advertiser*

One ship was sent away merely because no one would give bonds that the passengers . . . would not become a public charge . . . They come here to toil for their bread, not to become a public charge. *The Boston Pilot*

American citizens of Boston! The honorable Fathers of this City, have thought expedient to erect a HOSPITAL on Deer Island for the protection of FOREIGN PAUPERS! . . . AMERICAN CITIZENS BE IN AT THE DEATH. **Anti-Irish handbill, Boston**

Most of these foreigners are Roman Catholics. In the name of the religion of Him who rebuked the Pharisee's bigotry . . . let us resolve to purge away once and forever, all sectarian bias and preference in our charities. **Reverend Huntington, Protestant clergyman, South Congregational Church**

What is death to Ireland is but augmented fortune to America; and we are actually fattening on the starvation of another people. **General Irish Relief Committee, New York**

That measures be adopted for preventing . . . the sanitary evils arising from foreign emigration . . . involves one of the most momentous . . . social problems ever presented to us for solution. **Massachusetts Sanitary Commission Report**

Several convalescent patients under diet restrictions escaped from the wards at night, and gained access to a neighboring cornfield, where they partook freely of the unripe fruit. The fatal diarrhea followed, without mercy. **Dr. Upham, Deer Island Hospital**

The want of forethought in them to save . . . the indulgence of their appetites for stimulating drinks . . . and their strong love for their native land, which is characteristic with them, are the fruitful causes of insanity among them. **Massachusetts State Lunatic Hospital Annual Report**

The average age of Irish life in Boston, does not exceed fourteen years. **State Lunatic Hospital Report**

We should make ourselves American as much as we can . . . This is our country now. Ireland is only a recollection. **Bishop Fitzpatrick, Boston**

IRELAND

Emigration

The Celts are gone with a vengeance, the Lord be praised.

In a few years more a Celtic Irishman will be as rare in Connemara as is the Red Indian on the shores of Manhattan. *The Times*, **London**

The departure of thousands of papist Celts must be a blessing to the country they quit . . . Some English and Scots settlers have arrived. **Clarendon**

Although the population has been diminished in so remarkable a manner by Famine, disease and emigration between 1841 and 1851, and has been since decreasing, the results of the Irish census of 1851 are, on the whole, satisfactory, demonstrating as they do the general advancement of the country. **General Report Census Commissioners on 1851 Census of Ireland**

Politicians

If you are ambitious of a monument, the bones of a people, slain with the sword of Famine, piled into cairns more numerous than the ancient Pyramids, shall tell posterity the triumphs of your brief but disastrous administration. **Archbishop MacHale to Russell**

I consider the Union . . . was but a parchment and an unsubstantial union, if Ireland is not to be treated in the hour of difficulty and distress, as an integral part of the United Kingdom. **Russell**

The judgement of God . . . sent the calamity to teach the Irish a lesson, that calamity must not be too much mitigated. **Trevelyan**

We have tried to govern Ireland by conciliation and have failed . . . no other means are open except to . . . govern Ireland through Rome. **Russell**

The greatest evil we have to face . . . is not the physical evil of the Famine, but the moral evil of the selfish, perverse and turbulent character of the people. **Trevelyan**

I saw Trevelyan's claw in the vitals of those children. **Mitchel**

Posterity will trace up to that Famine . . . that on this, as on many other occasions, Supreme Wisdom has educed permanent good out of transient evil. **Trevelyan**

Ireland . . . is in your power. If you do not save her, she cannot save herself. I predict with the sincerest conviction that a quarter of her population will perish unless you come to her relief. **Daniel O'Connell (The Liberator), British House of Commons**

A neglect of public duty has occurred . . . some authority ought to be held responsible, or would long since have been held responsible had those things occurred in any union in England. **British Parliament Select Committee of Inquiry**

The Union; the dissolution of which would involve not merely the repeal of an act of parliament, but the dismemberment of this great empire. **Peel, 1843**

Ireland is the one deep blot on the brightness of British honour, Ireland is our disgrace. **Lord Grey, House of Lords**

We shall be equally blamed for keeping them alive or letting them die. **Clarendon**

The Lord Lieutenant had no power and Downing Street had no heart. *The Times*, London

I don't think there is another legislative in Europe that would disregard such suffering as now exists in the west of Ireland, or so coldly persist in a policy of extermination. **Clarendon**

The destitution here is so horrible and the indifference of the House of

Commons to it so manifest . . . a policy that must be one of extermination. **Edward Twistleton, Chief Poor Law Commissioner (resigned in March 1849)**

We must not complain of what we really want to obtain. If small farmers go, and their landlords are reduced to sell portions of their estates to persons who will invest capital, we shall at last arrive at something like a satisfactory settlement of the country. **Trevelyan to Twistleton**

What the patient now requires is rest and quiet and time for the remedies which have been given to operate.

God grant that the generation to which this great opportunity has been offered may rightly perform its part, and that we may not relax our efforts until Ireland fully participates in the social health and physical prosperity of Great Britain, which will be the true consummation of their union. **Trevelyan**

What can be more wicked . . . by talking of Ireland being a drain upon the English Treasury? If the Union be not a mockery, there exists no such thing as an English Treasury. The exchequer is the exchequer of the United Kingdom. If Cornwall had been visited with the scenes that have desolated Cork, would similar arguments have been used. **Isaac Butt, Professor of Political Economy, Trinity College, Dublin**

I have called it an artificial Famine . . . potatoes failed in like manner all over Europe; yet there was no Famine save in Ireland. The Almighty, indeed, sent the potato blight, but the English created the Famine. **Mitchel, 1860**

A fearful murder committed on the mass of the people. **Charles Gavan Duffy, Young Ireland leader, later Premier, State of Victoria, Australia**

The Irish people have profited much by the Famine, the lesson was severe; but so rooted were they in old prejudices and old ways, that no teacher could have induced them to make the changes which this Visitation of Divine Providence has brought about. **Lord George Hill, landlord, author, 1853**

They that die by Famine die by inches. **Matthew Henry, English author, 1662–1714**

TODAY'S POLITICAL LEADERS ON IRELAND'S GREAT FAMINE

IRELAND

The Famine is the defining moment in the evolution of modern Ireland and the Irish Diaspora. As such, we require the fullest possible understanding of it and its long-term significance. The Famine decimated our country and inflicted massive demographic, social, economic and cultural wounds. It teaches modern Irish people the lessons of compassion and of social inclusion, and of the need for constant vigilance on the issue of global hunger. **An Taoiseach Bertie Ahern, T.D. – August 1998**

AUSTRALIA

The Irish influence on Australia has been immense. About one third of all Australians can claim some Irish heritage. Irish culture and values have helped shape many aspects of contemporary Australian society, from literature and music through to politics and religion.

The Irish presence in Australia goes back to the first days of European settlement. One of the great catalysts for Irish emigration to the Australian colonies was the Great Irish Famine of 1845-52. Fleeing suffering and hardship, many thousands came to Australia to build a new life. It was a Famine which changed both Ireland and Australia. **Prime Minister John Howard – August 1998**

CANADA

Canada's and Ireland's histories have been closely linked. In 1847, tens of thousands of Irish people fleeing Ireland's Great Famine came to Grosse Île, Québec. Canadians received them with great generosity. These Irish settlers played a very important role in the early development of our country. Many of our most distinguished citizens have been of Irish descent. Today the descendants of these settlers are loyal Canadians, but they also look with great affection to the land of their ancestors. **Prime Minister Jean Chrétien – August 1998**

UNITED STATES OF AMERICA

The Famine was the greatest disaster in all the history of Ireland. Yet out of that horrible tragedy there emerged a blessing for our nation. The men, women, and children then crossed the ocean to build new lives in America.

Irish-Americans have . . . enriched America's way of life with the values of their heritage – love of family, faith, and hard work; devotion to community; and compassion for those in need. Perhaps the haunting memory of the Famine helps to explain the remarkable generosity of the Irish, at home and all around the world. **President Bill Clinton – May 1997**

UNITED KINGDOM

The Famine was a defining event in the history of Ireland and of Britain. It has left deep scars. That one million people should have died in what was then part of the richest and most powerful nation in the world is something that still causes pain as we reflect on it today. Those who governed in London at the time failed their people through standing by while a crop failure turned into a massive human tragedy. We must not forget such a dreadful event.

It is also right that we should pay tribute to the ways in which the Irish people have triumphed in the face of this catastrophe. Britain in particular has benefited immeasurably from the skills and talents of Irish people, not only in areas such as music, the arts and the caring professions but across the whole spectrum of our political, economic and social life.

Let us therefore today not only remember those who died but also celebrate the resilience and courage of those Irish men and women who were able to forge another life outside Ireland, and the rich culture and vitality they brought with them. Britain, the US and many Commonwealth countries are richer for their presence. **Prime Minister Tony Blair – May 1997**

BIBLIOGRAPHY

Over and above the books listed in the abridged bibliography which follows, I acknowledge a special debt to the following authors whose work I found particularly helpful with regard to scope and detail.

IRELAND

Christine Kinealy's two absorbingly analytical books *This Great Calamity: The Irish Famine 1845–52* (Gill & Macmillan, Dublin, 1994) and *A Death-Dealing Famine: The Great Hunger in Ireland* (Pluto Press, London/Chicago, 1997).

John Killen, ed., *The Famine Decade: Contemporary Accounts 1841–1851* (The Blackstaff Press Ltd., Belfast 1995).

Canon John O'Rourke's *The Great Irish Famine* (Veritas Publications, Dublin. First published 1874; abridged edn., 1989).

'The Visitation of God'?: The potato and the great Irish famine by Austin Bourke. Edited for Irish Historical Studies by Jacqueline Hill and Cormac Ó Gráda (Lilliput Press Ltd., Dublin, 1993).

Priests and People in Pre-Famine Ireland 1780–1845 by S.J. Connolly (Gill & Macmillan Ltd., Dublin/St. Martin's Press Inc., New York, 1982).

Mary E. Daly's *The Famine in Ireland* (Published for the Historical Association of Ireland by Dundalgan Press, Dundalk, 1986).

Donal A. Kerr's *'A Nation of Beggars': Priests, People and Politics in Famine Ireland 1846–1852* (Clarendon Press, Oxford, 1994).

Peter Gray's *The Irish Famine* (illustrated), (Thames and Hudson, London, 1995).

R. Dudley Edwards's and T. Desmond Williams's, eds., *The Great Famine: Studies in Irish History 1845–52* (Lilliput Press Ltd., Dublin, 1994).

Margaret Kelleher's *The Feminization of Famine: Expressions of the Inexpressible?* (Cork University Press, Cork, 1997).

Helen Litton's *The Irish Famine: An Illustrated History* (Wolfhound Press Ltd., Dublin/Irish Books and Media Inc., Minneapolis, 1994).

Chris Morash's and Richard Hayes's, eds., *Fearful Realities: New Perspectives on the Famine* (Irish Academic Press, Co. Dublin, 1996).

E. Charles Nelson's booklet 'The Cause of the Calamity: Potato blight in Ireland 1845–1847 and the role of the National Botanic Gardens, Glasnevin'

(The Office of Public Works, Government of Ireland, Dublin, 1995). Also, E. Charles Nelson's book with Eileen M. McCracken *The Brightest Jewel: A History of the National Botanic Gardens, Glasnevin, Dublin* (The Office of Public Works, Dublin, Boethius Press, Kilkenny, 1987) was invaluable for detail about David Moore, the then curator, and the Gardens themselves in the 1840s.

Cormac Ó Gráda's *The Great Irish Famine* (Gill & Macmillan Ltd., Dublin, 1989) was essential reading, as was Cathal Póirtéir's, *Famine Echoes* (Gill & Macmillan Ltd., Dublin, 1995) and *The Great Irish Famine – RTE Thomas Davis Lectures Series* (Mercier Press, Cork, published in association with Radio Telefís Éireann, 1995) edited by him.

AUSTRALIA

Joan Druett's book, *Petticoat Whalers: Whaling wives at sea 1820–1920* (Collins Publishers, New Zealand, 1991), was an important source for details of whaling, gamming, scrimshawing, and life in the Pacific Ocean in the 1840s.

Maritime Heritage Booklets from Polly Woodside, Melbourne Maritime Museum
— No. 4 'The Immigrants' by Barbara Cohen
— No. 6 'Life on the Cape-Horners' (no author named)
— No. 8 'Winds, Currents, and Trading Routes' (no author named)
— No. 12 'Port of Melbourne 1835–60' prepared by Dorothy Minkoff,
all also provided useful information and technical data.

Ronald Parson's book *Migrant Ships for South Australia 1836–1860* (Gould Books, Gumeracha, South Australia, 1988) and his booklet, 'Port Misery and the New Port' (early Port Adelaide) (R. H. Parsons, Lobethal, South Australia, reprint 1997) were extremely helpful with regard to landing conditions for immigrants and descriptions of the port of Adelaide.

For descriptions of The Barossa in the 1840s, the early Lutheran settlers and the first winemakers, the following all provided excellent source material: *Vineyard of the Empire: Early Barossa Vignerons 1842–1939* by Annely Aeuckens, Geoffrey Bishop, George Bell, Kate McDougall, and Gordon Young (Australian Industrial Publishers Pty., Ltd., Adelaide, 1988).

The Barossa: A Vision Realised, The Nineteenth Century Story by Reginald S. Munchenberg, Heinrich F.W. Proeve, Donald A. Ross, Anne Hausler, Geoffrey B. Saegenschnitter, Noris Ioannou; and Roger E. Teusner (Barossa Valley Archives & Historical Trust, South Australia, 1993).

And Heinrich F.W. Proeve's *A Dwelling Place at Bethany: The Story of a Village Church* (© H.F.W. Proeve (printed by Openbook Publishers, Adelaide, South Australia, 1996).

Graham Jenkin's prize-winning book *Conquest of the Ngarrindjeri – The Story of the Lower Murray Lakes Tribes* (Raukkan Publishers, Point McLeay, South Australia, 1995), was invaluable for 'understanding' (if that be the word) the dispossession of the Ngarrindjeri nation, and for providing detail on *tendi, lakalinyerar*, et al.

Aboriginal Studies 8–12. The Ngarrindjeri people: Aboriginal people of the River Murray, Lakes & Coorong (Education Department of South Australia, 1990) was also a source of much helpful information.

The South Australian Museum's 1989 booklet, 'Ngurunderi: An Aboriginal Dreaming, The Culture of the Ngarrindjeri People', text by Steve Hemming and Philip Jones with Philip Clarke, for providing valuable details on the story of the Dreaming Ancestor.

Michael Cannon's fascinating *Old Melbourne Town: Before The Gold Rush* (Loch Haven Books, Victoria, 1991) provided much factual information about streets, pubs, banks, Orange vs. Catholic riots and the 'Parades Commission' of 1847.

CANADA

I have already mentioned Marianna O'Gallagher's two books which provided a wealth of factual information on Grosse Île, to which must be added, *1847: Grosse Île: A Record of Daily Events* by André Charbonneau and André Sévigny (Canadian Heritage/Parcs Canada, Minister of Public Works and Government Services, Ottawa, 1997).

BOSTON

Thomas H. O'Connor's book *The Boston Irish: A Political History* (Back Bay Books, USA, 1995/Little, Brown & Company (Canada) Ltd., 1995) was most useful in providing a social, economic, and cultural backdrop to what Irish emigrants experienced in 1847, and also alerted me to 'Pope's night'.

ABRIDGED BIBLIOGRAPHY

IRELAND

Adelman, Paul, *Peel and the Conservative Party 1830–1850* (Longman Group UK, Ltd., 1989)

Barry, John, ed., *Historical Studies IX* (Papers read before the Irish Conference of Historians) (The Blackstaff Press Ltd., Belfast, 1974)

Berresford Ellis, Peter, *Celtic Women: Women in Celtic Society & Literature* (Constable and Company Ltd., London, 1995)

Bull, Philip, *Land, Politics and Nationalism: A Study of the Irish Land Question* (Gill & Macmillan Ltd., Dublin, 1996)

Campbell, Fr. Stephen J., *The Great Irish Famine: Words & Images from the Famine* (Famine Museum, Strokestown Park, Co. Roscommon, 1994)

Casey, Daniel J., & Rhodes, Robert E., eds., *Views of the Irish Peasantry 1800–1916* (Archon Books, Hamden, Connecticut, 1977)

Colville Scott, Thomas, *Connemara After The Famine: Journal of a Survey of the Martin Estate 1853*. Introduction by Tim Robinson, ed., (Lilliput Press, Dublin, 1995)

Corish, Patrick J., *The Irish Catholic Experience: A Historical Survey* (Gill & Macmillan Ltd., Dublin, 1985)
— *Maynooth College 1795–1995* (Gill & Macmillan Ltd., Dublin, 1995)

Crossman, Virginia, *Politics, Law and Order in Nineteenth-Century Ireland* (Gill & Macmillan Ltd., Dublin, 1996)

Dowley, Leslie J. & O'Sullivan, Eugene, 'Late Blight & the Potato in Ireland' (Teagasc, Oak Park Research Centre, Carlow, Ireland, 1995)

Engels, Frederick, & Marx, Karl, *Ireland and the Irish Question* (Progress Publishers, Moscow, 1971)

Evans, Eric J., *Sir Robert Peel: Statesmanship, Power and Party* (Routledge, London and New York, 1991)

Fitzpatrick, David, *Oceans of Consolation: Personal Accounts of Irish Migration to Australia* (Cork University Press, Cork, 1994)

Gallagher, Thomas H., *Paddy's Lament: Ireland 1846–1847: Prelude to Hatred* (Ward River Press, Co. Dublin, 1985)

Gavan-Duffy, Sir Charles, *Four Years of Irish History 1845–1849* (Gassell, Petter, Galpin & Co, London, Paris, New York, 1883)

Gillespie, Raymond & Moran, Gerard, eds., *A Various Country: Essays in Mayo History 1500–1900* (Foilseacháin Náisiúnta Teoranta, Westport, Co. Mayo, 1987)

Guinan, Rev. Joseph, P.P., 'The Famine Years' (Catholic Truth Society of Ireland, Dublin, 1921)

Hall, Mr. S.C., & Mrs. S.C., *Hall's Ireland: Mr. & Mrs. Hall's Tour of 1840*: Vol. 1 & 2 Michael Scott, ed. (Sphere Books Ltd., London, 1984)

Hamrock, Ivor, ed., compiled, *The Famine in Mayo 1845–1850: A portrait from contemporary sources* (Mayo County Council, Castlebar, Co. Mayo, 1998)

Hayden, Tom, ed., compiled, *Irish Hunger: Personal Reflections on the*

Legacy of the Famine (Wolfhound Press, Dublin/Roberts Rinehart Publishers, Boulder, Colorado, 1997)

Hughes, Harry, 'Croagh Patrick – An Ancient Mountain Pilgrimage' (Harry Hughes, Westport, Co. Mayo, 1991)

Jackson Hurlstone, Kenneth. *A Celtic Miscellany: Translations from the Celtic Literatures* (Penguin Books, UK, 1971)

Keating, Rev. Joseph, S.J., 'Souperism' (Catholic Truth Society of Ireland, Dublin, 1914)

Keenan, Desmond, *The Catholic Church in Nineteenth-Century Ireland: A Sociological Study* (Gill & Macmillan Ltd., Dublin/Barnes & Noble Books, New Jersey, 1983)

Kerr, Donal, A., *The Catholic Church and the Famine* (The Columba Press, Co. Dublin, 1996)
— *Peel, Priests and Politics: Sir Robert Peel's Administration and the Roman Catholic Church: Ireland 1841–1846* (Oxford University Press, UK/New York, 1982)

Kissane, Noel, *The Irish Famine: A Documentary History* (National Library of Ireland, Dublin, 1995)

Langan-Egan, Maureen, *Women in Mayo 1821–1851: 'A Historical Perspective'*. Thesis. (National University of Ireland, 1986)

Laxton, Edward, *The Famine Ships: The Irish Exodus To America 1846–51* (Bloomsbury Publishing Plc., London, 1996)

Luddy, Maria, *Women in Ireland, 1800–1918: A Documentary History* (Cork University Press, Cork, 1995)

Lyons, John, *Louisburgh: A History* (Louisburgh Traders Association, Louisburgh, Co. Mayo, 1995)

Lysaght, Patricia, *The Banshee: The Irish Supernatural Death-Messenger* (The O'Brien Press Ltd., Dublin, 1996)

McCarthy, Justin, M.P., *A Short History of Our Own Times: From the Accession of Queen Victoria to the General Election of 1880* (Chatto & Windus, London, 1897)

Miller, Kerby, & Vagner, Paul, *Out of Ireland: The Story of Irish Emigration to America* (Aurum Press Ltd., London, 1994)

Mokyr, Joel, *Why Ireland Starved: A Quantitive and Analytical History of the Irish Economy 1800–1850* (Allen and Unwin, London, 1985)

Morash, Christopher, *The Hungry Voice: The Poetry of the Irish Famine* (Irish Academic Press, Dublin, 1989)

Nicholson, Asenath, *Lights and Shades of Ireland, Annals of the Famine of 1847, 1848 and 1849* (New York, 1851)

O'Connor, John, *The Workhouses of Ireland: The fate of Ireland's poor* (Anvil Books, Dublin in association with Irish Books & Media Inc.,

Minneapolis, 1995)

O'Dwyer, Peter, O. CARM., *Mary: A History of Devotion in Ireland* (Four Courts Press, Dublin, 1988)
— *Towards A History of Irish Spirituality* (The Columba Press, Co. Dublin, 1995)

Ó Gráda, Cormac, ed., *Famine 150: Commemorative Lecture Series* (Teagasc/UCD, Dublin, 1997)

O' Hegarty, P.S., *A History of Ireland Under The Union 1801–1922* (Kraus Reprint Co., New York, 1969)

Ó' Ríordáin, John, J., C.Ss.R., *The Music of What Happens: Celtic Spirituality: A View From the Inside* (The Columba Press, Co. Dublin/Saint Mary's Press, Minnesota, 1996)

Percival, John, *The Great Famine: Ireland's Potato Famine 1845–51*. Foreword by Ian Gibson. (BBC Books, London, 1995)

Quinn, J. F., *History of Mayo* Vol. 1, 2 & 3 (Brendan Quinn, Ballina, Co. Mayo, 1993)

Scally, Robert James, *The End of Hidden Ireland: Rebellion, Famine and Emigration* (Oxford University Press Inc., New York, 1995)

Sharkey, Olive, *Old Days, Old Ways: An Illustrated Folk History of Ireland*. Foreword by Timothy P. O'Neill. (The O'Brien Press Ltd., Dublin, 1985)

Shaw Lefevre, G., The Right Hon., M.P., *Peel and O'Connell: A Review of the Irish Policy of Parliament from the Act of Union to the Death of Sir Robert Peel* (Kennikat Press, Port Washington, New York and London, reissued 1970)

Somerville, Alexander, *Letters From Ireland During The Famine of 1847*. Introduction by K. D. M. Snell, ed. (Irish Academic Press, Co. Dublin, 1994)

Sullivan, A.M., & Sullivan, T.D., eds., *Irish Readings* (M.H. Gill & Son Ltd., Dublin, 1913)

Thackeray, William Makepeace, *Paris, Irish and Eastern Sketches* (Smith, Elder & Co., London, 1872)

Thomson, David, ed., with McGusty, Moyra, *The Irish Journals of Elizabeth Smith 1840–1850* (Clarendon Press, Oxford, 1980)

Villiers-Tuthill, Kathleen, *Patient Endurance: The Great Famine in Connemara* (Connemara Girl Publications, Dublin, 1997)

Whyte, Robert T., James J. Mangan, ed., *1847 Famine Ship Diary: The Journey of an Irish Coffin Ship* (Mercier Press, Cork, 1994)

AUSTRALIA

Baglin, Douglass, & Mullins, Barbara, 'Aboriginals of Australia' (Shepp

Books, New South Wales in association with Mulavon Pty., Ltd., New South Wales, 1997)

Broome, Richard, *Aboriginal Australians – Black Responses to White Dominance 1788–1994* (Allen & Unwin Pty., Ltd., New South Wales, 1994)

Ebsworth. Rev. Walter, *Pioneer Catholic Victoria* (The Polding Press, Melbourne, 1973)

Geyer, Mary, *Behind The Wall: The Women of the Destitute Asylum Adelaide 1852–1918* (Axiom Publishers in association with the Migration Museum, Adelaide, 1994)

Havecker, Cyril (illustrations), 'Understanding Aboriginal Culture'. Foreword by Yvonne Malykke, ed. (Cosmos Periodicals, Sydney, 1994)

Hemming, S.J., & Clarke, P.A., 'Aboriginal Australia: Aboriginal People of South Australia' (Commonwealth of Australia, Canberra, 1992)

Hughes, Robert, *The Fatal Shore: A History of the Transportation of Convicts to Australia 1787–1868* (The Harvill Press, London, 1996)

Iwan, Wilhelm; Schubert, David, ed., trans., *Because of Their Beliefs – Emigration from Prussia to Australia* (H. Schubert, Highgate, South Australia, 1995)

O'Farrell, Patrick, *The Irish in Australia* (New South Wales University Press, 1987)

Richards, Eric, ed., *Visible Women – Female Immigrants in Colonial Australia: Visible Immigrants: Four* (Australian National University, Canberra, 1995)

Stokes, Deirdre, 'Desert Dreamings' (Rigby Heinemann, Victoria, 1993)

Whitelock, Derek, *Gawler, Colonel Light's Country Town: A History of Gawler and its region: The Hills, the Plains and The Barossa Valley* (Corporation of the town of Gawler, South Australia, 1989)

The Old Limerick Journal – No. 23 Spring 1988 (Australian edn.), Kemmy, Jim, T.D., ed.

Irish University Press Series of British Parliamentary Papers – Report from the Select Committee on Aborigines (British Settlements) (The Irish University Press, 1868)

CANADA

Dickinson, John A., & Young, Brian, *A Short History of Quebec* (Copp Clark Pitman Ltd., Toronto, 1993)

MacKay, Donald, *Flight from Famine: The Coming of the Irish to Canada* (McClelland & Stewart Inc., Toronto, 1990)

Tessier, Yves, *An Historical Guide to Québec* (La Société Historique de Québec, Québec, 1996)

Abbott, Edith, *Historical Aspects of the Immigration Problem: Select Documents* (The University of Chicago Press, Chicago, 1926)

Bergen, Philip, compiled, *Old Boston, in early photographs, 1850–1918, 174 prints from the collection of The Bostonian Society* (Dover Publications Inc., New York, 1990)

Handlin, Oscar, *Boston's Immigrants 1790–1880: A Study in Acculturation* (The Belknap Press of Harvard University Press, Cambridge, Massachusetts, 50th Anniversary edn., 1991)

Harrington, Edward T., Lord, Robert H., Sexton, John E., *History of the Archdiocese of Boston: In the Various Stages of Its Development 1604 to 1943 in Three Volumes: Volume 11.* Foreword by His Eminence William Cardinal O'Connell, Archbishop of Boston. (Sheed and Ward, New York, 1944)

Harris, John, *The Boston Globe: Historic Walks in Old Boston* (The Globe Pequot Press, Old Saybrook, Connecticut, 1993)